CONTENTS

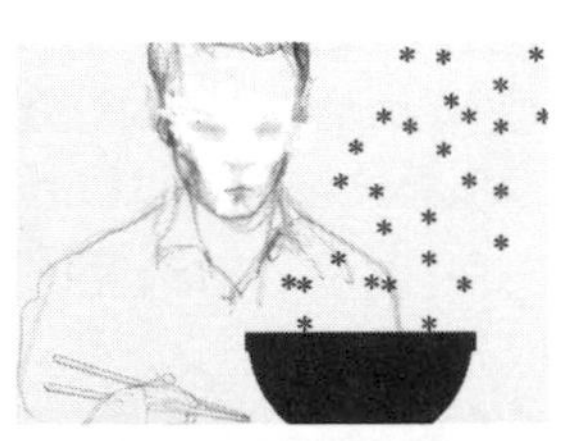

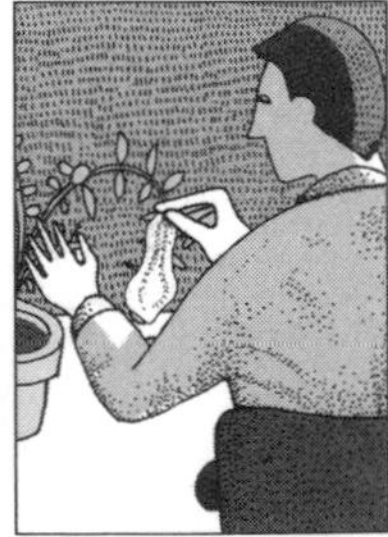

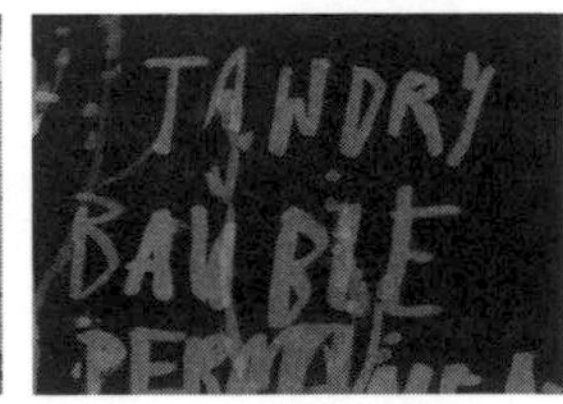

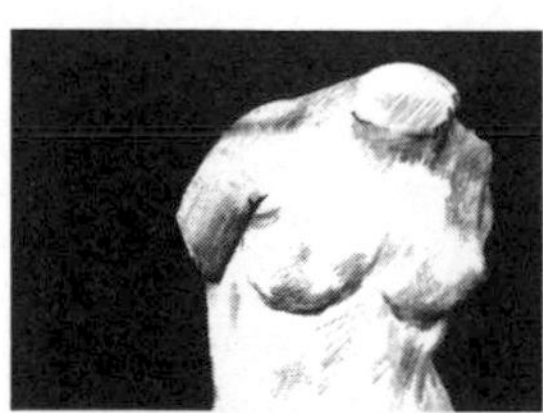

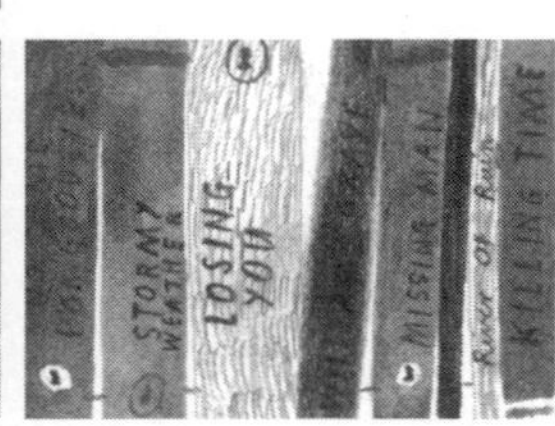
STORMY WEATHER
LOSING YOU
MISSING MAN
KILLING TIME

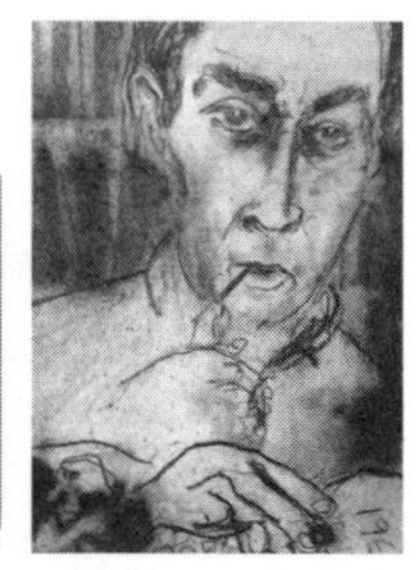

EDITOR'S LETTER | ALEX CLARK

Energetic failure

In 1979, when Bill Buford introduced his first issue of *Granta*, a penetrating, bravura survey of American fiction, he proclaimed his efforts to be 'a kind of energetic failure'. Thirty years later, I know what he means. Gathering together a magazine of new writing requires a certain amount of energy, although of an almost entirely pleasurable kind; sifting through short stories and novels-in-progress to provide an entertaining and illuminating sample of today's literary landscape is hardly work, by most people's standards. The prospect of failure is a different matter. But failure to do what?

That first issue of 1979 – a blend of fiction, interview material and critical writing – set out its stall clearly enough; to challenge the cultural hegemony and shortcomings of the contemporary British novel ('characterized by a succession of efforts the accomplishments of which are insistently, critically, and aesthetically negligible') by introducing the magazine's readership to writers from the United States who had, by and large, not yet garnered widespread attention.

Buford's tone was insistent, polemical, occasionally table-thumping; his line of argument at times academic, at times more impressionistic. His rather laudable demand – request, or suggestion, is too mild a word – was for British writing to notice the conversation that was going on in America, and to join in. Subsequent issues of *Granta*, most notably 'The End of the English Novel' (*Granta* 3), 'Dirty Realism' (*Granta* 8) and the once-a-decade 'Best of Young British Novelists' and 'Best of Young American Novelists' have attempted to encourage and to extend the

dialogue by providing snapshots of particular moments and by isolating emergent trends and movements.

This particular conversation has, of course, developed, not least because our literary discourse now encompasses far more readily writing that originates beyond the twin poles of America and Britain. But it might also be the case that the grand statement about literature, its provenance, its direction, its nature and its aim, has begun to seem anachronistic. Have we given up the idea of defining and characterizing contemporary literature because it has itself given up on the idea of a fictional project?

The counter to this argument is that the New American Writers, the Dirty Realists and so on, probably didn't see themselves as part of a group, and that writers – usually solitary, contemplative, dedicated to the expression of an individual sensibility – rarely do. Its reinforcement is that all writers work in a historical context, and their work will inevitably be inflected to a greater or lesser degree by the social, political and cultural climate of the time as well as by their personal circumstances or inclinations.

But labelling and categorizing have their perils as well as their undoubted uses. In the interview that Jhumpa Lahiri conducted with the great short-story writer Mavis Gallant for this issue, a portrait emerges of an artist determined to pursue her vocation at all costs, for whom the first step was to move continents and embark on a lifetime of what could be described as self-imposed exile. Her work subsequently draws heavily on the experience of emigration, isolation and cultural dislocation and disconnection; and on the specifics of French life and society following the Second World War. Gallant's fiction, and the perspective she provides on it here, bubble with glimpses into the period (the hostility of the English, for example, the first taste of French butter, the portrayal of Parisian cafe society as a flight from freezing apartments), with intriguing nods towards the shifting tectonic plates that form a writer. A question, however, remains: what would Gallant have written had she never moved from Montreal to Paris?

It is unanswerable, of course, although one feels that the attentive intelligence and commitment to language that characterize her stories mean that a different setting would have produced different work, but not necessarily an unrecognizably different writer, or no writer at all. But what the encounter between Gallant and Lahiri reveals is the extent to which a writer must first establish their own corner of ground from which to speak.

The stories we've chosen for this issue do not define an era nor encapsulate a literary movement. We have included work by several established writers – Paul Auster, Helen Simpson, Amy Bloom, Ha Jin and Nicola Barker – but we also alighted on writing by those who will likely be less familiar to our readers, for example the New Zealand writer Eleanor Catton, whose eerie story 'Two Tides' opens the issue, and William Pierce, who brings us a tale of mutual cultural incomprehension in the workplace in 'American Subsidiary'. We also feature a short graphic piece by Chris Ware, and an extract from a forthcoming novel by Adam Thirlwell, one of the last crop of Best of Young British Novelists. Beyond a certain kind of antic humour in evidence in several of the pieces, I would be hard pushed to identify a connecting thread, but that itself does not seem to constitute failure. It may turn out that fiction succeeds best when it represents nothing but itself. ■

POEM | FANNY HOWE

Seen

A real bungalow is stone
and snow white mud
on the inner walls,
a large grate
and a slate floor
and a picture of itself.

Every cupboard is old,
every glass and cup
wiped clean.
The wind cannot get in
so the flies are free
to buzz against the glass.

Outside, blue twine
is tied to a telephone pole
and a gate
to keep the brown cows
in their field.

Fuchsia hedges, clover
in full juice:
purple clover, purple heather.

There's a silver line
on the sea between
green sheer islands:

Now the sound of the wind
playing a foghorn,
enters forgotten.

DOUG BANVILLE

SUBJECT + OBJECT | JOHN BANVILLE

The music of the sphere

We never grow up – only older, then old – and our need for toys does not abate. I still remember with awful clarity the bitter, angry tears I shed as a little boy when, on a family outing one Sunday afternoon to the Cistercian Abbey at Mount Melleray in County Waterford, my mother refused to buy for me in the gift shop there a miniature missal bound in white calfskin on which I had fixed a longing eye. Nowadays I write my novels in manuscript books handmade for me by one of the great contemporary master bookbinders, Tony Cains. These beautiful volumes, covered in Cockerell paper with vellum spines, are more than toys, of course, but at one of the many levels on which we engage with our possessions I am sure I see in them a consolation for that original, never to be forgotten, missed missal.

Another time, another desired bauble. It was in Arles, twenty-some years ago, that I spotted it, in one of those bijou knick-knack shops the French do so well, presided over by a handsome, melancholy lady *d'un certain âge*. To look at, it was nothing much, a seamless silver sphere the size of a 'steeler', as we used to call those jumbo ball bearings that trundled unstoppably through our games of marbles; when picked up, however, it made a delightful musical sound, a cross between the tinkling of a tiny harpsichord and a glass harmonica's ethereal whisperings.

I wanted it – oh, I did so want it. But I also wanted a music box with a prancing Pierrot on the lid, which played a tune from *The Magic Flute*, and since I could not make up my mind I chose neither.

My friends hung back, however, and ten minutes later appeared at the outdoor cafe where I was sipping a *petit blanc* and presented me with the musical ball; they knew me better than I knew myself, they said, and were sure I would never forgive myself if I were to leave Arles without at least one trophy. And they were right.

I loved that little silly thing, extravagantly, shamefacedly, superstitiously. I would make no journey without it, would board no train, embark on no boat, buckle myself into no aeroplane seat, if it was not in my pocket or my bag. Strangely, it never set off a single security alarm; I would walk through screening gates beltless, shoeless, walletless but with a metal object in my pocket the shape of a miniature anarchist's bomb, and no bell would shrill. On reading tours, how many lonely hotel rooms in how many anonymous cities have I crawled into at the end of another day spent impersonating myself, and picked up and listened to that ball, like a lost and landlocked South Sea Islander pressing a seashell against his ear to catch the sound of home.

And then, one day, it was gone. I had been to Australia and when I got home I searched in my bags but could not find it. Australia! That haystack, and my precious needle somewhere in it! I tried to track it down. I contacted hotels in Sydney, Melbourne, Adelaide; I called friends whose houses I had visited; I pleaded with airline representatives. No good, no trace. In one of Nabokov's works – this is another of my lost trouvailles – a character tells of someone losing something, a ring, I think it was, in a rock pool somewhere on the Riviera and returning a year later to the day and finding it again in exactly the spot where it was lost, but that kind of thing only happens in the Russian enchanter's magical version of our sullenly acquisitive world.

Elizabeth Bishop did her best to comfort me, when in her wonderful and jauntily melancholy poem 'One Art' she assures that the art of losing is one that is not hard to master, and that so many things 'seem filled with the intent / to be lost that their loss is no disaster'. And she is right, I know she is, this sensible and practical poet – 'Lose something every day' – for anything as doted on as my musical talisman was bound to make a break for freedom. I only hoped it was happy, playing its little tune for the wallabies and the platypuses out there in the Outback.

I found a source on the Internet and got a new one; it was bigger, shinier, and played what to my ear was a coarser music. It was better than nothing, but just about. And then, a year ago, preparing for another trip abroad, I took down the bag I had not used since coming back from Australia and heard something as I did so, a faint, far, plaintive little chime. I delved in an inner pouch, thinking of kangaroos, and there it was, in its scuffed old velvet bag, my original and best-loved Arlesienne. Some toys, it seems, do return from the attic. ■

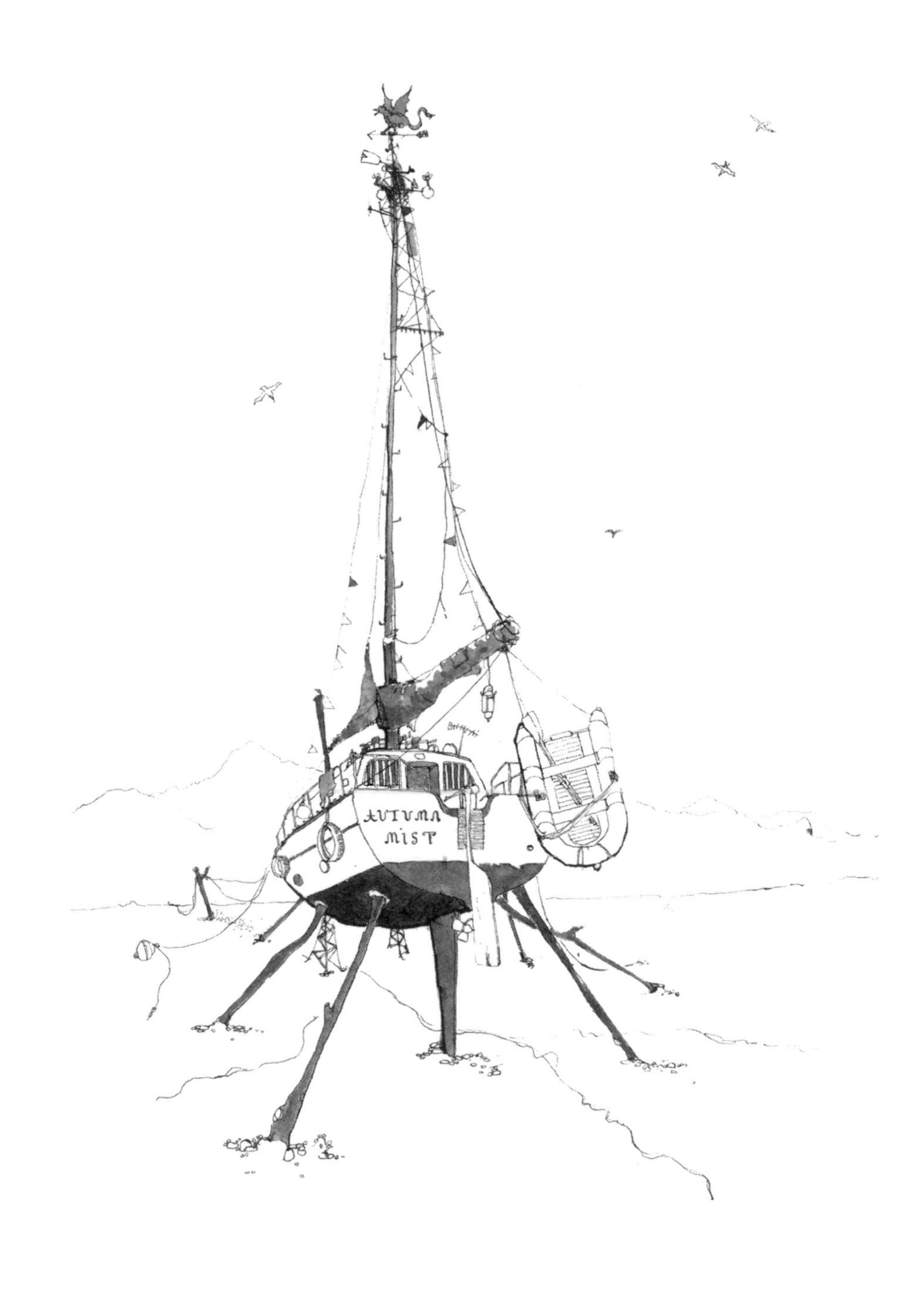
AUTUMN
MIST

TWO TIDES

Eleanor Catton

ILLUSTRATION BY GEORGE BUTLER

The harbour at Mana was a converted mudflat, tightly elbowed and unlovely at any tide but high. I had never been there when the tide was high. The birds were shags mostly. The fish were small. Low water showed the scabbed height of the yellow mooring posts, and the thick curded foam that shivered under the wharves, and the dirty bathtub ring on the rocks on the far side of the bay. The waves left a crust of sea lice and refuse and weed.

The marina was tucked into the crook of the elbow, facing back towards the shore. To make the hairpin journey from the shallow flats to open sea was dangerous, and so a central trench had been excavated in the seabed to create a channel deep enough for yachts to travel safely, even on the ugliest of tides.

'Bad luck to have a woman on board,' Craig said as I stepped down into the cockpit and took the tiller in my hand. 'That's the oldest in the book. But I'll tell you something else. There are grown men on this marina, educated men, who will never leave an anchor on a Friday. Grown men. Never leave on a Friday. It isn't just a quirk for them –

something runs deeper. And you know the reason why?'

I did: he'd told me this twice already, the first time at the yacht club with a gale wind thrashing at the door and the second time in the conical dry space beneath a fir tree on the Plimmerton domain, passing the last cigarette back and forth between us with our fingers cupped tight to keep it burning.

'No,' I said. I smiled at him. 'What's the reason?'

'*Vendredi* is French, that's Friday. Right? That's a word from way back when. And *Vendredi* means ruled by Venus. Right? And Venus is the ruler of women. And women are bad luck at sea. Right?' Craig sucked in the wind through his teeth. 'So never leave on a Friday.'

'Would you?' I said. 'Would you leave on a Friday?'

Craig thought for a moment.

'Say if the conditions were *perfect*,' I said. 'Say if the Strait was like *glass*.'

'Depends on the journey,' he said at last. 'If it was a day trip I would. But if it was some voyage – some huge beginning – I'd think twice. You don't want a curse on that.'

The limit was five knots inside the marina, impossibly slow. Even the speedboats seemed to drift. Once they passed the five-knot post you heard the grinding click and then the roar. The vessels ghosted by, passing close enough to whisper. I saw a seasick dog on a cabin roof and a charcoal smoker pouring steam and a scalloping basket hung like a flag from a boatswain's chair. It was still morning.

We left Mana with our faces turned back towards the harbour, watching the leading lights that showed the safe passage out of the bay. The leading lights comprised three colossal lengths of sewer pipe, diverging in three spokes and set into the hillside against the scrub. The central pipe was aligned with the excavated channel down the middle of the harbour, so if you were sailing safely you would be able to look cleanly up the length of the pipe and see the white light at the far end. If you strayed from your course you would no longer be looking down the unobstructed length of this middle pipe, and so the white light would disappear. Too far port and you would come into alignment with the left-hand pipe, which showed the warning red light; too far starboard and you would be aligned with the right-hand pipe, which showed a warning green.

There were two sets of leading lights in the harbour. The first was to guide you out of the marina and past the moored yachts, all shelved and slotted into the skeletal docks like a vast nautical library. Once these leading lights diminished in the distance and the light became difficult to see, you looked around to find the next set, fixed at an obtuse angle to the first and mounted on the shore above the motorway. The leading lights fascinated me. I drove the tiller to the right and left just to see over my shoulder the warning flash of green and then of red, leaping out from the hillside like a private flare.

Craig was smoking a cigarette and the ash was whipping off the butt and shredding whitely in the wind. The mainsail was up, but tightly reefed, and we hadn't yet switched off the diesel. He called the horsepower 'not quite enough to make a herd' and the description amused him so much that he had said it more than once, with minor variations. His foot was cocked, pinning a Primus stove upright against the hatch cover so it didn't fall and gutter as we bucked and rolled. The pale flame was invisible in the brightness of the day but I could see that the water in the billy was beading and ready to boil.

I was standing braced against the sides of the cockpit, half-turned and holding the tiller arm behind my back. 'Like backing a trailer,' Craig said. 'Just push the opposite to where you want to go.' I was not strong and my hand seemed to shiver on the tiller arm, the stout taper of teak wound around its length with a tight coil of waxed rope bleached grey by the salt and the sun. My awkwardness showed in the bunching lather of our wake. Craig's helming always left a crisp and minted streak; it conveyed a sense of purpose, a resolve. My wake was full of doubt. I looked back over my shoulder at the white spearhead stamp of our passing and watched the spume get sucked downward into the blue.

Craig flicked the end of his cigarette into the sea.

'That's what's missing,' I said. 'A dog.'

'You never met Snifter,' Craig said. 'Hell of a dog. He got so crook in the end, his skin just hung down. Kidneys. The boys said goodbye and I said I wanted to take him to the vet myself, in the truck, just him and me. But I took him out to our Foxton plot instead and we walked into the trees and I told him to sit, and I shot him. I bloody shot him. God, I cried that day. I cried. Could hardly see. That was a shit of a year. My dad died that year, and a bunch of other shitty stuff. Never found it in me to get another dog in place of Snifter. Buried him myself, under the trees.'

I'd seen the grave on his land at Foxton. There was a pine cross driven into the earth and a piece of aluminium was stapled to the upright spar like a plaque. With a shaky engraving tool Craig had written LOOK OUT, LOOK OUT, THERE'S A TERRIER ABOUT! and underneath, SNIFTER McNICHOL and a pair of dates. I'd come across it on my own, ducking off to take a piss behind a blackberry while Craig lopped Christmas trees with pruning shears and dragged them by their stump ends to make a pile. My hands were sticky from the sap. Later we sat on collapsible chairs on the Foxton drag and drank a case of beer and sold the trees for ten dollars, five for the ugly ones.

I thought about him sobbing as he dug the slender grave.

'Christ, I loved that dog,' Craig said. 'It's stupid. It's stupid. Hell of a dog.'

He reached down and pinched out the Primus flame. With one hand wrapped in a gutting glove he picked up the billy and poured out the hot water into two plastic mugs jammed tight between a cleat and the steel frame of the windshield. He was alert to the pitch and roll of the boat and he poured in steady, deliberate gulps. Nothing spilled. He tipped in coffee grains and milk and used the saw blade of his pocketknife to stir.

'It's bloody primitive,' he said as he passed the mug to me. 'Bloody primitive, savage really. The milk – I steal those creamers, anywhere I can. I can't offer – savage really. Acid in your mouth.'

He was embarrassed. I said, 'It's exactly right. It's great.' My hair was whipped across my face from the wind.

'It's bloody primitive,' he said, scowling now, and then backed swiftly down the narrow hatch into the saloon. I heard him sliding the panels behind the engine where his tools were stowed. The tiller leaped against my hand and I flexed my arm to hold her firm. I listened to him rummage and over the noise I said, more loudly, 'It's exactly what I feel like.'

Craig was nervous when he showed me the marina for the first time. I think I'd expected something charming and toothsome, some old glamour gone to seed, but his boat was capable and wifely and broad.

The causeway between the berths had a central grip of chicken wire stapled flat to the planking and it was ridged every metre with a strip of dowelling that made our handcart ring out sharply as we walked. *Sea Lady*, *Gracie*, *Taranui*, *Stoke*. Craig pointed and said, 'Wanker – wanker – he's an alright bloke but the boat's just for show – wanker – *that* boat's been all around the world, would you believe it – she's just changed hands, haven't met the new owner – *he's* a wanker – look at that, isn't she a beauty? – see this one? That's the boat I'd want if I downgraded to a sloop. *Precision*, she's a piece of work. Owner's a right prick though. And *here*,' as we finally stopped, third from the end, beside the *Autumn Mist*.

She slotted snug between a pair of gin palaces, shining white bridge-deckers with tinted glass and squared-off cabins that sat high and proud in the water and bobbed brightly in the crosswind. The *Autumn Mist* didn't bob. There was a weight to her, a low-slung gravity, a guarded economy of pitch and roll that seemed quietly to undermine the jouncing of the boats on either side. She was mute-coloured and scabbed with rust, trimmed with sky blue and antifouled with grey. I saw the new wind vane, mounted above the dented gutting tray at the stern, but the clean whiteness of the fin threw the rest of the boat into poor relief. Her sail covers were patched and tatted and fringed with loose threads. The gaskets hung slack. The cockpit windshield was coming apart from its steel framing. There was a dinghy strapped upside down on the bow and the triple bones of its keel showed darkly silver where a thousand landings had worn the paint away.

I thought about dogs that come to resemble their owners and turned to Craig with the tease already in my mouth, but I was startled to see that he was looking downright anxious. He had turned red and he was flapping his hand strangely, turning his wrist over and over.

'What do you make of it?' he said.

I put my hand up to shield the sun. 'Didn't you say once? Man can only have one mistress. Didn't you say that?'

'That's the truth.' He looked pleased, and ceased his flapping. After a moment he said, 'Meet the mistress,' and we stood in silence and bucked on our heels against the wind.

'I'm looking for scratches on the hatch,' I said.

'Don't say that when we get to Furneaux.'

'Too soon, you reckon.'

'All the boys in the yard been calling me Scott, or Mr Watson.'

'Yeah.'

'That keel's an inch thick and she's been to Tonga and back.'

'Yeah.'

'The name is from "Puff the Magic Dragon". Silly really.'

'Lived by the sea...'

Craig said, 'I know she needs a paint job.'

'Sorry,' I said, repenting. 'I shouldn't have said about the scratches.'

'But antifoul is a fuck of a business. It's best to find some shallow bay, somewhere that gives you a big margin between the tides, low and high. Got to pop her on blocks and then paint like mad until the tide comes back. Or you can pay for the crane and lift, but you'd be looking at five hundred just for the privilege.'

'She's lovely, Craig,' I said. 'Really she is.'

'I been thinking, a dragon on the wind vane,' he said. 'Some cheeky dragon with a spade on the end of his tail. I reckon I might like that. Always in my head I called that dinghy *Puff*.'

He leaned out over the water to grab the stainless braid of the shroud and haul the vessel closer to the marina where we stood. For a second she didn't move. Craig's biceps stood out on his arm. Then the great weight rolled towards us, against the grain of her keel, and slowly the gap of water between the marina and the boat narrowed and then closed. The low side of the deck touched the buffered planking with a thud.

'Jen – my wife,' Craig said suddenly, as I stepped over the braided rail on to the *Autumn Mist* and felt the slow dip as she rolled under my weight, 'she'd be white-knuckled. Any time I tried to take her – she'd sit and clamp. White-knuckled. It's the way she always was.'

He stepped past me on to the cabin roof to unlock the deadbolt on the hatch and the blond wool of his forearm touched my hand. I was disgusted at myself suddenly and I said, 'But the badminton, and cycling, and the half-marathon. It isn't like – I mean, she's got the things she loves.'

Craig's keyring was a plastic buoy, to keep his keys afloat if they ever fell in.

'My marriage,' he said. 'You wouldn't – you don't – Francie – it's just—' and then he shook his head and rattled his keys and breathed hard through his nose and said, 'Cunt-struck. I was cunt-struck when I married her. That's all.'

I watched a gannet make a free-fall dive. Craig reappeared, holding a spherical compass that rolled around like a weighted eyeball in his palm. I watched as he climbed one-handed out of the hatch and fitted the compass into a socket in the centre of the boom. It was about the size of an infant skull, heavy and wet-looking, and it sat just low enough to show the phosphorous degrees that spun around its equator beneath the glass. The red needle swung and hovered in its lolling underwater way.

'You got to have a compass above board,' he said as he dropped back into the cockpit and unwedged his coffee mug from beneath the windshield sill. 'If you got a steel hull you got to mount it up above. Makes the needle go funny below.'

We were flanking Mana Island now. I watched the red needle pitch back and forth and tried to hold her at twenty degrees. The northern fingers of the Sounds were still pale and fogged and flattened by the distance. I saw now that the surface of the sea had a pattern to it, a weave, and I could feel it through my arm and the arches of my feet as a push or a pull. The wind gusts showed a long way off before they struck; they approached like a little burnished patch of silver where the water was disturbed. You could predict exactly the moment when the flat hand of the wind would strike your face.

I said, 'How long would they have lasted, the bodies of those kids? If he pitched them over and weighed them down.'

They had made an arrest for the murders, Hope and Smart. We saw it on the news. There were fingernail scratches on the inside cover of the hatch, and a slender female hair on a swab in the saloon. The evidence was small. But the man was sour and dirty and he had a bad family like a killer ought. The story was he'd pitched them over, both of them, somewhere deep. He might have raped the girl. What were we doing that night, we all asked – that New Year's Eve, a few dark hours past the midnight toll, while somewhere north of Picton two lovers were stabbed, or brained, or strangled, while the boats all around them trembled back and forth on some dark sheet of oily calm? Lovers. It was too awful. The worst thing was that no one knew – no one knew the method of the kill.

Craig said, 'Thcy'd disappear. Flesh like that. Fish would eat them away in days, maybe a week. If he weighed them down all right. They'd disappear.'

Scott Watson's boat was called the *Blade*.

I said, 'The temptation would be to cover them in plastic. That's what I would want to do. Isn't that stupid? To want to preserve the bodies somehow. Like an instinct. To make them keep.'

Craig laughed and shot me a sly look. We didn't speak again for a long time. I finished my coffee and switched hands on the tiller and rolled my shoulder joint to feel it click. The cockpit floor was choked with empties, and mismatched sea boots, and the roped saltwater bucket, and a pair of life jackets that showed a fine spray of mould against the yellow. All of it shifted back and forth.

I watched him. Craig was short, five four. His hair had been reddish once but it was sandy now, white at the temples and the sides of his beard. He had a white scar above his left eye and a thick pink scar running down his left forearm like a vein. His hands were big. He was stocky and barrelled but his legs were slender and his calves were fine. I watched him watch the ocean and saw how his weathered squint had left the crinkles of his crow's feet untanned, so when his expression softened you could see two pale stars at the outer corners of his eyes. The tawny skin on the back of his neck was creased three times.

The first time I went to sea was as a child, when the replica of the *Endeavour* came to circumnavigate New Zealand and retrace Cook's voyage from the north. I sailed out to meet the great square-bellied ship in a restored yacht belonging to a friend of my father's. Lionel was a giant wrathful man who cursed at his children and ridiculed his wife, but from time to time he would lay his hands upon his boat with such a private, secret tenderness it was as if he believed himself to be alone on board.

Lionel kept the *Indigo* like a thoroughbred mare. A poor knot would turn him purple with fury. He screamed across the water at any vessel that flouted maritime law, and blacklisted any sailor who jammed the radio channels with ordinary talk. He would flare with a scarlet contempt if you said *rear* instead of *aft* or *back* instead of *stern*. He let nobody in the steering house when the *Indigo* was at sea, and he called for complete silence whenever he drove her glossy hips in or out of her marina berth, in case his concentration broke. We tucked ourselves against the mast on the aft cabin between his children and his wife and we tried to touch nothing, but he called us lubbers anyway. There was a brass plaque above the freshwater pump that read THE CAPTAIN'S WORD IS LAW.

Craig was generous with the *Autumn Mist*. He showed me every part of her. He watched while I fumbled with the tiller or dipped my hand down into the streaky black damp of the bilges or traced the fuel line to understand why the ignition wouldn't catch. He let me make the radio calls to the coastguard watch. He taught me to rope off the mooring line around the forward block and showed me how to cross the rope neatly over the top of the block so the knot could unravel with a single blow of an axe.

He said, 'Imagine if the boom clocked my temple and I went out cold. You have to know everything.'

When the *Endeavour* docked at Lyttelton we went aboard and marvelled at the five-foot ceilings and the swarming hammocks clustered tight and the giddy drop of the overboard latrines. They served limes. We touched the flayed catgut fingers of the cat-o'-nine-tails and learned how a single lash could shred a man. The crew were dressed in period costumes, rough linen for the seamen and covered buttons for the captain's men. Lionel hung back with his hands in his pockets and looked up the length of her mast. He said, 'Square-bottomed, now, and ship-rigged. Nothing much to look at. But what a life.'

The kauri shelves above the swabs in the *Autumn Mist*'s saloon were stuffed with faded thriller novels and food for the week ahead. In the morning before we left Mana I went below to stow my duffel bag in the V-shaped cabin underneath the bow and I saw that Craig had stuffed a box of Cadbury's chocolates into the stow hole beside the anchor chain. The box had been stowed so roughly: it was dented and a corner of the cellophane was pierced.

Craig was the full-time trucker and I worked weekends with the other girls in the store. The day that I came to work in hardware was the day that Craig became a kind of luminary in the timber yard. He shredded an order sheet in his customer's face, screamed, 'Don't you treat me like this shitty job is the only thing that makes my life worthwhile, you smug prick,' and then destroyed $600 worth of cement-board sheeting under the wheels of the delivery truck as he drove away with his middle finger out the driver's window of the cab. The ill fit of his leather working glove augmented the length of his finger by a withered inch where the glove sat thick and high on his hand.

This small detail, coupled with the fine Marxist flavour of his short speech, transformed the incident into an iconic protest, a movement on behalf of all the dirty timber boys who worked hard hours for a poor wage. He swiftly turned his celebrity to his advantage. He came to work blind drunk and slept through whole afternoons in the shade of the cab. He shaved each pallet-load of whatever he thought easiest to steal. He clocked false hours on his time card and often left inexplicably in the middle of the day, vaulting the fence and stuffing his red uniform into the scrubby tussock behind the gate. I think he only stayed on as a trucker to steal the diesel. Every morning he drove the truck home to his garage to siphon it into his own van, and when the van was full he filled whatever vessel was closest until the truck's tank ran close to dry. Every possible container in his garage was brimful of stolen diesel. There were drums and cans and barrels and buckets and jam jars lined up along his worktop bench. I even saw a sardine can – tiny, holding less than quarter of a cup.

The timber boys saw all of this and didn't rat on him once, even when they had to pick up the slack, or mop his sick, or cover for a lie. This was partly in recognition of Craig's heroic act of retail justice: he was a rebel darling now, and stood apart. But it was mostly from compassion, because everyone had heard the whisper that Craig was having trouble at home.

I was working weekends while I finished up with film school at the Newtown Polytech. When I took the job I'd just lost a lover for the first time. I was bitter. I drank a lot and cut my hair. I found in Craig a sympathetic streak of rawness, a muted anger, a grieving nostalgia that I thought I shared.

Craig said, 'I see a woman with a tattoo and I think, she's walked a little to the wild side. She's got spirit. I see a sense of adventure there.'

I said, 'It was stupid and now it's there for good.'

He turned my arm over to look at the bird again. 'All adventures are stupid,' he said. 'Anyone with any sense, they stay at home.'

Later, when I had spent more time at the yacht club, I came to understand that he spoke like a sailor. He talked often about mystery, and belief, and the deep and hallowed cradle of the sea. We were drunks together. I listened while he talked about his life, all the things he wanted and all the things he didn't have. He talked about the solo journeys he was planning, ten days to Fiji, three months to the bottom of Cape Horn. The parachute sail he wanted to buy, the anchor he couldn't afford. His depth sounder was broken. His mainmast needed to be stripped. His voice was always wistful. He talked about death by drowning, his brothers, his boys.

On the mainmast, each shackle was stamped with a stainless-steel tag that identified the lines: spinnaker, mainsail, jib. The stays and the halyards ran underneath the windshield and tied off on the two cleats behind the plastic sheeting, the main halyard on the starboard cleat and the jib halyards on port, so if the weather was foul and Craig was manning the boat on his own he could haul the sails without leaving the tiller. That was the first thing I noticed: the *Autumn Mist* was rigged for a solo crew.

I didn't meet Craig right away. One morning I was filling in at dispatch and the truck walkie fizzed and his voice came through saying, 'Top pair of tits in the trade office, get out here quick.' I buzzed back and said, 'Patrick's on lunch sorry Craig.' The handset fizzed again and Craig said, 'What's the use having a girl on the walkie line? That's a fine pair of tits wasted,' and then the light went out.

The hardware girls were doubtful.

Izzie said, 'Craig's drunk all the time.'

Gina said, 'He talks about sex.'

Laura said, 'He's gross. Patrick says he sleeps in the truck.'

In fact he slept on the *Autumn Mist* most nights, cuddled up on the swabs between a pair of sails. When I first stepped down into the saloon I saw the hollow that his body made between the sail sacks, one marked MIZZEN, the other MAIN. At nights he sat by the kerosene lamp that hung from a pivoted collar so it moved in rhythm with the swell. He filled the bilges with beer and the paper labels on the stubbies went soft in the water and peeled away. There was an extra fee for liveaboards so he left the marina early in the morning, before the yacht club opened and the fishers arrived. Showers were free.

After a while I asked about his wife.

'You'd be surprised,' he said. 'I lucked out with Jen. You wouldn't know to look at me but my wife is a very attractive woman. You wouldn't pick her from a line-up. You'd guess too low, I'd make a bet on that. She's a very attractive woman. I've had four affairs. Four affairs in thirty years. Christ, Francie, I'm a shit of a man.'

I asked about the women and he sucked on his lager and gazed up at the mounted row of trophy hoofs behind the bar, crooked downwards like tub faucets. He said, 'You would have liked the first one. Pat. She had a hell of a laugh. But I'll always remember: one night near the end I climbed up to her balcony to look in her bedroom window. She was there, with her husband, on her hands and knees. He was at her from behind and I'll never forget it, he had a blue magazine, a porno, open on her back. He was *turning the pages*. I remember it. As if she wasn't even there. God, she wasn't a beauty or anything. But *turning the pages*. And she just knelt there, rocking, hands and knees. Course I just crept away. But the image stayed. She got a job in Sydney after that.'

Craig liked to introduce me as his mid-life crisis to the salts at the yacht club. If anyone looked sceptical he'd just laugh and say I was actually his niece. That sounded worse, and he knew it.

At the yacht club there were lengths of waxed rope to practise knot work and Craig watched as I laid out the lengths on the tabletop and tried to copy the half-hitch and the Turk's head and the shroud.

'Pig's ear,' he said. 'Look at it! Jesus, do you have six thumbs? Remind me never to ask you for a handjob.'

He laughed and I laughed but the salts were quiet and they looked out the window or up at the television over the bar. Somebody coughed.

We both liked it, that nobody was sure.

At our Christmas party the store manager cocked his head at me and said, 'You and Craig are friends, I guess.'

I said, 'It's someone to share a drink with.'

He said, 'You're too young to be a cynic, Francie,' and handed me a beer. He must have kept watching from across the bar though, while I laughed at Craig's five-second pint, no hands (he dipped his nose into the glass and gripped the rim between his teeth, then lifted the glass with his jaw and threw his head back, and the pint disappeared in three open-throated slugs), because after a while he came back to me and said, 'What I mean to say is this. This is only a phase for you. This shitty job. Working weekends to earn a few bucks for a beer. But Craig is full-time. And he's a father. His kids—'

'His kids are grown up and they both live in Australia.'

'You got to understand. This isn't your *life*. Being a student is your life. Working here is just a phase for you. You don't—'

'It's a phase for him too.'

'Don't be a tourist. That's all I'm saying. It's not fair on him.'

I got to be mad at that, which was pleasant in its own way.

The fine-stemmed coral spray of the Sounds reached north as if it once had touched the other island, only to be knocked westward, out of true. Tory Channel, where the containers and the passenger ferries ran back and forth between the islands, was many miles to the east and from where I stood at the tiller I couldn't see a single craft in any direction. Even the fishing boats at Mana were out of sight now, hidden behind the island or melted flat against the diminishing coast. Wellington Harbour was invisible from this far west and there were no houses on the peninsula at all, just a dirty thread of a road that ran around the shoreline, long since swallowed by the distance and the mist of the sea. There was nothing. I couldn't even see any birds.

'I'm going to turn off the diesel,' Craig said. 'Turn those horses out to pasture for a spell.' He ducked back down the hatch and after a moment I heard a shuddering splat and then the sudden dead roar of the sea. I realized we'd been shouting. All at once the tiller lurched out of my hand and the boom swung right out over the water and the *Autumn Mist* pitched so violently that the edge of the starboard deck lapped under. A sheet of spray slammed into the windshield and hit my face. We spun like a coin and I saw the open mouth of Mana and the drunken whip of our wake, and then the sail snapped fatly and we spun back again. Craig lost his footing and fell back against the cockpit ladder. He laughed.

Craig had explained to me the concept of the sail ('You know how a plane lifts off? How a vacuum is created underneath the wing?') and the concept of the compression engine ('You know how a bike pump heats up if you pump it really fast?') but I simply couldn't hold the physics in my head. In practice I was utterly inept and growing hot with frustration as I hauled at the tiller and ducked under the boom again and again. The compass spun.

'See that?' Craig said every now and again. 'See? That's yawing, what we're doing now. And see that – how we're changing direction now? This is gybing. See how it swings? We're gybing now.' He didn't ask for the tiller. He kept low under the boom and turned his face to the sea.

Cook Strait is one of the most treacherous passages of open water in the world. The tropical bulk of the Tasman rushes in to meet head-on the fierce Antarctic rush of the Pacific, and in the narrow space between two islands the oceans vie for tidal supremacy, like two armies at a front. At French Pass, the narrow channel between d'Urville Island and the long arm of the outer Sounds, the seam between the two seas is so distinct that the water flows visibly downhill. Craig had seen it.

'Think of the whole of the Tasman trying to squeeze through that little gap. The water drops, clear as anything. I've seen boats on full throttle that can't make one bit of headway against the tide. It's amazing. It's bloody amazing. Never believed it until I saw it with my own eyes.'

He pointed out how the rat-tail threads on the mainsail showed the direction of the wind from the way they hung. Our course was about sixty degrees out and still weaving. My arm was sore.

'Tell you what,' he said. 'Sailing around d'Urville one time, just me on my own. I've got a mainsail up and that's all. Right? There I am nosing along, less than five knots probably, and then all of a sudden

Autumn Mist spun right around, like the minute hand on a clock coming round a full hour. She spins three hundred and sixty degrees, just like that, and then the wind picks her up again and she continues on. Looking back, there was only the tiniest of depressions in the water, like a fingerprint, to give any sort of clue. It was a whirlpool that spun me round.'

'Can you take the tiller?' I said. 'I think I'm going to be sick.'

'Bucket and chuck it,' Craig said. 'Get the wind on your face.'

On New Year's Eve Craig and I drove up to the dark hill above Wellington with a parcel of fish and chips and a crate of beer. We sat under the still blades of the wind turbine and as the sun went down we watched a tiny yacht tack its way right around the coast. The sky emptied over the narrow throat of the harbour. Even from the hilltop we could see whitecaps, which meant the sea was rough. The yacht blew back and forth. The slip of its sail stood out against the dark rumple of the sea.

'Hell's teeth. But still. They'll have a hell of a story if they make it,' Craig said.

'They're headed for Chaffers, anyway,' I said. 'They must be rich.'

'Too right,' Craig said.

He drank another six or seven beers and then he said, 'I'm not trying to get in your pants. That's the truth. It's just someone to talk to. Jen's got her sister. And her mum.'

There was a foam mattress in the back of his van. He slept there on the nights he was too tired to make it to the *Autumn Mist*. Behind the driver's seat was a twelve-pack of canned spaghetti, and a bulk stack of cigarette packets purchased duty-free, and a duffel bag full of underwear and socks. There were tools everywhere. It smelled of oil.

Sometime long after the faraway pop of the midnight fireworks we were both afflicted by a sudden flash of conscience and agreed that it was much too dangerous for him to drive. He always drove drunk. He'd driven drunk for years.

I remember Craig mumbling, 'I can sleep sitting up, the driver's seat is fine, it's fine,' but we just kept looking out over the ocean and he didn't move.

In the end we slept under the rough wool of his Swannie on the foam, tucked together so my head was on his shoulder and one leg was crooked up over his knee. In the morning I saw that the teeth of the Swannie zipper had left a bite mark along the bone of my arm.

The next morning was a Saturday and we were both rostered to work. My vision was bright and grainy and the skin on my face felt like sand. Craig's eyes were bloodshot and his breath was sour. He dropped me off three blocks from the store and then drove around for a while. I wasn't sober until after lunch. At afternoon smoko he waited for the other girls to stab out their cigarettes and walk away, and then when we were alone he asked me if I would like to take a trip to Mana where his boat was moored.

Olivia Hope and Ben Smart went to a New Year's party at Furneaux Lodge in Queen Charlotte Sound. The only access to the lodge is by water or over the walking tracks to the bays on either side. Sometime after midnight, they found that their accommodation plans had fallen through. It was too far, and too late, to get a water taxi back to Picton. They had been drinking. A local man offered them lodging on his yacht. (A sloop? A ketch? The detail would be crucial when both of them were dead.) When the police seized the *Blade* several weeks later the nail scratches seemed to clinch it: there had been a struggle, and someone had tried to escape. But Olivia Hope played the piano and her fingernails were always trimmed to the quick.

Furneaux Lodge is gorgeous. The cabins are weatherboard and stone and the lawns are lush. The bush comes right down to the water. It's a place for weddings. There's a pebbled beach and a wharf and the water is clear and warm.

The store manager in hardware said, 'Francie, don't you think it's bad taste? Going to Queen Charlotte, and everything. The very place. You know?'

I said, 'Come on. You can't think like that.'

'I'm just talking about respect,' he said.

The Watson counter-story was that the police had pounced too early. Their story was: Scott Watson was a dirty loner, but he was not a bad man.

Craig's patience with my helming had leached the afternoon away. With the diesel and the sail together we might have made the passage to Queen Charlotte in five hours, but without the diesel it could take as long as twelve. I realized that the light had paled. Sundown was at nine.

'See those islands?' Craig said now, pointing. 'Those two little teeth standing up out of the water there? We'll have a better view soon. They're called the Brothers.'

The Brothers were like dark chips of stone against the burnished blue of the Strait. One was taller and prouder: the elder and the heir. As we made our slow and arcing journey around them I marvelled at the deception of distance and space: the two rocks seemed to be constantly changing shape, revealing shoulders, elbows, knuckles, fusing together and then apart. The outermost fingers of the Queen Charlotte Sound slowly took a clearer shape before us. The hills were blue.

'You saw the *Endeavour* replica?' Craig said.

'Yeah. At Lyttelton though.'

'The place we're dropping anchor tonight is where Cook suffered the greatest disappointment of his lifetime,' Craig said. 'It was only when he climbed to the lookout on Arapawa Island that he saw how the Strait cleaved the two islands right through. Then he really knew the voyage was a failure. They were looking for the great southern continent. Right? The unknown southern land. It didn't exist.'

'I thought he came to record the transit of Venus.'

'Cover story,' Craig said. 'The official purpose was to look for the unknown southern continent, and claim it for the Brits.'

'Australia?'

'No. Something bigger,' Craig said. 'Some enormous land mass to balance out the top-heavy north. Something to give the world a symmetry. A kind of weight. In the beginning they thought the west coast of New Zealand was the edge of it. Not an island or a pair of islands. An edge.'

'And that's where we're headed.'

'Ship Cove,' Craig said. 'How's your stomach?'

'Empty,' I said.

The hills were darkest at the ridge. Their rims were sharp. The vivid purple faded into lightness where the hillside met the shore, so the still water seemed to give off a kind of luminosity, a haze. The winds died as the sun set and the Sound shimmered with perfect calm. Once we left the open water and entered the Sound we had to furl the mainsail and turn on the motor again.

Craig said, 'Six horses now. Not quite enough to make a herd.'

On that New Year's night above the bright lights of the city I asked him, 'Have you ever thought you might leave your wife?' I didn't mean for me. My bottle was beaded with moisture, and cold. We could no longer see the small white streak of the yacht below.

Craig said, 'My wife – my wife doesn't want an adventure. She draws a blank. Me, I'm restless. I'd rather quit a job and start again. I'd rather give the finger. And I can strike up anywhere. And – God. She's an attractive woman. You wouldn't think, to look at me. You wouldn't pick her for my wife.'

He fell silent. A bird called in the dark. Craig said, 'I don't know, Francie. How can I answer that? I left her before I even married her. There's nothing there to leave.'

'What's she doing now probably?' I said. 'Tonight, for New Year's Eve.'

'Waiting,' Craig said, and then he didn't speak again for a long time.

Night fell before we found our mooring. Like the leading lights at Mana, safe passage around the Sounds was navigable by another system of lights. Craig showed me how the nautical map of the outer

Sounds was studded with small lanterns, and beside each was a bracketed numeral in a tiny script. 'We wait for the flash and then count out the seconds,' he said. When we saw the white flare leap out of the darkness he began to count aloud until he saw the flash again. 'Thirteen,' Craig said, and consulted the map. There, on the outer edge of the slivered Arapawa Island, was a tiny lantern and the number thirteen. This meant that we could be sure that the light that we were seeing was indeed the Arapawa light, and so our position was confirmed; it also meant that the water between us and the island was clear, so if we sailed directly towards the flash we could be sure that we would not run aground.

'Think if we were *here*, and we had angled into this cove by mistake, thinking we were one bay over,' Craig said, stabbing at the map with his finger. 'We'd see the light flash, but then it wouldn't flash again because the lantern light would be obstructed by this flank here, and we wouldn't see it. Right? So we'd know we'd gone wrong somewhere. We'd retrace.'

The lights flashed, Craig said, so they could be distinguished from anchor lights, which were a constant white, and nav lights, which were a constant red and green. As we crept into Ship Cove I looked across the oily black of the water and saw a dull point of white shining out of the dark, and then another, and then a third.

'Oh, bad luck,' Craig said. 'That's bad luck. The moorings are taken. See here? Those three crosses? Show where the moorings are.'

'I definitely see three lights,' I said.

'So do I.' Craig looked back at the map at that moment and chewed his lip. He appeared older in the dark. 'Didn't think they'd be taken,' he said. 'But it's school holidays I guess. Damn.'

'Can't we share a mooring?' I said. I was holding the torch over the map for him but when I lifted it the yellow beam picked out the shrouds and they shone.

'You mean raft up,' Craig said. 'The way it's done, you shove a couple of buoys over the railing to keep from bashing together, and then you rope together tight, flank to flank.'

'Can't we do that?'

'You're only a metre apart then,' Craig said. 'With conversation and everything. It's worse than a hotel room.'

'But just to be safe.'

He rubbed at his chin with his forefinger as if he hadn't heard me. 'Plus, it's late,' he said. 'Be rude. We'd have to shout out over the water and they'd have to get up and help us motor up, to raft. No.'

'Should we go back?' I said uselessly.

'We'll motor close to the shore and drop an anchor. Hope she'll catch.'

She didn't catch. The seabed was rocky and too hard. Craig dropped thirty feet of chain and then another fifty. He said he hoped the weight of the chain would be enough. But he looked unhappy. We were thirty feet from the shore and if she dragged in the night the *Autumn Mist* would list on to the rocks.

He made stew from a can on the galley stove and scowled when I said it was good. After dinner we lit the kerosene lamp and played cribbage in the yellow light. Craig rummaged in the forward stow hole for the box of Cadbury's chocolates. He thrust it at me with a jerk and looked at the panelling above my head.

'May as well do a thing properly,' he said, which was funny, in the neglected seedy hole of the saloon, under the broken light fitting, in front of the unpainted stow holes, sitting on swabs that were stale and discoloured and patched. I didn't laugh. He watched me rip the cellophane and lift the lid.

'Turkish delight goes first in our family,' Craig said.

'With us it's the mint one,' I said.

'But we've got boys,' Craig said. 'That's a factor. Scrabble for the feed.'

I went topside to take a piss in the bucket and spit my toothpaste into the sea. When I came back down below, Craig was spreading a sleeping bag on the starboard swab. He said, 'This is for you. I'm going to watch the chain for a spell. Makes me uneasy. Thought of dragging. Couldn't sleep even if I tried.'

I fell asleep in my clothes against the sail bags and I think he must have tucked the sleeping bag around me where I was lying.

Craig was sitting in the cockpit boiling water for coffee when I woke up in the first gauze of dawn. The tide was high and the water was dull and flat. The *Autumn Mist* was hardly moving, but she rolled lazily under my weight when I climbed up the ladder out of the saloon. The ochre rocks at the water's edge showed like the rind of a fruit.

Craig moved his knees to let me past but I had to put my hand on his shoulder, for balance.

'We should have done a rolling watch,' I said. 'I feel bad.'

'You slept like a kitten. Your eyes.'

'Did the chain hold?'

'Hasn't dragged an inch. This is for coffee, if you want one.'

'Yeah. Have you slept?'

'No. Didn't mind,' Craig said. 'The stars were out. Wasn't cold.'

He was happy. He whistled a short little burst of something and then he said, 'This is what I wanted to show you. This – anyway. Here it is. Here it is. Dawn over the fiord.'

I sat down on the slats and drew my knees up to my chest and looked out over Ship Cove to the James Cook memorial and the mounted brass cannon on the shore. I could see the three moored yachts now, in the light, over the far side of the anchorage. They were all gin palaces, rich and smart, with swimming costumes pegged along the rails.

'Nothing stirred all night,' Craig said. 'They must be sleeping.'

IN THE CROSSFIRE

Ha Jin

ILLUSTRATION BY TILMAN FAELKER

The employees could tell that the company was floundering and that some of them would lose their jobs soon. For a whole morning Tian Chu stayed in his cubicle, processing invoices without a break. Even at lunchtime he avoided chatting with others at length, because the topic of layoffs unnerved him. He had worked here for only two years and might be among the first to go. Fortunately, he was already a US citizen and wouldn't be ashamed of collecting unemployment benefits, which the INS regards as something like discredit against one who applies for a green card or citizenship.

Around mid-afternoon, as he was typing, his cellphone chimed. Startled, he pulled it out of his pants pocket.

'Hello,' he said in an undertone.

'Tian, how's your day there?' came his mother's scratchy voice.

'It's all right. I told you not to call me at work. People can hear me on the phone.'

'I want to know what you'd like for dinner.'

'Don't bother about that, Mom. You don't know how to use the stove and oven and might set off the alarm again. I'll pick up something on my way home.'

'What happened to Connie? Why can't she do the shopping and cooking? You shouldn't spoil her like this.'

'She's busy, all right? I can't talk more now. See you soon.' He shut the phone and stood to see if his colleagues in the neighbouring cubicles had been listening in. Nobody seemed interested.

He sat down and massaged his eyebrows to relieve the fatigue from peering at the monitor screen. He yawned and knew his mother must feel lonely at home. She often complained that she had no friends here and there wasn't much to watch on TV. True, most of the shows were reruns and some were in Cantonese or Taiwanese, neither of which she could understand. The books Tian had checked out of the library for her were boring too. If only she could go out and chit-chat with someone. But their neighbours all went to work in the daytime, and she dared not venture out on her own, unable to read the street signs in English. This neighbourhood was too quiet, she often grumbled. It looked as if there were more houses than people. Chimneys were here and there, but none of them puffed smoke. The whole place was deserted after nine a.m., and not until mid-afternoon would she see traces of others – and then only kids getting off the school buses and padding along the sidewalks. If only she could have had a grandchild to look after, to play with. But that was out of the question, since Connie Liu, her daughter-in-law, was still attending nursing school and wanted to wait until she had finished.

It was already dark when Tian left work. The wind was tossing pedestrians' clothes and hair and stirring the surfaces of slush puddles that shimmered in the neon and the streetlights. The remaining snowbanks along the kerbs were black from auto exhaust and had begun encrusting again. Tian stopped at a supermarket in the basement of a mall and picked up a stout eggplant, a bag of spinach and a flounder. He knew that his wife would avoid going home to cook dinner because she couldn't make anything her mother-in-law would not grouch about. So these days he cooked. Sometimes his mother offered to help, but he wouldn't let her, afraid she might make something Connie couldn't eat – she was allergic to most bean products, especially to soy sauce and tofu.

The moment he got home, he went into the kitchen. He was going to cook a spinach soup, steam the eggplant and fry the flounder. As he was gouging out the gills of the fish, his mother stepped in.

'Let me give you a hand,' she said.

'I can manage. This is easy.' He smiled, cutting the fish's fins and tail with a large pair of scissors.

'You never cooked back home.' She stared at him, her eyes glinting. Ever since her arrival a week earlier, she'd been nagging him about his being henpecked. 'What's the good of standing six feet tall if you can't handle a small woman like Connie?' she often said. In fact, he was five feet ten.

He nudged the side of his bulky nose with his knuckle. 'Mom, in America, husband and wife both cook – whoever has the time. Connie is swamped with schoolwork these days, so I do more household chores. This is natural.'

'No, it's not. You were never like this before. Why did you marry her in the first place if she wouldn't take care of you?'

'You're talking like a fuddy-duddy.' He patted the flatfish on a paper towel to make it splutter less in the hot corn oil.

She went on, 'Both your dad and I told you not to rush to marry her, but you were too bewitched to listen. We thought you must've got her in trouble and had to give her a wedding band. Look, now you're trapped and have to work both inside and outside the house.'

He didn't reply; his longish face stiffened. He disliked the way she spoke about his wife. In fact, prior to his mother's arrival, Connie had always come home early to make dinner. She would also wrap lunch for him early in the morning. These days, however, she'd leave the moment she finished breakfast and wouldn't return until evening. Both of them had agreed that she should avoid staying home alone with his mother, who was lecturing her at every possible opportunity.

Around six-thirty his wife came back. She hung her parka in the closet; stepping into the kitchen, she said to Tian, 'Can I help?'

'I'm almost done.'

She kissed his nape and whispered, 'Thanks for doing this.' Then she took some plates and bowls out of the cupboard and carried them to the dining table. She glanced into the living room, where Meifen, her mother-in-law, lounged on a sofa, smoking a cigarette and watching the news aired by New Tang Dynasty TV, a remote control in her leathery hand. How many times Connie and Tian had told her not to smoke in here, but the old woman had ignored them. They dared not confront her. This was just her second week here. Imagine, she was going to stay half a year!

'Mother, come and eat,' Connie said pleasantly when the table was set.

'Sure.' Meifen clicked off the TV, got to her feet and stubbed out her cigarette in a saucer serving as an ashtray.

The family sat down to dinner. The two women seldom spoke to each other at the table, so it was up to Tian to make conversation. He mentioned that people in his company had been talking about layoffs. That didn't interest his mother or his wife; probably they both believed his job was secure because of his degree in accountancy.

His mother grunted, 'I don't like this fish, flavourless like egg white.' She often complained that nothing here tasted right.

'It takes a while to get used to American food,' Tian told her. 'When I came, I couldn't eat vegetables in the first week, so I ate mainly bananas and oranges.' That was long ago, twelve years exactly.

'True,' Connie agreed. 'I remember how rubbery bell peppers tasted to me in the beginning. I was amazed—'

'I mean this fish needs soy sauce, and so does the soup,' Meifen interrupted.

'Mom, Connie's allergic to that, I told you.'

'Just spoiled,' Meifen muttered. 'You have a bottle of Golden Orchid soy sauce in the cabinet. That's a brand-name product and I can't see how on earth it can hurt anyone's health.'

Connie's oval face fell, her eyes glaring at the old woman and then at Tian. He said, 'Mom, you don't understand. Connie has a medical condition that—'

'Of course I know. I used to teach chemistry in a middle school. Don't treat me like an ignorant crone. Ours is an intellectual family.'

'You're talking like an old fogey again. In America people don't think much of an intellectual family and most kids here can go to college if they want to.'

'She's hinting at my family,' Connie broke in, and turned to face her mother-in-law. 'True enough, neither of my parents went to college, but they're honest and hard-working. I'm proud of them.'

'That explains why you're such an irresponsible wife,' Meifen said matter-of-factly.

'Do you imply I'm not good enough for your son?'

'Please, let's have a peaceful dinner,' Tian pleaded.

Meifen went on speaking to Connie. 'So far you've been awful. I don't know how your parents raised you. Maybe they were too lazy or too ignorant to teach you anything.'

'Watch it – you mustn't bad-mouth my parents!'

'I can say whatever I want to in my son's home. You married Tian but refuse to give him children, won't cook or do household work. What kind of wife are you? Worse yet, you even make him do your laundry.'

'Mom,' Tian said again, 'I told you we'll have kids after Connie gets her degree.'

'Believe me, she'll never finish school. She just wants to use you, giving you one excuse after another.'

'I can't take this any more.' Connie stood and carried her bowl of soup upstairs to the master bedroom.

Tian sighed, again rattled by the exchange between the two women. If only he could make them shut up, but neither of them would give ground. His mother went on, 'I told you not to break with Mansu, but you wouldn't listen. Look what a millstone you've got on your back.'

Mansu was Tian's ex-girlfriend and they'd broken up many years before, but somehow the woman had kept visiting his parents back in Harbin.

'Mom, don't bring that up again,' he begged.

'You don't have to listen to me if you don't like it.'

'Do you mean to destroy my marriage?'

At last Meifen fell silent. Tian heard his wife sniffling upstairs. He wasn't sure whether he should remain at the dining table or go join Connie. If he stayed with his mother, his wife would take him to task later on. But if he went to Connie, Meifen would berate him, saying he was spineless and daft. She used to teach him that a man could divorce his wife and marry another woman any time whereas he could never disown his mother. In Meifen's words, 'You can always trust me, because you're part of my flesh and blood and I'll never betray you.'

Tian took his plate, half-loaded with rice and eggplant and a chunk of the fish, and went into the kitchen, where he perched on a stool and resumed eating. If only he'd thought twice before writing his mother the invitation letter needed for her visa. The old woman must still bear a grudge against him and Connie for not agreeing to sponsor his nephew, his sister's son, who was eager to go to Toronto for college. Perhaps that was another reason Meifen wanted to wreak havoc here.

Since his mother's arrival, Tian and his wife had slept in different rooms. That night he again stayed in the study, sleeping on a pull-out couch. He didn't go upstairs to say goodnight to Connie, afraid she'd demand that he send the old woman back to China right away. Also, if he shared the bed with Connie, Meifen would lecture him the next day, saying he must be careful about his health and mustn't indulge in sex. He'd heard her litany too often: some women were vampires determined to suck their men dry; this world had gone to seed – nowadays fewer and fewer young people were willing to become parents, and all avoided responsibilities; it was capitalism that corrupted people's souls and made them greedier and more selfish. Oh, how long-winded she could become! Just the thought of her prattling would set Tian's head reeling.

Before leaving for work the next morning, he drew a map of the nearby streets for his mother and urged her to go out some so that she might feel less lonesome – 'stir-crazy' was actually the expression that came to his mouth, but he didn't let it out. She might like some of the shops downtown and could buy something with the eighty dollars he'd just given her. 'Don't be afraid of getting lost,' he assured her. She should be able to find her way back as long as she had the address he'd written down for her – someone could give her directions.

At work Tian drank a lot of coffee to keep himself awake. His scalp was numb and his eyes heavy and throbbing a little as he was crunching numbers. If only he could have slept two or three more hours a day. Ever since his mother had come, he'd suffered from sleep deprivation. He'd wake up before daybreak, missing the warmth of Connie's smooth skin and their wide bed, but he dared not enter the master bedroom. He was certain she wouldn't let him snuggle under the comforter or touch her. She always gave the excuse that her head would go numb and muddled in class if they had sex early in the morning. That day at work, despite the strong coffee he'd been drinking, Tian couldn't help yawning and had to take care not to drop off.

Towards mid-morning Bill Nangy, the manager of the company, stepped into the large, low-ceilinged room and went up to Tracy Malloy, whose cubicle was next to Tian's. 'Tracy,' Bill said, 'can I speak to you in my office a minute?'

All eyes turned to plump Tracy as she walked away with their boss, her head bowed a little. The second she disappeared past the door, half a dozen people stood up in their cubicles, some grinning while others shook their heads. Tracy had started working here long before Tian. He liked her, a good-natured thirty-something, though she talked too much. Others had warned her to keep her mouth shut at work, but she'd never mended her ways.

A few minutes later Tracy came out, scratching the back of her ear, and forced a smile. 'Got the axe,' she told her colleagues, her eyes red and watery. She slouched into her cubicle to gather her belongings.

'It's a shame,' Tian said to her, and rested his elbow on top of the chest-high wall, making one of his sloping shoulders higher than the other.

'I knew this was coming,' she muttered. 'Bill allowed me to stay another week, but I won't. Just sick of it.'

'Don't be too upset. I'm sure more of us will go.'

'Probably. Bill said there'll be more layoffs.'

'I'll be the next, I guess.'

'Don't jinx yourself, Tian.'

Tracy put her eyeglass case beside her coffee cup. She didn't have much stuff – a few photos of her niece and nephews and of a Himalayan cat named Daffie, a half-used pack of chewing gum, a pocket hairbrush, a compact, a romance novel, a small Ziploc bag containing rubber bands, ballpoints, Post-its, dental floss, a chap stick. Tian turned his eyes away as though the pile of her belongings, not enough to fill her tote bag, upset him more than her dismissal.

As Tracy was leaving, more people got up and some spoke to her. 'Terribly sorry, Tracy.' 'Take care.' 'Good luck.' 'Keep in touch, Tracy.' Some of the voices actually sounded relieved and even cheerful. Tracy shook hands with a few and waved at the rest while mouthing 'Thank you.'

The second she went out the door, George, an orange-haired man who always wore a necktie at work, said, 'This is it,' as if to assure everyone that they were all safe.

'I don't think so. More of us will get canned,' Tian said gloomily.

Someone cackled, as if Tian had cracked a joke. He didn't laugh or say another word. He sat down and tapped the space bar on the keyboard to bring the monitor back to life.

'Oh, I never thought Flushing was such a convenient place, like a big county seat back home,' his mother said to him that evening. She had gone downtown in the morning and had a wonderful time there. She tried some beef and lamb kebabs at a street corner and ate a tiny steamer of buns stuffed with chives, lean pork and crabmeat at a Shanghai restaurant. She also bought a bag of mung bean noodles for only a dollar twenty. 'Really cheap,' she said. 'Now I believe it's true that all China's best stuff is in the US.'

Tian smiled without speaking. He stowed her purchase in the cabinet under the sink because Connie couldn't eat bean noodles. He put a pot of water on the stove and was going to make rice porridge for dinner.

From that day on, Meifen often went out during the day and reported to Tian on her adventures. Before he left for work in the morning, he'd make sure she had enough pocket money. Gradually Meifen got to know people. Some of them were also from the north-east of China and were happy to converse with her, especially those who frequented the eateries that specialized in Mandarin cuisine – pies, pancakes, sauerkraut, sausages, grilled meats, moo shu, noodles and dumplings. In a small park she ran into some old women pushing their grandchildren in strollers. She chatted with them, and one woman had lived here for more than a decade and wouldn't go back to Wuhan City any more because all her children and grandchildren were in North America now. How Meifen envied those old grandmas, she told Tian, especially the one who had twin grandkids. If only she could live a life such as theirs.

'You'll need a green card to stay here long enough to see my babies,' Tian once told his mother jokingly.

'You'll get me a green card, won't you?' she asked.

Well, that was not easy, and he wouldn't promise her. She hadn't been here for three weeks yet, but already his family was kind of dysfunctional. How simple-minded he and Connie had been when they encouraged Meifen to apply for a half-year visa. They should have limited her visit to two months or even less. That way, if she became too much of a pain in the ass, they could say it was impossible to get her visa extended and she'd have no choice but to go back. Now there'd be twenty-three more weeks for them to endure. How awful!

The other day Tian and Connie had talked between themselves about the situation. She said, 'Well, I'll take these months as a penal term. After half a year, when the old deity has left, I hope I'll have survived the time undamaged and our union will remain unbroken.' She gave a hysterical laugh, which unsettled Tian, and he wouldn't joke with her about their predicament any more. All he could say was, 'I'm sorry, really sorry.' Yet he wouldn't speak ill of his mother in front of his wife.

As Connie spent more time away from home, Tian often wondered what his wife was doing during the day. Judging from her appearance, she seemed at ease and just meant to avoid rubbing elbows with his mother. In a way, Tian appreciated that. Connie used to be a good helpmate by all accounts, but the old woman's presence here had transformed her. Then, who wouldn't have changed, given the circumstances? So he ought to feel for his wife.

One evening, as he was clearing the table while Connie was doing the dishes in the kitchen, his mother said, 'I ran into a fellow townswoman today and we had a wonderful chat. I invited her to dinner tomorrow.'

'Where are you going to take her?' Tian asked.

'Here. I told her you'd pick her up with your car.'

Connie, having overheard their conversation, came in holding a dishtowel and grinning at Tian. Her bell cheeks were pink while her eyes twinkled naughtily. Again Tian was amazed by her charming face. She was a looker, six years younger than he. He was unhappy about Meifen's inviting a guest without telling him in advance, but before he could speak Connie began, 'Mother, there'll be a snowstorm tomorrow – Tian can't drive in the bad weather.'

'I saw it on TV,' Meifen said. 'It will be just six or seven inches, no big deal. People even bike in snow back home.'

Tian told her, 'It's not whether I can pick up your friend or not, Mom. You should've spoken to me before you invited anyone. I'm busy all the time and must make sure my calendar allows it.'

'You don't need to do anything,' Meifen said. 'Leave it to me. I'll do the shopping and cooking tomorrow.'

'Mom, you don't get it. This is my home and you shouldn't interfere with my schedule.'

'What did you say? Sure, this is your home, but who are you? You're my son, aren't you!'

Seeing a smirk cross his wife's face, Tian asked his mother, 'You mean you own me and my home?'

'How can I ever disown you? Your home should also be mine, no? Oh heavens, I never thought my son could be so selfish. Once he has his bride, he wants to disown his mother!'

'You're unreasonable,' he said.

'And you're heartless.'

'This is ridiculous!' He turned and ambled out of the dining room.

Connie put in, 'Mother, just think about it, what if Tian already has another engagement tomorrow?'

'Like I said, he won't have to be around if he has something else to do. Besides, he doesn't work on Saturdays.'

'Still, he'll have to drive to pick up your friend.'

'How about you? Can't you do that?'

'I don't have a driver's licence yet.'

'Why not? You cannot let Tian do everything in this household. You must do your share.'

Seeing this was getting nowhere, Connie dropped the dishtowel on the dining table and went to the living room to talk with Tian.

However, Tian wouldn't discuss the invitation with Connie, knowing his mother was eavesdropping on them. Meifen, already sixty-four, still had sharp ears and eyesight. Tian grimaced at his wife and sighed. 'I guess we'll have to do the party tomorrow.'

She nodded. 'I'll stay home and give you a hand.'

It snowed on and off for a whole day. The roofs in the neighbourhood blurred and lost their unkempt features, and the snow rendered all the trees and hedges fluffy. It looked clean everywhere and even the air smelled fresher. Trucks passed by, giving out warning signals while ploughing snow or spraying salt. A bunch of children were sledding on a slope, whooping lustily, and some lay supine on the sleds as they dashed down. Another pack of them were hurling snowballs at each other and shouting war cries. Tian, amused, watched them through a window. He had dissuaded his mother from giving a multiple-course dinner, saying that here food was plentiful and one could eat fish and meat quite often. Most times it was for conversation and a warm atmosphere that people went to dinner. His mother agreed to make dumplings in addition to a few cold dishes. Actually, they didn't start wrapping the dumplings when the stuffing and the dough were ready, because Meifen wanted to have her friend participate in preparing the dinner, to make the occasion somewhat like a family gathering.

Towards evening it resumed snowing. Tian drove to Corona to fetch the guest, Shulan, and his mother went with him, sitting in the passenger seat. The heat was on full blast while the wipers were busy sweeping the windshield; even so, the glass frosted in spots from outside and fogged from inside. Time and again Tian mopped the moisture off the glass with a pair of felt gloves, but the visibility didn't improve much. 'See what I mean?' he said to his mother. 'It's dangerous to drive in such weather.'

She made no reply, staring ahead, her beaky face as rigid as if frozen and the skin under her chin hanging in wattles. Fortunately Shulan's place was easy to find. The woman lived in an ugly tenement, about a dozen storeys high and with narrow windows. She was waiting for them in the footworn lobby when they arrived. She looked familiar to Tian. Then he recognized her – this scrawny person in a dark blue overcoat was nobody but a saleswoman at the nameless snack joint on Main Street, near the subway station. He had encountered her numerous times when he went there to buy scallion pancakes or sautéed rice noodles or pork buns for lunch. He vividly remembered her red face bathed in perspiration during the dog days when she wore a white hat, busy selling food to passers-by. That place was nothing but a flimsy lean-to, open to waves of heat and gusts of wind. In winter there was no need for a heater in the room because the stoves were hot and the pots sent up steam all the time, but in summer only a small fan whirred back and forth overhead. When customers were few, the salespeople would participate in making snacks, so everybody in there was a cook of sorts. Whenever Tian chanced on this middle-aged Shulan, he'd wonder what kind of tough life she must have been living.

What vitality, what endurance and what sacrifice must have suffused her personal story? How often he'd been amazed by her rustic but energetic face furrowed by lines that curved from the wings of her nose to the corners of her broad mouth. Now he was moved, eager to know more about this fellow townswoman. He was glad that his mother had invited her.

'Where's your daughter, Shulan?' Meifen asked, still holding her friend's chapped hand.

'She's upstairs doing a school project.'

'Go get her. Let her come with us. Too much brainwork will spoil the girl's looks.'

Tian said, 'Please bring her along, Aunt.'

'All right, I'll be back in a minute.' Shulan went over to the elevator. From the rear she looked smaller than when she stood behind the food stand.

Tian and Meifen sat down on the lone bench in the lobby. She explained that Shulan's husband had come to the States seven years before, but had disappeared a year later. Nobody was sure of his whereabouts, though rumour had it that he was in Houston, manning a gift shop and living with a young woman. By now Shulan was no longer troubled by his absence from home. She felt he had merely used her as his cook and bed warmer, so she could manage without him.

'Mom, you were right to invite her,' Tian said sincerely.

Meifen smiled without comment.

A few minutes later Shulan came down with her daughter, a reedy, anaemic fifteen-year-old wearing circular glasses and a chequered mackinaw that was too big on her. The girl looked unhappy and climbed into the car silently. As Tian drove away, he reminded the guests in the back to buckle up. Meanwhile, the snow abated some, but the flakes were still swirling around the street lights and fluttering outside glowing windows. An ambulance howled, its strobe slashing the darkness. Tian pulled aside to let the white van pass, then resumed driving.

Tian and Connie's home impressed Shulan as Meifen gave her a tour through the two floors and the finished basement. The woman kept saying in a sing-song voice, 'This is a real piece of property, so close to downtown.' Her daughter, Ching, didn't follow the grown-ups but stayed in the living room fingering the piano, a Steinway, which Tian had bought for Connie at a clearance sale. The girl had learned how to play the instrument before coming to the United Sates, though she could tickle out only a few simple tunes, such as 'Jingle Bells', 'Yankee Doodle Dandy', and 'The Newspaper Boy Song'. Even those sounded hesitant and disjointed. She stopped when her mother came back and told her not to embarrass both of them with her 'clumsy fingers' any more. The girl then sat before the TV, watching a well-known historian speaking about the recent Orange Revolution in Ukraine and its impact on the last few Communist countries. Soon the four grown-ups began wrapping dumplings. Tian used a beer bottle to press the dough, having no rolling pin in the house. He was skilled but couldn't make wrappers fast enough for the three women, so Connie found a lean hot-sauce bottle and helped him with the dough from time to time. Meifen was unhappy about the lack of a real rolling pin and grumbled, 'What kind of life you two have been living! You have no plan for a decent home.'

Connie wouldn't talk back, just picked up a wrapper and filled it with a dollop of the stuffing seasoned with sesame oil and five-spice powder.

Shulan said, 'If I lived so close to downtown, I wouldn't cook at all and would have no need for a rolling pin either.' She kept smiling, her front teeth propping up her top lip a bit.

'Your place's pot stickers are delicious,' Tian said to her to change the subject.

'I prepare the filling every day. Meifen, next time you stop by, you should try it. It tastes real good.'

'Sure thing,' Meifen said. 'Did you already know how to make those snacks back home?'

'No way, I learned how to do that here. My boss used to be a hotel chef in Hangzhou.'

'You must've gone through lots of hardships.'

'I wouldn't complain. Life here is no picnic and most people work very hard.'

Tian smiled quizzically, then said, 'My dad retired at fifty-eight with a full pension. Every morning he carries a pair of goldfinches in a cage to the banks of the Songhua. Old people are having an easy time back home.'

'Not every one of them,' his mother corrected him. 'Your father enjoys some leisure only because he joined the Revolution early in his youth. He's entitled to his pension and free medical care.'

'Matter of fact,' Shulan said, 'most folks are as poor as before in my old neighbourhood. I have to send my parents money every two months.'

'They don't have a pension?' Meifen asked.

'They do, but my mother suffers from gout and high blood pressure. My father lost most of his teeth and needed new dentures. Nowadays folks can't afford to be sick any more.'

'That's true,' Tian agreed. 'Most people are the have-nots.'

The stout kettle whistled in the kitchen and it was time to boil the dumplings. Connie left to set the pot on, her waist-length hair swaying a little as she walked away.

'You have a nice and pretty daughter-in-law,' Shulan said to Meifen. 'You're a lucky woman, Elder Sister.'

'You don't know what a devil of a temper she has.'

'Mom, don't start again,' Tian begged.

'See, Shulan,' Meifen whispered, 'my son always sides with his bride. The little fox spirit really knows how to charm her man.'

'This is unfair, Mom,' her son objected.

Both women laughed and turned away to wash their hands.

Ten minutes later Tian went into the living room and called Ching to come over to the table, on which, besides the steaming dumplings, were plates of smoked mackerel, roast duck, cucumber and tomato salad, and spiced bamboo shoots. When they were all seated with Meifen at the head of the rectangular table, Tian poured plum wine for Shulan and his mother. He and Connie and Ching would drink beer.

The two older women continued reminiscing about the people they both knew. To Tian's amazement, the girl swigged her glass of beer as if it were a soft drink. Then he remembered she had spent her childhood in Harbin, where even children were beer drinkers. He spoke English with her and asked her what classes she'd been taking at school. The girl seemed too introverted to volunteer any information and just answered each question in two or three words. She confessed that she hated the Sunday class, in which she had to copy the Chinese characters and memorize them.

Shulan mentioned a man nicknamed Turtle Baron, the owner of a fishery outside Harbin.

'Oh, I knew of him,' Meifen said. 'He used to drive a fancy car to the shopping district every day, but he lost his fortune.'

'What happened?' Shulan asked.

'He fed drugs to crayfish so they grew big and fierce. But some Hong Kong tourists got food-poisoned and took him to court.'

'He was a wild man, but a filial son, blowing big money on his mother's birthdays. Where's he now?'

'In jail,' Meifen said.

'Obviously that was where he was headed. The other day I met a fellow who had just come out of the mainland. He said he wouldn't eat street food back home any more, because he couldn't tell what he was actually eating. Some people even make fake eggs and fake salt. It's mind-boggling. How can anyone turn a profit by doing that, considering the labour?'

They all cracked up except for the girl.

Sprinkling a spoonful of vinegar on the three dumplings on her plate, Shulan continued, 'People ought to believe in Jesus Christ. That'll make them behave better, less like animals.'

'Do you often go to church?' Meifen asked, chewing the tip of a duck wing.

'Yes, every Sunday. It makes me feel calm and hopeful. I used to hate my husband's bone marrow, but now I don't hate him any more. God will deal with him on my behalf.'

Ching listened to her mother without showing any emotion, as if Shulan were speaking about a stranger.

Meifen said, 'Maybe I should visit your church one of these days.'

'Please do. Let me know when you want to come. I'll introduce you to Brother Zhou, our pastor. He's a true gentleman. I've never met a man so kind. He used to be a doctor in Chengdu and still gives medical advice. He cured my stomach ulcer.'

Connie, eating focaccia bread instead of the dumplings that contained soy sauce, said under her breath, 'Ching, do you have a boyfriend?'

Before the girl could answer, her mother cut in, pointing her chopsticks at her daughter, 'I won't let her. It's just a waste of time to have a boyfriend so early. She'd better concentrate on her schoolwork.'

Ching said to Connie in English, 'See what a bitch my mom is? She's afraid I'll go boy-crazy like her when she was young.' The girl's eyes flashed behind the lenses of her black-framed glasses.

Both Connie and Tian giggled while the two older women were bewildered, looking at them enquiringly.

Tian told them, 'Ching's so funny.'

'Also tricky and headstrong,' added her mother.

When dinner was over, Shulan was eager to leave without having tea. She said she'd forgotten to sprinkle water on the bean sprouts in her apartment, where the radiators were too hot and might shrivel the young vegetables, which she raised and would sell to a grocery store. Before they left, Connie gave the girl a book and assured her, 'This is a very funny novel. I've just finished it and you'll like it.'

Tian glanced at the title – *The Catcher in the Rye* – as Meifen asked, 'What's it about?'

'A boy left school and goofed around in New York,' Connie answered.

'So he's a dropout?'

'Kind of.'

'Why give Ching such a book? It can be a bad influence. Do you mean to teach her to rebel against her mother?'

'It's a good book!' Connie spat out.

Tian said to the guests, 'Let's go.'

The moment they stepped out the door, he overheard his mother growl at Connie, 'Don't play the scholar with me! Don't ever talk back to me in front of others!'

'You were wrong about the book,' Connie countered.

Their exchange unsettled Tian, who knew they would bicker more when he was away. It got windy, the road iced over. He drove slowly. Before every lighted intersection he placed his foot on the brake pedal to make sure he could stop the car fully if the light turned red. Ching was in the back dozing away while her mother in the passenger seat chatted to Tian without pause. She praised Meifen as an educated woman who gave no airs. How fortunate Tian must feel to have such a clear-headed and warm-hearted mother, in addition to a beautiful, well-educated wife. Her words made Tian's molars itch and he wanted to tell her to shut her trap, but he checked himself. He still felt for this woman. Somehow he couldn't drive from his mind her image behind the food stand, her face steaming with sweat and her eyes downcast in front of customers while her knotted hands were packing snacks into Styrofoam boxes.

He dropped Shulan and Ching at their building and turned back. After he exited the highway and as he was entering College Point Boulevard, a police cruiser suddenly rushed out of a narrow street and slid towards him from the side. Tian slammed on the brakes, but the heads of the two cars collided with a bang; his Volkswagen, much lighter than the bulky Ford, was thrown aside and fishtailed a few times before it stopped. Tian's head had hit the door window, his ears buzzing, though he was still alert.

A black policeman hopped out of the cruiser and hurried over. 'Hey, man, are you okay?' he cried, and knocked on Tian's windshield.

Tian opened his door and nodded. 'I didn't see you, sorry about this, Officer.' He clambered out.

'I'm sorry, man.' Somehow the squarish cop chuckled. 'I hit you. I couldn't stop my car – the road is too damned slippery.'

Tian walked around and looked at the head of his sedan. The glass covers of the headlight and the blinker were smashed, but somehow all the lights were still on. A dent the size of a football warped the fender. 'Well, what should I do?' he wondered aloud.

The man grinned. 'It's my fault. My car slid into the traffic. How about this – I give you a hundred bucks and you won't file a report?'

Tian peered at the officer's cat-like face and realized that the man was actually quite anxious – maybe he was new here. 'Okay,' Tian said, despite knowing that the amount might not cover the repairs.

'You're a good guy.' The policeman pulled five twenties out of his billfold. 'Here you are. I appreciate it.'

Tian took the money and stepped into his car. The officer shouted, 'God bless you!' as Tian drove away. He listened closely to his car, which sounded noisier than before. He hoped there was no inner damage. On the other hand, this was an old car, worth less than a thousand dollars. He shouldn't worry too much about the dent.

The instant he stepped into his house, he heard his mother yell, 'Oh yeah? How much have you paid for this house? This is my son's home and you should be grateful that Tian has let you live here.'

'This is my home too,' Connie fired back. 'You're merely our guest, a visitor.'

Heavens, they'd never stop fighting! Tian rushed into the living room and shouted, 'You two be quiet!'

But Connie turned to him and said sharply, 'Tell your mother, I'm a co-owner of this house.'

That was true, yet his mother also knew that Connie hadn't paid a cent for it. Tian had added her name as a co-buyer because he wanted her to keep the home if something fatal happened to him.

His mother snarled at Connie, 'Shameless, a typical ingrate from un upstart's family!'

'Don't you dare run down my dad! He makes an honest living.'

Indeed, her father in Tianjin City was just scraping by with his used-furniture business.

'Knock it off, both of you!' Tian roared again. 'I just had an accident. Our car was damaged, hit by a cop.'

Even that didn't impress the women. Connie cried at Meifen, 'See, I told you there'd be a snowstorm, but you were too vain to cancel the dinner. Did you mean to have your son killed?'

'It was all my fault, huh? Why didn't you learn how to drive? What have you been doing all these years?'

'I've never met someone so irrational.'

'I don't know anyone as rude and as brazen as you.'

'Damn it, I just had an accident!' Tian shouted again.

His wife looked him up and down. 'I can see you're all right. It's an old car anyway. Let's face the real issue here: I cannot live under the same roof with this woman. If she doesn't leave, I will and I'll never come back.' She marched away to her own room upstairs.

As Tian was wondering whether he should follow her, his mother said, 'If you're still my son, you must divorce her. Do it next week. She's a sick, finicky woman and will give you weak kids.'

'You're crazy too!' he growled.

He stomped away and shut the door of the study, in which he was to spend that night trying to figure out how to prevent Connie from leaving him. He would lose his mind if that happened, he was sure.

On Monday morning Tian went to Bill Nangy's office. The manager looked puzzled when Tian sat down in front of him. 'Well, what can I do for you, Tian?' Bill asked in an amiable voice. He waved his large hand over the steaming coffee his secretary, Jackie, had just put on the desk. His florid face relaxed some as he saw Tian still in a gentle mood.

Tian said, 'I know our company has been laying off people. Can you let me go, like Tracy Malloy?' He looked his boss full in the face.

'Are you telling me you got an offer from elsewhere?'

'No. In fact, I will appreciate it if you can write me a good recommendation. I'll have to look for a job soon.'

'Then why do you want to leave us?'

'For family reasons.'

'Well, what can I say, Tian? You've done a crack job here, but if that's what you want, we can let you go. Keep in mind, you're not among those we plan to discharge. We'll pay you an extra month's salary and I hope that will tide you over until you find something.'

'Thanks very much.'

Tian liked his job but never felt attached to the company. He was pretty sure that he could find similar work elsewhere but might not get paid as much as he made now. Yet this was a step he must take. Before the noon break Jackie put a letter of recommendation on Tian's desk, together with a card from his boss that wished him good luck.

Tian's departure was a quiet affair, unnoticed by others. He was reluctant to talk about it, afraid he might have to explain why he had quit. He ate lunch and crunched some potato chips in the lounge with his colleagues as though he'd resume working in the afternoon, but before the break was over, he walked out with his stuffed bag and without saying goodbye to anyone.

He didn't go home directly. Instead, he went to a KTV joint and had a few drinks – a lager, a martini, a rye whiskey on the rocks. A young woman, heavily made up and with her hair bleached blonde, slid her hips on to the bar stool beside him. He ordered her a daiquiri but was too glum to converse with her. Meanwhile, two other men were chattering about Uncle Benshan, the most popular comedian in China, who was coming to visit New York, but the tickets for his show were too expensive for the local immigrants – as a result, his sponsors had been calling around to drum up an audience for him. When the woman placed her thin hand on Tian's forearm and suggested they spend some time in a private room where she could cheer him up, he declined, saying he had to attend a meeting.

Afterwards, he roamed downtown for a while, then went to a pedicure place to have his feet bathed and scraped. Not until the streets turned noisier and the sky darkened to indigo did he head home. But today he returned without any groceries. He went to bed directly and drew the comforter up to his chin. When his mother came in and asked what he'd like for dinner, he merely grunted, 'Whatever.'

'Are you ill?' She felt his forehead.

'Leave me alone,' he groaned.

'You're burning hot. What happened?'

Without answering, he pulled the comforter over his head. If only he could sleep a few days in a row. He felt sorry for himself and sick of everything.

Around six his wife came back. The two women talked in the living room. Tian overheard the words 'drunk', 'so gruff', 'terrible'. Then his mother whined, 'Something is wrong. He looks like he's in a daze.'

A few moments later Connie came in and patted his chest. He sat up slowly. 'What happened?' she asked.

'I got fired.'

'What? They didn't tell you anything beforehand?'

'No. They've been issuing pink slips right and left.'

'But they should've given you a warning or something, shouldn't they?'

'Come on, this is America. People lose jobs all the time.'

'What are you going to do?'

'I've no clue, I'm so tired.'

They continued talking for a while. Then he got out of bed and together they went up to Meifen in the living room. His mother started weeping after hearing the bad news, while he sprawled on a sofa, his face vacant. She asked, 'So you have no job any more?' He grimaced without answering. She went on, 'What does this mean? You won't have any income from now on?'

'No. We might lose the house, the car, the TV, everything. I might not even have the money for the plane fare for your return trip.'

His mother shuffled away to the bathroom, wiping her eyes. Connie observed him as if in disbelief. Then she smiled, showing her tiny, well-kept teeth, and asked in an undertone, 'Do you think I should look for a job?'

'Sure,' he whispered. 'But I shouldn't work for the time being. You know what I mean?' He winked at her, thin rays fanning out at the corners of his eyes.

She nodded and took the hint. Then she went into the kitchen to cook dinner. She treated her mother-in-law politely at the table that evening and kept sighing, saying this disaster would ruin their life. It looked like Tian and she might have to file for Chapter Eleven if neither of them could land a job soon.

Meifen was shaken and could hardly eat anything. After dinner, they didn't leave the table. Connie brewed tea and they resumed talking. Tian complained that he hadn't been able to stay on top of his job because his wife and his mother quarrelled all the time. That was the root of his trouble and made him too frazzled to focus on anything. In fact, he had felt the disaster befalling him and mentioned it to them several times, but they'd paid no attention.

'Can you find another job?' his mother asked.

'Unlikely. There're more accountants than pets in New York – this is the world's financial centre. Probably Connie can find work before I can.'

'I won't do that until I finish my training,' his wife said, poker-faced.

'Please, do it as a favour for me,' Meifen begged her.

'No, I want to finish nursing school first. I still have two months to go.'

'You'll just let this family go to pieces without lifting a finger to help?' her mother-in-law asked.

'Don't question me like that. You've been damaging this family ever since you came.' Connie glanced at Tian, who showed no response. She went on, 'Now your son's career is headed for a dead end. Who's to blame but yourself?'

'Is that true, Tian?' his mother asked. 'I mean, your career's over?'

'Sort of. I'll have to figure out how to restart.'

Meifen heaved a deep sigh. 'I told your sister I shouldn't come to America, but she was greedy and wanted me to get you to finance her son's college in Canada. She even managed to have the boy's last name changed to Chu so he could appear as your son on the papers. Now it's over. I'll call her and your father tomorrow morning and let them know I'm heading back.'

Connie peered at Tian's face, which remained wooden. He stood and said, 'I'm dog tired.' He left for the study.

Meifen wrapped Connie's hand in both of hers and begged, 'Please help him survive this crisis! Don't you love him? Believe me, he'll do everything to make you happy if you help him get on his feet again. Connie, you're my good daughter-in-law, please do something to save your family!'

'Well, I can't promise anything. I've never been on the job market before.'

Tian smiled and shook his head as he was listening in on them from the study. He was sure that his wife knew how to seize this opportunity to send his mother home.

For a whole week Tian stayed in while Connie called around and went out job hunting. She had several interviews. It wasn't hard for her to find work since she was already a capable nurse. The following Wednesday a hospital in Manhattan offered her a position that paid well, plus full benefits, and she persuaded the manager to postpone her start for a week. She showed the letter of the job offer to her husband and mother-in-law.

'Gosh,' Tian said, 'you'll make more than I ever can.'

Meifen perused the sheet of paper. Despite not understanding a word, she saw the figure $36. She asked in amazement, 'Connie, does this mean they'll pay you thirty-six dollars an hours?'

'Yes, but I'm not sure if I should take the job.'

'Don't you want to save this home?'

'This house doesn't feel like a home to me any more.'

'How can you be so cold-hearted while your husband is in hot water?'

'You made me and Tian always takes your side. So this house is no longer my home. Let the bank repossess it – I could care less.'

Tian said nothing and just gazed at the off-white wall where a painting of a cloudy landscape dotted with fishing boats and flying cranes hung. His mother started sobbing again. He sighed and glanced at his wife. He knew Connie must have accepted the job. 'Mom,' he said, 'you came at a bad time. See, I can't make you live comfortably here any more. Who knows what will happen to me if things don't improve. I might jump in front of a train or drive into the ocean.'

'Please don't think like that! You two must join hands and survive this blow.'

'I've lost heart after going through so much. This blow finished me off and I may never recover.'

'Son, please pull yourself together and put up a fight.'

'I'm just too heartsick to give a damn.'

Connie butted in, 'Mother, how about this? You go back to China next week and let Tian and me concentrate on the trouble here.'

'So I'm your big distraction, huh?'

'Yes, Mom,' Tian said. 'You two fought and fought and fought, and that made my life unbearable. I was completely stupefied and couldn't perform well at work. That's why they terminated me.'

'All right, I'll go next week, leave you two alone, but you must give me some money. I can't go back empty-handed, or our neighbours will laugh at me.' Her lips quivered as she spoke, her mouth as sunken as if she were toothless.

'I'll give you two thousand dollars,' Connie said. 'Once I start working, I'll send you more. Don't worry about the gifts for the relatives and your friends. We'll buy you some small pieces of jewellery and a couple packs of Wisconsin ginseng.'

'How about a pound of vegetable caterpillars? That will help Tian's father's bad kidneys.'

'That costs five thousand dollars! You can get them a lot cheaper in China. Tell you what, I can buy you five pounds of dried sea cucumbers, the Japanese type. That will help improve my father-in-law's health too.'

Meifen agreed, reluctantly – the sea cucumbers were at most three hundred dollars a pound. Yet her son's situation terrified her. If he declared bankruptcy, she might get nothing from the young couple, so she'd better take the money and leave. Worse, she could see that Tian might lose his mind if Connie left him at this moment. Meifen used to brag about him as a paragon of success to her neighbours and friends, and had never imagined that his life could be so fragile that it would crumble in just one day. No wonder people always talked about stress and insecurity in America.

Connie said pleasantly, 'Mother, I won't be able to take the job until I see you off at the airport. In the meantime, I'll have to help Tian get back on his feet.'

'I appreciate that,' Meifen said.

That night Connie asked Tian to share the master bedroom with her, but he wouldn't, saying they mustn't nettle his mother from now on. He felt sad, afraid that Meifen might change her mind. He remembered that when he was taking the entrance exam fourteen years back, his parents had stood in the rain under a shared umbrella, waiting for him with a lunch tin, sodas and tangerines wrapped in a handkerchief. They each had half a shoulder soaked through. Oh never could he forget their anxious faces. A surge of gratitude drove him to the brink of tears. If only he could speak freely to them again.

'*A Country in the Moon* is literary travel writing at its best: elegiac, informative and profound. It's probably the best travel book I will read this year'
Jim Blackburn, *Wanderlust* 'Book of the Month'

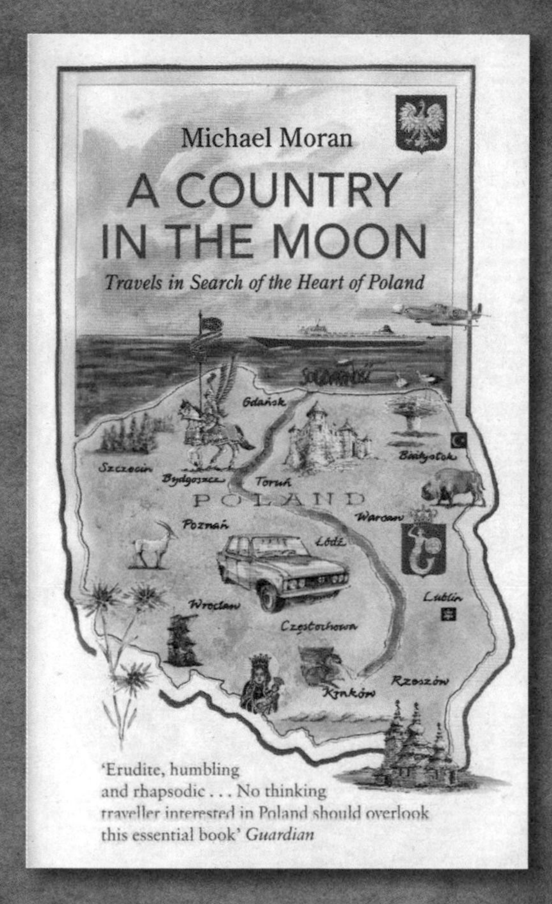

ISBN 9781847081049 • Paperback

'As much cultural history as conventional travel narrative . . . This lively and intelligent book is stuffed with original material that is both fascinating and quite new to most people in the West'
Robert Carver, *Times Literary Supplement*

'Wonderful' Giles Foden, *Condé Nast Traveller*

ILLUSTRATION BY CERI AMPHLETT

FOR THE EXCLUSIVE ATTN OF MS LINDA WITHYCOMBE

Nicola Barker

For the exclusive attn of
Ms Linda Withycombe –
Environmental Health Technician
Wharfedale District Council

The Retreat
Saxonby Manor
Burley Cross

21.12.2006

Dear Ms Withycombe,[1]

Here is the information as requested by yourself on Friday, December 19, during our brief conversation after the public meeting re. 'the proposal for the erection of *at least* [my itals] two new mobile phone

1. Are you one of the Cirencester-based Withycombes? If so, then I was extremely privileged to serve with the Royal Air Force in Burma (1961–63) alongside your late, maternal grandfather, Major Cyril Withycombe (although – on further reflection – Cyril may well have been a Withyc<u>oo</u>mbe).

masts in the vicinity of Wharfedale...' (I don't think it would be needlessly optimistic of me to say that the 'nay's definitely seemed to have the best of things that day[2] – so let's just hope those foolish mules[3] at the phone company finally have the basic, common sense to sit down and rethink what is patently a reckless, environmentally destructive and fundamentally ill-conceived strategy, eh?)

Might I just add (while we're on the subject of the meeting itself) that I sincerely hope you did not take to heart any of the unhelpful – and in some cases extremely offensive – comments and observations made by the deranged and – quite frankly – tragic subject of this letter: Mrs Tirza Parry, widow (as she persists in signing herself in all of our correspondence; although on one occasion she signed herself Mrs Tirza Parry, wi*n*dow,[4] by mistake, which certainly provided we long-suffering residents of The Retreat with no small measure of innocent amusement, I can tell you).

Because of her petite stature, advanced years and charmingly 'bohemian' appearance (I use the word bohemian not only in the sense of 'unconventional' – the white plastic cowboy boots, the heavy, sometimes rather coarse-seeming,[5] pagan-style jewellery, clumsily moulded from what looks like unfired clay,[6] the popsocks, the paisley headscarves – but also with a tacit nod towards Mrs Parry's famously 'exotic' roots, although – as a point of accuracy – I believe her parents were Turks or Greeks rather than Slovaks; Tirza being a derivation of 'Theresa', commonly celebrated as the Catholic saint of information which, under the circumstances, strikes me – and may well strike you

2. Hurrah!
3. *Sic.*
4. Transparency is definitely *not* one of Mrs Parry's main characteristics!
5. I'll make no bones about it, dear: *phallic.*
6. Norma Spoot works part-time at the local butcher's, and told me – in between hysterical gales of laughter – of how she overheard Mrs Parry boasting (while she was having a chicken deboned last Tuesday) that her jewellery 'sells like hot cakes' on the Internet.

– as remarkably ironic. *NB I am just about to close this scandalously long bracket, and apologize, in advance, for the rambling – possibly even inconsequential – nature of this lengthy aside. Pressure of time – as I'm sure you'll understand – prohibits me from rewriting/restructuring the previous paragraph, so it may well behove you to reread the first half of the original sentence in order to make sense of the second. Thanks*). Mrs Parry has it within her reach to create, if not a favourable, then at least a diverting first impression during fledgling social encounters (I remember falling prey to such an impression myself, and would by no means blame you if such had been your own). There is no denying the woman's extraordinary dynamism (it's only a shame, I suppose, that all this highly laudable energy and enthusiasm is being so horribly – one might almost say *dangerously* – misdirected in this particular instance).

I've often remarked on how wonderfully blue and piercing Tirza Parry's eyes are – my dear wife, Shoshana, calls them 'lavender eyes', which I think describes them most excellently (although – as she has also remarked, and very tellingly, I think, a 'blueing' of the eyes can often signify the onset of Alzheimer's, dementia and other sundry ailments related to the loss of memory/reason in old age – I mean nothing derogatory by this statement – none of us are getting any younger, after all![7]).

You will doubtless remember Shoshana (from the aforementioned meeting) as that fearless, flame-haired dominatrix (with the tightly bound arm – more of which, *anon*) who was acting as temporary secretary that day[8] – Wallace Simms, who usually fills this role,[9] having been bedridden by yet another severe bout of his recurrent sciatica.

7. I do not mean to include you in this sweeping statement. That would obviously be ridiculous.
8. People refuse to believe that she actually became eligible for a free bus pass last February.
9. And then some! The poor chap's tall as a doorhandle but weighs in at over seventeen stone!

It briefly occurs to me – by the by – that it may prove helpful at this point (especially in light of some of the wild accusations being thrown around by TP[10] herself in the course of said meeting) if I provide you with a short *précis* of some of the complex, logistical issues currently being employed by that cunning creature as a pathetic smokescreen to obfuscate the real – the critical – subject at the dark heart of this letter. If you – like Mandy Williamson, your charming predecessor[11] – are already fully convinced of my impartiality as a witness/informant on this delicate – and rather distasteful – matter then feel free to skip the next section of this letter and rejoin the narrative in two pages' time (I have taken the trouble to mark the exact spot with a tiny sticker of a Bolivian tree frog).

The Retreat (please see first document enclosed, labelled Doc. 1) is a charming – although rather Lilliputian – residence situated just inside the extensive grounds of Saxonby Manor (I have circled the residence – and its small garden – on the map provided with a fluorescent yellow marker).

My dear, late wife (Emily Baverstock, *née* Morrison) inherited said property over seventeen years ago from her great aunt – the esteemed Lady Beatrix Morrison – who was then resident full-time at Saxonby (although she generally preferred to overwinter in the South of France, where she kept an immaculate, art deco-style penthouse flat in the heart of Biarritz).

When The Retreat was initially built (in the late 1920s) the property's principal use was as a summer house/changing room (situated – as it was – directly adjacent to a fabulous, heated, Olympic-sized swimming pool – now long gone, alas). It was constructed with all mod cons (i.e. toilet, shower etc.; see second document – Doc. 2 – a photocopy of the original architectural plans) and although undisputedly *bijou*, The Retreat was always intended to be more than

10. I'll abbreviate Mrs Parry from this point onwards, if it's all the same to you.
11. Did she have it yet? Was it – as I predicted – a bonny little chap with a bright tuft of ginger hair on top?

a mere 'adjunct'. As early as 1933 they added a small kitchen and a bedroom to allow guests to stay there overnight in greater luxury, and it was eventually inhabited – full-time – by a displaced family (the Pringles, I believe[12]) for the duration of WWII.

After the war it became the home of Saxonby's gardener, the infamous Samuel Tuggs (he sang and played the washboard with local folk sensations The Thrupenny Bits[13]) who was subsequently implicated in the mysterious disappearance of his wife's fifteen-year-old niece, Moira (1974) and – rather sadly for Lady Morrison[14] – while he was never formally tried for the crime,[15] an atmosphere of intense social pressure eventually obliged him to flee the area.

The Retreat's already fascinating history[16] was consolidated further when it was rented out (1981–90) to a writer of books about the science of code-breaking (a fascinating old chap called John Hinty Crew – 'Hinty' to his pals – a promiscuous homosexual whose real claim to fame was his inflammatory adolescent correspondence with Anthony Blunt[17]).

12. The youngest child's initials are still scratched into the bark of our old apple tree.
13. His voice ranged over several octaves – although my late wife used to say that while he might *reach* a note with all apparent ease, he could never actually succeed in *holding* one for any extended period. I used to tell her that this was simply 'the rustic style' (I'm fairly well informed on the subject), but she refused to be convinced.
14. The topiary was never as good after he left.
15. I call it 'a crime' although a corpse was never discovered (there were signs of a struggle and several suspicious spots of blood, however).
16. Bertrand Russell, the famous philosopher and coward, apparently stayed there on several occasions.
17. In the early 1990s these letters were adapted into a play called *My Dear Hinty...* I can't remember, off-hand, who starred in it – possibly that game young lad who used to ride his bicycle up and down those steep, cobbled streets in the old Hovis adverts. Either way, a dear schoolfriend of mine – Hortensia Sandle, an RE teacher, charming lass – who lived in the Smoke and had a penchant for the theatre – was persuaded to attend the opening

Up until this point the cottage possessed no formal/legal rights as an 'independent dwelling'. Lady Morrison had – quite naturally – never felt the need to apply for any, and my late wife's ownership of the property was only ever made explicit by dint of a short caveat in the old lady's will which forbade the sale of the Manor at any future date without a prior agreement that The Retreat (and its tiny garden) were to remain exclusively in the hands of the Morrison family. Rights of access were, of course, a necessary part of this simple arrangement.

It is, I'm afraid, this worryingly fluid and vague 'rights of access' issue that is the source of all our current heartache.

As you will no doubt have already observed on the map provided, The Retreat was actually constructed within a short walking distance of an arched, medieval gate in the outer wall of the larger estate, and this gate has always been used as an entrance/exit (into the village of Burley Cross beyond) by the inhabitants of said dwelling (rather than the main entrance to the Manor, which lies approximately 500 yards – again, see Doc. 1 – to its right[18]).

It goes without saying that many times over the years my wife(s) and I have applied for some kind of permanent, formal, *legal* right of way, if only to establish the property as an independent dwelling (so that we might pay rates, raise a mortgage, or even consider selling[19] at some future date, perhaps).

night (I'd been given free tickets by Hinty himself, but was a martyr to chronic piles at the time so found it difficult to remain seated for extended periods). I still don't know for sure what she actually made of the production (one review I read said the direction was 'all over the shop'), because – for some inexplicable reason – she refused to ever speak to me again afterwards. *Very* odd.

18. To use the main entrance would actually involve cutting through a yew hedge and then swimming across a large, Japanese pond full of ornamental carp.
19. The Morrison line ended with Emily. We had no children of our own – 'though certainly not through want of trying! Rumour has it that an inappropriate liaison between two first cousins in 1810 caused a genetic

Unfortunately, the current owners of the Manor (the Jonty Weiss-Quinns[20]) have never been keen to support this application. The chief plank in their Crusoe-esque style raft of objections[21] is that the land which lies between The Retreat and the gate was once the site of an old monastery (see Doc. 1 – I have used a pink pencil to shade in the area) which is considered by – among others – the National Trust[22] and English Nature to be 'an important heritage site'.[23]

Were you to come along – in person – and take a good look at what actually remains of this 'Old Monastery', I think you would be

weakness in the Morrison gene pool which rendered all subsequent issue physically and reproductively flawed. Aside from her infecundity, Emily had the added distinction of a third nipple. In poor light it could be mistaken for a large mole, but she was very self-conscious about it and always wore a robe whilst lounging by the pool. Once, on holiday in Kenya, she allowed her guard (and the robe) to fall and the mark was spotted by a sharp-eyed cocktail waiter. We were subsequently evicted, unceremoniously, from the hotel. To protect Emily's feelings I determined to keep the real reason for our eviction hidden from her (and was relatively successful, to boot). She always naively believed that we were turfed out because I queried the bar bill (and gave me no end of stick about it, too!).

20. Who have always been extremely genial landlords and have never sought to interfere with our ready access to the property – although they did kick up quite a stink two years ago when we built our conservatory or 'sunroom'. Apparently the light reflects quite sharply off its glass roof and can be seen very clearly from the window of their dining room (an added complication is that this small but precious 'space' was added to the property with the intention of creating a safe/therapeutic environment for Shoshana to sunbathe, *au naturel.* The poor creature is prone to seasonal attacks of chronic eczema and constant exposure to gentle sunlight really is the best possible cure).
21. Which I won't bore you with here.
22. Little Hitlers. It beggars belief that these people actually have the right to claim 'charitable status'.
23. I am considering trying to claim this same status myself – I'll be seventy-three in February!

astonished (as, indeed, are we[24]) that so much fuss could be generated by what basically amounts to a scruffy pile of broken stones (approx. three feet in diameter – aka the 'Old Cloister') and a slight dip or indentation in the ground (just to the left of the gate) which is apparently all that's now left of the 'Old Monk's Latrine' (!).

As I'm sure you can imagine, Shoshana and I have grown rather depressed and frustrated by this unsatisfactory legal situation, not least because our non-payment of council tax has allowed less sympathetic/imaginative members of the Burley Cross community[25] to accuse us of tight-fistedness and a lack of social/fiscal responsibility.[26] Much of this unnecessary hostility (as you are probably no doubt already fully aware) centres around the disposal/collection of rubbish.

The situation has recently developed to such a pitch of silliness and pettiness[27] that the local binmen have been persuaded[28] to ignore the black bin bags deposited outside our gate. This means that we are now obliged to skulk around like criminals at dawn on collection day, furtively distributing our bags among those piles belonging to other – marginally more sympathetic – properties in the local vicinity. Worse still, many of these sympathetic individuals – while perfectly happy to help us out – must live in constant terror of incurring the (not inconsiderable) wrath of TP, who has tried her utmost to transform this mundane issue into what she loves to call a 'point of principle'.

24. And you could hardly call us philistines – Shoshana is actually treasurer of our local History Club!
25. A marvellous, generous, open-minded bunch of individuals (with the odd, notable exception).
26. Last April Shoshana single-handedly staged and organized a charitable quiz night (in conjunction with Radio Wharfedale DJ Mark Sweet) to raise money for repairs to the church organ (which she plays – very competently – whenever the resident organist is away on holiday).
27. Encouraged, in no minor part, by the poison tongue of you know who.
28. Money changed hands. It definitely changed hands. I'm almost one hundred per cent sure of it.

As I'm sure you can now understand more fully, this complex situation re. the disposal/collection of our rubbish feeds directly into the severe problems the village is currently experiencing with TP and her borderline obsessive interest in matters surrounding dog fouling.

You mentioned (during our brief exchange after the meeting) that I might benefit from reading the latest pamphlet on this subject published by EnCams: *Dog Fouling and the Law: a guide for the public*) which your department usually distributes free to interested parties (although due to a temporary snarl-up with the council's acquisitions budget you regretted that you had yet to acquire any for general distribution – or even, you confessed, to become better acquainted with the finer details of said document yourself). I didn't get a chance to tell you at the time that I already possess several copies of this useful booklet (and have – as you will doubtless have already noticed[29] – taken the liberty of enclosing one for your own, personal use[30]).

Among the more fascinating details contained therein are the extraordinary statistics that (pg 2) the UK's population of approximately 7.4 million dogs produces, on average, around 1,000 tonnes of excrement/day.

Burley Cross (human population: 210; dog population: 33; cat population: 47)[31] certainly produces its fair share of the above, but,

29. The cover photo of a booted foot suspended above a huge pile of steaming excrement is certainly eye-catching. Shoshana is very squeamish and will not allow me to keep my copies in the house (even wrong-side-up!) so I have been obliged to resort to storing them – and all correspondence relating to this issue – on a shallow back shelf inside our tiny garden shed.
30. No need to return it. The yellow marks on the back cover are nothing more sinister than grass stains (from where it accidentally fell into my lawnmower's clippings bin on retrieval).
31. Although felines – very helpfully, but with the odd exception – bury their own.

thanks to a – by and large – very responsible, slightly older[32] population, the provision of two, special poop-scoop bins within the heart of the village and the wonderful, wide expanses of surrounding heath and moorland lying beyond, the matter had never – until TP's sudden arrival in our midst[33] – become an issue of serious public concern.[34]

I confess that I have walked[35] Shoshana's pedigree spitz, Samson,[36] morning and evening, regular as clockwork, for almost five years now,[37] and during that time have rarely – if ever – had my excursions sullied by the unwelcome apprehension of a superfluity of dog mess. If Samson – in common with most other sensible dogs I know – feels the urge to 'do his business', then he is usually more than happy to 'perform' some short distance off the path (his modesty happily preserved by delicate fronds of feathery bracken) on the wild expanses of our local moor. Here, dog faeces – along with other animal faeces, including those of the moorland sheep, fox and badger – are able to decompose naturally (usually within – on average – a ten-day period, depending – of course – on the specific climatic conditions). If Samson is 'caught short' and needs to 'go' in a less convenient location then I automatically pick up his 'business' and dispose of it accordingly.

Further to a series of in-depth discussions with a significant number of the dog owners in this village (and its local environs), I think

32. The average age of your Burley Cross resident is fifty-nine (this is a quotable statistic – feel free to use it – I researched it myself).
33. Approximately eighteen months ago.
34. That said, I was utterly appalled by the filth I encountered on a day trip to Haworth in 'Brontë country' recently.
35. And not without occasional resistance – especially on icy winter mornings!
36. Shoshana's family have a tradition of naming their dogs after Biblical characters.
37. Samson actually turns eight this year – he was a rescue dog and three years old when we got him. But before Samson I regularly walked Shoshana's beloved Highland terrier, Hezekiah (or 'Zeke') – although we were not resident full-time in Burley Cross at that stage.

it would be fair to say that the model I follow with Samson is the model that most other reasonable people also adhere to *i.e.* the collection of dog mess is only appropriate within an 'urban/residential' setting, in public parks (where people are liable to picnic, stroll, relax, and children play) and finally – under very special circumstances – where your animal might be perceived to have 'despoiled' a well-used moorland path to the detriment of other walkers' enjoyment of it (although this last requirement is not legally binding but simply a question of community spirit).

I believe I am correct in saying that all of the above criteria tally perfectly with the procedures formally established by local government, and that – up until TP chanced to throw her very large (very filthy!) spanner into the works – these procedures were generally held to be not only just, but successful, necessary and universally beneficial.

With the arrival of TP, however, this fragile consensus was attacked, savagely mauled and rent asunder.[38] TP, as you may well know, owns four large German shepherds and prefers – rather eccentrically – to take them on long walks on the moor in the moonlight (I say 'them', although so far as I am aware she only ever walks one dog at any given time[39]). These four, large dogs are usually kept confined inside a concrete 'compound'[40] in the back garden of Hursley End – her dilapidated bungalow on Lamb's Green.

It was initially – she insists – due to the difficulties she experienced in negotiating/avoiding random dog faeces during these night-time

38. Like an innocent, young rabbit cruelly disembowelled by a savage fox (and this is an entirely pointless killing – the cruel fox is not hungry – it does not pause to eat the rabbit – it has already killed and consumed the mother – so attacks the young one purely for 'sport').
39. Pathetic creature. *Hugely* overweight. And I'm pretty convinced that it's always the *same* dog she walks – it seems to be lame in one of its back legs – although I've never had the chance to meet it – and so identify it – in daylight.
40. No judgement whatsoever is involved in my use of this word.

hikes that her bizarre habit of bagging other people's dogs' faeces and leaving them deposited on branches, walls and fence posts – apparently as a warning/ admonishment to others less responsible than herself – commenced.[41] This activity continued for upwards of six months before anyone either commented on it publicly or felt the urge to root out/apprehend the strange individual in our midst who had inexplicably chosen to enact this 'special service' on our behalf.[42]

Given the idiosyncratic nature of the bags employed (TP prefers a small, pink-tinged, transparent bag[43] – probably better adapted for household use i.e. freezing meat[44] – instead of the usual, custom-made, matt-black kind[45]) it was easy – from very early on – to understand that the person bagging up and 'displaying' these faeces was not only happy, but almost *keen* to leave some kind of 'signature' behind.

When the bags were eventually identified as belonging to none other than TP (and she was calmly – very *sensitively* – confronted with her crimes), rather than apologizing, quietly retreating, or putting a summary halt to her bizarre activities, she responded – somewhat perversely – by actively *redoubling* her poop-gathering efforts! In fact she went *still one stage further*! She began to present herself in public[46] as a wronged party, as a necessary – if chronically undervalued – environmental watchdog, as a doughty, cruelly misunderstood moral crusader, standing alone and defenceless – clutching her trademark, transparent poo-bag to her heaving chest – against the freely defecating heathen marauder!

41. Although one really has to wonder at her facility to locate these random faeces in order to bag them up when it's apparently so difficult for her to avoid stepping in them in the first place!
42. I'm guessing that this is because the habit took a while to become properly established and then suddenly snowballed after the first few months.
43. The contents are, therefore, always fully visible.
44. Chops, perhaps, or liver/kidney/tongue and other smaller cuts.
45. To be purchased at any large supermarket or pet shop.
46. Quite belligerently.

And it gets worse! She then went on the offensive (see Docs. 3+4 – copies of letters sent to the local press), angrily accusing the general body of responsible dog owners in Burley Cross of actively destroying the picturesque and historic moor by encouraging our animals to 'evacuate'[47] there.

One occasion, in particular, stands out in my mind. I met her – quite by chance – on a sunny afternoon, overburdened by shopping from the village store.[48] I offered to take her bags for her and during the walk back to her home took some pains to explain to her that there was *no actual legal requirement* for dog owners to collect their dog's faeces from the surrounding farm and moorland (The Dogs Fouling of Land Act, 1996). Her reaction to this news was to blush to the roots of her hair, spit out the word 'justifier!', roughly snatch her bags from me[49] and then quote, at length, like a thing possessed (as if reciting some ancient, biblical proverb[50]) from the (aforementioned) EnCams publication on the subject.[51]

To return to this useful document for just a moment, in *Dog Fouling and the Law,* EnCams provide an invaluable 'profile of a dog fouler' (page 4 – when you read it for yourself you will discover that it is an extremely thorough and thought-provoking piece of analysis). Apparently the average 'fouler' enjoys watching TV and attending the cinema but has a profound mistrust of soap opera, around half of them have Internet access – mainly at home – but 'are not particularly confident in its usage', and they are most likely to read the *Sun* and *Mirror* (but very rarely the *Daily Mail* or the *Financial Times*).[52]

47. *Her* word.
48. God only knows what she had in those damn bags – they weighed a tonne!
49. Lucky for TP we were only fifty or so yards from her front door at this stage.
50. And quite incorrectly, it later transpired.
51. I had yet to come across this valuable little booklet and so was, as you can imagine, somewhat confused and nonplussed by this attack.
52. We get the *Sunday Express* at The Retreat, but only for the sudoku.

EnCams have invented their own broad label to describe these irresponsible individuals: they call them 'justifiers' i.e. they justify their behaviour on the grounds of a) *Ignorance* ('I didn't realize it was a problem...' 'But nobody has ever mentioned this to me before...' etc.) and b) *Laziness* ('But nobody else ever picks it up, so why should I?').

EnCams insist that these 'justifiers' will only ever openly admit that they allow their dog to foul in public when placed under extreme duress. Their fundamental instinct is to simply pretend it hasn't happened or to lie about it.

Although I cannot deny that this profile is both interesting and – I don't doubt – perfectly valid in many – if not *most* – instances, TP was nevertheless entirely wrong to try and label me – of all people – with this wildly inappropriate nomenclature: I am neither ignorant, lazy nor in denial. Quite the opposite, in fact. I am informed, proactive and socially aware. And although I do dislike soaps,[53] I very rarely go to the cinema,[54] and my computer skills are – as this letter itself, I hope, will attest – universally acknowledged to be tip-top.

Since my acquisition of the EnCams document I have tried – countless times – to explain to TP (see Doc. 5 + Doc. 6: some valuable examples of our early correspondence) that not only am I a keen advocate of poop-scooping in residential areas and public parks, but that it shows *absolutely no moral or intellectual inconsistency on my part* to hold that allowing excrement to decompose naturally on the moor is infinitely more environmental than bagging it up and adding it, quite unthinkingly, to this small island's already chronically over-extended quantities of landfill. I have also told her that by simply bagging up the faeces she finds and then dumping them, willy-nilly, she is only serving to exacerbate the 'problem'[55] because the excrement cannot be

53. Shoshana, I must confess, is an avid *Corrie* fan.
54. The last film I saw was *The Full Monty*, and I only went to that because my late wife convinced me it was all about El Alamein.
55. Although – as I've already emphasized – there *wasn't* a problem before TP arrived on the scene – TP *is* the problem!

expected to decompose inside its plastic skin. Rather than helping matters she is actually making them infinitely worse – once bagged, the excrement is there forever: a tawdry bauble – a permanent, sordid testament to the involuntary act of physical evacuation!

As you will no doubt be aware, around two months ago Wharfedale's Dog Warden – the 'criminally over-subscribed'[56] Trevor Horsmith – was persuaded[57] to start to take an interest in the problems being generated by TP's activities on the moor. It will probably strike you as intensely ironic that *TP herself* was one of the main instigators in finally involving Trevor in this little, local 'mess' of ours.[58]

After familiarizing himself with the consequences of TP's 'work' (on the moor and beyond[59]) Horsmith announced (I'm paraphrasing here[60]) that while he fully condoned – even admired![61] – TP's desire to keep the moor clean, it was still perfectly legitimate for dog owners to allow their pets to defecate there, and that while excrement could not, in all conscience, be calibrated as 'litter' (it decomposes for heaven's sake! Same as an apple core!) once it has been placed inside plastic (no

56. I won't bore you with the details here as I am sure Mr Horsmith will already have bored you with them himself.
57. His words, not mine. Shoshana once observed – very wittily – that Mr Horsmith makes *Alice in Wonderland*'s Dormouse seem hyperactive!
58. By a flurry of phone calls, emails and at least half a dozen letters to the local press (two of which mentioned him by name).
59. Three of her bags were recently discovered in Lowsley Edge – over *seven miles* away as the crow flies!
60. His letter was full of the most appalling grammatical errors.
61. This struck me as an astonishingly irresponsible thing to say given the deranged nature of the character we are dealing with here. As I said to Horsmith myself (on one of the rare occasions he actually made a visit to the village), by encouraging TP to think that she's got moral right on her side he's only sharpening a stick for her to beat him (and the rest of us) up with.

matter how laudable the motivation[62]) then it *must necessarily* be considered so.[63]

Horsmith's pronouncement on this issue was obviously the most devastating blow for TP (and her cause), yet it by no means prompted her to desist from her antisocial behaviour. By way of an excuse for (partial explanation of/attempt to distract attention from) her strange, nocturnal activities, she suddenly changed tack and began claiming (see Doc. 6 again – last three paras) that – for the most part – whenever she goes on walks she generally bags up the vast majority of the faeces she finds and disposes of them herself ('double-wrapped', she writes – somewhat primly – inside her dustbin, at home[64]) and that on the rare occasions when she leaves the bags behind it is either because a) the 'problem' (as she perceives it) is so severe that she feels a strong, public statement needs to be made to other dog owners, b) the sheer volume of excrement is such that it is simply too much for her to carry home all in one go (while managing a large dog at the same time), and c) that she is sometimes prey to the sudden onset of acute arthritic 'spasms' in her fingers, which mean that she is unable to grip the bags properly and so is compelled to leave them *in situ*, while harbouring 'every earthly intention' of returning to collect them at a later date.

I am not – of course – in any way convinced by this pathetic, half-cocked hodge-podge of explanations. In answer to a) I say that other dog owners are completely within their rights to allow their dogs to defecate responsibly on the moor. They have the law on their side. It is a perfectly legitimate and natural way to proceed. In answer to b) I say that the volume of excrement on the moor is rarely, if ever – in my extensive experience of these matters – excessive (especially given the general rate of decomposition etc.). In answer to c) I say that it strikes me as rather odd that the same person who can apparently manage to

62. Ye gads!
63. A point I made myself to Mr Horsmith – but to no avail – over six long months before!
64. I will return to this important detail a little later!

'bag up' huge quantities of excrement when their fingers are – *ahem* – 'spasming'[65] is somehow unable to perform that superficially much less arduous act of transporting it back home with them![66]

Many of TP's bags lie around on the moor for months on end and no visible attempt is made to move them. Last Thursday, for example, I counted over forty-two bags of excrement dotted randomly about the place on my morning stroll.

Sometimes I come across a bag displayed in the most extraordinary of places. Yesterday I found one dangling up high in the midst of a thorny bush. It was very obvious that not only would the person who hung the bag there have been forced to sustain some kind of injury in its display (unless they wore a thick pair of protective gloves), but that so would the poor soul (and *here's* the rub!) who felt duty-bound to retrieve it and dispose of it.[67] This was – in effect – a piece of purely spiteful behaviour – little less, in fact, than an act of social/environmental terrorism.

Shoshana and I have both become so sickened, angered and dismayed by the awful mess TP has made of our local area (I mean who is to judge when an activity such as this passes from being 'in the public interest'[68] to a plain and simple public nuisance?[69]) that, in sheer desperation, we have begun to gather up the rotten bags ourselves.

On Friday, two weeks back,[70] Shoshana gathered up over thirty-six

65. A fiddly process at the best of times!
66. Let alone manufacture fashionable clay jewellery in such prodigious quantities!
67. I.e. Yours truly!
68. Which it never was, quite frankly.
69. This is intended as a purely rhetorical question – although, on further consideration, I suppose the person who might possibly be expected to make that vital judgement could very well turn out to be you, Linda.
70. There was a large convention of Girl Guides from Manchester and Leeds travelling to the moor for an orienteering weekend. Shoshana couldn't bear the idea of these lovely creatures being exposed to TP's vile 'handiwork'.

bags. On her way home – exhausted – from the village's poop-scoop bins[71] she tripped on a crack in the pavement, fell heavily, sprained her wrist and dislocated her collarbone.[72] I will not say that we blame TP *entirely* for this calamity, but we do hold her at least partially responsible.[73]

After Shoshana's 'accident' I marched over to TP's bungalow, fully intent on having it out with her,[74] but TP (rather fortuitously) was nowhere to be found. It was then – as I stood impotently in her front garden, seething with frustration – that I resolved[75] to take the opportunity to do a little private investigation of my own. If you remember,[76] TP had claimed that many – if not most – of the bags of excrement she retrieved from the moor, she automatically carried back home with her (only leaving the unmanageable excess behind) and placed them, double-wrapped, into her dustbin (alongside what I imagine would be the considerable quantities of excrement collected from her *own* four, chronically obese dogs which – as you know – she keeps penned up, 24/7,[77] inside that criminally small and claustrophobic, purpose-built concrete compound[78]).

71. Which could barely contain the sheer volume involved – amounting to almost 3,000 grams. If you have some difficulty imagining this weight in real terms, then it would be comparable to around twelve pats of best butter.
72. I have sent another letter to your colleague – Giles Monson – on this subject, along with directions from our lawyer.
73. Shoshana an angry seventy per cent, me, a more reasoned fifty-nine per cent (a broad, general majority, in other words).
74. Uncharacteristically hot-headed behaviour on my part.
75. Quite spontaneously. This was *in no way* premeditated.
76. But of course you do!
77. As the Yanks are wont to say.
78. Once again, I emphasize that *absolutely no judgement* is implied by my use of these words.

The day I visited Hursley End was a Monday, which is the day directly *before* refuse is collected in the village. I decided – God only knows why, it was just a random urge, I suppose – to peek inside her dustbin (literally deafened as I did so by the hysterical barks and howls of her four frantic German shepherds). By my calculation, I estimated that there would need to be *at least* forty-two dog faeces – from her own four animals – stored away inside there.[79] In addition to these I also envisaged a *considerable* number of stools collected from her nightly hikes on the 'filthy' moor.[80]

Once I'd made these quick calculations I steeled myself, drew a deep breath, grabbed the lid, lifted it high and peered querulously inside. Imagine my great surprise when I found *not a single trace of excrement within*! The bin was all but empty! I say again: the bin – *TP's* bin – was all but empty!! I quickly pulled on a pair of disposable gloves[81] and then gingerly withdrew the bin's other contents, piece by piece (just so as to be absolutely certain of my facts). I removed two large, empty Johnnie Walker bottles,[82] four family-size Marks and Spencer coleslaw containers, three packets of mint and one packet of hazelnut-flavoured Cadbury's Snaps biscuit wrappers, and the stinking remnants of two boil-in-the-bag fish dinners (Iceland) and one, ready-made, prawn biryani meal (from Tesco's excellent Finest range).

I stared blankly into that bin for several minutes, utterly confounded, struggling to make any sense of what I'd discovered. It then slowly dawned on me that TP might actually have *two* bins – one of which was specifically to be used for the storing of excrement. Bearing this in mind, I set about searching the untended grounds of

79. This figure was reached by estimating that, on average, each of TP's four dogs would be expected to defecate 1.5 times on any given day (an extremely conservative estimate, in actual fact).
80. Her word, obviously.
81. Which I just happened to have with me.
82. Not much of a recycler, then, our TP?!

her property[83] with a fine-tooth comb,[84] even going so far as to climb on to an upturned bucket and peer, trepidatiously, into the tiny concrete compound to the rear, where TP's four German shepherds barked and raced around – like a group of hairy, overweight banshees – frantic with what seemed to be a poignant combination of terror and excitement.[85]

No matter how hard I hunted, a second bin could not be found. I eventually abandoned my search on realizing how late it had grown[86] – Shoshana would definitely be worried, I thought, and if I tarried any longer I could be in serious danger of missing *Countdown*.[87] I left Hursley End, depressed and confused, only turning – with a helpless half-shrug – to peer back over towards the property once I'd reached the relative safety of the road beyond. It was then, in a blinding flash, that I had what I now refer to – somewhat vaingloriously, I'll admit – as my 'Moment of Epiphany'.[88]

83. TP is currently in the midst of having some major renovation work done to the external walls of her bungalow. If the rumours I hear about town are correct, she is trying to sue the former owners, Louise and Timothy Hamm, for some unspecified kind of 'negligence' – even though Timothy, an ex-GP and a truly inspirational human being, is in the final stages of Parkinson's and now lives in full-time residential care.
84. So to speak.
85. Probably thinking I was an animal-rights activist intent on releasing them from their hellish penury.
86. I'd been there for almost an hour!
87. I *didn't* miss it, which was most fortuitous as it was an especially good episode. One of the contestants came up with the high-scoring word 'toxocara', a term which refers to a type of roundworm which is responsible for generating the dangerous infection/disease called toxocariasis. This disease is produced when the toxocara roundworm's eggs are left to fester in the excrement of a dog for a period of two/three weeks after the faeces have been deposited. I was absolutely stunned when this word came up, and honestly believe it was some kind of message from 'The Beyond'!
88. Although Shoshana will insist on calling it my 'episcopy', the silly moo!

As I looked back at TP's property from a greater distance, I was able – with the benefit of perspective – to observe that recent renovation works to the bungalow had resulted in the temporary removal of large sections of the external fascia,[89] so that all that now remained of the property's original structure was the roof, the window frames and a series of basic, internal walls and supports, many of which had been copiously wrapped in thick layers of protective plastic (to safeguard the property against the worst of the weather, I suppose). By dint of this expedient – I suddenly realized, with a sharp gasp – TP's home had lately been transformed (voluntarily or otherwise) into a giant simulacrum of a *monstrous, semi-transparent poo-bag*![90]

As this – admittedly strange and somewhat hysterical – thought[91] caught ahold of me, a second thought – running almost in tandem with it – quickly overtook my mind: if no evidence of excrement could be found in TP's garden – not even faeces from her *own four dogs* – then where on God's earth might she actually be...?

What?!

I suddenly froze.

'*MARY, MOTHER OF JESUS!*' I bellowed, then quickly covered my mouth with my hand.[92] But wasn't it *obvious*?! Hadn't the simple answer to this most perplexing of questions been staring me in the face *all along*?!

89. Many of the more modest properties in this village – built within a particular time frame – were constructed out of a special, aluminium-based concrete which, while it poses only limited health risks to the residents, can, in certain instances, make it extremely difficult to raise a mortgage.
90. With TP – I hate to have to say it, but say it I *must* – representing the steaming turd of festering excrement within.
91. Remember that – in my own defence – I was still in somewhat of a state after Shoshana's tragic fall.
92. For fear of attracting the unwanted attentions of TP's neighbours – one of whom, a Mrs Janine Loose, has grown extraordinarily jumpy and paranoid of late, since a canny gang of local schoolchildren appropriated

The moor!

Our beautiful, unbesmirched, virgin moor!

TP had *not* – as she'd always emphatically maintained – been piously and dutifully collecting/bagging excrement left by other, irresponsible dog owners, during those long, dark, nightly hikes of hers. Oh no! Quite the opposite, in fact! TP had actually been carefully bagging prodigious quantities of HER OWN FOUR DOGS' EXCREMENT and then CHEERFULLY FESTOONING THE LOCAL FOOTPATHS WITH IT!!!

'Good *Lord*!' I can almost hear you howl, your smooth, firm cheeks flushed pink with rage and indignation.' But...but *why*?'

I'm afraid that this is a question which – for all of my age and experience – I cannot answer. I can only imagine that TP must derive some sick and perverse feeling of excitement/gratification from performing this debased act. Perhaps it is an entirely sexual impulse, or maybe she has some deep yet inexplicable grudge against the people of Burley Cross which she is 'acting out' through this strange and depraved pastime. Or perhaps the good people of this village have unwittingly come to 'represent' something (or someone) to TP from her tragic past and she feels the uncontrollable urge to punish/insult/degrade us all as a consequence of that. Or maybe – just maybe – a whole host of entirely *different* impulses are at play here. Shoshana had the fascinating idea that as a small child TP might've developed 'issues' during her anal phase[93] brought on by an overly strict and prohibitive potty-training regimen. She discussed this idea with a neighbour of ours who might properly be called an 'expert' in the field,

the disused greenhouse at the bottom of her garden and secretly cultivated marijuana plants in it. Their illegal activities were only brought to light after Mrs Loose discovered two boys spreadeagled on her lawn, 'completely monged', when she went to hang out her washing one blustery, autumn afternoon.

93. Who started – but never completed – a child psychology correspondence course a few years back (then swapped to aromatherapy).

and they explained to her – at some length – how as children we have an innocent, perfectly natural conception of our own faeces as a kind of 'gift'[94] which we generously share with our parents.

Shoshana wondered whether TP's emotional/psychological development as a child was halted/blocked at this critical stage, leading to an unusual fixation with faeces in adult life, which, many decades later, still gives TP the childlike compulsion to 'share' this 'precious' substance with all of her friends and neighbours.[95]

Whatever the real reasons for TP's extraordinary behaviour, the hard fact remains that she is currently posing a serious threat to the health and safety of the general public and must be stopped as a matter of some urgency. To this end I sent a lengthy email to Trevor Horsmith, insisting that he take some kind of positive action to deter TP from her foul and aberrant path.

Horsmith,[96] while professing himself to be 'very interested' in my theories, calmly informed me that unless he was able to catch TP red-handed (transporting faeces from her home and depositing them on the moor) then he would be unable to take any kind of prohibitive action against her. Given that TP prefers to walk only after dark and Trevor Horsmith's working hours finish promptly at five, the likelihood of this ever happening is – at best, I feel – extremely limited. Horsmith also went on to discourage me – and in no uncertain terms,[97] either –

94. Apparently – according to Ms Sissy Logan, an old Bluebell dancing girl turned colonic irrigation practitioner – Carl Gustav Jung has written quite extensively on this peculiar subject.
95. Lucky old us, eh?!
96. As he will no doubt have informed you.
97. I found his insinuations extremely hurtful. As I told you after the meeting, nine out of the ten charges were dropped through lack of evidence, and in the tenth instance a credible witness was able to verify that I had merely asked the girl for directions to the nearest Tesco Metro. I have visited Leeds for many years and know the town well, but the rejuvenation of the riverside area and recent changes to the one-way system are liable to catch even a seasoned old pro like myself on the hop.

from taking any kind of independent action myself, claiming that a matter this sensitive was – I quote – 'always better left in the hands of qualified professionals'.[98]

So there you have it, Ms Withycombe; a detailed summary of the complex web of problems our small – but perfectly formed – village is currently struggling to grapple with. Call me a foolish, old optimist (if you must!), but I have a strong presentiment that your input in this matter will prove most beneficial, and am keenly looking forward to bashing out some kind of joint plan of action with you at the start of the New Year.

Yours, in eager anticipation,

Jeremy – aka *Jez* – Baverstock

PS Merry Christmas! (I almost forgot!!)
PPS You will probably have noticed that I have taken the great liberty of enclosing a small, festive gift for your private enjoyment over the holiday season: an – as yet – unpublished book[99] I once wrote about my nefarious activities as a reconnoiter, black hat and mole inside the Royal Horticultural Society of Great Britain.[100]

XXJ

98. Although I remain a little confused as to what his 'professional' status might actually be.
99. This edition is limited to only thirty copies. Shoshana is wholly responsible for the wonderful, colourful, internal artwork.
100. An organization that has – over recent years – fallen prey to rank corruption, chronic inefficiency and levels of bovine complacency the like of which you can hardly dare to imagine. My lack of an independent publisher is, I believe, at least partly down to the fact that members of this powerful institution are currently rife within all – and I *mean* all – areas of the national media. It may shock you to discover that the Duchess of Windsor, Peter Sissons, and that queer little chap who owns Sainsbury's – or possibly ASDA – were former members and dabbled, quite seriously, in the organization for a while.

SORRY?

Helen Simpson

ILLUSTRATION BY MICHAEL KIRKHAM

'Sorry?' said Patrick. 'I didn't quite catch that.'

'SOUP OF THE DAY IS WILD MUSHROOM,' bellowed the waiter.

'No need to shout,' said Patrick, putting his hand to his troublesome ear.

The new gadget shrieked in protest.

'They take a bit of getting used to,' grimaced Matthew Herring, the deaf chap he'd been fixed up with for a morale-boosting lunch.

'You don't say,' he replied.

Some weeks ago Patrick had woken up to find he had gone deaf in his right ear – not just a bit deaf but profoundly deaf. There was nothing to be done, it seemed. It had probably been caused by a tiny flake of matter dislodged by wear-and-tear change in the vertebrae, the doctor had said, shrugging. He had turned his head on his pillow, in all likelihood, sometimes that was all it took. This neck movement would have shifted a minuscule scrap of detritus into the river of blood running towards the brain, a fragment which must have finished by blocking the very narrowest bit of the entire arterial system, the ultra-fine pipe leading to the inner ear. Bad luck.

'I don't hear perfectly,' said Matthew Herring now. 'It's not magic, a digital hearing aid, it doesn't turn your hearing into perfect hearing.'

'Mine's not working properly yet,' said Patrick. 'I've got an appointment after lunch to get it seen to.'

'Mind you, it's better than the old one,' continued Matthew Herring comfortably. 'You used to be able to hear me wherever I went with the analogue one, it used to go before me, screeching like a steam train.'

He chuckled at the memory.

Patrick did not smile at this cosy reference to engine whistles. He had been astonished at the storm of head noise which had arrived with deafness, the whistles and screeches over a powerful cloud of hissing just like the noise from his wife Elizabeth's old pressure cooker. His brain was generating sound to compensate for the loss of hearing, he had been told. Apparently that was part and parcel of the deafness, as well as dizzy episodes. Ha! Thanks to the vertigo which had sent him arse over tip several times since the start of all this, he was having to stay with his daughter Rachel for a while.

'Two girls,' he said tersely in answer to a question from his tedious lunch companion. He and Elizabeth had wished for boys, but there you were. Rachel was the only one so far to have provided him with grandchildren. The other daughter, Ruth, had decamped to Australia some time ago. Who knew what she was up to but she was still out there so presumably she had managed to make a go of it, something which she had signally failed to do in England.

'I used to love music,' Matthew Herring was saying, nothing daunted. 'But it's not the same now I'm so deaf. Now it tires me out; in fact, I don't listen any more. I deliberately avoid it. The loss of it is a grief, I must admit.'

'Oh well, music means nothing to me,' said Patrick. 'Never has. So I shan't miss *that*.'

He wasn't about to confide in Matthew Herring, but of all his symptoms it had been the auditory hallucinations produced by the hearing aid that had been the most disturbing for him. The low violent stream of nonsense issuing from the general direction of his firstborn had become insupportable in the last week, and he had had to turn the damned thing off.

At his after-lunch appointment with the audiologist, he found himself curiously unable to describe the hallucinatory problem.

'I seem to be picking up extra noise,' he said eventually. 'It's difficult to describe.'

'Sounds go into your hearing aid where they are processed electronically,' she intoned, 'then played back to you over a tiny loudspeaker.'

'Yes, I know that,' he snapped. 'I am awarc of that, thank you. What I'm asking is, might one of the various settings you programmed be capable of, er, amplifying sounds that would normally remain unheard?'

'Let's see, shall we?' she said, still talking to him as though he were a child or a halfwit. 'I wonder whether you've been picking up extra stuff on the Loop.'

'The Loop?'

'It works a bit like Wi-Fi,' she said. 'Electromagnetic fields. If you're in an area that's on the Loop, you can pick up on it with your hearing aid when you turn on the T-setting.'

'The T-setting?'

'That little extra bit of kit there,' she said, pointing at it. 'I didn't mention it before. I didn't want to confuse you while you were getting used to the basics. You must have turned it on by mistake from what you're saying.'

'But what *sort* of extra sounds does it pick up?' he persisted.

Rachel's lips had not been moving during that initial weird diatribe a week ago, he was sure of it, nor during the battery of bitter little remarks he'd had to endure since then.

'Well it can be quite embarrassing,' she said, laughing merrily. 'Walls don't block the magnetic waves from a Loop signal, so you might well be able to listen in to confidential conversations if neighbouring rooms are also on it.'

'Hmm,' he said. 'I'm not sure that quite explains this particular problem. But I suppose it might have something to do with it.'

'Look, I've turned off the T-setting,' she said. 'If you want to test what it does, simply turn it on again and see what happens.'

'Or hear,' he said. 'Hear what happens.'

'You're right!' she declared, with more merry laughter.

He really couldn't see what was so amusing, and said so.

Back at Rachel's, he made his way to the armchair in the little bay window and whiled away the minutes until six o'clock by rereading the *Telegraph*. The trouble with this house was that it had been knocked through, so you were all in it hugger-mugger together. He could not himself see the advantage of being forced to witness every domestic detail. Frankly, it was bedlam, with the spin cycle going and Rachel's twins squawking and Rachel washing her hands at the kitchen sink yet again like Lady Macbeth. Now she was doing that thing she did with the brown paper bag, blowing into it and goggling her eyes, which seemed to amuse the twins at least.

Small children were undoubtedly tiresome, but the way she indulged hers made them ten times worse. Like so many of her generation she seemed to be making a huge song and dance about the whole business. She was ridiculous with them, ludicrously over-indulgent and lacking in any sort of authority. It was when he had commented on this in passing that the auditory hallucinations had begun.

'I don't want to do to them what you did to me, you old beast,' the voice had growled, guttural and shocking, although her lips had not been moving. 'I don't want to hand on the misery, I don't want that horrible Larkin poem to be true.'

He had glared at her, amazed, and yet it had been quite obvious she was blissfully unaware of what he had heard. Or thought he had heard.

He must have been hearing things.

Now he held up his wrist and tapped his watch at her. She waved back at him, giving one last puff into the paper bag before scurrying to the fridge for the ice and lemon. As he watched her prepare his first drink of the evening, he decided to test out the audiologist's theory.

'Sit with me,' he ordered, taking the clinking glass.

'I'd love to, Dad, but the twins…' she said.

'Nonsense,' he said. 'Look at them, you can see them from here, they're all right for now.'

She perched on the arm of the chair opposite his and started twisting a strand of her lank brown hair.

'Tell me about your day,' he commanded.

'My day?' she said. 'Are you sure? Nothing very much happened. I took the twins to Rainbow, then we went round Asda…'

'Keep talking,' he said, fiddling with his hearing aid. 'I want to test this gadget out.'

'…then I had to queue at the post office and I wasn't very popular with the double buggy,' she droned on.

He flicked the switch to the T-setting.

'…never good enough for you, you old beast, you never had any time for me, you never listened to anything I said,' came the low growling voice he remembered from before. 'You cold old beast, Ruth says you're emotionally autistic, definitely somewhere on the autistic spectrum anyway, that's why she went to the other side of the world but she says she still can't get away from it there, your lack of interest, you blanked us, you blotted us out, you don't even know the names of your grandchildren let alone their birthdays…'

He flicked the switch back.

'…after their nap, then I put the washing on and peeled some potatoes for tonight's dinner while they watched CBeebies…' she continued in her toneless, everyday voice.

'That's enough for now, thanks,' he said crisply. He took a big gulp of his drink, and then another. 'Scarlett and, er, Mia. You'd better see what they're up to.'

'Are you okay, Dad?'

'Fine,' he snapped. 'You go off and do whatever it is you want to do.'

He closed his eyes. He needed Elizabeth now. She'd taken no nonsense from the girls. He had left them to her, which was the way she'd wanted it. All this hysteria! Elizabeth had known how to deal with them.

He sensed he was in for another bad night, and he was right. He lay rigid as a stone knight on a tomb, claustrophobic in his partially closed-down head and its frantic brain noise. The deafer he got the louder it became; that was how it was, that was the deal. He grimaced at the future, his other ear gone, reduced to the company of Matthew Herring and his like, a shoal of old boys mouthing at each other.

The thing was, he had been the breadwinner. Children needed their mothers. It was true he hadn't been very interested in them, but then, frankly, they hadn't been very interesting. Was he supposed to pretend? Neither of them had amounted to much. And he had had his own life to get on with.

He'd seen the way they were with their children these days – 'Oh that's wonderful darling! You *are* clever' and 'Love you!' at the end of every exchange, with the young fathers behaving like old women, cooing and planting big sloppy kisses on their babies as if they were in a Disney film. The whole culture had gone soft; it gave him the creeps. Opening up to your feminine side! He shuddered in his pyjamas.

Elizabeth was dead. That was what he really couldn't bear.

The noise inside his head was going wild: hooting and zooming and pressure-cooker hiss; he needed to distract his brain with – what had the doctor called it? – 'sound enrichment'. Give it some competition, fight fire with fire; that was the idea. Fiddling with the radio's tuning wheel in the dark, he swore viciously and wondered why it was you could never find the World Service when you needed it. He wanted talk but there was only music, which would have to do. Nothing but a meaningless racket to him, though at least it was a different *sort* of racket; that was the theory.

No, that was no better. If anything, it was worse.

Wasn't the hearing aid supposed to help cancel tinnitus? So the doctor had suggested. Maybe the T-setting would come into its own in this sort of situation. He turned on the tiny gadget, made the necessary adjustments, and poked it into his ear.

It was like blood returning to a dead leg, but in his head and chest. What an extraordinary sensation! It was completely new to him. Music was stealing hotly, pleasurably through his veins for the first time in his life, unspeakably delicious: at the same time it gave cruel pain, transporting inklings of what he had not known, intimations of things lovely beyond imagination which would never now be his as death was next. A tear crept down his face. He hadn't cried since he was a baby. Appalling! At this rate he'd be wetting himself. But it was so astonishingly beautiful, the music. Waves of entrancing sound were threatening to breach the sea wall. Now he was coughing dry sobs.

This was not on. Frankly he preferred any combination of troublesome symptoms to getting into this state. He fumbled with the hearing aid and at last managed to turn the damned thing *off*. Half-unhinged, he tottered to the bathroom and ran a basin of water over it, submerged the beastly little gadget, drowned it. Then he fished it out and flushed it down the lavatory. Best place for it.

No more funny business, he vowed. *That was that.* From now on he would put up and shut up, he swore it on Elizabeth's grave.

Back in bed, he once again lowered his head on to the pillow. Straight away the infernal noise factory started up; he was staggering along beat by beat in a heavy shower of noise and howling.

'It's not real,' he whispered to himself in the dark. 'Compensatory brain activity, that's what this is.'

Inside his skull all hell had broken loose. He had never heard anything like it.

STEVE MUREZ

Mavis Gallant at the Village Voice Bookshop, Paris, February 19, 2009

'USELESS CHAOS IS WHAT FICTION IS ABOUT'

Jhumpa Lahiri interviews Mavis Gallant

In 1997, I picked up a copy of Mavis Gallant's *Home Truths*, a collection of sixteen stories published in 1981, from a library book sale in the small New England town where I was raised. The first story I read, 'The Ice Wagon Going Down the Street', broke something in me – something about my prior understanding of what a story can do, and how. The story was a masterful chiaroscuro at once dense and nimble, urgent and orderly, light-hearted and dark; about experiences both pedestrian and profound. It was virtuosic without fuss, compassionate without sentimentality. It seemed to have been written in a radically different way than any story I'd read before, a live wire that crackled from start to finish on the page.

When my parents asked what I wanted for Christmas that year, I told them to get me *The Collected Stories of Mavis Gallant*, published in 1996. They honoured my request, and for the remainder of the winter I read little else but that volume, a total of 887 pages. The stories were mostly about North Americans and Europeans, many of them rootless either by circumstance or design. They were about uncovering the truth, about enduring disappointment and loss, about the recurrent shock of being alive. I was thirty years old that winter, a time when I was beginning to take the writing of stories seriously, but still lacked the conviction to regard myself as a writer. Reading those stories put an end to the questions, put the summit before me and put me on my path.

In November 2005, I met Mavis Gallant in person for the first time. The occasion was a celebration of her work held at Symphony Space in New York, in which I, along with Michael Ondaatje, Russell Banks and Edward Hirsch, took part. She had come from Paris, where she lives, to hear our tributes and then to give a reading. Mavis moved to Paris in 1950, when she was twenty-eight years old, in order to write fiction exclusively. Before that she worked as a journalist in Montreal, the city where she was born on August 11, 1922. She lost her father when she was ten years old, and was educated in a total of seventeen different convent, public and boarding schools. She married at the age of twenty and divorced five years later. In September 1951, her story, 'Madeline's Birthday', was published in *The New Yorker*. Since then, she has published more than one hundred short stories in the pages of that magazine. She has also published over a dozen collections of stories, two novels, a volume of non-fiction and a play. She is a Foreign Honorary Member of the American Academy of Arts and Letters, and among her numerous awards is the Rea Award for the Short Story, the Governor General's Award and the Order of Canada, which is the country's highest civilian honour.

By the time of our meeting at Symphony Space, Mavis was a writer I felt intimately connected to, whose work I'd read frequently and repeatedly and devotedly for close to a decade. I had never met a writer who has inspired me so greatly, and towards whom I felt such enormous debt. I was introduced to her backstage, sat with her along with the others and eventually mustered up the courage to ask her to sign one of her books. After the event there was a dinner, but because we were seated at separate tables, there had been no opportunity to talk.

The opportunity came in February 2009, when I travelled from

New York to Paris to conduct the following interview over three consecutive days. In preparing for our conversation, I decided to concentrate on three of her works. The first, *Green Water, Green Sky*, is her debut novel, published in 1959. Written in four parts, it centres on an American mother and daughter living in Europe. It is the first of many examples of the way Mavis has created a hybrid genre of complex narratives that are neither conventional chapters nor isolated stories, that are at once independent and connected and travel back and forth in time. She explores subjects that have remained preoccupations throughout her writing: foreigners in France, parents in absentia, the vicissitudes of marriage and the physical and emotional reality – as contradictory as any of her characters – of Paris itself. Each section unfolds from layered points of view, alighting, without the reader often being aware of it, from one character to the next. The result is a narrative that refuses to sit still, and the reward is the broad psychological perspective of many novels, concentrated in a relative handful of pages.

The second work I wanted to discuss, a long story called 'The Remission', published in 1979, is about an English family living in the south of France. A mature, unforgettable portrait of a dying man, 'The Remission' is thematically comparable, in my mind, to Tolstoy's 'The Death of Ivan Ilych'. The third work we discussed is a quartet of linked stories called 'The Carette Sisters', published in the mid-Eighties. Though similiar, structurally, to *Green Water, Green Sky*, the four sections of 'The Carette Sisters' do not constitute a novel. The grouping takes place, for the most part, in Montreal, and spans the lives of a widow and her two daughters over the course of half a century. My choice of the three texts was somewhat arbitrary, given that Mavis has written so many stories that may be considered paradigms of the form. Reading them together, I noted in each case, the bond – sometimes volatile, sometimes desperate, sometimes missing – between mothers and children. Representing, roughly, early, middle and late periods in Mavis's long-ranging body of work, they are three I happen to turn to again and again.

At eighty-six, Mavis remains an elegant woman. Each day she was impeccably dressed in a woollen skirt, sweater, scarf, stockings and square-heeled pumps. A medium-length coat of black wool protected her from the Paris chill and beautiful rings, an opal one among them, adorned her fingers. Her accent, soft but proper in the English manner, evoked, to my ear, the graceful and sophisticated speech of 1940s cinema. Her laughter, less formal, erupts frequently as a hearty expulsion of breath. French, the language that has surrounded her for over half a lifetime, occasionally adorns and accompanies her English. She is a spirited and agile interlocuter who tells stories as she writes them: bristling with drama, thick with dialogue, vividly rendered and studded with astringent aperçus.

We began talking at the Village Voice Bookshop, an English-language bookstore on rue Princesse in the neighbourhood of Saint-Germain-des-Prés. The shop, brightly lit and cheerfully utilitarian, has a winding metal staircase to one side, and is filled on two levels with books organized on black shelves. The owner, Odile Hellier, knows Mavis well, and warmly welcomed us both. Although Mavis suffers from osteoporosis and moves about, these days, with considerable difficulty, she ascended the metal staircase steadily on her own. Upstairs, the two of us sat by a window overlooking the dim, narrow street, on chairs wedged behind two square display tables piled with books. The view through the window was of a building covered with cloudy plastic and scaffolding. A folding table was set up between us, just large enough to hold a microcassette recorder and two glasses of water; a radiator affixed to the wall below the window kept us warm. While we were speaking, customers occasionally wandered upstairs to browse, but the atmosphere in the bookstore was tranquil, enough for us to agree to meet there the following day.

The third conversation was held at Le Dôme, a brasserie on the boulevard du Montparnasse, which is located in the neighbourhood where Mavis lives. She was greeted as a familiar when we arrived, and we were ushered to a yellow marble table set between two banquettes, where we sat beneath the glow of a hanging lamp. The atmosphere of the brasserie is old-fashioned and luxurious, with varnished wood-panelled walls, gold and amber-toned stained glass and wine-coloured velvet curtains. Mavis asked for a large cafe au lait and pointed out a cosy semi-circular banquette on the upper level, close to the bar, where Picasso liked to sit. Most of the other tables inside the restaurant were empty at that time of day and at one point a vacuum cleaner ran over the carpets. The head waiter, coming on for the night shift, also stopped by our table to say hello.

On Thursday, the day before my journey back to New York, Mavis and I read together at the Village Voice Bookshop. This time we sat side by side. Around her neck was a turquoise and dark blue silk scarf, a gift made in Brooklyn that I had presented to her at the beginning of our interview. Mavis read the story 'In Transit', followed by a scene from her play, *What is to be Done?* The crowd filled both levels of the store and each step of the staircase. As I told them before reading, that evening was the most thrilling moment of my life as a writer.

After answering questions and signing books, a small group of us walked a few doors down to have dinner at a Vietnamese restaurant. The wine was poured and conversation began to flow. I was seated directly across from Mavis, and though the interview was officially over, I kept asking her questions, about her travels, about certain scenes in her stories, about books we'd both read. When we parted, we promised to meet again one day at Le Dôme, this time for lunch, and sit at Picasso's table.

Jhumpa Lahiri, March 2009

JHUMPA LAHIRI: Was it winter when you first came to Paris?

MAVIS GALLANT: I arrived in October. I went to a hotel recommended to me by a musician I knew in Canada. It was just around the corner from here. This is only five years after the war, you see. So I lived there. The room was all red velvet. Not very clean, but I knew I had to get over that feeling. It was Paris, and I knew it was dirty. Let's see, what did I do? I unpacked, and I went for— oh yes, I went for a walk. I was coming from England, which, I have to tell you, I didn't like at all. Talk about illusion shattered.

JL: What didn't you like?

MG: I didn't like anything. I am more English than anything. I had an English father. My mother, being Canadian, was English, with, I think, some French mixed in. And I admired English writers very much, but I admired French painting more. I went for a walk, that's right, and it was still daylight. I had a large map of Paris in my apartment in Montreal, and had pasted this on my wall and studied it. I studied the Metro stops and all that. I knew them better than I know them now, because I don't take the train any more. I set out from my hotel down to the Seine and I reached the Ministry of Defence. A French sailor came over and asked for a direction in French, and I was able to give it to him. I said, '*Vous retraversez la pont, et vous verez le station Métro*', as if I'd lived here forever. I was so proud. And then I decided to have supper in a restaurant called Raffi. It wasn't recommended to me, I just looked at it. You had to go up some steps. I watched to see what people were eating. And I saw people eating radishes with butter on them, so I ordered that. For the first time in my life I tasted sweet butter, because we only had salted butter in Canada – it was called Jewish butter, and it was sold in the Jewish part of Montreal. I'd never tasted sweet butter. It was delicious! And I remember the radish didn't taste like our radishes, which were really just used for decoration. The bread was delicious, just lovely with sweet butter. And I had a pork chop.

JL: You remember.

MG: Oh, I do. And French fries. I think I had apple tart, but I'm not sure about that. I just looked at what people were eating. That I remember. Raffi's is now a Korean barbecue, and I recognize it only because there's still the steps. I've looked in – I've never eaten anything there – but the general skeleton of the place is still what it was in October 1950.

JL: Did anything disappoint you when you came here?

MG: I wouldn't say disappoint. I was very disappointed in London. I didn't like the people. I thought they were rude. They had a reputation for being polite, but they weren't. I didn't really understand. They were still rationed. They were bitter. They thought that we people from across the Atlantic were very well off, very spoiled; that we didn't know what a war was. And I became something I'm not really, which was nationalist. I don't like nationalism, and I thought, my God, every Canadian buried in a Commonwealth cemetery in the Second World War was a volunteer. There was no conscription in Canada for fighting. About halfway through the war, conscription was established for desk jobs, but service overseas was filled by volunteers. So there were all these people buried in France and Italy and Libya, taken at Hong Kong, taken at Singapore. I felt defensive of them because they were my generation. I didn't argue, but I didn't like it. They didn't like us. They took me for an American. I don't consider it an insult, and I was not looking to say, 'I'm one of these sweet Canadians everybody likes.'

JL: But Paris?

MG: To me it was literary.

JL: More than England?

MG: More than London. I'd read a great deal of French writers. I'd read a lot of Colette. François Mauriac. I'd always read French all my life, but I didn't prefer it to English, and I still don't. Not for writing, anyway. Oh, there were things I had to adjust to. I had been working on a newspaper, the *Standard* in Montreal, and suddenly I was in a large city. I had no more salary; I had no relatives here. I had introductions to people, but I didn't know anybody. I had all the expats somehow between me and France. It was a great time for expatriates. Five years after the war, everyone was dying to get to Europe. But what I loved in Paris itself – how can I explain it? Montreal at that time was a very cosmopolitan city because of the émigrés and refugees, which I liked, but there was hardly a bookstore you could rely on in English, and in Quebec there was a political oppression that I thought would never change. I had lived in New York so I didn't want to go back to New York. I wanted Europe. But here, there was a bookstore – many more, they're closing like mad – on every corner. There was something on every corner that was pleasing to me. I never made a move to meet anyone, to meet a writer. Whereas, when I came back from New York at eighteen, I found Montreal small, but as I lived in it and became a newspaper reporter I began to know the city and it was very complex; the French, the English, the Catholic, the Protestant. I made great efforts between eighteen and twenty-eight to meet every poet, every artist, every musician, because I seemed to need it. Once I got here I didn't need it. It was just there. I went to concerts, I went to the opera, sitting way up high in cheap seats. But I had no desire to meet them, to meet singers. It was the atmosphere.

JL: You had it.

MG: I had it here. So I got the feeling that Paris was like someone saying, 'You can have the run of the house, you can wander all over my house, you can open drawers and take books off the shelves, but we are apart.'

JL: 'We' being the French?

MG: Yes. But it was like a house where you could do anything you like.

JL: How long after you came here did you begin writing about it?

MG: I don't keep records, but I wrote a story called 'The Other Paris' [published in 1953], one of my first stories, and I wrote it that winter in Paris. It took me a long time to write. I left the hotel after a month because I realized I was seeing too many expatriates. I went to the Canadian Embassy and they had a book there of French people who wanted to rent rooms in their apartments. This was the hard-up French after the war. And they wanted – they didn't say this – but they wanted Canadians or Swedes or Swiss. Nice clean people. And I found a room that looked all right. The first man I talked to said, 'If this is a room, it's for you only, not *les copains, les copines'* because people would try to rent a room and squeeze all their friends in. I didn't like his tone, so I tried another phone number. I wanted a good bourgeois family who had roots in France – in Paris – so I could study them. I sound as if I was collecting butterflies, and I did. They lived on la rue de Monceau on the Right Bank, a very respectable street, infinitely respectable. It horrified the people I knew. 'You're going to live over there?' 'Yes, I am!' It was a youngish couple. They had two little boys. All of them became very fond of me. He was a civil servant and they were titled, but they were hard-up. They had beautiful furniture that they had inherited and they were very, very right wing, and if you wonder what I did, I kept my trap shut. I had no desire to argue. They were in their country, and I was friendly with them until they both died. Years and years and years.

JL: How long did you stay with them?

MG: In the spring I went for three months to the south, but I kept in touch with them, and they said, 'We always have a bed for you.' I rented something in the south of France because *The New Yorker* paid me for something.

JL: Were you here when you sold your first story to them?

MG: No, I sold one story when I was in Montreal. I gave my newspaper six months' leave – six months, what do you call it?

JL: Notice.

MG: Notice, thank you. It was funny, the men at the *Standard* were friendly in a brother-sister knockabout way, you know. But they just didn't want to work with women. One of them said to me, 'You're going over there? What are you going to do? What are you going to live on?' I said, 'Writing. I'm going to write.' He said, 'Write what?' I said, 'Stories'. He said, 'You know, you're like an architect who's never designed a garage.' That was his view of what I was going to do. But I had a lot of stories I'd never shown anyone, so I fished one out, typed it and sent it to *The New Yorker*. I didn't tell anyone. There was no note. There was my name and the address of my newspaper on the first page of the manuscript. It was up in the corner: St James Street West. And that came back, but with a letter, a very nice letter, saying we can't use this – they told me later why they couldn't – but is there anything else you can show us? So I sent a second one and they took it. They paid me six hundred dollars, which was more than I had ever had in the bank. I couldn't believe it. And I made the great mistake of showing my colleagues at the newspaper my letter of acceptance. It was a great mistake.

JL: Why?

MG: Because they were men.

JL: And they were upset?

MG: They were stupefied, first of all. And then, wishing they had the freedom to go away as I was going to go. They all had a mortgage and three kids. In a suburb.

JL: They were stuck.

MG: Stuck, yes. I had prepared three stories to show *The New Yorker*. They had rejected one and taken one. The third story, which was also accepted, I sent from Paris. At the beginning I wrote about foreigners, not understanding the French, or looking at them and getting it all wrong.

JL: And what interested you in that? Was it partly that you were going through it?

MG: Well, I'm a writer. That was the way I saw it, and I couldn't very well write about how the French looked at us. I couldn't get inside their skin. You have to be here for a long time, in a certain way. There was a story about the Americans in France called 'The Picnic'. Did you ever read that story?

JL: Yes. The picnic is concocted by an American magazine, an event to symbolize the unity between America and France. But there's no unity between the French and the American characters in the story. There's suspicion on both sides. The American woman worries that her children are being corrupted by French waywardness. And the French woman is appalled when the American throws out a wilting cauliflower. Which the French cook retrieves from the garbage.

MG: Those were situations I saw and felt and listened to, but I wanted to get into the French way of looking at us. So it began with 'The Other Paris' – the young woman expects so much from Paris and settles for something else. There's a story called 'Virus X' you may have come across. There are two Canadian girls. One of them has a fiancé in Canada. I've forgotten what she's doing here, but she's doing something.

JL: I believe she's writing a thesis about immigrants.

MG: The first wave of Asian flu was winter of 1952–53. And I caught it. I was in Strasbourg.

JL: Is that what the characters in 'The Cost of Living' also have, living in that hotel? Asian flu? You describe illness in a foreign place so effectively. I love the bit about the sister going out to get soup for everyone in a Thermos. 'Our grippe smelled of oranges, and of leek-and-potato soup.'

MG: Everybody got flu every winter. There was no vaccination in those days. First of all, the symptoms were like pneumonia, but nobody knew what it was. I mean, none of the doctors in the world knew what the first wave was about. That was why in France it was called Virus X. They were treating for pneumonia, which it turns out it wasn't at all, and there were a lot of deaths. I was in Strasbourg in a little hotel and at that point I had complicated my life with a dog. I was very very sick, had a very high temperature. There was a man in the next room, an elderly French man who lived there, and I was delirious. I thought I saw him walking through the wall. He used to say, *'Ma voisine, ma voisine!'* and he'd take my dog out. But in the story there's a girl – not me – and her boyfriend finally comes over to get her. And she is afraid that if she doesn't go back with him, she will be adrift. She's, on the contrary, very pleased to see him, and ready to go into a very restricted life because she's had a bad time with Virus X. *The New Yorker* ran that story. They would take a chance on things that others wouldn't.

JL: I asked you about the winter because I thought in many of those early stories, 'The Cost of Living' and 'The Other Paris', there's a very vivid experience of the season.

MG: The winters are rather dreadful.

JL: Differently from Montreal?

MG: In Montreal you're cold. You have sun on snow there.

JL: So it's the lack of sun.

MG: Lack of sun. That's why the first spring, I went for three months to Menton. I had never seen light in the south – I'd never been south of New York. I'd never seen the light that you get in the southern climate.

JL: And this made a big impression on you?

MG: I took a bus so that I could see a lot of France. Through Grenoble. We spent the night in Grenoble. Very interesting. Down, down, down to Nice. It was night when I arrived. I just asked in the bus station where I could find a hotel. I went to this hotel and my bed was facing a mirror, one of these big armoires with mirrored doors where you put your clothes, and the window was behind my head. And when I woke up in the morning, there was this fantastic sun in the window. I'd never seen that kind of light. Then I got a train and continued to Menton which was where my house was rented, my flat. And I carried my things and asked for directions and I found myself in the first old town I'd ever seen. It was medieval. In fact the old Roman road was the main street.

JL: Was that town partly inspiration for the setting of 'The Remission'?

MG: Much later. 'The Remission' is much later.

JL: But was it the same sort of place?

MG: No. I was in the old town. They collected the garbage with a horse and wagon. And the garbage man wore boots and stood in the middle of this unwrapped garbage. Just stood in the middle and people threw it out the window. It was really something. I loved it. I was very thrilled with it. Then I came back to Paris. I always came back to Paris. I spent ten years coming and going. I spent ten years, really, wandering through Western Europe.

JL: Your characters seem always to be comparing two ways of life in their minds. It's something I've grown up with, because my parents came from India and raised me in a place that was foreign to them.

MG: They didn't go home to live?

JL: No. They go to visit, but they've stayed in America. So I've been brought up with people who have that exchange rate going on in their brains, always converting and comparing.

MG: I don't compare.

JL: But your characters?

MG: I don't know. It depends.

JL: A lot of them have an idea of Paris, say, and then they come, and they're here, and it's not matching the image or the ideal, and they struggle with that.

MG: I remember one of the people around in that winter of 1950–51, and who I moved to the Right Bank to get away from, was Mordecai Richler. He was a bit of a brat. He was much younger. I'd met him in Montreal. The person who introduced me to him was the brother of the actor, Donald Sutherland. Anyway, he said, 'As you're going over to Europe, Mordecai Richler is going over and I'll have you meet him. He's very difficult, I warn you.' That winter everyone in the world was around Paris that I knew, practically. And I realized he didn't like it at all. For one thing, he couldn't speak any French. Though he came from Montreal, he couldn't say, 'Pass the salt.' He couldn't say anything.

JL: That's difficult for people, if they don't have the language. It affects you at every point.

MG: Well, it's a language you're able to learn. I mean, I didn't learn Finnish, I didn't even try, because it's not an Indo-European language, not anything I could cope with. I did speak English there, but I didn't live there. I rented a car, was just travelling along. But I didn't feel frustrated. It was their country, their language. But Mordecai resented having to speak French. He said, 'Anyway, what can you do in a country that's old and rotten and falling down?' Those were his words. Well at that time, it was burgeoning with writers, French writers. It was really the great period of the twentieth century. Colette was still alive, all these people were still alive, writing, producing. Gide had only just died that year. You breathed the air, the same air as these people I so admired. One day I was sitting reading in a cafe. And Mordecai came drifting over and he sat down and he grabbed the book out of my hand that I was reading. It was *The House in Paris*, Elizabeth Bowen's great novel.

JL: Which I just read.

MG: Oh it's wonderful. And he read some in a mocking voice. A mocking English voice which he didn't do very well. And he said, 'You know, if you go on reading this crap you're never going to get anywhere.' So I just took the book back.

* * *

JL: I want to talk about your first novel, *Green Water, Green Sky*, which consists of four parts. How did it begin?

MG: I had it pretty well in mind. It was my idea of a novel. *The New Yorker* published the first three parts. They didn't publish the fourth because you couldn't understand the fourth if you hadn't read the other three.

JL: It moves from Venice to Paris to Cannes, and then returns to Paris. Chronologically, it goes back and forth. Why did you decide to do that?

MG: I can't tell you. That's what I wanted.

JL: I find it so much more poignant because it's out of sequence. We know how things are going to turn out, and that they don't turn out well. Bob and Flor's marriage, for example. The first time I read this, I remembered being so haunted by the description, in the second section, of Flor staying alone in the apartment in August, when everybody in Paris famously goes away.

MG: This was someone with schizophrenia.

JL: When I reread it a few months ago, I remembered the moment she's wandering in the kitchen, looking for something to eat, and finds a sticky packet of dates. As I was reading that section, I suddenly remembered that that detail was approaching, and I dreaded it, because I knew how much it would unsettle me. That happens to me a lot when I read your stories. The smallest details are so incredibly resonant. And so memorable.

MG: Eating with her fingers.

JL: Yes, eating with her fingers. Eating mushrooms out of a tin.

MG: Well you see, that part of it is very dated, because now she would be cured with pills. Then there was no cure.

JL: Even with medication, people still suffer from schizophrenia these days. Flor's suffering is acute in the second part. She sees a psychiatrist, a relationship that threatens her family.

MG: Well, she has a mental argument with a psychiatrist, who is a woman – *you old frump, trying to tell me...* – and unaware of the way people will react to her. Completely unaware. She speaks to people and they don't know who she is. Being frightened by a stuffed horse in a window. That actually existed. There was a stuffed horse in a window at an antique store. I don't think anyone was meant to buy it. It was just there. She slides away.

JL: Did you know that this would be her mental state when you began the novel?

MG: I had roomed at school with a girl with schizophrenia. Her reaction was very different. Though she didn't like her mother, either. I remember she scribbled all over her mother's picture. I read Proust later on, and you get the thing about the lesbian making the other lesbian scribble all over her parents' picture. So I thought, 'That's true, that can happen, Mr Proust.' She ran around the room screaming. She had asked her mother for some money to buy a bathing suit. And her mother had written – I remember the letter – 'Buy a simple, modest number.' And she ran around the room.

JL: How old were you when you knew this girl?

MG: I was about fifteen. And I felt I should never tell anyone. I never told anyone about this rampage. I didn't think I should.

JL: But eventually, this girl inspired Flor's character.

MG: It was a determined ending. There was no other way out. I didn't know of any way out but going deeper and deeper. In her case, silence.

JL: The third section, which was published as a story called 'Travellers Must be Content', takes place in Cannes. Can you talk a little about the character of Wishart, a bachelor who comes to visit Flor and her mother, Bonnie? He's so horrible. A snob, a liar, an operator, a misogynist.

MG: I don't think people try so hard to shed their background now. In fact, they'll say, my father drove a bus, look where I've got. Wishart works to be accepted in America as an okay Englishman, and accepted in England as an okay American.

JL: So much dissimulation.

MG: I don't know if you've ever been with anyone like that. They abound. Then they'll make some mistake.

JL: He reminded me of a less benign version of someone like Jay Gatsby or Holly Golightly, one of those American characters who try fully to conceal who they are, and where they're from.

MG: His mistake is when he thinks that Flor's mother is offering her daughter. That's his social mistake.

JL: And he has such a terrible impression of the world of women. To him it's 'an area dimly lighted and faintly disgusting, like a kitchen in a slum... a world of migraines, miscarriages, disorder and tears'.

MG: Well, he's gay.

JL: I don't think being gay has anything to do with that.

MG: There are men like that, who have the depths of horror about what happens to women.

JL: Yet Wishart's also dependent on women, a parasite. He seeks them out.

MG: A leech, socially.

JL: But we can't fully condemn him. I can't. He's vulnerable in his own way, standing on his skinny legs. The story opens and ends with dreams. I like that you write about dreams. I was warned when I was just starting out writing, by a wonderful writer and teacher, never to write about people dreaming. He was against characters having dreams in stories.

MG: Well they're the people who think dreams are boring. I think they're fascinating.

JL: Have you kept a journal since childhood?

MG: I've stopped, except now and then. Up to 2000, I wrote regularly.

JL: When did you begin it?

MG: I had one when I was still in Canada, but I destroyed it when I left. I was going to a new life.

JL: So you wanted to destroy the evidence. Did you start it as a child? A teenager?

MG: I did as a teenager, sporadically. I had to be very careful, living with my mother. She went through my things like a beaver.

JL: But you always wrote in it honestly?

MG: At fourteen I wrote a poem called 'Why I am a Socialist'. It began, 'You ask?' Of course, no one had ever asked me if I even knew what socialism was. I had got hold of *A New Anthology of Modern Poetry*, published in 1938. I was fifteen and that was the Depression. Left-wing poetry I admired enormously. I liked the marching rhythm. There was Auden and company. There was Ezra Pound, so they weren't all left wing. I read this stuff over and over, knew it by heart. Muriel Rukeyser; the gang. And this inspired 'Why I am a Socialist'. It was a better world. And my mother found this. She wanted to know who I was mixed up with. Mothers then were very interested in preserving their daughters' sexual purity.

JL: Some mothers now, too.

MG: For the marriage market. She drove me cuckoo. She read everything. I never could keep anything to myself.

JL: So you destroyed the journal when you left Canada.

MG: In the building where I was living, in Montreal, you could burn garbage. People just threw things down a slot and there was a fire smouldering. I don't know why we weren't all asphyxiated.

JL: You've published some parts of your journal. I keep a journal as well, but it's never seen the light of day. It's hard for me to imagine having a part of it published. How does that feel?

MG: It feels – nothing. They're authentic. They sound different because it's where I am when I'm writing.

JL: One usually writes a journal with a different sensibility. You don't think of anyone reading it.

MG: But I think some things are interesting to read.

JL: You published a section of your journal in 1988 in the literary magazine *Antaeus* which I came across. On April 25, 1987 you wrote,

'I am thankful I do not have to live in a village, anywhere.'

MG: Oh, I would hate it.

JL: I was struck by that.

MG: I remember going to a dreary village outside Paris. They're very ugly. There's one street and everything is battleship grey. Awful colour. But that's the Ile de France. You go in to buy a newspaper and they all stop talking, to look at you. I love cities.

JL: Me too. But I wasn't raised in one. I was raised in pretty much a village. It's difficult as an adult, because I wasn't brought up in any other place, so all my memories of childhood are connected to a place I feel deeply ambivalent about. It wasn't until I got to a city, in my case New York, that I felt I could breathe properly and things were normal, even though it was a place that I didn't know at all. Until that moment, I really did feel that I was holding my breath.

MG: What I have noticed is how much you redo places and houses you've lived in when you were young. I think it was James Thurber who wrote a very funny essay called 'Mind's Eye Trouble', because you unconsciously take some house you lived in as a child and you redo it in your mind and there are these other characters, but it's not where you lived at all. It could be in a different city. Have you ever noticed that?

JL: I haven't lived in very many houses, but the ones I remember, I remember fairly well.

MG: To me the Chateauguay river, which is outside Montreal, has been everything. Even the Nile.

JL: It stands in for other things.

MG: They stand in. Whereas the characters don't do that. They come up – I don't know where they come from. They're just – they're there.

JL: In your journals and essays, you're such a shrewd observer of the world, and of world events. That section of your journal we were just discussing follows the Klaus Barbie trial.

MG: Don't forget, I was a journalist from age twenty-one to twenty-eight. That's a big chunk of your life.

JL: And you've maintained a journalistic connection with the world.

MG: Less now, because I'm physically hobbled. For example, in that journal – 'Paris '68' – I get up in the middle of the night, I get dressed, I go out to see somebody throwing stones. But now I stay home because I'm physically fragile. I could be knocked over. I could break all my bones.

JL: And yet some of your characters are so shamefully ignorant. I'm thinking of Marie and her mother, Madame Carette, in 'The Chosen Husband', who have never heard of Korea while a war is taking place there.

MG: 'There's a war on. Where? Not there, in Korea.'

JL: Do you think it's easier or harder to be a foreigner in France these days?

MG: It's hard for me to say. I'm not often taken for a foreigner.

JL: But in your observations?

MG: I wouldn't want to be a foreigner in the US, I can tell you.

JL: Even now?

MG: No.

JL: I actually think it's somewhat easier to be a foreigner there now. For some groups it's harder. But for the most part, I think America has gotten more accustomed to the idea of foreign populations arriving and settling and working their way into the culture. When I was growing up, most Americans had no real sense of India. But now, there's a relatively more informed sense of India, and of other parts of the world as well. And there's more of an effort, on the whole, to be inclusive. Obama is an obvious symbol for all this.

MG: We were all cuckoo for Obama.

JL: But have attitudes toward foreign populations in France changed or intensified? I was in Italy last summer, and the Italians seem really to be struggling in terms of what's happening to the identity of their country. There seems to be a real fear of the culture being watered down, tarnished somehow.

MG: In France there will be many, many foreign-born people who can carry on the culture. Which is declining, by the way. It's not declining because of foreigners. It's declining because the French school system is declining. I hear the French spoken around me and I say, no! The vocabulary is shrinking. With foreigners in Canada, they were left alone. They were there and they were working and paying taxes, and that's all. I was writer in residence for a year in Toronto.

JL: When was this?

MG: 1983–84.

JL: Did you enjoy that experience?

MG: I would never do it again. I think it's a dead loss. I'm opposed to it. You can't teach writing.

JL: Given that you were there, what did you teach them?

MG: They should know their language and read. Read, read, read.

JL: What did you have your students read?

MG: I was considered staff, so I had a markdown in the campus bookstore. I bought a lot of paperbacks, Penguins, with twenty per cent off. I had them on my desk. They'd say, 'Well I don't have any money on me.' And I said, 'No, I'm not selling them. If you like it, keep it. If you don't like it, give it to a friend or bring it back and I'll give it to someone else.' I gave them books I myself don't care for. I gave them Raymond Carver.

JL: Why did you give them books you didn't care for?

MG: I thought it my duty to open them up to different things. Otherwise I was there for nothing.

JL: Who was the person who first read your writing and told you that you should keep going?

MG: Just, 'Have you anything else you can show me?' Her name was Mildred Wood. She read the first story I sent to *The New Yorker*. I saw her twice, at *The New Yorker*, before I went to Europe.

JL: And she was the first person you ever showed your work to? Had you shown your writing to anyone else along the way? Any friend?

MG: Very seldom. I didn't want them to talk to me about it. There was one friend at the newspaper, Barbara. She wanted to be a poet, so we talked together and showed each other things, but that was it. I don't think anyone can help, you know. Now *Green Water* I showed – I had the proofs, and I was in hospital in Switzerland because of my back. I'd gone there instead of France, because in France they didn't know much about spines at the time. The owner of this clinic had studied psychiatry, this Swiss gentleman, but then he felt that most things are physical and he got interested in the brain, so he worked on brains and spines. And the proofs arrived in that clinic that I had to read and correct. And I still wasn't sure about the last story. I gave him just the last story to read.

JL: What were you unsure of?

MG: I wasn't sure if it was clinically correct. I didn't want something imaginative and poetic where she goes off into a dream. I asked, 'Do people like that commit suicide?' and he said, 'No, it's another thing altogether.' So that was really helpful. And I left it as I had it, where she goes into silence. He said she wouldn't have the initiative to pick up a gun or throw herself out the window. It's not despair – it's something up here [points to her head] – but she would have been unable to come to a decision.

JL: There's a real intimacy to the scenes. I would love for the novel to be reissued so that people could buy it and read it. I'd like to talk about the way you write about children.

MG: I like children. I had no desire to bring up children, that was a different thing. But I like them and I often feel sorry for them. The first time I ever saw children being hit in the face was when I came to France. I couldn't stand it. You'd go to a park and the mother's first gesture was to... I'd never seen that. The face slap.

JL: You often write about children who are profoundly neglected. Their parents are off doing things, living their lives. I think a degree of that is healthy, but so many children in your stories are just passing the time, wandering around, while difficult, grown-up things are happening, and the grown-ups are oblivious to their needs. The children in 'The Remission', for example.

MG: They're culturally dropped. I see it often happen with writers and artists who take their children to a village in Provence. They put them in the ordinary school, and they're culturally deprived, because they don't read what their parents read, and then it's too late.

JL: I didn't read what my parents read.

MG: But you had books around you. I can't remember not seeing books. And my books were separated from the grown-up books because my father had a lot of books of art and reproductions. I thought they were stories, illustrations for something I hadn't read. One book he was very careful of, an out-of-print book about Egyptian art. The colour pages had white behind them, that's how old a book it was. And then there were sepia photographs of different things, which were very interesting to me. What interested me was that you could colour this book, and I took it into my room and with wax crayons I coloured all the white sheets and made drawings. Then I tackled the black-and-white engravings and then I tackled the sepia photos and I put the book back. And once he had a friend in for something and he said, 'I'll just show you what I mean' and he pulled out the book, and it was ruined. So from that day on... I wasn't punished, but I was struck by his distress. 'You can do what you like, but don't touch anything else, ever!'

JL: I find children a particular challenge to write about. Do you feel the same way?

MG: In my house in the south of France I had a spare room for friends, and I sometimes had a child or two thrust into my care just so the parents could have a few days if they were travelling; nip down to Florence without them screaming in the back seat. I never had a problem with a child. I would say, 'Would you like to eat this, or not?' and they always said yes. We went up to an Italian place on the frontier and they had a choice of spaghetti or pizza, and then ice cream.

JL: I think children just like to be taken seriously. When I read your stories, I think you take them seriously, and that's the key. Because the parents don't.

MG: I had one little boy, Olivier. I was very fond of him. He would come up with the most astonishing things. One day – he was a very talkative little boy – I was trying to think of something. And I said, 'Olivier, sit down, don't talk, and don't talk for at least two minutes.' He didn't know if he should call me *vous* or *toi*. I left it up to him, and he'd say *vous-toi*. He said, '*Vous-toi*, you're not nice. *Tu n'est pas gentille*', and I said, 'I'm very nice indeed.' And he said, 'You're not as nice as you think you are.' Remarkable. And you think, I wonder if that's true? If they see clearly.

JL: My children teach me a lot. They'll say something and I really have to stop and look at things differently. The sense of childhood in your stories is really one of being in a prison. The children have no freedom. I felt that growing up.

MG: The prison of childhood used to come into my mind sometimes. Not when I was a child. Later.

JL: It's a phrase of yours, in the story 'In Youth is Pleasure'. Nabokov is an example of a writer who looks back on his childhood with such pure fondness.

MG: They had a high life.

JL: But many people, my own mother included, look back on their childhood and think of it as a liberating, dreamy, ideal period. My mother grew up and everything landed on her shoulders. I feel exactly the opposite way.

MG: Oh, me too.

* * *

JL: I'd like to ask you some questions about 'The Remission'. This is a story you wrote in the Seventies but that takes place in the Fifties. Can you talk about what inspired the story?

MG: I don't know. I just had an image of them getting down from the train, which I didn't use in the story, with the children.

JL: Can you talk about the experience of going back in time to write a story?

MG: They come with their clothes on, and he's going to die on National Health. No one would say that any more. Meaning social security. I've written a lot about the British on the Riviera after the war. I found them highly comic.

JL: In what way?

MG: Nylon skirts came in during that period. You could hang them up to dry and there was no ironing. Miraculous! I had a Black Watch tartan skirt with pleats. I'd wash it and dry it on a line and my British neighbour, whom I was renting my darling cottage from, came up when I was hanging it and she said, 'My dear, are you a Scot?' Actually there's a trace of Scot on my father's side, but I didn't go into that. And I said, 'No' and she said, 'You should not be wearing that kind of tartan you're putting up.' And I said, 'Why?' 'Well it's an insult to the family.' I said, 'I don't know much about Scots, we don't have them in Canada.' My dear, we have the largest number of Robbie Burns statues in the whole world! She said, 'It's just that the Scots take great objection to the wrong people wearing their tartans.'

JL: You talked yesterday about experiencing the light for the first time in the south of France. When I read this story, I'm always struck by the husband's and wife's separate relationships to the sun. Alec initially seeks the sun, moving from England to the south of France for it, but ends up hiding in the shadows. While Barbara is sunbathing nude, like something out of Greek mythology.

MG: She imagines the gardener looking up at her. But you know, she's not unkind to her husband. I don't think she's an unkind woman at all. She sits beside him as he's dying, she takes his hand. She talks about their future together. The fact that she has a lover doesn't come into it. She keeps that in another compartment.

JL: This is one of many examples in your stories where at some point or another we're in every character's head. It's an amalgam of points of view. It's what Tolstoy does in his novels, but you do it in the confines of a story. For me, it was very hard to get to that point. When I first started writing, I always wrote from a single person's point of view. But in your work, even in something early like *Green Water, Green Sky*, you're already dipping in and out of various characters' minds. Was this something that came easily?

MG: It must have, or I wouldn't have done it.

JL: I felt that I couldn't do it. I read your stories and other people's stories to learn. I didn't know how to go about it. But for you it felt natural?

MG. I never questioned it. The problem is getting it right.

JL: You're very funny, in this story, describing assiduous tourists. They struggle up steep hills to look at early Renaissance frescoes. Meanwhile, to Barbara's eyes, they're just 'some patches of peach-coloured smudge'. This must have been a time in Europe when a lot of tourists were arriving?

MG: I've never known it without tourists. Not like now, not like these mechanized hordes.

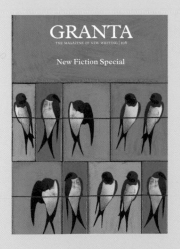

TEAR ALONG PERFORATION TO REMOVE

Gift subscription offer: take out an annual subscription as a gift and you will also receive a complimentary *Granta* special-edition MOLESKINE® notebook

GIFT SUBSCRIPTION 1

Address:

TITLE: INITIAL: SURNAME:

ADDRESS:

POSTCODE:

TELEPHONE:

EMAIL:

GIFT SUBSCRIPTION 2

Address:

TITLE: INITIAL: SURNAME:

ADDRESS:

POSTCODE:

TELEPHONE:

EMAIL:

YOUR ADDRESS FOR BILLING

TITLE: INITIAL: SURNAME:

ADDRESS:

POSTCODE:

TELEPHONE: EMAIL:

NUMBER OF SUBSCRIPTIONS	DELIVERY REGION	PRICE	
☐	UK	£34.95	All prices include delivery
☐	Europe	£39.95	YOUR TWELVE-MONTH SUBSCRIPTION
☐	Rest of World	£45.95	WILL INCLUDE FIVE ISSUES

I would like my subscription to start from:

☐ the current issue ☐ the next issue

PAYMENT DETAILS

☐ I enclose a cheque payable to '*Granta*' for £ ________ for ____ subscriptions to *Granta*

☐ Please debit my ☐ MASTERCARD ☐ VISA ☐ AMEX for £ ________ for ____ subscriptions

NUMBER ☐☐☐☐ ☐☐☐☐ ☐☐☐☐ ☐☐☐☐ SECURITY CODE ☐☐☐

EXPIRY DATE ☐☐ / ☐☐ SIGNED ____________ DATE ________

☐ Please tick this box if you would like to receive special offers from *Granta*

☐ Please tick this box if you would like to receive offers from organizations selected by *Granta*

Please return this form to: **Granta Subscriptions, PO Box 2068, Bushey, Herts, WD23 3ZF, UK, call Freephone 0500 004 033** or go to **www.granta.com**

Please quote the following promotion code when ordering online: **GBIUK106**

JL: One of the reasons Barbara seems pathetic to me is that she's so dependent on other people, other family members, for money. Things have changed so much since then, for women of my generation, certainly, in terms of more women being part of the workforce and being able to stand on their own.

MG: The sister-in-law is the pathetic one to me. She gives up part of her capital, which is tiny, so that her brother can go rest in the south of France. I don't think she's ever adequately thanked.

JL: Do you remember how long it took you to write this story?

MG: It took a very long time. I'm a very slow writer. There are things I've taken out, put away, taken out, put away. Other things, 'Across the Bridge', I wrote at great speed.

JL: Your writing is remarkable across the board, but I find 'The Remission' particularly first-rate. Do you have a sense of how strong it is?

MG: I don't compare stories. They're like the beads on this [fingers her necklace].

JL: But looking back, is there a point when you think, 'This was my earlier effort?' Are you aware of a progression?

MG: It's just a straight line to me.

JL: It's all connected, one off the next?

MG: I suppose so. There were years when I was doing nothing else. In the south of France I just wrote the whole time.

JL: Where did you work on this story? In Paris?

MG: Mostly in Paris.

JL: It ran in *The New Yorker*. Was it edited by Bill Maxwell?

MG: Yes. Then he had to leave because he was sixty-five. There's never been as good an editor. He was prudish, and I had trouble with his prudishness, not to speak of William Shawn's. They would say to me,

'Maybe those things go on in Canada, but they don't go on here.' The slightest hint of anything. I don't like pornography. But I'm very conscious of sexual tension. I think that's the most interesting thing to write about, the tension.

JL: There's a moment in this story that's so powerful. The children have come to see their father in the hospital, and he's about to die. After the visit, there's a description of them skipping down the stairway now that the obligation is over with, 'taking the hospital stairs headlong, at a gallop'. To me it's an example of why I love short stories. You can compress such enormous emotion and human experience into just a handful of words. It happens very seldom in novels. Novels have a more cumulative effect.

MG: There are novels sent to me by publishers to read. And I do try. And I can see where they had to fill a gap. I see it! I think, why did they need that? Take it out and tighten it.

JL: I'm working on a novel now, but I'm always conscious of that, of putting in something to fill the space between point A and point B. I just want to go, AB, not A, A-and-a-half, B.

MG: Exactly. Absolutely.

JL: I think that's the difference between stories and novels.

MG: Well, in the short story you can't fiddle around and wander. There are writers who do it, but I don't like it.

JL: Did you watch the Coronation on television the way the characters do in the story?

MG: Oh yes. I was living in the south. And the man who gets up to watch, the father… I realized years later that was my father. He didn't live beyond thirty-four. I don't mean he was crazy about the royal family: I never heard him talk about them – he died some twenty years before the Queen's coronation – but I recognized that he was that man.

JL: Does that happen often when you look back at things? You see something you didn't at the time of writing?

MG: Later. When I read, I think, my God. That's so deep in me.

JL: Do you look at your writing if you don't have to?

MG: If I have to give a reading I read a lot of things.

JL: How is that experience?

MG: It's completely mechanical, looking at the clock. I time them and I read them. There's a difference between speaking your work and reading. It's meant to be read silently, of course. So while I'm reading I'll change just a few words.

JL: Have you read 'The Remission' aloud?

MG: No. It's very long.

JL: Not even a part of it?

MG: I don't read parts of stories. Unless it's an evening where everything is in bits. Then I might. I don't prefer it, but if that's what they ask me to do.

JL: 'They'. The authorities.

MG: The police.

JL: I can't say I've read everything you've written, I haven't.

MG: Of course not. You're not writing a PhD, for God's sake.

JL: But every time I go back to one of your stories, it's absolutely fresh. It never tires. There's something so alive about your work. I can never just say, 'Oh, I've read that one.' No matter how many times I've read it. That experience is very rare.

MG: That's very good to hear for my age. My point in life. It's good to hear that you feel that.

JL: That's why I've read some of your stories literally a dozen or fifteen times. I keep turning to them. I can never fully take them in. I mean that in a good way.

MG: I had that experience with Elizabeth Bowen's 'Mysterious Kôr'.

I knew it almost by heart. It's one of her wartime London stories. It's a couple in the blackout with a bright moon. He's leaving, he's got one day's leave. They go hand in hand, they look at a park. They have nowhere to sleep together is what I'm trying to say. She starts to recite Andrew Lang's 'Mysterious Kôr' by moonlight. He's probably someone who's never heard a poem in his life, but he listens. And she is living in London with another young woman whose apartment it is and who is very – I can't say prudish because that was the period. So this girl is trying to get the girl who owns this apartment to go to a hotel for a night. And she says, 'Oh my dear, I don't think your mother would want me to do that. I don't mind playing gooseberry.' You know what a gooseberry was? The chaperone.

JL: What do you admire in particular about Bowen?

MG: Oh, I loved her stories.

JL: Did you ever meet her?

MG: I never tried to. But there's a book of her love letters to Charles Ritchie, and I did know him very well. He was Canadian. I knew his whole family. I was married from his aunt's house in Ottawa. Bowen was married to the head of the BBC and it was an unconsummated marriage. I don't know what happened. She wouldn't leave him to go marry Ritchie, the love of her life and her lover for years. And he got fed up with the situation. In the long run he may have felt it was humiliating for him to hang around.

JL: Have you kept count of how many stories you've written?

MG: There are over one hundred in *The New Yorker*. My files were always a big mess. When did we find out how many stories there were? Oh yes, when they were putting together what I call The Big Book [the *Collected Stories,* also called the *Selected Stories* in Britain and Canada]. There were over one hundred published in *The New Yorker* and then those that were published elsewhere. At the beginning they didn't take everything I sent so they appeared in other magazines like *Glamour* and *Esquire*. There weren't many outlets for fiction.

JL: Now even less so.

MG: I don't understand why they train students to write short stories when there's so little outlet for them.

JL: I think they're easier to respond to. My sense is that it's easier to tell a student what's working and not working in ten pages than in two hundred and fifty. When I first started writing, my efforts were just two or four pages. I didn't write more because I wanted to make sure those two or four pages were okay. I've crept incrementally toward longer work.

MG: I don't approve of writing classes for people with no talent.

JL: I don't know if I would ever have written fiction if I hadn't been in a class where someone encouraged me.

MG: Encouragement is different. But to teach them, how can you do that? And your teacher's only one person. There might be ten other people who read your work in ten different ways. I had a student in Toronto with talent and I had made her swear she wouldn't go to writing class after I'd gone back to Paris. I said, 'Above all don't go to one of those writing classes where other students criticize your work, because they're only going to look for things to pick on. Just read and read and go your own way.' It's not called a class, it's a writing—

JL: Programme?

MG: No, that's easy. Some junkie word.

JL: Workshop.

MG: Yes.

JL: Do you work on more than one thing at the same time?

MG: Yes, I've done that. Unless there's a point with the story when I can't do anything else. And at that point the flowers die because I don't change the water, dishes are in the sink. But that's when the story is almost ready and I stay with it.

* * *

JL: Last summer I visited the home of Marguerite Yourcenar, the Belgian-born French novelist who spent the latter part of her life in the United States. She had a house on Mount Desert Island, in Maine. It's called Petite Plaisance.

MG: Is it kept as a shrine?

JL: It's a sort of museum. They have everything preserved. Her rooms, her things, her books, her kitchen. She kept her refrigerator in a closet. It's a tiny little house, tiny rooms you walk in and out of. Her office is very lovely. She and Grace Frick sat at a single desk, facing one another.

MG: You mean she was able to work with someone else in the room?

JL: Apparently.

MG: What was Grace Frick working on?

JL: She was translating. When I came back from Maine, I read your essay on Yourcenar, 'Limpid Pessimist', in the *New York Review of Books*. You quote a phrase of hers: 'useless chaos'. And then you write that 'useless chaos is what fiction is about'. I keep turning that over in my head. I love her work, though I haven't read her in French.

MG: The translations are uniformly terrible. She would not accept anything that was not a word-for-word translation.

JL: And she collaborated on her own translations.

MG: Yes, but that was a tragedy. I don't think Yourcenar had a sense of English. Apparently Grace Frick didn't, either. If you translate French to English word for word, it goes on and on like a dead old spider web in the dust. I think that's one of the reasons she didn't have the Nobel. The committee only reads in Swedish translations or English. They probably got lost halfway through every book. Her lovely work was really her autobiographical work. They rang true and were wonderfully written.

JL: You grew up with your two distinct realities, privy to two languages, two ways of life, two sets of attitudes. It reminds me of my own upbringing. When I was growing up with that double life, I felt a lot of anxiety. Did you feel that?

MG: No. I spoke English at home and French when I was going to French schools.

JL: And you accepted it.

MG: I accepted most things like that. I don't look back at anything being very hard except the death of my father and my mother's remarriage and her abandonment of me. I found it very hard to be in the world without a father. I had no one to stick up for me. My one desire was to grow up and get away.

JL: Did you feel that you had a certain advantage, being able to speak the two languages?

MG: I remember we spent summers in a house in a town called Chateauguay, outside Montreal. I played with French-Canadian children on the farm where we bought eggs and chickens. Their name was Dansereau. I had English-speaking friends too, but I couldn't mix them. I remember my best friend was called Dottie Hill. She was so fair she looked albino: blue eyes and little stubby white lashes, flaxen hair. I remember a sister and brother from the farm came, peering through the vines that surrounded the gallery, and I said, 'Come on.' They didn't want to come because we were speaking English, and Dottie said, very prudently, 'Do you play with them?' And I said, 'Yes'.

JL: That's admirable of you. When I was a child I only wanted life to be a single way. I didn't appreciate knowing a second language. I wanted to hide the things that marked me as different.

MG: For me it was *comme ça*. There were things I didn't want to do. I didn't want to play the piano, I don't know why. I came from a family where everybody played instruments. My father, as a young man, played cello. He brought it with him from England as a young man. It was behind the sofa *chez nous*. You'd see the case lying on its side.

JL: Did he keep it up?

MG: By the time I became conscious of it, no, but before, apparently yes. My mother played the violin and my grandmother played the piano. They played together. When my mother was in a good mood and wanted to amuse me, she'd make it speak.

JL: The violin?

MG: I'd say, 'What is it saying?' And she'd say, 'It's saying it's time for Mavis to go to bed.' 'No it isn't!' That was when she was in a good mood.

JL: You were adamant about not wanting to play piano, but you love music.

MG: I love music. It's been part of my life. When I hear something on the radio in the middle of something, I'm a step ahead of them. I know the notes that are coming, I know the pauses. I just did not want, myself, to do it, and I don't know why. I was very stubborn about it and I would sit and cry. I married a musician, and he wanted to teach me the piano, but the moment he said, 'This is middle C,' I said, 'Don't do it! Please, no!' It seemed to me a lot of fiddling. It wasn't what I wanted to learn.

JL: What did you want to learn?

MG: I liked to read a lot. I painted with paintboxes. I had lovely paintboxes.

JL: When you were able to get around more easily, did you like going to museums here in Paris?

MG: One of the things I miss now is going to art galleries. Walking and standing – it's too difficult.

JL: Who are some of the painters you love?

MG: I love Goya. I'm not crazy about all the Impressionists, but I like Manet. I react to certain painters. De Staël I love. There's not much I turn away from. I don't like Dalí. It's fake. To me, anyway.

JL: Do you reread a lot?

MG: I was hospitalized for two months last year, and I was just thinking this morning, I wouldn't want to be back there, but I missed the time I had to read. Marilyn Hacker, the American poet, told me that every time she came to see me I was either reading or writing. She came two or three times a week. And I thought this morning, I wish I had that time again. My life – I'm not grumbling, I'm just telling you – is not quite in my hands, it's in the hands of visiting nurses, doctors and all that. It's chopped up. In the hospital, for hours, I just sat and read. Or I walked in the corridor for exercise, hanging on to something on the wall. I reread Tolstoy. My friends all bought me different kinds of books. As soon as I finished one, I'd take another. I hadn't read that way since I was an adolescent.

JL: I can't do that any more myself. I remember, a few months ago, I was on the subway in New York. I had a book in my hands. And I saw a young woman across the aisle with a book in her hands, but she was pouring her whole body into it.

MG: She was living it.

JL: It was incredible. I looked at her and for a moment I felt intense envy, because I can't attain that degree of connection with books in my life now. It's too difficult. What are you reading now?

MG: Different things. There's a pile on my kitchen table. But I can't just finish a book and pick up another one. I don't have that kind of time. For one thing, I'm slower physically.

* * *

JL: In a television interview you did in 2005 with the Canadian journalist, Stéphan Bureau, you said, 'One can't become something.' You were talking about one's origins.

MG: I'm not patriotic. Certainly not nationalist. You can't turn into something. I could have had an American passport. I could also have had a British one.

JL: I feel in my life that I'm always becoming something, because I never felt I was any one thing to begin with. I was born in London, and when my parents moved to the United States we had green cards, and I was appended to my mother's Indian passport.

MG: How old were you when you moved?

JL: I was two when we left London. My Indian passport always bothered me as a child, because I hadn't been born there. Then it was time to go to college, and for practical reasons, in terms of what it meant to be a resident alien versus a citizen, I was naturalized and received an American passport. Then eventually it began to bother me that I didn't have my English passport, because I was born there. So in my late twenties I applied, and the next thing I knew, the maroon thing embossed with a lion and a unicorn arrived.

MG: What do you use when going over a border?

JL: It depends on where I'm going. I always bring my UK passport when I'm in Europe now, since it's part of the European Union.

MG: In other words, the passport has no meaning any more.

JL: No. Mine never has. Though it does to other people, and I can understand that. I remember when my mother became a US citizen, it was a traumatic experience for her.

MG: She didn't have both?

JL: No.

MG: They let Canadians have both.

JL: America is full of people who feel they are becoming something. Because it's such a relatively young country, there's a process of becoming American. There's the possibility of it. I don't know if it happens in the same way in other countries. When I was growing up in the United States, I never felt American because I never felt I could get away with calling myself an American. People would question it, because of my name and appearance, and some still do. It's taken me about forty years to feel I can say that, and now I do feel more

American than I used to, but still with caveats.

MG: Are you married to an American?

JL: An American citizen, yes. My husband grew up in various parts of the world.

MG: I didn't feel I needed an extra passport. I can go anywhere in the world with a Canadian passport.

JL: You've lived here for so many years. How do the French regard you? Does it matter to you, how they regard you?

MG: Canadian. If they ask me I tell them, '*Je suis Canadienne.*' It is what I am, it's just a fact of life. It could have been another fact. I could have been something else. It's part of the deal, one of the cards they gave me when I was born. Then you don't think about it. That's that, that's settled.

JL: It never felt settled to me. I still sometimes wish I had the ability to say I'm from one place. That 'I'm X.' I always have to say, 'I'm XYZ.'

MG: I haven't any desire to get a French passport. I'm not French. I'm not British. You would have had to reject where you were born, and I didn't want to.

JL: I sometimes wonder what would have happened if my parents had never left India, or never left London. I think I might not have become a writer. Do you ever think about what would have happened if you hadn't come to Paris?

MG: I would not have stayed in Canada. The government in Quebec at that time was very right wing, under the heel of a particularly repressive Catholic Church. I told you about the Padlock Law, didn't I? There was a law passed while I was there, working for the *Standard*, that if anyone had left-wing literature, even private correspondence in their home, the police could enter – they didn't have to have a search warrant – and they could put you out of your home and padlock the door behind you. I couldn't get the English Canadians worried about this because it seldom happened to them. No one would come into an

'I would not have been happy if I had not tried.' Mavis Gallant in Paris in the 1960s.

English Canadian's home unless he was poor or unless he was left wing and Jewish. The majority of the French Canadians thought if you were in any way left wing there was something wrong with you. I covered a number of strikes as a reporter. I had very fixed ideas on the subject. And I thought, 'I can't go on living here, I'm going to end up with no soul, just me waving my hat or shutting up.' So I would not have stayed. But it seemed natural. I thought about living in France from the time I was fourteen or fifteen. But it came from films, pre-war films, and books.

JL: The idea to come to France?

MG: *La vie en France.* I would not have been happy if I had not tried. I had to try and I had to do it before I was thirty. I didn't want to marry again. I travelled alone most of the time. I liked it. When you're young you meet people very easily. You stand on a street corner and you have to beat them off with a baseball bat.

* * *

JL: How did you feel about John Updike's recent death? Did you like his work?

MG: I liked a lot of it. He didn't like me as a person. I don't know why. He once reviewed me nicely. He said I wrote nicely about men. I loved his first book, *The Poorhouse Fair*, and his short stories. He was a real writer – I mean that he could not have been anything else. I didn't like *Couples*. I thought he was a puritan in territory where he didn't belong.

JL: I liked him for always writing stories along with novels. For not abandoning them.

MG: And he wrote poetry, and he wrote criticism, and wrote about art.

JL: I agree with him that you write well about men. I admire Richard Yates, but when I read *Revolutionary Road* I thought to myself, 'This could only have been written by a man.' Do you ever think that about something you've read?

MG: Oh yes. One thing is, men don't know how women talk when they're together, just as we really don't know how men talk among themselves. You have to rather intuit it from something the man will let drop. And you'll think, 'Oh, so they do gossip.'

JL: People often ask me a question I find ridiculous. They ask why the main character of my novel is male. They think it's something radical I've done. And I want to say, 'Well have you ever read any Mavis Gallant? Every other story is from the point of view of a man.' Or, 'Have you read Chekhov, where every other story is from the point of view of a woman?'

MG: Not to speak of Flaubert.

JL: People seem to have no context about the history of writing and what writers have done all along.

MG: But you have to be careful. When I wasn't sure about something I'd written about a man I'd show it to a man friend, but never an intellectual.

JL: And did they ever say anything?

MG: Once. I had one scientific friend I'd ask to be a reader. Someone who didn't want to write himself. It was a story called 'Potter'. I wanted to make absolutely sure I wouldn't fall flat on my face because that was a tricky one. He was not only a man but he was another nationality.

JL: Polish?

MG: Polish, right. And it was set at the period of the Wall. I was very close to the Polish diaspora in Paris, the intellectuals who'd fled the communists. So I knew how they thought, but how to express their thoughts? So I gave it to this fellow who's actually German. And I said, 'If there's anything there that a man wouldn't say or do, in your opinion, tell me.' And there was one thing: it was a man who burst into tears on the street. And he said, 'I've never seen a guy do that.'

JL: What did you do? Did you take it out?

MG: I took it out. I just cut it out with scissors and pasted the page together with Scotch tape. It was just a sentence. I thought, I can't take a chance with this. But then, imagine what happened. I was in the post office here in Paris, and there was a fellow getting his mail from the Poste Restante. I went over, there was a ledge where you could put stamps on letters, and I was there stamping with stamps I'd just bought. And he was there next to me, and there fell out of an envelope a picture of a very young woman with a baby, and he burst into tears. And his tears were falling, and he didn't care if I was there or if anybody was there. And I thought, this is somebody looking for a job in France. I don't know where they come from. Tears were falling and I thought, 'I should have left it in, maybe.' On the other hand, many men reading might have said, 'What kind of person is this?' We have very little weeping in the streets. I'd never actually seen that myself, but I could imagine it. In 'Potter' he sees something that reminds him of her in the street, some oranges marked 'Venice'. I didn't mean he was standing there sobbing, just that he brimmed over. I've seen men wipe their eyes at funerals.

JL: Once I showed a story to my husband. I don't think we were married yet. I'd written a story from a male point of view and I wasn't sure about it. He said one thing. The story is about a husband and a wife, told from the husband's point of view. At one point the husband is looking at his wife's shoe. And my husband said, 'He wouldn't think of the shoe in such detail.'

MG: I don't agree with that.

JL: He said there was something too technical about my description of the shoe, something a man wouldn't know. That he would perceive it in other terms.

MG: So you took it out.

JL: I altered it. I made it less specific. Did you ever work in cafes?

MG: As a waitress?

JL: I meant to write in.

MG: No. People worked in cafes when their homes weren't heated.

Particularly in the war. That's when you had Simone de Beauvoir and all those people working in cafes, because they had a modicum of heat. There was a cafe near where I lived, on the corner of my street, but now, unfortunately, it's a restaurant. I used to be able to go in there at any hour and ask if there was something to eat. I could go in at three o'clock in the afternoon and say, 'Whatever you have, heat it up.' As long as it wasn't spinach, which I don't like. They would save it for me and they would let me have a marble-topped table for four next to a window. I'd bring proofs to correct. I was never bothered by the noise of people talking. But it's a restaurant now. And I miss it.

JL: I thought we could talk today about 'The Carette Sisters'. Here's a case where you group a few stories together, something you've done a number of times, something I like very much and tried doing myself in my last book. When was the first time you decided to do that?

MG: My dear, I don't know. You'd have to ask a *universitaire* for that. I have absolutely no idea when I thought of this. Usually I thought of a novel. And then I would not do the novel because, as we discussed, there are only certain points in a life that are turning points.

JL: And you wanted to stick to the turning points?

MG: Yes. Those are the important ones.

JL: In this case, did you write the sections as sections?

MG: I didn't write a whole novel, no. Some of it was already written. And the curve of the thing, I knew who they were, I knew what it was about. There's space between them, time between them, because sometimes I'd work on something else and come back to it.

JL: These were published in the 1980s. Was there any reason, when you were working on these stories, why you were going back to Montreal in your mind?

MG: I couldn't tell you. If I knew that I'd stop writing.

JL: Why?

MG: Because it has to come from something unknown in you. If I knew that I wouldn't bother writing. I'd be something else. I'd be a champion cricket player. Maybe I am a champion cricket player, in another life.

JL: The first story begins with an ending, with a husband dying. Madame Carette is twenty-seven years old and left with two young daughters. Yesterday we talked about 'The Remission', which is a story about a husband dying, and a soon-to-be widow with children. Madame Carette's life takes such a different path after her husband dies. She remains a widow and dresses in half-mourning, whereas Barbara, in 'The Remission', takes a lover before her husband is in the grave. Not knowing either of those times personally, and granting that they are very different characters, I wonder, how did society change for women between those periods? Specifically, for women who had lost their husbands?

MG: The circumstances are already different because the Carette girls were meant to work. They grew up with the idea of having jobs.

JL: And there's also the expectation for them to get married.

MG: That was universal in those days. I had it, not the same way, but I saw it. When I was seventeen I had a girlfriend, we were in school together. One day she told me a dreadful secret. She'd 'gone all the way', as we used to hear, with an older boy. And this was very secret. I said, 'You're not pregnant, are you?' She said, 'No'. And I said, 'You mustn't imagine your life is over.' But secretly I thought, 'Who ever will marry her?'

JL: That was the way it was.

MG: In the first place there was no birth control. There was a terrible risk all the time. To us condoms were for whores and sailors. Or soldiers. And so there was a terrible fear, I mean the fear of pregnancy was very real. There was no question of abortion, it wouldn't cross your mind. And you were cast out of society, the society you knew. We lived in fear. And it was up to women, girls, to prevent it going that far. If you didn't say hands off, they wouldn't be hands off. It was completely unnatural, but the consequences were dire. You can't imagine now. Babies being born and being given immediately up for adoption, back-street abortions. A girl who had a baby could be sent away, far from her family. So you have to put yourself back in that time.

JL: It's true that these stories are set in a time I haven't known. And yet 'The Chosen Husband', which is about finding Madame Carette's daughter, Marie, a suitable husband – arranging the match and chaperoning their meetings – reminds me of some of the old-fashioned expectations with which I was raised.

MG: Because of India?

JL: Because of the culture my parents came from, yes.

MG: But you came into a culture with birth control.

JL: I did. But throughout my adolescence the expectation in my family was for a young woman to remain sexually pure and then to get married, even though I was raised in a time and place when that was no longer the norm, and not at all how most of my peers were raised. The fact that I didn't get married until I was thirty-three was considered very old and unconventional by much of my parents' crowd.

MG: And they were worried about that?

JL: I think my parents tried not to worry, but it was there. My relatives in India were distressed when I would visit at the age of twenty-seven, twenty-eight, twenty-nine... 'Find her a husband, time's running out', etc. So my parents had to decide to trust me.

MG: Did they push you?

JL: There was some pressure, yes. I could never fully ignore it. When I was a teenager the idea of being married off to someone I didn't know or like was a real terror to me. But that's why, when I read these stories, I understand some of that attitude. The way the minute Madame Carette sees Louis Driscoll, Marie's suitor, and notes his ultramarine eyes, she immediately thinks ahead and hopes her grandchildren will inherit that colour. It's something I recognize.

MG: I can't imagine writing something that doesn't have a time attached and I don't like reading something that could happen anytime, anywhere. For example, in *Green Water*, the story when they're on the beach. It's early morning and the Vespas are starting. A translator who wanted to translate this into French said she wanted to take out any mention that it is the Fifties. And I said, 'No, I'm not making these changes.'

JL: What was her point?

MG: To bring it up to date.

JL: That's something I don't understand.

MG: She thought readers would not understand what a Vespa was. But one of the things I remember from that period is when they would start up in the morning. They'd rush along the roads. The Lambrettas too. When I'm reading, I like it if there's a mention of something that doesn't exist any more.

JL: I agree.

MG: Like a man giving a lady a light for her cigarette. It was very complex [leans over, imitating the gesture]. That was part of the seduction of the period, which I particularly noticed when I came to Europe. I'd been at a newspaper where they'd bang you on the back with the flat of the hand and say 'Hi, Mavis!' Then I came here where they were kissing my hand up to the elbow.

JL: The first of these stories begins in 1933, in Montreal. You would have been eleven years old that year.

MG: In 1936 I moved to New York, and when I came back at eighteen, I stayed with my old nurse. No one in Montreal knew I was coming. I got out at the railway station called Bonaventure, which doesn't exist any more, in Montreal, and I looked her up in the phone book. When I didn't find her, I searched the 'Red Book', a directory of Montreal addresses. I remembered her name and I took it for granted she would take me in. It never dawned on me that she might not even remember me. I had my last five dollars and I got into the taxi. It would have been sixty cents in the taxi. So I took a taxi to that address. It was the east end of Montreal. I went up some steep indoor stairs. Her house was very old and I trudged up those stairs. I was carrying two things: a suitcase and a typewriter that someone had given me. If you wanted to get any job at all, even as a hairdresser, as a woman, you had to learn to type, and I'd done that. I had left a trunk at the station. And she opened the door and she was smaller than I was! In my memory of her in my early childhood, I was always looking up. She didn't understand who I was, and I told her, and she said, '*Tu vis?*' 'You're alive?' And she let me in. At that point she did have a phone – I don't know why she wasn't in the phone book – and she called her daughter and she called her son and they came rushing to see me. They had been told I was dead. They'd been having a Mass said for me every birthday every year. They thought I was very tall: '*Tu est belle, tu est grande*!' I was five foot three.

JL: You write about this return to Montreal in the Linnet Muir stories.

MG: In disguise.

JL: But as you tell the story, I remember reading the fictional version, and Linnet going up the steep staircase.

MG: We had tea. She brought out a big pot of honey with pictures of bees on the outside. I remember picking up the honey pot to help her, and it was sticky and I said, '*C'est collant.*' I was speaking minimal French, but it began to come back. She asked what my plans were, and I said I was going to get a job. The very next day I looked for jobs. She gave me a room on the other side of the kitchen. It was a real room with a radiator, a dresser. It was clean as a whistle – she had a passion for cleaning. I think my rent was two dollars a week. When I started to get my pay we raised it to five. I was perfectly happy with her. We went over the past. I filled in what she didn't know and she filled in what I didn't know. They had adored me when I was a baby. Her son said, 'My mother and sister were so crazy about you that they used to watch you sleeping.'

JL: Those are the moments I feel the strongest love for my children, when I watch them sleeping. It all comes together then.

MG: I'm sure.

JL: Of course, they can't bother you in those moments.

MG: She was a widow, my nurse. She was a seamstress. In those days, bourgeois people had a seamstress come to the house who did the curtains, shortened the lengths on the winter coats or made one from scratch, worked a certain number of hours. She did work for my grandmother.

JL: Did she inspire the character of Madame Carette at all, a woman who takes in sewing after her husband dies?

MG: No, Madame Carette is something else altogether.

JL: The bond between Marie and Berthe, the sisters in these stories, is very strong. They protect each other all their lives. You were an only child. Did you ever feel the lack of a sibling?

MG: I thought it would be nice to have a brother. My father and mother both encouraged me to be friends with children from other families, go to their birthday parties, this and that. I was horrified because they were always quarrelling. I was bewildered by this.

JL: The relationship between Marie and Berthe is one of the most loving relationships, I think, in all your work.

MG: Wouldn't it be natural?

JL: It's not always the case. Marie and Berthe remain so devoted to each other. They almost have their own sort of marriage.

MG: They hold hands behind the groom's back.

JL: Berthe never marries. She earns her own money and buys her own fur coats.

MG: That was just beginning. Just the beginning of the change in Quebec.

JL: Raymond, Marie's son, loses his father as well. Not at such a young age as his mother loses her father, but still fairly young. And then he's raised by women. I saw a little of myself in Raymond.

MG: Why?

JL: The part in Florida, when his mother comes and he points out all the Canadian things in Florida. It's the sort of thing I would say to my mother if she came to visit me. I would go out of my way to find things in the US to remind her of Calcutta. I thought it would console her, to see signs of the place she missed. Also, the way they communicate. The coexistence of two languages, the separate but simultaneous conversations taking place. Raymond wants to tune out his mother speaking French, but he can't. He's a hybrid, like me.

MG: He's a high-school dropout.

JL: He goes to fight for the Americans in Vietnam, and meanwhile the Americans who didn't want to fight in that war were running to Canada.

MG: Did you think of that?

JL: At the end of the story, Marie and her daughter-in-law, Mimi, who is pregnant, have a surprising moment of connection. One minute Marie is suffering through Mimi's shrimp and rice, but then, when Raymond and Mimi fight and Raymond storms out, Marie physically enfolds Mimi and says, 'count on me'. It seemed very much a cycle of stories of the various bonds between women. Mothers, daughters, sisters. I found it very beautiful, looking at those connections.

MG: Well, I believe in that. There's a different kind of bond with men. It's a different thing altogether.

JL: I missed Madame Carette after she died. You don't mention her death, but I felt her absence. In those scenes when Louis comes to visit, there's something of the writer in her, the way she scrutinizes and sizes up a potential son-in-law. No detail escapes her.

MG: You think so? It wasn't meant to be. She would never write books. She would read newspapers.

JL: But she shares a certain trait with writers.

MG: You know, children have it. They lose it. They can come into a room and feel every tension between the adults. And not have the vocabulary for it, but they notice.

JL: Where did you come up with the idea of Marie being electric? Her thinking she's picking up a current?

MG: In Montreal there were all sorts of rumours about electricity, because when you came in out of the cold you could strike sparks. The doors in houses in Montreal had that brass letter drop where the postman puts the mail. It's brass all round, and there's a little flap that comes down. Children were always calling through the mailbox, 'I have to go to the bathroom, Mummy!' Otherwise they wouldn't let you in. They were having tea with cinnamon toast indoors, and we were out there freezing under grey skies. And they'd say, 'Don't put your tongue on the metal. It sticks.' But if you rubbed the metal, you might see a spark.

JL: I remember my mother telling me once that my grandmother was afraid of getting a shock from a light switch, and so she would protect her finger with the material of her sari when she turned the switch on and off. When I read this story, I remembered that detail my mother had told me about my grandmother.

MG: It depended on how cold your hands were, how cold it was outside, what it was like when you came in. And your feet shuffling on certain carpets.

JL: Did you ever know anybody like Marie, who was convinced she was electric?

MG: No, I just meant she was a bit dumb.

JL: It's idiotic, but it's also profound. 'We've got to make sure we're grounded,' she says at the end of the story. There's a meaning to that, even though she may not know what it is.

MG: I like '1933', the one where they're little girls. And the dog.

JL: The bilingual dog. There's a lot in this story about the specificity of origin. There's no such thing as simply Canadian. That really comes across.

MG: There's no such thing as a Canadian childhood. I've written about that in the introduction in The Big Book. You're Protestant or Catholic. You're East or West.

JL: Do you have any stories that you feel haven't been properly understood? Or do you not think about that?

MG: There's bound to be things that aren't understood. But you can still read a story. There's one, 'The Pegnitz Junction'.

JL: The characters in that story are German. What drew you to those characters?

MG: One of the things I wanted to know more about when I came to Europe was what really happened in Germany in the war. Because I could not understand how people so cultured – they have such extraordinary culture there – could do the things they let be done. And that came to me as a way of doing it. A great deal of it is satire on already published things. Kafka's *The Castle*. Wilhelm Busch. I used Busch names for the boys watching the train go by at a level crossing. Actually, only a German who had been given Busch as a child would spot that.

JL: Did you ever take a train journey like that?

MG: I took a very long journey. I've forgotten which year. On the German side – this was a long, long, long time ago – they changed to an old steam train. I started going to Germany in the Fifties but not right away. I didn't want to go there because I was distressed by what had happened. Did I tell you about my first seeing photographs?

JL: No.

MG: We really didn't know what was happening, that's the God's truth. I was working at the newspaper. I thought the Germans shot Jews by firing squad. That's what I believed. That any Jew who got out of handcuffs got shot. It was an enormous shock, and I had to write about it. The editor had the pictures face down on his desk. He turned them over very quickly and I didn't understand what I was seeing. I had to write eight hundred words and all the photo captions. I asked if I could take them home. He said, 'You can't show them to anybody,' because there was a fixed, international date for publication. But I had a friend, a young doctor in the army who was home on leave, and I showed him the pictures. 'What's wrong with these people?' I asked him. He said he thought they must be prisoners suffering from untreated tuberculosis. Actually, they had been systematically starved, but we couldn't imagine that. We couldn't take it in. Once I got on the subject, I wanted to go to the very end of it. The shorter stories in the collection *The Pegnitz Junction* are post-war. The book was published in 1973. I still think the title story is perhaps my best work. Everything is involved.

JL: Did you feel that as you were writing it?

MG: No. A lot of people didn't understand it but mostly they could read it for some sort of magic realism. I don't like magic realism at all. Like the girl on the train hearing this information. I didn't do anything else along that line. That is the book that's had the most written about it. MAs, that kind of thing. At least, the most who have come to me for help.

JL: Was the story too long for *The New Yorker*?

MG: It was returned to me because it was too long. William Maxwell said we can run the last sixteen pages and I said I wouldn't do it, because I knew this book was coming out anyway a year later. Years later, in the Nineties, not long before he died, he reread all my work and he wrote me a letter of apology. He said, 'I don't know what was wrong with me. My mind must have been out to lunch.' Imagine an editor saying that. He said also that he had felt bound by *The New Yorker*'s policy that fiction had to be linear. And this wasn't, it went all over the place.

JL: Do you still read *The New Yorker*?

MG: It's the one thing in life I've ever had free. I probably don't read every word now. Sometimes I come across a story that I think is marvellous. With some I read the beginning, the end, a bit in the middle, and I think, 'That to get to that?'

JL: It was a different magazine when you started appearing in it.

MG: You opened on to a story. It was a literary journal.

JL: How does your writing life change as you grow older?

MG: It changes in the sense that I have no hands any more.

JL: Holding a pen is difficult?

MG: I find it harder and harder.

JL: And the things you've been compelled to write about, to think about, to express – how does that evolve over the years?

MG: I'll tell you what happens when you get older. Things seem inevitable.

JL: In the writing?

MG: No, in life. They seem inevitable in some way. You feel less— I don't know what it is. You don't lose compassion. You know, *Men have died and worms have eaten but never I think for love*. Shakespeare had it.

JL: What are you working on now?

MG: I'm working on a story about my imaginary writer, Henri Grippes. And I do want to finish that. But it's massive, unreadable at the moment. I should have a clear mind, but ever since I came out of hospital everything seems a burden sometimes.

JL: Does the writing feel like a burden?

MG: Not the writing, but finding the time. I got to the point the other day, I said to myself, 'Are you sad because you left the hospital?'

JL: You were writing in the hospital, you said.

MG: I took up a journal because I didn't want to forget.

JL: What was happening to you?

MG: Not to me, but around me. Because I was eighty-five I was taken to a geriatric hospital. Some patients had gallstones, some chronic bronchitis and some had Alzheimer's. I'd never seen Alzheimer patients before. So I took notes. Rereading this set of notebooks, I found that I gave everybody a nickname because I was afraid the nurses or someone could read English and would recognize themselves.

JL: Do your journals ever give you ideas for writing stories?

MG: No, but they give me ideas of how things were. What was going on around that time. Sometimes descriptions of cities take you back. Not really people. Or they're people I've just had a glimpse of. I find them stuck back there in the brain. Like the Englishwoman I told you about yesterday, about the skirt. The one who said, 'My dear, are you a Scot?' I would not have remembered that if I hadn't written it. ■

AMERICAN SUBSIDIARY

William Pierce

ILLUSTRATION BY ADAM SIMPSON

One spring morning – it was early May, and sunlight had just reached the ivy at his shoulder – Joseph Stone leaped up at his boss's call, then slowly, so as not to remind himself of Pavlov's dog, tucked his chair back under the shelf that held his keyboard.

He did not have far to go: three steps, four at most, took him from his cubicle to Peter Halsa's pale, wood door.

'*Entschuldigung?*' he asked, pronouncing the German word slackly, as any American would. 'Excuse me?'

Herr Halsa was drying the inside of his ear with a white hand towel. This was nothing strange. It had seemed unusual at first, months ago, but then Joseph had asked himself why certain behaviours should be off-limits at work, especially to the boss. He tugged at his nose, waiting for Herr Halsa's answer.

He felt only mildly ridiculous thinking of his boss as Herr Halsa. Everyone else was required to use formal German address, and it seemed right, though he'd explicitly been asked to call him Peter, that Joseph not call too much attention to what was already unpleasantly obvious: the gratifying fact that his boss relied on him utterly.

Herr Halsa lifted his head, looked up – he was now drying the nape of his neck, having apparently rushed from home with his head still wet – and grunted in a German way that pleased Joseph, because it meant again that Joseph worked at a German company, among Germans, who might at any time release deep, Bavarian grunts.

'Nothing, no, you can return to your work. I was just saying good morning. Good morning.' Herr Halsa nodded, still rubbing his hair with his head aslant, and closed the office door. He preferred to give orders in his own good time, when he'd chanced across things that needed doing, and in the meantime he expected his employees to stay busy on their own.

Joseph returned to what he'd been doing. He was typing up another proposal for robots that would replace human workers in an engine factory.

No one else in the building, only Joseph Stone, could say that his cubicle opened on to the boss's door. The other cubicles, their short walls panelled in grey carpeting, were strung together to form two separate mazes, each of which closed in on itself and had a single entrance at the printers and copy machine, not far from the kitchen door. Herr Halsa's office took up the corner diagonally opposite.

To the gear-hobbing maze belonged seasoned American salesmen who were unable to sell machines, though not for want of escorting potential buyers to golf courses and strip clubs. For whatever reason, probably some sort of native laxness, the Americans were unsuccessful – and with them one German who was so good at selling gantries that he'd been transferred to raise the *Amerikaner* out of their slump, and had instead fallen into one himself. To the gantry maze belonged newcomers who had not sold anything before their arrival from Germany. They were young and hungry and German and knew how to browbeat their former colleagues at the *Automationsfabrik* to give them extremely large discounts. Why shouldn't the parent division sell its robots at a loss if it meant gaining a toehold in the prestigious American car market? These good *Kerle* had rubbed elbows in company showers with the very men they now called on for favours. The Americans in gear hobbing had visited Germany too, but only to try the Wiener schnitzel and spend a few days in seminar rooms.

Joe Stone was the exception. He was American and the company hadn't even sent him to Europe yet, but his was the cubicle that opened like a secret on to the boss's door. Despite various drawbacks, the arrangement suited him well. He preferred to be visible to no one, and at midday Herr Halsa would close his door and tighten the slats on the narrow shade covering the long, tall window beside it and (Joseph was fairly sure) nap. Herr Halsa idolized the chief of the Volkswagen company, and the chief of Volkswagen held as his guiding principle that nothing must remain on his desk overnight. So, to ensure that nothing violated this adopted dictum, Herr Halsa forbade everyone from putting papers or objects on his desk during the day also. Which left him with extraordinarily little to do.

Herr Halsa opened his door with the fresh snap of someone about to take the air and disappeared into the matrix of grey-walled cubicles. Joseph pasted another block of boilerplate just where it belonged, then plucked the lemon out of his iced tea to resqueeze it. The rind of a lemon, with its regular dimples and high yellow complexion, cheered him so extraordinarily that he plucked and resqueezed several times as he drank each glass. The sun warmed his back, the sky had receded higher than ever, it was an uncontainably beautiful day.

The silence broke.

'I don't care if the file is on your hard drive!' Herr Halsa cried. He was straining to yell as loudly as possible, no doubt to make an example for everyone in the building. 'I expect to see it in the next ten minutes, or your job will appear in tomorrow's classifieds!'

Whatever else one could say – such as 'Joseph Stone was badly paid' or 'Joe Stone the PhD was out of place here' – he did not forget to enjoy the small pleasures of his job.

Joseph held up his cutting and pasting and listened. He heard, of course, the soft scrapings made by the German receptionist, Roswitha, as she wiped each office plant's leaves with a handkerchief. But the dust-up seemed to be over.

It was no fault of the boss's that he knew nothing about computers. He'd never been shown how to use one, and his book learning, which pre-dated the era of workplace computers, was more in the nature of a technical apprenticeship.

Joseph considered the factory layout the company was proposing this time, but the German sales engineers, as they were called, knew plenty that he could not assess. It was a small marvel that the gantries could carry engine blocks not only high over the aisles but also through the women's room. Joseph's friend the mechanical draughtsman, an American, took great pleasure in formalizing the Germans' mistakes. 'I do *exactly* what I'm asked to,' he said. He liked to be challenged so he could repeat it.

'You might get a bigger raise if you—'

'I do exactly what I'm asked to.'

A few minutes later, the American salesman Alan Freedman – his name was spelled wrong according to Herr Halsa, who thought it should be *Friedmann* – ambled into the boss's office with his naked, silver hard drive and the large, sideburned service manager, Helmut Schall, who waved a screwdriver as he explained in German that he'd removed the hard drive at Freedman's insistence. Naturally anyone in Herr Halsa's position who had once been a service mechanic would hesitate before spending too much work time in the presence of a man who might, just by his rough familiarity, remind people where the boss had started out, so, pulling his suit jacket from the back of his chair, Herr Halsa excused Alan Freedman – 'All right, all right, go back to your phone calls!' – and closed the door on his friend Helmut Schall.

Joseph could easily sympathize with the boss on this occasion, for Herr Halsa's duke, his overlord, the very stylish Herr Doktor Hühne, who might as well have come from Berlin between the wars rather than any part of coarse *gemütlich* Bavaria, was scheduled to enter in the middle of this scene and, after half an hour, exit with nearly every German speaker to a gala welcoming lunch. Following this, Herr Doktor Hühne, without Joseph's boss, was to call on customers in

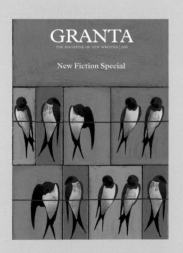

Yes, I would like to take out an annual subscription to *Granta* and receive a complimentary *Granta* special-edition **MOLESKINE**® notebook

YOUR ADDRESS FOR DELIVERY

Your address:

TITLE: INITIAL: SURNAME:

ADDRESS:

POSTCODE:

TELEPHONE:

EMAIL:

Billing address if different:

TITLE: INITIAL: SURNAME:

ADDRESS:

POSTCODE:

TELEPHONE: EMAIL:

NUMBER OF SUBSCRIPTIONS	DELIVERY REGION	PRICE	DIRECT DEBIT PRICE (UK ONLY)
☐	UK	£34.95	£29.95
☐	Europe	£39.95	
☐	Rest of World	£45.95	

All prices include delivery

YOUR TWELVE-MONTH SUBSCRIPTION WILL INCLUDE FIVE ISSUES

I would like my subscription to start from:

☐ the current issue ☐ the next issue

PAYMENT DETAILS

☐ I enclose a cheque payable to '*Granta*' for £ ______ for ____ subscriptions to *Granta*

☐ Please debit my ☐ MASTERCARD ☐ VISA ☐ AMEX for £ ______ for ____ subscriptions

NUMBER ☐☐☐☐ ☐☐☐☐ ☐☐☐☐ ☐☐☐☐ SECURITY CODE ☐☐☐

EXPIRY DATE ☐☐ / ☐☐ SIGNED DATE

Instructions to your bank or building society to pay by Direct Debit

DIRECT Debit

TO THE MANAGER:

(BANK OR BUILDING SOCIETY NAME)

ADDRESS:

POSTCODE:

ACCOUNT IN NAME(S) OF:

SIGNED: DATE:

BANK/BUILDING SOCIETY ACCOUNT NUMBER

SORT CODE

ORIGINATOR'S IDENTIFICATION

9 1 3 1 3 3

Instructions to your bank or building society Please pay Granta Publications Direct Debits from the account detailed on this instruction subject to the safeguards assured by the Direct Debit Guarantee. I understand that this instruction may remain with Granta and, if so, details will be passed electronically to my bank/ building society.

Banks and building societies may not accept Direct Debit instructions from some types of account

☐ Please tick this box if you would like to receive special offers from *Granta*

☐ Please tick this box if you would like to receive offers from organizations selected by *Granta*

Please return this form to: **Granta Subscriptions, PO Box 2068, Bushey, Herts, WD23 3ZF, UK, call Freephone 0500 004 033** or go to **www.granta.com**

Please quote the following promotion code when ordering online: **GBIUK106**

TEAR ALONG PERFORATION TO REMOVE

the afternoon. Herr Halsa had spent days revising a very smart, thoroughgoing agenda for the kick-off meeting.

When Hans Hühne arrived, he shook the beefy hand of his prime underling in the United States, Herr Halsa – who had in the meantime calmed himself and reopened his office for the grand arrival – accepted Roswitha's requisite offer of *Kaffee*, and promptly left the office to shake Joseph's hand and enter into private negotiations.

Joseph felt courted. Here was perhaps the most stylish suit-wearing man he had ever met – Herr Doktor Hans Friedrich Hühne crossed his legs even while standing, and turned his head gently to the side, not with any hint of arrogance but nevertheless with the suggestion of a long cigarette holder and a thin black tie – and, very consciously no doubt, he chose to address Joseph before anyone else. At this formal moment, the occasion of receiving a well-regarded superior who has just disembarked from a transatlantic flight, Peter Halsa could not very well emerge from his office. Herr Doktor Hühne had chosen to leave it and would return in his own time. But Herr Halsa clattered about – chairs, his empty outbox – to express impatience to Joseph in a language that Herr Doktor Hühne would not recognize.

'You translated the gantry catalogue, isn't it?' Hühne said. He spoke English with a smooth accent.

'*Das habe ich, ja*,' Joseph answered, wondering if he'd made any kind of mistake in his German.

'We have a new project in need of the highest-quality translation, and I'd like us to work on it together, you and me,' he went on, speaking German now.

Herr Halsa went so far as to clear his throat, but Joseph heard the softness in it, a touching womanliness that would mean to Herr Doktor Hühne, if he happened to hear, that Halsa intended nothing peremptory. On the contrary, it brimmed with comic lightness, the kind of mild rebuke that one might direct towards an old woman, perhaps a receptionist who had chosen this inopportune moment to dust the plants.

Joseph nodded with grave interest – he enjoyed being important;

who doesn't? – and stood up to match Herr Doktor Hühne's height, making certain in his American way to advance this relationship by allowing his arm to bump a few times against Herr Doktor Hühne's while they reviewed the as-yet-unreleased German prospectus for a new overhead-railcar system.

Herr Halsa appeared briefly at his door, then pulled back. Joseph saw his image there, the faintest double exposure, wearing the fine Italian jacket that usually hung behind the door.

Once Herr Doktor Hühne returned to Halsa's office, where the German salesmen were now gathered around the conference table, Herr Halsa grew expansive and host-like. At these times his bearing made Joseph proudest to have this unexpected opportunity, which had come up almost by accident six months before, to be the translator here instead of a mere secretarial temp. Joseph sat off to the side, his favourite fountain pen poised for note-taking. The Americans on staff were excluded from these meetings for the simple reason that the conversations were conducted in German, and for the complex reason that the Americans were American.

Not much happened during the meeting in terms of company business. But several important psychological or interpersonal things took place, and Joseph marvelled at how curious they were, and how lucky he was to be here to witness these intimate workings of an executive office – without having to suffer from any very significant attachment to the questions being discussed. First, the railcar system went unmentioned. Joseph felt fairly deep loyalty on this point and scratched out a reminder to tell Herr Halsa about the project as soon as the überboss left. Second, he noticed the obvious: the disappointment that caused Herr Halsa's eyes to shift nervously just ten minutes into the meeting, after the anecdotes and jokes and hellos. Charismatic Herr Doktor Hühne began to ask questions and guide the conversation – no guest-playing for him – and it became only too obvious that the written agenda would go unfollowed. Herr Doktor Hühne would have no chance to see, though tomorrow was another day, how tightly his next-in-command ran this important subsidiary.

Joseph, meantime, was smiling and nodding. He couldn't understand half of what was being said, the quick Bavarian retorts, the irony-drenched allusions to who knows what. But no matter. Joseph was the company translator and, with that credential, a fully vested German speaker. Even his mother said he wasn't a very good listener – how could anyone expect one hundred per cent comprehension here, where the salesmen were discussing technical matters foreign to Joseph even in English? Why should he squint or shrug or ask the others to repeat themselves when silence and a few well-timed laughs would carry him through?

Herr Doktor Hühne had worked himself into a bluster over the notion of *Handwerk*. Joseph took a few disjointed notes, hoping to record this fascinating paradox without scrambling it. *No matter how many 'machines' assemble our robots*, Herr Doktor Hühne seemed to be saying, *everything that the factory produces is 'handmade'*. Hühne was the kind of urbane man you might find in a pale linen suit smoking thin, stinking cigars, so his bluster did not throw him forward on to the points of his elbows, anxious and combative, but took him deeper into the chair, his fingers tepeed and restless and occasionally pressed against his lips. 'Customized production, gentlemen,' he said in English.

'Ah, customized production,' Herr Halsa joked. He didn't switch to English unless he had to. '*Kundenspezifische Fertigung*. I thought you wanted Reinhold to use handsaws and toilet plungers.'

Herr Halsa leaned back, trying to work himself as low in his chair as Herr Doktor Hühne, but of course it was impossible. Herr Halsa spent too many of his evenings in steakhouses.

'Let's leave American work to the Americans,' the highest-grossing salesman said.

Herr Hühne laughed. 'Yes, *Handwerk* in the manner of watchmakers, not plumbers.'

Joseph pulled at his upper lip and immediately read his own gesture. It was hardly-to-be-restrained pride. These men could tell their jokes about 'American work', their rather offensive jokes in which

'American' replaced what must have been 'Turk' back home, and altogether forget that Joseph was, in some ways – well, in every way – an American.

He liked to manoeuvre towards near-paradoxes, to insinuate himself into scenes that most could never hope to be part of.

At lunchtime, when the meeting broke up – Herr Doktor Hühne abruptly rose, declaring his hunger – the line of salesmen, and among them Herr Halsa, strolled towards the building's front door in twos and threes behind the visiting executive, who was a personal friend of the family that owned the company. Herr Doktor Hühne had walked ahead with the highest-grossing salesman, a curly-topped redhead far thinner than the rest and willing to make any kind of joke, transgress in any way, even to the point of yanking Hühne's tie, beeping like the Roadrunner, and calling the regent *Dingsbums*.

Joseph, too, proceeded to the front door. But this was where his deficiency cut him off. He could ride all of the other rides, but here at last he came upon a minimum height for the Tilt-a-Whirl, the requirement of actual Germanness, which he missed by a finger or two. It was his secret goal to grow into it, to convince Halsa next year or the year after, by silent competence – it would take just once to change the expectation permanently – and then he could board one of the cars departing for an inner-sanctum lunch.

Along behind the *Automationsabteilung*, as the only American invited to the restaurant, the sales rep Jack Wilson paddled out. He'd been talking all this while to Ted and Alan and the other non-German speakers in the hobbing area. Maybe he'd even done the rounds of the service department, the warehouse that occupied the back two-thirds of the building and marked the hunting grounds of the only birds lower than Americans in this peculiar aviary: the *Bauern*, Helmut Schall and his staff of Bavarian farmers who'd never had their moles removed. Joseph liked them, in fact they were some of the best men in the company, but the defensive jokes about their moles and so on – Herr Halsa's repertoire – any employee would have found funny, and Joseph felt justified in leaning back from his note-taking and giving a full-on laugh. Just the same, as he directed a quick salute to the sales rep Wilson, a slightly pleasant superciliousness washed over him, a feeling of gratitude to the fate that had given him cafes and saved him from the America of sports bars and chewing tobacco. Why shouldn't he enjoy some of the privileges conferred on him here and consider himself every bit as superior as the true Germans felt?

Joseph watched through the kitchen window and, like a basketball player who could dribble without looking, engineered a second iced tea blind. It did make sense, despite a tensing in his shoulders, that this man, Jack Wilson, would go to the restaurant. He was the one scheduled to escort Herr Doktor Hühne to the customer's plant that afternoon. Wilson and Hühne would tour the No. 3 Engine Plant in Cleveland, which had accepted the very first proposal that Joseph had written – an eleven-million-dollar project, the German factory's largest yet. And Herr Halsa was right to consider Hühne's impression of things. The previous executive vice-president had been recalled for capitulating too quickly to the American way of doing business – particularly by replacing German components with much cheaper substitutes.

In inviting Wilson to lunch there was no awkwardness, because Wilson did not work for the company. He was a kind of mercenary who agreed to play golf on the company's behalf exclusively and get drunk on the company's behalf exclusively and frequently with people who might or might not have purchasing clout at whatever plant Wilson had led the Germans to target. He was a go-between. A middleman. The aesthetics of the thing were less germane than the logic: it made sense for Wilson to liaise over popcorn shrimp. Nevertheless, when Alan Freedman walked into the lunch room, his hair full and proud, unlike all the monk-topped Germans, Joseph couldn't resist saying something conspiratorial.

'Look at Wilson out there laughing. Do you think he's drunk?'

Wilson soft-shoed into his son's minivan, the star of his own silent movie.

Freedman was forever in good spirits – he was a man of the highest, proudest, most natural spirits Joseph had ever known – and he pulled a Sam's Choice lemon-lime soda from the refrigerator along with his brown sack of lunch, and laughed with a gentle calm that put Wilson's bluster to shame. 'He deserves to be happy, no? A million and a half for the Cleveland plant, I'd be handing out tulips and Swiss chocolates.'

The pulp of Joseph's lemon went on spinning in his glass even after he'd stopped stirring, the swirls of dissolved sugar warping and turning like heatwaves coming up from a car. He often felt blessed by small things and now, with the young sun glinting off windshields and beckoning him outside with his lunch, he felt deeply fortunate to have this packet of sugar in his hand, to be already rolling the torn-off piece of it between his fingers, to be here in this job, a translator instead of a temp, twenty dollars an hour instead of eight-fifty.

A million and a half.

'And – do you get commissions when you sell?' he asked, expecting the worst. Every one of them must have been making too much money to care about anything. He was halfway back to his cubicle – a little-used door next to Herr Halsa's office led to the lawn behind the building – and Freedman was about to disappear into the gear-hobbing maze.

'Nope. I guess commissions are an American thing,' Freedman said wistfully. He was still smiling. He was almost laughing, and his hands were plunged so far into his pockets that his elbows were straight. Joseph thought he'd like to have him as an older brother or confidant who could advise on all the stages to come. 'It makes me think I should go out on my own. But damn, a drought's a drought when you're repping, and it doesn't matter how many daughters you have in school.'

What, Joseph asked himself as he sat on the cool May grass and looked out over the pond, is a million and a half dollars but an abstraction on a beautiful day like this, with a fresh iced tea, an egg salad sandwich with big pebbly capers, a slightly crunchy pear? The pond was a fire reservoir, man-made according to some code that required a certain-sized body of water for every so-and-so many feet of manufacturing space: the neighbouring company made baseballs, softballs, soccer balls, basketballs, volleyballs, all of inexpensive design and quality, for the use of small children. But even if their pond was square and covered across half its surface with algae, the jets that aerated the other half caught the light magnificently, scattering it like chips of glass, and the tiny green circles that undulated on the near side resembled stitches in a beautiful knitted shawl that the pond wore garishly in the sunlight. Joseph thought of his wife of less than a year, back in their apartment, studying by the window; his parents gardening five hundred miles away; his grandparents outside too, no doubt, mowing their tiny lawns just to walk under this magnificent sun.

When Joseph was back inside, Herr Doktor Hühne returned to pick up his briefcase, which he'd left in the middle of Herr Halsa's empty desk.

'Why didn't you join us for lunch?' he asked in German. 'That was unexpected. We arrived at the restaurant and I looked around myself, wanting to ask you a question, and what's this? He doesn't eat?'

Hühne left again with Wilson and the top-grossing salesman, and an hour passed by in welcome silence. Joseph worked steadily, with his usual dedication, no one but Roswitha interrupting. She sprayed Herr Halsa's window, his silk plants, his brass lamp, wiped and rubbed, a water spritzer in one hand, an ammonia bottle in the other, wiping, rubbing and spraying, holding the plant handkerchief between her cheek and shoulder and a roll of paper towel under her wing.

'I'm saying nothing, I'm saying nothing,' she said. 'Keep on with your work.' She spoke in heavily accented English and switched to German only when someone spoke in German to her. She was eighty or so, extremely short, with grey skirts that wrapped not far below her breasts. 'He keeps you busy too, I know that. With his whims,' she whispered, and shushed herself.

Joseph liked having a mercurial boss. *Mercurial* was a good word for him. He was pleased to have thought of it.

When Herr Halsa returned, it was clear where he'd gone after lunch – to the gym, as he often did. The advantages of a workout, not just for Herr Halsa's health but for the whole organization's well-being, so far outweighed any cause for criticism that Joseph wondered at his own momentary derision, the thought skittering into his head that these workouts seemed to follow on occasions of secret, carefully hidden stress. Who else was privy to Herr Halsa's fears and thoughts? Aside maybe from Frau Halsa and a few personal friends, no one but Joseph could have guessed at what was happening in the boss's mind.

On occasional weekend nights, with little notice, everyone at the company was invited to a German hall for drinks and music and laughing repetitions of the chicken dance. Herr Halsa would wrap his arm around every shoulder he came to and lift his beer *Krug* in a toast. *What? You have no beer?* He'd hesitate just long enough to show he regretted spending the company's money, then raise his finger to signal for another. By Monday, no one dared to remind or even to thank him.

Without exception, he returned from the gym with his face the deepest red, as if he were holding his breath through a heart attack. But in exchange, he was calm. His hair, as usual, remained wet, and he rubbed at it with the same towel that had started the day, bending his neck left and right, arching his back, and moving in other cat-like ways that would have seemed impossible an hour before. Joseph envied him his midday showers.

Then that was it for a while. Halsa retreated behind the closed door of his office and drew the shades of his tall, narrow windows – presumably so that others, instead of watching him eat an apple, might mistake this for his most productive hour. He would emerge afterwards, either confirmed in his good opinion of the day or reminded of some fresh inconvenience that needed a scapegoat.

Today, by the magic of endorphins, he was confirmed – his arms behind his back showed it immediately – and he took his flat expression from desk to desk and watched his employees' computer screens over their shoulders, occasionally nodding at what was for him the mystery of how things appeared and disappeared, moved, grew, changed and scrolled on the various monitors. Witnessing the growth of a letter on screen might have occupied him for hours if he hadn't realized, perhaps more acutely than anyone, that this rapt staring resembled ignorance.

'Come in here. Come in, come in,' Herr Halsa called from his office. Joseph had no idea who he was talking to. With the door open Joseph had a view into the room, but Herr Halsa was looking down at the things on his desk, reordering them according to some new, afternoon priority – name plate, lamp, telephone, pen stand. And Joseph could not see as far as Herr Halsa could along the hallway formed by the cubicle walls. Maybe someone was standing there: a petitioner. What's more, the boss was speaking not in German but in English. 'This is something you need to finish for the end of the day, so we must sit together. Quickly I think. Joe!'

Joseph hurried into the office with a notebook, two pens and some papers he'd finished the day before but not yet presented to Herr Halsa. 'Excuse me, I—'

'We're ready to send out a letter just now and offer this very good job. Inventory manager for the new production area,' Herr Halsa added, as if he'd forgotten that Joseph had sat in on every one of the interviews. The new 'production area' was an assembly room where this new employee would take robotic cranes out of their boxes, count the screws, assemble everything, test the completed system, then transfer it to a flatbed truck for shipment to the customer's plant. Joseph's attempt at a job description had muddled everything, though – no one asked if he'd ever written one before – so that several applicants showed up expecting to run an automated inventory system and a couple of others wanted a division reporting to them. But no matter. His influence held. After each interview, Herr Halsa would ask Joseph what the man (he couldn't help it that no women had been included) had meant by this and that, and very often what Herr Halsa wanted to know had nothing to do with the delta between languages at all.

The American salesmen liked to say that Peter Halsa was aptly named. He had risen beyond his competence and didn't know what to do with his time: the Peter Principle. Had anyone dared to repeat this to Herr Halsa, he would have said that he didn't need to understand his job – it was Joseph's responsibility to explain it to him.

Joseph sat while Herr Halsa paced, and here came a tremendous mistake that changed the course of the day. Even after five p.m., Joseph would resist thinking he'd made a mistake. But it was a mistake, and he knew it was a mistake, because a competent employee reads his boss's signs and does not transgress against the boss's most deeply held expectations.

Joseph believed he knew exactly what they'd be doing. They'd be writing to the candidate far more experienced than the others. And because it was a beautiful day and the sun was making use of each passing car's windshield to launch itself at the office walls, where long, overlapping triangles played across motivational posters framed in gold and black, Joseph nodded, looked Herr Halsa in the eye – calm Herr Halsa, for whom Herr Doktor Hühne's visit had been sweated out in the gym – and said, 'I'm happy to help.'

At first, nothing happened. And nothing seemed likely to happen. Why would it? Perhaps no one – least of all Joseph – would have expected anything to come of such innocuous or even friendly words on such a life-affirming day, where beyond the recirculating air of this boxy metal building the trillionth generation of bumblebees was unfurling from its hidden combs.

Herr Halsa smoothed a résumé like an angry mother pressing a shirt. 'This is the one we're hiring. Fred Wagner,' he said, still speaking in English.

Herr Halsa respected his translator, Joseph knew that. He felt the boss's admiration every day. There was the unusual latitude that Herr Halsa afforded him, and one day, when Joseph was off sick, Halsa had moved him into that cubicle by the door – the other Americans he pushed to the periphery and spied on. Of all the employees in the American subsidiary, German and English, Joseph Stone was the only person allowed to keep a real plant. All other plants were required to be silk or plastic. So when Herr Halsa tickled a file into his hand and sat down with a tired sigh, Joseph at some level did not hear the words he had just spoken. Frederick Lebeaux Wagner? Herr Halsa pronounced the name 'Vagna', the German way – though the underqualified good ol' boy with bobbing eyebrows and a love of dirty jokes was as American as Joseph himself.

Halsa placed his hand on Joseph's shoulder, then patted it. He leaned forward with whatever he had to say. 'Do you know why Hühne is a doctor?' he asked. Joseph couldn't get over how unusual this was: Herr Halsa speaking English to him in private. 'Hühne's a doctor because the owner's son, the old man's son, who went to *Gymnasium* with Hans, has a younger brother who became – chancellor, is it? – at the University Köpfingen. But a chancellor at the University Köpfingen doesn't give away free doctorates so easily, without work, so they arranged it in this way, that Hans Hühne, who couldn't rise so high on the technical side without a doctor's degree, would take his doctorate in insects, in *bugs*, and the university would confirm, yes, he's a doctor, with no diploma printed. He's a specialist in the dung beetle with his shit degree. I have only a certificate, but Doktor Schwanz Hühne has not even that much.' His face, which had cooled off since the gym, veered back towards plum as he spoke.

Joseph laughed because he thought Herr Halsa expected and even demanded a laugh from him – a good, strong, close-lipped laugh that said, *Wow, is that true? I won't ever tell anyone.* But on the table in front of him, Halsa's folder named the wrong man for inventory manager, very clearly and prejudicially wrong.

'What about Gary Jackson? For this job,' he said, tapping on the file. 'The applicant who did the same job before.' Also the applicant Joseph had recommended. Herr Halsa had nodded, and the other person in the room had nodded, and Joseph had in fact written the offer letter already, and it was in his hand here, behind the other papers for which he'd already, while Herr Halsa was talking about the shit doctorate, gotten his trusting signature, and he'd been planning to go up front after this meeting and drop it in the mail.

'Gary Jackson?' Herr Halsa said. 'The black one? I didn't know you wore white make-up to work.'

'You said on the phone with the lawyer that you need more minorities.'

'Do not refer to private conversations between me and my lawyer,' Halsa said, abruptly switching to German. 'You're in the room to explain his meaning when I'm lost in garbagey lawyer words. You're not supposed to remember any of it.'

'I'm just trying to help.'

Herr Halsa leaned in and pushed his chest hard against the table. He was speaking English again. 'I don't ask for your help,' he said, looking into Joseph's eyes but pressing his thumb against the table's high shine. 'I don't need your help ever, do you understand? I pay you!'

A truck flashed a stutter of sunlight across the posters again.

Joseph tried to think how to react like a German. Most of his German friends would have quit. The good, decent, strong-willed Germans would have argued, then quit. But what about the businessy Germans? The *Nieten in Nadelstreifen*, idiots in pinstripes? Or come to think of it, this bitter subversive feeling most closely matched his friend who drafted all the factory drawings here, that's who he felt most like. It was maybe pure American bitterness that welled up and spat a calculating line back at Herr Halsa in Joseph's most cordial tone of voice: something that would stab the boss without giving him grounds for firing.

'Herr Doktor Hühne just wants me to translate a new catalogue.'

This manoeuvre, once he'd completed it, did seem German to him – after all, his American friend, the draughtsman, had lived in Darmstadt for fifteen years. And Peter Halsa proved more adept at it.

'You're not the company translator waiting for everyone's work,' he said. 'You take your jobs from me. If anyone needs your time, tell them to ask first, they can knock on my door. But I won't give up my secretary's time for everybody's pet project.'

Without quite knowing how, Joseph retired from Herr Halsa's office to his own cubicle, where he could at least drink the melted ice at the bottom of his long-finished iced tea. He didn't buck forward or run. He walked upright, and he remembered squaring the signed papers on the boss's table in a very casual way before excusing himself. Halsa had already said, too, that there wasn't enough time to write to Fred Wagner before five and they should do it first thing in the morning. Joseph slipped his signed letter to Gary Johnson into a company envelope, affixed one of the personal stamps he kept in his top drawer and licked the envelope shut, exultant to have the last word. Sooner than face a lawsuit, they'd keep Johnson on – the most qualified man, a balm or salt to their racism, salutary either way.

The afternoon had lengthened the building's shadow more than halfway to the ball factory, nearly there, where the five o'clock shift had just arrived, bringing with it a fleet of cars vetted and certified to meet the arcane union rules for what it meant to be 'Made in the USA'.

Herr Halsa was hiring an inventory manager for one reason. He had fired two lawyers and with Joseph's help retained a third who'd given him the legal opinion that putting in the last few bolts in the production area would allow the company to pitch its robots as 'Assembled in the USA'. The lawyer before this latest had sent a long description in quotation marks, with his signature below: 'Final assembly done partially in the United States from some parts manufactured from metals mined and smelted partially in the USA.' And now, as Joseph squeezed another lemon into a fresh iced tea and breathed in the spray of lemon oil, he felt with decreasing urgency the embarrassment of having helped Herr Halsa turn away from the truth. Herr Halsa didn't want the truth of anything. He wanted whatever would seem to raise him up, well past his competence.

Meandering past Helmut Schall's test gantries, which flung an engine block back and forth ten, fifteen, twenty thousand times to prove their stamina, Joseph kept himself safe with an extra-wide margin, in case the many-worlds theory proved to be true and a few random quantums of difference in some conceivable world, leading to a stumble or a careless turn, put him fatally close. Whenever he approached a precipitous edge, or a car passed near enough to unsettle him, he wondered if in some other universe his mother would have cause to grieve now, and the thought of hurting her in that way, somewhere, saddened him.

He didn't pace for long. The company was paying. But he could feel how little that mattered now. He needed to finish the proposal by tomorrow and despite everything he couldn't help wanting it to be perfect, down to the indentations and centrings. Thirty pages' worth. But none of that was the main reason he sat at his desk again, resqueezing his lemon, dusting a few leaves of his ivy plant – a final act of defiance, since Herr Halsa's 'permission' was unspoken and grudging – and pasted in more blocks of pre-written text. These cubicles of words: he'd worried over them, like a boss getting a new job description right, and then, without testing it overmuch, he'd called the cut-and-paste system finished, suitable for all occasions, never to be questioned again. The main reason he dropped his disgust, gave up pacing and returned to his privileged corner was that he was bored.

At five o'clock Herr Halsa came out of his office and Joseph's pulse quickened. Towards or away? He glanced over: towards, and it was clear that Herr Halsa had forgotten everything, put it all behind him. He was wearing his smart suit jacket, finely tailored – Joseph took particular note of it. And he looked confident now. You couldn't think about the Peter Principle when Herr Halsa wore that suit jacket. Maybe Joseph should spend some of his paycheque on a hand-tailored suit. He didn't know what occasion he'd have to wear such a thing, but it seemed the perfect antidote to moulded rubber balls, a factory pond, the grey rugs climbing up the walls of his cubicle.

Herr Halsa laughed. He had a deep, hearty laugh when the day was done. And he told Joseph to go play a little.

Joseph chuckled and nodded. 'Good advice,' he said.

'*Das ist kein Ratschlag, das ist ein Befehl,*' Herr Halsa said. 'It's not advice. It's an order.'

Almost drunk now, Joseph gave a casual evening salute. '*Jawohl. Tschüß!*' he said familiarly. Swatting the envelope against his wrist, back and forth, he watched Herr Halsa swagger away, and noticed with a certain amount of unbecoming pleasure that even as the boss passed a trio of underperforming American salesmen he said nothing to them, lost in his pre-dinner whistling.

That was it. Without considering what was inside, or rather, thinking of it sidelong, as evidence of his importance here, Joseph raised the sealed envelope in a toast and shredded it, along with a few sensitive documents that Herr Halsa didn't want the others to see. He stood up and, with the last moments of the day – because Herr Halsa had left twenty-five seconds early – he wetted a square of paper towel in his melted ice and wiped the leaves of the ivy until they glowed.

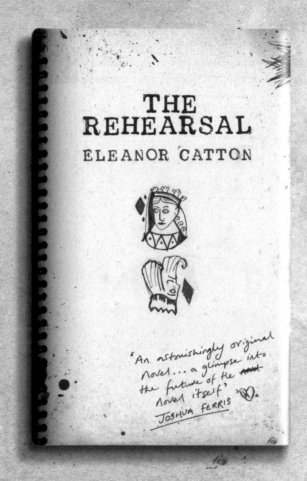

UNTITLED

Chris Ware

THE TOP OF HIS HEAD

PINK
FROM THE SUN.

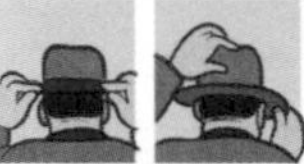

A KISS
GOODBYE

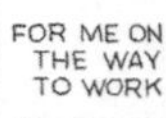
FOR ME ON
THE WAY
TO WORK

EVERY
DAY.

HIS COUGH:
A GRINDING
RASP, STIFLED
UNTIL HE'D
RETRIEVED HIS
HANDKERCHIEF
koff
kooff
koff kf

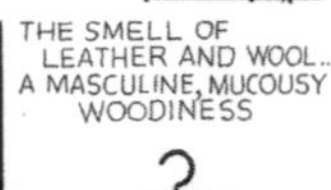
THE SMELL OF
LEATHER AND WOOL...
A MASCULINE, MUCOUSY
WOODINESS

STILL
FROM THE FOLDS
OF HIS COAT.

MOTHER,
RUNNING
THE
ELECTRIC
CARPET
SWEEPER

JUST TO
ANNOY ME.

WHY DID SHE HAVE
TO BOB HER HAIR
LIKE MINE, ANYWAY?
TRYING TO
LOOK YOUNG
WHILE I DO
EVERYTHING
I CAN

TO LOOK
GROWN UP.

IN THE
BATHROOM
HAMPER
PAPA'S
BLOODIED
NAPKINS
MIXED IN
WITH MINE.

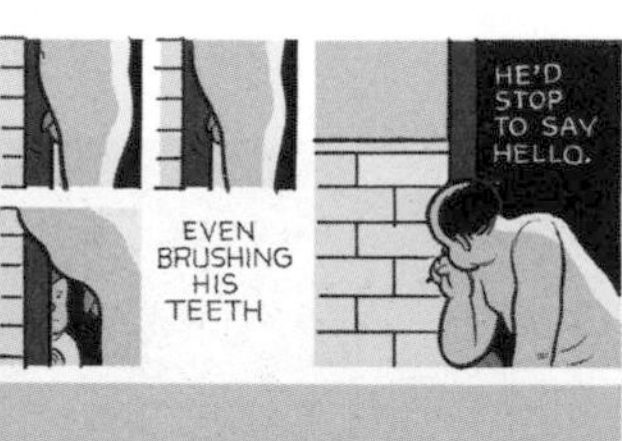

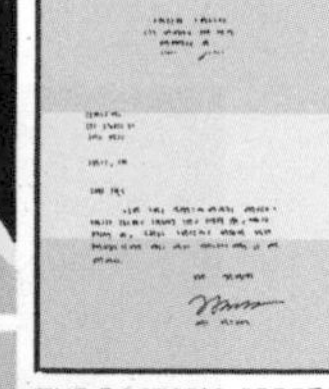

THE DOCTOR'S ORDERS THAT WERE TO SEND HIM AWAY FROM THE DAMP COLD OF CHICAGO.

THE ANTIBIOTICS INVENTED TWENTY YEARS TOO LATE TO SAVE HIM.

AND MAMA, PRETENDING LATER THAT THEY'D NEVER EXCHANGED HARSH WORDS

HOW COULD SHE LIE TO HERSELF LIKE THAT?

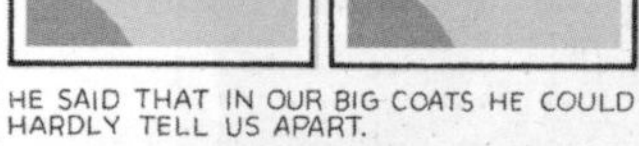

HE SAID THAT IN OUR BIG COATS HE COULD HARDLY TELL US APART.

AT AUNT GRACE'S HOUSE

THE CAMERA MAMA REFUSED TO TOUCH, AFRAID SHE WOULD "BREAK IT."

HE WOULD BE DEAD IN FORTY-EIGHT HOURS.

NO ONE COMFORTED ME.

THE LAST PICTURE OF US TOGETHER. I MUST BE STANDING ON ONE OF THE FENCE POSTS.

AND

THE FOOLISH THOUGHT OF HIM LOOKING DOWN ON ME FROM A CORNER OF THE CEILING IN THE LIVING ROOM

ALL THESE YEARS

WAITING

FOR ME

EXTRACT

HAFFNER

Adam Thirlwell

ILLUSTRATION BY RACHEL TUDOR BEST

1

And so the century ended: with Haffner watching a man caress a woman's breasts.

It was an imbroglio. He would admit that much. But at least it was an imbroglio of Haffner's making.

He might have been seventy-eight, but in Haffner's opinion he counted as young. He counted, in the words of the young, as hip. Or as close to hip as anyone else. Only Haffner, after all, would have been found in this position.

What position?

Concealed in a wardrobe, the doors darkly ajar, watching a woman be nakedly playful to her boyfriend.

This was why I admired him. Haffner Unbound! But there were other Haffners, too – Haffner Pensive, Haffner Abandoned. He tended to see himself like this; as in a dream, in poses: the Loves of Haffner. Like the panels of a classical frieze.

A tzigani pop album – disco drumbeats, accordions, sporadic

trumpets – was being broadcast by a compact-disc player above the minibar. This weakened his squinting concentration. He disliked the modern combination of sex and music. It was better, thought Haffner, for bodies to undress themselves in the quiet of the everyday background hum. In Naples once, in what, he had to say, could only be described as a dive, in the liberated city, the lights went suddenly out, and so the piano stopped, and in the ensuing silent twilight Haffner watched a woman undress so slowly, so awkwardly, so peacefully – accompanied only by the accidental chime of wine glasses, the brief struck fizz of matches – that she had, until this moment more than fifty years later, remained his ideal of beauty.

Now, however, Haffner was unsure of his ideals.

He continued looking at Zinka. It wasn't a difficult task. Her hair was dark; her nipples were long, and almost black, with stained pools of areolae; her stomach curved gently towards her hips, where the bone then steeply rose; her legs were slender. Her breasts and nose were cute. If Haffner had a type, then this was it: the feminine unfeminine. The word for her, in his heyday, would have been gamine. She was a *garçonne*. If those words were, he mused, at the end of his century, still used for girls at all.

They were not.

A suckling noise emerged from Niko, who was now tugging at Zinka's nipples with the pursed O of his mouth.

Haffner was lustful, selfish, vain – an entirely commonplace man. It was the unavoidable conclusion. He had to admit it. In London and New York he had practised as a banker. His life had been unremarkable. It was the twentieth century's idea of the bourgeois: the grey Atlantic Ocean. The horizontal placid waves of the grey Atlantic Ocean. With Liberty at one extreme, and the Bank of England at the other. But Haffner wasn't straddling the Atlantic any more. A hotel in a spa town was now Haffner's temporary home. He was landlocked – adrift in the centre of Europe, aloft in the Alps.

And now he was hidden in a wardrobe.

He was not, however, the usual voyeur. It was true that Niko was unaware of his presence. But Zinka, Zinka knew all about this spectral form in the wardrobe. Somehow, in a way that had seemed natural at the time, Zinka and Haffner had developed this idea of Haffner's unnatural pleasure. The causes were obscure, occasioned by some random confluence of Haffner's charm and the odd mixture Zinka felt of tenderness for Haffner and mischief towards her boyfriend. But however obscure its causes, the conclusion was obvious.

So, ladies and gentlemen, maybe Haffner was grand, in a way. Maybe Haffner was an epic hero. And if Haffner was a hero, then his wallet, with its creased photographs, was his mute mausoleum. Take a look! Haffner in Rome, wonkily crowned by the curve of the Coliseum, a Medusan pile of spaghetti in front of him; Haffner and Livia at a garden party in Buckingham Palace, trying to smile while hoping that Livia's hat – a plate on which lay a pile of flowers – would not erupt and blow away; Haffner's grandson Benjamin, aged four, in a Yankees baseball cap, pissing with cherubic abandon – a live renaissance fountain – in the gardens of a country house.

All photo albums are unhappy, in the words of the old master, in their own particular way.

2

And me? I was born sixty years after Haffner. I was just a friend. I went to see him, in a hospital on the outskirts of London. His finale in the centre of Europe was a decade ago. Now, Haffner was dying. But then Haffner had been dying for so long.

—The thing is, he said, —I just need to plan for the next forty-eight hours. We just need to organize the next few days of the new era.

And when I asked him what new era he meant, he replied that this was exactly what we had to find out.

Everything was ending. On the television, a panel was discussing the crisis. The money was disappearing. The banks were disappearing. The end, as usual, was continuing. I wasn't sorry for the money, however. I was sorry for Haffner. There was a miniature rose in bud on the table. Haffner was trying to explain.

Something, he said, had gone very very wrong. Perhaps, he said, we just needed to get this closed – pointing to a bedside cabinet, whose lock was gone.

He was lower than the dust, he told me. Lower than the dust. After an hour, he wanted to go to the bathroom. He started trying to undress himself, there in his armchair. And so I called a nurse and then I left him, as he was ushered into the women's bathroom, because that bathroom was closer to the room in which Haffner was busily dying.

Standing in the hospital's elliptical concrete drive, as the electric doors opened and closed behind me, I waited for the taxi to take me to the trains – back to the city. Across the silver fields the mauve fir trees kept themselves to themselves. It was neither the country nor the city. It was nowhere.

And as I listened to the boring sirens, I contemplated my memories of Haffner.

With my vision of Haffner – his trousers round his ankles, his hands nervous at his cream underwear – I began my project for his resurrection. Like that historian looking down at the ruins of Rome, in the twilight – with the tourists sketching their souvenirs, and the bells beginning, and the pestering guides, and the water sellers, and the sun above them shrinking: the endless and mortal sun.

3

His career had been the usual success story. After the war Haffner had joined Warburg's. He had distinguished himself with the money he made on the exchange crisis. But his true moment had arrived some years later, when it was Haffner who had realized, as the Fifties wore on, the American crisis with dollars. Only Haffner had quite understood the obviousness of it all. The obtuseness of Regulation Q! Naturally, more and more dollars would leave, stranded as they were in the vaults of the United States, and come to Europe. This was what he had explained to an executive in Bankers Trust, who was over in London to encourage men like Haffner to move to New York. In 1963, therefore, Haffner left Warburg's for America, where he stayed as a general manager for eight years. He was the expert in currency exchange: doyen of the international. Then, in 1974, he returned as Chief General Manager in the London office of Chase Manhattan. Just in time for the birth of his grandson – who had promised so much, thought Haffner, as another version of Haffner, and yet delivered so little. Then, finally, there came Haffner's final promotion to the board of directors. His banishment, joked Haffner.

Haffner, I have to admit, didn't practise the usual art of being a grandfather. Cowardice, obscenity, charm, moral turpitude: these were the qualities Haffner preferred. He had bravado. And so it was that, a decade ago, in the spa town, when everything seemed happier, he avoided the letters from his daughter, the telephone calls from his grandson, the metaphysical lamentation from his exasperated family. Instead, he continued staring at Zinka's breasts, as Niko clumsily caressed them.

Since Zinka was the other hero of Haffner's finale, it may be useful to understand her history.

To some people, Zinka said she was from Bukovina. This was where she had been born, at the eastern edge of Europe – on a night, her mother said, when everything had frozen, even the sweat on her forehead. Her mother, as Zinka knew, was given to hyperbole. To other people, Zinka said she was from Bucharest; and this was true too. It was where she had grown up, in an apartment block out to the north of the city: near the park. But to Haffner, she had simply said she was from Zagreb. In Zagreb, she had trained in the corps de ballet. Until History, that arrogant personification, decided to interrupt. So now she worked here, in this hotel in a spa town, in the unfashionable unfrequented Alps, north of the border with Italy – as a health assistant to the European rich.

This was where Haffner had discovered her – on the second day of his escape. Sipping a coffee he had seen her – the cute yoga teacher – squatting and shimmying her shoulders behind her knees, while the hotel guests comically mimicked her. She was in a grey T-shirt and grey tracksuit trousers: a T-shirt and trousers that could not conceal the twin small swelling of her breasts, borrowed from an even younger girl, and their reflection, the twin swelling of her buttocks, borrowed from an even younger boy. Then she clasped her hands above her back, in a pose that Haffner could only imagine implied such infinite dexterity that his body began to throb, and he felt the old illness return. The familiar, peristaltic illness of the women.

Concealed in a bedroom wardrobe, he looked up at what he could see of the ceiling: where the electric bulb's white light was converted by a dusty trapezoid lampshade into a peachy, emollient glow.

He really didn't want anything else. The women were the only means of Haffner's triumph – his ageing body still a pincushion for the multicoloured plastic arrows of the victorious kid-god: Cupid.

4

Reproductions of these arrows could now be found disporting on Niko's forearms, directing the observer's gaze up to his biceps, where two colourful dragons were eating their own tails – dragons which, if he could have seen them in detail, would have reminded Haffner of the lurid mythical beasts tattooed on the arms of his CO in the war. But Haffner could not see these dragons in detail. Gold bracelets tightly gilded Niko's other wrist. Another more abstract tattoo spread over the indented muscles of his stomach – a background, now, to his erect penis, to which Zinka – dressed only in the smallest turquoise panties – was attending.

Situations like these were Haffner's habitat – he lived for the women, ever since he had taken out his first ever girl, to the Ionic Picture Theatre on the Finchley Road. Her name was Hazel. She let him touch her hand all through the feature. The erotic determined him. The film they had seen had been chosen by Hazel: a romance involving fairies, and the spirits of the wood. None of the effects – the billowing cloths, the wind machines, the fuzzy light at the edges of each frame, the doleful music – convinced sarcastic Haffner of their reality. Afterwards, he had bought her two slices of chocolate cake in a Lyons tea house, and they looked at each other, softly – while in a pattern that would menace Haffner all his life he began to wonder when he might acceptably, politely, try to kiss her.

He was mediocre, he was unoriginal. He admitted this freely. With only one thing had Haffner been blessed – with the looks. There was no denying, Haffner used to say, mock-ruefully, that Haffner was old – especially if you took a look at him. In the words of his favourite comedian. But Haffner knew this wasn't true. He was unoriginal – but the looks were something else. It was not just his friends who said this; his colleagues acknowledged it too. At seventy-eight, Haffner possessed more hair than was his natural right. This hair was blond. His eyes were blue, his cheeks were sculpted. Beneath the silk weave of his polo necks, his stomach described the gentlest of inclinations.

Now, however, Haffner's colleagues would have been surprised.

Haffner was dressed in waterproof sky-blue tracksuit trousers, a sky-blue T-shirt, and a pistachio sweatshirt. These clothes did not express his inner man. This much, he hoped, was obvious. His inner man was *soigné*, elegant. His mother had praised him for this. In the time when his mother praised him at all.

—Darling, she used to say to him, —you are your mother's man. You make her proud. Let nobody forget this.

She dressed him in white sailor suits, with navy stripes curtailing each cuff. At the children's parties, Haffner tried to forget this. As soon as he could, he preferred the look of the gangster: the Bowery cool, the Whitechapel raciness. Elegance gone to seed. His first trilby was bought at James Lock, off Pall Mall; his umbrellas came from James Smith & Sons, at the top of Covent Garden. The royal patent could seduce him. He had a thing for glamour, for the mysteries of lineage. He could talk to you for a long time about Haffner's lineage. The problem was that now, at the end of the twentieth century, his suitcase had gone missing. It had vanished, two weeks ago, on his arrival at the airport in Trieste. It had still not been returned. It was imminent, the airline promised him. Absolutely. His eyesight, therefore, had been forced to rely on itself – without his spectacles. And he had been corralled into odd collages of clothes, bought from the outdoor clothes shops in this town. He walked round the square, around the lake, up small lanes, and wondered where anyone bought their indoor clothes. Was the indoors so beyond them? Was everyone always outdoors?

He was a long way, thought Haffner, sadly, from the bright lights of the West End.

Zinka leaned back, grinned up at Niko, who pushed strands of her hair away from her forehead: an idyll. He began to kiss her, softly. He talked to her in a language that Haffner did not know. But Haffner knew what they were saying. They were saying they loved each other.

It was midsummer. He was in the centre of Europe, as high as Haffner could go. As far away as Haffner could get. Through the slats on the window he could see the blurred and Alpine mountains, the vague sky and its clouds, backlit by the setting sun. The view was pricked by conifers.

And Haffner, as he watched, was sad.

He lived for the women, true. And Haffner would learn nothing. He would learn nothing and leave everyone. That was what Barbra had said of him, when she patiently shouted at him and explained his lack of moral courage, his pitiful inadequacy as a husband, as a father, as a man. He would remain inexperienced. It seemed an accurate description.

But as Zinka performed for her invisible audience, Haffner still felt sad. He thought he would feel exultant, but he did not. And the only explanation he could think of was that, once again, Haffner was in love. But this time there was a difference. This, thought Haffner, was the real thing. As he had always thought before, and then had always convinced himself that he was wrong.

5

The mute pain of it perturbed him. To this pain, he also acknowledged, there was added the more obvious pain in his legs. He had now been standing for nearly an hour. The difficulty of this had been increased by the tension of avoiding the stray coat hangers Haffner had not removed. It was ridiculous, he thought. He was starting to panic. So calm yourself, thought Haffner. He tried to concentrate on the naked facts – like the smallness of Zinka's breasts, but their smallness simply increased his panic, since they only added to the erotic charge with which Haffner was now pulsing. They were so little to do with function, so much to do with form – as they hung there, unsupported. The nipple completed them, the nipple exhausted them. They were dark with areola. Their proportions all tended to the sexual, away from the neatly maternal.

Haffner wasn't into sex, after all, for the family. The children were the mistake. He was in it for all the exorbitant extras.

No, not for Haffner – the normal curves, the pedestrian features. His desire was seduced by an imperfectly shaved armpit, or a tanning forearm with its swatch of sweat. That was the principle of Haffner's mythology. Haffner, an admirer of the classics. So what if this now made him laughable, or ridiculous, or – in the newly moralistic vocabulary of Benji, his orthodox and religious grandson – sleazy. As if there should be closure on dirtiness. As if there should ever be, thought Haffner, any shame in one's lust. Or any more shame than anyone else's. If he could have extended the epic of Haffner's lust for another lifetime, then he would have done it.

In this, he would confess, he differed from Goldfaden. Goldfaden would have preferred a happy ending. He was into the One, not the Many. In New York once, in a place below Houston, Goldfaden had told him that some woman – Haffner couldn't remember her name, some secretary he'd been dealing with in Princeton, or Cambridge – was the kind of woman you'd take by force when the world fell apart.

Not like his wife, said Goldfaden: nothing like Cynthia. Then had downed his single malt and ordered another.

At the time, helpful Haffner's contribution to the list of such ultimate women was Evelyn Laye, the star of stage and screen. The most beautiful woman he had ever laid eyes on, when she accompanied her husband to his training camp in Hampshire, in 1939 – the year of Haffner's manhood. They arrived in a silver Wolseley 14/16. Goldfaden, however, had contradicted Haffner's choice of Evelyn Laye. As he contradicted so many of Haffner's opinions. She was passable, Goldfaden argued, but it wasn't what he had in mind.

And Haffner wondered – as now, so many years later, he watched while Niko stretched Zinka's slim legs apart, displaying the indented hollows inside her thighs, the tattooed mermaid's head protruding from her panties – whether Goldfaden would have agreed that in Zinka he had finally found this kind of woman: the unattainable, the one who would be worth any kind of immorality. If Goldfaden was still alive. He didn't know. He didn't, to be honest, really care. Why, after all, would you want anyone when the world fell apart? It was typical of Goldfaden: this macho exaggeration.

But Haffner no longer had Goldfaden. Which was a story in itself. He no longer had anyone to use as his mute audience.

This solitude made Haffner melancholy.

The ethos of Raphael Haffner – as businessman, raconteur, wit, jazzman, reader – was simple: no experience could be more pleasurable than its telling. The description was always to be preferred to the reality. Yet here it was: his finale – and there was no one there to listen. In the absence of this audience, in Haffner's history, anything had been known to take its place; anything could be spoken to in Haffner's intimate yell: himself, his ghosts, his absent mentors, even – why not? – the more neutral and natural spectators, like the roses in his garden, or the bright impassive sun.

He looked at Zinka, who suddenly crouched in front of Niko, with her back to Haffner, and allowed her hand to be elaborate on Niko's penis.

As defeats went, thought Haffner, it was pretty comprehensive. Even Papa never got himself as messed up as this.

Was it too late for him to change? To undergo one final metamorphosis? I am not what I am! That was Haffner's constant wish, his mantra. He was a man replete with mantras. He would not act his age, or his Age. He would not be what others made of him.

And yet; and yet.

The thing was, said a friend of Livia's once, thirty years ago, in the green room of a theatre on St Martin's Lane, making smoke rings dissolve in the smoky air – a habit that always reminded Livia of her father. The thing was, he was always saying that he wanted to disappear.

She was an actress. He wanted this actress, very much. Once, in their bedroom with Livia before a party, he had seen her undress; and although asked to turn away had still fleetingly seen the lavish shapeless bush between her legs. With such memories was Haffner continually oppressed. It wasn't new. With such memories did Haffner distress himelf. But he couldn't prevent the thought that if she'd undressed in front of him like that then it was unlikely that she looked on him with any erotic interest – only a calm and uninterested friendliness.

Yes, she continued, he was always saying how he'd prefer to live his life unnoticed, free from the demands of other people.

But let me tell you something, Raphael, said Livia's friend. You don't need to disappear.

Then she paused; blew out a final smoke ring; scribbled her cigarette out in an ashtray celebrating the natural beauty of Normandy; looked at Livia.

—Because no one, she said, —is ever looking for you.

How Haffner had tried to smile, as if he didn't care about her jibe! How Haffner continued to try to smile, whenever this conversation returned to him.

Maybe, he thought, she was right: maybe that was the story of his life, of his century.

And now it was ending – Haffner's twentieth century. What had Haffner done with the twentieth century? He enjoyed measuring himself like this, against the grand categories. But that depended, perhaps, on another question. What had the twentieth century done with him?

6

The era in which Haffner's finale took place was an interregnum: a pause. The British Empire was over. The Hapsburg Empire was over. Over, too, was the Communist Empire. All the ideologies were over. But it was not yet the time of full aromatherapy, the era of celebrity: of chakras, and pressure points. It was after the era of the spa as a path to health, and before the era of the spa as a path to beauty. It was not an era at all.

Everything was almost over. And maybe that was how it should be. The more over things were, the better. You no longer needed to be troubled by the constant conjuring with tenses.

In this hiatus, in the final year of the previous century, occurred Haffner's finale.

The hotel where Haffner was staying defined itself as a mountain escape. It had the normal look. It was all white – with a roof that rose in waves of red tile and green louvred shutters on all three floors, each storey narrower than the one below. The top storey resembled a little summerhouse with a tiny structure made of iron shutters on the roof, like an observation post or a weather station with instruments inside and barometers outside. On top of it all, at the very peak, a red weathercock turned in the wind. Every window on every floor had a balcony entered through a set of French doors. Behind it rose the traces of conifered paths, ascending to a distant summit; in front of it pooled the lake, with its reflections. Beside this lake, on the edge of the town, there was a park, with gravel diagonals, and a view of a distant factory.

Once, the town had been the main location for the holidays of the central European rich. This was where Livia's family had spent their summers, out of Trieste. They had gone so far, in 1936, as to purchase a villa, with hot and cold water, on the outskirts of the town. In this town, said Livia's father, he felt happy. It had style. The restaurants were replete with waiters – replete, in their turn, with eyebrow. Then, in the summer of 1939, when she was seventeen, Livia and her younger brother Cesare had not come to the mountains, but instead had made their way to London. And they had never come back. Seven years later, in a hotel dining room in Honfleur, where Haffner had taken her for the honeymoon that the war had prevented, she described to Haffner – entranced by the glamour – the dining rooms of her past: the spa's sophisticated restaurants. Crisp mitres of napkins sat in state on the tables. The guests were served the classics of their heritage: schnitzel Holstein, and minestrone. The Béarnaise sauce was served in a silver boat, its lip warped into a moue. There was the clearest chicken soup with the lightest dumplings.

And now, when this place belonged to another country, here was Haffner, her husband: alone – to claim the villa, to claim an inheritance which was not his.

The hotel still served the food of Livia's memory. This place was timeless: it was the end of history. The customer could still order steak Diane, beef Wellington – arranged on vast circles of china, with a thin gold ring inscribing its circumference. Even Haffner knew this wasn't chic, but he wasn't after the chic. He just wanted an escape. An escape from what, however, Haffner could not say.

No, Haffner could never disappear.

In 1974, in the last year of his New York life, when Barbra – who was twenty-nine, worked in the Wall Street office as his secretary and smoked Dunhills which she kept in a cigarette holder, triple facts that made her desirable to Haffner as he passed middle age – asked him why it was he still went faithfully back every night to his wife, he could not answer. It didn't have to be like that, she said. With irritation, as he looked at Barbra, the steep curve between her breasts, he remembered his snooker table in the annexe at home, its blue baize built over by Livia's castles of unread books. He knew that the next morning he would be there, at home: with his breakfast of Corn Chex, morosely reading the Peanuts cartoons. He knew this, and did not want to know it. So often, he wanted to give up, and elope from his history. The problem was in finding the right elopee. He only had Haffner. And Haffner wasn't enough.

Zinka turned in the direction of the wardrobe. Usually, she wore her hair sternly in a ponytail. But now she let it drift out, on to her shoulders. And Haffner looked away. Because, he thought, he loved her. He looked back again. Because, he thought, he loved her.

No, there was no escape. And because this is true, then maybe in my turn I should not always allow Haffner the luxury of language. He was burdened by what he thought was love. But therefore he did not express it in this way. No, trapped by his temptations, Haffner simply sighed.

—Ouf, he exhaled, in his wardrobe. —Ouf: ouf: ouf. ■

LOST
sleep
HURT
HAVEN
THE MISSING PERSON
NO-ONE
BLACK
RUNNING BLIND
HARD TRUTH
KILLING TIME
HOUSE OF Blues
DEAD SILENCE
ALONE with the DEAD
WILLIAM'S GRAVE
Shattered
NO TIME FOR GOODBYE
STORMY WEATHER
LOSING YOU
MISSING MAN
River of Ruin
KILLING TIME

COMPASSION AND MERCY

Amy Bloom

ILLUSTRATION BY LAURA CARLIN

No power.

The roads were thick with pine branches and whole birch trees, the heavy boughs breaking off and landing on top of houses and cars and in front of driveways. The low, looping power lines coiled on to the road and even from their bedroom window, Clare could see silver branches dangling in the icy wires. Highways were closed. Classes were cancelled. The phone didn't work. The front steps were slippery as hell.

William kept a fire going in the living room and Clare toasted rye bread on the end of fondue forks for breakfast, and in the early afternoon they wrapped grilled cheese sandwiches in tinfoil and threw them into the embers for fifteen minutes. William was in charge of dinner and making hot water for Thai Ginger Soup-in-a-Bowl. They used the snowbank at the kitchen door to chill the Chardonnay.

They read and played Scrabble and at four o'clock, when daylight dropped to a deep indigo, Clare lit two dozen candles and they got into their pile of quilts and pillows.

'All right,' William said. 'Let's have it. You're shipwrecked on a desert island. Who do you want to be with – me or Nelson Slater?'

'Oh my God,' Clare says. 'Nelson. Of course.'

'Good choice. He did a great job with the firewood.'

William kept the fire going all night. Every hour, he had to roll sideways and crouch and then steady himself and then pull himself up with his cane and then balance himself, and because Clare was watching and worried, he had to do it all with the appearance of ease. Clare lay in the dark and tried to move the blankets far to one side so they wouldn't tangle William's feet.

'You're not actually helping,' he said. 'I know where the blankets are, so I can easily step over them. And then, of course, you move them.'

'I feel bad,' Clare said.

'I'm going to break something if you keep this up.'

'Let me help,' Clare said.

When the cold woke them, Clare handed William the logs. They talked about whether or not it was worth it to use the turkey carcass for soup and if they could really make a decent soup in the fireplace. William said that people had cooked primarily in hearths until the late eighteenth century. William told Clare about his visit to his cardiologist and the possible levels of fitness William could achieve ('A lot of men your age walk five miles a day,' the doctor said. 'My father-in-law got himself a personal trainer, and he's eighty.'). Clare said maybe they could walk to the diner on weekends. They talked about Clare's sons Adam and Danny and their wives and the two grandchildren and they talked about William's daughter Emily and her pregnancy and the awful man she'd married ('I'd rather she'd taken the veil,' William said. 'Little Sisters of Gehenna.'). When the subject came up, William and Clare said nice things about the people they used to be married to.

It had taken William and Clare five years to end their marriages. William's divorce lawyer was the sister of one of his old friends. She was William's age, in a sharp black suit with improbably black hair and blood-red nails. Her only concession to age was black patent flats, and

William was sure that for most of her life this woman had been stalking and killing wild game, in stiletto heels.

'So,' she said. 'You've been married thirty-five years. Well, look, Dr Langford—'

'Mister is fine,' William said. 'William is fine.'

'Bill?' the woman said, and William shook his head no and she smiled and made a note.

'Just kidding. It's like this. Unless your wife is doing crack cocaine or having sex with young girls and barnyard animals, what little you have will be split fifty/fifty.'

'That's fine, Mrs Merrill,' William said.

'Not really,' the woman said. 'Call me Louise. Your wife obviously got a lawyer long before you did. I got a fax today, a list of personal property your wife believes she's entitled to. Oil paintings, a little jewellery, silverware.'

'That's fine. Whatever it is.'

'It's not fine. But let's say you have no personal attachment to any of these items. And let's say it's all worth about twenty thousand dollars. Let's have her give you twenty thousand dollars and you give her the stuff. There's no reason for us to just roll over and put our paws up in the air.'

'Whatever she wants,' William said. 'You should know, I'm not having sex with a graduate student. Or with porn stars.'

'I believe you,' Mrs Merrill said. 'You may as well tell me, as it'll all come out in the wash. Who are you having sex with?'

'Her name is Clare Wexler. She teaches. She's a very fine teacher. She makes me laugh. She can be a difficult person,' he said, beaming as if he was detailing her beauty. 'You'd like her.' William wiped his eyes.

'All right,' said Louise Merrill. 'Let's get you hitched, before we're all too old to enjoy it.'

A year later, when they could finally marry, Clare called her sons.

Her oldest said, 'You might want a prenup. I'm just saying.'

Her youngest said, 'Jeez, I thought Isabel was your friend.'

William called his daughter Emily and she said 'How can you do this to me? I'm trying to get pregnant' and her husband Kurt had to take the phone because she was crying so hard. He said 'We're trying not to take sides, you know.'

Three days after the storm had passed, classes resumed, grimy cars filled slushy roads and Clare called both of her sons to say they were essentially unharmed.

'What do you mean, essentially?' Danny said, and Clare said, 'I mean my hair's a mess and I lost at Scrabble seventeen times and William's back hurts from sleeping near the fireplace. I mean, I'm absolutely and completely fine. I shouldn't have said "essentially".'

William laughed and shook his head when she hung up.

'They must know me by now,' Clare said.

'I'm sure they do,' William said, 'but knowing and understanding are two different things. *Verstehen und erklären*.'

'Fancy talk,' Clare said and she kissed his neck and the bald top of his head and the little red dents behind his ears, which came from sixty-five years of wearing glasses. 'I have to go to Baltimore tomorrow. Remember?'

'Of course,' William said.

Clare knew he'd call her the next day to ask about dinner, about Thai food or Cuban or would she prefer scrambled eggs and salami and then when she said she was on her way to Baltimore, William would be, for just a quick minute, crushed and then crisp and English.

They spoke while Clare was on the train. William had unpacked his low-salt, low-fat lunch. ('Disgusting,' he'd said. 'Punitive.') Clare had gone over her notes for her talk on *Jane Eyre* ('In which I will reveal my awful, retrograde underpinnings') and they made their night-time phone date for ten p.m., when William would still be at his desk at home and Clare would be in her bed at the University Club.

Clare called William every half-hour from ten until midnight and then she told herself that he must have fallen asleep early. She called him at his university office on his cellphone and at home. She called him every fifteen minutes from seven a.m. until her talk and she began calling him again, at eleven, as soon as her talk was over. She begged off the faculty lunch and said that her husband wasn't well and that she was needed at home; her voice shook and no one doubted her.

On the train, Clare wondered who to call. She couldn't ask Emily, even though she lived six blocks away; she couldn't ask the pregnant woman to go see if her father was all right. By the time she'd gotten Emily to understand what was required, and where the house key was hidden and that there was no real cause for alarm, Emily would be sobbing and Clare would be trying not to scream at her to calm the fuck down. Isabel was the person to call but Clare couldn't call her. She could imagine Isabel saying, 'Of course, Clare, leave it to me,' and driving down from Boston to sort things out; she'd make the beds, she'd straighten the pictures, she'd gather all the overdue library books into a pile and stack them near the front door. She'd scold William for making them worry and then she would call Clare back to say that all broken things had been put right.

Clare couldn't picture what might have happened to William. His face floated before her, his large, lovely face, his face when he was reading the paper, his face when he'd said to her, 'I *am* sorry,' and she'd thought, 'Oh, Christ, we're breaking up again, I figured we'd go until April at least,' and he'd said, 'You are everything to me, I'm afraid we have to marry,' and they cried so hard, they had to sit down on the bench outside the diner and wipe each other's faces with napkins.

Clare saw that the man in the seat across from her was smiling uncertainly; she'd been saying William's name. Clare walked to the little juncture between cars and called Margaret Slater, her former cleaning lady. There was no answer. Margaret's grandson Nelson didn't get home until three so Margaret might be running errands for another two hours. They pulled into Penn Station. If Margaret had a cellphone, Clare didn't know the number. Clare called every half-hour, home and then Margaret's number, leaving messages and timing herself, reading a few pages of the paper between calls. 'Goddammit, Margaret,' she thought, 'you're retired. Pick up the fucking phone.'

Clare pulled into their driveway just as the sun was setting and Margaret pulled in right after her. Water still dripped from her gutters and the corners of the house and it would all freeze again at night.

'Oh, Clare,' Margaret said, 'I just got your messages. I was out of the house all day. I'm so sorry.'

'It's all right,' Clare said, and they both looked up at the light in William's window. 'He probably unplugged the phone.'

'They live to drive us crazy,' Margaret said.

Clare scrabbled in the bottom of her bag for the house key, furiously tossing tissues and pens and chap sticks and quarters on to the walk, and thinking with every toss, 'What's your hurry? This is your last moment of not knowing, stupid, slow down.' But her hands moved fast, tearing the silk lining of the bag until she saw, out of the corner of her eye, a brass house key sitting in Margaret's flat, lined palm. Clare wanted to sit down on the porch and wait for someone else to come. She opened the door and wished she could turn around and close it behind her.

They should call his name, she thought, it's what you do when you come into your house and you haven't been able to reach your husband, you go, *William, William, darling, I'm home*, and then he pulls himself out of his green-leather desk chair and comes to the top of the stairs, his hair standing straight up and his glasses on the end of his nose. He says, relief and annoyance clearly mixed together, *Oh, darling, you didn't call, I waited for your call.* And then you say, *I* did *call, I called all night, but the phone was off the hook, you had the phone off*, and he says that he certainly did not and Margaret watches, bemused. She disapproved of the divorce (she all but said, I always thought Charles would leave you, not the other way around) but gave herself over on the wedding day when she'd brought platters of devilled eggs and put Nelson in a navy blue suit, and cried, shyly.

'Fulgent,' William said after the ceremony, and he said it several times, a little drunk on champagne. 'Absolutely *fulgent*.' It wouldn't have mattered if no one had been there, but everyone except William's sister had been, and they got in one elegant foxtrot before William's ankle acted up. William will call down, 'I'm so sorry we inconvenienced you, Mrs Slater,' and Margaret will shake her head fondly and go, and you drop your coat and bag in the hall and he comes down the stairs, slowly, careful with his ankle, and he makes tea to apologize for having scared the shit out of you.

Margaret waited. As much as she wanted to help, it wasn't her house or her husband and Clare had been in charge of their relationship for the last twenty years; this was not the moment to take the lead. Clare walked up the stairs and right into their bedroom, as if William had phoned ahead and told her what to expect. He was lying on the bed, shoes off and fully dressed, his hand on *Jane Eyre*, his eyes closed and his reading glasses on his chest. ('He is not to them what he is to me,' Jane thought. 'While I breathe and think, I must love him.') Clare lay down next to him, murmuring, until Margaret put her hand on Clare's shoulder and asked if she should call the hospital or someone.

'I have no idea,' Clare said, lying on the bed beside William, staring at the ceiling. These things get done, Clare thought, whether you know what you're doing or not. The hospital is called, the funeral home is contacted, the body is removed, with some difficulty, because he was a big man and the stairs are old and narrow. Your sons and daughters-in-law call everyone who needs to be called, including the terrible sister in England who sent William one note, explaining that she could not bring herself to attend a wedding that so clearly should not be taking place.

Margaret comes back the next day and makes up one of the boys' bedrooms for you, just in case, but when your best friend flies in from Cleveland, you are lying in your own room, wrapped in William's bathrobe, and you wear his robe and his undershirt while she sits across from you, her sensible shoes right beside William's wingtips, and she helps you decide chapel or funeral home, lunch or brunch, booze or wine, and who will speak. Your sons and their wives and the babies come and it's no more or less terrible to have them in the house. You move slowly and carefully, swimming through a deep but traversable river of shit. You must not inhale, you must not stop, you must not stop for anything at all. Destroyed, untouchable, you can lie down on the other side when they've all gone home.

Clare was careful during the funeral. She didn't listen to anything that was said. She saw Isabel sitting with Emily and Kurt, a little cluster of Langfords; Isabel wore a grey suit and held Emily's hand and she left as soon as the service ended. At the house, Clare imagined Isabel beside her; she imagined herself encased in Isabel. Even in pyjamas, suffering a bad cold, Isabel moved like a woman in beautiful silk. Clare made an effort to move that way. She thanked people in Isabel's pleasant, governessy voice. Clare straightened Danny's tie with Isabel's hand and then wiped chocolate fingerprints off the back of a chair. Clare used Isabel to answer every question and to make plans to get together with people she had no intention of seeing. She hugged Emily the way Isabel would have, with a perfect degree of appreciation for Emily's pregnant and furious state.

Clare went upstairs and lay down on the big bed and cried into the big, tailored pillows William used for reading. Clare held his glasses like a rosary. Clare walked over to the dresser and took out one of William's big Irish linen handkerchiefs and blotted her face with it. (Clare and Isabel did their dressers the same way, William said: odds and ends in the top drawer, then underwear, then sweaters, then jeans and T-shirts and white socks. Clare put William's almost empty bottle of Tabac in her underwear drawer.) She rearranged their two, unlikely stuffed animals.

'Oh, rhino and peckerbird,' William had said. That's how he saw them and two years ago Clare had found herself in front of a fancy toy store in Guilford on a spring afternoon buying a very expensive plush grey rhino and a velvety little brown and white bird and putting the pair on their bed that night.

'You're not so tough,' William had said.

'I was,' Clare said. 'You've ruined me.'

*

Clare wanted to talk with Isabel about Emily; they used to talk about her all the time. Once, after William's second heart attack, when he was still Isabel's husband, Isabel and Clare were playing cards in William's hospital room and Emily and Kurt had just gone off to get sandwiches and Clare had stumbled over something nice to say about Kurt and Isabel slapped down her cards and said, 'Say what you want. He's dumb in that awful preppy way and a Republican and if he says "no disrespect intended" one more time, I'm going to set him on fire.' William said, '*De gustibus non disputandum est*', which he said about many things, and Isabel said, 'That doesn't help, darling.'

Clare looked at William's lapis cufflinks and at the watch she'd given him when they were in the third act of their affair. 'You can't give me a watch,' he'd said. 'I already have a perfectly good one.' Clare took his watch off his wrist, laid it on the asphalt and drove over it, twice. 'There,' she'd said. 'Terrible accident, you were so careless. You had to replace it.' William took that beautiful watch she'd bought him out of the box and kissed her in the parking lot of a Marriott halfway between his home and hers. He'd worn it every day until last Thursday. Clare walked downstairs holding William's jewellery and when she passed her sons pouring wine for people, she dropped the watch into Danny's pocket. Adam turned to her and said, 'Mom, do you want a few minutes alone?' and Clare realized that the time upstairs had done her no good at all. She laid the lapis cufflinks in Adam's free hand. 'William particularly wanted you to have these,' she said, and Adam looked surprised, as well he might, Clare thought.

Clare took the semester off. She spent weeks in the public library, crying and wandering up and down the mystery section, looking for something she hadn't read. A woman she didn't know popped out from behind the stacks and handed her a little ivory pamphlet, the pages held together with a dark blue silk ribbon. On the front it said: GOD NEVER GIVES US MORE THAN WE CAN BEAR. The woman ran off and Clare caught the eye of the librarian, who mouthed the words 'ovarian cancer'. Clare carried it with her to the parking lot and looked over her shoulder to make sure the woman was gone and then she tossed it in the trash.

After the library, Clare went to the coffeehouse or to the Turkish restaurant where they knew how to treat widows. Every evening at six, men would spill out of the church across the street from the coffeehouse. A few would smoke in the vestibule and a few more would come in and order coffee and a couple of cookies and sit down to play chess. They were not like the chess players Clare had known.

One evening, one of the older men, with a tidy silver crew cut and pants yanked up a little too high, approached Clare. (William dressed beautifully. Clare and Isabel used to talk about how beautifully he dressed; Clare said he dressed the way the Duke of Windsor would have if he'd been a hundred pounds heavier and not such a weenie and Isabel said, 'That's wonderful. May I tell him?')

The man said, gently, 'Are you waiting for the meeting?'

Clare said, in her Isabel voice, that it was very kind of him to ask, but there was no meeting she was waiting for.

He said, 'Well, I see you here a lot. I thought maybe you were trying to decide whether or not to go to the next meeting.'

Clare said that she hadn't made up her mind, which could have been true. She could just as soon have gone to an AA meeting as to a No Rest for the Weary meeting or a People Sick of Life meeting. And Clare did know something about drinking, she thought. Sometime after she and William had decided, for the thousandth time, that their affair was a terrible thing, that their love for their spouses was much greater than their love for each other, that William and Isabel were *suited*, just like Charles and Clare were suited, and that the William and Clare thing was nothing more than some odd summer lightning that would pass as soon as the season changed, Clare found herself having three glasses of wine every night. Her goal, every night, was to climb into bed early, exhausted and tipsy, and fall deeply asleep before she could say anything to Charles about William. It was her version of One Day at a Time and it worked for two years until she woke up one night, crying in her sleep and saying William's name into her pillow over and over again. Clare didn't think that that was the kind of reckless behaviour that interested the people across the street.

The man put *AA for the Older Alcoholic* in front of Clare and said, 'You're not alone.'

Clare said, 'That is *so* not true.'

She kept the orange and grey pamphlet on her kitchen table for a few weeks, in case anyone dropped in, because it made her laugh, the whole idea. Her favourite part (she had several, especially the stoic recitation of ruined marriages, dead children, estranged children, alcoholic children, multiple car accidents (pedestrian and vehicular), forced resignations, outright firings, embezzlements, failed suicides, diabetic comas), her absolute favourite in the category of the telling detail, was an old woman carrying a fifth of vodka hidden in a skein of yarn. She finally put the pamphlet away so it wouldn't worry Nelson Slater when he came for Friday-night dinner. Margaret dropped him off at six and picked him up at eight-thirty, which gave her time for Bingo and Nelson and Clare time to eat and play checkers or cribbage or Risk.

Nelson Slater didn't know that William's Sulka pyjamas were still under Clare's pillow, that the bedroom still smelled like his cologne (and that Clare bought two large *flacons* of it and sprayed the room with it, every Sunday), that his wingtips and his homely black sneakers were in the bottom of the bedroom closet. He knew that William's canes were still in the umbrella stand next to the front door and that the refrigerator was filled with William's favourite foods (chicken liver pâté, cornichons, pickled beets, orange marmalade and Zingerman's bacon bread) and there were always two or three large Tupperware containers of William's favourite dinners, which Clare made on Friday, when Nelson came over, and then divided in half or quarters for the rest of the week. Nelson didn't mind. He had known and loved Clare most of his young life and he understood old-people craziness. His great-aunt believed that every event in the Bible actually happened and left behind physical evidence you could buy, like the splinter from Noah's Ark she kept by her bed. His Cousin Chick sat on the back porch, shooting the heads off squirrels and chipmunks and reciting poetry. Nelson had known William Langford since he was five years old and Nelson had got used to him. Mr Langford was a big man with a big laugh and a big frown. He gave Nelson credit for who he was and what he did around the house and he paid Nelson, which Clare never remembered to do. ('A man has to make a living,' he said one time, and Nelson did like that.) Nelson liked the Friday-night dinners and until Clare started doing something really weird, like setting three places at the table, he'd keep coming over.

'Roast pork with apples and onions and a red-wine sauce. And braised red cabbage. And Austrian apple cake. How's that?'

Nelson shrugged. Clare was always a good cook, but almost no one knew it. When he was six years old and eating gingerbread in the Wexler kitchen one afternoon, Mr Wexler came home early. He reached for a piece of the warm gingerbread and Nelson told him that Clare had just baked it and Wexler looked at him in surprise. 'Mrs Wexler doesn't really cook,' he said, and Nelson had gone on eating and thought, 'She does for me, Mister.'

Clare put the pork and apples on Nelson's plate and poured them both apple cider. When Nelson lifted the fork to his mouth and chewed and then sighed and smiled, happy to be loved and fed, Clare left the kitchen for a minute.

After a year, everything was much the same. Clare fed Nelson on Friday nights, she taught half-time, she wept in the shower and at the end of every day, she put on one of William's button-down shirts and a pair of his socks and settled herself with a big book of William's or an English mystery. When the phone rang, Clare jumped.

'Clare, how are you?'

'Good, Lauren. How are you? How's Adam?'

Lauren would not be deflected. She tried to get her husband to call his mother every Sunday night but when he didn't (and Clare could just hear him, her sweet boy, passive as granite: 'She's okay, Lauren. What do you want me to do about it?') Lauren, who was properly brought up, made the call.

'We'd love for you to visit us, Clare.'

I bet, Clare thought. 'Oh, not until the semester ends, I can't. But you all could come out here. Any time.'

'It really wouldn't be suitable.'

Clare said nothing.

'I mean, it just wouldn't,' Lauren said, polite and stubborn.

Clare felt sorry for her. Clare wouldn't want herself for a mother-in-law, under the best of circumstances.

'I'd love to have you visit.' This wasn't exactly true but she would certainly rather have them in her house than be some place that had no William in it. 'The boys' room is all set, with the bunk beds, and your room, of course, for you and Adam. There's plenty of room and I hear Cirque du Soleil will be here in a few weeks.' Clare and Margaret will take Nelson, before he's too grown-up to be seen in public with two old ladies.

Lauren's voice dropped. Clare knew she was walking from the living room, where she was watching TV and folding laundry, into a part of the house where Adam couldn't hear her.

'It doesn't matter how much room there is. Your house is like a mausoleum. How am I supposed to explain that to the boys, Clare? Grandma loved Grandpa William so much she keeps every single thing he ever owned or read or *ate* all around her?'

'I don't mind if that's what you want to tell them.'

In fact, I'll tell them myself, Little Miss Let's-Call-a-Spade-a-Gardening-Implement, Clare thought, and she could hear William saying, 'Darling, you are as clear and bright as vinegar but not everyone wants their pipes cleaned.'

'I don't want to tell them that. I want, really, we all want, for you just to begin to, oh, you know, just to get on with your life, a little bit.'

Clare said, and she thought she never sounded more like Isabel, master of the even, elegant tone, 'I completely understand, Lauren, and it is very good of you to call.'

Lauren put the boys on and they said exactly what they should:

Hi, Grandma, thanks for the Lego. (Clare put Post-its next to the kitchen calendar and at the beginning of every month, she sent an educational toy to each grandchild, so no one could accuse her of neglecting them.) Lauren walked back into the kitchen and forced Adam to take the phone and Clare said to him, before he could speak, 'I'm all right, Adam. Not to worry,' and he said, 'I know, Mom,' and Clare asked about Adam and his work and Lauren's classes and she asked about Jason's karate and the baby's teeth and when she could do nothing more, she said, 'Oh, I'll let you go now, honey,' and she sat on the floor, with the phone still in her hand.

One Sunday, Danny called and said, 'Have you heard about Dad?' And Clare's heart clutched, just as people describe, and when she didn't say anything, Danny cleared his throat and said, 'I thought you might have heard. Dad's getting married,' and Clare was so relieved she was practically giddy. 'Oh, wonderful,' she said. 'That nice tall woman who golfs?' Danny laughed. Almost everything you could say about his future stepmother points directly to the ways she's not his mother – particularly nice, tall and golfs. Clare got off the phone and sent Charles and his bride – she doesn't remember her name, so she sends it to Mr and Mrs Charles Wexler, which has a nice old-fashioned ring to it – a big pretty Tiffany vase of the kind she'd wanted when she married Charles.

The only calls Clare makes are to Isabel. She calls in the early evening, before Isabel has turned in. (There's nothing she doesn't know about Isabel's habits. They shared a beach house three summers in a row and she'd slept in their guest room in Boston a dozen times. She knows Isabel's taste in linens, in kitchens, in moisturizer and make-up and movies. There's not a single place on earth that you could put Clare that she couldn't point out to you what would suit Isabel and what would not.) She dials her number, William's old number, and when Isabel answers she hangs up, of course.

Clare calls Isabel about once a week, after watching *Widow's Walk*, the most repulsive and irresistible show she's ever seen. Three, sometimes four women sit around and say things like, 'It's not an ending; it's a beginning.' What makes it bearable to Clare is that the women are all ardent Catholics and not like her, except the discussion leader, who is so obviously Jewish and from the Bronx that Clare has to google her and discovers that she has a PhD in philosophical something and converted to Catholicism after a personal tragedy. Clare gets to hear a woman who sounds a lot like her great-aunt Frieda say, 'I pray for all widows and we must all keep on with our faith and never forget that Jesus meets every need.' Clare waits for the punchline, for the woman to yank her cross off her neck and say, 'And if you believe that, bubbeleh, I've got a bridge I'd like to sell you,' but she never does. She does sometimes say, in the testing, poking tone of a good rabbi, 'Isn't it interesting that so many women saints came to their sainthood through being widows? They were poor and desperate, alone in the world with no protection, but the sisters took them in and even educated their children. Isn't it *interesting* that widowhood led them to become saints and extraordinary women, to know themselves and Jesus better?' The other widows, the real Catholics, don't look interested at all. The good-looking one, in a red suit and red high heels, keeps reminding everyone that she is very recently widowed (and young and pretty) and the other two, a garden gnome in baggy pants and black sneakers which don't touch the floor and a tall woman in a frilly blouse with her glasses taped together at the bridge, talk, in genuinely heartbroken tones, about their lives now that they are alone. They rarely mention their husbands, although the gnome does say, more than once, that if she can forgive her late husband, anyone can forgive anyone.

Clare dials, as soon as the organ music dies down, and Isabel picks up after one ring. Clare doesn't speak.

'Clare?'

Clare sighs. Hanging up was bad enough.

'Isabel.'

Isabel sighs as well.

'I saw Emily a few weeks ago. I dropped off a birthday present for the baby. She's beautiful. Emily seems very happy. I mean, not to see me, but in general.'

'Yes, she told me.'

'I shouldn't have gone.'

'Well. If you want to offer a relationship and generous gifts, it's up to Emily. Kurt's mother's dead. I guess it depends on how many grandmothers Emily wants Charlotte to have, regardless of who they are.' There was no one like Isabel.

'I guess it does. I mean, I'm not going to presume. I'm not going to drop in all the time with a box of rugelach and a hand-knit sweater.'

'I wouldn't think so. Clare—'

'Oh, Isabel, I miss you.'

'Goodnight, Clare.'

When Clare gets off the phone, there's a raccoon in her kitchen, on the counter. It, although Clare immediately thinks *he*, is eating a slice of bacon bread. He's holding it in his small, nimble and very human black hands. He looks at her over the edge of the bread, like a man peering over his glasses. A fat, bold, imperturbable man with a twinkle in his dark eyes.

Even though she knows better, even though William would have been very annoyed at her for doing so, Clare says softly, 'William.'

The raccoon doesn't answer and Clare smiles. She wouldn't have wanted the raccoon to say 'Clare' because then she would have had to call her boys and have herself committed, and although this is not the life she hoped to have, it's certainly better than being in a psychiatric hospital. The raccoon has started on his second slice of bacon bread. Clare would like to put out the orange marmalade and a little plate of honey. William never ate peanut butter, but Clare wants to open a jar for the raccoon. She's read that they love peanut butter and she doesn't want him to leave.

In an ideal world, the raccoon would give Clare advice. He would speak to her like Quan Yin, the Buddha of Compassion and Mercy. Or he would speak to her like St Paula, the patron saint of widows, about whom Clare has heard so much lately.

Clare says, without moving, 'And why is St Paula a saint? She dumps her four kids at a convent, after the youngest dies. She runs off to *hajira* with St Jerome. How is that a saint? You've got shitty mothers all over America who would love to dump their kids and travel.'

The raccoon nibbles at the crust.

'Oh, it's very hard,' Clare says, sitting down slowly and not too close. 'Oh, I miss him so much. I didn't know. I didn't know that I would be like this, that this is what happens when you love someone like that. I had no idea. No one says, there's no happy ending at all. No one says, if you could look ahead, you might want to stop now. I know, I know, I know I was lucky. I was luckier than anyone to have had what I had. I know now. I do, really.'

The raccoon picks up two large crumbs and tosses them into his mouth. He scans the counter and the canisters and looks closely at Clare. He hops down from the counter to the kitchen stool and on to the floor and strolls out the kitchen door.

Clare told Nelson about the raccoon and they encouraged him with heels of bread and plastic containers of peanut butter leading up the kitchen steps but he didn't come back. She told Margaret Slater who said she was lucky not to have gotten rabies and she told Adam and Danny, who said the same thing. She bought a stuffed animal raccoon with round black velvet paws much nicer than the actual raccoon's, and she put him on her bed with the rhino and the little bird and William's big pillows. She told little Charlotte about the raccoon when she came to babysit (how could Emily say no to a babysitter six blocks away and free and generous with her time?). She even told Emily who paused and said, with a little concern, that raccoons could be very dangerous.

'I don't know if you heard,' Emily said. 'My mother's getting married. A wonderful man.'

Clare bounced Charlotte on her knee. 'Oh, good. Then everyone is happy.' ■

1967

EXTRACT

INVISIBLE

Paul Auster

ILLUSTRATION BY SAM MESSER

I shook his hand for the first time in the spring of 1967. I was a second-year student at Columbia then, a know-nothing boy with an appetite for books and a belief (or delusion) that one day I would become good enough to call myself a poet, and because I read poetry, I had already met his namesake in Dante's hell, a dead man shuffling through the final verses of the twenty-eighth canto of the *Inferno*. Bertran de Born, the twelfth-century Provençal poet, carrying his severed head by the hair as it sways back and forth like a lantern – surely one of the most grotesque images in that book-length catalogue of hallucinations and torments. Dante was a staunch defender of de Born's writing, but he condemned him to eternal damnation for having counselled Prince Henry to rebel against his father, King Henry II, and because de Born caused division between father and son and turned them into enemies, Dante's ingenious punishment was to divide de Born from himself. Hence the decapitated body wailing in the underworld, asking the Florentine traveller if any pain could be more terrible than his.

When he introduced himself as Rudolf Born, my thoughts immediately turned to the poet. Any relation to Bertran? I asked. Ah, he replied, that wretched creature who lost his head. Perhaps, but it doesn't seem likely, I'm afraid. No *de*. You need to be nobility for that, and the sad truth is I'm anything but noble.

I have no memory of why I was there. Someone must have asked me to go along, but who that person was has long since evaporated from my mind. I can't even recall where the party was held – uptown or downtown, in an apartment or a loft – nor my reason for accepting the invitation in the first place, since I tended to shun large gatherings at the time, put off by the din of chattering crowds, embarrassed by the shyness that would overcome me in the presence of people I didn't know. But that night, inexplicably, I said yes, and off I went with my forgotten friend to wherever it was he took me.

What I remember is this: at one point in the evening, I wound up standing alone in a corner of the room. I was smoking a cigarette and looking out at the people, dozens upon dozens of young bodies crammed into the confines of that space, listening to the mingled roar of words and laughter, wondering what on earth I was doing there, and thinking that perhaps it was time to leave. An ashtray was sitting on a radiator to my left, and as I turned to snuff out my cigarette, I saw that the butt-filled receptacle was rising toward me, cradled in the palm of a man's hand. Without my noticing them, two people had just sat down on the radiator, a man and a woman, both of them older than I was, no doubt older than anyone else in the room – he around thirty-five, she in her late twenties or early thirties.

They made an incongruous pair, I felt, Born in a rumpled, somewhat soiled white linen suit with an equally rumpled white shirt under the jacket and the woman (whose name turned out to be Margot) dressed all in black. When I thanked him for the ashtray, he gave me a brief, courteous nod and said *My pleasure* with the slightest hint of a foreign accent. French or German, I couldn't tell which, since his English was almost flawless. What else did I see in those first moments? Pale skin, unkempt reddish hair (cut shorter than the hair of most men at the time), a broad, handsome face with nothing particularly distinctive about it (a generic face, somehow, a face that would become invisible in any crowd), and steady brown eyes, the probing eyes of a man who seemed to be afraid of nothing. Neither thin nor heavy, neither tall nor short, but for all that an impression of physical strength, perhaps because of the thickness of his hands. As for Margot, she sat without stirring a muscle, staring into space as if her central mission in life was to look bored. But attractive, deeply attractive to my twenty-year-old self, with her black hair, black turtleneck sweater, black miniskirt, black leather boots, and heavy black make-up around her large green eyes. Not a beauty, perhaps, but a simulacrum of beauty, as if the style and sophistication of her appearance embodied some feminine ideal of the age.

Born said that he and Margot had been on the verge of leaving, but then they spotted me standing alone in the corner, and because I looked so unhappy, they decided to come over and cheer me up – just to make sure I didn't slit my throat before the night was out. I had no idea how to interpret his remark. Was this man insulting me, I wondered, or was he actually trying to show some kindness to a lost young stranger? The words themselves had a certain playful, disarming quality, but the look in Born's eyes when he delivered them was cold and detached, and I couldn't help feeling that he was testing me, taunting me, for reasons I utterly failed to understand.

I shrugged, gave him a little smile, and said: Believe it or not, I'm having the time of my life.

That was when he stood up, shook my hand, and told me his name. After my question about Bertran de Born, he introduced me to Margot, who smiled at me in silence and then returned to her job of staring blankly into space.

Judging by your age, Born said, and judging by your knowledge of obscure poets, I would guess you're a student. A student of literature, no doubt. NYU or Columbia?

Columbia.

Columbia, he sighed. Such a dreary place.

Do you know it?

I've been teaching at the School of International Affairs since September. A visiting professor with a one-year appointment. Thankfully, it's April now, and I'll be going back to Paris in two months.

So you're French.

By circumstance, inclination, and passport. But Swiss by birth.

French Swiss or German Swiss? I'm hearing a little of both in your voice.

Born made a little clucking noise with his tongue and then looked me closely in the eye. You have a sensitive ear, he said. As a matter of fact, I *am* both – the hybrid product of a German-speaking mother and a French-speaking father. I grew up switching back and forth between the two languages.

Unsure of what to say next, I paused for a moment and then asked an innocuous question: And what are you teaching at our dismal university?

Disaster.

That's a rather broad subject, wouldn't you say?

More specifically, the disasters of French colonialism. I teach one course on the loss of Algeria and another on the loss of Indochina.

That lovely war we've inherited from you.

Never underestimate the importance of war. War is the purest, most vivid expression of the human soul.

You're beginning to sound like our headless poet.

Oh?

I take it you haven't read him.

Not a word. I only know about him from that passage in Dante.

De Born was a good poet, maybe even an excellent poet – but deeply disturbing. He wrote some charming love poems and a moving lament after the death of Prince Henry, but his real subject, the one thing he seemed to care about with any genuine passion, was war. He absolutely revelled in it.

I see, Born said, giving me an ironic smile. A man after my own heart.

I'm talking about the pleasure of seeing men break each other's skulls open, of watching castles crumble and burn, of seeing the dead with lances protruding from their sides. It's gory stuff, believe me, and de Born doesn't flinch. The mere thought of a battlefield fills him with happiness.

I take it you have no interest in becoming a soldier.

None. I'd rather go to jail than fight in Vietnam.

And assuming you avoid both prison and the army, what plans?

No plans. Just to push on with what I'm doing and hope it works out.

Which is?

Penmanship. The fine art of scribbling.

I thought as much. When Margot saw you across the room, she said to me: Look at that boy with the sad eyes and the brooding face – I'll bet you he's a poet. Is that what you are, a poet?

I write poems, yes. And also some book reviews for the *Spectator*.

The undergraduate rag.

Everyone has to start somewhere.

Interesting...

Not terribly. Half the people I know want to be writers.

Why do you say *want*? If you're already doing it, then it's not about the future. It already exists in the present.

Because it's still too early to know if I'm good enough.

Do you get paid for your articles?

Of course not. It's a college paper.

Once they start paying you for your work, then you'll know you're good enough.

Before I could answer, Born suddenly turned to Margot and announced: You were right, my angel. Your young man is a poet.

Margot lifted her eyes towards me, and with a neutral, appraising look, she spoke for the first time, pronouncing her words with a foreign accent that proved to be much thicker than her companion's – an unmistakable French accent. I'm always right, she said. You should know that by now, Rudolf.

A poet, Born continued, still addressing Margot, a sometime reviewer of books, and a student at the dreary fortress on the heights, which means he's probably our neighbour. But he has no name. At least not one that I'm aware of.

It's Walker, I said, realizing that I had neglected to introduce myself when we shook hands. Adam Walker.

Adam Walker, Born repeated, turning from Margot and looking at me as he flashed another one of his enigmatic smiles. A good, solid American name. So strong, so bland, so dependable. Adam Walker. The lonely bounty hunter in a CinemaScope Western, prowling the desert with a shotgun and six-shooter on his chestnut-brown gelding. Or else the kind-hearted, straight-arrow surgeon in a daytime soap opera, tragically in love with two women at the same time.

It sounds solid, I replied, but nothing in America is solid. The name was given to my grandfather when he landed at Ellis Island in 1900. Apparently, the immigration authorities found Walshinksky too difficult to handle, so they dubbed him Walker.

What a country, Born said. Illiterate officials robbing a man of his identity with a simple stroke of the pen.

Not his identity, I said. Just his name. He worked as a kosher butcher on the Lower East Side for thirty years.

There was more, much more after that, a good hour's worth of talk that bounced around aimlessly from one subject to the next. Vietnam and the growing opposition to the war. The differences between New York and Paris. The Kennedy assassination. The American embargo on trade with Cuba. Impersonal topics, yes, but Born had strong opinions about everything, often wild, unorthodox opinions, and because he couched his words in a half-mocking, slyly condescending tone, I couldn't tell if he was serious or not. At certain moments, he sounded like a hawkish right-winger; at other moments, he advanced ideas that made him sound like a bomb-throwing anarchist. Was he trying to provoke me, I asked myself, or was this normal procedure for him, the way he went about entertaining himself on a Saturday night? Meanwhile, the inscrutable Margot had risen from her perch on the radiator to bum a cigarette from me, and after that she remained standing, contributing little to the conversation, next to nothing in fact, but studying me carefully every time I spoke, her eyes fixed on me with the unblinking curiosity of a child. I confess that I enjoyed being looked at by her, even if it made me squirm a little. There was something vaguely erotic about it, I found, but I wasn't experienced enough back then to know if she was trying to send me a signal or simply looking for the sake of looking. The truth was that I had never run across people like this before, and because the two of them were so alien to me, so unfamiliar in their affect, the longer I talked to them, the more unreal they seemed to become – as if they were imaginary characters in a story that was taking place in my head.

I can't recall whether we were drinking, but if the party was anything like the others I had gone to since landing in New York, there must have been jugs of cheap red wine and an abundant stock of paper cups, which means that we were probably growing drunker and drunker as we continued to talk. I wish I could dredge up more of what we said, but 1967 was a long time ago, and no matter how hard I struggle to find the words and gestures and fugitive overtones of that initial encounter with Born, I mostly draw blanks. Nevertheless, a few vivid moments stand out in the blur. Born reaching into the inside pocket of his linen jacket, for example, and withdrawing the butt of a half-smoked cigar, which he proceeded to light with a match while informing me that it was a Montecristo, the best of all Cuban cigars – banned in America then, as they still are now – which he had managed to obtain through *a personal connection* with someone who worked at the French embassy in Washington. He then went on to say a few kind words about Castro – this from the same man who just minutes earlier had defended Johnson, McNamara and Westmoreland for their heroic work in battling the menace of communism in Vietnam. I remember feeling amused at the sight of the dishevelled political scientist pulling out that half-smoked cigar and said he reminded me of the owner of a South American coffee plantation who had gone mad after spending too many years in the jungle. Born laughed at the remark, quickly adding that I wasn't far from the truth, since he had spent the bulk of his childhood in Guatemala. When I asked him to tell me more, however, he waved me off with the words *Another time*.

I'll give you the whole story, he said, but in quieter surroundings. The whole story of my incredible life so far. You'll see, Mr Walker. One day, you'll wind up writing my biography. I guarantee it.

Born's cigar, then, and my role as his future Boswell, but also an image of Margot touching my face with her right hand and whispering: Be good to yourself. That must have come towards the end, when we were about to leave or had already gone downstairs, but I have no memory of leaving and no memory of saying goodbye to them. All those things have been blotted out, erased by the work of forty years. They were two strangers I met at a noisy party one spring night in the New York of my youth, a New York that no longer exists, and that was that. I could be wrong, but I'm fairly certain that we didn't even bother to exchange phone numbers.

I assumed I would never see them again. Born had been teaching at Columbia for seven months, and since I hadn't crossed paths with him in all that time, it seemed unlikely that I would run into him now. But odds don't count when it comes to actual events, and just because a thing is unlikely to happen, that doesn't mean it won't. Two days after the party, I walked into the West End Bar following my final class of the afternoon, wondering if I might not find one of my friends there. The West End was a dingy, cavernous hole with more than a dozen booths and tables, a vast oval bar in the centre of the front room, and an area near the entrance where you could buy bad cafeteria-style lunches and dinners – my hang-out of choice, frequented by students, drunks, and neighbourhood regulars. It happened to be a warm, sun-filled afternoon, and consequently few people were present at that hour. As I made my tour around the bar in search of a familiar face, I saw Born sitting alone in a booth at the back. He was reading a German newsmagazine (*Der Spiegel*, I think), smoking another one of his Cuban cigars, and ignoring the half-empty glass of beer that stood on the table to his left. Once again, he was wearing his white suit – or perhaps a different one, since the jacket looked cleaner and less rumpled than the one he'd been wearing Saturday night – but the white shirt was gone, replaced by something red – a deep, solid red, midway between brick and crimson.

Curiously, my first impulse was to turn around and walk out without saying hello to him. There is much to be explored in this hesitation, I believe, for it seems to suggest that I already understood that I would do well to keep my distance from Born, that allowing myself to get involved with him could possibly lead to trouble. How did I know this? I had spent little more than an hour in his company, but even in that short time I had sensed there was something off about him, something vaguely repellent. That wasn't to deny his other qualities – his charm, his intelligence, his humour – but underneath it all he had emanated a darkness and a cynicism that had thrown me off balance, had left me feeling that he wasn't a man who could be trusted. Would I have formed a different impression of him if I hadn't despised his politics? Impossible to say. My father and I disagreed on nearly every political issue of the moment, but that didn't prevent me from thinking he was fundamentally a good person – or at least not a bad person. But Born wasn't good. He was witty and eccentric and unpredictable, but to contend that war is the purest expression of the human soul automatically excludes you from the realm of goodness. And if he had spoken those words in jest, as a way of challenging yet another anti-militaristic student to fight back and denounce his position, then he was simply perverse.

Mr Walker, he said, looking up from his magazine and gesturing for me to join him at his table. Just the man I've been looking for.

I could have invented an excuse and told him I was late for another appointment, but I didn't. That was the other half of the complex equation that represented my dealings with Born. Wary as I might have been, I was also fascinated by this peculiar, unreadable person, and the fact that he seemed genuinely glad to have stumbled into me stoked the fires of my vanity – that invisible cauldron of self-regard and ambition that simmers and burns in each one of us. Whatever reservations I had about him, whatever doubts I harboured about his dubious character, I couldn't stop myself from wanting him to like me, to think that I was something more than a plodding, run-of-the-mill American undergraduate, to see the promise I hoped I had in me but which I doubted nine out of every ten minutes of my waking life.

Once I had slid into the booth, Born looked at me across the table, disgorged a large puff of smoke from his cigar, and smiled. You made a favourable impression on Margot the other night, he said.

I was impressed by her too, I answered.

You might have noticed that she doesn't say much.

Her English isn't terribly good. It's hard to express yourself in a language that gives you trouble.

Her French is perfectly fluent, but she doesn't say much in French either.

Well, words aren't everything.

A strange comment from a man who fancies himself a writer.

I'm talking about Margot—

Yes, Margot. Exactly. Which brings me to my point. A woman prone to long silences, but she talked a blue streak on our way home from the party Saturday night.

Interesting, I said, not certain where the conversation was going. And what loosened her tongue?

You, my boy. She's taken a real liking to you, but you should also know that she's extremely worried.

Worried? Why on earth should she be worried? She doesn't even know me.

Perhaps not, but she's gotten it into her head that your future is at risk.

Everyone's future is at risk. Especially American males in their late teens and early twenties, as you well know. But as long as I don't flunk out of school, the draft can't touch me until after I graduate. I wouldn't want to bet on it, but it's possible the war will be over by then.

Don't bet on it, Mr Walker. This little skirmish is going to drag on for years.

I lit up a Chesterfield and nodded. For once I agree with you, I said.

Anyway, Margot wasn't talking about Vietnam. Yes, you might land in jail – or come home in a box two or three years from now – but she wasn't thinking about the war. She believes you're too good for this world, and because of that, the world will eventually crush you.

I don't follow her reasoning.

She thinks you need help. Margot might not possess the quickest brain in the Western world, but she meets a boy who says he's a poet, and the first word that comes to her is *starvation.*

That's absurd. She has no idea what she's talking about.

Forgive me for contradicting you, but when I asked you at the party what your plans were, you said you didn't have any. Other than your nebulous ambition to write poetry, of course. How much do poets earn, Mr Walker?

Most of the time nothing. If you get lucky, every now and then someone might throw you a few pennies.

Sounds like starvation to me.

I never said I planned to make my living as a writer. I'll have to find a job.

Such as?

It's difficult to say. I could work for a publishing house or a magazine. I could translate books. I could write articles and reviews. One of those things, or else several of them in combination. It's too early to know, and until I'm out in the world, there's no point in losing any sleep over it, is there?

Like it or not, you're in the world now, and the sooner you learn how to fend for yourself, the better off you'll be.

Why this sudden concern? We've only just met, and why should you care about what happens to me?

Because Margot asked me to help you, and since she rarely asks me for anything, I feel honour-bound to obey her wishes.

Tell her thank you, but there's no need for you to put yourself out. I can get by on my own.

Stubborn, aren't you? Born said, resting his nearly spent cigar on the rim of the ashtray and then leaning forward until his face was just a few inches from mine. If I offered you a job, are you telling me you'd turn it down?

It depends on what the job is.

That remains to be seen. I have several ideas, but I haven't made a decision yet. Maybe you can help me.

I'm not sure I understand.

My father died ten months ago, and it appears I've inherited a considerable amount of money. Not enough to buy a chateau or an airline company, but enough to make a small difference in the world. I could engage you to write my biography, of course, but I think it's a little too soon for that. I'm still only thirty-six, and I find it unseemly to talk about a man's life before he gets to fifty. What, then? I've considered starting a publishing house, but I'm not sure I have the stomach for all the long-range planning that would entail. A magazine, on the other hand, strikes me as much more fun. A monthly, or perhaps a quarterly, but something fresh and daring, a publication that would stir people up and cause controversy with every issue. What do you think of that, Mr Walker? Would working on a magazine be of any interest to you?

Of course it would. The only question is: why me? You're going back to France in a couple of months, so I assume you're talking about a French magazine. My French isn't bad, but it isn't good enough for what you'd need. And besides, I go to college here in New York. I can't just pick up and move.

Who said anything about moving? Who said anything about a French magazine? If I had a good American staff to run things here, I could pop over every once in a while to check up on them, but essentially I'd stay out of it. I have no interest in directing a magazine myself. I have my own work, my own career, and I wouldn't have the time for it. My sole responsibility would be to put up the money – and then hope to turn a profit.

You're a political scientist, and I'm a literature student. If you're thinking of starting a political magazine, then count me out. We're on opposite sides of the fence, and if I tried to work for you, it would turn into a fiasco. But if you're talking about a literary magazine, then yes, I'd be very interested.

Just because I teach international relations and write about government and public policy doesn't mean I'm a philistine. I care about art as much as you do, Mr Walker, and I wouldn't ask you to work on a magazine if it wasn't a literary magazine.

How do you know I can handle it?

I don't. But I have a hunch.

It doesn't make any sense. Here you are offering me a job and you haven't read a word I've written.

Not so. Just this morning I read four of your poems in the most recent number of the *Columbia Review* and six of your articles in the student paper. The piece on Melville was particularly good, I thought, and I was moved by your little poem about the graveyard. *How many more skies above me / Until this one vanishes as well?* Impressive.

I'm glad you think so. Even more impressive is that you acted so quickly.

That's the way I am. Life is too short for dawdling.

My third-grade teacher used to tell us the same thing – with exactly those words.

A wonderful place, this America of yours. You've had an excellent education, Mr Walker.

Born laughed at the inanity of his remark, took a sip of beer, and then leaned back to ponder the idea he had set in motion.

What I want you to do, he finally said, is draw up a plan, a prospectus. Tell me about the work that would appear in the magazine, the length of each issue, the cover art, the design, the frequency of publication, what name you'd want to give it, and so on. Leave it at my office when you're finished. I'll look it over, and if I like your ideas, we'll be in business.

Young as I might have been, I had enough understanding of the world to realize that Born could have been playing me for a dupe. How often did you wander into a bar, bump into a man you had met only once, and walk out with the chance to start a magazine – especially when the *you* in question was a twenty-year-old nothing who had yet to prove himself on any front? It was too outlandish to be believed. In all likelihood, Born had raised my hopes only in order to crush them, and I was fully expecting him to toss my prospectus into the garbage and tell me he wasn't interested. Still, on the off chance that he meant what he'd said, that he was honestly intending to keep his word, I felt I should give it a try. What did I have to lose? A day of thinking and writing at the most, and if Born wound up rejecting my proposal, then so be it.

Bracing myself against disappointment, I set to work that very night. Beyond listing half a dozen potential names for the magazine, however, I didn't make much headway. Not because I was confused, and not because I wasn't full of ideas, but for the simple reason that I had neglected to ask Born how much money he was willing to put into the project. Everything hinged on the size of his investment, and until I knew what his intentions were, how could I discuss any of the myriad points he had raised that afternoon: the quality of the paper, the length and frequency of the issues, the binding, the possible inclusion of art, and how much (if anything) he was prepared to pay the contributors? Literary magazines came in numerous shapes and guises, after all, from the mimeographed, stapled underground publications edited by young poets in the East Village to the stolid academic quarterlies to more commercial enterprises like the *Evergreen Review* to the sumptuous *objets* backed by well-heeled angels who lost thousands with every issue. I would have to talk to Born again, I realized, and so instead of drawing up a prospectus, I wrote him a letter explaining my problem. It was such a sad, pathetic document – *We have to talk about money* – that I decided to include something else in the envelope, just to convince him that I wasn't the out-and-out dullard I appeared to be. After our brief exchange about Bertran de Born on Saturday night, I thought it might amuse him to read one of the more savage works by the twelfth-century poet. I happened to own a paperback anthology of the troubadours – in English only – and my initial idea was simply to type up one of the poems from the book. When I began reading through the translation, however, it struck me as clumsy and inept, a rendering that failed to do justice to the strange and ugly power of the poem, and even though I didn't know a word of Provençal, I figured I could turn out something better working from a French translation. The next morning, I found what I was looking for in Butler Library: an edition of the complete de Born, with the original Provençal on the left and literal prose versions in French on the right. It took me several hours to complete the job (if I'm not mistaken, I missed a class because of it), and this is what I came up with:

I love the jubilance of springtime
When leaves and flowers burgeon forth,
And I exult in the mirth of bird songs
Resounding through the woods;
And I relish seeing the meadows
Adorned with tents and pavilions;
And great is my happiness
When the fields are packed
With armoured knights and horses.

And I thrill at the sight of scouts
Forcing men and women to flee with their belongings;
And gladness fills me when they are chased
By a dense throng of armed men;
And my heart soars
When I behold mighty castles under siege
As their ramparts crumble and collapse
With troops massed at the edge of the moat
And strong, solid barriers
Hemming in the target on all sides.

And I am likewise overjoyed
When a baron leads the assault,
Mounted on his horse, armed and unafraid,
Thus giving strength to his men
Through his courage and valour.
And once the battle has begun
Each of them should be prepared
To follow him readily,
For no man can be a man
Until he has delivered and received
Blow upon blow.

In the thick of combat we will see
Maces, swords, shields, and many-coloured helmets
Split and shattered,
And hordes of vassals striking in all directions
As the horses of the dead and wounded
Wander aimlessly around the field.
And once the fighting starts
Let every well-born man think only of breaking
Heads and arms, for better to be dead
Than alive and defeated.

I tell you that eating, drinking, and sleeping
Give me less pleasure than hearing the shout
Of 'Charge!' from both sides, and hearing
Cries of 'Help! Help!,' and seeing
The great and the ungreat fall together
On the grass and in the ditches, and seeing
Corpses with the tips of broken, streamered lances
Jutting from their sides.

Barons, better to pawn
Your castles, towns, and cities
Than to give up making war.

Late that afternoon, I slipped the envelope with the letter and the poem under the door of Born's office at the School of International Affairs. I was expecting an immediate response, but several days went by before he contacted me, and his failure to call left me wondering if the magazine project was indeed just a spur-of-the-moment whim that had already played itself out – or, worse, if he had been offended by the poem, thinking that I was equating him with Bertran de Born and thereby indirectly accusing him of being a warmonger. As it turned out, I needn't have worried. When the telephone rang on Friday, he apologized for his silence, explaining that he had gone to Cambridge to deliver a lecture on Wednesday and hadn't set foot in his office until twenty minutes ago.

You're perfectly right, he continued, and I'm perfectly stupid for ignoring the question of money when we spoke the other day. How can you give me a prospectus if you don't know what the budget is? You must think I'm a moron.

Hardly, I said. I'm the one who feels stupid – for not asking you. But I couldn't tell how serious you were, and I didn't want to press.

I'm serious, Mr Walker. I admit that I have a penchant for telling jokes, but only about small, inconsequential things. I would never lead you along on a matter like this.

I'm happy to know that.

So, in answer to your question about money… I'm hoping we'll do well, of course, but as with every venture of this sort, there's a large element of risk, and so realistically I have to be prepared to lose every penny of my investment. What it comes down to is the following: How much can I afford to lose? How much of my inheritance can I squander away without causing problems for myself in the future? I've given it a good deal of thought since we talked on Monday, and the answer is twenty-five thousand dollars. That's my limit. The magazine will come out four times a year, and I'll put up five thousand per issue, plus another five thousand for your annual salary. If we break even at the end of the first year, I'll fund another year. If we come out in the black, I'll put the profits into the magazine, and that would keep us going for all or part of a third year. If we lose money, however, then the second year becomes problematical. Say we're ten thousand dollars in the red. I'll put up fifteen thousand, and that's it. Do you understand the principle? I have twenty-five thousand dollars to burn, but I won't spend a dollar more than that. What do you think? Is it a fair proposition or not?

Extremely fair, and extremely generous. At five thousand dollars an issue, we could put out a first-rate magazine, something to be proud of.

I could dump all the money in your lap tomorrow, of course, but that wouldn't really help you, would it? Margot is worried about your future, and if you can make this magazine work, then your future is settled. You'll have a decent job with a decent salary, and during your off-hours you can write all the poems you want, vast epic poems about the mysteries of the human heart, short lyric poems about daisies and buttercups, fiery tracts against cruelty and injustice. Unless you land in jail or get your head blown off, of course, but we won't dwell on those grim possibilities now.

I don't know how to thank you…

Don't thank me. Thank Margot, your guardian angel.

I hope I see her again soon.

I'm certain you will. As long as your prospectus satisfies me, you'll be seeing as much of her as you like.

I'll do my best. But if you're looking for a magazine that will cause controversy and stir people up, I doubt a literary journal is the answer. I hope you understand that.

I do, Mr Walker. We're talking about quality…about fine, rarefied things. Art for the happy few.

Or, as Stendhal must have pronounced it: *ze appy foo*.

Stendhal and Maurice Chevalier. Which reminds me… Speaking of chevaliers, thank you for the poem.

The poem. I forgot all about it—

The poem you translated for me.

What did you think of it?

I found it revolting and brilliant. My faux ancestor was a true samurai madman, wasn't he? But at least he had the courage of his convictions. At least he knew what he stood for. How little the world has changed since 1186, no matter how much we prefer to think otherwise. If the magazine gets off the ground, I think we should publish de Born's poem in the first issue.

I was both heartened and bewildered. In spite of my doleful predictions, Born had talked about the project as if it was already on the brink of happening, and at this point the prospectus seemed to be little more than an empty formality. No matter what plan I drew up, I felt he was prepared to give it his stamp of approval. And yet, pleased as I was by the thought of taking charge of a well-funded magazine, which on top of everything else would pay me a rather excessive salary, for the life of me I still couldn't fathom what Born was up to. Was Margot really the cause of this unexpected burst of altruism, this blind faith in a boy with no experience in editing or publishing or business who just one week earlier had been absolutely unknown to him? And even if that was the case, why would the question of my future be of any concern to her? We had barely talked to each other at the party, and although she had looked me over carefully and given me a pat on the cheek, she had come across as a cipher, an utter blank. I couldn't imagine what she had said to Born that would have made him willing to risk 25,000 dollars on my account. As far as I could tell, the prospect of publishing a magazine left him cold, and because he was indifferent, he was content to turn the whole matter over to me. When I thought back to our conversation at the West End on Monday, I realized that I had probably given him the idea in the first place. I had mentioned that I might look for work with a publisher or a magazine after I graduated from college, and a minute later he was telling me about his inheritance and how he was considering starting up a publishing house or a magazine with his newfound money. What if I had said I wanted to manufacture toasters? Would he have answered that he was thinking about investing in a toaster factory?

It took me longer to finish the prospectus than I'd imagined it would – four or five days, I think, but that was only because I did such a thorough job. I wanted to impress Born with my diligence, and therefore I not only worked out a plan for the contents of each issue (poetry, fiction, essays, interviews, translations, as well as a section at the back for reviews of books, films, music, and art) but provided an exhaustive financial report as well: printing costs, paper costs, binding costs, matters of distribution, print runs, contributors' fees, news-stand price, subscription rates, and the pros and cons of whether to include ads. All that demanded time and research, telephone calls to printers and binders, conversations with the editors of other magazines, and a new way of thinking on my part, since I had never bothered myself with questions of commerce before. As for the name of the magazine, I wrote down several possibilities, wanting to leave the choice to Born, but my own preference was *The Stylus* – in honour of Poe, who had tried to launch a magazine with that name not long before his death.

This time, Born responded within twenty-four hours. I took that as an encouraging sign when I picked up the phone and heard his voice, but true to form he didn't come right out and say what he thought of my plan. That would have been too easy, I suppose, too pedestrian, too straightforward for a man like him, and so he toyed with me for a couple of minutes in order to prolong the suspense, asking me a number of irrelevant and disjointed questions that convinced me he was stalling for time because he didn't want to hurt my feelings when he rejected my proposal.

I trust you're in good health, Mr Walker, he said.

I think so, I replied. Unless I've contracted a disease I'm not aware of.

But no symptoms yet.

No, I'm feeling fine.

What about your stomach? No discomfort there?

Not at the moment.

Your appetite is normal, then.

Yes, perfectly normal.

I seem to recall that your grandfather was a kosher butcher. Do you still follow those ancient laws, or have you given them up?

I never followed them in the first place.

No dietary restrictions, then.

No. I eat whatever I want to.

Fish or fowl? Beef or pork? Lamb or veal?

What about them?

Which one do you prefer?

I like them all.

In other words, you aren't difficult to please.

Not when it comes to food. With other things yes, but not with food.

Then you're open to anything Margot and I choose to prepare.

I'm not sure I understand.

Tomorrow night at seven o'clock. Are you busy?

No.

Good. Then you'll come to our apartment for dinner. A celebration is in order, don't you think?

I'm not sure. What are we celebrating?

The *Stylus*, my friend. The beginning of what I hope will turn out to be a long and fruitful partnership.

You want to go ahead with it?

Do I have to repeat myself?

You're saying you liked the prospectus?

Don't be so dense, boy. Why would I want to celebrate if I hadn't liked it?

I remember dithering over what present to give them – flowers or a bottle of wine – and opting in the end for flowers. I couldn't afford a good enough bottle to make a serious impression, and as I thought the matter through, I realized how presumptuous it would have been to offer wine to a couple of French people anyway. If I made the wrong choice – which was more than likely to happen – then I would only be exposing my ignorance, and I didn't want to start off the evening by embarrassing myself. Flowers on the other hand would be a more direct way of expressing my gratitude to Margot, since flowers were always given to the woman of the house, and if Margot was a woman who liked flowers (which was by no means certain), then she would understand that I was thanking her for having pushed Born to act on my behalf. My telephone conversation with him the previous afternoon had left me in a state of semi-shock, and even as I walked to their place on the night of the dinner, I was still feeling overwhelmed by the altogether improbable good luck that had fallen down on me. I remember putting on a jacket and tie for the occasion. It was the first time I had dressed up in months, and there I was, Mr Important himself, walking across the Columbia campus with an enormous bouquet of flowers in my right hand, on my way to eat and talk business with *my publisher*.

He had sublet an apartment from a professor on a year long sabbatical, a large but decidedly stuffy, over-furnished place in a building on Morningside Drive, just off 116th Street. I believe it was on the third floor, and from the French windows that lined the eastern wall of the living room there was a view of the full, downward expanse of Morningside Park and the lights of Spanish Harlem beyond. Margot answered the door when I knocked, and although I can still see her face and the smile that darted across her lips when I presented her with the flowers, I have no memory of what she was wearing. It could have been black again, but I tend to think not, since I have a vague recollection of surprise, which would suggest there was something different about her from the first time we had met. As we were standing on the threshold together, before she even invited me into the apartment, Margot announced in a low voice that Rudolf was in a foul temper. There was a crisis of some sort back home, and he was going to have to leave for Paris tomorrow and wouldn't return until next week at the earliest. He was in the bedroom now, she added, on the telephone with Air France arranging his flight, so he probably wouldn't be out for another few minutes.

As I entered the apartment, I was immediately hit by the smell of food cooking in the kitchen – a sublimely delicious smell, I found, as tempting and aromatic as any vapour I had ever breathed. The kitchen happened to be where we headed first – to hunt down a vase for the flowers – and when I glanced at the stove, I saw the large covered pot that was the source of that extraordinary fragrance.

I have no idea what's in there, I said, gesturing to the pot, but if my nose knows anything, three people are going to be very happy tonight.

Rudolf tells me you like lamb, Margot said, so I decided to make a *navarin* – a lamb stew with potatoes and *navets.*

Turnips.

I can never remember that word. It's an ugly word, I think, and it hurts my mouth to say it.

All right, then. We'll banish it from the English language.

Margot seemed to enjoy my little remark – enough to give me another brief smile, at any rate – and then she began to busy herself with the flowers: putting them in the sink, removing the white paper wrapper, taking down a vase from the cupboard, trimming the stems with a pair of scissors, putting the flowers in the vase, and then filling the vase with water. Neither one of us said a word as she went about these minimal tasks, but I watched her closely, marvelling at how slowly and methodically she worked, as if putting flowers in a vase of water were a highly delicate procedure that called for one's utmost care and concentration.

Eventually, we wound up in the living room with drinks in our hands, sitting side by side on the sofa as we smoked cigarettes and looked out at the sky through the French windows. Dusk ebbed into darkness, and Born was still nowhere to be seen, but the ever-placid Margot betrayed no concern over his absence. When we'd met at the party ten or twelve days earlier, I had been rather unnerved by her long silences and oddly disconnected manner, but now that I knew what to expect, and now that I knew she liked me and thought I was *too good for this world,* I felt a bit more at ease in her company. What did we talk about in the minutes before her man finally joined us? New York (which she found to be dirty and depressing); her ambition to become a painter (she was attending a class at the School of the Arts but thought she had no talent and was too lazy to improve); how long she had known Rudolf (all her life); and what she thought of the magazine (she was crossing her fingers). When I tried to thank her for her help, however, she merely shook her head and told me not to exaggerate: she'd had nothing to do with it.

Before I could ask her what that meant, Born entered the room. Again the rumpled white pants, again the unruly shock of hair, but no jacket this time, and yet another coloured shirt – pale green, if I remember correctly – and the stump of an extinguished cigar clamped between the thumb and index finger of his right hand, although he seemed not to be aware that he was holding it. My new benefactor was angry, seething with irritation over whatever crisis was forcing him to travel to Paris tomorrow, and without even bothering to say hello to me, utterly ignoring his duties as host of our little celebration, he flew into a tirade that wasn't addressed to Margot or myself so much as to the furniture in the room, the walls around him, the world at large.

Stupid bunglers, he said. Snivelling incompetents. Slow-witted functionaries with mashed potatoes for brains. The whole universe is on fire, and all they do is wring their hands and watch it burn.

Unruffled, perhaps even vaguely amused, Margot said: That's why they need you, my love. Because you're the king.

Rudolf the First, Born replied, the bright boy with the big dick. All I have to do is pull it out of my pants, piss on the fire, and the problem is solved.

Exactly, Margot said, cracking the largest smile I'd yet seen from her.

I'm getting sick of it, Born muttered, as he headed for the liquor cabinet, put down his cigar, and poured himself a full tumbler of straight gin. How many years have I given them? he asked, taking a sip of his drink. You do it because you believe in certain principles, but no one else seems to give a damn. We're losing the battle, my friends. The ship is going down.

This was a different Born from the one I had come to know so far – the brittle, mocking jester who exulted in his own witticisms, the displaced dandy who blithely went about founding magazines and asking twenty-year-old students to his house for dinner. Something was raging inside him, and now that this other person had been revealed to me, I felt myself recoil from him, understanding that he was the kind of man who could erupt at any moment, that he was someone who actually *enjoyed* his own anger. He swigged down a second belt of gin and then turned his eyes in my direction, acknowledging my presence for the first time. I don't know what he saw in my face – astonishment? confusion? distress? – but whatever it was, he was sufficiently alarmed by it to switch off the thermostat and immediately lower the temperature. Don't worry, Mr Walker, he said, doing his best to produce a smile. I'm just letting off a little steam.

He gradually willed himself out of his funk, and by the time we sat down to eat twenty minutes later, the storm seemed to have passed. Or so I thought when he complimented Margot on her superb cooking and praised the wine she had bought for the meal, but it proved to be no more than a temporary lull, and as the evening progressed, further squalls and gales came swooping down on us to spoil the festivities. I don't know if the gin and burgundy affected Born's mood, but there was no question that he packed away a good deal of alcohol – at least twice the amount that Margot and I downed together – or if he was simply out of sorts because of the bad news he had received earlier in the day. Perhaps it was both in combination, or perhaps it was something else, but there was scarcely a moment during that dinner when I didn't feel that the house was about to catch on fire.

It began when Born raised his glass to toast the birth of our magazine. It was a gracious little speech, I thought, but when I jumped in and started mentioning some of the writers I was planning to solicit work from for the first issue, Born cut me off in mid-sentence and told me never to discuss business while eating, that it was bad for the digestion and I should learn to start acting like an adult. It was a rude and unpleasant thing to say, but I hid my injured pride by pretending to agree with him and then took another bite of Margot's stew. A moment later, Born put down his fork and said to me: You like it, Mr Walker, don't you?

Like what? I asked.

The *navarin*. You seem to be eating it with relish.

It's probably the best meal I've had all year.

In other words, you're attracted to Margot's food.

Very much. I find it delicious.

And what about Margot herself? Are you attracted to her as well?

She's sitting right across the table from me. It seems wrong to talk about her as if she weren't here.

I'm sure she doesn't mind. Do you, Margot?

No, Margot said. Not in the least.

You see, Mr Walker? Not in the least.

All right, then, I answered. In my opinion, Margot is a highly attractive woman.

You're avoiding the question, Born said. I didn't ask if you found her attractive, I want to know if *you* are attracted to *her*.

She's your wife, Professor Born. You can't expect me to answer that. Not here, not now.

Ah, but Margot isn't my wife. She's my special friend, as it were, but we aren't married, and we have no plans to marry in the future.

You live together. As far as I'm concerned, that's as good as being married.

Come, come. Don't be such a prude. Forget that I have any connection to Margot, all right? We're talking in the abstract here, a hypothetical case.

Fine. Hypothetically speaking, I would hypothetically be attracted to Margot, yes.

Good, Born said, rubbing his hands together and smiling. Now we're getting somewhere. But attracted to what degree? Enough to want to kiss her? Enough to want to hold her naked body in your arms? Enough to want to sleep with her?

I can't answer those questions.

You're not telling me you're a virgin, are you?

No. I just don't want to answer your questions, that's all.

Am I to understand that if Margot threw herself at you and asked you to fuck her, you wouldn't be interested? Is that what you're saying? Poor Margot. You have no idea how much you've hurt her feelings.

What are you talking about?

Why don't you ask her?

Suddenly, Margot reached across the table and took hold of my hand. Don't be upset, she said. Rudolf is only trying to have some fun. You don't have to do anything you don't want to do.

Born's notion of fun had nothing to do with mine, alas, and at that stage of my life I was ill-equipped to play the sort of game he was trying to drag me into. No, I wasn't a virgin. I had slept with a number of girls by then, had fallen in and out of love several times, had suffered through a badly broken heart just two years earlier and, like most young men around the world, thought about sex almost constantly. The truth was that I would have been delighted to sleep with Margot, but I refused to allow Born to goad me into admitting it. This wasn't a hypothetical case. He actually seemed to be propositioning me on her behalf, and whatever sexual code they lived by, whatever romps and twisted dalliances they indulged in with other people, I found the whole business ugly, off-kilter, sick. Perhaps I should have spoken up and told him what I thought, but I was afraid – not of Born exactly, but of causing a rift that might lead him to change his mind about our project. I desperately wanted the magazine to work, and as long as he was willing to back it, I was prepared to put up with any amount of inconvenience and discomfort. So I did what I could to hold my ground and not lose my temper, to absorb *blow upon blow* without falling from my horse, to resist him and appease him at the same time.

I'm disappointed, Born said. Until now, I took you for an adventurer, a renegade, a man who enjoys thumbing his nose at convention, but at bottom you're just another stuffed shirt, another bourgeois simpleton. How sad. You strut around with your Provençal poets and your lofty ideals, with your draft-dodger cowardice and that ridiculous necktie of yours, and you think you're something exceptional, but what I see is a pampered middle-class boy living off daddy's money, a poseur.

Rudolf, Margot said. That's enough. Leave him alone.

I realize I'm being a bit harsh, Born said to her. But young Adam and I are partners now, and I need to know what he's made of. Can he stand up to an honest insult, or does he crumble to pieces when he's under attack?

You've had a lot to drink, I said, and from all I can gather you've had a rough day. Maybe it's time for me to be going. We can pick up the conversation when you're back from France.

Nonsense, Born replied, pounding the table with his fist. We're still working on the stew. Then there's the salad, and after the salad the cheese, and after the cheese, dessert. Margot has already been hurt enough for one night, and the least we can do is sit here and finish her remarkable dinner. In the meantime, maybe you can tell us something about Westfield, New Jersey.

Westfield? I said, surprised to discover that Born knew where I had grown up. How did you find out about Westfield?

It wasn't difficult, he said. As it happens, I've learned quite a bit about you in the past few days. Your father, for example, Joseph Walker, age fifty-four, better known as Bud, owns and operates the Shop-Rite supermarket on the main street in town. Your mother, Marjorie, aka Marge, is forty-six and has given birth to three children: your sister, Gwyn, in November 1945; you in March 1947; and your brother, Andrew, in July 1950. A tragic story. Little Andy drowned when he was seven, and it pains me to think how unbearable that loss must have been for all of you. I had a sister who died of cancer at roughly the same age, and I know what terrible things a death like that does to a family. Your father has coped with his sorrow by working fourteen hours a day, six days a week, while your mother has turned inward, battling the scourge of depression with heavy doses of prescription pharmaceuticals and twice-weekly sessions with a psychotherapist. The miracle, to my mind, is how well you and your sister have done for yourselves in the face of such calamity. Gwyn is a beautiful and talented girl in her last year at Vassar, planning to begin graduate work in English literature right here at Columbia this fall. And you, my young intellectual friend, my budding wordsmith and translator of obscure medieval poets, turn out to have been an outstanding baseball player in high school, co-captain of the varsity team, no less. *Mens sana in corpore sano*. More to the point, my sources tell me that you're a person of deep moral integrity, a pillar of moderation and sound judgement who, unlike the majority of his classmates, does not dabble in drugs. Alcohol yes, but no drugs whatsoever – not even an occasional puff of marijuana. Why is that, Mr Walker? With all the propaganda abroad these days about the liberating powers of hallucinogens and narcotics, why haven't you succumbed to the temptation of seeking new and stimulating experiences?

Why? I said, still reeling from the impact of Born's astounding recitation about my family. I'll tell you why, but first I'd like to know how you managed to dig up so much about us in such a short time.

Is there a problem? Were there any inaccuracies in what I said?

No. It's just that I'm a little stunned, that's all. You can't be a cop or an FBI agent, but a visiting professor at the School of International Affairs could certainly be involved with an intelligence organization of some kind. Is that what you are? A spy for the CIA?

Born cracked up laughing when I said that, treating my question as if he'd just heard the funniest joke of the century. The CIA! he roared. The CIA! Why on earth would a Frenchman work for the CIA? Forgive me for laughing, but the idea is so hilarious, I'm afraid I can't stop myself.

Well, how did you do it, then?

I'm a thorough man, Mr Walker, a man who doesn't act until he knows everything he needs to know, and since I'm about to invest twenty-five thousand dollars in a person who qualifies as little more than a stranger to me, I felt I should learn as much about him as I could. You'd be amazed how effective an instrument the telephone can be.

Margot stood up then and began clearing plates from the table in preparation for the next course. I made a move to help her, but Born gestured for me to sit back down in my chair.

Let's return to my question, shall we? he said.

What question? I asked, no longer able to keep track of the conversation.

About why no drugs. Even the lovely Margot has a joint now and then, and to be perfectly frank with you, I have a certain fondness for weed myself. But not you. I'm curious to know why.

Because drugs scare me. Two of my friends from high school are already dead from heroin overdoses. My freshman room-mate went off the rails from taking too much speed and had to drop out of college. Again and again, I've watched people climb the walls from bad LSD trips – screaming, shaking, ready to kill themselves. I don't want any part of it. Let the whole world get stoned on drugs for all I care, but I'm not interested.

And yet you drink.

Yes, I said, lifting my glass and taking another sip of wine. With immense pleasure, too, I might add. Especially with stuff as good as this to keep me company.

We moved on to the salad after that, followed by a plate of French cheeses and then a dessert baked by Margot that afternoon (apple tart? raspberry tart?), and for the next thirty minutes or so the drama that had flared up during the first part of the meal steadily diminished. Born was being nice to me again, and although he continued to drink glass after glass of wine, I was beginning to feel confident that we would get to the end of the dinner without another outburst or insult from my capricious, half-crocked host. Then he opened a bottle of brandy, lit up one of his Cuban cigars, and started talking about politics.

Fortunately, it wasn't as gruesome as it could have been. He was deep in his cups by the time he poured the cognac, and after an ounce or two of those burning, amber spirits, he was too far gone to engage in a coherent conversation. Yes, he called me a coward again for refusing to go to Vietnam, but mostly he talked to himself, lapsing into a long, meandering monologue on any number of disparate subjects as I sat there listening in silence and Margot washed pots and pans in the kitchen. Impossible to recapture more than a fraction of what he said, but the key points are still with me, particularly his memories of fighting in Algeria, where he spent two years with the French army interrogating *filthy Arab terrorists* and losing whatever faith he'd once had in the idea of justice. Bombastic pronouncements, wild generalizations, bitter declarations about the corruption of all governments – past, present, and future; left, right, and centre – and how our so-called civilization was no more than a thin screen masking a never-ending assault of barbarism and cruelty. Human beings were animals, he said, and soft-minded aesthetes like myself were no better than children, diverting ourselves with hair-splitting philosophies of art and literature to avoid confronting the essential truth of the world. Power was the only constant, and the law of life was kill or be killed, either dominate or fall victim to the savagery of monsters. He talked about Stalin and the millions of lives lost during the collectivization movement in the Thirties. He talked about the Nazis and the war, and then he advanced the startling theory that Hitler's admiration of the United States had inspired him to use American history as a model for his conquest of Europe. Look at the parallels, Born said, and it's not as far-fetched as you'd think: extermination of the Indians is turned into the extermination of the Jews; westward expansion to exploit natural resources is turned into eastward expansion for the same purpose; enslavement of the blacks for low-cost labour is turned into subjugation of the Slavs to produce a similar result. Long live America, Adam, he said, pouring another shot of cognac into both our glasses. Long live the darkness inside us.

As I listened to him rant on like this, I felt a growing pity for him. Horrible as his view of the world was, I couldn't help feeling sorry for a man who had descended into such pessimism, who so willfully shunned the possibility of finding any compassion, grace, or beauty in his fellow human beings. Born was just thirty-six, but already he was a burnt-out soul, a shattered wreck of a person, and at his core I imagined that he must have suffered terribly, living in constant pain, lacerated by the jabbing knives of despair, disgust, and self-contempt.

Margot re-entered the dining room, and when she saw the state Born was in – bloodshot eyes, slurred speech, body listing to the left as if he was about to fall off his chair – she put her hand on his back and gently told him in French that the evening was over and that he should toddle off to bed. Surprisingly, he didn't protest. Nodding his head and muttering the word *merde* several times in a flat, barely audible voice, he allowed Margot to help him to his feet, and a moment later she was guiding him out of the room towards the hall that led to the back of the apartment. Did he say goodnight to me? I can't remember. For several minutes, I remained in my chair, expecting Margot to return in order to show me out, but when she didn't come back after what seemed to be an inordinate length of time, I stood up and headed for the front door. That was when I saw her – emerging from a bedroom at the end of the hall. I waited as she walked towards me, and the first thing she did when we were standing next to each other was put her hand on my forearm and apologize for Rudolf's behaviour.

Is he always like that when he drinks? I asked.

No, almost never, she said. But he's very upset right now and has many things on his mind.

Well, at least it wasn't dull.

You comported yourself with great discretion.

So did you. And thank you for the dinner. I'll never forget the *navarin.*

Margot gave me one of her small, fleeting smiles and said: If you want me to cook for you again, let me know. I'll be happy to give you another meal while Rudolf is in Paris.

Sounds good, I said, knowing I would never find the courage to call her but at the same time feeling touched by the invitation.

Again, another flicker of a smile, and then two perfunctory kisses, one on each cheek. Goodnight, Adam, she said. You will be in my thoughts.

I didn't know if I was in her thoughts or not, but now that Born was out of the country, she had entered mine, and for the next two days I could barely stop thinking about her. From the first night at the party, when Margot had trained her eyes on me and studied my face with such intensity, to the disturbing conversation Born had provoked at the dinner about the degree of my attraction to her, a sexual current had been running between us, and even if she was ten years older than I was, that didn't prevent me from imagining myself in bed with her, from wanting to go to bed with her. Was the offer to give me another dinner a veiled proposition, or was it simply a matter of generosity, a desire to help out a young student who subsisted on the wretched fare of cheap diners and warmed-over cans of precooked spaghetti? I was too timid to find out. I wanted to call her, but every time I reached for the phone, I understood that it was impossible. Margot lived with Born, and even though he had insisted that marriage wasn't in their future, she was already claimed, and I didn't feel I had the right to go after her.

Then she called me. Three days after the dinner, at ten o'clock in the morning, the telephone rang in my apartment, and there she was on the other end of the line, sounding a little hurt, disappointed that I hadn't been in touch, in her own subdued way expressing more emotion than at any time since we'd met.

I'm sorry, I lied, but I was going to call you later today. You beat me to it by a couple of hours.

Funny boy, she said, seeing right through my fib. You don't have to come if you don't want to.

But I do, I answered, meaning every word of it. Very much.

Tonight?

Tonight would be perfect.

You don't have to worry about Rudolf, Adam. He's gone, and I'm free to do whatever I like. We all are. Nobody can own another person. Do you understand that?

I think so.

How do you feel about fish?

Fish in the sea or fish on a plate?

Grilled sole. With little boiled potatoes and *choux de Bruxelles* on the side. Does that appeal to you, or would you rather have something else?

No. I'm already dreaming about the sole.

Come at seven. And don't trouble yourself with flowers this time. I know you can't afford them.

After we hung up, I spent the next nine hours in a torment of anticipation, daydreaming through my afternoon classes, pondering the mysteries of carnal attraction, and trying to understand what it was about Margot that had worked me up to such a pitch of excitement. My first impression of her had not been particularly favourable. She had struck me as an odd and vapid creature, sympathetic at heart, perhaps, intriguing to look at, but with no electricity in her, a woman lost in some murky inner world that shut her off from true engagement with others, as if she were some silent visitor from another planet. Two days later, I had run into Born at the West End, and when he told me about her reaction to our meeting at the party, my feelings for her began to shift. Apparently she liked me and was concerned about my welfare, and when you're informed that a person likes you, your instinctive response is to like that person back. Then came the dinner. The languor and precision of her gestures as she cut the flowers and put them in the vase had stirred something in me, and the simple act of watching her move had suddenly become fascinating, hypnotic. There were depths of sensuality in her, I discovered, and the bland, uninteresting woman who seemed not to have a thought in her head turned out to be far more astute than I had imagined. She had defended me against Born at least twice during the dinner, intervening at the precise moments when things had threatened to fly out of control. Calm, always calm, barely speaking above a whisper, but each time her words had produced the desired effect. Thrown by Born's prodding insinuations, convinced that he was trying to lure me into some voyeuristic mania of his – watching me make love to Margot? – I'd assumed that she was in on it as well, and therefore I had held back and refused to play along. But now Born was on the other side of the Atlantic, and Margot still wanted to see me. It could only be for one thing. I understood now that it had always been that one thing, right from the moment she'd spotted me standing alone at the party. That was why Born had behaved so testily at the dinner – not because he wanted to instigate an evening of depraved sexual antics, but because he was angry at Margot for telling him she was attracted to me.

She cooked us dinner for five straight nights, and for five straight nights we slept together in the spare bedroom at the end of the hall. We could have used the other bedroom, which was larger and more comfortable, but neither one of us wanted to go in there. That was Born's room, the world of Born's bed, and for those five nights we made it our business to create a world of our own, sleeping in that tiny room with the single barred window and the narrow bed, which came to be known as the love bed, although love finally had nothing to do with what happened to us during those five days. We didn't fall for each other, as the saying goes, but rather we fell into each other, and in the deeply intimate space we inhabited for that short, short time, our sole preoccupation was pleasure. The pleasure of eating and drinking, the pleasure of sex, the pleasure of taking part in a wordless animal dialogue that was conducted in a language of looking and touching, of biting, tasting, and stroking. That doesn't mean we didn't talk, but talk was kept to a minimum, and what talk there was tended to focus on food – *What should we eat tomorrow night?* – and the words we exchanged over dinner were wispy and banal, of no real importance. Margot never asked me questions about myself. She wasn't curious about my past, she didn't care about my opinions on literature or politics, and she had no interest in what I was studying. She simply took me for what I represented in her own mind – her choice of the moment, the physical being she desired – and every time I looked at her, I sensed that she was drinking me in, as if just having me there within arm's reach was enough to satisfy her. What did I learn about Margot during those days? Very little, almost nothing at all. She had grown up in Paris, was the youngest of three children, and knew Born because they were second cousins. They had been together for two years now, but she didn't think it would last much longer. He seemed to be growing bored with her, she said, and she was growing bored with herself. She shrugged when she said that, and when I saw the distant expression on her face, I had the terrible intuition that she already considered herself to be half-dead. After that, I stopped pressing her to open up to me. It was enough that we were together, and I cringed at the thought of accidentally touching on something that might cause her pain.

Margot without make-up was softer and more earthbound than the striking female object she presented to the public. Margot without clothes proved to be slight, almost meagre, with small, pubescent-like breasts, slender hips, and sinewy arms and legs. A full-lipped mouth, a flat belly with a slightly protruding navel, tender hands, a nest of coarse pubic hair, firm buttocks, and extremely white skin that felt smoother than any skin I had ever touched. The particulars of a body, the irrelevant, precious details. I was tentative with her at first, not knowing what to expect, a bit awed to find myself with a woman so much more experienced than I was, a beginner in the arms of a veteran, a fumbler who had always felt shy and awkward in his nakedness, who until then had always made love in the dark, preferably under the blankets, coupling with girls who had been just as shy and awkward as he was, but Margot was so comfortable with herself, so knowledgeable in the arts of nibbling, licking, and kissing, so unreluctant to explore me with her hands and tongue, to attack, to swoon, to give herself without coyness or hesitation, that it wasn't long before I let myself go. If it feels good, it's good, Margot said at one point, and that was the gift she gave me over the course of those five nights. She taught me not to be afraid of myself any more.

I didn't want it to end. Living in that strange paradise with the strange, unfathomable Margot was one of the best, most unlikely things that had ever happened to me, but Born was due to return from Paris the next evening, and we had no choice but to cut it off. At the time, I imagined it was only a temporary ceasefire. When we said goodbye on the last morning, I told her not to worry, that sooner or later we'd figure out a way to continue, but for all my bluster and confidence Margot looked troubled, and just as I was about to leave the apartment, her eyes unexpectedly filled with tears.

I have a bad feeling, she said. I don't know why, but something tells me this is the end, that this is the last time I'll ever see you.

Don't say that, I answered. I live just a few blocks from here. You can come to my apartment anytime you want.

I'll try, Adam. I'll do my best, but don't expect too much from me. I'm not as strong as you think I am.

I don't understand.

Rudolf. Once he comes back, I think he's going to throw me out.

If he does, you can move in with me.

And live with two college boys in a dirty apartment? I'm too old for that.

My room-mate isn't so bad. And the place is fairly clean, all things considered.

I hate this country. I hate everything about it except you, and you aren't enough to keep me here. If Rudolf doesn't want me anymore, I'll pack up my things and go home to Paris.

You talk as if you want it to happen, as if you're already planning to break it off yourself.

I don't know. Maybe I am.

And what about me? Haven't these days meant anything to you?

Of course they have. I've loved being with you, but we've run out of time now, and the moment you walk out of here, you'll understand that you don't need me anymore.

That's not true.

Yes, it is. You just don't know it yet.

What are you talking about?

Poor Adam. I'm not the answer. Not for you – probably not for anyone.

It was a dismal end to what had been such a momentous time for me, and I left the apartment feeling shattered, perplexed, and perhaps a little angry as well. For days afterward, I kept going over that final conversation, and the more I analysed it, the less sense it made to me. On the one hand, Margot had teared up at the moment of my departure, confessing that she was afraid she would never see me again. That would suggest she wanted our fling to go on, but when I proposed that we begin meeting at my apartment, she had become hesitant, all but telling me it wouldn't be possible. Why not? For no reason – except that she wasn't as strong as I thought she was. I had no idea what that meant. Then she had started talking about Born, which quickly devolved into a muddle of contradictions and conflicting desires. She was worried that he was going to kick her out, but a second later that seemed to be exactly what she wanted. Even more, perhaps she was going to take the initiative and leave him herself. Nothing added up. She wanted me and didn't want me. She wanted Born and didn't want Born. Each word that came out of her mouth subverted what she had said a moment earlier, and in the end there was no way to know what she felt. Perhaps she didn't know herself. That struck me as the most plausible explanation – Margot in distress, Margot pulled apart by equal and opposite forces – but after spending those five nights with her, I couldn't help feeling hurt and abandoned. I tried to keep my spirits up – hoping she would call, hoping she would change her mind and come rushing back to me – but deep down I knew it was finished, that her fear of never seeing me again was in fact a prophecy, and that she was gone from my life for good.

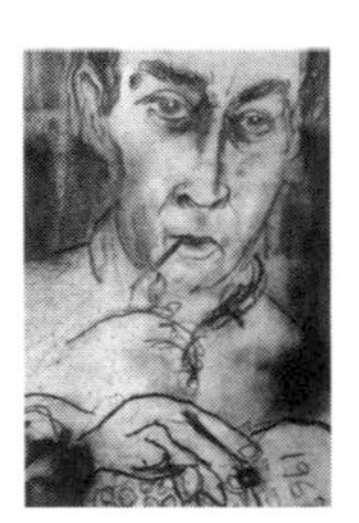

CONTRIBUTORS

Paul Auster is the bestselling author of, among other titles, *Man in the Dark*, *The Brooklyn Follies* (part of which appeared in *Granta* 87) and *The Book of Illusions*. He has also appeared in the magazine with 'The Red Notebook' (*Granta* 44), 'Dizzy' (*Granta* 46), 'The Money Chronicles' (*Granta* 58) and 'It Don't Mean a Thing' (*Granta* 71). 'Invisible' is an extract from his new novel of the same title, which will be published in November 2009.

John Banville was awarded the Man Booker Prize in 2005 for *The Sea*. His new novel, *The Infinities*, will be published in the autumn. He last appeared in *Granta* 56 with 'The Enemy Within'.

Nicola Barker's most recent novel, *Darkmans*, was shortlisted for the Man Booker and Ondaatje prizes, and won the Hawthornden Prize. In 2003 she was named as one of *Granta*'s Best of Young British Novelists. 'For the Exclusive Attn of Ms Linda Withycombe' will be published in *Burley Cross Postbox Theft*, an epistolary novel to be published in 2010. She lives in London.

Amy Bloom is the author of one novel, *Away*, and two books of short stories. 'Compassion and Mercy' is taken from a new collection, *I Love to See You Coming, I Hate To See You Go*, to be published in 2010. She is at work on a new novel.

Eleanor Catton was born in 1985 in Ontario, Canada and raised in New Zealand. Her first novel, *The Rehearsal*, won the 2007 Adam Award from the International Institute of Modern Letters. It will be published in the UK in July 2009 and in the USA in 2010. She is currently a student at the Iowa Writers' Workshop.

Mavis Gallant was born in Montreal in 1922. When she was twenty-eight she gave up her job as a journalist, moved to Paris and devoted herself to writing fiction. In 1951 she published her first short story in *The New Yorker* and since then she has established an international following as one of the world's greatest short-story writers. She is the author of over twelve collections of stories, two novels, a volume of non-fiction, *Paris Notebooks: Essays and Reviews*, and a play. A selection of her work from

1951–71, *The Cost of Living*, will be published in autumn 2009.

Fanny Howe's poetry collections include *On the Ground*, shortlisted for the Griffin Poetry Prize, and *The Lyrics*. *The Winter Sun: Notes on a Vocation*, a book of essays, was published earlier this year.

Ha Jin was born in Liaoning, China, in 1956, and moved to America in 1984. His books include the novel *Waiting*, winner of the PEN/Faulkner Award and the National Book Award; *War Trash*, which won the PEN/Faulkner Award; *Under the Red Flag*, which won the Flannery O'Connor Award for Short Fiction; and *Ocean of Words*, which won the PEN/Hemingway Award. A new collection of stories, *A Good Fall*, will be published in November 2009. He is a professor of English at Boston University.

Jhumpa Lahiri is the author of *The Namesake*, a novel, and two collections of stories, *Interpreter of Maladies*, which won the Pulitzer Prize, the PEN/Hemingway Award and *The New Yorker* Debut of the Year, and *Unaccustomed Earth*, winner of the Frank O'Connor International Short Story Award. She lives in Brooklyn, New York.

William Pierce is Senior Editor of the American literary and cultural magazine *AGNI*, and publishes a series of essays there called 'Crucibles'. He is currently at work on a novel, *A Man of Restraint*.

Helen Simpson is the author of five collections of short stories: *Four Bare Legs in a Bed*, *Dear George*, *Hey Yeah Right Get a Life* (*Getting a Life* in the US), *Constitutional* (*In the Driver's Seat* in the US) and *In-Flight Entertainment*, which will be published later this year. In 1993 she was chosen as one of *Granta*'s Best of Young British Novelists. 'In-Flight Entertainment' was published in *Granta* 100. She lives in London.

Adam Thirlwell was born in 1978 and named one of *Granta*'s Best of Young British Novelists in 2003. His story, 'The Cyrillic Alphabet', appeared in the issue of that title. His first novel, *Politics*, was followed by an essay on the art of fiction, *Miss Herbert*, published in 2007 and winner of The Somerset Maugham Award in 2008. His second novel,

The Escape (from which 'Haffner' is taken), will be published in 2010.

Chris Ware lives in Oak Park, Illinois, and is the author of *Jimmy Corrigan – The Smartest Kid on Earth.* He has guest-edited *Timothy McSweeney's Quarterly Concern* and Houghton-Mifflin's *The Best American Comics*, and was the first cartoonist chosen to regularly serialize an ongoing story in the *New York Times*. A contributor to *The New Yorker* and *The Virginia Quarterly Review*, his work was included in the 2002 Whitney Biennial and later enjoyed an exhibit of its own at the Museum of Contemporary Art Chicago.

ILLUSTRATORS

Ceri Amphlett's commissions include the artwork for the album *Thunder, Lightning, Strike* by British band The Go! Team. She has also shown her work internationally, most recently as part of *The Art of Lost Words* exhibition.

Rachel Tudor Best draws on the rich and diverse experience of her home life and travels to provide the source and inspiration for her work, developing ideas through the playful use of art materials, photographs and books.

George Butler has been a freelance illustrator since 2007. The majority of his work could be described as reportage illustration but he has also undertaken commercial jobs for Descent ski holidays and has been named Illustrator in Residence at *The Globalista Travel Journal*.

Laura Carlin won a V&A Illustration Award for her contribution to Barbara Toner's piece 'Inside a Rape Trial' (*Guardian*). While at the Royal College of Art she twice received the Quentin Blake Award, and her recent clients include British Airways and the *New York Times*.

Tilman Faelker lives in Stuttgart, Germany, and has been a freelance illustrator since the beginning of 2009. His work has appeared in *Beef* – the magazine of the Art Directors Club of Germany – and the Italian cultural quarterly *Drome*.

Michael Kirkham won the D&AD 'Best New Blood' award in 2006 and the Association of Illustrators' 'New Talent' Gold award in 2007. His commissions have included work for the Folio Society, Random House and *The Times*.

Sam Messer is an artist and teacher whose work is exhibited and collected internationally. He has also collaborated with writers including Denis Johnson, Jonathan Safran Foer and Paul Auster, with whom he published *The Story of My Typewriter*.

Adam Simpson's clients include Conran and the *LA Times*. His work encompasses design, animation and illustration, but always with an emphasis on drawing. He has exhibited internationally and has lectured on art and design at the Universities of Derby and Plymouth.

THE POETRY SOCIETY

NATIONAL POETRY COMPETITION 2009

JUDGES
Daljit Nagra, Ruth Padel & Neil Rollinson

DEADLINE
31 October 2009

FIRST PRIZE
£5000

Submit online or download an entry form at www.poetrysociety.org.uk

ROYAL LITERARY FUND

FINANCIAL ASSISTANCE
FOR WRITERS

The Royal Literary Fund

Grants and Pensions are available to
published authors of several works
who are in financial difficulties due to
personal or professional setbacks.
Applications are considered in confidence
by the General Committee every month.
For further details please contact:
Eileen Gunn, General Secretary
The Royal Literary Fund
3 Johnson's Court,
London EC4A 3EA
Tel 0207 353 7159
Email: egunnrlf@globalnet.co.uk
website www.rlf.org.uk
Registered Charity No 219952

CHARLESTON FESTIVAL

Charleston Festival

15th to 24th of May 2009

including...

Eileen Atkins
Kate Atkinson
Alain de Botton
A.S. Byatt
Vince Cable
Margaret Drabble
Patrick Gale
Robert Harris
Richard Holmes
Michael Holroyd
Tristram Hunt
Steve Jones
David Lodge
Hilary Mantel
Michael Morpurgo
James Naughtie
Jeremy Paxman
Grayson Perry
Prunella Scales
Graham Swift
Colm Toibin
Tim West
Jeanette Winterson
Markus Zusak

Charleston, Firle, Lewes BN8 6LL
For more information call 01323 811626
or visit www.charleston.org.uk

charleston

CELEBRATE 20 YEARS OF THE CHARLESTON FESTIVAL 1989–2009

GRANTA | 107

IN THE NEXT ISSUE

Mary Gaitskill meditates on how we measure varieties of loss after the disappearance of her rescued cat; **Will Self** walks through Tehran thirty years on from the revolution; **Timothy Phillips** uncovers a story of espionage in London between the wars; and **Rana Dasgupta** reports from Delhi on the emergence of India's super rich.

Plus: **Ariel Leve** visits the American town revitalized by immigration and **Xan Rice** among the Polisario rebels fighting for the disputed territory of the western Sahara; and the best new fiction from emerging and established writers.

www.granta.com

The magazine's website has relaunched. It now provides an accessible and responsive forum for writers and readers. For the first time, visitors to the site can comment on, and add tags to, all of our articles and online-only content. Users can also get updates on new material appearing on granta.com via RSS and every issue is available for purchase on the site. As well as online exclusives, www.granta.com will make freely available to subscribers the entire archive of the print magazine, with five new back issues added each month. Non-subscribers can receive access to our archives for the special offer of £3.50. Visit www.granta.com to find out more and explore.

The UK financial system

Theory and practice

second edition

Mike Buckle and John Thompson

Manchester University Press

Manchester and New York
distributed exclusively in the USA and Canada by St Martin's Press

Published by Manchester University Press
Oxford Road, Manchester M13 9NR, UK
and Room 400, 175 Fifth Avenue, New York, NY 10010, USA

Distributed exclusively in the USA and Canada
by St Martin's Press, Inc., 175 Fifth Avenue, New York, NY 10010, USA

British Library Cataloguing-in-Publication Data
A catalogue record for this book is available from the British Library

Library of Congress Cataloging-in-Publication Data applied for

ISBN 0 7190 4815 X *hardback*
0 7190 4816 8 *paperback*

First published 1995
First edition published 1992

99 98 97 96 95 10 9 8 7 6 5 4 3 2 1

Printed by Biddles Ltd, Guildford & King's Lynn

Contents

Preface to the second edition

In writing this second edition we are conscious of the many changes that have taken place in the UK financial system since 1990. To take just one example, the failures of BCCI and Barings have led to new practices in the prudential control of banks. Whilst we have endeavoured to incorporate most of the recent developments, we are aware that the financial system is never static so that by the time this text is published further changes will have taken place. This necessitates the reader keeping abreast of future developments through reading the financial sections of the quality press. At the time of writing, four features are worth future attention:

(i) In April 1995, the Bank of England will carry out a further survey of the London foreign exchange market. The coverage of this survey is likely to be wider than that of earlier surveys. Details of the results of the survey are to be published in the autumn. A commentary on the results of this survey will be available on request from either of the authors towards the end of 1995.
(ii) Prudential legislation is currently passing through Parliament and the outcome may differ from the details contained in the white paper.
(iii) Building society legislation is likely to be amended.
(iv) Further European integration and legislation are likely.

We would like to reiterate our thanks contained in the Preface to the first edition to the various colleagues who have helped us in the preparation of this text. We are particularly grateful to Professor Peter Franklin, who contributed the appendix to chapter 6 dealing with Lloyd's insurance market.

Mike Buckle
John Thompson
June 1995

Preface to the first edition

In recent years there have been extensive developments in the UK financial system. This book presents a review of these developments for second/third-year students of Accountancy, Business Studies, Economics and Finance. Chapters 1 to 6 are concerned with the various financial institutions comprising the British financial system. Chapters 7 to 13 discuss the different financial markets located in the UK. The remaining chapters deal with a number of issues including the management of risk, the development of a single European market in financial services, the efficiency and regulation of the UK financial system.

We are grateful to Peter Franklin, Nottingham Polytechnic, Bryn Gravenor, European Business Management School, Richard Harrington, University of Manchester, Ken Holden, University of Liverpool, and Kent Matthews, Cardiff Business School, for their help in the preparation of the book. Any errors and omissions are the responsibility of the authors.

To Margaret and Fiona

Mike Buckle
John Thompson
January 1992

Chapter 1

Introduction to the financial system

1.1 Introduction

We begin our study of the UK financial system with an introduction to the role of a financial system in an economy. We start this introduction with a very simple model of an economy and then extend the analysis throughout the rest of this and the next chapter. A second objective is to establish some of the basic financial concepts which will be drawn upon throughout this book. Finally, we hope to introduce readers to the many sources of data available relating to the UK financial system. In particular we explain the relationships between the various sets of financial statistics.

1.2 The role of the financial system

To help us to understand the role played by a financial system in a mature economy such as that of the UK we start by constructing a simplified model of an economy. In this model the economy is divided into two distinct groups or sectors. The first is the household sector, which is assumed to be the ultimate owner of all the resources of the economy. In the early stages of development of an economy the household unit would have undertaken production of any goods consumed. As economies developed, a form of specialisation has generally taken place so that the proximate ownership and control of much of the productive resources of the economy, such as land, buildings and machinery, have been vested in units making up the second sector, which we call the firms sector. We will examine the financial relationships between these two sectors later. In our simple model it is the firms sector which organises the production of goods and services in the economy. In exchange for these goods and services, households hire out their resources of land, labour, etc. At this stage we ignore the role of the government and we assume that the economy is closed, so that there is no

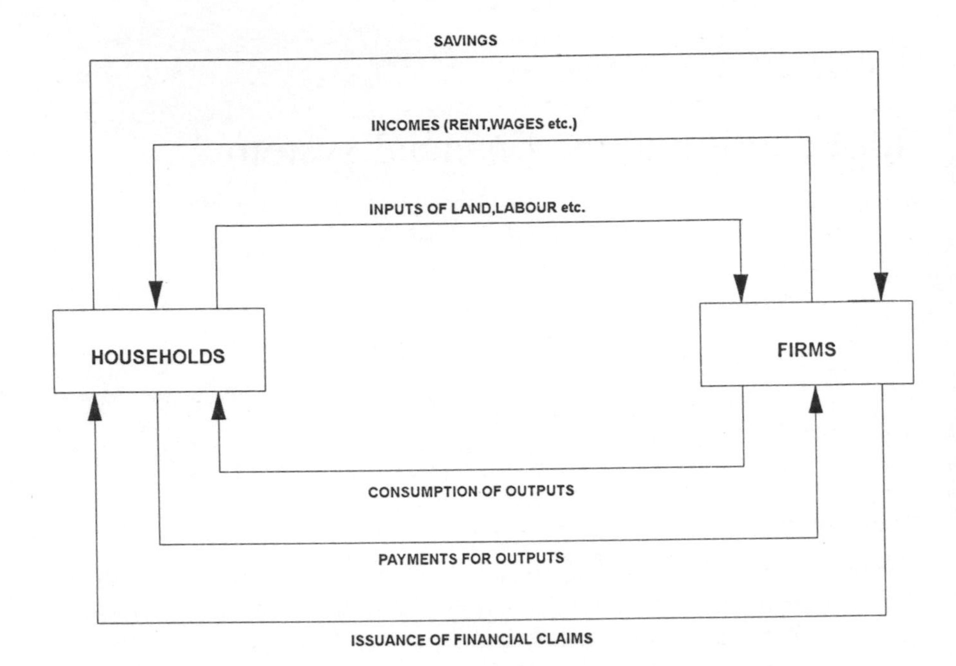

Figure 1.1

exchange of goods and services with other economies. The real flows in this simple economy are set out in the inner loop of figure 1.1.

In this simple economy it would not be an easy task for households to attempt to satisfy their wants. The greater the number of commodities available in the economy, the greater would be the task. This can be seen by considering the choices open to households. Households can consume the commodities they own, they can exchange these commodities for commodities owned by other households or they can use these commodities as inputs to create new commodities. In the last situation the household would have to hire out the commodities to an existing firm in exchange for the firm's output or alternatively create a new firm. In the case of exchanging commodities with other households there would clearly be many difficulties. For a successful transaction to take place between two parties in such a barter economy, it is necessary for each of the two parties to want simultaneously that which the other party is offering to exchange. This requirement is termed 'double coincidence of wants'. There would be considerable costs involved both in searching for a suitable party with which to trade and also in reaching an agreement over the terms of the trade. Such costs would limit the amount of trade taking place and would eventually lead to pressure for general agreement to use a single commodity as a standard unit of exchange into which all other commodities can be converted. The commodity used as the unit of exchange is known as money and various commodities have been used as money over time including cowrie shells, cattle, gold, silver, and cigarettes. The main criteria for development of a commodity as money is that it is generally acceptable in exchange for other commodities. With the development of money, the act of sale can be separated from the act of purchase.

We can now introduce money into our simple economy so that households are paid in money for the resources they hire out to firms and in turn households use that money to purchase the outputs of firms. These monetary flows are denoted by the middle circuit in figure 1.1 and are the flows corresponding to the real flows of goods and services occurring in the opposite direction. We should note that by aggregating all firms into one sector we are considering flows taking place only between firms and households and are therefore ignoring the considerable flows which take place between firms. That is to say, we are considering only inter-sector flows and ignoring intra-sector flows.

In this simple economy any expenditure in excess of current income by a household or a firm could occur only if the household or firm had accumulated money balances by not spending all of its income received in past periods. This is clearly a constraint on economic development since firms need to invest, that is, replace, maintain or add to existing real assets such as buildings and machinery. As the economy becomes more sophisticated, investment requires larger amounts of accumulated funds. Various expedients were developed to enable firms to overcome such constraints. For example, partnerships were formed so that accumulated savings could be pooled. The next major stage in the development of financing arrangements came with borrowing. Those households which did not spend all of their current income on consumption, that is, saved some of their income, could lend these funds to firms who in turn could use these funds to finance investment. In exchange for these funds, firms would issue claims which are effectively sophisticated IOUs which promise some benefits to the lender of funds at some date or dates in the future. The nature of financial claims and the various types of claims in existence are discussed in the next section. The ability to finance investment through borrowing undoubtedly encourages economic development and the existence of financial claims would also stimulate household saving. The investment and saving flows in our simple economy are represented by the outer loop of figure 1.1. The non-spending of income (or saving) by households can be regarded as a leakage of funds from the circular flow of income and expenditure captured in the middle loop of figure 1.1. This household saving, though, finds its way into firms' investment and firms' investment involves the purchase of capital equipment from other firms, so the leaked funds are injected back into the circuit.

We can now see one of the main roles of a financial system, which is to provide the mechanisms by which funds can be transferred from those with surplus funds to those who wish to borrow. In other words, the financial system acts as an intermediary between surplus and deficit units. In terms of figure 1.1 this function is represented by the outer loop. It is clear therefore that the financial system plays an important role in the allocation of funds to their most efficient use amongst competing demands. In a market system such as the UK financial system this allocation is achieved through the price mechanism, with the various prices being set within the relevant financial markets, which are themselves part of the financial system. The existence of financial markets also enables wealth holders to alter the composition of their portfolios. A secondary role for a financial system is to provide the mechanisms for the inner money flows, that is, the payments mechanism. A further function of a financial system is the provision of special financial services such as insurance and pension services.

Before we consider in more detail the lending and borrowing flows represented by the outer loop of figure 1.1, we examine in the next section the nature of the financial claims which underlie these flows.

1.3 Financial claims

A financial claim can be defined as a claim to the payment of a sum of money at some future date or dates. A borrower of funds issues a financial claim in return for the funds. The lender of funds holds the borrower's financial claim and is said to hold a financial asset. The issuer of the claim is said to have a financial liability. By definition therefore the sum of financial assets in existence will exactly equal the sum of liability. To take an example, a bank deposit is a sum of money lent by an individual or company to a bank. The deposit is therefore a liability of the borrower of funds, which is the bank. The depositor holds a financial asset, that is, a financial claim on the bank. Another term commonly used to denote a financial claim is a financial instrument.

The existence of a wide variety of financial instruments in a mature financial system, such as the UK system, can be explained by reference to consumer theory. Traditional consumer theory explains the demand for a commodity in terms of utility and a budget constraint, with the implication that a particular good can be identified as separate from other goods. In contrast Lancaster [1966] argues that:

(i) all goods possess objective characteristics, properties or attributes,
(ii) these characteristics form the object of consumer choice.

In the same way, a financial instrument can be considered to be a 'bundle' of different characteristics. Because individual agents place different emphasis on the various characteristics, a wide range of financial instruments are supplied. It is now necessary to examine the different characteristics possessed by financial instruments. The most important of these are risk, liquidity, real value certainty, expected return, term to maturity, currency denomination and divisibility.

Risk

Risk is a fundamental concept in finance and it is one which we will return to many times throughout the book. What follows is a brief introduction to the nature of financial risk. When we talk about risk in relation to a financial instrument we are referring to the fact that some future outcome affecting that instrument is not known with certainty. The uncertain outcome may, for example, be changes in the price of the security, or default with respect to repayment of capital or income stream. Although such outcomes are uncertain, an individual may have some view about the likelihood of particular outcomes occurring. Another way of stating this is that the individual will view some outcomes as more likely than others. Such views are likely to be formed on the basis of past experience of such outcomes occurring although other relevant information may also be used. The next step in assessing the particular risk of the financial instrument is to assign subjective probabilities to the different outcomes that may occur. The resulting probability distribution provides us with the individual's view as to the most likely outcome, that is, the expected value of the distribution. The spread of the distribution indicates the degree to which the outcome will be much greater or much less than expected. The greater the spread, the greater the risk that an outcome far removed from that expected will occur. The most common measure of risk is in fact the standard deviation of the probability distribution, a measure which increases as the spread widens.

To take an example, a person invests £1,000 in the ordinary shares of a company. The value of the shares in one year's time, that is, the price of those shares plus any income received from them in the form of dividends, is uncertain. The value may have risen or fallen; however, this person will believe some range of values are more likely than others. For example he or she may believe that there is a 50 per cent chance that the value of the shares in one year's time will be in the range £1,000 to £1,200. Figure 1.2 illustrates one possible distribution of likely values.

The expected value of this distribution is £1,090 and the standard deviation, or measure of risk, is 161. A larger spread, that is, a larger standard deviation, would indicate the potential for a larger reward and, conversely, the potential for a larger loss around a particular expected value. In these

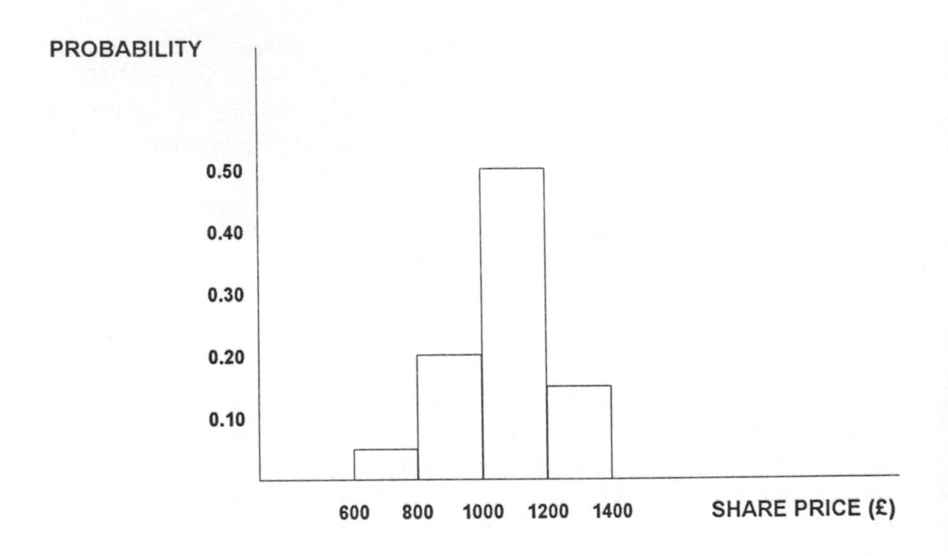

Figure 1.2

introductory remarks on the nature of risk, two types of risk were mentioned, namely price risk (or market risk, i.e. the risk that the price of the security will change) and the risk of not being repaid the sum lent or any interest promised in the claim, known as default risk. During the course of this book we will consider many other types of financial risk.

Liquidity

Liquidity refers to the ease and speed at which a financial instrument can be turned into cash without loss. This will depend upon on the asset being redeemable or marketable on an organised market. Thus for example a bank sight deposit can be withdrawn or redeemed on demand and is therefore very liquid. In contrast listed shares can be sold on the stock exchange but the precise amount of cash obtained will depend on the market valuation at the time of sale. Hence listed shares are less liquid than sight deposits. As a final example a bank loan is an agreement between two parties, the bank and the borrower, and so there is unlikely to be a third party willing to purchase the loan from the bank before it matures. That is to say, the bank loan is not marketable. (Note that over the 1980s there was a growing trend towards packaging loan-type assets, such as mortgages, to make them marketable so they can be sold on; this process is part of a larger phenomenon termed securitisation – for further discussion see chapter 12). The existence of an organised market for an instrument and the ability to deal at short notice therefore enhances the instrument's liquidity. It is possible to devise a spectrum of liquidity along which different financial instruments can be positioned. Such an analysis is crude and subject to a number of exceptions but is still illustrative. At the very liquid end we would find short-term deposits, moving through longer-term deposits, where funds are tied up for longer periods, through bonds and shares, where their marketability provides some degree of liquidity, to long-term loans, life policies and pension rights. Life policies and pension rights are considered to be very illiquid when they are held to maturity, although it has become increasingly easier to turn them into cash at short notice, albeit at considerable financial penalty, the further the date of encashment is from the maturity date.

Real value certainty
A third distinguishing characteristic of financial instruments is real value certainty, which refers to their susceptibility to loss due to a rise in the general level of prices. The maintenance of real value of an asset is likely to be an important consideration for those who are lending funds over a long time period. An individual acquiring assets to draw upon in retirement will want to ensure that the purchasing power of those assets is at least as great in retirement as when the assets were acquired. Financial instruments whose values are fixed in money terms, for example a bank deposit, will find their real value eroded when the rate of inflation exceeds the rate of interest earned. Over most of the 1970s, inflation exceeded the interest rate earned on bank and building society deposits in the UK and as a consequence the real value of such deposits was eroded. Ordinary shares are an instrument which, if held over a few years, have tended to increase in value in line with or above the rise in the general price level. The asset which has tended to provide the best protection against erosion in value by inflation is not a financial asset but the physical asset of property. This is not to say that there are not times when the real value of property does decrease, and an example of this is the decline in the real value of residential property in recent years. Rather, it is to say that if held over a number of years, the increase in value of property has tended to exceed inflation. This, as we shall see in chapter 6, explains why the long-term investment institutions are significant holders of property in their portfolios.

Expected return
Most financial instruments offer an explicit cash return to their holders. This return takes the form of a rate of interest or dividend and, for those instruments subject to changes in their market price, there is an additional element of return in the form of an appreciation in their value. Instruments subject to changes in price are termed capital uncertain and include bonds

and equities. For such capital uncertain instruments it will be the expected return (see above section on risk) that is used to determine whether to purchase or hold on to the instrument. *Ceteris paribus,* the higher the expected return the greater the demand for the instrument. In practice, however, a high return on an asset may also indicate that there is a premium component to the return to compensate the holder for some disadvantage such as illiquidity or high risk.

Term to maturity

Financial instruments vary widely according to the characteristic of term to maturity. Sight deposits at banks have zero term to maturity as they can be withdrawn on demand. At the other end of the spectrum 'consols' (a type of government bond) and equity have no redemption date and therefore possess an infinite term to maturity. Between these two extremes financial instruments are issued with a wide range of maturities. In general, returns on instruments identical except for their term to maturity will reflect (i) expectations of future interest rate changes and (ii) the loss of liquidity in holding long-term as opposed to short-term instruments. This is examined in more detail in chapter 9.

Currency denomination

With the general reduction in restrictions on the movement of capital across national boundaries, the currency denomination of a financial instrument has assumed greater importance. This adds a further component to the return on non-domestic instruments in the form of the appreciation or depreciation of the relevant exchange rate.

Divisibility

This characteristic reflects the degree to which the instrument can be subdivided into small units for transaction purposes. For example, a sight deposit is fully divisible whereas Treasury bills are sold in minimum denominations and hence not divisible. The degree of divisibility is therefore an additional determinant of an instrument's liquidity.

The characteristics approach to analysing financial instruments can also provide some indication of why an economic agent, such as an individual or company, will desire to hold more than one type of financial asset. It is likely that economic agents will hold their wealth in different forms so as to meet a number of different financial objectives. For example, an individual may be uncertain about her or his level of income or consumption in the near future and so can meet this uncertainty by holding wealth in a form which can be drawn on at short notice. That is, some wealth will be held as liquid assets such as bank deposits. The individual may also have the objective of holding wealth over a long period of time, for the purpose of providing income in retirement, and will want these funds to keep their purchasing power. This may lead to the holding of some funds in the form of ordinary shares. From this analysis we can see that an economic agent is likely to hold a collection or portfolio of assets, where the mix of characteristics underlying the assets in the portfolio will satisfy the various objectives of the agent.

We have referred to some specific types of financial instruments in this section, such as a bank deposit and an ordinary share. These are examples of the two general types of claim, namely debt and equity, which dominate the types of financial instruments in existence. We shall finish this section with a look at the characteristics of these two general types of claim.

Debt

Debt is a financial claim which is normally due to be repaid on a specified future date with interest being paid at regular intervals until the claim is repaid. Examples of debt instruments are deposits, loans, bills and bonds.

A deposit is a claim which records the liability of a financial institution to repay a sum of money in the future to the depositor (the lender of funds to the institution). A variety of deposit types exist, differing mainly in the arrangements for repayment; so for example, a sight deposit with a bank would be repayable on demand whilst a time deposit is repayable after a given period of notice. Deposits are generally considered to be at the liquid end of the spectrum of liquidity, although there are some exceptions to this where a deposit may have a repayment date of up to five years from the date of issue. Deposits are susceptible to default risk, though such risk is considered to be low as financial institutions rarely default. Deposits can also be classified according to their size, so that retail deposits are small and wholesale deposits are large. Financial institutions have also issued certificates of deposits (CDs), which are instruments acknowledging the existence of a deposit for a fixed period but which can be sold in the money markets (i.e. possess the characteristic of marketability – see chapter 10 for further discussion).

The majority of loans are made by financial institutions and generally specify a fixed date for repayment. The term to maturity of the loan generally varies according to the purpose for which the finance is required, and may be up to 30 years hence in the case of a mortgage. Most bank loans though have a repayment date of under ten years from the date they are issued. Loans are susceptible to default risk, although, as we shall see in the next chapter, financial institutions attempt to minimise such risks through a variety of methods. Loans which are secured, such as a mortgage on property, have a lower default risk than unsecured loans, as in the event of non-repayment the holder of the claim can sell the security to recover the debt. Loans are generally considered to be illiquid as they are agreements between two parties and therefore not marketable.

Bills of exchange can be considered to be promises to pay a certain sum of money at a fixed date and are analogous to postdated cheques. Commercial bills are used to finance trade and help to reconcile the competing interests of (i) the buyer of the goods who wishes to delay payment and (ii) the seller who desires prompt payments. The buyer issues a bill which promises to pay in the future but the seller receives a financial instrument which can be resold in the money markets (i.e. it is negotiable). The price received from the sale is less than the face value of the bill on maturity and so the bill is said to be discounted. For example, if a £1,000 bill due for redemption in three months' time is sold for £950, the rate of discount over three months is 5.3 per cent ((50/950)×100), or approximately 21 per cent per annum. Bills are also issued by central government (Treasury bills) and local authorities.

Deposits and loans are claims which generally pay variable rates of interest. In contrast, a bond is a claim which pays a fixed rate of interest, known as a 'coupon payment', at regular intervals. The bond may have a known repayment date, at which time the bond's par value, which is generally £100, is repaid. Some bonds though have no definite repayment date and are known as undated bonds, for example 2.5 per cent consolidated stock (consols) issued by the UK government in 1888. In the UK, bonds are issued by central government, local government, public boards and companies. Bonds issued by the UK government are commonly known as 'gilt edged', as the risk of default on such stocks is as close to zero as is possible on a financial instrument. Bonds issued by companies, known as debentures or loan stocks, do carry some risk of default, as do bonds issued by some foreign governments. Another type of bond traded in London is the eurobond. These are issued by international companies, governments and government agencies and are distinguished by not being subject to the tax and other regulations of the country in whose currency they are issued. This freedom from restrictions has led to many innovations in the characteristics of eurobonds and so there exists a wide variety of interest, currency denomination and repayment terms for these bonds (see chapter 12 for further detail on this). All bonds have the characteristic of marketability, which enhances their liquidity. The yield to maturity on a bond can be defined as the rate of discount which equates the current market price of the bond with the future coupon payments and the repayment of the principle. Thus, for example, the yield to maturity on a five-year £100 bond with a coupon of ten per cent paid once a year can be calculated by solving for i (the yield to maturity) in the following formula:

$$\text{Market price of bond} = \frac{10}{(1+i)} + \frac{10}{(1+i)^2} + \frac{10}{(1+i)^3} + \frac{10}{(1+i)^4} + \frac{10}{(1+i)^5} + \frac{100}{(1+i)^5}$$

The price at which bonds trade in a market will change as yields on other financial instruments change. It can be seen from the above formula that there is an inverse relationship between the price of a bond and its yield to maturity. If yields on competing financial instruments change then, given that the coupon is fixed, changes in the market price of a bond keep its yield in line with that of similar financial instruments. Consequently, if a bond is not held to maturity, there is a risk that the price at which the bond is sold is less than the price at which the bond was bought; that is, bonds are subject to price risk.

A final point about the characteristics of debt instruments is that they are normally susceptible to a reduction in real value due to general price inflation (when the nominal rate of interest is less than the rate of general price inflation). There are some exceptions to this where debt instruments have been issued with yields that are linked to the retail price index. In the UK two examples of such instruments are index-linked government bonds and index-linked national savings certificates.

Equity

Equities differ from the types of financial instruments so far described in that they represent a claim to a share in the ownership of a company, rather than evidence of debts. The principal type of equity instrument is the ordinary share issued by limited companies. The main characteristic of ordinary shares is that the income to be received from them is not fixed in any way. This income payment, known as dividends, constitutes a share in the profits earned by the company. The amount of the total profits earned by the company which is distributed to shareholders is determined by the company's management. The factors determining the dividend payment will include the financial performance of the company and the extent to which the company wishes to retain profits to finance investment. In addition to uncertainty about the income payments on ordinary shares, known as income risk, ordinary shares are also subject to price risk. Ordinary shares are marketable, although it is easier to trade listed shares in the larger, well known companies than it is in small companies. The liquidity of the particular ordinary share will therefore depend on its degree of marketability. In times of panic in share markets, for example October 1987, it may not be possible to sell a share without incurring a significant loss. One characteristic of ordinary shares which is highly valued is their real value certainty, that when held over a sufficiently long period of time the value of shares has generally increased at a rate in excess of the rate of inflation.

1.4 Sectoral analysis of the financial system

In the simple circular flow model of the economy introduced in section 1.1 the economy was assumed to be made up of two separate groups of decision makers, or sectors, namely households and firms. To take our analysis of the financial system further we need to consider both a further disaggregation of these two sectors and an extension of the economy to introduce a government and trade with overseas economies. The further disaggregation involves splitting the firms sector into industrial firms and firms whose primary activity is financial. The other changes introduce a public sector and an overseas sector. We have now achieved a sectoral breakdown of the economy which roughly corresponds to that used by the Central Statistical Office (CSO) for the UK economy. The CSO in fact identifies five main sectors of the UK economy, with a further breakdown of two of these sectors:

(i) personal,
(ii) industrial and commercial companies (ICC),
(iii) financial institutions –
    banks,
    building societies,
    life assurance and pension funds,
    other financial institutions,
(iv) public –
    central government,
    local government,
    public corporations,
(v) overseas.

The personal sector consists mainly of households, along with some other groups such as unincorporated businesses, charities, universities etc. which the statisticians find difficult to separate out. Ideally we would like data relating solely to households; however, it is not thought that these other groups distort the overall picture of household behaviour to any significant degree. As described above, the firms sector is split into industrial and commercial firms and financial companies. The CSO then disaggregates further the latter group in the construction of sector financial accounts. The public sector represents government institutions and in most analysis by the CSO this is further split into central government, local government and public corporations.

1.5 National wealth

We begin our examination of the financial relationships within the UK economy with a look at the extent of national wealth. We will then move on to examine a breakdown of this wealth by sector. The first assessment of wealth relating to the UK was the Domesday Book which, just over 900 years ago and using a census approach, set out the value of the land, animals and mills of England. Over the last 30 years government statisticians and academics have adopted statistical techniques to provide an assessment of the nation's wealth today.

The tangible wealth of a nation consists of its national resources and its stocks of goods, which includes buildings, durable equipment which provides services to consumers and producers, stocks of finished goods, raw materials and work in progress. In addition, a nation also possesses intangible wealth, which includes the skill, knowledge and character of its people, otherwise described by economists as human capital. The final component of a nation's wealth is its claims on wealth in other countries net of other countries' claims on its own wealth. The statisticians have encountered many problems in estimating the value of these various components of national wealth and these are discussed in detail in an article in *Economic Trends* written by Bryant [1987]. The main problems identified by Bryant are those of putting a value on natural resources such as oil, coal and gas and on valuing human capital. As a consequence these items are left out of the final national accounts published by the CSO. The complete UK national balance sheet for the end of 1993 is summarised in table 1.1.

From table 1.1 we can note that the net national wealth of the UK at the end of 1993 was approximately £2,700 billion. This is just over four times gross domestic product for the UK for that year. This figure for net national wealth is of course only an estimate because of the exclusion of certain items, mentioned above, and because many of the included items are measured with error.

Table 1.1 *UK national balance sheet for 1993 (£billion)*

Tangible assets		2,462.5
Intangible assets[a]		188.4
External assets of the UK	1,376.6	
External liabilities of the UK	1,358.1	
Net external financial wealth		18.5
Net national wealth		2,668.4

[a] Non-marketable tenancy rights (includes housing and agricultural tenancy rights).
Source: CSO, *UK National Accounts*, 1994 edn, table 12.1.

Table 1.2 *Ownership of the national wealth by sector, 1985*

Sector	*% share of wealth*
Personal	71.5
Industrial and commercial companies	11.3
Monetary sector	1.5
Other financial institutions	2.1
Total private sector	86.4
Total public sector	13.6

Source: Bryant [1987], table 6.

In a capitalist economy such as the UK most of the appropriable wealth is owned privately. The breakdown by sector of the ownership of national wealth for 1985 is given in table 1.2.

Thus private sector ownership of net national wealth was estimated to be just over 86 per cent at the end of 1985. Persons are in fact the ultimate owners of most private sector wealth (i.e. more than the 71.5 per cent owned directly) through the equity claims they hold, either directly or indirectly, on the other parts of the private sector.

1.6 Sector balance sheets

The national balance sheet shown in table 1.1 hides most of the financial wealth held by the various groups which make up the UK economy. A person may be wealthy without possessing any of the wealth counted in national wealth. This is because, to take an example, wealth held in the form of a bank deposit by a person (i.e. an asset to that person) will have a corresponding liability held by the bank. So, assuming that the bank deposit is not held outside the UK, aggregation of the net wealth of the personal sector (which contains the person's bank deposit as an asset) with the net wealth of the monetary sector (which contains the bank deposit as a liability) to form national wealth causes the asset and liability to cancel each other out. The financial relationship between the person and the bank is said to be 'netted out'. It therefore follows that the only financial wealth appearing in the national balance sheet is those assets held by UK residents which are claims on the overseas sector (i.e. the corresponding liability is held overseas). These are included in the item 'External assets' in table 1.1. As we move down to the sectoral level of the economy, the more financial wealth is revealed. In this connection, balance sheets are now constructed for the domestic sectors of the UK economy identified in the earlier section and it is to these that we now turn our attention.

Table 1.3 *Personal sector balance sheet for 1993 (£billion)*

Tangible assets	1,234.8
Intangible non-financial assets	188.4
Financial assets	1,664.3
Financial liabilities	505.7
Net financial wealth	1,158.7
Net total wealth	2,581.7

Source: CSO, *UK National Accounts*, 1994 edn, table 12.2.

(i) *Personal sector*

The personal sector balance sheet showing how its wealth is made up at the end of 1993 is shown in table 1.3. Tangible assets of the personal sector are principally houses. Intangible assets are as defined in table 1.1. The financial assets and liabilities of the personal sector are many and varied and will be examined more closely later in this chapter, when financial accounts are considered.

There are a number of important points to note about the personal sector's balance sheet. First, its financial assets greatly exceed its financial liabilities; therefore the sector has been a net lender of funds to other sectors of the economy. This is not to say that all members of the personal sector have been net savers but that in aggregate the personal sector has been a net saver. This highlights again the point about aggregation hiding information and that a disaggregation of the households of the personal sector by, for example, age would reveal more information about the ultimate lenders and ultimate borrowers in the economy. A second point not revealed by the figures in table 1.3 is that over the period 1975 to 1987, when personal sector net wealth rose by over £2,200 billion, over four-fifths of this increase was due to price changes of its tangible assets (mainly houses) and financial assets (mainly equities, held directly and indirectly). Therefore most of the increase in personal sector wealth was due to positive changes in the value

Table 1.4 *Personal sector balance sheet 1993 (£billion): conventional format*

Liabilities		*Assets*	
Net wealth	2,581.7	Tangible assets	1,234.8
Financial liabilities	505.7	Intangible non-financial assets	188.4
		Financial assets	1664.3
	3,087.4		3,087.4

Table 1.5 *Industrial and commercial companies balance sheet 1993 (£billion)*

Liabilities		*Assets*	
Net wealth	-135.1	Tangible assets	760.2
Financial liabilities	1,378.1	Financial assets	482.9
	1,243.0		1,243.0

Source: CSO, *UK National Accounts*, 1994 edn, table 12.3.

of assets already held rather than increases in the quantity of assets held; this has not been so in more recent years.

The balance sheet described in table 1.3 can be rewritten in a more conventional format as in table 1.4, which shows us that net wealth, sometimes known as 'net worth', is the item that brings assets and liabilities of the sector into balance. This format of balance sheet is the one we adopt for the rest of this chapter.

(ii) *Industrial and commercial companies*

The balance sheet for the ICC sector for 1993 is shown in table 1.5. Tangible assets for the ICC sector are mainly the buildings, plant and machinery which provide the means of production along with any stocks of raw materials, finished goods and work in progress. Financial assets held by this sector are mainly funds held to meet short-term needs, loans to subsidiaries and trade credit provided. On the liabilities side the main item is issued share capital or equities, with the rest made up of loans from banks and trade credit received (this is approximately balanced by trade credit provided). The ICC sector, in contrast to the personal sector, has generally been a net borrower, as evidenced by the excess of financial liabilities over financial assets outstanding at the end of 1993. It should be noted that as equities are a liability of companies then the value of these liabilities can change as the prices of shares change. This can lead to the rather curious result, seen over the 1980s, of an increase in equity prices, as the equity markets enjoyed a long period of boom, leading to an increase in the liabilities of companies greater than an increase in their assets, resulting in a reduction in the net wealth of the ICC sector. Indeed, the total net wealth of this sector was negative for 1993.

(iii) *Financial institutions sector*

For the purpose of this analysis of sectoral wealth we will take the four financial subsectors together as they are sufficiently similar in respect of their wealth structure. The balance sheet for this sector is summarised in table 1.6.

Table 1.6 *Financial institutions balance sheet 1993 (£billion)*

Liabilities		*Assets*	
Net wealth	86.6	Tangible assets	90.7
Financial liabilities	3,126.9	Financial assets	3,122.8
	3,213.5		3,213.5

Source: CSO, *UK National Accounts*, 1994 edn, table 12.4.

The striking points about the balance sheet of this sector are the substantial financial assets and liabilities alongside a comparatively low net wealth. This follows from the nature of their activities as financial intermediaries. Their business is to lend and borrow funds, hence their substantial holdings of financial assets and liabilities. The near equality of the financial asset and liability positions again reflects the nature of their business as intermediaries. Unlike companies in the ICC sector they do not need substantial investment in plant, equipment and stocks to undertake this business, hence the relatively low level of tangible assets. These tangible assets are mainly buildings, for example the branch networks of the banks and building societies, and equipment such as computers.

(iv) *The public sector*
As with financial institutions, for this analysis we examine the combined public sector balance sheet, shown for 1993 in table 1.7.

The public sector's tangible assets rose only slowly in value over the 1980s and hence its share of national wealth declined from 18 per cent in 1980 to under 14 per cent in 1985 (see table 1.2). This was due in the main to the policies of privatisation (sales of public corporation assets) and sales of council houses (sales of local authority tangible assets) initiated by the Conservative administration over this period.

Table 1.7 *Public sector balance sheet 1993 (£billion)*

Liabilities		*Assets*	
Net wealth	135.9	Tangible assets	376.5
Financial liabilities	435.8	Financial assets	195.2
	571.7		571.7

Source: CSO, *UK National Accounts*, 1994 edn, table 12.12.

1.7 Sector financial transactions

The analysis of sectoral financial relationships has so far examined balance sheets. These show the breakdown of wealth by sector and the financial relationships between sectors at one point in time – the day the balance sheet is constructed. In addition to information on stocks of assets and liabilities it is also useful to have information on financial transactions in these stocks, recorded over periods of time. By comparing the balance sheets of a sector at two different points in time and noting the changes that have taken place, balance sheet data can be converted from stock to flow form. However, the changes in stocks of assets and liabilities observed from this process could have come about either by transactions in those assets/liabilities or by revaluations of the stocks (i.e. price changes). The sector financial transactions accounts published by the CSO are not, at present, reconciled with the published sector balance sheets. The financial transactions accounts that are published are part of the national accounting framework which relates sector accounts for income, expenditure, capital and financial transactions. Thus, for a sector we have:

	Income	Income and
+	Inter-sector transfers	expenditure
-	Expenditure	account
=	Saving	
-	Capital transactions	Capital account
=	Financial surplus/deficit	

The income and expenditure accounts describe the economic identity of income, and income less expenditure gives the residual of saving. Capital transactions are mainly investments in physical goods. The financial surplus/deficit is then the link between the real transactions of the sector and its financial transactions. If a sector has a financial surplus then it has funds available to add to its financial assets or to reduce its financial liabilities. A financial deficit implies the sector needs to raise funds by selling financial assets or increasing its financial liabilities by borrowing.

To introduce the construction of sector financial transaction accounts we will consider a simple two-sector economy – households and firms – which has two financial instruments available for transactions – trade credit and equity. Trade credit is an asset of firms, that is, it represents funds lent from firms to households. Equity on the other hand is an asset of households. At 31 December 1993 our imaginary household sector is described by the balance sheet in table 1.8.

Table 1.8 *Example of household sector balance sheet at 31 December 1993 (£million)*

Liabilities		*Assets*	
Net wealth	1,400	Tangible	800
Financial	200	Financial	800
	1,600		1,600

Over 1994 the household sector undertakes the following transactions:

income, £500 million,
expenditure, £300 million,
saving, £200 million,
investment, £100 million,
financial balance, £100 million.

So for 1994 the household sector has a financial surplus of £100 million, which implies that it has funds available to enable it to acquire additional financial assets or reduce existing liabilities or both. For this example we take the situation where households acquire £200 million of company-issued equities as well as increasing their liabilities by £100 by borrowing from companies through the medium of trade credit. Any other collection of financial transactions is possible as long as the net transactions are consistent with the financial surplus. As a result of these transactions the household sector balance sheet for the end of 1994 will be as shown in table 1.9.

The increase in tangible assets is the result of investment over the period. The value of financial assets and liabilities have increased by the value of the transactions over the period. The change in the value of net wealth comes about to bring the balance sheet of households back into balance. Another way to see the increase in net wealth is that it is equal to the value of saving over the period. Saving, which is the value of funds coming into

Table 1.9 *Example of household sector balance sheet at 31 December 1994 (£million)*

Liabilities		*Assets*	
Net wealth	1,600	Tangible	900
Financial	300	Financial	1,000
	1,900		1,900

Table 1.10 *Example of a firms sector balance sheet at 31 December 1993 (£million)*

Liabilities		*Assets*	
Net wealth	300	Tangible	500
Financial	400	Financial	200
	700		700

the sector which are not consumed, is one way in which the size of the balance sheet of the sector can increase. The other way is for the value of assets already held to increase. In the case of households, the value of housing may increase as a result of an increase in house prices. So it is possible for the net wealth of a sector to increase without it saving any funds out of its income. However, changes in the value of assets are not captured within financial transaction accounts.

If we now consider the firms sector in our imaginary economy, its balance sheet for the end of 1993 is given in table 1.10.

The firms sector flows over 1994 are given below:

income, £200 million,
consumption, –
saving, £200 million,
investment, £300 million,
financial balance, £-100 million.

The firms sector has retained earnings of £200 million over 1994 but invests £300 million, leaving it with a financial deficit of £100 million. This implies that firms must sell existing assets or borrow new funds to finance the deficit. The financial decisions of the firms sector are implied by the household sector flows described earlier. This is because in a two-sector economy, as one sector increases its asset holdings the other sector

Table 1.11 *Example of a firms sector balance sheet at 31 December 1994 (£million)*

Liabilities		*Assets*	
Net wealth	500	Tangible	800
Financial	600	Financial	300
	1,100		1,100

Table 1.12 *Financial account matrix for a two-sector economy (£million)*

	Households	*Firms*
Saving	200	200
Investment	100	300
Financial balance	100	-100
Trade credit	-100	100
Equities	200	-200
Net financial transactions	100	100

must be increasing its liabilities by the same amount, for reasons explained in section 1.3. The financial decisions of firms are therefore to borrow funds through the issue of £200 million of equities and at the same time to increase holdings of financial assets by £100 million. The resulting balance sheet for the firms sector for the end of 1994 is given in table 1.11.

The financial transactions for the two sectors can be brought together in a financial account as shown in table 1.12.

The convention of financial accounts is:

a positive value implies an increase in financial assets or a decrease in financial liabilities,
a negative sign implies an increase in financial liabilities or a decrease in financial assets.

So in the financial account in table 1.12, a negative sign on trade credit transactions for the households sector implies that this sector is increasing its liabilities, that is, it is borrowing more from companies through the medium of trade credit. It should be clear from this example that in order to interpret a particular figure in the financial transactions account we need to know not only the convention stated above, but whether the instrument transacted is an asset or liability of that sector.

From this simple financial account we can discern the accounting rules which underlie its construction and the construction of all financial accounts. First, the sum of the financial surpluses and deficits equals zero, which reflects the fact that the financial assets of one sector are by definition the financial liabilities of another. Second, the net financial transactions of a sector will equal its financial balance. Third, the sum of transactions in a particular financial instrument will equal zero. This again follows from the fact that increased holdings of an asset of one sector will be balanced by increased liabilities of another. Finally, the sum of saving across sectors, that is, for the economy, will equal the sum of investment across sectors. In other words all saving will find its way into investment.

We now turn to examine the financial account for the complete UK economy.

1.8 Financial accounts for the UK economy

The CSO publishes financial accounts for the UK on a quarterly basis in *Financial Statistics* and annually in *National Accounts* (*The Blue Book*).

The financial accounts matrix for the second quarter of 1994 is presented in table 1.13. This matrix is fully disaggregated into the ten sectors described earlier. The total number of financial instruments is 55. Whilst the matrix in table 1.13 is larger and more disaggregated than the matrix for our imaginary economy in table 1.12, its structure is essentially the same although the full matrix only shows the financial account (lines 1 to 5 showing the capital account are not included).

There are problems with the data used to construct both national income and financial accounts. The figures making up these accounts are recorded with varying degrees of error. A sector's overall financial position, after calculating all income, expenditure and capital flows, is shown in its financial balance. If these flows were accurately recorded and if the sector's financial transactions were likewise identified in full, then the sum of financial transactions, shown in line 39 of table 1.13, should equal the financial balance. The effects of the errors and omissions in the flows recorded above and below line 5 leads to a difference between the financial balance and the sum of financial transactions. This difference is recorded in line 40 as the balancing item although its appearance adjacent to the financial transactions account should not be interpreted as implying that all or even most of the errors occur in this account. The sum of the balancing items across each sector is equal, necessarily, to the residual error which accounts for the discrepancy between the recorded national income and expenditure flows. For the public sector and financial institutions, where most transactions have to be accurately recorded for policy or supervisory purposes, then the balancing items have generally been small. For the other sectors, where there is less direct collection of statistics, the balancing items are large and were particularly large in the latter part of the 1980s although fell in the early 1990s as the CSO has devoted more resources to the compilation of these statistics. This can be seen in table 1.14, which shows the balancing items for the three sectors most prone to this problem.

There are other deficiencies with the published financial accounts although none as serious as that just described. One problem, which can be seen from the matrix in table 1.13, is that the available data do not allow a separation of the capital account transactions of the four subgroups of

Table 1.13 *Financial account: analysis by sector and type of asset, second quarter 1994 (£million)*

	Line no.	Public sector			Financial companies and institutions				Industrial commercial companies	Persons	Overseas
		Central govern-ment	*Local auth-orities*	*Public corpor ations*	*Banks*	*Building societies*	*Life assur-ance and pension funds*	*Other financial institutions*			
Financial balance	5	-14,190	870	864	–	–	–	–	4,716	7,331	1,599
Notes and coins	6	1,166		-13	-827	-48		1	-22	-405	148
Sterling Treasury bills	7	-3,491	-6	47	2,553	436	-8	429	6	–	34
British government securities	8	-6,091	6	11	1,294	352	2,654	2,108	-199	1,498	-1,633
National savings	9	-1,450	–	7		–	–		–	1,443	
Tax instruments	10	126		–	-1	–		–	-102	-23	
Net government indebtedness to Banking Department	11	1,340			-1,340						
Northern Ireland central government debt	12	-1			–	–		–	–	1	
Government liabilities under exchange cover scheme	13	16	-10	–					-6		
Other public sector financing	14										
non-marketable debt	14.1	-120		120	–			–	–		
short-term assets	14.2		199	147		-73		21	2	-296	–
Issue Department transactions in bills, etc.	15	-3,250			–			835	1,897		518
Goverment foreign currency debt	16	9			-1,059	-76	1	-590			1,715
Other government overseas financing	17	–									–
Official reserves	18	286									-286
Local authority debt:	19										
temporary	19.1	270	-507	77	-1	64	15	-32	34	80	–
foreign currency	19.2		38		–			–			-38
sterling sercurities	19.3	–	-5	–	–	–	10	-1		-4	–
other sterling debt	19.4	-648	645	11	-35	20	13	–	–	4	-10

Table 1.13 *Continued*

	Line no.	Public sector			Financial companies and institutions				Industrial commercial companies	Persons	Overseas
		Central govern-ment	Local auth-orities	Public corpor ations	Banks	Building societies	Life assur-ance and pension funds	Other financial institutions			
Public corporation debt:	20										
foreign currency	20.1			26	–			–			-26
sterling	20.2	-56	-16	101	-37		-11	2	–	18	-1
Deposits with banks:	21										
sterling	21.1	115	-412	60	434	-225	-2,461	1,345	1,304	418	-578
foreign currency	21.2	16	17	34	-7,194	-24		3,301	1,148	201	2,501
sterling money-market instruments	21.3		–	–	-1,413	531	141	741	43	-27	-16
foreign currency money-market instruments	21.4				-1,745		-2	445	21	4	1,277
Deposits with building societies:	22										
sterling	22.1				-347	-1,712	-118		79	1,868	499
sterling money-market instruments	22.2				-904	-6		481	152	101	176
foreign currency money-market instruments	22.3					74		1	–	–	-75
Bank lending (excluding public sector)	24										
foreign currency	24.1				12,157			-515	838	-73	-12,407
sterling	24.2				1,827	-135	-836	346	768	-1,442	-528
Credit extended by retailers	25			–					-20	20	
Identified trade credit:	26										
domestic	26.1	–	1,800	270				259	-2,006	-323	
import and export	26.2	–		-5				-3	1		7
Loans secured on dwellings:	27										
building societies	27.1					3,089				-3,089	
other	27.2	8	-57	1	1,701		-45	151		-1,759	

Other public sector lending	28	104	12	-1	–	–		–	-12	-69	-34
Other lending by financial institutions	29										
finance leasing	29.1	3	-3	-2	21			-84	61	4	
other forms of lending	29.2			–		213	105	618	-575	-361	
Unit trust units	30						243	-2,473		2,230	
UK company securities	31	-594	-	1	-495	-1,349	3,884	-819	-4,469	-1,863	5,704
Overseas securities	32	–			-1,520	12	-641	-8,069	1,970	-23	8,271
Life assurance and pension funds	33	-239					-4,254			4,493	
Miscellaneous domestic instruments	34	-156	-1	1	–	193	203	-245	-687	369	323
Direct and other investment abroad	35			–	182		-2	253	2,078	8	-2,519
Overseas direct and other investment in UK	36				-193		–	318	-2,734	-75	2,684
Miscellaneous overseas instruments	37	-492		–	-30		-346	156	1,497		-785
Accruals adjustment	38	-1,656	-905	-137	93	-420	31	-557	2,223	1,264	64
Total financial transactions	39	-14,785	795	756	3,121	916	-1,424	-1,796	3,290	4,192	4,935
Balancing item	40	595	75	108		93			1426	3139	-3336

Acquisition of assets or reduction in liabilities is shown positive: sale of assets or increase in liabilities negative.

Table 1.14 *Balancing items (at 1994) (£billion)*

	1988	*1990*	*1992*	*1993*
Personal	-8.1	-8.9	-8.3	-2.3
ICCs	9.1	5.0	5.4	3.4
Overseas	5.6	0.8	6.5	2.0

Source: *Financial Statistics*, December 1994, table 8.1L.

financial institutions. A further problem is that the data are published on a net basis, that is, a figure presented in the financial transactions account represents the net result of purchases and sales (new borrowing and repayments) of an asset (liability). We cannot therefore infer whether a larger than normal figure for, say, acquisition of company securities by other financial institutions is due to more purchases or fewer sales during the period.

However, despite these drawbacks there are still many interesting points that can be drawn from a study of a financial account. One fundamental thing that the accounts show is that those people who save in an economy are not the same as those people who invest in physical assets. The financial account thus demonstrates one of the reasons for the existence of financial institutions, which is to channel funds from savers to investors, and it shows the various routes by which the funds flow. This will be considered in more detail in the next chapter. The financial account, by setting the flows for each sector together in a consistent framework, also allow us to obtain a more complete picture of financial relationships when compared with looking at each sector's flows individually. For example, if we examine row 21.1 in the account for the second quarter of 1994 in table 1.13, we can see each sector's transactions in bank sterling deposits. Here we see that the net flows into bank sterling deposits over this quarter were negative, that is, more funds were withdrawn than deposited, hence the positive sign on the amount shown in the column for banks – reduction in liabilities for banks. Whilst persons, industrial and commercial companies, other financial institutions, central government and public corporations all made deposits these were outweighed by the withdrawals of life assurance and pension funds, overseas, local authorities and building societies. The largest withdrawal came from the life assurance and pension funds, which generally build up liquid assets, like bank deposits, when the investment climate is uncertain and then switch out of liquid assets into long-term investments when the investment climate improves. By looking down the column for life assurance and pension funds we can see that the principal investments by these institutions in this quarter were UK company securities and UK government securities.

Another interesting feature of the financial picture in second quarter of 1994 is revealed in line 32. This shows that other financial institutions, primarily unit and investment trusts, were massively net sellers of overseas securities. Banks, life assurance and pension funds, and persons were also net sellers, although not to the same extent. The purchases of overseas securities by industrial and commercial companies is explained by the acquisitions of European companies by UK companies in that period. The use of the proceeds from the sale of overseas assets by other financial institutions can be seen by looking down the column for that sector. Thus we see an increase in purchases of UK government securities and an increase in deposits with banks, primarily foreign currency deposits.

This discussion of some of the features of the second quarter 1994 financial accounts matrix was intended to show that, bearing in mind the caveat on data deficiencies, some interesting insights into changing financial relationships can be obtained from a study of such accounts.

1.9 Conclusion

In this chapter we have started our examination of the role of a financial system in an economy, established some fundamental concepts of finance and have introduced data on wealth and financial transactions in the UK and shown the relationship between these. In the next chapter we build on this and examine further the role of a financial system in mediating between savers and investors before looking at how financial systems evolve.

Chapter 2

Financial intermediation

2.1 Introduction

In this chapter we aim, first of all, to describe the process of financial intermediation, a process which provides the *raison d'être* for financial institutions. Our second aim is to examine the general evolution of financial systems and in particular distinguish between the more bank-oriented financial systems of Germany and Japan and the more market-oriented systems of the United States and the UK. Our final aim is to provide an overview of the many significant changes that have taken place in the UK financial system over the last 20 years and the 1980s in particular. This will provide a framework for the more specific discussion of changes to financial institutions and financial markets which makes up the remainder of this book.

2.2 Financial intermediation

In developed economies, decisions to invest are often taken separately from decisions to save. There are some exceptions to this; for example, firms which do not distribute all profits as dividends but retain some to finance investment are both saving and investing. However, even when saving and investment are carried out by the same economic agent, the timing of the decisions will often be different. Saving may precede the investment as sufficient funds are accumulated, or the saving may follow the investment as debts used to finance it are paid off. However, it is a general feature of developed economies that a high proportion of saving is not used immediately by the saver but is made available to investors elsewhere. In the last chapter, one of the roles of a financial system was described as the channelling of funds from those who save to those who invest. To be more precise, we are concerned with the channelling of funds from those economic agents with a financial surplus (lenders) to those economic agents with a

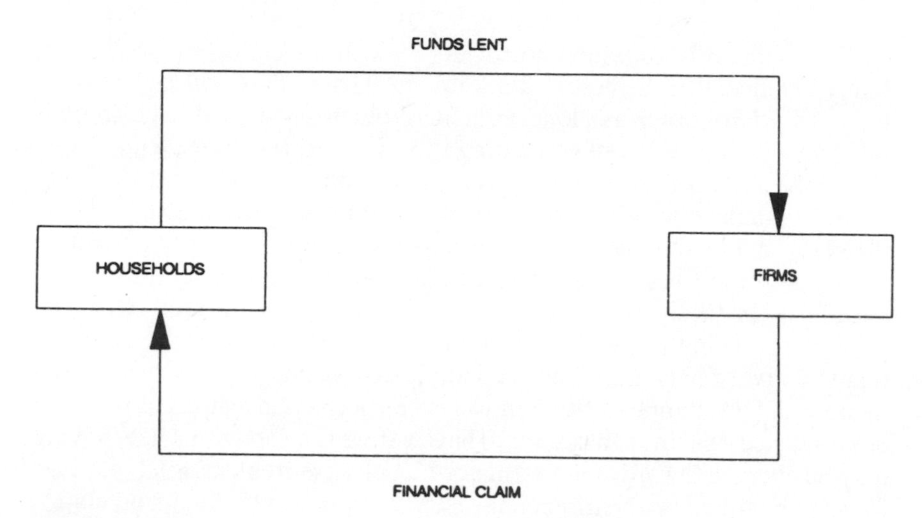

Figure 2.1

financial deficit (borrowers). Whilst most borrowing is used to finance investment, this more precise statement acknowledges that there will be some economic agents who borrow to finance a deficit which has arisen not from investment but from an excess of consumption over income.

A financial system essentially consists of financial markets and financial institutions. In this section we will examine in some detail the role of financial markets and institutions in the process of channelling funds from lenders to borrowers. To begin the analysis we will return to our simple economy, introduced in section 1.2, which consists of households and firms only. This highlights more clearly the benefits which a financial system brings to this process. Assuming that households in aggregate are lenders and firms in aggregate are borrowers, then the only way in which funds can flow from lenders to borrowers is directly, as shown in figure 2.1.

In this simple economy, firms will finance some part of their investment by borrowing funds from households and in return households will hold the financial claims issued by firms. Investment, which takes the form of the acquisition of durable real assets such as buildings or machinery, will generally be long term in nature so that the returns to the firm generated by the investment will take some time to meet the promised repayment to the claim holder. Further to this, investment by firms is an inherently risky activity. The returns produced by the investment are uncertain. The firm making the investment may have misjudged the market for the product, or the costs of producing the product may be higher than anticipated. Both these factors would cause returns to be less than the anticipated level. Furthermore, the acquired real assets are generally highly specialised, making them difficult to sell, if problems occur, except at a loss.

The characteristics which borrowers seek in the claims they issue are likely to reflect these features of investment. That is, they will seek to issue long-term claims, such as a long-term loan, which will provide a reasonable prospect of the investment generating sufficient returns to repay the claim. Given the uncertainty of the returns from investment, firms are also likely to seek to finance some part of the investment in the form of equity, where the claim can be remunerated according to the profitability of the firm.

Whilst some (wealthy) lenders will be happy to hold long-term, risky claims, it is likely that the majority of lenders will seek different characteristics in the claims they hold. As we saw in chapter 1, there are many motives for saving. Some economic agents save in order to even out income and consumption flows or to provide a cushion against unforeseen circumstances and in such cases will have a short time horizon. Other saving may be directed towards long-term needs such as retirement. Such motives for saving will have a bearing on the characteristics of the financial claims that savers will seek to hold. For most savers an important characteristic will be safety, that is, the risk of loss of the sum lent should be low. For savings directed towards short-term purposes the characteristic of liquidity will be important.

It is clear from the preceding discussion that the requirements of borrowers and lenders are in general different. Borrowers are looking to issue long-term, risky claims. Lenders will be seeking to hold low-risk and, in many cases, short-term claims. In addition, borrowers are likely to be seeking a sum of money greater than the sum provided by one lender. In the absence of organised financial markets or financial institutions, as presented in figure 2.1, lending/borrowing will occur as a result of direct negotiation between two parties. The claims that occur as a result of such transactions will be highly illiquid since it would be difficult to sell them to a third party in the absence of an organised market. There will also be significant search costs as borrowers seek out willing lenders and vice versa. For the borrower seeking a large loan such costs will be greater, as a number of lenders will have to be found. There will also be costs relating to the drawing up of any agreement confirming the terms of the transaction. There are also additional costs involved in carrying out a financial transaction which are generally not encountered in trade in physical goods and services. This is because the potential lender will have to assess whether the borrower can meet the promises of future payments over the relatively long time period which are inherent in financial claims. Thus, the lender will have to assess the financial standing of the borrower and also whether the use to which the loaned funds are put is likely to generate sufficient returns to repay the claim. A particular problem here is that borrowers have more information about the likely return and riskiness of the investment project than a direct lender. This problem is one of a class of general problems of trade in financial markets referred to since Akerlof [1970] as that of asymmetric information. A related problem is that of moral hazard, which here refers to the incentive for borrowers to exaggerate the returns or play down the risks involved in the use of the borrowed funds; that is, they may behave differently when using borrowed rather their own funds. Therefore a lender will incur costs in acquiring information and the information obtained may not be complete or honest. In addition, after the loan is made, the lender will incur further costs relating to monitoring the performance of the borrower until the loan is repaid.

We now consider the situation where an organised financial market emerges, where standard equity-type instruments are issued and acquired. Such a market is called a capital market as it deals in claims which are used to finance the acquisition of capital or physical assets. A capital market where claims are first issued is called a primary market, as distinct from a secondary market, which deals in the purchase and sales of existing claims. We shall consider this distinction in more detail in chapter 8. The existence of organised primary and secondary capital markets overcomes some of the obstacles to the flow of funds from lenders to borrowers.

The ability to sell on claims in a market will enhance the liquidity of such claims and so encourage more lending of funds. In addition, a central feature of organised markets is the existence of specialist brokers who bring together buyers and sellers and so reduce the search costs outlined above. However, many of the problems which reduce the incentive to lend and borrow remain; in particular the risk of the claims on offer to lenders is

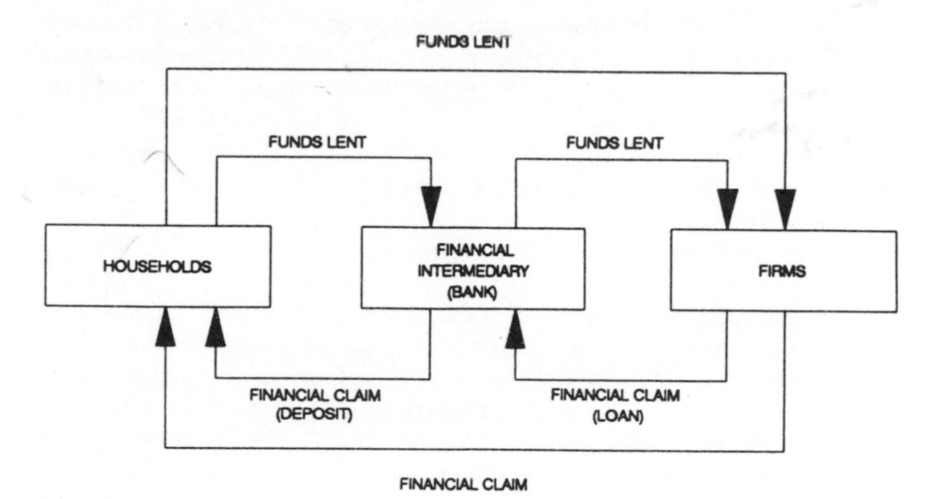

Figure 2.2

still high. It is the existence of financial institutions which provides the means to overcome such problems and so stimulate and smooth the flow of funds from lenders to borrowers. Financial institutions achieve such an intermediation by holding the long-term, risky claims of borrowers whilst financing the lending that accompanies this by issuing claims which are attractive to lenders. For example, a financial institution such as a bank lends funds in the form of loans, which are generally risky and long term, whilst at the same time borrows funds in the form of low-risk, short-term deposits – see figure 2.2.

So, instead of households being able to deal only directly with firms, they can now also deal indirectly through an intermediary such as a bank. To acknowledge the indirect nature of the flow of funds from households to firms in this example, households can be labelled the ultimate lenders and firms the ultimate borrowers. We now turn to discussing how such an indirect financing process benefits the economy.

2.3 Implications of financial intermediation

The two-period investment/consumption model

In this section we examine the implications of financial intermediation for the economy. As a starting point for this analysis we use the Hirschleifer model (see e.g. Hirschleifer [1958]). The initial assumptions of this model are:

(i) two-period analysis;
(ii) the existence of a perfect capital market, implying that (a) the individual can borrow or lend what he or she wishes at the same ruling rate of interest, (b) there is perfect knowledge of the investment and borrowing opportunities open to the individual and (c) access to the capital market is costless;
(iii) there are no distorting taxes;
(iv) the individual allocates consumption expenditure over the two periods so as to maximise utility;
(v) investment opportunities are infinitely divisible.

The first important component of the analysis is the physical investment opportunities line (PIL) depicting the physical investment opportunities available to the firm/individual in period 0. These are ranked in descending order of profitability. This is shown in figure 2.3, where the vertical axis represents period 1 and the horizontal axis period 0. We assume for sake of ease of exposition that the individual has an initial endowment of goods equal to Y_0 and none in period 1. Hence any consumption in period 1 must be financed by saving goods in period 0 and investing them. Thus, point A

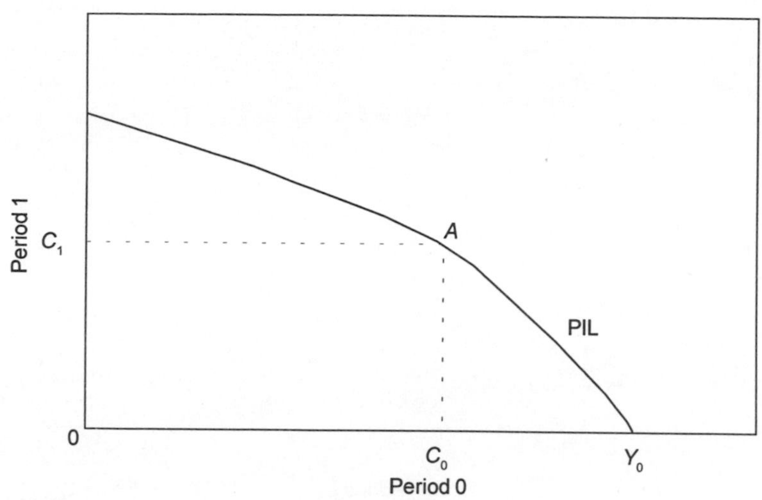

Figure 2.3

represents a consumption of C_0, with $Y_0 - C_0$ being invested to produce consumption goods of C_1 for consumption in period 1. The slope of the PIL curve reflects diminishing returns to investment.

Consequently, given the amount of resources in period 0, say Y_0, without a capital market the individual's consumption in period 1 is restricted to the proceeds from investment in period 0. Similarly any investment reduces the level of consumption in period 0. The optimum allocation of consumption between the two periods occurs at the familiar point of tangency between the PIL and the individual's indifference curve (i.e. point B in figure 2.4). At this point the marginal return on investment equals the individual's time preference as indicated by the slope of the indifference curve. Note the return is given by C_1 and the cost of the investment by $Y_0 - C_0$.

The introduction of the capital market changes the situation since the individual can borrow or lend so as to rearrange her or his investment opportunities. The borrowing/lending opportunities can be represented diagrammatically using the financial investment opportunity line (FIL), as shown in figure 2.5. The straight line represents the perfect capital market assumption that borrowing and lending can be achieved at the same rate of interest. The slope of the FIL line is given by $-(1 + r)$ where r is the market rate of interest. The individual can move up and down the FIL; for example, investment of *0A* funds in the financial market in period 0 would produce *0B* in period 1 $\{0A(1+r)\}$. Similarly investment of *DA* in the financial market in period 0 would produce *0E* in period 1$\{DA(1 + r)\}$.

The impact of the introduction of a capital market (i.e. financial intermediation) can be seen by combining the information given in figures

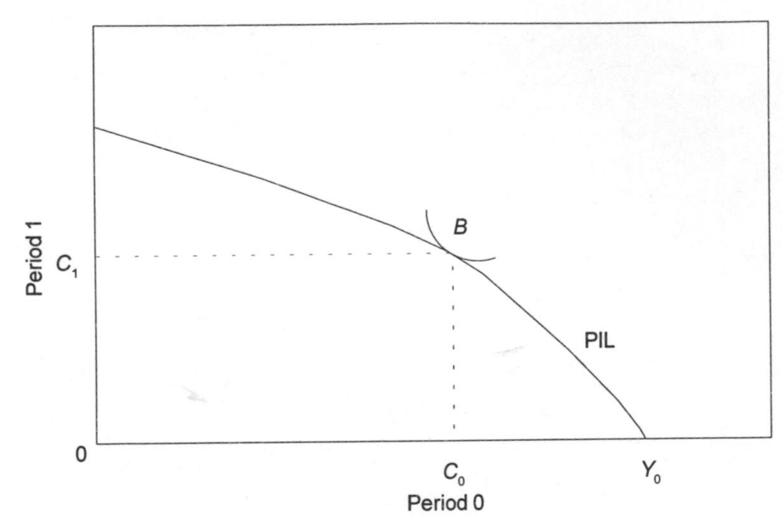

Figure 2.4

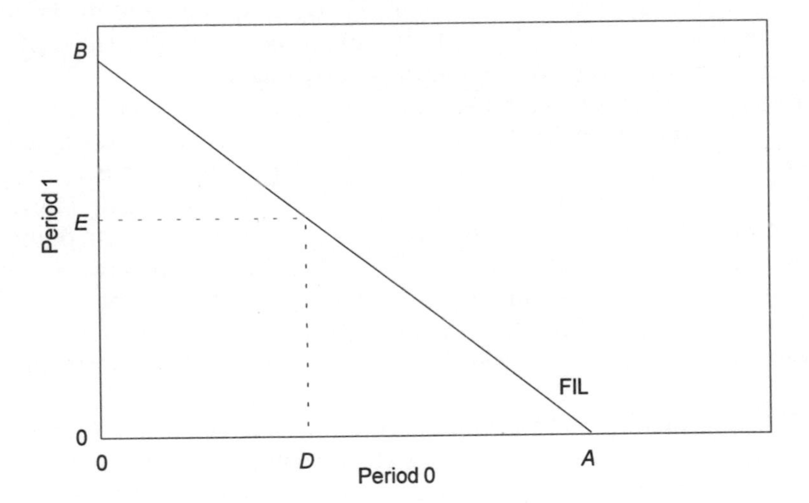

Figure 2.5

2.4 and 2.5 to arrive at figure 2.6. The individual can separate the two decisions (production and consumption) so that:

(i) The present value of production is maximised at point *A*, where the marginal return on investment equals the capital market rate of interest, that is, where the PIL is tangential to the FIL furthest from the origin. Optimal production in the two periods is then C^*_0 and C^*_1 respectively.

(ii) Utility is maximised where the individual's time preference equals the capital market rate of interest. This occurs where the individual's indifference curve is tangential to the FIL so that the market rate of interest is also equal to the individual's time preference. This can occur by one of two means

(a) Borrowing against further production to finance present consumption. This is illustrated in figure 2.6a where $(C^*_0 - C_0)$ is borrowed in period 0, with consumption being C_0. In period 1 consumption is C_1, with $(C^*_1 - C_1)$ being the debt repayment.

(b) Lending to finance future consumption. This is illustrated in figure 2.6b, where $(C^*_0 - C_0)$ is lent in period 0, with consumption

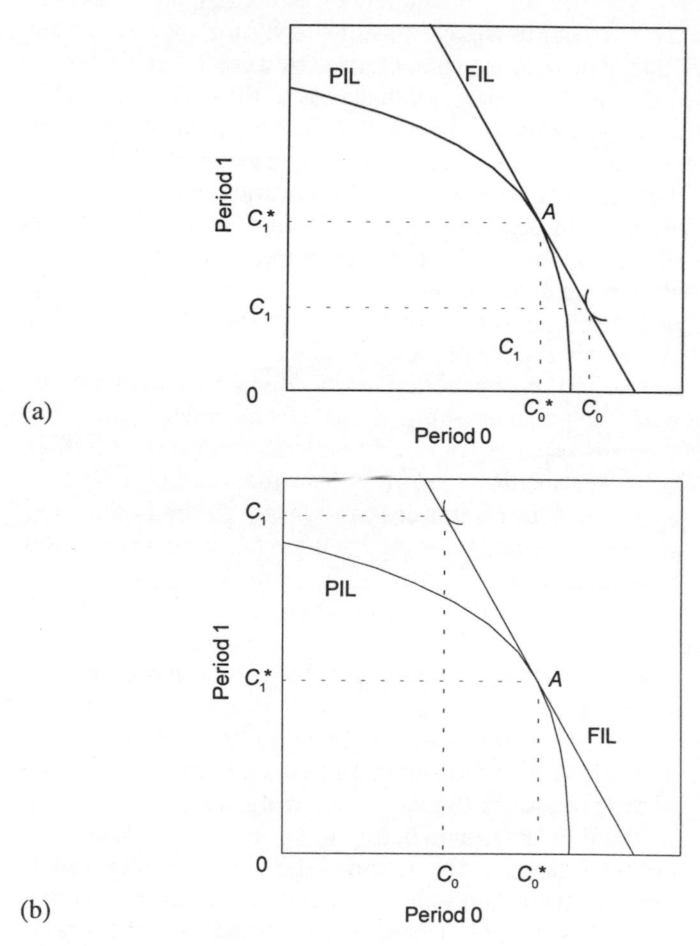

Figure 2.6

being C_0. In period 1 consumption is C_1, with $(C^*_1 - C_1)$ being the proceeds of loan repayment.

Consequently utility has been increased by the introduction of a financial intermediary since the individual could have always remained at point A, with consumption equal to C^*_0 and C^*_1 in the two periods respectively; that is, he or she is on either a higher or the original indifference curve following the introduction of a capital market. This analysis is however only as good as its underlying assumptions. It is apparent that these are very (perhaps overly) restrictive. The perfect capital market is unlikely to occur in the real world for three reasons. First, in all markets borrowers pay a higher rate of interest than that earned by lenders or depositors. Hence the slopes of the FIL will differ for the borrower and lender. Second, many operators will not possess the perfect knowledge postulated by the capital market assumption and financial markets are characterised by a considerable degree of uncertainty. Third, it is also apparent that access to the capital market is not costless and, as we shall see in chapter 8, the costs of raising finance are not negligible. Furthermore, taxes do exist and consequently distortions are introduced in the raising of finance. Also, the assumption of two-period analysis may also appear to be restrictive but, in fact, is merely used to simplify the exposition. Similar results could be obtained from multi-period analysis but would be more complicated to derive.

As we noted in the discussion following figure 2.2, the process of financial intermediation, that is, the process by which financial institutions intermediate to reconcile the conflicting requirements of lenders and borrowers, involves not only a channelling of funds from lenders to ultimate borrowers but also a transformation of the characteristics of those funds as they pass through the intermediary. We now turn to examine in greater detail the ways in which financial institutions can achieve this transformation of the characteristics of funds and how they reduce the transaction costs involved in channelling funds from lenders to borrowers.

Maturity transformation

On average, financial intermediaries have liabilities with a shorter term to maturity than that possessed by their assets. A good illustration of this phenomenon is provided by the practice of building societies, which accept deposits largely repayable on demand and make loans repayable over 25 or 30 years (note that this overstates the degree of maturity transformation since many mortgages are in fact repaid before maturity). This is known as mismatching their balance sheets, or borrowing ‘short’ and lending ‘long’. Mismatching exposes the institution to liquidity risk, which is the risk that it has insufficient liquidity to meet its commitments. Financial institutions can accomplish such mismatching by relying on the ‘law of large numbers’ and holding a structured asset portfolio. The law of large numbers applied here means that a bank, for example, by attracting a large number of depositors, knows that in any period whilst some depositors will be withdrawing funds, others will be making new deposits, thus keeping the net withdrawal of funds small in relation to total liabilities. Banks can then cover against the potential net withdrawal by holding some assets in liquid form, which it can turn into cash at short notice if required. This is not the only method by which banks can manage liquidity risk and further discussion of this problem is left until chapter 3.

Risk transformation

Financial institutions such as banks hold mainly loans in their asset portfolio, but issue mainly deposits to finance these assets. Loans inevitably carry some risk of default yet bank deposits are generally considered to be of low risk. Financial institutions can transform risky assets into virtually riskless deposits by minimising the risk of the individual loans it takes on, spreading the risks over a large number of loans and by holding sufficient capital to meet any unexpected losses.

There are many ways in which a bank can control the risk of any individual loan it takes on going into default. First of all the bank can consider the purpose of the loan and allow funds to be lent only for what the bank considers to be legitimate. Secondly it can consider the financial circumstances of the borrower. An important consideration here would be the borrower's income, although other factors are also taken into account for consumer lending, where credit scoring is increasingly used. Such factors include other financial commitments, age and whether the borrower is a home owner. Under credit scoring, on the basis of their answers to a standard set of questions, borrowers are given a score which determines the risk involved and therefore whether to make the loan. The use of credit scoring has largely replaced judgement in determining loan entitlement, and can indeed be automated, so reducing costs of acquiring information to judge borrower suitability. A third method of reducing individual loan risk is for the bank to ask for security over the borrower's assets. In the event of the borrower getting into difficulties and being unable to meet the loan repayments the bank can sell the secured assets and recover the loan. A well known type of secured lending is mortgage lending, where the property is used as security.

Even when such methods of risk control are used there is still some residual risk of loan default. Further techniques of risk management can be used by banks to manage such risks. One particular technique is to pool risks by making a large number of small loans rather than a small number of large loans. In addition, financial intermediaries can spread their loans across different types of borrowers and geographical region. If, for example, a bank lent funds only to firms involved in the construction industry then it is open to the risk of a large number of defaults if there is a recession in the construction industry. By spreading its loans across different types of firms, firms in different regions and consumers as well as firms, then it achieves a greater independence of default risks. Of course if the whole economy goes into recession then it will incur a relatively large number of defaults. International diversification of its loans may help to reduce this problem.

Use of these techniques of risk management increases the accuracy of the bank's predictions of its loan losses in any one period. Knowledge of its probability distribution of loan losses allows the bank to incorporate a charge in its lending rate to cover the expected value of such losses. Any loan losses in excess of its expected losses, that is, any unexpected losses, are then covered by the institution's own capital and it is only in the event of losses in excess of the institution's capital that the depositors' funds are threatened. Hence it is quite rare for a bank or similar financial institution to default on its deposits and hence deposits are considered to be safe financial instruments. There are occasions when a loss of confidence may lead to large net withdrawals from an institution or a particular group of institutions. For example, Kindleberger [1978] reports that in the US over the depression years of 1930–33, such a loss of confidence occurred leading to 9,096 bank suspensions. This is known as systemic risk and is one of the reasons for the detailed prudential controls over financial institutions seen in most countries. This is discussed in chapter 17.

Another type of risk transformation is carried out by financial institutions which hold mainly ordinary shares in their asset portfolios. In the UK such institutions are unit trusts and investment trusts. These institutions hold portfolios of ordinary shares, which as we saw in section 1.3 are particularly risky assets. By holding a large number of different shares in the portfolio, particularly if these shares are spread over different types of company and even different countries, as with bank loans described above, the overall riskiness of the portfolio can be reduced without any corresponding loss in the overall return of the portfolio. An additional advantage held by institutions such as unit trusts and investment trusts over all but the most wealthy individuals in constructing a portfolio is that the proportionate transaction costs in buying and selling shares are smaller for larger blocks of shares. The claims issued by such institutions therefore offer the advantage of the lower risk that comes from a diversified portfolio with lower costs of achieving and maintaining the portfolio.

Collection and parcelling

When describing the requirements of lenders and borrowers above it was noted that lenders tend to lend smaller amounts of funds relative to the amounts that borrowers generally wish to borrow. A third feature of financial intermediation then is the way in which many financial institutions collect the small amounts of funds made available by lenders and parcel these into the larger amounts required by borrowers. Institutions such as banks and building societies achieve this collection by convenient location of their branches in high streets but more generally the various institutions achieve this collection by offering claims which are tailored to meet the lenders' requirements. The convenient location of institutions and the standard products offered by such institutions can reduce the search and information costs to both lenders and borrowers. Related to this feature of collecting small amounts to lend as larger amounts is the feature of size intermediation. This refers to the process by which financial intermediaries can offer the small lender the benefits which would come from lending large amounts. An example of size intermediation was referred to in the last section on risk transformation whereby institutions such as unit trusts provide the advantages which arise from a diversified portfolio to the small lender. Another example is the money market deposits provided by most banks in the UK and many other countries. Such accounts offer the high rates of interest available on large, wholesale money market deposits to lenders without the requirement of providing the large outlay.

2.4 Rationale for the existence of financial intermediaries

We will now attempt to bring together the various strands of the analysis introduced above and so provide the main reasons suggested to explain the existence of financial intermediaries. One of the main obstacles to direct financing of ultimate borrowers by ultimate lenders was presented as the conflicting requirements of lenders and borrowers in terms of the characteristics of the financial claims sought by lenders and the characteristics of the financial claims that borrowers would prefer to issue. Financial institutions are therefore able to find a role in bridging this gap by holding the primary claims issued by borrowers but financing these by issuing secondary claims which have characteristics which are more attractive to lenders. Financial intermediaries therefore in effect transform the characteristics of the funds as they pass from ultimate lender to ultimate borrower.

The costs involved in ultimate lenders transacting with ultimate borrowers are likely to be high. There are various types of costs involved in such direct transactions, including (i) searching out suitable agents to transact with, (ii) drawing up contracts, (iii) screening borrowers to enable an assessment of the likelihood of repayment of the loan, and (iv) monitoring and enforcing the terms of the contract. Where a lender and borrower have agreed to transact at a particular rate of interest, the existence of transaction costs implicitly reduces the return earned by the lender below that of the agreed interest rate and increases the charge paid by the borrower to above the agreed rate. The existence of a differential between the net return to lending and the total cost of borrowing provides additional scope for the emergence of financial intermediaries. Many reasons have been presented in the discussion above to suggest that the involvement of financial intermediaries reduces these transaction costs, including convenient location and provision of standard products. In general though there are two main advantages that financial intermediaries bring to the process that are likely to lead to lower transaction costs. First, their size brings economies that generally accompany a large scale of operations. Second, by specialising they obtain expertise and experience in obtaining and interpreting information, which enable them to assess and manage the various risks involved. By significantly reducing transaction costs the intermediary is able to enter the market and earn a profit on its operations by charging an interest rate on its lending (loan rate) which is higher than that paid on its borrowing (deposit rate). As long as the differential between the financial intermediary's lending and borrowing rates is lower than the differential created by transaction costs in the process of direct transacting then all parties gain from the existence of intermediaries. More formally, defining the rate of interest as R and the search transaction costs as TL and TB for the lender and borrower respectively (note that these costs are calculated as a percentage on the loan):

$$\begin{array}{lrl} \text{the net return for the lender} & (RL) & = R - TL \\ \text{the cost for the borrower} & (RB) & = R + TB \\ \text{then} & RB - RL & = TB + TL \end{array}$$

Introduction of a financial intermediary introduces a new element of cost, C, which we, for convenience, assume is paid by the borrower and is again expressed in percentage terms. Thus, now:

$$RL = R - TL'$$
$$RB = R + TB' + C$$

where the prime indicates search/transaction costs after the introduction of the intermediary. Hence:

$$RB - RL = TB' + TL' + C$$

The gap between lending and borrowing rates will be lower and benefit both parties provided:

$$(TB + TL) - (TL' + TL') > C$$

That is, providing the introduction of the intermediary has lowered search/transaction costs by more than its charge.

Competition between intermediaries serves to keep down operating costs and therefore the margin charged by the intermediaries. The competitive pressures have increased over the 1980s following widescale deregulation within the financial system and we will return to this topic later in this chapter.

It is likely that the reduction in costs involved in lending and borrowing through financial intermediaries has increased the level of lending and hence saving and borrowing and hence investment compared with a situation of no intermediation. The stimulation of investment has also been achieved through the improvement in the characteristics of financial instruments available, which is likely to have made saving more attractive, again increasing the level of aggregate saving.

In addition to conflicting requirements of borrowers and lenders and transaction costs, a further reason to explain the existence of financial intermediaries which is increasingly stressed in the literature is the existence of informational asymmetries. Direct lenders do not have the experience or skills necessary to gather information on borrowers and monitor their performance and so lenders delegate these functions to an intermediary which can specialise in this role. Leland and Pyle [1977] and Diamond [1984] analyse such market imperfections as a basis for the existence of intermediaries.

The effects of a reduction in transaction costs is represented diagrammatically in figure 2.7. The demand for credit is represented by the curve *D–D*, with the normal downward slope. The supply of credit is considered to respond positively to increases in interest rates and is represented by the curve *S–S*. Note that two effects operate here: the substitution effect, leading to a substitution of saving for consumption; and the income effect, which could lower saving. We are assuming the substitution effect dominates, so that saving increases as the rate of interest rises. In the absence of transaction costs and so on (the perfect capital market assumption), equilibrium would occur at point *A*, where both the quantity demanded and supplied are equal to *0Z*. Clearly, transaction costs do occur and, in the absence of a financial intermediary, we assume that the transaction costs summarised above equal *CD*, so that the quantity of credit demanded and supplied equals *0Y*. This gap between the rates paid by the borrower and received by the lender is termed the spread. The introduction of a financial intermediary reduces these costs so the spread narrows to *EF* from *CD* and the quantity of credit demanded and supplied rises to *0X*. Provided the increase in credit leads to increased investment, it is reasonable to suppose that real gross domestic product (GDP) has also increased. In any case, if the increased consumption has been used to finance consumption, it is also reasonable to assume that utility has also risen.

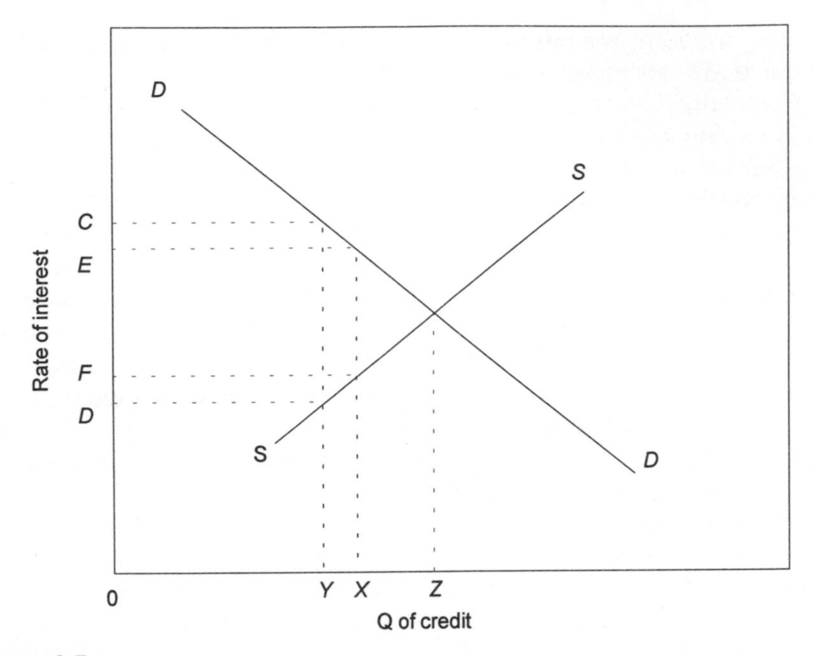

Figure 2.7

The traditional theory of financial intermediation described above is based on the presence of economies of scale and specialised intermediaries (Gurley and Shaw [1960]). More recent analysis has tended to emphasise the advantages banks and other financial intermediaries possess in reducing the informational asymmetries and moral hazard inherent in the financing process. Direct lenders do not have the experience or skills necessary to gather information on the borrowers and monitor their performance. Hence it may be more efficient for lenders to delegate these functions to an intermediary which can specialise in this role. Leland and Pyle [1977] and Diamond [1984] analyse such market imperfections as a basis for the existence of intermediaries. Diamond stresses that portfolio diversification will lead to a reduction in the cost of making loans due to the ability to spread risk. This also enables financial intermediaries to repay fixed debt claims to depositors. Diamond [1989, 1991] also suggests that borrower reputation is important in the financing process. Where a borrower has no reputation, then imperfect information and the moral hazard problem will mean the borrower is likely to be dependent on banks for finance. Once a reputation is established, allowing the borrower future access to a cheaper source of funds through other financial markets (e.g. equity, bond or commercial paper issues – these are discussed in chapters 8, 9 and 10 respectively), reputation becomes a capital asset. Consequently, firms are more likely to select safe rather than risky investments to protect their capital asset, thus reducing the adverse selection problem.

The standard view of finance discussed above sees the emergence of financial intermediaries as the final stage in the evolution of a financial system. A new view has been presented though (see for example McCulloch [1981] and Tobin [1984]) which argues that financial intermediaries can in some circumstances distort the workings of the system and further that they should be seen as a transitory phase in this evolutionary process. The final phase under the new view is a complete set of spot, futures and options markets embracing all commodities and all contingencies. Such markets are referred to as complete or Arrow–Debreu markets, following the Arrow–Debreu general equilibrium model (for a theoretical exposition of this see Arrow and Hahn [1971] or for an introduction to the concepts see Flood [1991]), and are markets characterised by negligible transaction costs. The nature of futures and options markets are covered later in this book (see chapter 13). Essentially though futures markets allow trade in commodities for delivery in the future. The existence of a complete set of such markets allows borrowing to take place by selling goods now for delivery at a future date. Similarly lending takes place by buying goods now for future delivery. Options markets are essentially markets in contingent claims; that is, they provide the holder of an option with insurance against the risk of a particular contingency occurring. The existence of a complete set of such contingent markets removes the uncertainty from transactions. With negligible transaction costs and little risk involved in lending and borrowing, there is no role for financial intermediaries and transactions would return again to direct barter. The existence of a complete set of options and futures markets with negligible transaction costs is of course a theoretical construct. Such markets however are expanding in both volume of transactions and number of products traded. Advances in computer and telecommunications technology are reducing costs of financial transactions. This new view of finance may therefore provide some indication of the likely future direction of financial systems. Indeed, there is some evidence of a move away from financial intermediation by large companies to raising funds directly through international capital markets. This phenomenon is referred to as securitisation and is discussed in more detail in chapter 12.

2.5 Evolution of financial systems

The financial systems that have emerged in the major developed countries of the world have some important differences in structure. The differences that exist, in particular the different relationships between the financial system and the corporate sector, have been suggested as one explanation for the different economic performances of these countries since the Second

World War. We will examine this debate in some detail in chapter 16; however, to provide some background to this debate we will consider here the relationship between the evolution of a financial system and the different phases of economic growth (see Rybczynski [1988] for further discussion).

In the early stages of the growth of an economy, that is, when an economy transforms itself from agrarian to industrial, it is banks which act as the main intermediary providing the external finance for the investment required for this restructuring. During this bank-oriented phase of the financial system, ownership of the productive resources of the economy is concentrated in few hands and there is little separation of ownership and control of these resources. As industrialisation continues it is usual for firms to obtain a larger proportion of their externally raised funds through the capital markets. This inevitably leads to a separation of ownership from control of firms, with ownership (i.e. holders of the equity claims issued by firms through the capital market) held by households both directly and increasingly indirectly through non-bank financial companies. The control of firms is delegated to professional managers subject to satisfactory performance of the company. In this market-oriented phase of the financial system the role of the banks in providing finance for firms is less important and generally passive. As industrialisation reaches a peak, there is greater restructuring of economic activity, that is, redirection of resources in the economy through a change in the ownership and control of firms. This active restructuring takes place through the capital markets. As the economy moves into what has been termed the de-industrialisation phase, where the relative importance of the traditional manufacturing industries declines and the relative importance of service industries increases, there is a much greater level of economic restructuring. This places greater demands on the financial system, which, it is argued, moves into the securitised phase. The functions of the financial system expand under this phase so that enhanced capital and credit markets emerge along with markets for corporate control and venture capital. The financial system is more complete under the securitised phase and more importantly plays an active role in the restructuring of the economy. This restructuring takes place through the new markets in corporate control and venture capital. The market for corporate control is concerned with changing the ownership and control of existing firms and is increasingly carried out through the use of takeovers. Such takeovers are often hostile (i.e. the bid from the company proposing the takeover is opposed by the target company's management) but the takeover process may be seen as providing a discipline on companies, allowing control to be transferred from inefficient to efficient management – see chapter 16 for further discussion of this. The market for venture capital is concerned with the provision of finance to the new firms which emerge in this restructuring process.

The preceding description of the evolution of financial systems was very general and does not apply to all countries. The description is probably most applicable to the US and the UK, with the transformation to a securitised financial system taking place earlier in the US. In contrast, countries such as Germany, Japan and to a lesser extent France have continued to operate with a financial system which more closely represents the bank-oriented system. In such countries banks can and do act in an active way in industrial restructuring, providing risk capital (equity) to companies and then working closely with those companies. This close relationship also involves performance monitoring of the management of the company and where necessary banks may initiate a change in the management or ownership of companies. Such changes, in contrast to the market or securitised systems, are generally carried out without hostile confrontation.

The foregoing discussion of the evolution of financial systems presents a clear-cut distinction between bank-oriented and market-oriented or securitised systems. In recent years certain developments have blurred this distinction. As countries loosely associated with bank-oriented systems have moved into the de-industrialisation phase, the accompanying increased level of restructuring has tended to encourage a transition to more market-oriented or securitised financial systems. Countries experiencing such a transition are France and Italy. Also companies in both Germany and Japan are now increasingly making greater use of capital markets, with a greater proportion of risk capital being provided by non-bank institutions. Finally countries more strongly associated with bank-oriented systems have recently experienced hostile takeover activity, although the regulatory and institutional impediments to hostile takeovers in such countries suggest that such activity is unlikely to grow at a significant rate.

2.6 Recent developments in the UK financial system

In the last section we identified the UK system as one that has recently moved into a securitised type of financial system. There has in fact been a vast amount of change in the UK financial system in recent years, and in particular over the 1980s. The changes that have taken place are not random and can be analysed in a systematic way. In this section we will provide an overall perspective of the main forces leading to change and the major changes that have taken place. This analysis (adapted from Llewellyn [1985, 1991]) will provide a framework for assessing and interpreting the more specific discussion of events in the various financial markets and institutions throughout the rest of this book.

Some of the main forces leading to change in any financial system are:

(i) changes in the market environment,
(ii) changes in the portfolio preferences of the users of financial intermediation services,
(iii) changes in the portfolio preferences of and constraints on the providers of financial intermediation services.

The interaction of these forces produces financial innovation, which is essentially the development of new financial instruments, markets and techniques of intermediation, and changes in the structure of the financial system, with new markets appearing and changes in the organisation and behaviour of institutions. With this general framework in mind we can now examine the main changes in the financial system.

Over the post-war period up to the end of the 1960s the UK financial system was characterised by strict demarcation between the various types of financial institution. So, for example, it was rare for the banks to operate in the housing finance market, which was seen as the sole province of the building societies. There was therefore very little competition between the different types of financial institution. There was also little internal competition within a particular financial market as, for example, banks and building societies operated cartels which controlled the setting of interest rates. Similarly within the stock market, restrictive practices, in particular the existence of minimum non-negotiable commissions, had the effect of reducing competition. Towards the end of the 1970s, however, the first competitive pressures were felt by banks as the relaxed requirements of entry to the City of London saw penetration by foreign banks into the UK banking system. In 1971 the first substantial official reforms of the financial system, known as competition and credit control, were introduced. These reforms were aimed at the banking system and were designed to remove the banking cartel and encourage competition between banks. These reforms heralded the beginning of a long period of deregulation of the financial system, mostly officially sanctioned, which has increased competition throughout the financial system. Most of the deregulation of the financial system has though taken place over the 1980s and has been a feature of financial systems in most other countries. Before we analyse the changes that have taken place, we will first of all examine the broad forces inducing change, referred to above.

Changes in the market environment

The main environmental factors over the 1970s and 1980s which brought about changes in the financial system can be summarised as follows.

(i) There was a strong trend over this period, particularly the 1980s, towards deregulation of the financial system. The aim here was to introduce

Table 2.1 *Key events in the market environment since 1970*

Year	*Event*
1971	Introduction of competition and credit control – banking cartel removed
1973/4	Secondary bank crisis – led to rethink of bank regulation
1975	'May Day' at the New York Stock Exchange – deregulation
1979	Exchange controls abandoned
1979	Banking Act – introduced a system of controls by which the Bank of England could monitor and control banks' activities
1980	Medium-term financial strategy – new system of monetary control – also controls on bank lending ('the corset') abandoned
1983	Building Societies Association cartel abandoned
1984	Collapse of Johnson Mathey bank – further rethink of bank regulation
1986	'Big Bang' at the London Stock Exchange – deregulation
1986	Building Societies Act – deregulation of building societies
1986	Financial Services Act – investor protection
1987	Banking Act
1988	Convergence Accord – international agreement on measuring banks' capital

greater competition into the financial system with a view to increasing efficiency. Alongside this deregulation was a parallel trend to tighten up the prudential regulation of the financial system, with the aim of protecting the user of financial intermediation services. So, this period has seen deregulation as far as pricing of services is concerned, accompanied by increased regulation for purposes of prudential control and investor protection. The key events in this process are presented in table 2.1.

The deregulation of banking in 1971 was the starting point for the wave of deregulation that was to come later in the 1980s. The delay before the deregulation of building societies is partly explained by the controls that were intermittently placed on banks, for example 'the corset', over the 1970s. With the removal of these controls in 1980, banks were free to compete with building societies in the market for housing finance. The competitive pressures on building societies led in 1983 to the breakdown in the cartel arrangement, whereby interest rates were set, and in 1986 to the Building Societies Act, which allowed societies to pursue a much wider range of financial services. The pressure for deregulation in the stock market arose partly from competitive pressures following the deregulation of the New York Stock Exchange in 1975, which led to lower costs of transacting in New York, and also from the general philosophy of the Conservative administration from 1979 in favour of unrestricted markets. The abolition of exchange controls in 1979, allowing the big institutional investors to invest funds abroad, particularly using the lower-cost New York Exchange, led to some loss of business for London. Preparations for deregulation of the London Stock Exchange began in 1979, following the decision of the Director General of Fair Trading to take the rule book of the Exchange before the Restrictive Practices Court, but it was not until 1986 that full deregulation occurred.

(ii) The economic environment, particularly in the 1970s and 1980s, was very volatile. High and volatile rates of inflation and interest rates led to great uncertainty in financial decision taking. This led to changes in the portfolio preferences of users and the development of new financial instruments to manage the greater risks. These are discussed below.

(iii) A substantial rise in domestic and international imbalances led to a greater demand for financial intermediation services. International imbalances on a large scale occurred following the oil price increases of 1973/74 which led to surpluses in countries in the Organization of Petroleum Exporting Countries (OPEC) and balance of payments deficits for many developing countries. In the 1980s Germany and Japan, continuing a long-term trend, accrued large surpluses and the US and to a lesser extent the UK had balance of payments deficits.

(iv) The taxation system played a major role in determining the portfolio preferences of the users of the financial system. One obvious example of this were the tax incentives provided to saving through life assurance (up until 1984) and pension funds. This led to a greater proportion of personal sector investment being directed through investment institutions.

Changing portfolio preferences of users

Here we examine the main changes in the portfolio preferences of the three domestic sectors which use the financial intermediation services provided by financial institutions.

(i) *The personal sector.* The personal sector went into financial deficit over the period 1987–89 (shown in table 2.2), reversing a long run of financial surpluses since the early 1970s. After 1989 the sector returned to its more normal position of financial surplus, recording a record surplus in 1992. However, some caution is needed here because, as explained in chapter 1, the figures for saving and financial transactions for the personal sector are subject to a wide degree of error.

Table 2.2 *Financial surplus/deficit of the personal sector (£million)*

1985	*1986*	*1987*	*1988*	*1989*	*1990*	*1991*	*1992*	*1993*
9,860	3,618	-3,720	-14,599	-6,232	2,879	19,123	34,312	34,012

Source: CSO, *Financial Statistics*, various issues.

It is likely though that significant changes took place in personal sector behaviour over the 1980s and a number of reasons have been suggested to explain these developments. First, personal sector saving reduced over this period (see table 2.3), so that a savings ratio of 13.4 per cent in 1980 fell to 5.7 per cent by 1988 before recovering again to figures in 1992 and 1993 roughly equivalent to that for 1980 as interest rates rose and the recession set in.

One suggested explanation for the decline in savings over the 1980s is the decline in inflation over the same period, which means that households do not need to save as much to maintain the real value of their nominal assets such as bank deposits. A second possible explanation is the growth in the wealth of the personal sector resulting from large rises in the prices of housing and equities (up to the stock market crash of 1987). It can be argued that the greater feeling of wealth created by these capital gains may lead households to decide to save less. Another factor is that households are borrowing more following the liberalisation of financial markets, particularly the mortgage market, early in the 1980s. The growth in their assets and liabilities over the 1980s is shown in table 2.4. As households have found it easier to borrow they have used this to finance an increase in consumption. Some of the finance for consumption expenditure may have 'leaked' out of the equity built up in housing through the phenomenon of equity withdrawal (explained further in chapter 5).

(ii) *The companies sector.* The sources of finance for companies over the 1970s and the 1980s are compared in table 2.5 (refer to table 8.1 in chapter 8 for more detail). It is clear from these figures that whilst internally generated funds are the dominant form of company finance, externally raised finance became more important over the 1980s. Issues of ordinary

Table 2.3 *Savings ratio of the personal sector (%)*

1985	*1986*	*1987*	*1988*	*1989*	*1990*	*1991*	*1992*	*1993*
10.7	8.7	7.1	5.7	7.2	8.4	10.5	12.8	12.2

Source: *Economic Trends,* 1995 annual supplement, table 1.6.

Table 2.4 *Components of personal sector net wealth (£billion)*

	1981	*1991*	*% growth 1981–91*
Dwellings	401	1130	182
Financial assets	340	1348	297
Financial liabilities	108	473	338

Source: CSO, *Financial Statistics*, various issues.

shares increased over the 1980s, taking advantage of a bull market in shares until the stock market crash in October 1987. In fact in the year of the stock market crash, issues of ordinary shares were the main source of externally raised finance. After the stock market crash, companies turned increasingly to bank-raised funds to finance the large numbers of takeovers that occurred in 1988 and 1989. As a consequence, companies' gearing ratios increased with capital gearing, defined as the stock of borrowing as a percentage of total capital, rising from 8 per cent in 1980 to 25 per cent in 1991. However, the gearing of UK companies has typically been lower than that in other industrialised countries, in particular Germany and Japan. As the UK economy moved into recession in 1990, bank borrowing slowed down dramatically and in 1991, 1992 and 1993, firms were net repayers of bank debt. The main source of external capital in these years was issues of shares. The reduction in debt issues and greater use of equity finance has had a stabilising effect on companies' capital gearing. Debentures and preference shares, essentially fixed-interest marketable debt, declined in importance over the 1970s as historically high interest rates discouraged issues. Issues of this type of debt showed some signs of recovery in the 1980s and issues in 1989 exceeded issues of ordinary shares. The growth in issues of company fixed-interest debt at the end of the 1980s is partly explained by investors

Table 2.5 *Company sources of finance (% of total)*

	Internal funds	*Bank loans*	*Ordinary shares*	*Debentures and preference shares*	*Other*
1970s	69	15	2.8	0.7	12.5
1980s	55	24	7.2	1.6	11.4
1990–93	57.3	-7.2	15.1	5.5	29.3[a]

[a] Of this figure 11.7 percentage points represented overseas funding.
Source: CSO, *Financial Statistics*, various issues – see table 8.1 for more details.

seeking alternative types of fixed-interest debt following the reduction in the amount of government debt (see below). Overseas funding also increased in importance, so that for the years 1990–93, it formed 11.7 per cent of total funding.

(iii) *The public sector.* In 1980 the government introduced the medium-term financial strategy which stressed the need to reduce public expenditure. The original aim was to reduce the public sector borrowing requirement (PSBR) to one to two per cent of GDP. This aim was exceeded towards the end of the 1980s as the policy of reducing public sector spending combined with greater revenues from a growing economy over the mid-1980s, together with proceeds from privatisation sales, brought about a government budget surplus over the period 1987–90 resulting in the PSBR giving way to a public sector debt repayment (PSDR). The existence of the PSDR permitted the government to redeem maturing debt without making new issues and to buy in outstanding debt. This reduced the amount of debt available for investing institutions to hold. A downturn in the UK economy from 1990/91 led to an end to the run of budget surpluses. The PSBR for 1991 came in at £7.7 billion, rising to £28.7 and £42.5 billion respectively for the years 1992 and 1993. The last figure is equal to 6.7 per cent of GDP, which is considerably above the original target for the PSBR set in 1980.

Changing portfolio preferences of the suppliers of financial intermediation services

The banks were the first institutions to be affected by the waves of deregulation described above and as a consequence banks have gone through more change and produced more innovation than other financial institutions. The removal of controls on bank activity in 1971 led to greater competition between banks, which became more growth oriented, more profit conscious and more innovative. An early development involved the switch from a strategy of asset management, whereby the asset portfolio is managed on the basis of a given level of deposits, to a strategy of liability management, whereby liabilities are managed to fund a desired level of assets. In response to a more volatile economic environment and the changing nature of portfolio preferences of companies, banks developed term loans, which came to replace fixed-interest debt issued by companies. The growing international financial imbalances, largely arising from the oil price rises in the 1970s, saw banks substantially increasing their role as international financial intermediaries. This however turned out to be an unsuccessful episode in the history of international banking as the high interest rates and slowdown in world trade in the early 1980s produced the sovereign debt crisis (examined in chapter 4). In response to capital controls imposed on banks and the greater competitiveness of traditional banking business of taking in deposits and making loans, banks have increasingly undertaken fee-generating business such as underwriting security issues. A large proportion of this business does not appear on the balance sheet and, in response to the growth of off-balance-sheet business, the regulatory authorities have had to rethink the capital controls on banks. Greater international competition between banks led to pressure for these new capital controls to be harmonised across borders to create a 'level playing field', resulting in the 'Convergence Accord' in 1988. These issues are considered in more detail in chapter 17. Another development, mentioned above, was the move by banks into the mortgage market, previously dominated by building societies, following the removal of lending constraints on banks. This in turn contributed to pressures for the deregulation of building societies, to allow them to compete in the more competitive climate created by banks. A development affecting the portfolio preferences of the investing institutions, namely life assurance companies and pension funds, was the abandonment of exchange controls in 1979, which led to a greater proportion of foreign securities in the asset portfolios of these institutions.

The interaction of the forces described above led to changes in market structure and financial innovation. The main developments are summarised below.

2.7 Market structure and financial innovation

Financial conglomeration

Deregulation and the greater competition it produced have resulted in a steady erosion of the traditional demarcation between different types of financial institutions. Over the 1980s we have seen banks enter the housing finance market, traditionally dominated by building societies, and building societies lending on an unsecured basis and offering cheque-book accounts, activities traditionally associated with banks. This diversification of the activities of the different financial institutions, largely encouraged by the authorities, is leading to the development of financial conglomerates, or financial supermarkets. Banks again are furthest along this road, with interests in broker-dealer firms operating on the stock market, insurance companies, foreign currency dealing, unit trusts, and so on. Whilst the development of financial conglomerates brings greater competition to the financial markets and can reduce search costs for users of financial intermediation services, it also poses difficulties. One problem that has been identified is the greater potential for conflict of interest. An example is the new market-making entities on the Stock Exchange which combine the old (separate) functions of broking and market making. The broking section of these bodies may advise a client to buy the shares held by its market-making section even though these shares may not be the best available for that client. A further problem posed by conglomeration is that

Table 2.6 *Growth of assets of UK financial institutions (£billion)*

	1976	*1980*	*1984*	*1988*	*1992*	*% growth (1976–92)*
Banks[a]	70.8	117.4	271.4	401.8	552.1	680
Building societies	28.1	54.3	103.3	189.8	266.6	849
Unit and investment trusts	8.7	12.5	31.1	61.6	92.5	963
Insurance companies:						
general		11.5	19.9	39.6	53.8	
life	29.9[b]	53.7	114.2	198.3	327.2	1358[c]
Pension funds	16.9	52.6	130.3	214.5	392.6	2223

[a] Combined retail, merchant and other British banks.
[b] Figure for combined life and general insurance assets.
[c] Growth of combined life and general insurance.
Source: CSO, *Financial Statistics*, various issues.

of the appropriate regulatory authority for the different activities of the conglomerate. A related problem is that of cross-infection, where the failure of a bank's subsidiary operating in a non-banking field and regulated by a different authority to the regulator of banks may lead to difficulties for the parent company.

Growth of non-bank financial institutions

Over the 1970s and 1980s the non-bank institutions grew at a rapid rate. This is illustrated by the figures in table 2.6, which show all the main non-bank financial institutions achieving a higher rate of growth of assets than the banks.

The growth of all the financial institutions reflects the greater need for intermediation services as a result of the growing domestic financial imbalances. The slower growth of banks is partly explained by the greater role of off-balance-sheet and other fee-paying business as banks have sought to diversify their income base (this is examined in more detail in chapter 4). The growth of building societies and investment institutions also reflects certain tax advantages which are obtained by the use of the services of these institutions. Tax relief on mortgage interest payments is one of the factors which has contributed to the steady growth in home ownership over the 1970s and 1980s and hence to the assets of building societies. Contributions to pension schemes and life assurance policies (up to 1984) also benefited from tax advantages. The consequent growth in funds flowing to these institutions from the personal sector has resulted in greater indirect investment in company shares and other marketable securities by the personal sector at the expense of direct investment.

Growth in use of new technology
Developments in computing and telecommunications technology applied to financial intermediation services have been both a consequence of the greater competition fostered by deregulation, as institutions have sought to cut costs and introduce new products, and at the same time an enabling factor, allowing the development of new products and services. One of the main areas where new technology has so far had the most impact is in the area of payments and cash dispensing systems. Banks and building societies have introduced greater numbers of automated teller machines (ATMs) into their branches. It is argued that the development of ATMs makes the branch networks of banks and building societies largely redundant. However, the diversification of the product base of these institutions, described above, provides one reason for these institutions holding on to these high street financial supermarkets where the range of products they provide can be marketed. The numbers of staff involved in the payments services side of banks and building societies are likely to decrease though, as more of the service is automated. The greater automation of payments services should reduce entry costs into this traditional area of banking activity. Further developments in automation of banking services, for example EFTPOS (electronic funds at point of transfer) and home banking through a computer/ modem link, have not been introduced as quickly as forecast. Another area where new technology has found an application is in the automation of dealing in stock markets. In the London Stock Exchange the SEAQ (stock exchange automatic quotation) system is at present only a price information system. Automated dealing is, however, possible on the foreign exchange and future markets.

Internationalisation
Another trend in the provision of intermediation services is internationalisation. London has always had relaxed entry requirements in relation to foreign banks. This helped London to develop as one of the main centres for international banking, in particular euro-banking (discussed in chapters 4 and 7). Some of the foreign banks which established themselves in London, however, have increasingly competed for domestic UK business in the area of wholesale banking, mortgage lending and securities trading. At the same time UK-based banks have increasingly sought business in other countries. The development of a European single market in a wide range of financial services (see chapter 15) should encourage greater cross-border activity and therefore greater international competition in financial services. The removal of exchange controls in the UK in 1979 has increased cross-border investment by UK investment institutions. This development, the reforms of the London Stock Exchange and London's time zone position in the 'golden triangle' of New York, London and Tokyo have enabled

London to become one of the major centres in international equities trading. The developments in new technology, enabling prices to be transmitted around the world in seconds, has also contributed to the globalisation of equities trading.

Financial innovation
In addition to the structural changes in the financial system, described above, the last 20 years have also seen considerable innovation in financial instruments, techniques and markets. Many of the innovations have been mentioned in the above discussion. For example, the volatility and high level of interest rates in the 1970s saw companies withdraw from issuing fixed-interest debt and banks develop term loans to fill the gap. Gap filling is one of the many determinants of financial innovation and at the risk of over-simplification can be seen as institutions and markets combining the various characteristics that make up financial instruments to create a new instrument for which there is a demand.

Growth of the UK financial services industry
The 1980s saw a rapid growth in the UK financial services industry, which mirrored the decline in the manufacturing sector. This is reflected in table 2.7, which shows the relative contributions to GDP and employment by manufacturing and (a widely defined – see notes to table) financial services sector over the 1980s.

Table 2.7 *Gross domestic product (at constant factor cost) and employment by industry as a percentage of total*

	1982	*1983*	*1984*	*1985*	*1986*	*1987*	*1988*	*1989*	*1990*	*1991*
Gross domestic product										
Manufacturing	25.0	23.8	23.5	23.6	23.7	23.0	23.0	22.6	22.1	21.0
Financial services	12.1	13.3	13.1	14.2	15.7	16.5	16.8	18.8	18.2	17.7
Employment										
Manufacturing	27.4	26.2	25.5	25.0	24.4	23.9	23.3	22.9	22.5	21.7
Financial services	8.4	8.9	9.3	9.7	10.1	10.6	11.1	11.5	12.0	12.1

Financial services are defined as banking, finance, insurance, business services and leasing. This definition includes accounting and computing services and is therefore wider than the traditional perception of financial services. However, it is the narrowest category to which GDP data refer.
Financial services' contribution to GDP includes net interest receipts. In the aggregate measure of GDP (where net interest flows within the economy must sum to zero) these interest receipts are excluded.
Source: CSO, *UK National Accounts*, 1992.

This provides support for the hypothesis that the UK has been going through a process of de-industrialisation, as described in section 2.5, with a relative decline in the manufacturing sector and a relative growth in the services sector.

2.8 Conclusion

In this chapter we have described the role of a financial system in intermediating between lenders and borrowers and set out in broad terms the tremendous changes that have taken place in the UK financial system in recent years. In the next two chapters of this book we will describe in greater detail the changes to the various institutions and markets that make up the UK financial system.

Chapter 3

Retail banking

3.1 Introduction

In this chapter we examine the nature of retail banking as distinct from wholesale banking. Whilst such a distinction has in recent years become less relevant in practice as most retail banks also undertake wholesale business, we feel there is still some advantage to be gained from some aspects of retail banking being considered separately from wholesale banking. In particular we examine why retail banks combine payments services with intermediation services, the risks inherent in retail banking, and the strategies adopted by banks to manage these risks. We then finish this chapter by outlining the main functions of the Bank of England. Wholesale banking will be discussed in chapter 4.

3.2 Nature of retail banking in the UK

The traditional business of banking involves taking in deposits which are then packaged and on-lent as loans. Retail banking refers to the large-volume, low-value end of this business, where deposits are typically attracted from individuals and small businesses and loans are made to the same groups. This is in contrast to wholesale banking, where transactions are typically small volume but large value. In practice it is difficult to distinguish between retail and wholesale banks in the UK as most of the banks operating in the retail markets also operate in the wholesale markets. In fact one of the issues we focus upon in section 3.4 is why retail activities are typically combined with wholesale activities.

To operate in the retail markets, banks require an extensive branch network. The Bank of England in fact defines retail banks, with a few exceptions, as those banks 'which either have extensive branch networks in the United Kingdom or participate directly in a UK clearing system'. At 31 December 1993, the Bank of England classified 22 banks as retail. The

Table 3.1 *The combined balance sheet of UK retail banks at 31 December 1993 (£billion)*

Liabilities		*Assets*	
Notes outstanding	2.2	Notes and coins	4.7
Total sterling deposits	336.8	Balances with Bank of England	1.1
(of which sight deposits	168.7)	Market loans	73.9
		Total bills	8.9
Foreign currency deposits	118.9	Investments	28.7
Items in suspense and transmission plus capital and other funds	75.1	Advances	265.9
		Other currency and miscellaneous assets	155.2
		Banking Department lending to central government (net)	-5.4
Total liabilities	533.0	Total assets	533.0
(Eligible liabilities	274.5)		

Source: *Bank of England Statistical Abstract*, 1994, table 2.4.

largest of these are the four London clearing banks, namely, Barclays, Lloyds, Midland and National Westminster, along with the recently transformed Trustee Savings Bank and the Abbey National which in 1989 transferred from the mutual status of a building society to p.l.c. status (public limited company), and hence a bank. The rest include banks whose operations are largely confined to Scotland (Bank of Scotland, Clydesdale and the Royal Bank of Scotland) and Northern Ireland (Bank of Ireland, Ulster and Northern).

By examining the combined balance sheet for retail banks in the UK (table 3.1) we can discern their main activities.

Examining the liabilities side of retail banks' balance sheet, first we find the small item of 'Notes outstanding', which refers to private bank notes issued by Scottish and Northern Ireland banks. The bulk of a bank's liabilities are deposits, accounting for 85 per cent of total retail bank liabilities, with 26 per cent of these deposits being in foreign currency. There are no figures available for the retail banks as a whole showing a breakdown of sterling deposits into retail and wholesale deposits (which are deposits mainly raised through the inter-bank market – see section 3.4) although some indication is provided by table 3.2, which shows 64 per cent of London clearing banks' group sterling deposits at the end of 1985 were wholesale. It should be noted however that the figures in table 3.2 are likely to misrepresent to some extent the position of the retail banking sector as a whole as, firstly, they relate to both parent and the wholesale

Table 3.2 *The balance between wholesale and retail funding for London clearing banks*

Year	*Retail funds as a % of total sterling deposits*	*Wholesale funds as a % of total sterling deposits*
1976	59	41
1978	56	44
1980	56	44
1982	43	57
1984	38	62
1985	36	64

Source: Committee of London Clearing Banks, *Abstract of Banking Statistics*, 1985.

subsidiaries of clearing bank groups and, secondly, since 1985 the clearing banks have more actively competed for retail deposits, seeing these as a base for selling other financial products (see chapter 5). The other main liabilities are items in suspense and transmission, which refer for example to cheques drawn and in the course of collection, and capital and other funds, which refer mainly to banks' issued share capital, long-term debt and reserves. These latter capital funds are important items when it comes to assessing a bank's capital adequacy in relation to the risks it faces. Finally, eligible liabilities are essentially defined as non-bank sterling deposit liabilities with an original maturity up to two years, plus net sterling inter-bank transactions plus any sterling resources obtained by switching foreign currencies into sterling.

Turning now to the assets side of the balance sheet, we find a small item referring to balances with the Bank of England. This relates to a compulsory 'cash ratio' requirement whereby all banks with eligible liabilities greater than £10 billion are required to hold 0.35 per cent of their eligible liabilities in a non-interest-bearing account at the Bank of England. This has little relevance to any prudential assessment of a bank but is simply a tax on banks which is used to finance the various activities of the Bank of England. The cash balances held outside of the Bank of England (notes and coins) account for roughly 0.9 per cent of total assets, which is a very low cash base. Additional liquidity is provided by market loans, which refer to short-term loans made through the money markets. Traditionally banks' market loans were call or overnight loans to the discount houses. These loans are used to even out cash positions within the banking system. However, the retail banks' involvement in the inter-bank markets since 1971 has reduced the importance of this function and inter-bank loans now account for approximately 72 per cent of total market loans. Dealings between banks and the discount houses, however, continue to take place in order to smooth out shortages or surpluses of cash arising out of dealings between the banking system as a whole and non-banks as, clearly, the inter-bank market cannot perform this function. This is dealt with in more detail in chapter 10. Further liquidity is provided by the next item on the assets side, which is bills. These are mainly Treasury bills and bank bills eligible for re-discounting at the Bank of England via discount houses. The item of investments refers to retail banks' holdings of marketable securities. These are mainly government bonds or government guaranteed stocks and therefore have the characteristics of low default risk and marketability. The main assets of retail banks are sterling advances, which accounted for approximately 50 per cent of total assets or 70 per cent of sterling assets. The majority of advances are the traditional 'overdraft facility' made to business borrowers. However, since the mid-1970s banks have increasingly made term loans to businesses, with an average original term to maturity of around seven years. In addition, over the 1980s, following the removals of controls on bank lending, the banks have increasingly targeted personal sector customers with both long-term mortgage lending and unsecured term loans. The next items on the assets side of the retail banks' balance sheet are 'other currency and miscellaneous assets'. Of the 'other currency' assets, around 20 per cent is accounted for by advances, with the remainder being made up of mainly market loans and investments. Miscellaneous assets include the banks' physical assets, mainly premises and equipment, which provide the infrastructure of the business. The final item is Banking Department lending to central government, which refers to the Banking Department of the Bank of England which is included in the retail banks classification owing to its involvement in the clearing system. We consider the function of the Banking Department and the other functions of the Bank of England in section 3.5.

It follows from the Bank of England's definition of a retail bank, quoted above, that in addition to providing intermediation services, most retail banks provide transaction or payments and cash distribution services. In the next section we examine the nature of the payments system in the UK and consider why it is that banks combine payments with intermediation services.

3.3 Payments services

Banks until very recently have been the sole provider of payments services. A payments service is merely an accounting procedure whereby transfers of ownership of certain assets are carried out in settlement of debts incurred. Payments facilities generate a desire for instruments that (i) serve as a medium of exchange enabling consumers to acquire goods, (ii) serve as a medium of payment to effect payment of the good acquired, and (iii) act as a temporary store of purchasing power, since income receipts and payments are generally not synchronised. As we saw in chapter 1, a commodity that takes on these three characteristics is termed money and any commodity can act in this role as long as it generally accepted. In most developed economies the payments system that has evolved is based on government-issued paper money and cheques drawn on a bank deposit. The reasons for this are covered adequately in most texts on money and banking. What we propose to examine here are some recent developments in the UK payments system. Recent financial innovation has made it possible to 'unbundle' the three functions of money so they can be separately carried out using different instruments. So, for example, a credit card may serve as the medium of exchange enabling goods to be purchased. A direct debit from a bank deposit account may then be used to effect payment at a later date and in between the purchase and payment the funds used for payment may be held in a high-yielding account. Developments in technology are also bringing about changes in the payments system. In particular the ongoing developments in electronic funds transfer, whereby electronic signals replace paper cheques in undertaking the accounting transfers, are lowering the entry barriers to the provision of payments systems.

As we have noted above, payments services are generally provided together with portfolio services by an institution. This is because there are certain advantages in combining the two services. The funds which are held in bank accounts before being used to finance purchases – although customers will attempt to keep these at a minimum as they can most likely obtain a higher return by lending them elsewhere – can in aggregate be used to on-lend profitably. Thus, intermediation emerges as a byproduct of payments services. The profits from the intermediation services have generally been used to cross-subsidise the costs of providing the payments service. Various schemes have been adopted by banks in the past to enable the profits earned by the bank from the use of the idle balances of a customer to reduce or eliminate charges for the use of the payments service. For example, customers who kept a positive minimum and average account balance were then exempt from charges for payments services. Another method used was the calculation of implicit interest on a customer's idle balances which was used to offset charges. The policy of deregulation of the financial system over the 1980s has affected these arrangements. In particular, deregulation of the building societies – covered in chapter 5 – allowed them to offer payments services. A number of building societies have to date set up deposit accounts with a cheque-book facility and the feature of paying interest on the idle funds in the account whilst at the same time not charging for the payments service. This additional competition for banks has induced them to introduce cheque accounts which either pay interest or involve no bank charges. Deregulation and the increased competition it brings has so far not led to the removal of cross-subsidisation whereby explicit rates of interest are paid on account balances but payments services are fully charged for (as suggested by e.g. Fama [1980]), but instead appears to have reduced the overall profitability of retail banking-type services. The providers of payments services, though, obtain certain advantages which enable them to be more efficient in their intermediation operations. In particular, they will obtain valuable information about the financial circumstances of the customer. This enables them to judge whether it is suitable to extend that customer credit and once the loan is extended the transactions account can be used as a source of information in the monitoring process. Such specialised information, as we saw in chapter 2, provides part of the explanation for the existence of financial intermediaries. Also, the access to transactions details enables an institution to target other financial services at customers. These advantages therefore partly explain why institutions such as building societies have sought to introduce payments services.

3.4 Risks in retail banking

Banks, like all financial intermediaries, as we saw in chapter 2, are involved in managing risk. The principal risks that are managed by retail banks are:

(i) liquidity risk – this is a consequence of issuing liabilities that are largely payable on demand or at short notice whilst holding assets which have a longer term to maturity;
(ii) asset risk – the risk that assets held by the bank may not be redeemable at their book value due to default, price risk or forced-sale risk.

Two additional sources of instability in the banking system stem first from the nature of the payments system and secondly from banks' increasing undertaking of business which involves contingent commitments. The payments system risk arises from the exposures created when funds are committed by a bank before final settlement. This is a feature of payment systems where settlement occurs at the end of the day. The last risk arises from transactions termed 'off balance sheet' as they do not appear on the balance sheet until the contingency arises. This is a feature of banking which relates more to the wholesale side although it is relevant to retail banking to the extent that most retail banks also undertake wholesale business. We leave discussion of the nature of off-balance-sheet business and its implications for regulation until the next chapter.

In this section we will examine first the nature of the two risks inherent in retail banking, identified above, and briefly examine the methods used by banks in their management. We will also consider the nature of payments risk and recent moves by the Bank of England to tackle this problem.

Liquidity risk

Bank deposits can be withdrawn at call or very short notice, whereas a large proportion of a bank's assets are illiquid (advances make up 70 per cent of sterling assets – see above). This practice of mismatching or maturity transformation, discussed further in chapter 2, exposes the bank to liquidity risk and as a consequence it is important that banks manage the inflow and outflow of their funds. The inflows and outflows of much of the funds passing through a bank are uncertain. Deposit inflows and outflows are largely uncertain and, on the assets side of the balance sheet, overdraft commitments introduce another element of uncertainty. The inflow and outflow of funds through a bank will be predictable to some extent on the basis of what has happened in the past. However, there will be a stochastic element to these flows and banks will have to structure their balance sheet in such a way that they can manage this uncertainty. A fundamental element in a bank's management of this uncertainty comes from the large scale of its operation and more importantly from a diversified base of deposit accounts. When a large number of uncertain net flows (deposit accounts) are combined then a greater degree of predictability is achieved. The basic principle here is that it is better to have a large number of small accounts than a small number of large accounts. This reduces the uncertainty of the bank's cash flows but the remaining uncertainty still needs to be managed.

We will examine the requirements set out by the Bank of England to ensure that banks adequately cover this liquidity risk in chapter 17. What we concentrate on here are the two main strategies that banks can adopt to manage this liquidity problem.

(i) *Reserve asset management*. Figure 3.1 simply illustrates the reserve asset management approach to liquidity risk.

Inflows in the form of new deposits and loan repayments are added to the holdings of cash and liquid assets. Loan repayments will clearly be a more predictable element of cash inflows, determined by the loans made in the past, although the bank will have to allow for potential default on repayment of the loan. The outflows, in the form of deposit withdrawals and new loans made, will deplete the holdings of cash and liquid assets. The illiquid loan portfolio is protected from an unexpectedly large net outflow of funds by the holding of a buffer stock of cash and liquid assets. That is, it will hold cash and liquid assets at a level above that which is required to meet the expected volatility of cash flows.

The assets held in liquid form do not have to be comprised only of cash with a zero rate of interest, and a tiering or maturity ladder approach is generally adopted whereby some of the reserve assets held are short term

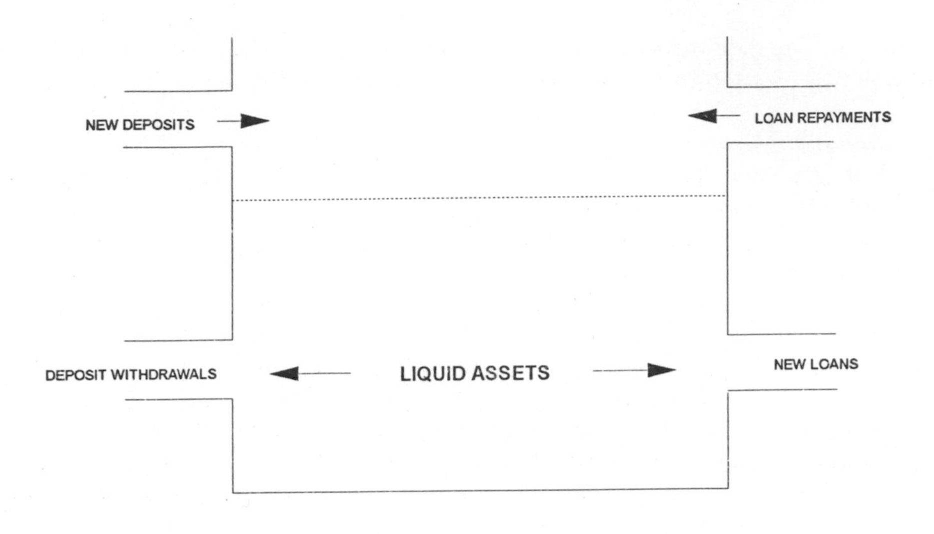

Figure 3.1

and therefore easily realisable assets, such as callable or overnight deposits, and others are longer term and therefore less easy to realise but still liquid because of their marketability, such as bills, certificates of deposit, government securities, and so on. By holding these liquid assets rather than just cash the bank is obtaining at least some return on its funds. However, the return is still less than that it would obtain on its main earning asset, which is advances.

(ii) *Liability management.* Liability management involves relying on instruments bearing market rates of interest to fund activity. At its most general it involves determining a desired quantity of assets and then adjusting interest rates to attract in the desired level of deposits to fund this. This is in contrast to reserve asset management, where interest rates are held constant, at least in the short term, and the scale of the asset portfolio is adjusted in line with the quantity of deposits attracted at that rate. The form that liability management takes depends on the market for funds where existing deposits are drawn. If a bank is reliant on retail deposits then, leaving aside its ability to vary other characteristics of the deposits such as term, in order to attract new deposits it has to increase the interest rate on all deposits. This makes the marginal cost of the additional funds raised high. The existence of a market for deposits where the bank is effectively a price taker, so its borrowing does not lead to a rise in the interest rate, means the marginal cost of the funds raised is reduced. As we describe in chapter 10, the inter-bank market is such a market in the UK. Banks can therefore use the inter-bank market as a marginal source of funds and for the marginal use of funds, so that at the end of a working day if the bank has a shortage of funds it can borrow short term from the inter-bank market, or if the bank has a surplus of funds it can lend short term. The existence of an inter-bank market means that banks can raise additional funds at a lower marginal cost than raising interest rates across the board and also more quickly than from retail sources. As a consequence, retail banks in the UK have largely moved away from reserve asset management to liability management as a technique of managing liquidity risk. It has to be noted though that inter-bank markets are not perfect and that banks are not pure price takers in these markets. There is therefore some uncertainty about the quantity and price of funds raised through these markets and hence banks still require some level of reserve assets as a back up. Note also that if there is a net shortage of funds in the banking system then banks have to look outside the inter-bank market to relieve this shortage.

Asset risk

The Bank of England (*Bank of England Quarterly Bulletin*, May 1980) identifies three ways in which a bank's assets are subject to the risk of a fall in value below that recorded in the balance sheet (their 'book value'). First, and most important in terms of the structure of the bank's assets, is the risk of default on the part of borrowers on the advances made by the bank. In chapter 2 we examined the ways in which a bank can manage the risk of default on its advances and we summarise these again here. As a first step a bank can minimise the risk of default on an individual advance by, for example, considering the use of the loaned funds and the financial circumstances of the borrower. Second, a bank can increase the predictability of default by spreading its loan portfolio over many borrowers, therefore enabling it to incorporate a premium in its lending interest rate to cover the effects of default. Finally, a bank can minimise the overall risk of default on its loan portfolio by diversifying over different types and regions of borrower.

A second asset risk considered by the Bank of England is investment risk, which relates to capital uncertain assets and refers to the risk of a price fall, thus reducing the value of the asset. The main capital uncertain asset held by banks are government securities and if the general level of interest rates increases then the value of the bank's government securities will decline.

The final risk considered by the Bank of England is forced-sale risk, which refers to the risk that the realisable value of the asset may fall below its book value if the asset has to be sold at short notice.

A bank's exposure to these risks is an important consideration in determining its solvency and we consider this in detail in chapter 17, which examines regulation and prudential control of banks by the Bank of England.

Payments risk

As we saw in section 3.3, a payments system provides for the transferring of funds between accounts at different institutions. In the UK, on an average day the payment systems process 16 million transactions with a total value of over £160 billion. We can separate payment systems into two types: wholesale and retail. Of the wholesale type, dealing with large-value, same-day, sterling transfers, the main system is the Clearing House Automated Payments System (CHAPS). CHAPS regularly processed daily payments of £100 billion through its 16 member banks in 1994. Of the retail payment systems, the cheque clearing and credit clearing systems deal with cheques and paper items, respectively. In addition, there is the Bankers' Automated Clearing Services (BACS), which is an electronic clearing house for items such as standing orders and direct debits.

CHAPS allows a bank to make guaranteed and irrevocable sterling credits to other banks in the system, either on its own account or on behalf of customers. At the end of the day, final debit and credit balances for each member bank are calculated and net settlements are made through settlement accounts held at the Bank of England. One type of risk that arises with this type of system is known as receiver risk. This arises when a system member provides funds to its customers, having received a payment instruction from another member but before final settlement. The receiving bank that has offered irrevocable funds to its customers is exposed to the sending bank until final settlement occurs at the end of the day. Those customers receiving funds prior to settlement may then initiate further transfers, creating additional obligations for their settlement banks. This may be repeated several times during a day, building up large exposures. If one of the settlement banks were to fail before final settlement the other members would be deprived of the funds needed to fund their own payments. Thus, a failure at one bank may lead to settlement failures at other banks and create a systemic crisis.

One solution to this problem is to move from end-of-day net settlement to real-time gross settlement. This requires that all inter-bank transactions are recorded in the accounts of the central bank as they occur. It is then possible to structure the system so that a settlement bank receives an incoming payment instruction only once the payment has been settled by the central bank. Thus, there is little scope for them to pass funds to their customers before final settlement. Such a system is due to be implemented in the UK by the end of 1995 (see *Bank of England Quarterly Bulletin*, May 1994).

3.5 The role of the Bank of England

The Bank of England (hereafter just termed the Bank) performs a wide range of activities in the UK financial system. In the remainder of this

Table 3.3 *Bank of England: balance sheet as at 29 December 1993 (£million)*

Liabilities		*Assets*	
Issue Department			
Notes in circulation	19,378	Government securities	5,924
Notes in Banking Department	12	Other securities	3,466
Banking Department			
Public deposits	3,330	Government securities	1,076
Special deposits[a]	0	Advances and other accounts	9,674
Bankers' deposits	1,458	Premises, equipment and other securities	444
Reserves and other accounts	6,433	Notes and coins	11

[a] This item refers to additional interest-bearing deposits which the Bank reserves the right to call from banks. Such deposits constitute an additional instrument in the Bank's armoury for monetary control purposes but have not been used since the early 1980s, hence the 0 entry.

Source: *Bank of England Statistical Abstract*, 1994, table 1.

chapter we will outline these activities, some of which we will discuss in greater detail in later chapters.

The Bank of England was formally recognised as a central bank by the 1946 Bank of England Act, which effectively nationalised the Bank. Prior to this Act, from its establishment in 1694, the Bank had carried out the functions of a central bank, but operated as a private concern. Under the Act the subordinate status of the Bank to the Treasury was statutorily established. In practice, whilst the Bank and the Treasury may arrive at policies, for example on when to cut interest rates, by discussion, it is ultimately the politically controlled Treasury which holds sway. This has led to some discussion as to whether the Bank should be made independent of the government, as some other central banks operate, and we will briefly examine the arguments later in this section. First of all though we will describe the structure of the Bank and then outline its main functions.

The Bank is separated into two departments for accounting purposes (see table 3.3): the Issue Department, which is treated as being part of the government, and the Banking Department, which is a public corporation. The Issue Department has as liabilities notes in circulation or held by the Banking Department. Whilst it was possible to call upon the Bank to redeem these notes for gold up until 1931, since that date the note issue has been a fiduciary one backed by securities. These securities, held as assets by the Issue Department, include government securities as well as privately issued securities such as commercial bills.

The Banking Department obtains its deposits from two main sources. First, acting as banker to central government, it has the item referred to as 'public deposits', which represents the consolidated accounts of the various revenue collecting and spending departments of the government. Second, it has 'bankers' deposits', which include the mandatory deposits of UK banks, set at 0.35 per cent of eligible deposits – discussed in section 3.2, as well as additional balances held by retail banks which form part of their cash reserves as they are redeemable for notes and coins on demand. The remainder of the Banking Department's liabilities are made up of accounts held by other bodies such as overseas governments and central banks, capital and reserves. The assets of the Banking Department include: first, government securities, which comprise government bonds, Treasury bills and ways-and-means advances to the government; second, advances and other accounts, which include short-term loans to discount houses and holdings of commercial bill; and third, notes and coins, which represent the reserve held by the Bank to meet any deposit withdrawals.

Bankers' bank

By holding balances at the Bank of England, banks are able to settle any inter-bank indebtedness in a convenient way. This works through the operation of a clearing house, so that at the end of a working day, the net debts between any two banks are settled by means of an appropriate transfer of funds between the two banks' accounts at the Bank of England. A further role played by the Bank under this heading is that of note issuing. If the general public increase their demand for notes then this will show up as a decrease in notes held by the banks. The banks can then replenish their stocks by exchanging for notes their balances held at the Bank. The Banking Department in turn can replenish its stock of notes, if required, by authorising a change in the fiduciary issue from the Issue Department. The resulting transfer of notes from the Issue Department to the Banking Department will generate a corresponding balancing transfer of securities in the opposite direction.

Lender of last resort

The Bank's role here works on two levels. On a day-to-day basis, when the banking system as a whole runs short of cash then it is ultimately the Bank which restores the cash position of the banks. However, unlike in many other countries, the banks do not borrow cash directly from the Bank but receive assistance via the discount houses. Thus, a cash shortage for the banks would be reflected by the banks recalling loans made to the discount houses. The discount houses obtain the cash to pay the banks from the Bank, which stands ready to offset any cash shortages by open market purchases of bills from, or by lending to, the discount market. As the Bank is acting as lender of last resort in this situation, then the terms at which the Bank is prepared to lend have implications for the level of short-term interest rates and ultimately for the level of interest rates generally. We examine the operation of the discount market in greater detail in chapter 10.

The Bank also adopted the role of lender of last resort to any bank or group of banks experiencing liquidity problems. The Bank's aim here is to maintain the stability of the banking system. As the banking system is based on confidence then the failure of one or more banks can rapidly lead to a collapse in confidence in the banking system generally. A classic example of the Bank acting in this role was the operation of the 'lifeboat' to help a number of secondary banks in 1974/75. We examine the 'lifeboat' operation in more detail in chapter 17.

Regulation of banks

As the Bank ultimately guarantees the stability of banking through its role as lender of last resort then in order to minimise any moral hazard which may result from this, that is, banks acting imprudently as they know they will be bailed out if they get into difficulties, the Bank also undertakes prudential regulation of banks. Prudential regulation in the UK is based on flexible supervision of individual banks. Supervision by the Bank has tended to concentrate on two areas of banking: (i) the entry and establishment of banks, and (ii) the risks of the activities undertaken by banks. With regard to the first aspect of supervision, the Bank has required authorisation of banks subject to specified criteria, and has the ability to revoke such authorisation in the event of wrongdoing. Supervision of the risks of banks' activity has focused on monitoring the liquidity and capital adequacy of banks. We consider such prudential regulation in chapter 17.

Managing monetary policy

The Bank is the agent of government policy. In this role it manages the marketable securities, mainly government bonds, which form the bulk of the outstanding government debt. It regulates the redemption of maturing issues and the issue of new securities so as to preserve an orderly market. The main techniques of the Bank's operations in this regard are considered in chapter 9. The other channel through which the Bank pursues government monetary policy is through its operations in the discount market. As we have indicated above, the Bank can alter the level of short-term interest rates through its dealings with the discount houses. Government international monetary policy is administered by the Bank's management of the Exchange Equalisation Account (EEA). This account comprises the nation's gold and foreign currency reserves and by intervention in the foreign exchange markets, that is, by buying or selling sterling through this account, the official policy on the exchange rate can be pursued.

Independence of the Bank of England

As we have noted above, the politically controlled Treasury has the ultimate say on the monetary policy objectives which are pursued by the Bank. In such a situation there is a temptation for a government to finance its current borrowing requirement and to reduce its real burden of accumulated debt through increasing the money supply, thereby leading to inflation. There are also some suggestions that over the 1980s the government has relaxed monetary policy at politically convenient times, for example in the period leading up to a general election, rather than pursued the monetary policy most appropriate for reducing or controlling inflationary pressures. This has prompted serious consideration of the question of central bank independence. Examples of independent central banks are the German Bundesbank, established in 1957, and the US Federal Reserve System ('the Fed'), established in 1913. The legislation governing both these central banks includes the pursuit of price stability. However, this is just one of many economic and monetary objectives in the governing legislation and neither central bank is legally required to make price stability its prime concern. The legislation does assign a great deal of power over economic and monetary policy to these unelected bodies, which inevitably brings them into conflict with the elected government of the country. Indeed, the lack of accountability of an independent central bank is often cited as a counter-argument to independence. However, this argument fails to take into account the fact that the independence of a central bank is not permanently guaranteed, as the government could introduce new legislation to remove its independence. Central banks such as the Bundesbank and the Fed maintain their autonomy by being accepted as legitimate. The Bundesbank obtains its legitimacy through the widespread popular support it enjoys in Germany, which has come from its achievement of low and stable inflation, and this has assisted the economic success of the country. The legitimacy of the Fed has been achieved largely as a result of successive Fed chairmen exploiting the conflict between President and Congress built into the US constitution.

In recent years many countries have adopted or made progress towards adopting legislative proposals removing their central banks from government control. Between 1989 and 1991 the central banks of New Zealand, Chile and Canada were made independent. From 1992, following the agreement in Europe of the Maastricht Treaty, the central banks of the European Union (EU) (except for Denmark and the UK, which have reserved the right not to join the monetary union) have introduced legislation or are committed to introducing legislation to make their central banks more independent. In 1993 the governments of Brazil and Mexico announced proposals to make their central banks more independent. In view of these developments it is therefore helpful to examine the empirical evidence on the relationship between central bank independence and economic performance.

One of the first empirical studies of this kind was that of Bade and Parkin [1988], who examined the relationship between the degree of central bank independence and inflation for 12 countries of the Organization for Economic Co-operation and Development (OECD) in the post-Bretton Woods era. Central bank independence was split into two types: financial independence, as measured by the government's ability to set salary levels for members of the governing board of the central bank, to control the central bank's budget and to allocate its profits; and policy independence, as indicated by the government's role in appointing members of the governing board of the bank, government representation on the board and whether the government was the final policy authority. Bade and Parkin found that financial independence was not a significant determinant of inflation outcome, but policy independence had a role to play. Alesina [1989] extended the Bade and Parkin study by adding four more countries to the analysis and also found an inverse relationship between the degree of central bank independence and inflation outcome. Grilli *et al.* [1991] separated independence into two categories: economic and political. The political measure was similar to the Bade and Parkin measure of policy independence whilst the economic measure included factors such as the government's ability to borrow from the central bank and the policy instruments under the control of the central bank. For the 1970s they found both measures of independence were significantly and inversely correlated with inflation whilst for the 1980s only the economic measure was significant. Alesina and Summers [1993] constructed a measure of independence based on an average of the indexes used by Bade and Parkin and Grilli *et al.* and found a negative relationship between independence and inflation over the full sample period of 1955–88 and for the post-Bretton Woods era. A more comprehensive study has been undertaken by Cukierman [1992] for the period 1950–89. He extended the work of the previous studies by using not only legal or de jure measures of independence but also practical measures which attempt to capture the actual or de facto independence of the central bank. The measures of de facto independence included the frequency of turnover of central bank governors and the responses to a questionnaire from qualified individuals from central banks. In addition, Cukierman extended the study to 70 countries by including less developed countries in addition to the developed countries included in previous work. Cukierman also found that the degree of central bank independence affects the rate of inflation in the expected negative direction, with the relationship being stronger for developed countries.

Most of the empirical evidence therefore suggests that creating an independent central bank will improve a county's inflation performance.

There are however a number of weaknesses with studies of this kind, as highlighted by Pollard [1993]. Most of the studies create indexes of independence by identifying a relevant set of factors and then looking for compliance with the factors in the central bank charters, with each factor being given an equal weight in constructing the index. Thus, in the study by Grilli *et al.* the factor that the governor's term of office must exceed that of the political term of office is given the same weighting as the factor that no government approval is required for the central bank in setting monetary policy. Clearly, the latter factor has more bearing on the central bank's actions. The only study that attempts a weighting of the criteria is that of Cukierman but here the weights are subjective. Another problem with the analysis is that most of the studies use a legal or de jure measure of independence, which may not reflect the actual or de facto experience of the central banks. Cukierman in fact examines the relationship between a legal index of independence and a measure of de facto independence based on his questionnaire results. A correlation between the legal and de facto measures of 0.33 for developed countries suggests that a legal measure may give misleading results. A further concern with these studies is that most of them consider only central bank independence as a determinant of inflation. When other determinants of inflation are included in the analysis it is possible that central bank independence may have no role to play. As a final point, a negative correlation between central bank independence and inflation does not necessarily imply causality. Countries averse to inflation, such as Germany, may formalise this aversion through the creation of an independent central bank. Thus, it is inflation aversion in a country which is the causal factor in explaining low inflation and the policy of making a central bank independent in a country where there is not sufficient aversion to inflation among the public and policy makers may not yield the desired outcome in the long run.

3.6 **Conclusion**

In this chapter we have considered the nature of retail banks, the risks involved in retail banking and the strategies available to banks to manage these risks. We have also outlined the main roles of the Bank of England and discussed the merits of making it more independent of government. We pointed out at the beginning of this chapter that it has become increasingly difficult to separate retail banks from wholesale banks in practice as most retail banks also undertake wholesale banking operations. To complete our picture of banking we therefore turn in the next chapter to consider the nature of wholesale and international banking and some of the issues that have affected such banking over the 1980s and 1990s.

Chapter 4

Wholesale and international banking

4.1 Introduction

In the last chapter we examined the nature of retail banking in the UK and noted that the distinction between this type of banking and wholesale banking has become increasingly blurred over recent years. To complete our discussion of banking we therefore turn in this chapter to examine the nature of wholesale banking. This type of banking can be further separated into domestic and international. We begin by examining the general nature of wholesale banking in section 4.2. This examination relates to activities which are captured on the balance sheet. An increasing amount of business of wholesale banks does not appear on the balance sheet and is termed 'off-balance-sheet' business. We discuss the nature, causes and consequences of this type of business in section 4.3. In section 4.4 we discuss the nature of eurocurrency banking, which is now the most dominant form of international banking. Finally in section 4.5 we consider the issue of sovereign lending, that is, lending by banks to sovereign countries. A boom in this type of lending over the 1970s led to consequences which blighted the international banking system over the 1980s, although recent initiatives appear to have provided a framework for a lasting solution.

4.2 Nature of wholesale banking

A large number of banks which operate in the UK do not come under the category of retail banks as defined in the last chapter. These banks are a heterogeneous group and the Bank of England, in its statistical analysis, separates them on the basis of the country where the headquarters are located and then for the non-retail UK banks further subdivides these to identify those operating as merchant banks. At 31 December 1993 the breakdown of non-retail banks operating in the UK was as follows:

(i) British merchant banks (27) – members of the British Merchant Bankers and Securities Houses Association (formerly the Accepting Houses Committee). Merchant banks have traditionally financed commerce and trade by the 'accepting' of bills. Their activities are now much broader and include direct lending to industry, underwriting new issues and providing advice on mergers, acquisitions, portfolio management, and so on.
(ii) Other British banks (114). This group captures all financial institutions registered as banks which are not included in the retail and merchant bank categories. As a consequence the activities of these institutions are diverse, ranging from small regional banks to finance houses, leasing companies and other specialised institutions, some of which are the subsidiaries of retail banks.
(iii) American banks (35).
(iv) Japanese banks (37).
(v) Other overseas banks (242).

Most banks today are to some degree multi-product banks. As we noted in chapter 3, most retail banks also operate in the wholesale markets, but the converse is not true since the non-retail banks tend to operate solely or mainly in wholesale markets. We now examine the balance sheets of these different categories of wholesale banks, so as to identify some of the aspects of wholesale banking and in particular those features which distinguish it from retail banking. The sterling and foreign currency breakdown of the deposits of the different categories of banks is provided in table 4.1.

One salient feature of wholesale banking, revealed in table 4.1, which contrasts with retail banking is the large size of deposits and loans and

Table 4.1 *Sterling and foreign currency breakdown of the deposits of non-retail banks (as at end December 1993) (£million)*

	Sterling	*Foreign currency*	*Sterling sight as a % of total sterling*
British merchant banks	26,271	22,683	23
Other British banks	30,437	7,878	14
Japanese banks	31,331	196,580	6
American banks	15,411	87,839	26
Other overseas banks	100,973	356,528	10

Source: *Bank of England Statistical Abstract*, 1994, tables 2.5, 2.6, 2.7, 2.8, 2.10.

Table 4.2 *Assets of non-retail banks operating in the UK at 30 December 1993 (£million)*

	Merchant banks	*Other UK banks*	*Japanese banks*	*American banks*	*Overseas banks*
Sterling					
Notes and coins and balances at the Bank of England	65	91	98	178	267
Market loans	11,009	6,715	12,603	5,256	41,390
Bills	44	279	179	38	244
Advances	12,678	28,639	14,796	9,062	55,175
Investments	13,059	1,549	2,505	2,085	7,568
Total sterling assets	29,768	37,137	30,040	16,638	104,744
Foreign currency[a]					
Market loans	10,591	6,891	145,774	55,245	218,294
Advances	5,924	2,217	35,861	18,127	78,241
Bills, investments etc.	12,351	2435	21,955	17,184	76,667
Total foreign currency[a]	28,786	11,543	203,590	90,556	373,202

[a] Selected foreign currency assets – some miscellaneous assets excluded.
Source: *Bank of England Statistical Abstract*, 1994, tables 2.5, 2.6, 2.7, 2.8, 2.10.

consequently the smaller number of depositors and borrowers. Minimum values for sterling deposits and loans are typically £250,000 and £500,000, respectively. The structure of the sterling deposits of these wholesale banks is also quite different from retail banks. For sterling deposits, the sight element is considerably lower for non-retail banks, with merchant banks and American banks showing the largest proportions at 23 per cent and 26 per cent respectively (see table 4.1), compared with 50 per cent for retail banks. This reflects the absence of these banks from retail banking. Approximately 30 per cent of sterling wholesale deposits are inter-bank (i.e. deposits of one bank placed with another bank – see chapter 10 for further discussion), the remainder being mainly time deposits from UK private companies and overseas companies and banks. For the foreign currency business a much larger proportion (approximately 70 per cent) of wholesale deposits are inter-bank.

One other feature of wholesale banking, indicated in the table 4.1, is the greater extent of foreign currency business for both British and overseas banks when compared with retail banks (where foreign currency deposits accounted for approximately 26 per cent). The overseas banks though, whilst engaging in a considerable amount of sterling wholesale business, are more heavily involved in foreign currency business. The reasons why overseas banks locate in the UK but deal mainly in foreign currencies is explored in section 4.4.

The assets held by non-retail banks are summarised in table 4.2, again broken down by type of bank.

Non-retail banks, because the nature of their business is low-volume, large-value and hence unlikely to be conducted through cash transactions, require little in the way of cash balances. Much of the first item in table 4.2 is made up of the compulsory cash balance which the Bank of England requires of all banks. In terms of sterling assets, market loans are clearly important, with the main item here being inter-bank loans – the counterpart to inter-bank deposits. Compared with retail banks, a larger proportion of sterling assets of non-retail banks is accounted for by market loans. The extent to which overseas banks based in the UK have become involved in domestic UK activity is revealed in table 4.2. Taken together, overseas banks accounted for 19 per cent of total sterling lending to the UK private sector. A significant part of this lending was directed towards large construction projects, including the Canary Wharf development in the London Docklands and the Channel Tunnel. As is also the case for the liabilities side of the balance sheet, foreign currency assets form a significant proportion of total assets. This is particularly pronounced for non-British banks. Reference back to table 4.1 illustrates a fair degree of currency matching, since foreign currency assets for each category of bank are similar in total to foreign currency liabilities.

A common hypothesis about wholesale banks is that they aim to 'match' the term to maturity of their liabilities and assets. So, for example, a £100,000 three-month certificate of deposit in its liability portfolio may be used to finance the purchase of a three-month commercial bill of value £100,000. Under this hypothesis wholesale banks are simply liquidity distributors or brokers of liquid assets and do not produce liquidity by undertaking maturity transformation. It is sometimes argued that wholesale banks cannot mismatch because, unlike retail banks, they typically have a small number of large-value deposits and therefore cannot rely on the law of large numbers effect which comes from having a large number of small-value deposits. This effect, as we saw in chapter 3, makes net withdrawals of deposits more predictable so that, it is claimed, in the face of uncertainty wholesale banks will aim to match the maturity of its assets with those of its liabilities. If wholesale banks are simply distributing liquidity then the justification for the existence of such banks is dependent solely on their ability to reduce the costs of liquidity distribution to a lower level than would exist if borrowers and lenders sought out each other directly. As we saw in chapter 2, banks can reduce costs in credit markets through specialisation, which enables them to achieve economies of scale in their lending and borrowing operations. However, unlike the normal type of financial intermediation described in chapter 2, there will be no reflection of the liquidity generated by the bank in its interest rate margin as no liquidity is being generated. Of course this does not preclude other types of transformation, such as risk transformation.

We now turn to examine whether there is any evidence to support the hypothesis of matching by wholesale banks. The Bank of England has published the results of a survey of retail and non-retail banks operating in London, which show the maturity profiles of the aggregate asset and liability portfolios at the end of January 1987. These results (also presented in Lewis and Davis [1987]) are shown in table 4.3.

It should be noted that the figures in table 4.3 refer to business with non-banks, that is, the inter-bank positions are netted out, as these positions will be matched positions in aggregate. The figures for business with non-banks reveal considerable mismatching by wholesale banks, with the overwhelming majority of deposits having a maturity of under three months whilst a majority of assets have a maturity of over one year. The main features of this mismatching are: (i) similarity in the degree of maturity mismatching between sterling and foreign currency business; (ii) wholesale banks whilst significantly mismatching appear do this to a lesser extent than retail banks – for example, for retail banks roughly 84 per cent of deposits fall in the category 0–7 days and 66 per cent of assets have a maturity of over three years, whereas for British merchant banks the figures are 53 per cent and 42 per cent respectively; and (iii) British wholesale banks appear to mismatch to a greater extent than overseas banks – in their operations in London.

This evidence therefore does not support the view that wholesale banks are only liquidity distributors but rather that they transform the maturity characteristic of the funds flowing through the institution, albeit to a lesser extent than for retail banks. This result begs the question of how they are able to engage in maturity transformation and hence liquidity production for their non-bank customers when they do not have the advantage of the retail banks of the law of large numbers effect. That is, how do wholesale banks manage their liquidity risks? A related problem is that, given the small number of advances on the assets side of the balance sheet, there is less scope for pooling and diversifying default risks than with retail banking. The solution to the problem of liquidity risk is provided first by the practice of liability management, which, as we discussed in chapter 3, involves banks having access to inter-bank borrowings and other market-based deposits as an immediate source of funds to replace any shortfall in the event of maturing or withdrawn deposits. A second strategy, which has become increasingly available to banks since the mid-1980s, is the securitisation or marketisation of assets. This involves transforming

Table 4.3 *Maturity analysis of sterling and foreign currency business with non-bank customers of retail and wholesale banks in the UK as at end January 1987 (%)*

	Sterling						*Foreign currency*			
	Retail banks		*British non-retail banks*		*Overseas banks*		*All banks*		*British banks*	
	A	*L*	*A*	*L*	*A*	*L*	*A*	*L*	*A*	*L*
0–7 days	3.54	83.51	13.98	52.83	12.64	41.29	11.96	38.15	11.11	47.95
8 days–1 month	3.49	7.89	3.09	18.74	12.75	21.97	11.00	23.97	8.20	20.70
1–3 months	6.18	6.28	6.27	15.61	15.35	20.88	13.71	18.15	10.21	17.19
3–6 months	5.01	1.00	6.19	4.36	5.69	5.16	9.33	6.87	7.86	6.71
6 months–1 year	5.91	0.67	10.42	4.70	7.20	4.03	6.09	2.68	6.61	2.29
1–3 years	10.21	0.24	18.11	1.83	12.65	2.37	13.11	2.02	15.20	1.74
Over 3 years	65.68	0.41	41.94	1.93	33.72	4.30	34.80	8.16	40.81	3.42

A = Assets.
L = Liabilities.
Source: Bank of England, *Sterling Business Analysed by Maturity and Sector*, March 1987; Bank of England, *Maturity Analysis by Sector of Liabilities and Claims in Foreign Currencies*, March 1987.

previously illiquid assets such as mortgages into marketable instruments which can then be sold on to a third party. This phenomenon is discussed in more detail under 'Asset-backed securitisation' below and is one aspect of the more general process of securitisation, which refers to the switch away from indirect, bank financing to direct financing through the capital markets observed since the mid-1980s (discussed in chapter 12). The solution to the problem of default risk has been for wholesale banks to form 'syndicates' to spread the default risk of a large loan over a number of banks. This is examined further in section 4.4.

The discussion of wholesale banking so far has focused on the activities which appear on the balance sheet. We now examine the growing phenomena of off-balance-sheet business.

Asset-backed securitisation

An asset-backed security (ABS) is a tradeable instrument supported by a pool of loans. The main type of ABS created in recent years is one based on a pool of residential mortgages. The creation of an ABS in the UK involves the bank removing some of its loans from its balance sheet, placing them with a special purpose vehicle which finances its holdings by selling ABSs to investors. This process, also known as securitisation, adds marketability to assets which would otherwise have very little liquidity. A detailed discussion of the ABS market in the UK can be found in Twinn [1994].

The first issue of an ABS was in the US during the 1970s. The first issue in the UK came in 1985 and the UK ABS market is now the second largest in the world. However, in the UK only a small proportion of lending has been securitised. The total number of issues by December 1993 was 94, with a principal of £16 billion compared with a total amount lent by banks and building societies of £640 billion. Nevertheless, the UK market is growing rapidly and the structure of lending is likely to change as a consequence.

The main advantage of ABSs for the lender is that by removing assets from the balance sheet (provided the relevant risks are transferred to the investors) the institution frees up capital for other uses. Securitisation also allows an institution to concentrate on those aspects of the lending business in which it has a comparative advantage. Thus, for example, a small building society may feel it is more efficient at originating loans and so once the loans are obtained can securitise the assets and sell them to institutions more efficient at securing the necessary funding. Another use of securitisation to a lender is that when it feels overexposed to a particular sector or set of borrowers it can securitise part of its lending. The main attraction of ABSs to an investor is the margin they offer over other highly rated bonds. They also allow investors an opportunity to diversify their portfolios, increasing their exposure in areas to which they may not have direct access.

The common structure for an ABS issue in the UK is similar to the US 'pass through'. Here an originator separates suitable assets from its portfolio, normally assets of similar quality and repayment calendar. These assets are then sold to a special purpose vehicle (SPV), thus providing a legal separation of the assets from the originator. The SPV then sells securities to investors to fund the purchase of the assets which it holds in a trust on their behalf. The issued securities will normally have at least one credit rating in order to make them attractive to investors (see chapter 9, section 9.5). In addition, most issues have credit enhancement in order to boost the credit rating. A credit enhancement provides a degree of assurance to investors that the principal and coupon payments will be paid in a timely manner. Various methods of credit enhancement are used, with the most common, until recently, being an insurance contract. An ABS is normally issued as a floating-rate note (see chapter 12), paying the London inter-bank offer rate plus a margin.

As mentioned above, the UK ABS market is small but growing. Recently a wider range of assets than mortgages have been securitised. It is anticipated that as banks and building societies expand their lending and come up against capital constraints, ABS issues may be an attractive alternative to an equity issue if retained earnings cannot be accumulated quickly enough.

4.3 **Off-balance-sheet business**

Off-balance-sheet business refers to business undertaken by a bank which generates a contingent commitment and generally an income to the bank without the business being captured on the balance sheet under conventional accounting procedures. This type of business has long been undertaken by banks but has grown rapidly in both volume and scope over the 1980s. In this section we will examine the nature of off-balance-sheet business and the reasons for its growth in recent years. In order to consider the latter we broaden the picture to examine more generally the causes of financial innovation. Finally we examine some of the implications of off-balance-sheet business, in particular its implications for the regulation of banks.

Types of off-balance-sheet business

If we consider first of all the narrow definition of off-balance-sheet business, that is, activities giving rise to contingent commitments, then four broad areas can be identified.

(i) *Loan commitments*. This covers any advance commitment by a bank to provide credit. Examples are: revolving lines of credit, where a bank provides a line of credit to which it is committed often for several years ahead; overdrafts, where a bank has agreed a facility but can withdraw it in certain circumstances; and note issuance facilities (see chapter 12), where the bank provides credit only in the event of others being unable to. Provision of these commitments generates a fee income for banks.

(ii) *Guarantees.* This involves a bank in underwriting the obligations of a third party, thus relieving the counterparty from having to assess the ability of the customer to meet the terms of the contract. Examples of such guarantees are acceptances, whereby the bank guarantees payment of a customer's liability to a holder of her or his debt, and performance bonds, which support the good name of a customer and her or his ability to perform under a particular contract. The bank receives a fee for providing such guarantees.

(iii) *Swap and hedging transactions.* These involve the bank in a transaction using one of the recently developed 'derivative' instruments such as swaps, forward contracts, options, financial futures, interest caps, collars, and so on. Many of these instruments are discussed further in chapters 11, 13 and 14. The transaction can be hedged (to neutralise a position exposure) or unhedged (left open to exposure).

(iv) *Securities underwriting.* Investment banks and merchant banks are involved in underwriting issues of securities, whereby they agree to buy a set amount of the securities which are not taken up in an issue. This guarantees the issuer that the whole of the issue is taken up and a fee is paid to the banks providing the underwriting service.

All the above examples involve the bank in a commitment which may or may not lead to a balance sheet entry in the future. There are a wide range of other financial services provided by banks which generate fee income and where the business does not lead to a balance sheet entry. These include loan origination, trust and advice services, brokerage and agency services and payments services such as the provision of credit cards

Table 4.4 *Fee or commission income*[a] *as a percentage of net interest income for Barclays Bank Group*

1980	*1982*	*1984*	*1986*	*1988*	*1989*
29	34	41	45	52	53

[a] Fee or commissions from banking and related services plus foreign exchange trading income plus securities trading income (since 1986 when, after Big Bang, banks have been allowed to own a securities trading firm).
Source: Published accounts.

and cash management systems. The total income of a bank can be roughly split into net interest income, that is, the margin between its lending and borrowing rates, and fee or commission income. The relative growth in fee or commission income and other non-interest income (excluding capital gains from selling investments) over the 1980s for Barclays Bank Group, shown in table 4.4, illustrates a general trend for the UK clearing banks.

The relative growth in fee or commission income reflects both a growth in contingent commitment business and attempts by banks to diversify into related financial services such as selling insurance policies and securities trading. In the remainder of this section we concentrate on the nature of contingent commitment banking, which we will call off-balance-sheet business whilst recognising that this term covers a wider range of activities.

Nature of contingent commitment banking

It is traditional to view a bank as a collection of assets and liabilities making up its balance sheet. We have already discussed in chapters 2 and 3 why banks engage in the traditional business of borrowing and lending, in terms of lenders delegating the collection and use of information to banks and sharing risks with banks, in return for a charge obtained from the interest rate spread. Banks are able to perform these services at a lower cost than ultimate lenders by specialising in collecting and skilfully using information about credit risks, thereby leading to a better selection of risks and, because of their size of operations, enabling them to pool and diversify risks more effectively. Lewis [1987] argues that banks perform similar information and risk sharing roles when they undertake off-balance-sheet activities. For example, the establishment of a loan commitment, such as an overdraft, reduces the liquidity risk faced by the customer but exposes the bank to greater liquidity risk, which it is better able to bear through its size of operations and access to the wholesale markets. When a bank provides a guarantee of a customer's ability to meet her or his debts, as with a bill acceptance, then this leads to a lower interest rate being required by the market. When looked at from the lender, or bill holder, viewpoint the effect is akin to a depositor accepting a lower rate of interest from a bank because of the safety provided by the bank compared with holding a primary security. Other transformations of asset characteristics performed on the balance sheet have their equivalent off the balance sheet. Note issuance facilities provide an example of maturity transformation, where issues of short-term paper generate longer-term funding. When banks make available a syndicated loan, the borrower can negotiate the terms of the loan, including the interest rate basis, the currency and the date at which the loan is to be drawn down. All these choices can be made off balance sheet as well by means of currency swaps, interest rate basis swaps and financial futures contracts to alter draw down dates.

Factors ...
The moti ... y.
One mot ... he
that this ... se.
More ge ... he
liberalis ... as
allowed ... he
conting ... of
comme ... the
banks h ... es.
Other p ... ons
trading ... ng,
have er ... ged
positio ... ce-
sheet b ... ent
and th ... r to
examin ... n to
consider the factors determining financial innovation.

As we saw in chapter 1, a financial instrument can be described by its underlying characteristics of liquidity, risk, and so on. Financial innovation, as related to financial instruments, can be defined as the process of unbundling the characteristics and repackaging them to create new instruments. Indeed, recent developments have made it easier to unbundle and repackage the characteristics of an instrument even after it has been issued. For example, a ten-year, fixed-rate, dollar-denominated eurobond represents a particular package of characteristics. Any of these characteristics can be unpackaged and traded separately. The holder of the bond can swap the currency to yen or swap the fixed-interest stream to a floating rate. This example illustrates the fungibility of financial instruments compared with physical products. The demand for financial innovation can be explained by reference to a number of factors, which are discussed below (see Bank for International Settlements [1986] for further discussion).

(i) *Changes in the financial environment*. Changes of policy regimes over the last 20 years have led to greater volatility of asset prices. In particular, the general move to floating exchange rates in the early 1970s after the breakdown of the Bretton Woods agreement and the adoption of monetary aggregates as intermediate policy targets have increased the scope for fluctuations in exchange rates and interest rates (see figures 14.1 and 14.2 for an illustration of this). The greater the volatility of asset prices and other prices, such as commodities, the greater is the uncertainty about future prices and hence the greater demand for instruments for hedging exchange rate and interest rate risk. We examine hedging strategies in greater detail in chapter 14.

(ii) *Greater perception of credit risks*. There was a deterioration in the credit standing of banks which had large exposures to the debts of less developed countries (LDCs) following the onset of the debt crisis in 1982 – discussed in section 4.5. One consequence of this was a desire by some banks to sell or swap some problem debts to diversify extreme exposures, and so a secondary market in LDC debt emerged (although not used to a significant extent to date). A further consequence of the decline in the credit standing of many banks was that investors were more wary of lending to banks and therefore were more willing to hold the direct securities of ultimate borrowers. In addition, large borrowers with good credit standing found they could obtain better terms by issuing their own securities through the capital markets rather than borrowing directly from banks. One result of this was some shift away from bank intermediation and towards capital market instruments as a source of financing – a process known as securitisation and discussed in chapter 12. Banks, however, sought to benefit from this trend by securitising packages of their own loans so they could be sold on and by expanding their role in guaranteeing and underwriting securities issues so as to increase their fee income.

(iii) *Arbitrage opportunities in capital markets*. The existence of barriers, such as exchange controls, interest rate controls and reserve ratios, separating banking markets in different countries led to the development of eurocurrency banking. This in turn put pressure on domestic markets to lessen controls, thus eventually creating a global short-term money market. A similar process is occurring in the capital markets. Barriers separating capital markets have led to the emergence of eurobond and euronote markets (see chapter 12). However, the process of globalisation of capital markets is still incomplete, leaving banks to exploit arbitrage opportunities. The use of the swap transaction (see chapter 13) has enabled a borrower to raise funds in the capital market in which it has a comparative advantage and then swap the principal and interest on those funds to the currency in which it wishes to borrow. For example, a UK company which has a comparative advantage with its issues of sterling bonds but wanting to raise US dollars can issue a sterling eurobond and then swap with a US company wishing to raise sterling but with a comparative advantage in the issue of dollar bonds.

Two factors which have had a major influence on the supply of innovations have been increased regulatory pressures and developments in technology.

(i) *Increased regulatory pressures*. One consequence of the deterioration in bank credits over the 1980s (see above) has been greater pressure from bank regulators for increased levels of capital in banking. The need to operate on higher capital ratios and the greater cost of raising additional capital due to their reduced credit standing led banks to pursue business that was not subject to capital adequacy controls, that is, off-balance-sheet business. Thus, banks actively contributed to the development and growth in use of instruments such as swaps, options, note issuance facilities etc. Another consequence of increased capital pressures was the development of securitisation, whereby banks packaged up parts of their loan portfolio (e.g. mortgages) so that they could be sold on in markets.

(ii) *Technology*. Advances in computing, information processing and telecommunications technology have enabled more complex instruments to be designed and priced on a continuous basis. In particular, they have enabled the complex financial engineering of already issued financial products, as described above, to take place.

Implications of the growth in off-balance-sheet business

The growth in off-balance-sheet business has been largely the result of the interaction of the demand and supply factors described above. An important implication of this growth stems from one factor in particular, which is the desire of banks to escape capital adequacy controls. This has concerned the regulatory authorities as banks have taken on risks which are not explicitly related to the bank's capital. These risks are similar to the risks faced by banks in their on-balance-sheet activities but are heightened by the greater uncertainty arising from the novelty of many of the instruments traded. Such risks include: first, liquidity risk, which is the risk of banks having insufficient funding to meet its obligations as they fall due; second, credit risk, which covers both the risk of default by a loan counterparty and the risk of a customer whose performance is guaranteed by the bank failing to deliver; third, position risk, which is concerned with exposure to adverse movements in interest rates and exchange rates (in relation to swap and hedging transactions, banks are exposed to position risk when they take up an unhedged position); and fourth, price risk. There was concern that banks may be underpricing new services in the sense that the income derived may not be sufficient to cover costs, including profit, over the long term. This fear was heightened by (i) keen competition which could force prices down to uneconomic levels and (ii) lack of experience of sufficient duration on which an assessment of the risks could be made.

Regulators have addressed the credit risk of off-balance-sheet transactions in their construction of a new risk assets ratio (a capital ratio where the capital of a bank is related to the risk-adjusted value of its assets – see chapter 17). In the construction of this ratio, off-balance-sheet instruments are converted to a credit equivalent and then risk weighted along with the on-balance-sheet instruments. An illustration of banks' greater exposure to position risk as a consequence of the growth of off-balance- sheet business is provided by the case of Midland Montague, the investment banking arm of the Midland Bank Group. Their treasury operations in 1989 were positioned towards declining interest rates which failed to materialise and as a consequence the net interest income of the group was considerably reduced. A further risk of off-balance-sheet business is related to the novelty and complexity of the new instruments. This risk was highlighted in the swap market in 1989 when banks suffered sizeable losses following the ruling of the UK High Court that swap deals undertaken by local authorities, in excess of their underlying borrowing, were *ultra vires*. The banks which had entered into these swap arrangements had clearly not fully considered the risks arising from the special legal status of the local authorities.

4.4 International banking

As we have indicated in section 4.2, much of the business of wholesale banks based in the UK is not concerned with domestic sterling borrowing and lending, but with borrowing and lending in foreign currencies. The Bank of England defines international banking as all banking transactions in foreign currency – both cross-border and with local residents – plus cross-border transactions in domestic currency. From this definition we can identify two distinct types of international banking. The first is traditional foreign banking, which, for UK-based banks, involves transactions in sterling with non-residents. The second type of international banking is termed eurocurrency banking, which, for UK-based banks, involves transactions in currencies other than sterling with both residents and non-residents. Traditionally the location of a bank determined the currency in which it would make loans, so to obtain dollar loans you would go to a US-based bank. Whilst such traditional foreign banking still exists, it has been largely replaced by eurocurrency banking, where the location of the bank is unrelated to the currency of its transactions.

Eurocurrency banking

In this section we first of all define the term 'eurocurrency' and then examine the nature and operation of eurocurrency markets. We then discuss eurocurrency lending before reaching a conclusion on the role of these markets in the international financial system.

A eurocurrency can be defined as a deposit or loan denominated in a currency other than that of the host country where the bank is physically located. Thus, for example, a deposit denominated in dollars placed with a bank located in London is a eurocurrency. In a similar manner, a deposit denominated in sterling placed with a bank located in Paris is a eurocurrency. Consequently the existence of eurocurrency markets permits the separation of location of the market and the currency and therefore political and currency risks. It is not surprising that the main currency employed in eurocurrency markets is the dollar (about 75 per cent of the total market),

Table 4.5 *Eurobank A receives a payment of $1 million as a demand deposit: impact on the two sets of balance sheets ($million)*

	Liabilities	*Assets*
Consolidated US banking system		
US resident demand deposit	-1	0
Eurobank A demand deposit	+1	0
Net change	0	0
Eurobank A		
UK company time deposit	+1	+1
Net change	+1	+1

given the importance of the dollar in the international payments mechanism. Because of this dominant role, much of the following exposition will be in terms of the eurodollar market, though it can easily be extended to other currencies.

In order to demonstrate the operation of the eurodollar market we will trace the effect of a series of hypothetical transactions on the balance sheets of (i) the consolidated US banking system and (ii) two eurobanks, designated A and B. Assume initially that a UK customer of eurobank A receives a payment of $1 million in respect of the sale of goods and he places this as a demand deposit with the bank. The impact of this on the two sets of balance sheets is as shown in table 4.5.

These changes represent the first round, with the customer lodging the receipt of dollars with his own bank as a time deposit. Suppose for sake of exposition that eurobank A has no immediate use for the funds, so they are placed in the market via a broker with eurobank B in the form of a time deposit earning a rate of interest higher than that paid to the bank's UK customer. The second-round impact of these changes on the various balance sheets is shown in table 4.6.

If eurobank B then lends the $1 million to a customer, the only changes recorded to the balance sheets would refer to the consolidated US banking system and eurobank B recording the change of ownership of the demand deposit and the loan. These would be as shown in table 4.7.

This completes the chain of transactions in our hypothetical example. Note these changes are simplified to the extent that we have assumed that the total sum, that is, the $1 million, has been moved around the system whereas in practice the various banks will have retained some portion as a reserve for their own protection. Secondly, we have not included the situation after the customer has used the loan. If this is paid to a US exporter for

Table 4.6 *Eurobank A places funds with eurobank B: impact on balance sheets ($million)*

	Liabilities		*Assets*
Consolidated US banking system			
Eurobank B demand deposit	+1		0
Eurobank A demand deposit	-1		0
Net change	0		0
Eurobank A			
		Demand deposit with US bank	-1
		Time deposit with eurobank B	+1
Net change			0
Eurobank B			
Time deposit with Eurobank A	+1	Demand deposit with US bank	+1
Net change	+1		+1

goods then the demand deposit at the US bank will have reverted back to a US resident and the chain completed. These caveats do not invalidate the general principle of the analysis. The points to note are that (i) no extra demand deposits have been created on the US banking system, and (ii) total eurodollar deposits are now $2 million (original customer with eurobank A, eurobank A with eurobank B), so that an extra $1 million deposit has been created by the operation of the eurobanks. This demonstrates the tiering in the eurocurrency markets, with the original demand

Table 4.7 *Recorded changes to balance sheet if eurobank B lends the $1 million to a customer ($million)*

	Liabilities		*Assets*
Consolidated US banking system			
Customer	+1		0
Eurobank B	-1		0
Net change	0		0
Eurobank B			
		Demand deposit with US bank	-1
		Loan to customer	+1
Net change	0		0

deposit creating an additional deposit of $1 million. In practice the quantity of extra deposits created would depend on the ratio of the reserves held by eurobanks in the form of deposits in banks within the US banking system against eurodollar deposits. Also illustrated by this example is the difference between gross and net measures of the size of the eurocurrency markets. The gross size is $2 million but the net size is $1 million dollars, that is, the gross size less the quantity of inter-bank lending.

The interesting question posed is why did the market develop outside the US since, in our example, the original recipient of the deposit could have held it with a US bank rather than eurobank A. A number of reasons have been put forward. One suggestion is that the Eastern bloc countries wished to hold dollar deposits for international payment purposes but were reluctant to hold them in the US for fear that they could be 'blocked' in time of dispute. A second reason put forward is the existence of regulations in the US covering interest rates payable on deposits and capital flows.

Since their development in the early 1960s the markets have experienced a fast rate of growth. One of the main reasons for this is an advantage in terms of cost. As noted above, US banks were restricted in terms of interest rates that could be paid on bank deposits and this restraint became more onerous as interest rates rose worldwide. Furthermore, other regulations in the form of reserve requirements and deposit insurance raised the cost of banking in the US as compared with a centre such as London where prudential control was more relaxed. Banks' costs were also lower in the eurocurrency markets since they operated as wholesale banks with no branch network. The effect of these cost advantages was that eurobanks could offer rates on deposit and charges on loans that were marginally more attractive than those relevant to similar transactions with banks located in the US. This raised the attractiveness of the eurocurrency markets and stimulated a fast rate of growth. A second factor was the growth in international banking itself. This was stimulated by: first, the growth in world trade, necessitating a corresponding growth in the international payments system; and second, a growth of financial imbalances worldwide. In particular, the vast surpluses earned by OPEC countries following oil price increases in the early 1970s were an important factor. OPEC members placed their surplus dollar revenue from the sale of oil with eurobanks. It is often claimed that the large US balance of payments deficits over recent years also aided the development of the market. The importance of this factor may be overestimated since, whilst it increased the total quantity of dollars, it does not explain why these dollar balances were held outside the US. The main reason for the continued growth of the market appears to be the cost advantage and it remains to be seen whether the market will continue to grow as quickly once the relative advantage of offshore centres is reduced following harmonisation of prudential regulation noted in chapter 17.

We now briefly examine the general nature of the market. The first point to note is that it is a wholesale market with transactions typically of $1 million or more. As illustrated in our hypothetical example, the second point to note is that there is a significant volume of inter-bank lending, so that the gross size of the market is larger than the net size obtained when the inter-bank transactions are netted out. Interest rates are clearly related to those charged in domestic markets. Thus, the rate charged on dollar loans by banks situated in the US sets an upper limit to the rates charged for similar loans in the eurocurrency markets. Similarly, there is a relationship between the rates ruling in a particular location. Interest rate parity requires the following relationship to hold between rates on sterling in the domestic market and those on dollars in the London eurodollar market for transactions of similar maturity and risk, and so on:

Nominal rate of interest on sterling	=	Nominal rate of interest on eurodollars in London	=	Expected appreciation/ depreciation of the dollar versus sterling

Arbitrage will ensure that this relationship holds provided the market is efficient – see chapter 7 for a fuller discussion of this point.

The market is essentially a market for short-term deposits, with the average maturity of a deposit being in the region of three months. The main depositors and borrowers are governments, multinational corporations and banks from a wide range of countries, including the US. Lending appears on the other side of the bank's balance sheet. It is estimated by the Bank for International Settlements that at the end of 1989 approximately 80 per cent of outstanding gross international bank lending was of the eurocurrency type. The reasons for this dominance of eurocurrencies in international lending follow from those discussed above for the growth of the eurocurrency markets. It is difficult to obtain separate figures for net eurocurrency lending, so the figures reported below refer to total international lending. The figures for the volume of new international lending over the 1980s are presented in table 4.8.

The net international lending figures exclude lending between banks and so provide us with a view of new international lending to companies, governments and government agencies. The eurocurrency part of this net international lending figure can be further separated into syndicated loans, which are large, long-term loans, and the rest, which are mainly shorter-term credits for financing trade and so on. The figures for international syndicated credits, which are mainly eurocurrency syndicated credits, are presented in table 4.9.

Eurocurrency loans and syndicated loans in particular were the method of financing the international imbalances of the 1970s following the oil

Table 4.8 *Gross and net international lending, 1981–89 (figures in $billion adjusted to exclude estimated exchange rate effects)*

	1981	*1982*	*1983*	*1984*	*1985*	*1986*	*1987*	*1988*	*1989*	*1990*	*1991*	*1992*	*1993*
Gross international lending	336	229	127	152	297	657	760	511	807	714	-103	164	261
Net international lending[a]	165	95	85	90	105	200	300	260	410	465	80	195	165

[a] Net figure excludes interbank lending but allows for banks' own use of external funds for domestic lending.
Source: Bank for International Settlements annual report – various issues.

Table 4.9 *International syndicated lending, 1981–89*

	1981	*1982*	*1983*	*1984*	*1985*	*1986*	*1987*	*1988*	*1989*
International syndicated credits	101	88	38	30	19	30	89	102	149

Source: Allen [1990].

price rises of 1973/74. Sovereign borrowers from the LDCs and the newly industrialising countries (NICs) in Latin America became important borrowers in this market. When the debt crisis broke in 1982 (see section 4.5) this had two main effects on the syndicated loan market. First, banks became reluctant to lend new money to LDCs and NICs unless forced to as part of an restructuring package of the International Monetary Fund (IMF) ('involuntary lending'). Second, those banks with a high ratio of sovereign debt to capital found their credit rating reduced, which made raising funds in the capital markets more costly, leading to higher lending charges. One consequence of this was that highly rated borrowers found they could raise funds at lower cost through the international capital markets than through borrowing from banks. This led to the phenomenon known as securitisation, which is discussed in chapter 12. The overall effect of the debt crisis was to bring about a dramatic reduction in the volume of new syndicated lending which continued until 1985. From 1986 to 1989 the market grew again, reversing the trend of the early 1980s which many commentators predicted would continue. Most of the growth of syndicated credits in the late 1980s has come from a greater use of this type of financing by industrial borrowers. By 1989 industrial borrowers accounted for over 80 per cent of total syndicated credits, compared with approximately 60 per cent in the early 1980s.

Syndicated loans are loans spread among many, sometimes over 100, banks. They are generally medium-term loans with maturities ranging from three to fifteen years, although the average maturity of new loans is around six to eight years. Interest rates on the loans are floating, with the interest rate related to a reference rate such as the LIBOR, plus a margin representing risk and so on, and adjusted several times a year. Syndicated loans can be denominated in any currency although the US dollar is the most popular. Given the large number of banks involved in syndicated lending, it is natural that one bank will act as a 'lead' bank organising the arrangements of the loan. The lead bank will receive a fee for this service in addition to the normal interest rate charge. There are a number of advantages for borrowers using the syndicated credits market compared with international capital markets. First, the loan provides a steady source of funds, unlike some of the short-term underwritten instruments of the euronote markets (considered in chapter 12). Second, borrowers can generally raise larger sums of money than through the capital markets. For example, a $13.6 billion credit was raised for Kohlberg Kravis Roberts for the leveraged takeover of RJR Nabisco in 1989. Third, deals can be arranged quickly. For example, in 1987 BP sought to raise a syndicated loan to finance its offer to purchase the remainder of the stock of Standard Oil. A consortium of banks, led by Morgan Guaranty, took just five days to arrange $15 billion, which was $10 billion more than BP actually required. The syndication of a loan across many banks also brings advantages compared with a loan from one bank, in that an individual bank in the syndicate will be less affected by a default. The lower risk implies that the cost of a syndicated loan should be lower.

The surge of corporate restructuring in the late 1980s using the vehicle of mergers and acquisitions, particularly in the US and UK, has been one of the driving forces behind the growth of syndicated lending. An increasing proportion of the financing of such activity has been debt, partly marketable debt in the US ('junk bonds') but largely loans raised through the method of syndicated lending. The advantage of syndicated loans in this activity is the speed with which funds can be raised and the ability to raise these funds more discreetly than through the capital markets.

Another development in the syndicated credit market over the 1980s has been the emergence of a secondary market, in particular of LDC debt. This involves banks securitising the debt so that it can be sold on to a third party. The Basle agreement on capital adequacy (see chapter 17) means that banks have either to raise more capital or remove some assets from the balance sheet. A number of banks have chosen the latter course and this raises the prospect of the emergence of a general secondary market in syndicated credits. Allen [1990] states that this 'could be regarded as part of a more general process in the euromarkets, where in recent years innovation and securitisation have led to gradual dissolving of the boundaries between money, credit and capital markets'.

Finally in this section we consider the consequences of the development of the eurocurrency market. The market clearly carries out many of the facets of financial intermediation discussed in chapter 2. Maturity transformation is obviously present, with loans being of a longer term than deposits. Similarly, asset transformation is evidenced by the change of almost riskless deposits into more risky loans. This creates some dangers for the financial system given the interdependence of the operators within the market due to the presence of inter-bank lending built on a relatively small base of deposits held in US banks. Failure of one bank may have a large knock-on effect, creating problems for national supervisors of the domestic monetary system. In fact, as we have argued earlier for the parallel sterling markets, such operations may enjoy 'de facto' support since national supervisory authorities are loathe to allow a major bank to default on its liabilities. There is also a concern arising from the overhang of sovereign lending financed by borrowing in the eurocurrency markets. Furthermore, it is sometimes argued that the creation of such a large pool of acceptable currencies creates the potential for movement of funds which could lead to the destabilisation of exchange rates and the frustration of monetary policy.

A final concern has been expressed over the role of the eurocurrency markets in the propagation of inflation on a worldwide basis. It is sometimes argued that the creation of these markets has led to an expansion of the world money supply, which in turn leads to higher world inflation rates. However, an examination of the hypothetical examples at the outset of this section suggests that there was no expansion in the quantity of US dollars held at US banks but that secondary deposits were created in the manner of non-bank financial intermediaries building up credit on the base of bank deposits. This analogy suggests that the existence of the eurocurrency markets has permitted a growth of credit rather than the money supply *per se,* and as such may have increased the efficiency of the allocation of credit worldwide. This is also evidenced by the existence of syndicated lending, which permits the sharing of the risks of international lending amongst different banks from different locations.

In the next section we examine one of the consequences of the growth of international lending over the 1970s.

4.5 Sovereign lending crisis

In the 1960s and early 1970s most lending to developing countries was carried out by official institutions such as the World Bank and the IMF. This position changed, largely as a result of oil price increases between October 1973 and January 1974, which saw oil prices rise by over 400 per cent. These price increases were initiated by OPEC, a cartel whose member countries as a consequence experienced a dramatic increase in their foreign currency receipts. Oil-importing countries, however, experienced balance of payments deficits. Some of the developed countries were supported by direct capital flows from OPEC countries; for example $6 billion was placed in investments in the UK in the years shortly after the oil price rises. The oil-importing developing countries suffered the most problems, and those with access to the international financial markets generally chose to borrow to cover their balance of payments deficits in order to sustain growth. However, unlike the borrowing of the period prior to the oil price rises, developing countries turned increasingly to commercial banks. Developing countries were reluctant to borrow from the IMF because any funds provided were usually given as part of a reconstruction package which, because they were generally deflationary, were politically unpopular. The international agencies such as the IMF and the World Bank would in any event have been unable to support the scale of lending required, as the basis of their funding was the developed countries' governments, in particular the US, which were themselves experiencing problems. Since oil is priced in dollars, the commercial banks received a massive flow of liquid funds from the OPEC countries in the form of eurodollar deposits and therefore had the ability to meet the developing countries' demands for funds. Much of this lending was to governments or was government guaranteed and was therefore termed sovereign lending. There was a widespread belief amongst the banking community that this lending was relatively safe, as countries could not go bankrupt. As a consequence any credit assessment was superficial and there was little monitoring by the banks as to the purpose to which the funds were put. Part of the blame for the crisis which came later can therefore be placed with the banks which were imprudent in their lending. However, in mitigation, the banks were encouraged by Western governments to recycle the OPEC surpluses to offset the effects of higher oil prices on the world economy. Much of this lending was to the newly industrialising countries of Latin America. The poorer developing countries, particularly in the sub-Saharan region of Africa, generally did not have sufficient credit standing to gain access to loans from commercial banks.

To sum up this section, the developing countries borrowed heavily in dollars at floating rates of interest to finance balance of payments deficits (i.e. consumption) rather than investment. Consequently, adjustment to the higher oil prices was delayed and servicing the debt necessitated current-account balance of payment surpluses to earn the required dollars to meet the interest payments and repayment of principal.

There was little sign of problems resulting from this sovereign lending over the rest of the 1970s, partly because of negative real interest rates on the debt. Over the latter half of the 1970s though, the surpluses of the OPEC countries reduced as a result of dramatically increased imports. In 1979, OPEC decided on a further sharp rise in the price of oil, which more than doubled the spot price, from $11 to $24 a barrel. Further increases also occurred in 1980. The response of the developed countries to this second round of oil price rises, however, was different. Around this time the governments elected in the UK, US and Germany adopted monetarist policies and so attempted to control inflation arising from higher oil prices by monetary restraint. This time there was no attempt to borrow and spend a way out of the problem. The policy of monetary restraint, however, contributed to a world recession, making it much more difficult for developed countries to expand exports to earn foreign currency. As part of the policy of monetary restraint, interest rates were increased, which led to a further deterioration in the debt servicing capacity of the debtor countries. Thus, the combination of higher interest payments yet declining exports led to increased pressure on debtor countries. The first public sign of a crisis though did not occur until 1982, when Mexico, one of the leading borrowers and a country with proven reserves of oil which had achieved rapid economic growth in the previous four years, announced a moratorium on principal payments until the end of 1983. Pressure from the IMF on commercial banks with exposure to Mexico to provide new money prevented an actual default. However, the incident brought home to the international banking system the nature of the risks of sovereign debt. The years between 1982 and 1985 have been termed the years of debt crisis management, with the IMF orchestrating commercial bank loan reschedulings along with 'concerted' lending packages. At the same time the debtor countries receiving help from the IMF were forced to accept politically unpopular austerity programmes. Whilst this period of management achieved stability for the international banking system, it did little to help the problems faced by the debtor countries. Whilst there was some narrowing of the balance of payments positions for many debtor countries, this was at the expense of a sharp fall in investment and growth. Net resource transfers to Latin American countries over the period 1982 to 1985 were in fact away from these countries to the developed countries, as debtors paid back more than they received in new loans (table 4.10).

The next initiative came in 1985, when James Baker, the US Secretary to the Treasury, announced a new package which was aimed at improving economic growth in the debtor countries. With this package, additional funds were to be provided to finance supply-side reforms, such as encouraging inward investment, tax reform and the encouragement of competition in their economies. The Baker plan was aimed at 15 heavily indebted countries, mostly based in South America, with a total of $29 billion targeted over three years. Of this additional funding, $20 billion was to come from commercial banks and $9 billion from international

Table 4.10 *Net resource transfers to Latin America, 1981–85 ($billion)*

Year	*Net capital inflow*	–	*Interest repayments and foreign profits*	=	*Net resource transfer*
1981	49.1		27.8		21.3
1982	27.6		36.8		-9.2
1983	6.1		34.9		-28.8
1984	11.6		37.1		-25.5
1985	4.1		36.7		-32.6

Source: Inter American Development Bank.

agencies. However, as Sachs [1986] states, 'The Baker plan was significant not as a new policy, but rather an admission by the United States that the debt strategy up to 1985 had not generated adequate economic growth in the debtor countries'. Whilst the commercial banks cautiously welcomed the Baker plan there were a number of problems identified. In particular, the smaller banks which had already been withdrawing credit lines or writing off LDC loans since the crisis broke, were not anxious to increase their exposure again. This meant that the burden of new lending had to be taken up by the larger banks already heavily exposed. At the same time, these banks were being put under pressure by their central banks to increase capital ratios because of the greater risks. As the new lending under the Baker plan envisaged 'soft' terms, these new loans would likely be classified as high risk, thereby requiring greater capital backing. As a consequence, little new lending, from either official institutions or commercial banks, materialised. In addition, the supply-side reforms proved difficult to sustain and continuing high interest rates increased the pressure on debtor countries. To prevent defaults, banks were forced to agree to extensive rescheduling of the debt. Many debtor countries, faced with growing social problems and political unrest, began to impose conditions on the servicing of the debt. In March 1987, Brazil, the largest debtor country, declared a moratorium on interest payments on $68 billion of its outstanding foreign private sector debt. Against this background the commercial banks began to acknowledge the serious consequences of default. To illustrate the potential for insolvency of UK banks in the mid-1980s the exposure of the four main clearing banks to the four largest Latin American debtors, as a percentage of their capital base, is shown in table 4.11.

Citicorp became the first bank, in May 1987, to establish substantial reserves against poorly performing LDC debt. Other US banks with large exposures quickly followed the example of Citicorp. UK banks, led by National Westminster and under pressure from the Bank of England and the stock market, which had started to mark down the price of bank shares, also announced substantial provisions. Further substantial provisions were

Table 4.11 *UK banks' exposure to outstanding debt of Mexico, Argentina, Brazil and Venezuela as a percentage of capital (end 1984)*

Barclays	62
Lloyds	165
Midland	205
National Westminster	73

Source: Estimate in Lever and Huhne [1985].

Table 4.12 *Exposure to debt and provisions for debt of the clearing banks*

	Provisions as a % of exposure			*Exposure to debt in 1989 (after deduction of provisions) as a % of shareholders' funds*
	1987	*1988*	*1989*	
Midland	29	33	50	80
Lloyds	34	34	72	50
Barclays	35	40	70	8
National Westminster	33	35	75	7

Source: published accounts.

set aside in 1989 in response to a deterioration in debt servicing by many debtor countries, discussed below. Whilst this provisioning acknowledged the dangers of default of LDC debt, it did not in itself help the debtor countries, as the provisions represented funds set aside in case of default rather than any write-off of the debt. The effect of the provisions was to improve substantially the financial health of the banks, so that by the end of 1989 the four largest UK clearing banks had exposure to developing countries' debt, after allowing for provisions, of below 100 per cent of the core capital of the bank (table 4.12).

Over the latter half of the 1980s, a number of market-based solutions were used by the banks to reduce their exposure to LDC debt. Three of the solutions which have been often used are discussed below.

(i) *Selling the debt in the secondary market in LDC debt*

A secondary market in LDC debt began in late 1983, and although much of the activity in this market is inter-bank trading, with banks having the aim of adjusting their portfolio of risks, it has also been used as a basis for

Table 4.13 *Secondary market prices for selected LDC debt (price in $ for $100 claim)*

Country	*August 1986*	*April 1987*	*October 1987*	*March 1989*	*May 1990*	*December 1992*
Argentina	66	60	34	17	76	63
Brazil	76	63	38	34	25	30
Mexico	56	59	47	41	46	59

Source: Sachs and Huizinga [1987], *Barclays Bank Review*, August 1990, and Clark [1993].

debt buy-backs by the debtor countries and as an intermediate stage for debt–equity swaps. The price of a country's debt in the market does provide some indication of the current and future performance of the debt, and table 4.13 illustrates the generally deteriorating position for the three main Latin American debtors over the latter half of the 1980s, followed by an improvement in the early 1990s, the reasons for which are discussed below.

The fact that a debtor's servicing record can influence the secondary market price of its debt introduces a moral hazard problem to the extent that any debt relief is tied to the secondary price of the debt, and debtor countries can 'engineer' a reduction in the price to obtain greater relief.

(ii) *Debt–equity swap*

This involves a debt denominated in a foreign currency being paid by the debtor in local currency, at an agreed discount, to the debt's face value. The bank then uses the local currency to invest in the debtor country, thereby acquiring a claim on a real asset, with the potential of capital gain as well as income return. For example, Midland Bank in 1989 swapped $63 million of debt owed by Chile for a $53 million investment in a Chilean copper mine. The discount in the swap was 16 per cent, which is better than the 35 per cent discount which would have resulted from selling through the secondary market.

(iii) *Debt–debt swap*

This involves a bank exchanging the debt for bonds issued by the debtor country's government, where the bonds are either issued at a discount on the par value but with a market rate of interest or at par value with a lower than market rate of interest.

It has been estimated that, by 1989, the 15 countries targeted in the Baker plan had reduced their bank debt by 13 per cent using these and other methods. Despite some success in reducing debt burdens it was accepted that the debt burdens of debtor countries remained too high. A further initiative came in March 1989 in the form of a set of proposals announced by US Treasury Secretary Nicholas Brady. These proposals represented a shift from the earlier approaches to the debt problem in that they recognised the need for official backing of schemes designed to achieve voluntary reduction of market-based debt or debt service. However, the proposals also represent a continuation of the Baker approach in that participation is based on the pursuit of an IMF-approved economic adjustment programme and that new money is to be provided by the banks. Under these proposals debt relief is provided by the methods described in (i) to (iii) above. Official money to back the initiative is also provided primarily from the IMF and World Bank but also from the governments of developed countries such as

Japan. At the time of writing (1994) eight Brady deals have been completed or agreed in principle. These were with Mexico, Costa Rica and the Philippines in 1989, Venezuela and Uruguay in 1990, Nigeria in 1991 and Argentina and Brazil in 1992. A typical deal was that arranged with Mexico, covering $48.5 billion of its debt, where 88 per cent of the banks with exposure to Mexico opted for debt reduction (roughly half for bonds at a discount and half for bonds at par with a reduced interest rate), with only 12 per cent of banks opting to provide new money. The amount of new money provided fell well short of the amount targeted. This deal though has provided some help to Mexico, both directly in terms of a $1 billion reduction in interest payments per year (out of $8 billion in total) and more indirectly with the reduction in debt overhang increasing investor confidence, reducing domestic interest rates and increasing foreign direct investment and capital repatriation. The eight deals agreed have in fact reduced the present value of debt service obligations by $65 billion, or just over one-third of the existing bank debt. The banks have also obtained some benefit from the deal as the average secondary price of debtor countries' debt has increased from approximately 40 cents in the dollar before 1989 to around 57 cents in the dollar in 1993, effectively boosting the value of the residual debt left on the balance sheets of banks. Another indicator of the improving financial position of debtor countries has been the tremendous increase in private capital flows into those countries, particularly those that have agreed a Brady deal. Table 4.14 shows the upward trend for most Brady-deal countries in net capital flows made up of direct and portfolio investment through equity and bond markets and repatriation of flight capital.

Table 4.14 *Net capital inflows to Brady deal countries ($billion)*

Country	*1989*	*1990*	*1991*	*1992*	*1993*
Mexico	4.5	10.4	21.9	24.0	23.9
Costa Rica	0.6	0.3	0.5	0.5	0.7
Venezuela	-1.1	-3.4	0.7	2.2	1.3
Uruguay	-0.1	-0.1	0.1	0.2	0.3
Nigeria	0.1	-2.5	-0.6	-6.0	1.3
Philippines	1.9	2.3	3.0	2.7	3.7
Argentina	-0.5	1.2	4.9	12.8	12.7
Brazil	-0.1	2.7	0.9	2.9	2.8

Source: International Monetary Fund, international financial statistics.

Despite the positive developments following the Brady initiative, significant problems still remain for the debtor countries. Despite the permanent improvements in debtor countries' positions, debt service obligations remain heavy and whilst re-entry to the private capital markets is helpful, the key to long-term recovery is improvement in the real economy, which occurs more slowly than improvement in the financial economy. The debtor countries have also been helped since 1990 by significant reductions in US interest rates. The LIBOR for US deposits, to which most loan contracts were linked before the Brady deals, declined by about 500 basis points between 1990 and 1993. Those countries that agreed a deal early on obtained interest savings on that portion of their debt that was left at floating rates. Countries agreeing later will have obtained much larger interest savings. Indeed, the relationship between the decline in international interest rates and the improvement in secondary market prices has been found to be very strong (see Dooley *et al.* [1994]) and thus a reversal of these interest rates may bring back debt servicing problems.

4.6 **Conclusion**

In this chapter we have examined the nature of wholesale banking in general and its international dimension in particular. Attention has also been focused on two developments concerning the wholesale banking sector, namely off-balance-sheet business and the sovereign lending problem. As we have noted in this chapter, the former development has implications for the way banks are regulated and we consider this issue further in chapter 17. The problems that have arisen out of sovereign lending appear to have been mitigated since the latter part of the 1980s, in the sense that large defaults on the debt will not now threaten the solvency of the main banks involved. The position of the debtor countries, although much improved for those that have agreed Brady deals, remains vulnerable to an upturn in international interest rates.

Chapter 5

Other deposit-taking institutions

5.1 Introduction

In this chapter we examine two other deposit-taking institutions, namely building societies and finance houses. In view of their greater importance in the financial system and the recent significant changes affecting them, the major proportion of this chapter will be directed towards the building societies.

The building societies have traditionally been mutually owned, specialist financial institutions, borrowing from the personal sector and lending back to the personal sector in the form of a mortgage to finance house purchase. Up until the beginning of the 1980s the building societies enjoyed a virtual monopoly in the mortgage market. On the borrowing side, although experiencing some external competition for personal sector deposits from banks and national savings, there was little internal competition between different building societies owing to a cartel arrangement on the setting of interest rates. Over the 1980s, however, building societies experienced a considerable degree of change as various liberalisation measures stimulated competition in the mortgage and personal savings markets. In the second half of the 1980s the Building Societies Act 1986 allowed for progressive deregulation of the products that building societies can offer on both sides of the balance sheet. The specialist institutions which began the decade are, as a consequence of these changes, more able to emulate banks as general providers of financial services. A slowdown in mortgage demand in the early 1990s is one of the factors behind the government's rethink of the legislation governing building societies announced in 1994. Further liberalisation measures have been announced and the general direction of reform appears to be towards a more permissive regime and away from the prescriptive framework of the 1986 Act. However, if any of the larger building societies feels that too many restrictions remain then the 1986 Act also provides a procedure for a society to transfer from mutual to company (i.e. bank) status. The Abbey National was the first to follow this route, in 1989, although other large societies are considering incorporation, with the proposed merged Halifax/Leeds institution announcing plans to incorporate at the time of writing (1995).

In this chapter, after providing a brief history of building societies (section 5.2), we concentrate on an examination of the pressures for change and the actual changes that have taken place in building society activity over the 1980s and early 1990s (sections 5.3 to 5.6). Finally, in section 5.7 we provide a brief survey of finance houses.

5.2 History of the building society movement

The first building societies were founded in the late eighteenth century. These early societies were set up by a group of around 20 to 30 people who contributed on a weekly basis to a fund which financed the purchase of land and the building of houses. These early societies were known as terminating societies, because when all the contributing members had been housed, the society terminated. The next stage came with the development of permanent societies, which increasingly borrowed from those who did not wish to buy a house and lent to those who both financed the construction of new homes and purchased existing homes. By 1912 approximately half the building societies were of this permanent type and no new terminating societies have been formed since 1953.

Up until the early 1980s there was little change in the activities of building societies, which had a specialist role involving intermediation within the personal sector, borrowing in the form of deposits and lending in the form of a mortgage to finance house purchase. Nevertheless, the structure of the industry has significantly changed in two respects. First, the branch networks of the societies have expanded; and second, the concentration of building societies has increased. This is illustrated in table 5.1.

The 2,286 building societies in existence at the beginning of this century were in the main small in size and operated over a limited local area. The inter-war period saw the beginning of branching, as societies sought to expand their catchment area for personal savings. Expansion of the building societies' branch networks appears though to have come to an end over the last half of the 1980s. Concentration of the building society sector has proceeded at a rapid pace in the period since 1960, with the majority of mergers between societies taking the form of a smaller society transferring its engagement to a larger society. The largest ten societies now account for around 80 per cent of total assets compared with approximately 70 per cent in 1980. These developments were accompanied by a large expansion of the business of building societies, as evidenced by the figures shown in

Table 5.1 *Changes to the structure of the building society industry*

Year	*Number of societies*	*Number of branches*
1900	2,286	
1920	1,271	
1940	952	640
1960	726	985
1980	273	5,684
1982	227	6,480
1984	190	6,816
1986	151	6,954
1988	131	6,912
1990	117	6,051
1992	105	5,765
1993	101	5,054

Note: Figures for number of branches for 1940 and 1960 are estimates.

table 5.2 for the level of personal sector deposits with the banking sector and total shares and deposits of building societies. The figures terminate at the end of 1988, to exclude the complications caused by the transfer of Abbey National from building society to bank status.

The figures in table 5.2 illustrate the success of building societies in the competition for personal sector deposits compared with banks. We consider this competition in more detail in the next section. What we are concerned with here is the controversy which has arisen as to whether the growth of building society deposits adversely affected the banks to any extent. The traditional argument followed the rationale that since building societies maintain their own deposits with the banking sector, the growth of building society deposits did not entail deposit losses for the banking sector, but rather a change in ownership. A second argument put forward noted that the societies lent exclusively on mortgages whereas banks conducted little mortgage lending and hence there was little competition between these two classes of institution on the assets side of the balance sheet.

The first argument is of an extremely dubious nature. To the extent that building societies keep reserves in the form of public sector debt (see table 5.8 for further details), funds are lost to the banks in precisely the same manner as any other open market sale of government securities. The second argument is certainly no longer true. As we will discuss in the next section,

Table 5.2 *Stocks of personal sector savings held with banks and building societies (£million)*

	Bank deposits[a]	*Building society shares and deposits*[b]	*Ratio of a to b*
1963	6,232	4,057	0.65
1965	7,210	5,211	0.72
1970	10,036	10,194	1.02
1975	19,206	22,748	1.18
1980	36,598	50,002	1.37
1985	61,488	104,922	1.71
1988	94,129	152,700	1.62

Source: CSO, *Financial Statistics*, various issues.

banks have become extremely active lenders in the mortgage market over the 1980s. Even more significant is the fact that the traditional argument ignored the effect of competition on the terms under which banks raised deposits. Increased competition for retail deposits must have raised to some extent the cost to banks of obtaining such deposits. These costs could arise, apart from the direct impact on interest rates, in a variety of ways, including reversion to Saturday opening, innovative time deposit schemes and reduction of charges on the operation of current accounts. Building societies' entry into the wholesale money markets – discussed in the next section – has also increased the demand for wholesale funds, which must have again raised to some extent the cost of funds for banks in this market. Finally there is the evidence in table 5.7, which shows the withdrawal of equity from house ownership. In effect this provided indirect finance from building societies for the purchase of consumer goods at the expense of other financial institutions which would normally have provided such finance.

5.3 Competitive pressures on building societies

Building societies have experienced greater competition in both their funding and lending activities since the end of the 1970s. As noted above, the main competitors to building societies in the personal sector savings market have been banks in particular and, to a lesser extent, national savings, although over the latter half of the 1980s building society deposits have also come under competition from equity instruments following a number of privatisation issues, the growth of unit trusts and the growth in equity prices (temporarily reversed by the stock market crash of 1987). Table 5.3 illustrates the competition for personal sector liquid assets since 1977.

Table 5.3 *Competition for personal sector liquid assets since 1977 (additions to liquid assets as a percentage of the total)*

Year	*Building society deposits*	*Bank deposits*	*National savings*
1977	70.7	10.1	19.1
1978	47.8	35.9	16.3
1979	41.3	47.6	11.1
1980	45.1	43.9	10.9
1981	44.9	28.4	26.8
1982	57.8	22.2	19.9
1983	61.2	20.9	17.9
1984	64.9	18.8	16.3
1985	64.8	23.0	14.4
1986	52.5	37.4	10.0
1987	57.9	32.6	9.5
1988	52.7	43.6	3.7
1989	48.0	64.0	-12.0
1990	51.9	45.4	2.0
1991	71.4	19.8	8.9
1992	51.5	24.0	24.5
1993	61.7	12.0	26.8

Bank deposits includes Trustee Savings Bank deposits.
National savings includes national savings investment account.
Abbey National transferred from building society to bank status in 1989.
Source: *Housing Finance*, various issues.

Over much of the 1970s the building societies faced little competition from other institutions for personal sector deposits. As we saw in chapter 3, the banks changed the balance of their funding from the retail market towards the wholesale market over the 1970s. Banks, however, did make an adjustment to this balance at the end of the 1970s and targeted personal savings for a few years. This was repeated in the early 1990s, illustrating the ability of banks to move between the retail and wholesale markets for funding, according to relative availability and cost of funds. Further competitive pressures to building societies' funding came from the government when, from 1979, greater emphasis was placed on funding the PSBR through national savings. At this time the government introduced an index-linked retirement issue of national savings certificates and with an inflation rate of around 18 per cent in 1979/80 this issue proved very popular. Also, in 1980 the rate of interest on the national savings investment account was raised to a very competitive rate of 15 per cent. The competitiveness of this rate was maintained throughout 1981 and a new issue of index-linked national savings certificates without an age restriction was introduced at the end of this year. From mid-1982, however, national savings have provided less competition to building societies as inflation and hence the popularity of index-linked certificates has fallen, and because the government has placed less emphasis on funding through national savings. However, over the last few years of the 1980s building societies also faced greater competition from banks in the personal sector savings market. Reasons for this are (i) that banks have increasingly viewed retail funding as a base for selling other retail financial services and (ii) perhaps by this time banks had realised that competition from building societies did impose costs on themselves. A more specific reason for the greater competition though was the decision to put banks and building societies on the same footing in terms of deducting tax from depositors' interest at source at a composite rate of 25.25 per cent from April 1985 (abolished for both banks and building societies from April 1991). It was believed that the effect of quoting bank interest rates net of tax rather than gross would be to make their uncompetitiveness more obvious. In response to these pressures banks introduced high-interest deposit accounts similar to the building societies' short-notice and instant-access accounts. Later in the 1980s banks offered high-interest cheque accounts and more recently cheque accounts free of bank charges. As a consequence banks have regained some of the share of personal sector liquid asset holdings they had lost to building societies.

Up until the early 1970s the majority of the building societies' funding came from the ordinary share account. Building societies then introduced, in 1973, term accounts, which offered a guaranteed differential over the ordinary share rate in exchange for the depositor leaving the deposit untouched for a certain length of time. Term accounts were generally for two years up to five years. These accounts grew very rapidly over the 1970s and by 1982 accounted for just over 23 per cent of building society personal sector funding. The next main innovation from building societies came in the early 1980s, in response to the greater competition described above, with the introduction of the short-notice account and later the instant-access account, where a higher rate of interest than the ordinary share rate is paid in exchange for a short period of notice or some minimum level of deposit. By the end of 1989, these short-notice and instant-access deposits accounted for just over 83 per cent of the total of personal sector deposits with building societies.

Another major development in building society funding over the 1980s was the greater volume of funds raised from wholesale sources. A series of changes in the taxation position of building societies from 1983 allowed them to pay interest gross of tax on various wholesale instruments, thereby making the issue of such instruments more appealing to investors and hence making wholesale funding a more viable proposition for building societies. The 1986 Building Societies Act placed an upper limit on wholesale funding of 20 per cent although this was raised to 40 per cent 1988 and then 50 per cent in 1994 following representations from building societies. The percentage breakdown of retail and wholesale funding for building societies is shown in table 5.4.

Although building societies in aggregate are well below the upper limit for wholesale funding, the figures in table 5.4 do not reveal that many of the larger societies in 1994 were approaching 30 per cent wholesale funding. The three main wholesale instruments issued by societies are certificates of deposit (CDs), eurobonds and bank borrowing. The largely floating-rate assets (mortgages) of societies means that they would prefer to hold floating-rate liabilities. Therefore the most attractive eurobond for societies (in cost terms as well) has been the floating-rate note (see chapter 12 for further discussion). These issues have largely been eurosterling floating-rate notes. Since March 1986, though, societies have been able to enter into interest rate swaps and so have started raising funds through the fixed-rate note market. The ability of societies to enter into currency swaps since the beginning of 1987 has added further flexibility, allowing societies to raise wholesale funds in a variety of currencies.

Access to the wholesale markets has allowed societies to practise liability management (see chapter 3). As with banks, which switched to liability management over the 1970s, societies have been able to reduce the level of liquid assets they hold – see section 5.5 below.

Table 5.4 *Breakdown of building society funding (%)*

Year	*Retail funds*	*Wholesale funds*
1982	100	0
1983	99	1
1984	98	2
1985	93	7
1986	90	10
1987	88	12
1988	86	14
1989	84	16
1990	81	19
1991	80	20
1992	80	20
1993	80	20

Source: *Housing Finance,* various issues.

On the lending side, the building societies had a virtual monopoly on mortgage lending over the 1970s and accounted for some 82 per cent of the outstanding stock of mortgages at the end of 1979. Over the 1970s banks, although involved to a limited extent in mortgage lending, were restricted by direct controls on their lending which impinged most directly on the personal sector. Building societies, as mutual organisations, were not profit maximisers but instead attempted to reconcile the conflicting demands of borrowers for low interest rates and savers for high interest rates by maintaining a relatively stable path for interest rates over time. This was made possible by the cartel arrangement which existed whereby the Building Societies Association (BSA) recommended rates of interest to be charged to borrowers and savers. Such an institutional structure minimised the role played by interest rates in equilibrating supply and demand for mortgages. The stickiness of rates offered by building societies on shares and deposits meant that at times the rates were uncompetitive, thus reducing inflows (see figure 5.1). This shortage of funds for lending that occurred at times could be made up by the societies running down liquid asset stocks. However, this provided only a temporary solution and, given that societies would not raise interest rates to reduce the demand for

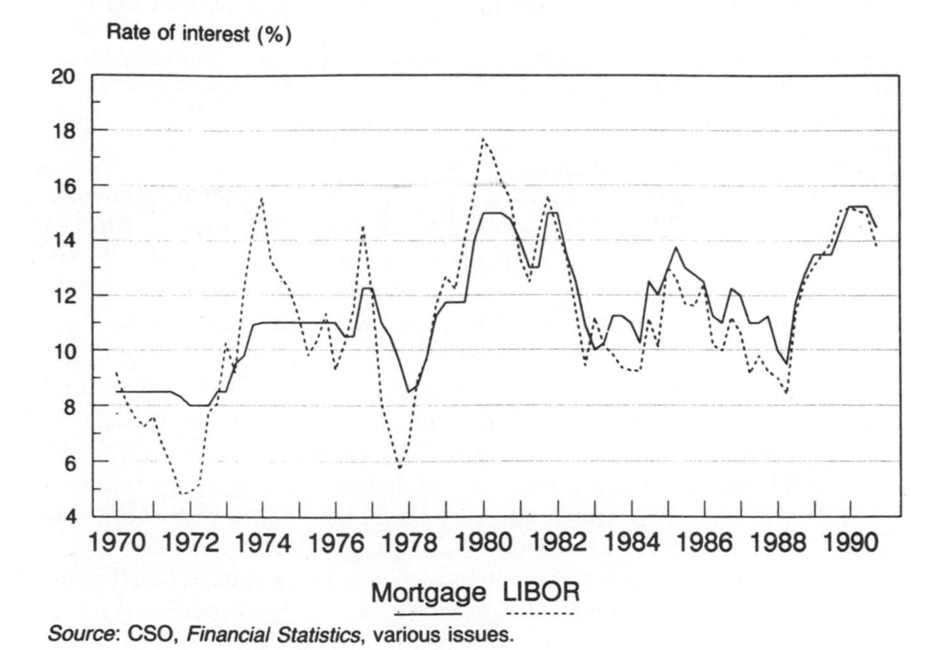

Source: CSO, *Financial Statistics*, various issues.

Figure 5.1 *Building society mortgage rate and LIBOR*

Table 5.5 *Shares of net new mortgage lending (%)*

Year	*Building societies*	*Banks*	*Miscellaneous institutions*[a]	*Others*[b]
1979	82	9		9
1980	78	8		14
1981	67	26		7
1982	58	36		6
1983	75	24	1	0
1984	85	12	3	0
1985	77	22	2	0
1986	72	19	9	0
1987	50	35	14	1
1988	59	27	12	2
1989	71	21	8	0
1990	73	19	9	-1
1991	81	18	8	-7
1992	76	35	-9	-2
1993	58	61	-16	-3

[a] Miscellaneous institutions refers to specialised mortgage lenders funded exclusively from wholesale sources.
[b] Others refers to insurance companies and pension funds, local authorities and other public sector.
Source: *Housing Finance*, various issues.

mortgages, other means of rationing were pursued. These included queues and changes in lending arrangements. The latter generally took the form of lowering (i) the ratio of loan to borrower's income or (ii) the ratio of loan to the value of the associated property. Another criticism of the cartel arrangement was that the rates of interest set were designed to protect the smaller, less efficient societies. This had the effect of allowing the larger societies to operate on margins which would not occur in a competitive environment and therefore provided no incentive for them to cut costs, so that the industry as a whole operated at a higher cost. However, a defence of the cartel that was often made was that because the mortgage rate was often kept below market rates, the cartel kept the cost of borrowing low (although at the expense of savers).

The market structure just described began to break down shortly after the start of the 1980s. In mid-1980 direct controls on bank lending (known as the 'corset') were lifted and the banks immediately strove to develop new areas of business. In particular they entered the mortgage market (see table 5.5) and by 1982 they had achieved a market share of new mortgage lending of 36 per cent. After this initial expansion bank mortgage lending slowed down, though picked up in the 1990s, reaching a peak of 61 per cent in 1993 despite a depressed mortgage market. This illustrates that banks can enter and leave the mortgage market freely as factors such as demand and relative profitability change.

5.4 Consequences of the competitive pressures

Greater competition in the mortgage market following the entry of banks and in the retail deposit markets has had a number of consequences. First of all it made societies more sensitive to interest rate changes, which in turn led to the breakdown in the cartel arrangement between societies, precipitated by the decision of Abbey National to leave the cartel in September 1983. The BSA recommendation of rates came to an end in October 1983, although the BSA continued to advise rates until November 1984. The greater competition in the mortgage market and the breakdown of the cartel led to both a greater availability of mortgage funds and price clearing in the market and therefore to an end to non-price rationing. Mortgage rates now move more in line with money-market interest rates and for much of the 1980s have been above them (see figure 5.1). This has induced into the market specialised mortgage lenders which are funded completely from wholesale sources (the miscellaneous institutions in table 5.5). A rapid expansion in mortgage lending therefore occurred over the 1980s and this is reflected in the growth of home ownership, as illustrated in table 5.6.

Whilst the main explanation of the growth in home ownership, particularly over the 1980s, is likely to be the greater availability of mortgage funding, other factors include the policy of tax relief earned on mortgage

Table 5.6 *The stock of dwellings in Britain: distribution by tenure (as a percentage of total)*

	1960	*1970*	*1980*	*1990*	*1992*
Owner occupied	42.0	50.0	56.1	65.8	66.1
Rented from local authority or new town corporation	26.6	30.4	31.1	21.9	20.7
Rented from private owners and others	31.4	19.6	12.7	12.3	13.2

Source: *Housing Finance*, 1994.

interest payments, the sale of council houses and the decline of the private rented housing stock.

The buoyancy in the mortgage market has also led to lending institutions, particularly building societies, extending the type of lending. Traditionally, mortgages have been predominantly in the form of first advances for the purchase of a house. In the latter part of the 1980s, second mortgages and further advances, not directly connected with home improvements, have been available. It is now relatively easy for owner-occupiers to withdraw cash from the equity built up in their property, without moving house, simply by increasing the debt on the property. This led to a rapid growth in equity withdrawal in the late 1980s as house prices increased at a rapid rate. Equity withdrawal is defined as the difference between the net increase in the stock of loans for house purchase and the private sector's net expenditure on additions to the stock of owner-occupied housing, including improvements. Estimates of equity withdrawal are provided in table 5.7.

Whilst the estimates of equity withdrawal provided in table 5.7 may exaggerate the position because of the likely under-recording of housing improvement expenditure, there is still likely to have been a growing leakage of funds from housing into consumption expenditure over the 1980s contributing to the consumption boom in the latter half of that decade. As noted in section 5.2, this implies that societies have been indirectly providing finance for consumption expenditure. The fall in house prices in the early 1990s with the consequent fall in equity built up in houses is likely to have slowed down this process.

Table 5.7 *Equity withdrawal by the personal sector (£million)*

Year	*Net loans for house purchase*	*Private sector net investment in housing*[a]	*Equity withdrawal*
1980	7,368	5,952	1,416
1981	9,483	6,353	3,130
1982	14,127	7,606	6,520
1983	14,520	6,887	7,633
1984	17,030	7,888	9,142
1985	19,032	8,926	10,106
1986	26,979	10,640	16,339
1987	29,521	12,456	17,065
1988	40,834	16,171	24,663

[a]Private sector residential fixed investment + council house sales - government capital grants to the private sector for housing purposes.
Source: Miles [1989].

The greater competition faced by building societies led the government to recognise that new legislation was required to enable building societies to compete with other financial institutions on a more equal basis. In 1981 the BSA established the 'Nature of a building society' working group, under the chairmanship of John Spalding, who was the chief general manager of the Halifax Building Society. This led to a report in 1983 entitled *The Future Constitution and Powers of Building Societies.* The two key proposals of this report were (i) that the mutual status of building societies should continue but that a procedure should be established whereby a society could convert to p.l.c. status and (ii) that societies should be permitted to undertake a wider range of business, but which should be related to the mainstream business. After a period of consultation the BSA published its final proposals in February 1984 in a report entitled *New Legislation for Building Societies.* In July 1984, the government published its proposals in a green paper, *Building Societies: A New Framework.* This largely followed the proposals put forward by the BSA. This finally led to the publication of the Building Societies Bill, which received Royal Assent in 1986 with most of its provisions taking effect from 1 January 1987.

Under the Building Societies Act and subsequent revisions, societies are permitted to offer additional services which fall into the categories of 'financial or 'land related'. Under the former category are:

(i) banking services –
    money transmission (including providing cheque-book accounts),
    credit cards,
    unsecured lending (up to a maximum – see below),
    foreign currency services,
(ii) investment services –
    manage investments,
    establish personal equity plans,
    operate a stock broking service,
    provide investment advice,
(iii) insurance services –
    underwrite insurance,
    provide insurance.

Under the category of land-related services are services relating to the acquisition, development, management or disposal of land primarily for residential purposes, in particular the provision of estate agency services, conveyancing and estates management.

A further provision under the Act allows a society to convert from mutual status to p.l.c. status. A society following this route ceases to be a building society and effectively becomes a bank. Therefore as part of the conversion procedure the society would have to obtain approval from the Bank of England. The Act also allows societies to operate in the other member states of the European Union (EU). Finally the Act introduced a new supervisory body for building societies, namely the Building Societies Commission, which took over the majority of the functions of the Registrar of Friendly Societies.

5.5 After the Act

The new services which societies have most actively taken up are in the category of banking services. In general though it is only the larger societies which have the capital and the size of operations to enter into competition with banks. The Nationwide Anglia was the first society to offer, in the spring of 1987, an interest-bearing current account with chequing facilities, called the 'FlexAccount'. The other large building societies now also offer similar current account services. Most of the larger societies have also introduced a credit card although the credit card market has been saturated since the end of the 1980s and so most societies that have introduced credit cards have lost money on their operations so far. Many societies offer an automatic teller machine (ATM) service through the Link network. The Link network of machines (which includes the machines that formerly belonged to the Halifax and the rival Matrix network) is, however, still outstripped by the combined networks of the banks. A further development in 1990 was the expansion into banking services by the National and Provincial Building Society through the acquisition of Girobank.

A second area of expansion by the larger building societies is into estate agency operations. These societies saw estate agencies as an additional channel for the distribution of their mortgages. However, this expansion occurred in the final stages of a housing boom, so that when the market went into depression in the early 1990s an excess capacity in estate agency operations was revealed and most agency chains have made substantial losses. This has prompted a number of societies to sell their estate agency businesses, generally at a significant loss. However, some societies which have built up estate agency chains appear to be holding on to their investment as they see them as closely tied to their principal operation of mortgage lending in the long term.

A third area of expansion for the large societies has been the selling of insurance. Under the polarisation rules of the Financial Services Act, an institution selling insurance had to opt for either tied or independent status. The majority of the larger societies have opted for tied status.

The smaller societies, not having sufficient capital to diversify into banking services, have in the main concentrated on their traditional business of savings and mortgages. Merger activity continues as some societies have attempted to achieve a size which allows them to take advantage of more of the diversification possibilities provided by the Act. Some smaller societies have diversified into specialist services allowed under the Act that do not require such a large amount of capital. For example, some have set up a subsidiary to handle mortgage administration for other new lenders such as foreign banks.

For one building society, the Abbey National, the Building Societies Act was perceived as not going far enough in removing restrictions. In July 1989 it became the first building society to take advantage of the relevant provision in the Act and convert to p.l.c. status. There are two main advantages to converting to p.l.c. status. First, it provides an escape from restrictions imposed on building societies. For example, building societies are not permitted to undertake corporate banking and there are limits on the extent of unsecured lending they can carry out (see below). International operations for building societies are still limited to the UK and other EU countries. Secondly, it is argued that societies need to convert in order to obtain additional capital, which they may use to diversify more quickly. The act of conversion itself leads to an injection of capital from the new shareholders and would, by increasing the primary capital of the company, enable other forms of capital to be increased commensurately.

After the incorporation of Abbey National there was a gap of five years before the next major development, which was the proposal to transfer the business of the Cheltenham and Gloucester Building Society to Lloyds Bank (effectively a bank takeover of a building society). This transfer is still to be voted on at the time of writing (1995). Also in late 1994 came the proposal of a merger between the Halifax and Leeds Permanent building societies with an eventual incorporation of the merged institution. It is likely that merger activity and incorporation will increase in pace as competition in the retail financial services markets continues to intensify in the 1990s.

The government in 1994 addressed some of the concerns of building societies about the restrictive nature of the building society regulatory framework by (i) increasing the limit on wholesale funding from 40 per cent to 50 per cent, (ii) allowing societies to establish subsidiaries to make unsecured loans to businesses and (iii) giving societies the right to wholly own general insurance companies which offer housing-related products such as building and contents insurance. At the same time the government announced a more wide-ranging review of building society legislation, in particular considering whether to move from the prescriptive regulatory framework introduced by the 1986 Act, where everything is prevented unless powers are granted to allow an activity, to a permissive regime where everything is allowed unless specifically prohibited. New legislation has yet to be formulated at the time of writing (1995). Allowing building societies more scope for diversification is clearly needed in the 1990s as house purchases and hence mortgage demand have slowed down considerably compared with the boom years of the 1980s. This is mainly a consequence of falling house prices in the early 1990s, which have reduced the equity in houses for home owners and at the extreme has left a large number of households (approximately 1.2 million in early 1994) in a position of negative equity. This is a situation where the value of the mortgage exceeds the value of the house. Home owners in this position are clearly unlikely to move house, thus depressing the housing market.

5.6 The balance sheet of building societies

We now turn to examine some of the effects of the changes previously described as revealed by the aggregate balance sheet position of building societies at the end of 1993 (table 5.8).

The balance between wholesale and retail funding for building societies has been discussed in section 5.3. The other part of liabilities is made up of the societies' capital, which is mainly reserves. As building societies are

Table 5.8 *Building societies balance sheet (end 1993) (£million)*

Liabilities		*Assets*	
Retail shares and deposits	200,694	Notes and coins	458
Wholesale funds:		Sterling bank deposits	
CDs	7,349	(including CDs)	30,164
Term deposits and		Bank bills	864
commercial paper	22,106	Building society CDs	2,325
Syndicated		British government stocks	5,177
borrowing	3,272	Other public sector debt	1,081
Bonds	17,374		
Foreign currency	6,601	Other liquid assets	7,047
	50,431		
		Commercial assets:	
Other liabilities		Class 1	214,951
and reserves	29,872	Class 2	8,204
		Class 3	5,924
		Other assets	4,388
Total liabilities	279,857	Total assets	279,857

Source: CSO, *Financial Statistics*, 1994, tables 4.3A, 4.3B.

mutual organisations, owned by their depositors and borrowers, they do not make profits on their operations in the sense of an amount available for distribution for shareholders. Any surplus that is made on their operations is added to reserves. Specific capital adequacy requirements for building societies have been introduced by the Building Societies Commission. These requirements set down a separate capital ratio for each category of asset as well as for off-balance-sheet items (see chapter 4 for further discussion). The capital ratios for each category held by a society are then aggregated and the desired capital ratio is this aggregate plus a margin of at least 0.5 per cent.

On the assets side of the balance sheet the first seven items make up societies' liquid assets. Up until the Building Societies Act, societies were required to operate with a minimum of seven per cent of their assets in liquid form. The Act abolished this minimum requirement and instead stated that societies should keep sufficient assets in a form which enables them to meet liabilities as they fall due. However, a maximum level of liquid assets was set by the Act at 33⅓ per cent. With the ability to raise up to 50 per cent of deposits from wholesale sources, building societies are now more able to practise liability management – see chapter 3 for a discussion of this concept – and as a consequence there is less need to hold a large cushion of liquid assets. An adjustment has therefore occurred so that, in 1982, building societies' liquid assets amounted to approximately 20 per cent of total assets whilst at the end of 1993 this had declined to just under 17 per cent. The composition of building societies' liquid assets portfolio has also changed over the 1980s; in particular, there has been a decline in holdings of government securities and an increase in holdings of short-term deposits and CDs. Part of the explanation for this is a change in the interpretation of the law regarding capital gains in 1984 which led to societies being taxed at the normal corporate rate whereas previously gains had generally been tax free. A further reason is that the greater volatility of societies' retail inflows in the latter half of the 1980s as a result of greater competition from banks and equities led societies to prefer short- rather than long-term assets.

Building societies' commercial assets are divided into three classes by the Act. Broadly, speaking, class 1 assets are first mortgage loans to owner occupiers of residential property. Class 2 are other loans secured on property and class 3 are unsecured loans, investment in residential property and investments in subsidiaries and associates. Initially the limits for these three classes of commercial assets were set so that not less than 90 per cent of assets must be in class 1 and not more than 5 per cent in class 3. In addition, smaller societies are prohibited from owning certain class 3 assets. Following representations from societies these limits were reviewed and the limits have been progressively relaxed, so that from 1 January 1993 the limits are 25 per cent maximum for class 2 and class 3 assets combined, with a maximum of 15 per cent in class 3.

The introduction of class 3 unsecured lending allowed societies to offer credit cards and cheque accounts with overdraft facilities. At the end of 1993 building societies in aggregate were well below the prescribed limits, with class 2 lending at 3 per cent and class 3 lending at just over 2 per cent.

5.7 The finance houses

Finance houses (or non-bank credit companies) comprise a rather heterogeneous group of financial institutions which include subsidiaries of UK banks and overseas financial institutions and several independent institutions. Their activities are specialised and they account for a very small proportion of total lending by financial institutions. At the end of 1993 they had total assets of £10.5 billion, compared with £280 billion for building societies and £533 billion for retail banks. The combined balance sheet for finance houses at the end of 1993 is shown in table 5.9.

Table 5.9 reveals the nature of the business of these institutions. Nearly 70 per cent of their funds are raised by way of loans from banks and other financial institutions. On the asset side, their main business is the provision of instalment credit, with the majority of this going to the personal sector. Finance companies also provide a significant amount of finance to companies in terms of instalment loans as well as through leasing and factoring. Leasing involves the finance company (the lessor) purchasing a

Table 5.9 *Non-bank credit companies balance sheet as at end 1993 (£million)*

Liabilities		*Assets*	
Commercial bills	737	Cash and balances with banks	99
Bank loans	6,373	CDs	0
Loans from other		Other current assets	869
financial institutions	51	Block discounts	0
Other UK loans	231	Finance leases	1,322
Loans from overseas	44	Loans and advances to:	
Sundry current liabilities	467	UK companies	1,753
Capital	2,646	UK persons	6,296
		Other financial assets	54
		Physical assets (own use)	105
		Physical assets (for hiring)	51
	10,549		10,549

Source: CSO, *Financial Statistics*, 1994, table 5.2B.

physical asset which is subsequently leased out to a firm (the lessee) in return for a series of rental payments over a term which usually approximates its economic life. As the lessee is in the same position as if the asset had been purchased outright then finance leases are equivalent to raising a loan. Factoring involves a finance company taking over all or some of the debts owed to a company. The purchase price represents less than the book value of the debts and the gap represents the profit, including a risk element, for the finance company. As far as the company whose debts have been taken over is concerned, the gap is equivalent to the interest on an equivalent loan, with the benefit being an immediate acquisition of funds as compared with the delay before debts are normally paid.

This brief survey illustrates the nature of finance houses acting as financial intermediaries by obtaining funds mainly from banks, and therefore ultimately individuals and companies, and lending to individuals and companies. These institutions undertake a transformation of the characteristics of the funds as they pass through the institution. The transformation of risk is evident from the risky nature of their main lending activity, that is, consumer credit, as compared with the perceived nature of their liabilities. This transformation is of course reflected in the relatively high interest charges on their instalment loans.

5.8 **Conclusion**

In this chapter we have concentrated our attention on the significant changes that have taken place in building society activity over the 1980s. These changes were brought about largely by deregulation of the banking sector in 1980, which led to greater competition between banks and building societies on both sides of the balance sheet. This led to the breakdown in the building society cartel on interest rate setting and a virtual end to non-price rationing in the mortgage market. The Building Societies Act 1986 enabled building societies to undertake many more activities and so compete more effectively in the new environment subject, however, to severe restraints on the quantity of non-mortgage lending. Whilst the government took steps to relax some of these restrictions in 1994 it is likely that a number of large societies will wish to escape these restrictions altogether by following the lead of Abbey National and converting to bank status. Also, as restrictions on societies are relaxed the demarcation between banks and the larger building societies becomes blurred and the distinctive nature of building societies is lost. Whether a role remains in the medium term for a distinct specialist institution providing housing finance is therefore an open question. A related issue commented upon in this chapter is that building societies are facing a significant degree of competition in their traditional business of mortgage lending. Furthermore, there has been some

Table 5.10 *Percentage of owner occupation in the industrialised world*

Ireland	81
Norway	79
Greece	77
Spain	76
New Zealand	74
Australia	73
Finland	68
UK	68
Italy	67
Belgium	65
Luxembourg	64
Canada	63
US	63
Japan	61
Portugal	58
Austria	55
Sweden	55
France	54
Denmark	51
Netherlands	45
Germany	38
Switzerland	30

Source: *Observer* newspaper, 15 January 1995, from Council of Mortgage Lenders.

doubt expressed as to whether the rate of home ownership, illustrated in table 5.6, will continue to grow as rapidly as it has done in recent years, with the consequence that the demand for mortgages may not grow as rapidly. However, although population growth is expected to slow down in the late 1990s, the slowdown in the rate of household formation is likely to be much less marked, assuming incomes and rents continue to grow at recent rates. The long-run outlook for home ownership and hence mortgage demand may therefore not be as gloomy as some have predicted. Further support for this view is provided by the figures shown in table 5.10, which indicates that the proportion of home ownership is lower in the UK than in a number of other industrialised countries. This suggests that owner occupation may not have reached saturation point.

Chapter 6

Investment institutions

6.1 Introduction

The investment institutions are a class of financial intermediary which enable small investors to participate in collective investment funds. These institutions pool together a large number of small-value contributions into a fund which is used to finance the acquisition of a diversified portfolio of assets. The small investor thus obtains the benefit of the lower risks that come from a large diversified portfolio at a lower outlay than would be required if investing directly. Such indirect investment in capital market instruments has long since replaced direct investment by individuals, so that investment institutions now dominate the capital markets. This type of financial institution contrasts with deposit-taking institutions such as banks and building societies principally in the nature of its liabilities. Investment institutions, unlike deposit-taking institutions, have long-term liabilities and this is reflected in the nature of their asset portfolios. In the next section we examine the different types of investment institutions and the growth of these institutions in recent years. The remainder of this chapter is concerned with the nature of the activities of the different types of investment institutions. We also include two appendices to this chapter. The first appendix provides an introduction to Lloyd's insurance market and the second a short description of the so-called 'hedge funds'. Both these topics are outside the main thrust of financial intermediation but are of sufficient current interest to warrant some discussion.

6.2 Types of investment institution

There are four main types of investment institution:

(i) pension funds,
(ii) life assurance companies,

Table 6.1 *Assets of investment institutions for selected years (£billion)*

	1982	*1984*	*1986*	*1988*	*1990*	*1993*	*% growth 1982–93*
Pension funds	83.6	130.3	190.5	214.5	302.7	463.9	454.9
Life assurance companies	79.9	114.2	158.6	198.3	232.3	412.9	416.8
Investment trusts	10.1	15.2	20.5	19.3	20.3	39.4	290.1
Unit trusts	7.8	15.1	32.1	41.6	41.6	89.5	1047.4
Total	181.4	274.8	401.7	473.7	596.9	1,005.7	454.4

Source: CSO, *Financial Statistics*, various issues.

(iii) investment trusts,
(iv) unit trusts.

We do not include the category of general insurance companies in the class of investment institutions for reasons which we outline in the next section.

At the end of 1993 the combined assets of these four types of institution were £1,005.7 billion. This compares with total assets for building societies of £279.9 billion and £1,198.9 billion for all banks reporting to the Bank of England. As we noted in chapter 2, investment institutions have shown rapid growth in recent years and this illustrated in table 6.1.

Of the investment institutions, unit trusts have shown the most rapid growth over the period covered by table 6.1, albeit from a low base. Of the two largest investment institutions, namely pension funds and life assurance companies, it is the pension funds which have achieved the greatest growth over this period. We will examine the reasons for the growth of these different institutions in later sections. First of all we discuss the nature of general insurance and in particular the reasons why we do not consider it to be an investment intermediary.

6.3 General insurance

The 1982 Insurance Companies Act separates the business of insurance companies into two categories: general insurance and long-term business. The former category encompasses a wide variety of business, all of which is concerned with providing insurance against specific contingencies, for example fire, accident, and theft. Such insurance is provided over a fixed period of time, generally one year. The general insurance companies hold

Table 6.2 *Assets of general insurance companies at the end of 1993*

Asset	*£million*
Short term (net)	3,661
British government securities	11,990
UK ordinary shares	10,454
UK other company securities	4,124
Overseas securities	9,744
Local authority	36
Unit trusts	229
Loans and mortgages	1243
Property	2,125
Other	21,170
Total	64,776

Source: CSO, *Financial Statistics*, various issues.

funds, or reserves, to enable them to meet claims on the insurance policies they have issued. As most of these policies are effective for one year and claims are usually made very soon after the event giving rise to the claim, general insurance companies' liabilities are mostly short term. Even where claims take a number of years to settle, a reserve is maintained to cover possible payments. The short-term nature of their liabilities is partly reflected in the assets making up the funds of general insurance companies – see table 6.2.

The majority of the long-term assets of general insurance companies are also marketable, and so can be called on at short notice, but they also provide a return to compensate for any underwriting loss – a common situation in the competitive general insurance industry where premium income is less than claims and the shortfall has to be found out of earnings on the investments. However, we are concerned in this chapter (and this book) with financial intermediaries which, as we described in chapter 2, channel funds from savers through to investors. The premium income which flows into general insurance companies is essentially a payment for a consumption service (indemnity against loss) and therefore cannot really be classified as savings. Also, whilst general insurance companies hold financial assets, these are more a byproduct than a central feature of their business. We therefore conclude that general insurance companies are not strictly financial intermediaries and we do not consider them further in this chapter.

6.4 Nature of the liabilities of pension funds and life assurance companies

Life assurance companies

The long-term, or life assurance, business of insurance companies can be separated into three broad categories.

(i) *Term assurance.* A term assurance policy provides insurance cover, for a specified period, against the risk of death during that period. If the insured survives the specified period then no payment is made. These term policies, which can be characterised as pure insurance policies, do not provide large sums for investment.

(ii) *Whole-of-life policies and endowment policies.* With a whole-of-life type of policy the insurance company pays a capital sum on the death of the person assured, whenever that event occurs. With an endowment policy a capital sum is paid out at the end of some specified term or earlier if the assured dies within the term. Both these types of policies provide cover against premature death and provide a vehicle for savings. The premiums for both these types of policy will be higher than for term assurance because the company is committed to paying out a capital sum at some point in time. As a consequence the life insurance company has to accumulate a substantial fund out of which payments can be made as they fall due. Both these types of policies may be 'without profits', in which case the money value of the benefit is fixed in advance, or 'with profits', where a minimum sum assured may be augmented by bonuses declared by the company. These bonuses will be related to the performance of the fund over the life of the policy and so the 'with profits' policies have the effect of transferring some of the risk of building up sufficient benefits to the policyholder when compared with 'without profits' policies. In some cases a policy may be 'unit linked', where the premiums paid are used to purchase units in a chosen unit trust and the final payment is then dependent on the performance of that trust.

The role of endowment policies has been recently subject to criticism on two counts. First, there is the level of commission paid to the insurance sales person at the time of initial sale of the policy. These initial costs incurred by the insurance company have caused such policies to have a low 'surrender' value, that is, the price the insurance company will pay the policyholder on cancellation of the policy in respect of payments already made on the policy. This problem is mainly in respect of the early years of a policy, when such commission charges are large relative to payments on the policy. Companies are required to be more open now and commission payments have to be disclosed to the potential policy purchaser. The second criticism concerns the use of endowment policies with respect to house purchase, whereby the capital sum is paid directly to the mortgage company on maturity of the policy. As indicated earlier in this section, such policies can be with or without profits. Originally the policy value was fixed so as to be equal to the mortgage debt on maturity so that any profits connected with the policy provided a windfall gain to the policyholder. However, the practice arose of assuming profit levels and taking out a policy which matched the mortgage debt only if the assumed profits were actually achieved. Consequently if the profits attached to the policy were less than the assumed level when the mortgage expired, the policyholder was left with a shortfall which had to be met from her or his own pocket. In some cases the mortgagee was unable to make the required payments.

(iii) *Annuities*. Annuities generally involve a policyholder paying an initial lump sum which is used by the insurance company to provide an agreed income until death. In this case the insurance company will immediately create a fund which is then run down as payments are made to the policyholder.

Pension fund liabilities

Pension provision in the UK comes from three basic sources: (i) the state scheme, (ii) an occupational scheme and (iii) a personal pension. The state scheme consists of a first tier of a flat-rate pension, paid since 1925, and a second tier which is earnings related. We will examine recent developments in the provision of state pensions later in this section. Occupational pensions are provided by employers in both the public and private sector. It is these pension schemes which involve the build up of an investment fund and which form the pension funds we refer to in this chapter. Personal pensions are pensions tailored to an individual's requirements and until recently were provided only by life assurance companies. As a consequence such pensions are counted as part of life assurance business. Recent reforms, outlined later in this section, have however widened the range of institutions which can provide personal pensions.

There are two basic types of pension scheme: the unfunded or pay-as-you-go scheme, and the funded scheme. Many of the public sector schemes are unfunded schemes, whereby the costs of providing benefits are met out of current contributions. In such schemes, therefore, there is no build up of an investment fund and little impact on the capital markets. All the state pensions are run on an unfunded basis, with benefits provided out of the general revenue of the government. The occupational schemes of the Civil Service, the National Health Service, teachers, police and other parts of the public sector are also unfunded, although in some instances a notional fund is maintained. The public sector industries and local authorities, however, run funded schemes. The disadvantage of unfunded schemes is that if the number of contributing members declines or the number of people receiving benefits increases relative to contributors (due, for example, to medical advances leading to longevity, decline in birth rate, etc.) then the burden on contributors can become excessive. There is also a risk with occupational unfunded schemes that the company may be wound up, thus making the pensions provided by the company insecure. In the private sector it is therefore the funded pension scheme which is the norm. With the funded scheme, the contributions of working members, along with in most cases the contributions of employers, are paid into a fund which is invested to yield income and capital gain, out of which benefits are paid. With most funded schemes, benefits are determined by a contributing member's length of service and final salary upon retirement.

Growth of pension funds and life assurance companies

We noted in section 6.2 that the assets of pension funds and life assurance companies have increased in value at a rapid rate over the 1980s and 1990s. In this section we examine the reasons for this growth. First of all we analyse the nature of the growth of these institutions by separating their growth into two categories: (i) net receipts and (ii) changes in price of the assets held (revaluations).

It is clear from table 6.3 that revaluations of assets held by the funds have accounted for a slightly larger proportion of the growth in funds over the whole period. This is explained by the strong growth in equity prices (company shares making up a substantial part of the funds' total asset portfolio, as we shall discover in the next section) both in the UK and overseas over this period. This revaluation effect is strongest in 1986 and 1992 but almost disappears in 1987 as a result of the stock market crash. The growth in net receipts also reflects the strong performance of the assets

Table 6.3 *Growth of life assurance and pension funds (£billion)*

	1986	*1987*	*1988*	*1989*	*1990*	*1991*	*1992*	*Total*
Net receipts[a]	18.7	20.2	20.6	28.1	27.8	29.0	28.9	173.3
Revaluations[b]	39.2	3.7	19.3	28.4	25.0	32.1	40.6	188.3

[a] Contributions of employers and employees + life assurance premiums + investment income of funds + current grants from government - pensions and other benefits - transfers to other pension schemes - administration costs. These are the net receipts of funded schemes only.

[b] Change in holding of personal sector equity in life assurance and pension funds - net receipts. The figure for revaluations may therefore also include any unidentified transactions.

Source: CSO, *National Income Accounts*, 1993, table 4.10 (for net receipts), and *Financial Statistics*, 1993, table 14.5 (for personal sector holdings of equity in life assurance and pension funds).

held by the funds feeding through into investment income in the form of dividends, interest and rent.

The contractual nature of premiums for life policies and contributions for pension schemes provides stability for the funds. Most life policies and pension schemes are paid into over a period of many years and, as we have noted above, there are penalties involved in cashing in life policies in the first few years after commencement. Life policies as a vehicle for long-term savings were encouraged up to 1984 by the existence of tax relief on premiums, at 15 per cent. A further development was the introduction of mortgage interest relief at source (MIRAS) in 1982, which gave a boost to endowment policies linked to mortgages (i.e. only the interest is paid on the mortgage over the term it is taken out for, with the maturing endowment policy used to pay back the capital sum at the end of the term). Building societies have been active in selling endowment mortgages, in order to earn commissions, and the strong marketing of endowment mortgages continued after 1984 when the ending of tax relief increased the costs of this type of mortgage relative to the straight repayment mortgage. We have already indicated potential problems with the use of endowment policies as a vehicle for house purchase. Another boost for insurance companies has come from the recent changes in the state pension system (described below) which have made personal pensions more attractive. As noted above, insurance companies had a monopoly in this type of pension scheme until recently and, despite attempts to broaden the range of providers, are still the main source.

The important factors explaining the growth of pension funds over the last 20 years are related to government policies. The first of these is the taxation treatment of 'approved' occupational pension schemes. The contributions of both employers and employees are deductible from taxable income. The investment returns achieved by a fund are also exempt from taxation. Finally the benefits payable by a fund are subject to the pensioners' rate of personal income tax, except for any lump sum paid up to a set limit, which is tax exempt. Such fiscal privilege has undoubtedly had a positive impact on the growth of occupational funds. Government policies with regard to the state pension have also had an effect on occupational schemes. In 1978 the government introduced the State Earnings Related Pension Scheme (SERPS), which provided greater benefits than the second-tier state earnings-related scheme it replaced. At the same time tougher minimum requirements on benefits paid out by occupational schemes were laid down if employers were to contract out of the state scheme. Most schemes in fact chose to contract out, which in many cases meant that benefits had to be raised. It has been estimated though that, in 1988, approximately 13 million people were contracted into SERPS and were not in an occupational scheme. After a review of social policy in the mid-1980s, the government argued that with increasing longevity and a declining birth rate the burden on the working population in supporting pensioners when SERPS matured early in the twenty-first century would become intolerable. As a consequence SERPS was reformed and the central feature of the new pension arrangements, which came into force in April 1988, was to transfer the responsibility for pension provision from the state to the private sector. To achieve such a transfer, first, benefits available from SERPS were curtailed in order to provide an incentive to take out a private pension or join an occupational scheme and, secondly, the procedures for contracting out of SERPS were made easier and financial incentives were provided to individuals to take up a personal pension and to employers to start up occupational schemes. The monopoly on provision of personal pensions held by insurance companies was also removed to allow other financial institutions such as banks and building societies to become providers. The aim here was to encourage competition in provision. Such developments are likely to lead to an expansion of both personal pensions and occupational funds. One consequence of the competition in selling pensions was that, in some cases, customers were sold pensions which were not appropriate to the individual circumstances of the customer. This situation is being unravelled at the moment and it is likely that compensation will be paid to a quite a large number of the purchasers of pension schemes. In the spring of 1995, the industry watchdog, the Personal Investment Authority (PIA) (see chapter 17 for a discussion of the role of the PIA in the financial regulatory system), reported that there were about 350,000 priority cases which must be examined by the life assurance companies by the end of 1996. Estimates of the total compensation likely to be paid are in excess of £2.5 billion.

6.5 Portfolio investment of pension funds and life assurance companies

The portfolio investment of both life assurance companies and pension funds is determined by the nature of their liabilities and the return and availability of the various types of financial asset. In the previous section we noted that the liabilities of both life assurance companies and pension funds are long term. In evidence to the Wilson committee in 1977, the insurance companies stated the objectives of their investment strategy as being to maximise return, subject to risk, within an asset structure that takes the term structure of their liabilities into account. A particular risk faced by life assurance companies is that when a contract is written, certain sums are guaranteed to be paid in the future and these sums exceed the value of the premiums over the life of the contract. For example, in the case of an endowment policy, a guaranteed sum is assured at the outset. This sum will have been determined by reference to actuarial calculations about mortality and a prediction of likely returns on investment of the premiums. There is therefore a risk that outcomes of mortality, investment returns and so on may prove worse than the life assurance company's assumptions. In order to protect itself against such a risk the life assurance company can 'match' the term structure of its assets and liabilities. In this situation the assets should have a given yield which should be at least equal to the investment returns assumed in the calculation of the sum assured. The ideal type of asset for matching purposes is the British government (gilt-edged) security. As we saw in chapter 1, this asset possesses the characteristics of safety, known term to maturity, fixed interest rate and known redemption value if held to maturity. By carefully selecting gilts with terms to maturity which match the term to maturity of its liabilities, a life assurance company can immunise itself against changes in investment returns and so be in a position to meet its contractual requirements. However, there are several disadvantages with this strategy of matching. First, life assurance companies also write 'with profits' policies and the holders of these policies will expect bonuses to paid. To achieve the returns necessary to pay bonuses, life assurance companies will need to hold some proportion of their asset portfolio in assets which yield higher returns than gilts. Indeed, competition between life assurance companies will encourage them to hold high-yielding assets such as equities. Second, there is a practical constraint to life assurance companies holding portfolios constructed only of gilts, which is that there are insufficient quantities of gilts across the range of maturities required for matching. However, the matching strategy provides a benchmark for life assurance companies in that the further away the fund is from a fully matched position, the greater the risk for the life assurance company of not meeting its contractual requirements.

The liabilities of pension funds, whilst being long term, are also different in nature to those of life assurance companies, as in most cases benefits to be paid out are not known with certainty. As we noted in the last section, the benefits of most occupational pension schemes are related to the final salary of the contributor, which is not known in advance. Wage inflation complicates matters further as it increases the benefits to be paid by the fund, which has been accumulated from lower contributions over past periods. Index linking of final benefits, which occurs with some schemes, provides an additional uncertainty. As a consequence, the concept of matching is less relevant to pension funds. A greater consideration is to achieve funds in excess of the rate of inflation. Hence pension funds will look to hold assets which, over the long term, yield positive real returns. Examples of such assets are equities and property. Index-linked gilts, introduced in the early 1980s, provide a benchmark in this regard.

We now turn to examine the actual investments made by life assurance companies and pension funds over the 1980s and early 1990s. We consider

Table 6.4 *Asset portfolio of life assurance companies and pension funds at end 1993 (%)*

	Life assurance companies	*Pension funds*
Short term	3.4	3.2
UK government securities	16.5	6.8
(of which index linked)[a]	(12.4)	(48.2)
UK local authority	0.2	0
UK ordinary shares	39.2	53.5
Other UK company securities	7.5	1.5
Overseas securities	12.2	19.7
Unit trusts	8.8	2.5
Property, loans and mortgages	9.5	4.8
Other	2.2	7.9
Debtors	0.4	0

[a] Percentage of holdings of gilts not total assets.
Column totals may not sum to 100 due to rounding errors.
Source: CSO, *Financial Statistics*, 1994, tables 5.1A & 5.1B and related earlier tables.

first the actual holdings of the main categories of assets for the two institutions at the end of 1993. We then examine the investment strategies of the institutions over the recent past as revealed by net investment of cash flows, which represent the conscious investment decisions of the institutions.

The figures in table 6.4 reveal that life assurance companies held a greater proportion their portfolio as UK government securities than did pension funds. This follows from the discussion above where we noted that the principle of matching is more relevant to life assurance companies. Pension funds have placed greater attention on index-linked gilts, which make up a larger proportion of their total holdings of gilts compared with life assurance companies. Index-linked gilts are perhaps more relevant to pension funds, as we noted above. Whilst equities are the main asset held by both life assurance companies and pension funds, they make up a greater proportion of the portfolio of pension funds. This reflects the greater requirement on the part of pension funds to achieve positive real returns. When we take into account overseas securities, which are mainly ordinary shares of overseas listed companies, then the proportion of equities held by pension funds is approximately 70 per cent of the portfolio. Another asset which generally yields positive real returns over the long term is property. Surprisingly, life assurance companies have been more active investors in property than pension funds, with the latter concentrating their investment attentions mainly on equities in recent years. We can observe this more

Table 6.5 *Investment of life assurance companies' and pension funds' net receipts 1986–93 (% of total)*

	1986	*1987*	*1988*	*1989*	*1990*	*1991*	*1992*	*1993*
Life assurance companies								
Short term	6.5	13.9	8.0	5.6	35.7	4.5	11.3	-2.8
UK government securities	7.2	10.0	9.4	-5.7	-4.6	13.1	46.6	29.3
UK ordinary shares	48.0	46.0	36.9	17.5	32.5	33.3	14.1	39.6
Other UK company securities	9.4	10.7	16.4	16.7	8.5	12.9	13.4	11.9
Unit trusts				13.9	0.5	4.6	-0.3	7.0
Local authority				0.0	-0.5	0.1	0.0	0.3
Overseas securities	9.7	0.4	8.5	24.3	17.3	21.5	5.8	10.6
Property	7.8	7.3	10.8	7.2	6.0	6.6	3.1	1.8
Loans and mortgages	4.1	7.1	9.0	13.0	2.4	0.6	2.4	-0.9
Other	7.2	4.5	1.1	15.2	2.3	2.7	2.8	2.8
Debtors net of creditors				2.3	0.0	0.0	0.8	0.3
Pension funds								
Short term	16.5	36.9	14.6	23.5	17.0	-48.9	0.4	36.6
UK government securities	13.6	-21.3	-13.7	-32.9	-19.9	-18.4	35.6	39.6
Local authority				-0.2	-0.2	0.0	0.0	0.4
UK ordinary shares	34.9	81.0	50.5	4.0	59.0	66.1	7.3	-23.3
Other UK company securities	4.5	4.5	5.9	10.5	3.7	9.8	0.0	-5.2
Overseas securities	26.7	-0.7	28.7	81.6	48.5	73.1	7.6	25.8
Unit trust				3.5	0.6	1.8	9.9	11.0
Property	3.8	1.5	2.8	0.7	-3.6	3.7	13.8	5.3
Loans and mortgages				0.0	-0.2	0.0	-0.9	-0.1
Other	0.0	4.5	11.4	9.3	5.7	12.7	31.0	9.5
Debtors net of creditors				0.0	-10.8	0.0	-4.6	0.3

Column totals may not sum to 100 due to rounding errors.
Source: CSO, *Financial Statistics*, 1994, tables 5.1A, B and related earlier tables.

clearly by examination of each institution's cash flow investment over the period 1986 to 1993, which is summarised in table 6.5.

The figures in table 6.5 reveal the importance of UK equity investment for both types of institution, which had taken advantage of the rising equity market in the 1980s (see figure 8.1). For life assurance companies the figures portray a picture of allocation of funds to UK company securities over the whole period. The position for pension funds is more variable, with a particularly large proportion of funds being allocated to UK company securities in 1987 and a withdrawal of funds in 1993. The stock market crash of 1987 has brought about a slowdown in equity investment, although the proportion of investment directed towards equities in the year after the crash was in fact greater than the proportion in the first five years of the decade. The popularity of equities for institutions is mainly explained by the fact that the real return (i.e. nominal return less the rate of inflation) on UK equities averaged approximately 13 per cent per year (compared with -1 per cent over the 1970s). The attractiveness of equities also partly explains the decline in investment in UK government securities by both types of institutions over the 1980s. The real return on gilts averaged at about 8 per cent per year over this period. The dramatic fall in investment in gilts in 1986–88 also reflects the decision by the authorities to buy back gilts following budget surpluses (see chapter 9 for further discussion). Property investment by both types of institution also declined over the 1980s as property returns slowed over this period. The real return on property was, on average, approximately 4 per cent per year over the 1980s. The slump in property values towards the end of the decade resulted in property investment virtually ceasing for pension funds.

Investment in overseas securities was high in the early 1980s as the institutions sought to restructure their portfolios following the removal of exchange controls in 1979. A second increase in investment in overseas securities occurred in the middle of the decade as institutions sought to take advantage of the worldwide boom in equity prices. As was the case for domestic equities, the stock market crash of 1987 led to a dramatic slowdown in investment in overseas securities and some repatriation of funds by UK institutions. Following a recovery in world stock markets in 1988, investment in overseas securities picked up again. The purchase of overseas securities was more pronounced in the case of pension funds than for life assurance companies.

A final comment on investment strategies concerns the variable inflows into short-term assets. Investment institutions have relatively low liquidity requirements and although short-term assets provide some return, this is generally lower than the main assets held by these institutions. Short-term assets therefore represent a depository for funds awaiting investment in the main earning assets. High investment in short-term assets generally implies uncertainty about the future returns on the main earning assets. Thus, for example, we note high investment in short-term assets in 1987, particularly by pension funds, reflecting a slowdown in equity investment in the final quarter following the stock market crash and an increase in receipts following the buy back of gilts by the authorities.

We now turn to an examination of the future investment behaviour of pension funds. During the early 1990s two major scandals hit the pension fund industry. In 1991, directors of Belling, the UK cooker manufacture, bought a Belling subsidiary for the pension scheme with £5.5 million of pension assets and also borrowed £2.1 million from the fund. On liquidation the subsidiary was valued at £2.5 million (*Financial Times*, 25 and 26 June 1994). This however pails into insignificance when compared with the disappearance of £440 million from pension funds controlled by the late Robert Maxwell. Legal moves are still continuing to recover some or all of this sum. As a result of the Maxwell deficit, the government set up the Goode committee to review the legal and general environment of pension funds. A number of recommendations were introduced and in the summer of 1994 the government produced its proposals in a white paper. These include:

(i) The establishment of a pensions regulator with the power to discipline schemes which break the rules. The regulator would be financed by a levy on the pension funds industry.
(ii) The setting up of a compensation scheme which would cover loss of assets due to fraud or misappropriation. Note that the limitation of the cover is similar in principle to that applied to deposit insurance for banks discussed in chapter 17, section 17.4. The basic idea is presumably an attempt to induce fund members to exert some control over the behaviour of the fund whereas 100 per cent compensation would remove this incentive (the 'moral hazard' problem). We have doubts as to the efficacy of such an arrangement. The fund would also be financed by levies on the pension fund industry.
(iii) Minimum solvency standards introduced initially in April 1997. These standards aim to ensure that a fund has adequate assets to meet its liabilities, that is, pension obligations. Schemes were permitted five years to meet fully these requirements. A further three years' grace would be allowed to schemes which meet at least 90 per cent of the standard by the year 2002.
(iv) Members of the scheme would have the right to appoint at least one-third of the board of trustees and importantly these trustees cannot be removed by the employer. In the case of small funds, the employees are guaranteed at least one member trustee.

The legislation when fully implemented should make pension funds more transparent and also provide a means of compensation to employees in respect of misappropriation of the fund assets. The measures are currently (spring 1995) being debated in Parliament.

6.6 Unit trusts and investment trusts

Unit trusts and investment trusts are institutions which allow individuals or companies to purchase a stake in a larger and more diversified portfolio than they would normally be able to hold directly and at the same time to obtain the benefits of a sophisticated portfolio management service.

A unit trust is a fund to which individuals and companies may contribute in order to obtain a share in the returns generated by the fund. The institution is legally constituted as a trust, where a trustee acts as guardian of the assets on behalf of the beneficial owners and a separate management company is responsible for investment decisions. The terms and conditions governing these investment decisions are specified in the trust deed under which the institution operates. The trustee company is generally a bank or insurance company.

The industry of fund management underwent diversification over the 1980s and many institutions, including retail banks, merchant banks, stockbrokers and insurance companies have become more involved. At the end of the decade insurance companies accounted for the largest share of ownership of unit trust management companies.

A contributor to a unit trust purchases 'units' at a price which reflects the aggregate value of the trust's net assets divided by the number of units outstanding. The funds are termed 'open ended', which means that the fund can expand by issuing new units at the same value as existing units at that point in time, or it may contract, through unit holders selling back their units to the fund at the prevailing price. There is no secondary market in units, with all sales and purchases of units being made with the trust managers, although another intermediary may act as agent to the transaction. The price at which an investor purchases units is known as the offer price and the price at which he or she sells them back to the trust is known as the bid price. To determine these prices the trustee will request the investment manager to value the assets held at bid or offer price. The price of units is then calculated by adding to the offer price stamp duty, stockbroker's commission, VAT and managers' charges. With managers' charges typically in the region of 5 per cent and a dealing spread (the difference between the bid and offer prices on the underlying assets) of 2 per cent then the difference between unit offer and bid prices can be around 9 per cent. The prices of most units are calculated on a daily basis and the changing prices therefore reflect the changing prices of the underlying assets. The calculation of bid and offer prices just described represents a maximum spread. The quoted spread is normally much lower as fund managers do not always have to buy or sell the underlying securities when they are buying and selling units but match a certain proportion of buying and selling orders. The quoted price will therefore lie within the maximum calculated spread so that during periods of net sales of units the quoted offer price will be at the calculated offer price, with the quoted bid price at a higher price than the calculated bid price. Conversely, during periods of net redemption of units, the quoted bid price will be equal to the calculated bid price, with the quoted offer price lower than the calculated offer price.

Traditionally the price at which the unit trust managers have transacted with investors has been the price related to the last valuation – known as historical or backward pricing. An alternative method, known as forward pricing, means that units are sold at prices that prevail at the valuation (a few hours after the order is processed). The Department of Trade and Industry has recently implemented new rules that give unit trust managers the choice of pricing on a forward or backward basis, with the investor being informed of the chosen method. The advantage of forward pricing is that investors are sold units at (almost) current rather than historical prices. The disadvantage is that investors do not know the transaction price when the order is made.

We noted in section 6.2 that unit trusts have grown rapidly over the 1980s and at the end of 1988 had assets of just over £41 billion. They can invest in a wide variety of assets including bank deposits, UK and overseas company shares and government securities. As we can observe from table 6.6, the main asset held is company shares, both UK and overseas.

A shake-up in the UK investment industry is likely to occur early in 1996. The Treasury has intimated that it is prepared to countenance the introduction of open-ended investment companies in 1996. These are a more flexible form of collective investment institution as they will enable the same fund to provide a wider variety of investments through differing charging structures and in different currencies. Such funds are fairly common in Continental Europe and North America. The timetable for their introduction envisages discussions during the summer of 1995 with the requisite enabling legislation being introduced during the autumn/winter of 1995/96. The Securities and Investment Board will also be required to prepare draft regulations for investor protection during this period. It is thought the open-ended investment institutions (their precise title was not yet determined at the time of writing – early 1995) will be bought and sold at a single price. This will create pressure also for single pricing of unit trusts, that is, abandoning the bid/offer spread noted above. In fact it is

Table 6.6 *Investments held by unit trusts at end 1993 (%)*

Short-term securities	3.1
British government securities	1.0
UK company securities	57.0
Other sterling assets	1.4
Overseas ordinary shares	36.6
Other overseas securities	0.9

Source: COS, *Financial Statistics*, 1994, tables 5.2D and related earlier tables.

quite likely that there will be a movement of funds from unit trusts to these new institutions for two reasons. First, a number of fund managers are understood to be considering transferring from unit trusts to the new institutions. Second, competition from open-ended investment trusts will attract new funds at the expense of unit and possibly investment trusts.

In contrast to unit trusts, investment trusts are public limited companies whose business is the investment of funds in financial assets. Investment trusts raise their finance like any other company, through the issue of shares and debentures, by retaining income and so on. Therefore if an investor wishes to acquire an interest in an investment trust he or she must acquire its shares either by subscribing to a new issue or by purchasing the shares on the stock market. These shares can be sold on to a third party through the stock market.

The investments held by the investment trust industry are summarised in table 6.7. Ordinary shares make up the overwhelming majority of securities held. In contrast to unit trusts, overseas shares form the larger proportion of total equity holdings.

The existence of borrowed funds, as opposed to equity, in the capital structure of an investment trust means that if the value of the underlying securities fluctuates there is a 'gearing' effect on the value of the shares issued by the trust. To illustrate this effect we will consider a simple example of an investment trust which has a capital structure comprising £8 million in shareholders' equity claims, attributable to 4 million issued shares, and £2 million of outstanding debt. The total value of funds invested by the trust is therefore £10 million, which we assume is invested only in ordinary shares. The net asset value (NAV) per share (the value of assets less debt divided by the number of issued shares) is thus £2. Now if the value of the investment trust asset portfolio were to double to £20 million then the NAV per share would increase to £4.50. Therefore a 100 per cent increase in the value of assets held has led to an increase in the NAV per share of

Table 6.7 *Investments held by investment trusts at end 1993 (%)*

British government securities	2.8
Shares of UK listed companies	41.3
Shares of UK unlisted companies	2.1
Other sterling assets	1.5
Overseas company shares	50.8
Other overseas securities	1.5

Source: COS, *Financial Statistics*, 1994, table 5.2C and related earlier tables.

125 per cent. The gearing effect of course can work to the detriment of shareholders when the assets of the investment trust fall in value. There is also a gearing effect on the income to be distributed to shareholders resulting from a change in the net income (before interest) derived from the investment trust's asset portfolio. Whilst the gearing effect is always of benefit to shareholders, in terms of NAV of their shares, in a rising stock market, the effect from income generation will be of benefit only if the return from utilising the borrowed funds is greater than the interest cost. The actual gearing of investment trusts in aggregate in recent years has been relatively modest, averaging around 8 per cent.

A particular curiosity of investment trusts is that the share price of most of them is at a significant discount to the NAV per share. The price of shares is of course determined by demand and so the existence of a discount would imply that demand for the investment trust's shares is lower than the demand for its portfolio of shares bought independently. We noted in section 6.2 that investment trusts have not grown as rapidly as unit trusts over the 1980s. This lower demand for the services of investment trusts may be because, unlike unit trusts, investment trusts cannot advertise themselves through the media. Another factor which discourages investors may be the greater risk of the investment which comes from the gearing effect. The existence of a discount makes investment trusts vulnerable to takeover, especially when a trust owns an appreciable stake in a target company. The potential bidder can acquire up to 30 per cent of the trust and therefore the shares owned by it at a discount. The full bid for the remainder will have to reflect the NAV. An example of such a process includes, in 1979, Lonhro's agreed acquisition of the Scottish and Universal Trust, which held 10.29 per cent of the shares in House of Fraser, which Lonhro went on to bid for.

6.7 The performance of institutional investors

Rising equity markets around the world over most of the 1980s resulted in historically high performances, with regard to returns, by UK fund managers. The discussion that follows, which examines the nature of this performance over the 1980s and some recent developments in fund management techniques, relates specifically to pension funds but the main points broadly apply to other parts of the UK fund management business.

Average annual returns on pension fund investments over the 1980s were 19.5 per cent, which compares favourably with average inflation and wage inflation, over the same period, of 6.9 per cent and 9.5 per cent respectively. The figure for wage inflation represents a form of target return for those pension funds where benefits are linked to final salary. This performance over the 1980s contrasts strongly with performance over the

1970s, where pension fund investment returns underperformed wage inflation by, on average, approximately 6 per cent per year. The consequence of this was that pension fund actuarial deficits had to be met by higher contributions from employers. The considerably higher investment income over the 1980s has resulted in actuarial surpluses for many funds, which have allowed companies to take 'contribution holidays'.

The investment performance by pension funds over the 1980s was largely a consequence of rising equity markets, which, as we noted in section 6.5, were tapped by funds which invested most of their cash flows into equities. The diversification into overseas equities, where growth has at times been stronger in particular markets than in the UK, has also been a contributory factor. However, the diversification into overseas equities has not been as successful as it could have been, as evidenced by a failure of funds to match closely the index in overseas equity markets. The return on UK equities was on average 23.2 per cent per year over the 1980s, compared with a 23.6 per cent return on the FT index – a close match after taking costs into account. In contrast there was underperformance of the indexes in the US by, on average, 3.6 per cent and in Japan by, on average, 2.5 per cent. This underperformance has led to consideration by fund managers of index-tracking funds. These are funds which are constructed according to a chosen index, with the shares making up that index included in the fund according to the weightings in the index. Such an index has the advantage of low transaction costs, as shares are bought and sold only to keep the fund in line with the index. Depending on how well the index has been tracked, this type of passive management yields returns in line with returns on the index. Index funds were first established in the US and have only been slowly taken up in the UK. However, it has been estimated that about 8 per cent of UK pension funds are now of the index-tracking type (reported in a *Financial Times* survey of pension funds, 3 May 1990).

A recent development affecting the investment strategy of pension funds and unit trusts is the removal in 1990 of a tax restriction on trading derivative products such as futures and options. Prior to this, futures trading which was not for hedging purposes was liable to corporation tax. This allows fund managers to use derivative products to adjust exposure to the market without having to buy or sell the underlying securities. The recent introduction of new rules also makes it easier for fund managers to create futures funds.

A final comment concerning fund management relates to the way the performance of managers is assessed. Performance of fund management is conventionally assessed on a quarterly basis. This is not to say that managers are hired and fired on such a timescale but it is argued that subtle pressures may be introduced. Such pressures may lead managers to focus on short-term objectives. If a hostile takeover attempt is made and a fund manager holds shares in the target company in her or his portfolio then it is argued that the manager may accept the offer to boost short-term performance. We consider the general debate about 'short termism' in more detail in chapter 16.

6.8 Conclusion

In chapter 2 we noted the significant growth of assets held by investment institutions in recent years when compared with the growth of assets held by the deposit-taking institutions. In this chapter we have shown that the principal reason for this is that the main assets held by investment institutions are equities, which have achieved substantial returns, in terms of both income and capital gain, over the 1980s. Other reasons suggested to explain the growth of investment institutions relate to government policy and include tax-privileged contributions to pension funds and changes in the state pension scheme which have encouraged private provision.

We have indicated the nature of forthcoming legislation which is designed to prevent future pension fund scandals. It is also interesting to note that some large firms are giving up in-house pension fund management teams and contracting the business to outside professional fund managers. This is just one example of the current tendency for firms to concentrate on their core business and to contract out peripheral business. We also noted the criticisms that have been levied against the life assurance industry. The scale of the problem is indicated by a survey by actuaries AKG, who report that 20 per cent of pension policies and 15 per cent of life assurance policies sold in 1992 were terminated within the first year (*Financial Times*, 3 January 1995). It is also believed that industry-wide compensation for mis-selling of pensions could amount to between £2 billion and £2.7 billion.

We have now completed our discussion of financial institutions and so in the next section of this book we turn our attention to financial markets.

Appendix 1: Lloyd's of London

This appendix has been contributed by Professor Peter Franklin, Bass Leisure Dean, Nottingham Business School, Nottingham Trent University.

Introduction

Lloyd's of London is a unique institution. Based in architecturally distinct, high-tech, state-of-the-art premises in the heart of the City of London, Lloyd's sources its worldwide insurance business by operating through international insurance brokers accredited to Lloyd's and by being capitalised by wealthy individuals known as 'names'.

Historically, the unique structure of Lloyd's has been a source of competitive advantage and a base for continuing curiosity about the potential longevity of a worldwide business which depends significantly on private capital. Before we look at recent and prospective developments at Lloyd's, it is sensible to understand the role of names within Lloyd's and then appropriate to go on to outline some of the underlying business transactions which distinguish Lloyd's from other non-life insurers.

Names

Names are wealthy individuals who are recruited to Lloyd's to provide the capital which supports the underwriting activities of the Lloyd's insurance market. Lloyd's names are introduced by a members' agent. The principal role of a members' agent is first to advise its members (i.e. its names) on the choice of Lloyd's syndicates which operate within the market and secondly to administer the names' Lloyd's affairs.

Names normally join a number of different underwriting syndicates, each of which specialise in different sorts of risks. Each of these syndicates is managed by a managing agent and the profits or losses made by the syndicate are shared among the names in proportion to the names' shares in the syndicate. Names are required to accept the principle of unlimited liability, so that if an underwriting member (i.e. name) sustains a substantial underwriting loss, the member is liable to meet these losses from other (i.e. non-LLoyd's) assets.

Following substantial losses incurred by some syndicates, the efficacy of an insurance market entirely dependent on wealthy individuals' capital has again become an issue, and in 1993 Lloyd's made arrangements governing the admission of corporate capital.[1] Corporate capital gives Lloyd's a welcome opportunity to increase its overall underwriting capacity; it is also likely to enhance Lloyd's overall capital adequacy.

In the meantime, Lloyd's has had to deal with the difficult situation caused by the losses incurred by some syndicates. Whilst names are required to assume unlimited liability, in practice Lloyd's has generally not caused underwriting members to declare bankruptcy. Indeed, Lloyd's has set up a hardship fund to help members who have been particularly badly affected. This action, and others outlined later in this appendix, aims to give confidence to past, current and future names in the potential benefits of being an underwriting member at Lloyd's.[2]

Having looked at the capital base supporting the Lloyd's insurance market, it is now appropriate to look at some of the fundamental business and financial transactions which characterise the operations of the market.

Underwriting: the fundamental transaction

At Lloyd's, underwriting involves an exchange between two parties: one a professional underwriter who acts on behalf of her or his names; the other a Lloyd's broker who acts on behalf of the insured.

In simple terms we can imagine an insurance broker being instructed by a manufacturing group to obtain buildings insurance for its factories and offices. Acting on behalf of the insured, the duty of the broker is to obtain the best cover possible at least cost, and as a result the broker will need to search the insurance market to find one or more underwriters who are willing to accept the implied risks.

Being a broker accredited by Lloyd's gives the broker a greater number of prospective underwriters to choose from. Not only can the broker approach non-life insurance companies (such as Eagle Star or General Accident), but as a Lloyd's broker the risk can now be offered to Lloyd's underwriters. Indeed, the Lloyd's broker may well come to the initial view that Lloyd's is most likely to offer the best deal; alternatively, the broker may judge that it is essential that Lloyd's is seen to take the lead in the market, and set the premium rate.

So, going back to our simulation, the Lloyd's broker enters the Underwriting Room at Lloyd's and approaches one of the underwriters known to have expertise in buildings insurance for factories and offices. The underwriter interrogates the broker about the details of the prospective liability, including any specific terms and conditions, and makes three judgements:

(i) whether or not to accept the risk,
(ii) and if so, what proportion,
(iii) at what premium rate.

The fundamental insurance transaction, therefore, is an agreement between the Lloyd's broker and the underwriter about:

(i) the details, terms and conditions relating to the insurance policy,
(ii) the premium rate,
(iii) the proportion of the risk accepted by the underwriter.

Assuming the first underwriter takes only a small fraction of the overall risk, the process and agreement reached between the broker and the first underwriter is replicated with others. The broker therefore moves from the 'leading' underwriter to a second and a third and so on until 100 per cent cover has been obtained for the risk.

The financial transaction

With the risk now covered, the next transaction is a financial one. The broker is now committed to forward the premiums he or she has agreed; the underwriters are committed to accept the risk and, in return for the premium payments, authorise the issuing of an insurance policy to the insured through the broker.

This relatively simple financial transaction masks significant changes in the assets and liabilities of the parties associated with the transaction. These changes are outlined in table 1.

Table 1 *Changes in the assets and liabilities of the participants in the insurance transaction*

Insured	*Broker*	*Underwriter/name*
Impact on liabilities		
The insured company has covered its property risks	The broker assumes the costs of placing the business with an under-writer	The underwriter has now assumed the risk and is liable in the event a claim is incurred
Impact on assets		
A premium payment has been made and as a result the company's financial assets have reduced	To offset costs, the broker receives commission from the underwriter for the business placed	The underwriter receives a premium payment (net of commission and reinsurance) which is added to existing insurance funds

As table 1 indicates, the insurance transaction has the *net* effect that the underwriter's balance sheet changes, such that both liabilities and assets increase.

Asset portfolio management, Lloyd's and financial intermediation

So far we have seen two transactions: one an *insurance* transaction; the second a *financial* one. This exchange of money for insurance cover, however, has one other effect: the alteration of the underwriters' assets and liabilities, and by extension, the continuing changes in their asset portfolios.

Asset portfolio management is consequently an integral feature of the day-to-day operations of Lloyd's underwriters. In practice, asset portfolio management is delegated to the agents who manage an underwriting member's (i.e. names') Lloyd's business. These managing agents act on behalf of names, crediting premiums and, in profitable times, disbursing profits.[3] Managing agents therefore play an important if secondary role, and by managing the funds attributable to names act as a specialised form of financial intermediary.[4]

Two measures of the asset portfolio management activity are worth recording. According to Lloyd's most recent figures, given in their *Global*

Results for 1993, the premium trust funds managed by members' managing agents amounted to £19,650 million, and other funds (held at Lloyd's on behalf of members) £4,718 million.

The investment income earned on names' assets is another measure of financial intermediation at Lloyd's. Using the same source,[5] this shows that gross investment income plus capital appreciation amounted to £714 million in 1991, the last closed year of account.[6]

The importance of Lloyd's
Having examined the unique character of Lloyd's of London it is right to put the importance of Lloyd's into context. For this purpose we will consider just four measures:[7]

(i) the volume of business undertaken by Lloyd's,
(ii) Lloyd's share of the UK insurance market,
(iii) Lloyd's share of worldwide premiums written by UK authorised insurers,
(iv) Lloyd's contribution to invisible exports.

The volume of business undertaken by Lloyd's
In its accounts, Lloyd's distinguishes between premiums obtained during a calendar year (calendar year premium income) and premiums associated with an accounting year.

Data published in Lloyd's 1993 *Global Results* indicate that Lloyd's has continued to write increasing amounts of non-life business, with calendar year premium income rising from £5,584 million in 1989 to £8,606 million in 1993. Closed accounting years show a similar trend, with net premiums rising from £3,966 million in 1989 to £6,014 million in 1991.

Share of the UK non-life insurance market
According figures produced by Lloyd's,[8] Lloyd's holds 18 per cent of UK general liability business, and 15 per cent of UK motor insurance. Comparing these data with statistics published by the ABI,[9] in 1992 Lloyd's overall share of the UK domestic market in 1992 is given as 8 per cent, equivalent to about £1.5 billion.

Lloyd's share of worldwide premiums written by UK authorised insurers
A less reliable statistic is Lloyd's share of worldwide premium written by UK authorised insurers, where the ABI report indicates that Lloyd's accounts for about 20 per cent of this measure. A later report, also published by the ABI,[10] estimates that Lloyd's accounts for over 25 per cent of net premiums written in the UK, amounting to approximately £8 billion.

Lloyd's contribution to invisible exports
The final measure of the importance of Lloyd's is the market's contribution to invisible exports. Figures for 1988–92 indicate something of the difficulties faced by Lloyd's underwriters over this period, with net contributions to invisible exports falling from £681 million in 1988 to -£645 million in 1992.[11] Over the same period returns on overseas investments of Lloyd's rose from £321 million to £912 million.[12] And on a related theme, the contributions of brokers (including Lloyd's brokers) rose from £690 million to £1,034 million over the same years.

The future for Lloyd's
Over the last 30 years Lloyd's has gone through turbulent times and a number of well publicised crises. Of particular note is the fact that Lloyd's has incurred significant aggregate underwriting losses, as indicated in table 2.

Table 2 *The profitability of Lloyd's[13] (£million)*

	Closed underwriting years					
	1986	*1987*	*1988*	*1989*	*1990*	*1991*
Underwriting profit/(loss)	745	412	(549)	(1,902)	(2,418)	(1,993)
Gross investment return	550	796	789	736	746	714

The losses shown in table 2, however, conceal the significant variations between syndicates, with some remaining in profit whilst others have incurred heavy losses. Those Lloyd's members who have been affected by these losses have been particularly critical about the stewardship of their affairs, arguing that these losses could have been avoided, by not writing loss-making business or by setting better premium rates or by adopting different policy guidelines within the market as a whole.

Some Lloyd's members have felt sufficiently aggrieved to begin legal proceedings against the Society of Lloyd's itself, seeking to annul their underwriting obligations on the grounds of negligent or fraudulent misrepresentations alleged to have been made by the Society through its agents. Others are pursuing legal action against managing agents, claiming compensation for underwriting liabilities which they allege would not have been incurred but for the negligent actions of the agents.[14] On its behalf, Lloyd's is endeavouring to reach a settlement outside the courts by agreement with the names, and simultaneously Lloyd's is 'ring fencing' past losses so as to protect future investors from incurring liabilities attributable to past losses.

Behind the headlines there remain serious issues concerning:

(i) stewardship – the stewardship of names' assets; the adequacy of existing regulations; the integrity and thoroughness of their implementation; and the willingness to accept accountability in policy formation *and* implementation within the Lloyd's community;
(ii) the financial basis of Lloyd's – the extent to which Lloyd's can continue to rely on individual private wealth and unlimited liability; the extent to which Lloyd's will be forced into accepting corporate capital and limited liability owing to its current and prospective liability portfolio;
(iii) the underwriting portfolio – the extent to which the underwriting portfolio appropriately matches the sources and durability of the assets which underpin Lloyd's members' insurance liabilities; the extent to which its niche will or can continue to be associated with innovative, difficult or syndicated risks, whether for direct or reinsurance business;
(iv) the economic contribution of Lloyd's – to the global insurance market and, as knock-on consequences, Lloyd's contribution to GNP and the UK balance of payments.

Each and all of these issues represent a profound strategic challenge facing the leaders and opinion formers within Lloyd's. Much has been debated since the publication of the Cromer report in 1968; much has been achieved in the form of more open disclosure and accountability; much is being achieved in bringing Lloyd's attitudes into the realities of the late twentieth century.[15]

Concluding remarks

In this short exposition it is not possible to deal fully with the rich texture of life at Lloyd's, nor to give a satisfactory or entirely justified view about its future potential. Yet, as a final observation, one of the enduring features of Lloyd's is its very endurance: its ability to survive unimagined and unexpected geological, political, technical and social shocks. One would be a fool to write off Lloyd's future. However, it needs to reform and reform urgently in preparation for the next century.[16]

Endnotes

1 In Lloyd's *Global Results 1993*, published in 1994. The report indicates that at the beginning of 1994 there were 17,526 names and just 95 corporate members.
2 Over the ten-year period 1984–93 Lloyd's underwriting capacity rose from £5,090 million to a peak of £11,382 million in 1991 and fell to £8,878 million in 1993.

3 Profits arise from two sources. Underwriting profits arise from the difference between claims and premiums. They are supplemented by any investment income earned from the financial assets held by Lloyd's or the members' agents acting on behalf of Lloyd's names.
4 Strict and limiting regulations govern the composition and balance of the asset portfolios which the managing agents control. As a consequence, the scope of financial intermediation is much more limited than (say) for a merchant bank advising a personal client.
5 *Global Results 1993*, Lloyd's of London.
6 Until recently, Lloyd's has operated a three-year system of accounting such that an account is closed only after three years has elapsed. Thus, the 1993 revenue accounts refer to business initiated in 1991 or earlier.
7 The calculation of Lloyd's share of worldwide business is a further measure outside the scope of this appendix.
8 *Planning for Profit: A Business Plan for Lloyd's of London*, Lloyd's of London, April 1993, pages 63 and 64.
9 Association of British Insurers, *Insurance Statistics 1988–1992*, ABI, London, page 14.
10 Association of British Insurers, *UK Market Statistics 1984–1992*, ABI, London, February 1994, pages 11 and 6.
11 Association of British Insurers, *Insurance Statistics 1988–1992*, ABI, London, page 25.
12 Association of British Insurers, *Insurance Overseas Earnings 1984–1991*, ABI, January 1994, London, page 6.
13 Source: *Global Results 1993*, Lloyds of London, 1994, page 20.
14 *A Guide to Corporate Membership*, Lloyd's of London, September 1993, pages 97 and 98.
15 A useful reference available from the Corporation of Lloyd's is *Planning for Profit: A Business Plan for Lloyd's of London*, Lloyds of London, April 1993.
16 The *Post Magazine* of 26 May 1994 reported that if returned to power at the next general election, the Labour Party 'would bring Lloyd's under full statutory control' rather than regulation via the Lloyd's Act of 1982.

Appendix 2: Hedge or leveraged funds

This section draws heavily on 'Hedged or leveraged funds' (*Bank of England Quarterly Bulletin*, May 1994).

'Hedge fund' is a rather vague term used to describe an investment fund drawn up in a manner which permits exemption from the investor protection requirements. Little hedging is, in fact, carried out, as the fund managers tend to take a positive view on future market movements and act accordingly by taking long or short positions. The funds are, however, leveraged, by both borrowing and trading in the derivative markets (see chapter 13 for a discussion of derivative markets). Hence the term 'leveraged funds' may be more appropriate. The degree of leverage obtained by the funds depends on the extent that the funds can borrow without collateral security and the margin requirements imposed by their counterparties in the derivative markets (again see chapter 13 for a discussion of margins). The effect of this degree of leverage is to make the returns on the fund's position highly sensitive to marginal movements in the prices of the relevant assets.

The precise number of such funds is not known but the Bank of England reports that 'conservative estimates nevertheless indicate that there are around 800 leveraged funds world wide handling investment funds of $45 billion' (*Bank of England Quarterly Bulletin*, May 1994). The size of the individual funds vary considerably, with a handful of the largest being responsible for roughly half of the total funds handled. The main direction of their operations is directed towards US markets and US citizens but the Bank states that leveraged fund activity is growing in Europe.

A leveraged fund is typically managed by a small group of key individuals whose reputation is critical for the success of the fund in obtaining capital and so on. Some funds, particularly the larger ones, require long-term commitment of capital, for example for three years or more. These larger funds seem to resort to a lower degree of leverage as compared with the smaller funds, which the Bank reports may be leveraged 'up to forty times or more'.

These funds obviously influence the pattern of behaviour of financial markets. It can be argued that because they are quick to perceive anomalies they increase the efficiency of financial markets, to which the following chapters are devoted.

Chapter 7

Financial markets: introduction

7.1 Introduction

With this chapter we begin our look at the main financial markets making up the UK financial system. All of the markets we consider in subsequent chapters are located in London and, although they serve the domestic economy, a substantial amount of transactions through these markets are international. In the case of markets such as foreign exchange (see chapter 11) and euro-securities (chapter 12) the majority of transactions conducted through London are for non-UK residents. We therefore begin this chapter by considering the importance of London as an international financial centre and some of the reasons for this. We then turn to consider in sections 7.3 and 7.4 some general issues relating to the nature of financial markets, including types of trading systems and types of trading activity. We then finish this chapter with a discussion of the nature of an efficient financial market.

7.2 London as an international financial centre

Three international centres dominate the financial scene. These are New York, London and Tokyo. The main exception to the dominance of the so-called golden triangle which these three centres make up lies within the sphere of exchange-traded futures and options, where Chicago dominates. During 1989 the major markets in Chicago (the Chicago Board of Trade and the Chicago Mercantile Exchange) accounted for 65 per cent of total world trade in these increasingly used financial instruments. At this time London and the rest of Europe attracted 6.25 per cent and 7.14 per cent respectively. It is, however, pertinent to note that the US share is decreasing and by 1993 the Chicago exchanges together accounted for just 35.4 per

Table 7.1 *International banking: analysis by centre (% of total international claims outstanding)*

	December 1980	*December 1985*	*September 1989*	*December 1993*
Belgium	4.2	3.8	3.2	4.2
Luxembourg	6.7	4.1	4.0	6.6
France	10.8	7.1	6.4	10.3
Germany	5.5	3.2	3.7	8.9
Switzerland	4.5	6.4	5.5	7.2
UK	27.0	25.4	19.3	21.1
Japan	5.0	10.8	21.5	18.4
United States	13.4	13.3	9.4	10.9

Source: *Bank of England Quarterly Bulletin*, various issues.

cent of total world trade. This compares with 15.7 per cent through London (the largest centre in Europe) and 16.5 per cent for the rest of Europe. Since London occupies a position mid-way between the eastern and western time zones, it is no surprise to find a large number of financial institutions and markets present in London.

With reference to banking, London has long been a major international banking centre and has developed since the 1960s as a eurocurrency banking centre. At the beginning of the 1980s, London was by far the largest international banking centre in the world, accounting for 27 per cent of total international lending. Table 7.1 shows that by the end of the 1980s the figure had declined to just over 19 per cent and London had lost its

Table 7.2 *International banks in London: share of international lending through London (%)*

	End 1975	*End 1989*	*End 1993*
US	38	13	9
Japan	13	35	23
UK	22	17	18
Other European	6	22	25
Other overseas	22	13	25

Source: *Bank of England Quarterly Bulletin*, various issues.

dominance to Japan, which accounted for 21.5 per cent. However, in the early 1990s Japanese banks began withdrawing from international banking following a decline in Japanese stock markets which reduced the capital of the banks and a decline in Japanese property prices which reduced profits. Thus, by 1993 the positions of London and Japan in the ranking of international banking had reversed.

The 1980s saw a marked increase in Japanese international banking conducted both through Tokyo and its overseas establishments in London, the USA and elsewhere. This growth largely reflects the growth in Japanese international trade and investment. London, in fact, is the most important centre for Japanese banks outside of Japan. The decline in Japanese banks' international lending, referred to above, is therefore reflected in the decline in Japanese bank lending through London in the early 1990s – see table 7.2. The US banks were the dominant international banks in London over the 1960s and 1970s. However, over the 1980s and early 1990s the US banks have experienced a decline in their share of total international lending, both generally and through London. This partly reflects a retrenchment by US banks, to concentrate on domestic business, following the sovereign debt crisis which broke in 1982. However, whilst the on-balance-sheet business of US banks operating in London has declined, these banks continue to be the main players in international off-balance-sheet activities, such as foreign exchange dealing and swaps. The other main source of growth of international banks based in London is other European banks, particularly German banks, which in 1993 accounted for 16 per cent of international lending through London.

The dominance of London in international banking is reflected in the fact that, in 1993, 520 foreign banks were established in London. This compares with 340 in New York, 170 in France and 150 in Germany. In addition, there are 173 securities houses established in London, underlining London's lead not only in securities transactions (discussed below) but also in investment banking.

The markets located in London include (i) the sterling money markets, (ii) the capital markets, both primary and secondary, (iii) the foreign exchange market, (iv) financial futures, (v) the commodity markets, (vi) the eurocurrency and eurobond markets, and (vii) the derivative markets in options, futures swaps and so on. In fact it is more than a case of existence of these markets in London because, as we shall see, London occupies a dominant position as an international financial centre. The London foreign exchange market is the largest in the world. As far as equities are concerned, whilst only the third largest equity market, London's importance as an international centre for equity dealing is evidenced by the fact that there are more foreign companies listed on the London Stock Exchange and turnover in foreign company equities is larger than on any other world equity market. In 1993, 64 per cent of all foreign equity trading carried out on national exchanges was done through the London Stock Exchange.

Given its importance in international banking business and foreign exchange dealing, it is not surprising that London is one of the major centres for dealing in eurocurrencies and eurobonds. An indication of London's dominance of the secondary trading of eurobonds is given by the fact that 80 out of 114 dealers reporting daily or weekly prices to the International Securities Markets Association (ISMA) were located in London. London is also one of the two primary centres (the other being New York) for dealing in swaps, which are a rapidly growing market closely linked to eurobonds. The various markets are discussed in more detail in chapters 8 to 13.

The emergence of London as an international financial centre can be explained with reference to a number of factors apart from the time-zone factor briefly noted above. London has a long tradition of international business, arising from the development of the Empire and the accompanying international trade. International financial institutions have been attracted to London because of the existence of a number of features. These include a suitable pool of experienced and skilled labour, relatively light restrictions on access to financial markets, a tax regime which is not hostile to financial innovation, the absence of exchange controls since 1979, relatively light reserve requirements, a stable political regime and the English language. This last factor is an important consideration for US institutions setting up a European base. A more detailed discussion is provided by Davis and Latter [1989] and Davis [1990], with the latter paper examining the development of international financial centres from a more theoretical perspective. The growing concentration of financial firms in London due to these factors will have attracted to London new firms which are likely to have been the more innovative financial institutions, at the forefront of the development of new instruments and techniques. This in turn will have reinforced the importance of London as a financial centre.

All the markets mentioned above are both global and 'wholesale' markets and only deal in large-value transactions between both domestic and foreign institutions. The retail markets are linked to these markets via banks and other financial institutions. Thus, for example, a private individual buying foreign currency for a holiday would go along to a high street bank which would have obtained the currency originally on the London foreign exchange market. The markets are also organised in the sense that trading there requires operators to conform to rules specified within a 'rule' book and/or those imposed by the supervisory authority. These markets, together with the financial institutions which use the markets, are known colloquially as 'the City'. In the next section we examine in more detail the nature of markets.

7.3 The nature of markets

In the past, it was easy to define a market according to the geographical location where deals were made; for example, the Stock Exchange was a building where interested traders could meet and strike bargains. In many cases the growth of screen-based information systems has changed all of this. This has removed the need to meet fellow traders and deals can be made over the telephone or on the screen itself. Up to now this has not been true of all markets since, for example, financial futures have tended to maintain the 'open outcry' system of trading, but the Chicago Board of Trade (CBOT) and the Chicago Mercantile Exchange (CME) along with Reuters in 1992 introduced GLOBEX, an electronic matching system alongside the open outcry system. This is discussed further below. The London International Financial Futures and Options Exchange (LIFFE) also provides a system of automated trading outside normal trading hours. This raises the question of how to define an organised market, since asset prices are now publicly available via the payment of a subscription to an information system (the pricing function is said to be 'transparent'). Three core functions can be identified. First, there is the price discovery system whereby demand for and supply of the particular asset are brought together to determine the equilibrium price. The trading rules of the market determine how this function is to be carried out. The second core function is the surveillance function through which the public can be guaranteed as far as possible that any deal is fair. The market is, in effect, giving its stamp of approval. This latter function is also ensured through the trading rules by such means as regulations concerning disclosure, settlement and so on. Third, an organised market provides either a meeting place where, or a network through which, interested parties can be brought into contact with each other. The problem for the organised market is that both the first two functions are in the nature of public goods. Consequently there is little to stop individuals extracting the information and dealing on their own account (i.e. 'piggy-backing').

Markets can be characterised in a number of ways. First, a distinction can be drawn between continuous and batch markets. In a continuous market, as the name suggests, buyers and sellers are in continuous contact with each other throughout the period the market is open and deals can be concluded at any time. On the other hand, in a batch market, orders for purchases and sales are accumulated and are executed together at particular points of time. A second distinction can be made between auction and dealers' markets (sometimes these two market types are called 'order-driven' and 'quote-driven' markets respectively). An example of an auction market are the markets for futures, where an 'open outcry' system is used for dealers to strike individual bargains between each other. Open outcry is characterised by the presence of traders in close physical proximity, in a trading pit, who must verbally or publicly announce their bids and offers. To execute a trade a trader must establish eye contact with the trader bidding or offering and say 'sold'. At any given time only the best bid and offer price are valid for execution. Another feature of the open outcry system is the presence of a type of trader known as a local. Local traders are members of the exchange but have limited capital compared with the institutional members of the exchange. Locals will trade primarily for their own personal account and generally trade by taking small, short-horizon (e.g. seconds or minutes) positions. The role of locals is important in this type of market and this is reflected in the fact that they generally account for more then 50 per cent of total trading volume in the market. The existence of locals means that customer orders arriving in a trading pit usually find a two-sided market that can accommodate their trades immediately. Thus, locals provide liquidity in the market.

As referred to above, a number of futures markets with the open outcry trading system have in recent years introduced or begun evaluating electronic trading systems. An electronic matching system is made up of a set of computer terminals connected via high-speed communication links to a central host computer. Bids and offers are entered into a remote terminal and sent to the host computer, which queues them according to price and for bids/offers at the same price, according to time received by the host. Only the host computer has complete information on the market. A trader will see only the best bid or offer. All trades take place through the host. On GLOBEX, the electronic matching system referred to above, a transaction occurs when a bid arrives at a price that equals or exceeds the best offer or an offer arrives at a price that equals or is less than the best bid. Massimb and Phelps [1993] consider the relative merits of open outcry and electronic matching systems and find that electronic matching improves the operational efficiency of the market in terms of customer order delivery, accurate record keeping and so on but, because the costs of trading with such a system are higher for locals than open outcry, a market with electronic matching only is likely to have fewer operating locals and thus reduced liquidity.

In the case of the dealers' markets, market makers exist and they guarantee to operate throughout the time the market is open. They publicise two prices for an asset throughout the market. The first is known as the 'bid' price and refers to the price at which the market maker is prepared to buy the asset. The second and higher price is termed the 'ask' price and is the price at which the market maker is prepared to sell the relevant asset. The gap between the two prices is known as the 'bid–ask spread' (or more simply the 'spread') and provides funds to meet the market maker's operating costs and the provision of profits. Normally there is some slight variation between quotes by different market makers and the spread between the highest bid price and the lowest ask price is termed the 'market touch'. This provides an indication of the liquidity of the market. A market is said to be 'tight' if prices are close to the true market value for small transactions and 'deep' if this applies to large transactions. Thus, for example, a market for which the bid–ask spread is small for large and medium transactions but widens substantially for small transactions would be said to be deep but not tight. A final attribute of a market is termed 'immediacy', which is the speed with which a proposed transaction can be completed. In the case of continuous dealers' markets, immediacy is present provided the dealers do not suspend trading for any reason.

Financial markets provide opportunities for many different types of activity and we now consider three specialist activities, namely hedging, speculation and arbitrage.

7.4 Hedging, speculation and arbitrage

These techniques originally developed in the commodity markets and we shall use a hypothetical example of the sale/purchase of grain in the following discussion to illustrate their role.

The term 'hedging' refers to the purchase of a financial instrument or portfolio of instruments in order to insure against a possible reduction in wealth caused by unforeseen economic fluctuations. For example, a producer of grain may wish to hedge against a fall in the price of grain over some future period. One method of achieving such a hedge is to find a party who wishes to hedge against the opposite risk, that of a price rise. One example of such a person would be a bread producer who wishes to avoid a rise in price of future purchases of grain. The two parties can then agree on the price of grain for future delivery and this removes the risk of adverse price changes for both parties. This type of transaction would take place in a futures market where trade is highly organised. Such markets exist for all major commodities traded and for many financial assets, including foreign currency, short-term deposits, bonds and equities. At this stage it is worth emphasising that both traders have gained certainty of price rather than made a profit. For example, if the price of grain does fall the purchaser has foregone profits which would have been obtained if he or she had deferred purchasing grain until later. The converse would apply in the case of a price rise.

A second hedging possibility for the grain producer is to transfer the risk to a party who is less risk averse than the hedger. Such a party is a speculator who would purchase (or sell goods) for later resale (or purchase) in the hope of profiting from any intervening price changes. In this example, the speculator would purchase the grain at a set price for delivery in the future (the 'futures' price) in the expectation that the market price at that time (the future 'spot' price) had risen above the purchase price. If speculators make accurate forecasts they improve the efficiency of markets. They buy when prices are perceived to be low and sell when prices are perceived to be high, thus evening out price fluctuations. However, inexpert speculators (and in some instances rational speculators) can destabilise markets – for further discussion see Newberry [1989]. Speculative activity is prevalent in all the major commodity and financial markets.

An arbitrage opportunity is an investment strategy that, in a particular situation, guarantees a positive pay off with no possibility of a negative pay off occurring. Thus, arbitrage takes advantage of price or yield differentials in different markets (geographically or over time) in a riskless transaction. A simple example of an arbitrage transaction would be to borrow at one rate and lend at a higher fixed rate of interest when there was virtually no risk of default. Given the growth of informational technology such differentials would not be expected to exist for any significant period of time, since the action of arbitrageurs serves to eliminate them.

7.5 The efficient markets hypothesis

At this stage it is also useful to examine in general terms the nature of the term 'efficiency' as applied to markets. Efficiency can take three meanings: (i) operational efficiency, (ii) allocative efficiency and (iii) informational efficiency. The first type of efficiency is concerned with whether the market operates at the lowest level of cost or whether excessive resources are allocated to the operation of the market. In this connection it is likely that absence of price competition and presence of cartels will lead to economic inefficiency. This is one of the motives behind the drive to liberalise financial markets seen in recent years. The second facet refers to the role of the market in the allocation of resources. The third aspect deals with the question of whether market prices reflect all available information. The 'efficient markets hypothesis' is restricted to this narrow and technical meaning of the term efficiency but it is, however, worth noting that it would be difficult to conceive how allocative efficiency is possible if informational efficiency is not present.

If market efficiency is present anywhere, it is likely to be in the context of some financial markets. This is so for a number of reasons. First, financial assets are akin to durable assets in the sense that they are not purchased for immediate consumption. In fact, as we noted in chapter 1, they are purchased because of both the running yield or return they offer and, probably what is more important, the expectation of a capital gain, which may occur due to price change. Second, continuous trading is a feature of financial markets and in many cases this is international rather than just national continuous trading. Consequently prices are free to move to eliminate any imbalance between demand and supply. It may be expected that, given these two features, dealing between sophisticated traders would force financial asset prices to reflect all available information. There will be clearly some dispersion in the interpretation of information but, on average, the market will arrive at the 'correct' view. The idea of market efficiency embodies two components. First, the belief that an equilibrium market price exists. Second, the actual observed market price of the asset will adjust to this equilibrium price quickly. Two predictions follow from these observations: (i) that prices will alter only if new information is received on the market – this is technically known as 'news'; and (ii) since all information within the designated information set is reflected in the price, all knowable above-normal profits will have been eliminated by trading, or 'arbitrage' in the technical jargon. This second prediction carries with it the belief that trying to outperform the market by forecasting is not worthwhile because the market price will contain an accurate prediction in the light of current conditions. The qualification concerning above-normal profits is particularly important. Trading on financial markets is risky and, unless it is assumed that operators are risk neutral or indifferent to the degree of risk, it is natural to assume that a relatively high level of profit is necessary to induce them to enter the market. However, it is very difficult to quantify a precise numerical value for this element of profit necessary to compensate for the high degree of risk (or 'risk premium' as it is called in the literature), so that the 'efficiency' of the financial markets is still a controversial issue.

A formal definition of the 'efficient markets hypothesis' is that a specific market may be termed efficient if the prices of the assets traded on that market instantaneously reflect all available information. Fama [1970] neatly defines three types of empirical test of market efficiency defined according to the extent of the information set available:

(i) weak efficiency – in this category the asset price is tested to see that it reflects fully the information concerned in the history of both the price and volume of trading of that asset;
(ii) semi-strong efficiency – in this instance the asset price is required to reflect fully all publicly available information; the information set here would include all reports and statistics available in the media;
(iii) strong efficiency – this embodies the requirement that the asset price should reflect all information, whether publicly available or not; this category would include all privileged (inside) information.

Clearly, these categories are interdependent. Thus, a market which is strongly efficient must also satisfy the semi-strong and weak tests. Similarly, a market which satisfies the semi-strong test must also satisfy the weak test. It is unlikely that any market will fully satisfy the requirements of efficiency on all occasions but, conversely, it is difficult to conceive of a market which is perfectly inefficient – that is, a market in which asset prices never reflect any available information! Consequently the important question is whether markets approximate efficiency for all practical purposes.

Empirical testing of the efficient markets hypothesis is fraught with problems. Normally at least two hypotheses coexist in any efficient-markets test: first, that expectations are formed in the manner prescribed in the particular test and are used to arrive at the information set; and second, that the market uses these expectations in an efficient way in the price-setting process. Thus, failure to find support for the efficient markets hypothesis may be due to failure of either (or both) of the sub-hypotheses. A further difficulty arises because we observe price data at discrete periods, generally at the end of the day, which is the trading price reported most often in the media. The assumption underlying most empirical work is that the process of arbitrage has been completed during the trading period, so that the end-of-trading price reflects all the information in the prescribed test.

The plan of the rest of this section on financial markets is as follows. In chapters 8 and 9 we discuss the equity and bond markets before proceeding in chapter 10 to examine the money markets. In chapters 11 to 13 we examine the foreign exchange market, the international financial markets based in London and the traded options and financial futures market respectively. In chapter 14 we finish the section with a discussion of how these markets may be used to manage risk. Generally in each chapter we will not only describe the institutional detail but also the extent to which the market concerned conforms to the efficient markets hypothesis.

Chapter 8

The market for equities

8.1 Introduction

The market for equities is part of the capital market, which refers to the market for long-term finance, as distinct from the money markets, which are markets for short-term funds. Clearly, this distinction is difficult to draw at the margin as there is no clear-cut time rule to differentiate between the two classes of market. In principle the capital market can be divided into two segments: (i) the primary market, where new capital is raised, and (ii) the secondary market, where existing securities are sold and bought. Again, this distinction is blurred since new capital can be raised via a stock exchange and existing securities sold on the same market. Furthermore, the existence of a secondary market is necessary to support the primary market since an essential prop to the market for long-term capital is the existence of a market where these long-term claims can be sold if the holder needs to obtain liquidity. A further distinction can be made, between private sector finance and public sector finance. We can also distinguish between fixed-interest securities and equities. In this chapter we discuss the equity market and in chapter 9 the market for fixed-interest securities. We commence by examining in section 8.2 the raising of finance by private firms and in section 8.3 the secondary market for private sector finance. In section 8.4 we examine the degree to which the stock market conforms to the efficient markets hypothesis. Our conclusions are presented in section 8.5.

8.2 The primary market

At the outset of this section it is worth examining the ways in which private firms can raise long-term finance. The main methods in recent years have been the following:

(i) long-term bank loans,
(ii) equipment leasing,
(iii) issues of fixed-interest securities,
(iv) issues of equities,
(v) retained profits,
(vi) finance obtained from official sources.

We have discussed the nature of bank loans in chapter 1, so no further comment will be made in this section other than to draw the reader's attention to the importance of this source of finance. Equipment leasing is a substitute for firms' raising finance, inasmuch as they lease the equipment instead of raising finance themselves for the purchase. Categories (iii) and (iv) are discussed below. An important source of finance to firms comes from the profits they have attained from trading but have not distributed to shareholders in the form of dividends. Finally it is possible for firms to obtain government assistance, for example the award of investment grants in connection with the regional selective assistance policy of the UK government. Table 8.1 shows the pattern of finance raised by British firms over the period 1963–93.

A few explanatory remarks concerning table 8.1 are necessary. First, a negative figure indicates a repayment of the debt. Second, the item marked 'Sundries' comprises three items: accruals, capital transfer, and import and other credit. Accruals refer to items where the change of ownership has occurred but payment has not been made. Third, 'Other loans and mortgages' refers to instalment credit received, loans from financial institutions other than banks and from the public sector.

The statistics contained in table 8.1 show differences in the relative importance of the various components over time. Over the whole period, however, the importance of internal funds as opposed to external funds is patently obvious, with just under 57 per cent of total funds raised being generated from within the companies. Of the external funds, bank loans are the most important component. Issues of ordinary shares contributed only 7.6 per cent of total funds over the period although this figure was significantly higher in the later part of the period compared with the 1970s as firms took advantage of the rising equities market. However, this figure includes shares issued to finance takeovers, so the additional or new corporate finance raised by firms through equity issues during this period was considerably smaller and was, in fact, negative during the period 1970 to 1985 (Mayer and Alexander [1990]). Debentures showed a large drop for a time after 1973 owing no doubt to the rises in the rate of interest to levels not experienced before. As firms became accustomed to these levels, issues of debentures and preference shares picked up again. Note also the rising importance of overseas funding towards the end of the period.

Table 8.1 *Identified sources of capital funds of industrial and commercial companies, 1963–93 (£million, current prices)*

	Internal funds	*Bank loans*	*Other loans and mortgages*	*Ordinary shares*	*Debentures and preference shares*	*Sundries*	*Overseas funds*
1963	2,522	554	121	123	212	51	165
1964	2,887	745	158	158	254	50	106
1965	2,978	514	228	63	345	23	115
1966	2,659	197	124	124	452	22	172
1967	2,655	411	108	65	350	212	236
1968	3,194	672	159	303	183	472	261
1969	3,733	749	213	177	362	716	140
1970	3,813	1,183	302	39	193	652	377
1971	4,724	888	236	149	285	741	342
1972	5,859	3,032	113	296	267	785	17
1973	8,710	4,688	429	98	87	971	538
1974	9,330	3,126	375	38	27	1,058	1,285
1975	9,609	504	505	954	257	678	1,016
1976	12,325	2,700	213	770	56	1,271	1,188
1977	16,280	2,460	404	710	-46	876	1,159
1978	18,750	2,402	500	797	-41	991	533
1979	25,339	3,962	780	879	5	2,030	397
1980	18,938	6,321	176	896	152	463	1,865
1981	20,794	5,672	715	1,660	739	2,056	1,025
1982	18,310	6,635	857	1,033	243	1,137	1,223
1983	25,932	1,619	750	1,872	610	1,204	1,630
1984	30,323	7,082	575	1,127	248	451	-2,826
1985	32,250	7,454	876	3,522	816	695	572
1986	27,903	9,096	1,450	5,608	490	563	3,627
1987	36,642	12,141	2,720	13,338	534	606	5,434
1988	36,959	31,064	3,771	4,817	1,207	1,147	5,475
1989	30,810	33,945	7,964	2,694	2,980	832	10,353
1990	31,266	19,756	9,436	2,851	3,627	7,780	11,554
1991	32,022	-922	6,015	9,761	5,673	6,006	9,210
1992	31,112	-1,974	2,681	5,272	2,179	8,414	3,094
1993	48,172	-11,284	4,858	14,372	2,900	6,286	10,330
Total	556,800	155,392	47,812	74,566	25,646	49,239	70,613
%	56.8	15.9	4.9	7.6	2.6	5.0	7.2

Source: CSO, *Financial Statistics*, various issues, and ESRC Data Bank.

We now turn to the main subject of this section, which is new issues. New issues can be made by firms whose shares are already quoted on the Stock Exchange or by those companies seeking a listing on the Exchange. In this latter case the company must meet a list of requirements concerning its financial status and past trading record. In 1980 these requirements were relaxed for small and growing companies, which could then seek access to the unlisted securities market (USM). When the USM opened, 12 companies had their shares quoted. By the end of 1986 this figure had risen to 368. In 1987 a third tier was provided for small untested companies to have access to a 'third' market. This three-tier structure changed at the end of 1990 in response to European Community directives to harmonise listing requirements. These are summarised in the *Bank of England Quarterly Bulletin* of May 1990 and effectively lower the requirements for the main market which, in turn, has led to lower requirements for the USM. At the same time the requirements for the third market would have to be tightened, making the difference between this market and the USM minimal. Consequently the third market closed down at the end of 1990. At the time of writing (January 1995), the future of the USM itself is uncertain as it is to be merged into the listed securities market at the end of 1996, although a new market called the 'alternative investment market' (AIM) is to be established for the trading of small companies' shares alongside the main 'official list'. The opening date was 19 June 1995. It is anticipated that many of the companies whose shares are currently quoted on the USM will transfer to full Stock Exchange listing for a number of reasons. First, the cost differential of coming to the USM as opposed to the main market has almost disappeared; for example, it is reported that it only cost Metal Bulletin, one of the first firms to join the USM, £50,000 to make the move on to the official list. Second, it was often felt that listing on the USM made the company a second-class citizen. It is hoped that the AIM will provide a market for shares of companies that do not wish to transfer, as well as providing facilities for other small companies which wish to obtain listing on a stock exchange. For this reason the new market is likely to be lightly regulated, thus lowering costs for companies whose securities are listed on this market. It is also envisaged that the AIM will have low entry barriers because no thresholds are envisaged at the moment for market capitalisation, length of trading or the percentage of shares in public hands. Sponsorship will be optional in the AIM. Sponsorship, typically carried out by a bank or stockbroking firm, is the process by which the firm is shepherded through its various flotation obligations. The sponsor is also responsible for ensuring that the firm's affairs are in order and that its documentation has been adequately prepared. However, the applicant will be required to find a minimum of one market maker prepared to deal in its shares. Similar to the requirements for inclusion in the official list, the applicant will be required to provide price-sensitive information to the market (including unaudited interim accounts), which will be disseminated in the normal manner. The aim of the new market is to facilitate the obtaining of finance by small companies whilst still maintaining a satisfactory degree of investor protection. It was originally envisaged that companies on the AIM would be required to pay an annual fee of only £1,000, though this has yet to be finalised.

Every new issue will involve a stockbroking concern and is generally managed by an issuing house which, in these days of financial conglomerates, may be part of the same company. The main issuing houses are members of the Issuing Houses Association and are generally merchant banks. Their function is to manage the new issue by (i) offering advice concerning the timing and the terms attached and (ii) handling the publicity and administration involved. The issuing house may act as a principal by buying the shares from the company and then disposing of them on its own account, or it may act as an agent. Even in the latter case, some risk is involved since the issuing house normally provides a guarantee that a specified sum will be raised. In order to spread this risk of a failure to sell the whole issue to the public, the issuing house will normally arrange for the issue to be 'underwritten'. This involves an institution guaranteeing that the whole issue will be sold at the price indicated. If the issue is taken up by the public the underwriter has no further liability. If, on the other hand, only part of the issue is sold to the public (i.e. 'partly subscribed'), the underwriter will purchase the remainder of the issue herself or himself. In return for this service the underwriter will obtain a commission on the issue in the region of 1 to 2 per cent of the capital raised. In the case of rights issues, the new shares are generally offered to existing shareholders at a discount of around 15 per cent of the market price and the charge for underwriting appears, for the last 30 years or so, to have been fixed at 2 per cent irrespective of the quality of the issuer and has, therefore, attracted the attention of the Office of Fair Trading (OFT). Currently (spring 1995) the OFT is reported to be planning to refer the whole system of equity capital raising in London to the Monopolies and Mergers Commission ('OFT Plans to Refer City Share Issue System to MMC', *Financial Times*, 2 February 1995). The main underwriters of new issues are the long-term investment institutions, that is, the insurance companies, the pension funds and investment trusts.

The main methods for new issues are the following:

(i) *Placings*. The issuing house purchases the securities from the issuer and places the shares with investors. Normal prudence dictates that the major proportion of these placings will be replaced with the investors who are generally the long-term investment institutions. In addition to the quantity replaced, one-quarter of the new issue must be made available for the general public. This method of new issue was restricted to issues up to £15 million. These restrictions were modified with effect from December 1993. Initial public offerings up to £25 million may now be placed entirely with clients of the sponsor subject to a minimum of 5 per cent being placed with at least one independent market maker. For offers between £25 million and £50 million (defined as medium-size offers), up to 75 per cent of the offer may be placed with the sponsoring broker's clients. At least 5 per cent of the shares being placed direct must be offered to two independent market makers of the shares concerned. All offers greater than £50 million must be made by way of an offer for sale. In this case, a sponsor will be permitted to place or underwrite 50 per cent of the issue with its clients. As in the case of medium-size offers, there must be at least two independent market makers and they must be offered at least 5 per cent of the shares placed or underwritten.

(ii) *Offers for sale by tender.* In this case the public is invited to purchase shares at any price over a publicised minimum price. A single so-called striking price is established at which it is believed that the issue will be fully subscribed and all tenders at that or a higher price will receive an allotment at this striking price irrespective of whether the tender was at a higher price or not. This system of allocation is called a 'common price tender'.

(iii) *Offers for sale.* Here the issuing house purchases the whole issue at a specified price and then offers the issue for sale to the general public.

(iv) *Offers for sale by subscription.* This method is a variation of number (iii) above whereby the company rather than the issuing house offers the shares to the public.

(v) *Rights issue.* This method is restricted to companies whose shares are already quoted on the Stock Exchange (i.e. a secondary issue). Existing shareholders have the right to purchase additional shares in proportion to their existing holdings at a fixed price. The price is normally at a discount to that currently quoted on the Stock Exchange so that the issuing price is unlikely to be higher than the price quoted on the Stock Exchange at the time of the issue due to price fluctuations. The shareholder does not have to take up the rights issue and may, in fact, sell the right. If it so wishes the issuing company may avoid the need for the issue to be underwritten by making the right at a large discount compared with the current market price (at a 'deep' discount) so as to make the offer attractive. Such rights issues must be approved by the shareholders and protection for existing shareholders against dilution of their holdings is afforded by the Companies Act 1985 and Stock Exchange rules. These are termed pre-emption requirements. As part of the reorganisation following 'Big Bang' (discussed later in this chapter), the Stock Exchange decided to withdraw the pre-emptive rights requirement for listed companies. Other methods of raising equity finance are now more common for secondary issues as funds are more speedily obtained than for rights issues. The Stock Exchange has followed this path mainly because it wished to reduce the possibility that new member firms would bypass the London market and issue securities through other world capital markets.

The method of issue adopted by an individual firm will depend on the costs involved relative to the total funds being raised. These costs include administrative expenses, advertising and, in the case of an issue by a company new to the Stock Exchange, any discount on the nominal price of the share. In the case of a secondary issue, this cost is not applicable since the total value of outstanding stock will remain the same. The Bank of England carried out a survey of new issues for period 1983 to 1986 which was updated to 1989 (*Bank of England Quarterly Bulletin*, 1986 and 1990).

In the period 1985–89, £24 billion of equity was raised in initial public offerings in the main stock market. The number and sizes of the various methods of initial public offerings during this period are show in table 8.2.

The most common method of initial public offering over the last half of the 1980s was the method of placing although the table shows the importance of offers for sale in large-value issues. Over this period, there has not been a tender issue since 1986 and offers for sale have been a declining method. This trend follows the raising of the limit on placings to £15 million in 1986.

The broad conclusions of the early survey carried out by the Bank of England were that for initial offerings for small amounts placing is the cheapest method and is invariably followed in the USM and third market. Costs of issue were lower on the USM than the listed market. Substantial economies of scale were evident and issue expenses (excluding the under-pricing cost) were in the region of 11 per cent for placings and 17.8 per

Table 8.2 New issues of equity 1985 to 1989

	Sums raised (£million)	*Number*
Offers for sale	5,855	94
Tenders	361	11
Placings	725	120
Privatisations	16,661	15
Total	23,602	240

Initial public offerings do not include rights issues.
The large sizes of issues associated with the privatisation of nationalised industries has meant that slightly different methods of issuing techniques have been used. Most of the privatisation offers have contained elements of placing and offers for sale.

cent for offers for sale for amounts up to £3 million but falling to 4.7 per cent for amounts over £10 million in the case of offers for sale. Comparative figures on the unlisted market were 10 per cent for placings and 16.6 per cent down to 2.3 per cent for offers for sale. Rights issues were cheaper than those for initial issues on the listed market and were estimated to be in the region of 3.9 per cent for issues during 1985. Deep discount issues were cheaper, again because of the absence of the need for the issue to be underwritten. This method of raising new capital is rarely used (only five issues during 1985 as compared with 82 other issues) and the average cost was estimated to be 1.5 per cent. The later survey, restricted to the main market, found that the proportionate costs of placings and offers for sale changed little over the last half of the 1980s except for small issues (under £5 million) which rose since Big Bang in 1986.

8.3 The secondary market for private securities

Nature of the market

Stock exchanges are subject to ever-increasing internationalisation. For example, according to the Bundesbank non-residents own more than 20 per cent of all shares issued by German companies. Similarly, dealing in non-domestic shares is an important component of trading on the London Stock Exchange (LSE). There is a considerable degree of actual and potential competition with the LSE in dealing in UK equities from such channels as:

(i) American depository receipts (ADRs) traded on US exchanges – US financial institutions purchase blocks of shares in UK companies and then issue titles to the underlying shares which are traded on the New York Stock Exchange and the National Association of Securities Dealers' automated quotations system (NASDAQ), an electronic securities exchange;
(ii) index futures traded equity options available on LIFFE (see chapter 13 for a full description of these instruments);
(iii) over-the-counter dealing in equities between institutions;
(iv) over-the-counter equity derivatives;
(v) off-exchange systems such as the proposed electronic share interchange system, which is to be launched in 1995. This is an electronic share-dealing system which enables anyone with a personal computer and modem to buy and sell shares; the intention is to create a UK-wide share-dealing system at low cost, specialising in small-company equity.

It is apparent, therefore, that the LSE faces competition which should stimulate market efficiency in its broadest context. In comparison with other European stock exchanges the LSE is the largest in terms of total

Table 8.3 *Comparison of major stock exchanges at end of 1989*

	Market value of domestic equity (£billion)	*Number of companies*		*Turnover (£billion)*	
		Domestic	*Foreign*	*Domestic*	*Foreign*
Tokyo	2,639	1,597	119	1,436	12
New York	1,800	1,634	87	957	n/a
London	507	2,015	544	198	85
NASDAQ	241	4,026	267	249	14
German Federation of Exchanges	227	628	535	218	11
Paris	227	462	223	69	3
Zurich	107	117	229	n/a	n/a
Milan	106	211	0	27	0

Source: LSE, *Quality of Markets Quarterly*, spring 1990.

turnover (i.e. domestic and foreign) but smaller than the New York or Tokyo exchanges. On the other hand, the non-domestic business is larger than any of the other exchanges'. Details are shown in table 8.3.

The LSE is a market for private sector securities and public sector debt. Table 8.4 shows that in terms of turnover trading in gilt-edged securities is the main component.

The figures also show that whilst the percentage of turnover attributable to gilt trading is just over 63 per cent for the whole period, that for number of transactions is only 10.3 per cent. This implies that the average size of order is much larger for gilts than equities.

The LSE is a continuous dealers' market using screens to display prices but not for actual trading. It is termed a 'quote-driven system' since market makers registered with the Exchange indicate firm quotes for buying and selling specific securities up to a specific size. The alternative system is an 'order-driven auction market'. The rules applying to auction markets are quite different from those applying to the quote-driven market. There is the complete absence of market makers indicating firm prices at which they are prepared to deal. In this case orders are executed on the basis of price and time. Consequently orders at the best price will be executed first. Two types of order exist: 'limit' and 'market fill' orders. In the former case the deal only takes place at a price indicated as the limit. In the latter case the deal takes place at the best price displayed in the market at that time. The price is kept near the equilibrium price by a steady flow of orders. Deviations from the perceived equilibrium price will stimulate offsetting intervention by speculators.

Table 8.4 *Transactions on the London Stock Exchange, 1974–93*

	Value (£million)		*Number of bargains (thousands)*	
	Total	*Gilts*	*Total*	*Gilts*
1974	56,753	38,263	5,026	538
1975	94,037	67,246	6,030	688
1976	106,435	81,925	4,868	766
1977	173,334	135,759	6,085	978
1978	138,770	103,678	5,489	751
1979	168,941	128,950	5,457	883
1980	192,687	151,699	5,708	996
1981	190,665	146,057	5,287	951
1982	260,045	203,389	5,385	1,073
1983	287,587	210,754	6,007	867
1984	364,675	268,679	6,049	822
1985	390,472	261,527	6,711	758
1986	646,263	424,416	8,847	797
1987	1,757,493	1,148,358	15,399	1,098
1988	1,602,804	1,129,112	9,191	909
1989	1,627,265	975,211	10,680	683
1990	1,655,028	961,164	9,868	655
1991	1,813,905	1,112,716	11,218	622
1992	2,088,966	1,238,792	11,988	799
1993	2,830,051	1,598,417	14,462	783
Total	16,446,176	10,386,112	159,755	16,417
%		63.2		10.3

At the moment actual deals are made by telephone though there are plans to extend the facilities to a paperless trading system. Originally this was to be implemented by 1993 through the Taurus computer system with the consequent elimination from share trading of paper certificates. However, the project ran into difficulties and was eventually abandoned. A project team to design a replacement electronic book-entry settlement system, CREST, was set up in August 1993 under the auspices of the Bank of England. It is intended that the new system will be operated and owned by the users rather than the Bank of England. Accordingly a new company will be set up, called 'Crestco', to own and operate the system. The Bank of England aims to produce tested software by the end of 1995 and this will then be handed over to Crestco to implement the new system and make the necessary commercial decisions such as level of charges and development strategy. Presumably the method of operation will be similar to that for gilts via the Central Gilts Office (CGO) – see chapter 9 for a description of the CGO.

At the same time the system of settlement is being changed. All transactions executed at the LSE over a 14-day account period were settled on a single day six working days after the end of the account period. A new rolling settlement was introduced in July 1994 whereby each day's transactions are to be settled 10 business days after the transactions take place (a so-called T+10 rule). It is intended that the rolling settlement should move to T+5 early in 1995 and eventually T+3. The introduction of CREST will lead to a reduction in costs and an improvement in settlement arrangements. However, whilst the bulk of trades will not involve share certificates, the Bank of England expects that some investors who rarely trade may wish to retain the use of certificates. Consequently the new system will permit this at a reasonable charge.

The price information is distributed through the Stock Exchange automated quotations system (SEAQ), which supports two market segments: (i) domestic and (ii) international. A new system, SEQUENCE, is due to replace the SEAQ in 1996. Quoted prices are indicated to the market via the Stock Exchange's own 'Topic' or other information service such as Reuters' 'Equity 2000'. At the time of writing (spring 1995) the LSE has intimated it does not intend to update Topic and will allow it to be replaced by independent market information systems.

The former categorisation of domestic shares (alpha, beta, gamma and delta) has been abolished and, from January 1991, shares are allocated to bands according to their 'normal market size' (NMS), based on market turnover. A well informed equity market requires public disclosure of information relevant to the pricing of shares. This information includes such items as price quotations, prices at which deals are made, and trade volumes, in addition to general macroeconomic information and specific information relating to individual companies. The technical term for the presence of such information in the market is 'transparency'. Transparency can be subdivided into two categories: 'pre-trade' and 'post-trade' transparency. Pre-trade transparency is provided by SEAQ price quotations and the requirement for companies to provide the market with relevant information. The requirement for post-trade transparency is met through the publication of details of the prices at which deals have been made. Deals for all shares with a NMS greater than 2,000 shares must be reported to the system within three minutes of the trade taking place, provided the transaction is less than six times the NMS of that share. A delay of 60 minutes is allowed before reporting in the case of deals greater than six times the NMS of that share. A third reporting class occurs in the case of 'block deals' between market makers. These are defined as trades greater than 75 times the NMS of that share. In this latter case notification must be carried out after five days or after the market maker has offset 90 per cent of the trade (whichever is the earlier). Note that the LSE monitors closely the unwinding of the block trade. All 'agency crosses' (in-house deals) must be reported, irrespective of the NMS of the equity concerned. A further example of the lack of transparency concerns the permission of market makers to avoid disclosure of the quantity of any given stock owned by them. This applies to ownership greater than the 3 per cent threshold above which any other purchaser is required to make its identity known.

The justification of the delay in reporting large trades is based on the view that details concerning the large trades provides competitors with information on which to base their strategies. Thus, for example, knowledge that there was a large seller in the market following a block trade may lead to a fall in prices and hence losses for the market maker. The example of three years of losses following Big Bang under a more transparent regime are cited as example of the problems faced by market makers. It is argued that loss of this privilege may lead to the withdrawal of market makers on which the system depends and its consequent replacement by an 'order-driven' system. This raises the question whether the quote-driven system adopted by the LSE is better than the alternative of the order-driven system. A further query with respect to delayed publication of trade details concerns the impact of the lack of information on derivatives exchanges since the derivative price may not reflect accurately the price of the underlying shares. This may be driving derivative trade away from London to Continental exchanges. The question of delayed reporting is currently the subject of investigation by both the Securities and Investment Board (see chapter 17 for discussion of this body) and the Office of Fair Trading.

The LSE also operates a screen-based market for shares which is restricted to market makers; this is termed the inter-dealer broker (IDB) market. Transactions for this market executed on inter-dealer broker screens are also disclosed.

The analogous system for leading international stocks which are traded by international market makers operating in London is the SEAQ International. Reporting of transactions are less onerous in this market, which, given the degree of international competition, seems reasonable.

The system is backed up by the SEAQ automatic execution facility (SAEF), enabling member firms to buy and sell, automatically matching the order against the best bid or ask quote within the system. This facility is mainly used for small orders and enables the avoidance of telephone calls to execute orders.

Illiquid stocks have presented a problem to the LSE since the fall in trading volume consequent upon the 1987 stock market crash. 'The bottom 50% of listed stocks (about 1200 issues) represent just 1.2% of LSE turnover' (Securities and Investment Board [1994]). This makes it difficult to devise a trading structure which meets the needs of both the market makers and potential buyers and sellers and in particular the LSE's requirement for the existence of at least two market makers. The LSE has attempted to deal with this problem through the creation of the Stock Exchange alternative trading service (SEATS). This is a combination of a 'bulletin' service with permission for there to be a single trader or market maker. The market maker is required to make continuous two-way prices (i.e. for purchase and sale of shares). Investors will also be able to post on the bulletin orders to buy or sell stocks. The market maker is obliged, on trading, to fulfil orders on the bulletin which are at the same price or at better prices than those at which it is proposing to trade. At the same time brokers must show proposed trades to a market maker before matching orders within their office. This will permit the market maker and investors to have first chance of meeting the order.

Changes in trading arrangements: Big Bang

The arrangements at the LSE were subject to a fundamental change on 27 October 1986, the so-called 'Big Bang'. Prior to this date the LSE was subject to a number of restrictive practices. In particular, three practices were important. First, there was single capacity, since the market makers in shares, termed jobbers, were able to deal only on their own account. All contact with the jobbers was to be conducted via stockbrokers who, in turn, were unable to deal in shares. In other words, stockbrokers were purely agents acting as intermediaries between the ultimate customer and the jobber. Second, a cartel arrangement applied whereby minimum commissions were fixed for all trades irrespective of size. Third, ownership of brokers and jobbers was restricted to private partnerships until 1969. In that year brokers and jobbers were permitted to form limited companies and further relaxation occurred in 1971 when ownership of corporate members could be held by outside members but subject to the severe restraint that no one shareholder could hold more than 10 per cent of the capital of a single firm. Economic theory predicts that cartels have the effect of raising members' income and consequently it is certain that the minimum commission arrangement raised dealing costs. On the other hand, it was suggested that it protected the interest of the public since there was no conflict of interest because the market makers could not deal directly with the public and brokers could not deal in shares. Thus, each party had no motive to act against the interests of the public.

There were two separate motives for change. First, after 1979, the Conservative government was interested in increasing the degree of competition throughout the economy. This resulted in a referral of the Stock Exchange rule book to the Restrictive Trade Practices Court in 1979. Within this motive was, perhaps, the feeling that the government was providing excessive commission incomes on dealings in gilts. Second, the LSE was losing business following the abolition of controls on movements of capital for UK residents in 1979. Share dealings have become dominated to an increasing extent by the institutions. These are the agents most likely to suffer from minimum prices since their deals would be of a large size. A significant development at this time was the growth of American deposit receipts (ADRs), discussed earlier. Costs of trading were lower in New York, which had experienced its equivalent to Big Bang ('May Day') in 1975. Consequently large dealings in UK shares tended to move to New York at the expense of London.

Agreement was reached in 1983 between the LSE and the government which led to the dropping of the referral to the court. Three important components of the agreement were: (i) the abolition of minimum commissions, (ii) the permission of dual capacity and (iii) relaxation of the rules of outside ownership. With regard to point (ii), there is now a single form of institution called a broker-dealer who can either operate on her or his own account or as an agent for another institution/person. Within this category there is a subset who are registered to act as market makers or dealers. These market makers may specialise in a particular group of shares. Restraints operate where broker-dealers who are not market makers are acting as an agent, inasmuch as they can deal on their own account or match an order with another client only if they can show that they can execute the order at a superior price than by going to a market maker. Similarly, market makers can act as an agent only if they can deal at a price at least as good as that which could be obtained from another market maker.

The three components of the agreement were closely interconnected. Abolition of minimum commissions would place income of brokers under great pressure, so that they would be likely to seek alternative sources of income. One such source would be market making. Second, dealing is a high-risk industry and new sources of capital would be needed in view of the likely fall in incomes. Thus, outside interests were permitted to own 100 per cent of the share capital of single-member firms as from 1 March 1986. This led to a scramble to buy up firms and to form financial conglomerates, such as Barclays de Zoete Wedd.

Along with changes brought about by 'Big Bang', the screen information system described above was introduced, so that the old 'face-to-face' discussions between LSE members were quickly eliminated. What effect did these change have on share dealing? First, the level of commissions have fallen on deals. In February 1987 the Bank of England (*Bank of England Quarterly Bulletin*) suggested that, for an equity deal in the region of £10,000 to £1 million, commission rates fell from 0.4 per cent to 0.2 per cent. Larger falls were reported in larger deals, with the largest fall being

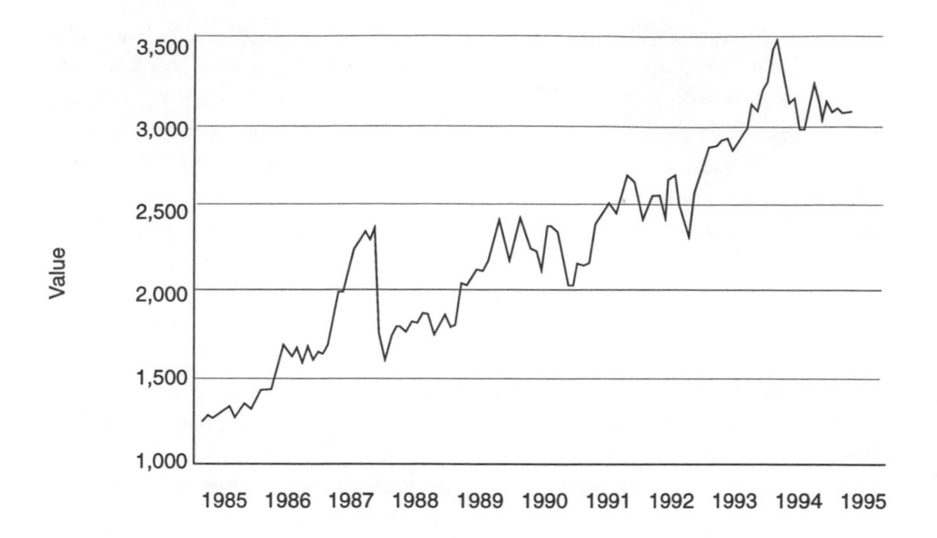

Figure 8.1 *FT-SE 100 Share Index*

obtained in deals carried out by the institutions, which have conducted a large part of their business net of commission. It also appeared that commissions on small transactions did not rise to any great extent and might have actually fallen slightly. The evidence also suggested that the market touch had fallen for beta and gamma shares and remained the roughly same for alpha shares. There was also anecdotal evidence that the touch does not widen significantly for larger quotes; in other words the market is deeper than before. As would be expected from the elementary theory of demand and supply, lower prices stimulated demand and increased turnover was observed on both the listed and unlisted markets immediately after Big Bang. Increases of the order of 20 per cent were obtained and this, together with the trend increase in share prices experienced during the early months of 1987, enabled profitable trading to continue. Reference to table 8.4 demonstrates the dramatic growth in turnover in the years after 1986. However, this situation did not last for any length of time and substantial falls in share prices occurred on a global basis during October 1987. This is demonstrated in figure 8.1.

The graph reveals a steady rise in the share index from 1985 to the middle of 1987, when the dramatic fall in prices occurred. It is also noticeable that the rise in the index was particularly pronounced during the early months of 1987. As is demonstrated in table 8.4, the fall in prices was accompanied by a decrease in the volume of turnover, resulting in a dramatic loss in profitability for the dealer-brokers. In fact this decrease in trading was far more pronounced in the number of transactions than in turnover. As noted above, the larger orders were subject to falls in commission rates and this enhanced the general loss of profitability in the market. In other words there was large-scale excess capacity, which led to some firms giving up market making altogether. Following Big Bang there were some 32 domestic equity market makers but by 1990 this had fallen to 26 firms. Reductions in capacity also came from other firms restricting their market-making activities.

Stock market crash

There is no consensus concerning the reasons for the dramatic fall in stock market prices which began on Monday 19 October 1987 ('Black Monday') when the New York Stock Exchange suffered a drop of 22.6 per cent (its largest ever in a single day) which quickly spread to most exchanges around the world, including London. Four possible causes have been suggested.

First, there was uncertainty over the international payments situation. Recent years had seen the persistent balance-of-payments disequilibria. The USA and the UK had experienced large deficits, which had been matched by large surpluses obtained by Japan and Germany. At the same time corrective measures for the US federal budget deficit also seemed to be proving inadequate. Perhaps the perception of the serious nature of these problems was enhanced by the continued problem of sovereign debt (see chapter 4). It could be argued therefore that bad US trade figures on the Thursday before the crash provided the trigger for the fall in stock prices. Two problems remain with this approach. First, the worldwide nature of the 'crash' across a wide number of exchanges in different countries seems to be out of keeping with the weight of news. On the other hand a look at the 'fundamentals' suggests that share prices should be sensitive to changes in expectations. By definition:

$$\text{expected rate of return} = (E_t P_{t+1} + E_t D_t - P_t)/P_t \qquad (8.1)$$

where P refers to the share price at the beginning of the period, D to the dividend paid during the period and E the expectation operator, so that $E_t P_{t+1}$ refers to the forecast of the price at the beginning of the next period.

Solving equation 1 for the current price and noting that, in equilibrium, the required rate of return is equal to the required rate of discount:

$$P_t = \frac{E_t P_{t+1} + E_t D_t}{(1 + R)} \qquad (8.2)$$

where R is the required rate of discount.

Note that in equation 8.2 investors have to forecast the price of stock and future dividends, that is, expectations of future events are important. This is often termed the intrinsic value of the stock. If it is assumed that dividends will grow at a constant annual rate (g) and also the discount rate is constant, equation 8.2 can be solved to produce the 'Gordon' growth model:

$$\text{Current price} = \frac{E_t D_t}{(R - g)} \quad (8.3)$$

Note that equation 8.3 requires the required discount rate (R) to be larger than the expected growth rate of dividends (g). If values of £0.30 for forecast of dividends and 8 per cent and 6 per cent for the two growth rates are assumed, then the share value will be £15. If the expected growth rate of dividends falls to 5 per cent, the price of each share falls to £10. This explanation would, therefore, require investors to revise downwards their expected rate of growth of dividends (or equivalently the forecast of dividends) or to revise upwards the required rate of discount in the light of uncertainty about future events due to the international financial problems. A problem with this approach is that survey evidence in the US suggested that investors regarded the equity market as being overvalued before the crash. This evidence was, however, collected after the crash and may be tainted with wisdom after the event.

The second potential cause for the crash has been identified with 'speculative bubbles'. The basis of the belief in the existence of speculative bubbles is that rises in share prices induce expectations that the price will rise even further. This has been dubbed 'the greater fool theory' in the sense that each purchaser believes that he or she will find an even bigger fool who will buy the equity at a higher price, which, by definition, is not related to the 'fundamentals'. This cause implies market failure in the sense that shares become increasingly overvalued until the bubble bursts at a particular point of time for what may seem a trivial reason. Examination of the time pattern of share price index in figure 8.1 shows the index increasing at a fast rate throughout the early months of 1987 and this might be taken as casual support for the 'speculative bubble' hypothesis. However, existence of speculative bubbles would require that sequences of price changes are related but Santoni [1987] presents evidence that suggests that this requirement was absent from daily data for the US for the period 2 January 1986 to 25 August 1987. Two tests were applied to the Dow-Jones index for this period: (i) based on an examination of the autocorrelation coefficients and (ii) and on runs of positive and negative changes. Neither of these tests supported the rejection of the hypothesis that the data conformed to a random walk.

The third possible cause lies in the belief that there may have been a temporary market failure triggered by an initial price decline. Suggested causes of this failure include: (i) value-insensitive trading due to automatic computer trading, (ii) false price signals resulting from the abnormally heavy trading observed, and (iii) the absence of countervailing price-sensitive market traders acting from a viewpoint of the fundamentals. It could be argued that the heavy price falls themselves induced a change in market expectations which then validated the new, lower prices. It may also be argued that the growth of high-speed communications and trading mechanisms increased the possibility of such crises and this has led to a demand for the introduction of circuit breakers in markets. These would have the effect of suspending trading when prices fell (or rose) beyond a specific amount during the day. The idea is that a 'cooling-off' period may restore calmer conditions during the subsequent trading period. Two problems arise with such proposals. First, if traders wish to trade, they may well do so off the market. Second, is it just to suspend trading just at the time when the public has a strong desire to trade?

A fourth reason for the crash, suggested by the Brady commission, concerns the use of the futures market to obtain portfolio insurance. Discussion of the futures market takes place in chapter 12 but it is possible to outline here the main thread of the argument. If it were possible to enter into a series of put options (i.e. the right to sell all the securities in the portfolio at predetermined prices) then the risks of adverse price changes would be reduced. Portfolio insurance replicates this position by taking a simultaneous position in a risky portfolio and a synthetic put option by shifting funds from the risky portfolio into a safe liquid asset on the basis of the Black/Scholes option pricing model. This involves selling shares when prices are falling and, if used by sufficient operators, will increase the volatility of prices on the market. In the USA portfolio insurers bought and sold futures contracts on a share index rather than the shares themselves. This has the obvious advantage of lower cost since it would be difficult, and therefore costly, to carry out the alternative of entering into contracts to purchase or sell shares across the whole range of securities in a share price index. A second facet of the argument concerns the practice of arbitraging between shares making up the index and the relevant futures contract. For example, if the futures contract falls below the share price by a sufficient amount then it is possible to make a profit by purchasing the futures contract and selling the shares making up the index. Clearly, the futures price discount must be sufficiently large to offset the transactions costs. During the week preceding the crash, portfolio insurers were selling futures heavily and this induced index arbitrage purchasing futures and selling shares. It appears that at certain critical times the volume of this trading accounted for up to 66 per cent of transactions. In addition, the underlying techniques of portfolio insurance are well known on the market so that other operators could identify when insurers were likely to sell securities. This would lead them to try to sell in advance of the insurers in the hope of buying stock back later at the lower price induced by the sales of the insurers.

It is claimed that the volume of sales on the futures market was so large on the Monday and Tuesday of the crash that index arbitrageurs were unable to absorb the pressure by purchasing futures, but the falling futures price still provided a guide as to the likely price of the shares making up the market, thus inducing more sales and price falls.

The causes of the crash are still controversial and we are unable to come to any firm conclusion. We now move on to consider the empirical evidence concerning the efficiency of the stock market.

8.4 The Stock Exchange and the efficient markets hypothesis

In this section we briefly survey the literature on the informational efficiency of the stock market. As the literature on this topic is extensive, some degree of selection is inevitable. We therefore concentrate on representative studies. At this stage we would, however, like to stress the practical importance of this. If the stock market conforms to the efficient market hypothesis, then forecasting future movements in share prices is not likely to be worth the effort involved because the market price reflects all available information. Thus, on average it will not be possible to outperform the market consistently. The caveat applying to this statement is that of risk aversion and it may be that the operator's degree of risk aversion is less than that ruling in the market.

Most early studies tended to support the hypothesis that the Stock Exchange was efficient. One interesting approach was to consider the role of filter rules. Basically a filter rule is an automatic instruction to buy a stock after it rises x per cent above a recent trough and sell again after it falls y per cent below a recent peak. The object of the rule is to identify cycles from which it is hoped to make profits. The size of x and y (which may be the same) is determined empirically from past data. If the two filters are small a large number of transactions will be undertaken. This increases cost but at the same time, hopefully, identifies profitable trading opportunities. Thus, there is a trade off between costs and the identification of potential for profit. An early study by Alexander [1954] suggested that filter rules did offer scope for obtaining profits above those realised from a buy and hold strategy. These conclusions were modified in the light of biases in the original study. A subsequent study, by Fama and Blume [1966], investigated the profitability of a wide range of filters for the 30 individual securities in the Dow-Jones index. The period involved was between 1957 and 1962 and the total number of observations ranged between 1,200 and 1,700 per share. After taking commissions into account, filter rules failed to provide as profitable a strategy as that obtained from buying and holding the securities. Thus, it appears that the market is 'weakly' efficient.

The evidence against the efficient market hypothesis as applied to the stock market comes from three different sources. These are (i) the records of some forecasters, (ii) the volatility of the prices of stocks and (iii) the so-called anomaly literature. First, regarding predictive evidence, Dimson and Marsh [1984] describe a study covering 3,364 share one-year horizon forecasts by a number of brokers for a large UK investment institution during the calendar years 1981 and 1982. They found that acting on these forecasts produced profitable trading. Similarly Bjerring *et al.* [1983] examined the profitability of the recommendations of a Canadian brokerage house for forecasts involving both US and Canadian stocks. After allowing for transaction costs Bjerring *et al.* calculate that an investor who followed the recommended list would make 9.3 per cent more than those who bought and held the market. Finally, Value Line in the US categorises stocks according to the expected performance over the next 12 months. The prediction of Value Line is good – see for example Stickel [1985].

The second attack on the efficient market came from the observed volatility of share price changes. This work is particularly associated with Shiller (e.g. [1981]). Shiller studied the aggregate dividends and earnings of the Standard and Poor (S&P) index from 1871 to 1979. This information was used to calculate what the price of the index should be if investors possessed perfect foresight. The actual value of the index was more volatile and this led Shiller to conclude that the market was excessively volatile, which could only be explained by irrational behaviour of the operators. The method involved may be illustrated quite easily with reference to a single share. Define the perfect foresight market value (V^*) as:

$$V^*_t = \Sigma \delta^{t+k} D_{t+k} \tag{8.4}$$

where $\delta = 1/(1 + R)$ is the discount factor.

The rational expected value of V^*_t is equal to the observed value V_t plus a random uncorrelated error term e_t, that is:

$$V^*_t = V_t + e_t$$

This leads to the variance bound:

$$\text{Var}(V^*) > \text{Var}(V) \tag{8.5}$$

However, it has been argued (see Kleidon [1986]) that it is inappropriate to use time series data from one economy to construct variance bounds and that the correct method would be to derive cross-section statistics for expectations and realisations from identical economies.

The third criticism involves the anomaly literature discovering that prices vary according to an unusual pattern. Typical examples are the fact that returns measured from the close of Friday to the close of Monday are typically negative over a wide range of securities (see e.g. Gibbons and Hess [1980]). Blume and Friend [1974] showed that there were large differences between the returns on large firms and those on small firms and these differences were not explainable by models of security pricing. It was also noticed that the majority of these differences occurred in January (Keim [1986]). These anomalies are difficult to explain within the context of acceptance of the efficient markets hypothesis.

The efficiency of the stock market is still an open question but a growing volume of evidence may point to a refutation of this hypothesis in its extreme form. The question of whether this evidence is sufficient to claim that the Stock Exchange does not approximate an efficient market remains a question of judgement.

8.5 Conclusion

In this chapter we have discussed the market in London for equities. We have shown that only a small proportion of new finance is raised by way of new issues of equities and the major source of finance for UK firms is the ploughing back of profits. This does not imply that the secondary market is irrelevant or a mere gambling casino since it provides liquidity for holders of equity. We have also discussed a number of problems that are currently facing the LSE. First, there is the question of transparency or to what extent information on actual trades should be immediately made available. Second, there is the development of CREST and the extent to which the LSE should operate the settlements system. Finally, the twin problems of lightly traded shares and small companies has yet to be resolved. A more fundamental issue concerns the role of 'quote-driven' versus 'order-driven' markets. In order-driven markets, no participant is required to make a market and details are provided immediately a deal is struck. Consequently investors would know the true prices of all trades. 'Just over half the largest share deals (those worth more than £1m) were struck at prices better than the best publicly available prices' (*Financial Times*, 3 August 1994). This complaint is enhanced by the allegation that many market makers do not really make markets but register as market makers to attract the benefits of no stamp duty and lack of transparency. It is claimed that 'although there are 29 registered market makers, only seven are recognized as genuine' ('Transparency or Opacity', *Financial Times,* 20 January 1995). Change of the system would, it is argued, increase investor confidence. In contrast, the LSE points out the success of SEAQ International in attracting business in Continental shares despite the fact that most other European exchanges are of the order-driven type. The LSE argues that the greater liquidity arises from the fact that market makers are prepared to risk their capital for share dealing. It is apparent that there is a connection between this issue and the earlier discussion of transparency.

The extent to which the equities market conforms to the efficient markets hypothesis was also examined and we were unable to reach an unambiguous conclusion in one direction or another.

Chapter 9

Interest rates and the bond market

9.1 **Introduction**

In this chapter the main foci of discussion are the bond market (in particular the market for gilt-edged securities) and the term structure of interest rates. We have linked these two topics together because the discussion of the term structure of interest rates is mainly conducted in the context of government securities. As an introduction we briefly survey the differing theories of the level of interest rates in section 9.2 before discussing the market for gilt-edged securities as regards both new issues (section 9.3) and the secondary market (section 9.4). A brief discussion of the corporate bond market and the role of credit rating agencies in this market is provided in section 9.5. The determinants of the term structure are considered in sections 9.6 to 9.8 before the empirical evidence is summarised in section 9.9.

Quotations of interest rates in the press take the form of publishing two rates. The lower figure represents the rate at which funds are accepted on deposit (the 'bid' rate) and the higher figure the rate at which the institution is prepared to lend out funds (the 'offer' rate). At the outset of the discussion it is necessary to emphasise that interest rates differ for a number of reasons, in particular:

(i) the risk of default,
(ii) cost of administering the loan,
(iii) tax arrangements,
(iv) term of the loan.

Discussion of the last factor is carried out in the main body of the chapter. Clearly, the risk of default is an important feature of the determinant of the

Table 9.1 *Selected money market rates (offer rates)*

Treasury bills	*Local authority*	*Bank bills*	*Sterling CDs*
$6^1/_8$	$6^1/_2$	$61^5/_{32}$	$6^5/_8$

Source: *Financial Times,* 'London Money Market Rates', 27 January 1995.

difference between interest rates charged to different borrowers. Market arbitrage should equalise the risk-adjusted rate of return rather than the actual rate itself. The role of risk can be illustrated with reference to the structure of rates for three-month securities on the London money markets at close of trading on 27 January 1995, shown in table 9.1. It can be seen that these short rates rise slightly as the risk of default (itself almost non-existent on the first security) increases.

The other factors are fairly easily dealt with. Very small loans at, say, pawnbrokers incur not only a high risk but are also costly to administer, with the result that the interest rate charges involved are also high. Tax arrangements differ between financial securities, with some being tax exempt and others bearing taxes at the normal rates. Clearly, it would be anticipated that the rates charged would differ in such circumstances.

A final distinction must be made between nominal and real rates of interest. The nominal rate is the rate paid on the loan or security whereas the real rate is the rate paid after making allowance for inflation. The relation between these two rates is shown below:

$$(1 + R) = (1 + i)(1 + E\Delta p) \qquad (9.1)$$

where R is the nominal rate and i is the real rate (both rates applying to a single period) and $E\Delta p$ is the rate of inflation expected during the period to maturity.

Simplifying equation 9.1 produces:

$$R = i + E\Delta p + iE\Delta p \qquad (9.2)$$

Since the last term on the right-hand side is the product of two decimals which are both likely to be small, the relationship may be approximated by:

$$R = i + E\Delta p \qquad (9.2a)$$

Equation 9.2a is the normal formula used to link the real rate of interest and the nominal rate. Market efficiency suggests that short-term, nominal rates of interest for differing maturities should therefore be a function of (i) the real rate for the relevant maturity and (ii) the level of inflation expected during the maturity of the security. We shall return to this topic in section 9.9.

9.2 The level of interest rates

The level of interest rates can be considered to be an index or some average value around which individual interest rates vary according to the factors discussed above. This is the approach taken in basic macroeconomic textbooks which discuss the determination of 'the' rate of interest via IS and LM curves. In this connection two distinct theories can be discerned: (i) the monetary approach and (ii) loanable funds theory.

The monetary (not monetarist) approach explains the level of interest rates in terms of the demand for and supply of money. Typically money demand equations depend on factors such as real income, rate(s) of interest on money (this may be implicit or a convenience yield) and alternative assets and possibly inflation, and incorporate some form of dynamic adjustment to the desired long-run equilibrium. Money supply is normally specified to depend on (i) a variety of rates of interest, such as those paid on deposits and earned on bank loans and (ii) the monetary base. Non-domestic factors can be allowed for by the inclusion of foreign rates of interest in both the demand and supply functions. The equilibrium rate of interest then follows from the equality of the demand for and the supply of money. In terms of the economy as a whole these are of course only the proximate determinants of the level of interest rates because the levels of real income and other explanatory variables will themselves be determined within the context of a simultaneous model, at the same time as the interest rate. Notice this explanation is in terms of stocks. Increases in the rate of interest can be due to either an increased demand for money or a reduction in the supply of money.

In contrast the loanable funds approach emphasises flows in the form of the demand and supply of credit by the various sectors, including the overseas sector. In turn savings come from the financial surpluses of the various sectors in the form of excess of income over expenditure. The main sources of savings come from personal savings and retained profits by firms. At times, however, the overseas sector provides credit by way of balance-of-payments capital inflows. Borrowings are required to finance either consumption or investment expenditure. For ease of exposition in the following narrative we shall assume that borrowing to finance consumption expenditure can be considered as negative saving and that all borrowings are made for the purpose of financing investment. Links to the monetary sector are introduced via increases in the money supply being representative of an additional source of credit but provided by the banks. Similarly, increases in the demand for money (technically known as hoarding) are akin to a demand for loanable funds. Hence the supply of loanable funds can be defined to be the sum of saving (S) plus increases in the money supply (ΔM) whereas the demand for loanable funds is specified as investment (I) plus increased demand for money (ΔH). Thus, the equilibrium rate of interest is determined by the equality of the demand and supply schedules for loanable funds, that is, where:

$$I + \Delta H = S + \Delta M \tag{9.3}$$

It is argued that both investment and saving are functions of the rate of interest, with savings increasing and investment declining as the domestic rate of interest rises. The allocation of savings to and borrowings from overseas as opposed to domestic sources will depend on the relative levels of domestic and foreign rates after taking into consideration the prospects of exchange rate changes during the period of the loan. The other two components may in the main reflect changes in taste (hoarding) and government policy and so can be considered as an addition to the interest rate components. However, this is not a vital assumption since, if anything,

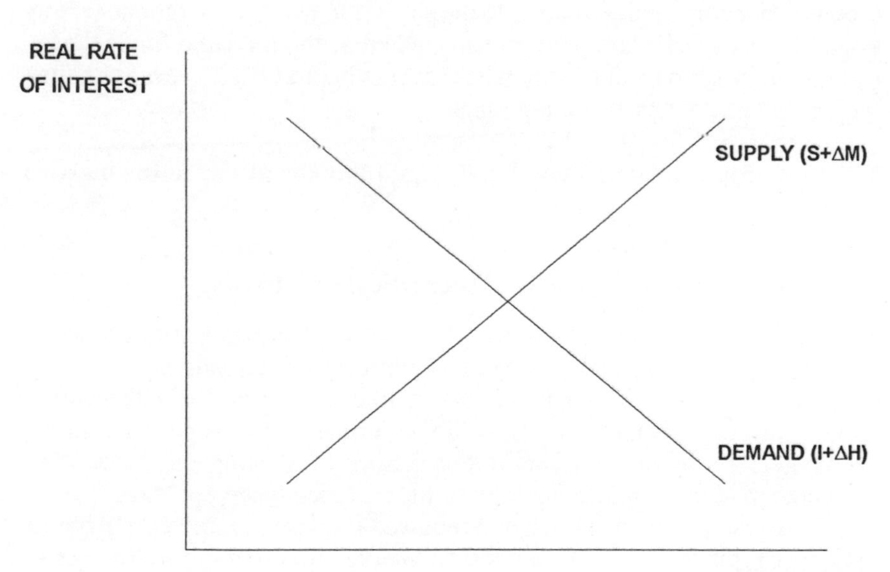

Figure 9.1 *Equilibrium in the credit market*

the money supply is likely to increase and hoarding to decrease as domestic interest rates rise in the same manner as savings and investment.

Equilibrium in the credit market is demonstrated in figure 9.1. Increases in the rate of interest can, according to this approach, be caused by an increase in the demand for loanable funds attributable to increased investment or hoarding or a reduction in the supply due to reduced saving or a reduction in the money supply. A rise in the foreign rate of interest (given expectations of future interest rate changes) would also cause a rise in domestic rates through a reduction in supply of, and an increase in demand for, domestic loanable funds. It should be noted that this explanation of the level of interest rates emphasises real factors, such as productivity determining investment opportunities and saving as a function of thrift, so that the rate of interest is the real rate.

Although the two theories have a different rationale, they are consistent with each other to a considerable degree. First, long-run equilibrium requires that both (i) savings equals investment (using the broad definitions adopted in this section) and also (ii) changes in the money supply equal changes in the demand for money. Second, the predictions of the two theories are the same following, for example, an increase in the quantity of money. Similarly, an increase in investment will raise the rate of interest directly in the case of the loanable funds theory and indirectly in the case of the liquidity preference (i.e. monetary) theory via the resulting increase in income raising the demand for money. A possible reconciliation is that the liquidity preference theory applies mainly to the short run, where for example factors in the money market are predominant, whereas the loanable funds theory is more relevant to the long run, where agents have sufficient time to adjust their expenditure and financing plans.

We now turn to examining the gilt-edged market in the following two sections.

9.3 The market for gilt-edged securities: new issues

The central government requires finance to meet the surplus of its expenditure over revenue and to meet the cost of refinancing debt as it matures. Further funds may be necessary to cover the cost of intervention in the foreign exchange markets. If the government intervenes to push the exchange rate down, this entails the selling of sterling on the foreign exchange markets in return for convertible currency reserves. Thus, finance has to be raised over and above that required for purely domestic purposes. In contrast, intervention to push the exchange rate up involves the loss of convertible currency reserves and a gain of sterling finance, thus reducing the amount of finance that needs to be raised for purely domestic purposes.

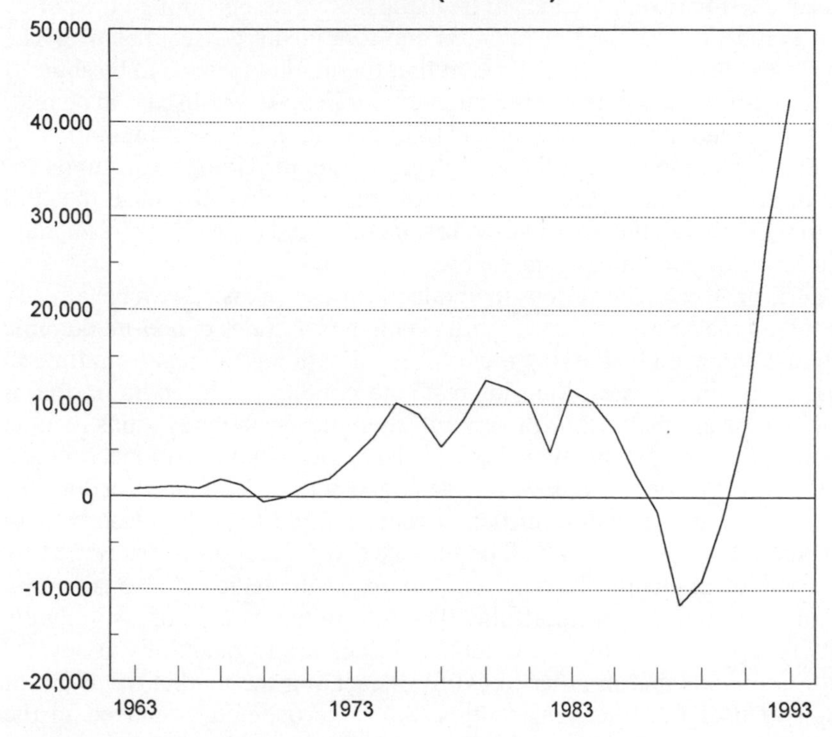

Figure 9.2 *Financial position of the public sector: 1963 to 1993*

Consequently, even if the central government is in fiscal balance during any one year, new issues of debt may be necessary to refinance maturing existing debt and to finance intervention in the foreign exchange market though, of course, this last component may be negative. Any finance that may be necessary is obtained through the issue of new securities of a variety of types and maturities including:

(i) bonds termed 'gilt-edged' securities,
(ii) non-marketable debt such as national savings and tax reserve certificates,
(iii) Treasury bills.

Figure 9.2 shows the financial position of the public sector over the period 1963 to 1993. The salient feature is the move into surplus in the period 1988–90 although the PSBR rose dramatically in the early 1990s, reaching £45 billion in the financial year 1993/94. Some of this surplus was due to the revenue achieved from the sale of assets through the policy of privatisation but the remainder is due to a positive fiscal balance. The surpluses shown in figure 9.2 meant that the markets tended to be short of funds, causing upward pressure on interest rates. As we discuss in chapter 10, this forced the Bank of England to intervene in the discount market by purchasing commercial bills of exchange, thus providing extra funds for the discount market. The other side of this coin was of course the 'bill mountain', that is, the stock of commercial bills held by the Bank of England as a result of purchases in the market.

Turning now to the various methods of raising finance, we have already discussed the nature of Treasury bills in chapter 1. Sales of non-marketable debt are achieved by varying the returns on national savings from time to time according to prevailing interest rate conditions. In addition, major innovations are made, though very infrequently. Such innovations include the introduction of (i) premium bonds and (ii) index-linked national savings.

We now consider the issue of gilt-edged securities. The procedure for the issue of gilt-edged securities is more simple than that described in chapter 8 for company debt. The underwriting function is performed by the Bank of England, which not only manages the issue but also takes any unsold debt into its own portfolio. The traditional method of issuing new gilts is to offer debt by public tender. Issues are in quantities of several million pounds and in order to avoid dislocating the market the Bank of England uses the following tactics. An advertisement is placed in the financial media advertising the terms of the issue (fixed coupon value, date of maturity, payment dates etc.) and the minimum price acceptable and inviting tenders for specified amounts of stock. If the issue is undersubscribed the stock is allocated at the minimum price with the Bank of England taking the balance into its own portfolio. The stock will then be made available to the market when the Bank believes there is demand for it and when it suits the Bank to make further sales. Stock available for issue in this way is known as tap stock. If, on the other hand, the issue is oversubscribed, the bids are accepted in descending order of price offered until the whole issue is allocated. A second method of issuing new stock is by way of additional supplies of existing stock, known as 'tranchettes'. These are taken directly into the portfolio of the Bank of England and made available to the market in the same way as tap stock.

Both these methods involve the Bank of England subsequently selling stock via the market. The Bank of England is also involved in the purchase of short-dated stock as it nears maturity. We shall discuss the methods of purchase and sale in our examination of the secondary market for government debt (section 9.4). In recent years the Bank of England has increasingly used the method of auctioning government stock without indicating a minimum price. In this case all stock would be sold according to the highest bids without the Bank of England performing an underwriting function. The Bank has, however, reserved the right to intervene in the case of extremely abnormal market conditions though, in fact, has not found it necessary to do so. In 1993 about half the issues of government stock were by auction with the other half being sold on tap to the gilt-edged market makers (see above). Finally, in this connection, the Bank has also carried out what are called 'reverse auctions'. A central government surplus, as in the late 1980s, implies a reduction in the total stock of gilt-edged securities and so the Bank has invited tenders to sell to it specific quantities of gilts.

9.4 The market for gilt-edged securities: the secondary market

Changes in the market for gilts mirrored those occurring in the market for private securities, discussed in chapter 8. Prior to 'Big Bang' there were eight gilt-edged jobbers, of whom two accounted for 75 per cent of the turnover. The new system of trading created an institution known as a 'gilt-edged market maker' (GEMM), who acted in a dual capacity as market maker and agent. GEMMs have an obligation to communicate, on demand, to other market participants continuous and effective bid–ask prices for a wide range of gilts in any trading conditions. GEMMs have a direct dealing arrangement with the Bank of England in gilts such that the Bank will bid to buy gilts from the GEMMs at prices of its own choosing and will respond to bids for gilts from the GEMMs at its discretion. This is of course the counterpart to the arrangements for issue of gilts discussed in section 9.3, whereby the Bank of England took into its own portfolio any unsold stock. The GEMMs are subject to the Bank's prudential control, in particular with reference to capital adequacy, which is required to be 'dedicated' to the operation in gilts. GEMMs have also approved borrowing facilities at the Bank.

A special facility is that the GEMMs have sole access to the inter-dealer broker mechanism. Inter-dealer brokers (IDBs) are subject also to the Bank of England's prudential control and supervision in order to ensure that the system works satisfactorily. The essential purpose of the IDBs is to enable the market makers to unwind their stock positions as and when required without trading directly with each other whenever they wish this dealing to be anonymous. A further important support to the market making function is provided by Stock Exchange money brokers (SEMBs), who both lend stock to the GEMMs and also money generated from their equity lending operations at rates which are competitive with those in the money market.

The Bank of England has announced plans for the operation of an open gilt repo market from 2 January 1996 (see chapter 10, section 10.2, for a discussion of the facilities for repo, i.e. repurchase agreements in the discount market). This would permit repo activity to be widened beyond the existing GEMMs. It is claimed that this will allow all market operators to adopt a wider range of trading strategies, including 'shorting' the market – selling stock which they do not own – and financing 'long' positions by lending stock. By making trading more flexible this development is also expected to attract more international investors to the gilt market. The resulting increased demand for gilts will lead to the additional benefit of lower funding costs for the government by several basis points. It is estimated that a reduction in yields of one basis point will eventually lead to an annual reduction in public spending of £25 million.

The impact of these changes was similar to those described for Big Bang. Prices of dealing fell. The Bank of England reports (*Bank of England Quarterly Bulletin*, February 1989) that typical spreads before the change were 2–4 ticks (£2/32 – £4/32) for shorts and 4–8 ticks for longs and these fell to 1–2 ticks and 2–4 ticks respectively. Similar falls were observed on index-linked stocks. In addition, the size of deal that could be transacted at normal prices also increased. Transaction costs fell because commissions largely disappeared on the wholesale market. These factors lead to an increase in turnover (see table 8.4 in the previous chapter). The Bank also reported that trading rose from around £1 billion a day to around £4 billion per day, out of which about half was intra-market, between GEMMs dealing primarily via IDBs. By 1993 trading had increased to £16.7 billion per day. Competitive pressures on the market operators became quite severe after these changes. The number of GEMMs increased from the eight quoted above to 27. Not unnaturally many of these firms made substantial losses given the fall in trading prices. At the time of writing 20 firms remain. The Bank of England also reports (*Bank of England Quarterly Bulletin*, February 1994) that the financial performance of the GEMMs has improved over the 1990s, with most firms making a profit after experiencing considerable losses in the two years after Big Bang.

This improved performance comes from an improved operating environment since 1991, with greater supply of gilts and improved investor confidence. The size of the gilt-edged market declined between October 1988 and January 1991, when net issues of gilts were negative as the authorities purchased stock. Consequently the total gilt-edged stock available in the market fell by 9 per cent, from £142 billion to £129 billion, during 1989. The service provided by the IDBs was new to the gilt market and six firms started although only three firms remained by 1994. The number of SEMBs increased at the time of Big Bang from six to nine, with eight firms remaining in 1994.

Following substantial issues of gilts in 1993 the total nominal value of gilt-edged stock outstanding rose to £190 billion (£224 billion at market

Table 9.2 *Sectoral holdings of gilt-edged stock at end 1993 (%)*

Total UK holdings	80.3
of which:	
Banks	6.0
Building societies	2.8
Insurance companies	37.2
Pension funds	18.2
Other financial institutions	1.4
Personal	11.9
Industrial and commercial companies	2.0
Public sector (other than official holdings)	0.3
Overseas holdings	19.7

Source: *Bank of England Quarterly Bulletin*, February 1994.

prices) at the end of that year. The market holdings of gilts were made up of approximately 35 per cent 0–7 years of outstanding maturity, 35 per cent 7–15 years, 15 per cent 15 years and above, 15 per cent index-inked stock and 0.7 per cent undated stock. The estimated sectoral holdings of gilts are given in table 9.2.

This completes our discussion of the gilt-edged market and we now turn to examine briefly the corporate bond market and the importance of credit ratings in this market.

9.5 The corporate bond market and credit ratings

Gilt-edged securities are perceived by investors as having virtually zero risk of default as the UK government is the guarantor and is very unlikely to default. Bonds issued by the governments of developing countries are likely to have a higher associated risk of default, as are issues of bonds by companies. The main domestic issuers of sterling bonds other than gilts are UK companies and local authorities. The volume of issues has been variable over the last 20 years and reference to table 8.4 will give some idea of the magnitude of recent issues. A wide variety of bonds exist. The typical bond offers a fixed return each year (i.e. the coupon) and has a fixed date for redemption. Some bonds are secured by specific assets of the issuer, so that in the case of bankruptcy the proceeds from the sale of those assets accrue to the bond holders. Other bonds carry what is termed a negative pledge, which commits the company to refrain from subsequently issuing bonds which carry greater security or preference in the event of default by the company. Some bonds also carry the right to convert into equity of the company at specific dates and terms. These are called 'convertibles'.

The risk of default clearly differs for different borrowers and so the returns demanded by investors to induce them to hold different bonds will also differ. Investors can obtain information on the likelihood of default or delayed payment of a security from the rating assigned by a credit ratings agency. Originally these ratings were applied solely to corporate bond issues but over recent years coverage has extended to a wide variety of debt instruments: local authority bonds, asset-backed securities, medium-term note programmes (see chapter 12), commercial paper programmes and bank certificates of deposit. The main rating agencies are the US-based Moodys Investors Service and Standard and Poors (S&P) although many smaller, more specialised agencies have emerged in recent years. Most agencies use their own system of symbols to rank securities according to risk of default. For example, for S&P the highest-quality ranking is AAA and the lowest is D, with a further 19 grades between these two extremes. A distinction is usually made between investment-grade ratings and speculative-grade ratings, with bonds graded BBB or above under the S&P system designated as investment grade. Generally the rating agency charges a fee to the issuer related to the size and type of the issue. Increasingly regulators, particularly in the US, have used the ratings applied to bonds and other debt instruments to simplify their prudential control of financial institutions. For example, the Basle Committee on Bank Supervision proposed in its 1993 market risk guidelines that internationally active commercial banks dealing in securities should hold extra capital against their non-investment-grade bonds.

Table 9.3 *Spreads between corporate bonds and US Treasury bonds, 1973–87 averages*

Rating	Basis points
AAA	43
AA	73
A	99
BBB	166
BB	299
B	404
CCC	724

Source: Cantor and Packer [1994].

Given the growth in the credit ratings industry and the increasing reliance being placed on ratings they produce it is important to consider their reliability. One study of the reliability of credit ratings, by Cantor and Packer [1994], found that the two main agencies referred to above do a reasonable job of assessing relative credit risks, so that lower-rated bonds were found to default more frequently than higher-rated bonds. However, they also found that assessment of absolute credit risks have been less reliable, as default probabilities associated with specific rankings have drifted over time. This latter result suggests that the use of a specific grade as a cut-off to determine which securities are investment-grade securities, and therefore should be assigned less capital for prudential purposes, is suspect. Cantor and Packer also report the fact that for US corporate bonds the yields are closely related to the rating grade. Table 4 from their article is reproduced as table 9.3 to illustrate this point. Clearly, the yield increases as the credit rating falls and this helps explain why companies are prepared to pay fees to credit rating agencies for this service. However, an important caveat is necessary. The figures in the table do not prove that there is any causal relationship between credit ratings and yields, or in other words the credit ratings may not provide any information in addition to that contained in market prices. It may be that the market had assimilated the available information and produced results similar to those derived by the credit rating agencies.

9.6 The expectations theory of the term structure

First of all we need to define the term 'yield to maturity' as the return on securities which are held to maturity. Thus, if we take as an example a three-year bond, redeemable at par (£100) and returning a coupon of £X paid once a year and with a current market price of £V, then solving the following equation for R provides the yield to maturity on that bond:

$$V = X/(1+R) + X/(1+R)^2 + X/(1+R)^3 + 100/(1+R)^3 \qquad (9.4)$$

Notice in this example that we are assuming the interest received is immediately reinvested in the security. The term structure then refers to the differences in yields to maturity on securities which are identical except for the outstanding (not initial) maturity. The yield curve itself is a representation of the term structure in a graphical form.

It is difficult to find examples of securities identical in all respects save for the outstanding term to maturity, with one major exception. This is for government securities, where the risk of default is virtually zero but more crucially the same on all issues. For example, the UK government has just over 90 different issues of gilt-edged securities with similar terms, although

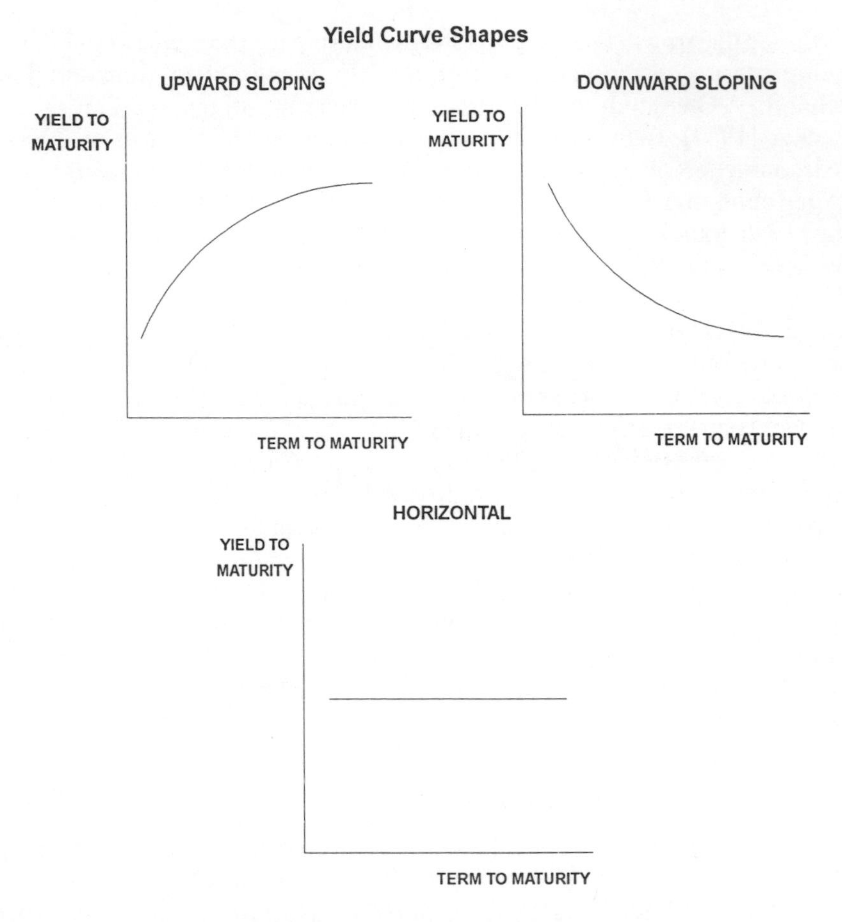

Figure 9.3 *Observed yield curve shapes*

differences do occur (e.g. index-linked, undated stock, etc.). Thus, the quantity of different stocks issued are sufficient to derive yield curves. This contrasts with issue of bonds by companies although, in principle, their debt issues would be subject to the same term structure plus a risk premium which might vary over time and between different companies. Figure 9.3 depicts the patterns of yield curves which have been observed over time.

In addition, combinations of the general patterns illustrated in figure 9.3 can also be seen from time to time. Consequently any credible theory of the term structure must be able to explain a wide variety of patterns of yield curves observed over time. So far our discussion has been in terms of yields but it should be noticed that quotations in the market or media refer to security prices. There are intrinsically no differences between these two approaches since, given a coupon value and outstanding term to maturity, a yield to maturity on a bond implies the market price and, similarly, the market price implies the yield to maturity.

The expectations theory explains the term structure of interest rates as being a function of rates of interest expected to exist in the future. Thus, for example, if short-term interest rates were expected to rise in the future, it would be reasonable to assume that long-term rates encompassing the period of those future short-term rates would be higher than current short-term rates. According to this theory, arbitrage ensures that the return for holding different securities for a specific period will be the same irrespective of their outstanding maturity. This is the basis of the expectations theory and in the following paragraphs we critically examine this theory. We make the following preliminary assumptions:

(i) agents possess perfect foresight, so they know all current and future interest rates;
(ii) a perfect capital market exists;
(iii) interest is paid once a year and is immediately reinvested in the same bonds;
(iv) two classes of bonds only are available:
(a) a one-year bond,
(b) a three-year bond,
both types of bond are issued at par;
(v) the investor has a holding period of three years, that is, he or she wishes to invest funds for three years.

Assumptions (iii) to (v) are merely simplifying assumptions to facilitate the exposition. Assumption (i) is clearly unrealistic and is made as a temporary aid to the explanation and will be relaxed later in this section. The second assumption is one normally made in the analysis and implies the absence of transaction costs, a spread between buying and selling prices and so on. It is a useful approximation to the truth as long as it is realised that the resulting predictions are likely to be less precise in practice.

Investors then have a choice of investment strategies. They can either buy a three-year bond or alternatively buy a sequence of one-year bonds, reinvesting the proceeds as the first two bonds mature. The choice of which strategy to follow will depend on which offers the higher return. Consequently arbitrage and market clearing will force the yields on the two strategies to be equal. For example, if the yield on the three-year bond is higher then agents will buy three-year bonds at the expense of one-year bonds. This raises the yield on one-year bonds (lowers the price) and lowers the yield (raises the price) on three-year bonds. The converse would apply if the yield on one-year bonds was higher than that on three-year bonds. Thus, given the assumptions made, market clearing ensures that:

$$(1 + {}_tR_3)^3 = (1 + {}_tR_1)(1 + {}_{t+1}R_1)(1 + {}_{t+2}R_1) \tag{9.5}$$

where the first subscript applied to R refers to the time the interest rate pertains (i.e. t represents year 1, t + 1 represents year 2 etc.) and the second subscript the time period of the rate (e.g. 1 is the one-year rate and 3 the three-year rate). The term on the left-hand side represents the return from purchasing a three-year bond at time t and that on the right-hand side the return from investing in a succession of one-year bonds for three years. Consequently the three-year rate can be expressed as the geometric average of the current and subsequent one-year rates. Note also that we have ignored the redemption of the bonds at the end of year three because the sum obtained would be the same in both cases.

Patently, the assumption of perfect foresight is absurd if applied to the real world and must therefore be relaxed. This entails replacing the known future rates with their expected values, denoted as $E_{t\ t+1}R_1$ and so on. The first subscript (t) refers to the time period at which expectations are formed and the second subscript the time period at which the rate is to hold. At this stage we introduce another assumption at the same time as relaxing that of perfect foresight. This is the assumption that the agents are risk neutral, that is, they are indifferent to risk due to the uncertainty of the future (not default) and motivated solely by the return on the security. In this case market equilibrium would for all practical purposes be the same as that given perfect certainty but with the expected values replacing the perfect foresight variables, and would therefore be represented by:

$$(1 + {}_tR_3)^3 = (1 + {}_tR_1)(1 + E_{t\ t+1}R_1)(1 + E_{t\ t+2}R_1) \tag{9.5a}$$

So now the three-year rate is the geometric average of the known one-year rate and the expected future one-year rates. More generally, any long-term rate can be decomposed into a series of short-term rates and for the one-period rates (R) the equilibrium condition can be shown as:

$$(1 + {}_tR_n)^n = (1 + {}_tR_1)(1 + E_{t\ t+1}R_1)(1 + E_{t\ t+2}R_1) \ldots (1 + E_{t\ t+n-1}R_1) \tag{9.6}$$

Solving for R_n gives:

$$R_n = \{(1 + {}_tR_1)(1 + E_{t\ t+1}R_1)(1 + E_{t\ t+2}R_1) \ldots (1 + E_{t\ t+n-1}R_1)\}^{1/n} - 1 \tag{9.7}$$

showing that the long-term rate will be the geometric average of the current known and future expected short-term rates into which it can be decomposed.

This result is perfectly general and is not restricted to the one-period rates used for the above demonstration.

We now look at the predictions of the expectations theory. First, the shape of the yield curve reflects expectations of future interest rates. Thus, if interest rates are expected to rise in the future, the yield curve will slope upwards, whereas if they are expected to fall, a downward-sloping yield curve will be observed. The second prediction follows from this dependence on expectations of future interest rate movements. The relative supply of securities with different maturities will not affect the yield curve. This has implications for government policy. If the expectations theory is correct, it is irrelevant for the impact on the economy whether the authorities intervene at the short or long end of the market. Arbitrage will cause the shape of the yield curve to remain the same in either case, since the long rates will retain the same relationship to short-term rates given by expectations. Arbitrage will also ensure that inflation expectations are incorporated into the term structure via their impact on current and expected short-term rates. Finally, external effects would also be included via the interest rate parity condition applying to the various term rates.

The expectations theory is open to a number of objections. First, over long periods of time upward-sloping yield curves are more commonly observed in the markets than other shapes. Whilst it is certainly true that interest rates have tended to rise since the 1950s, this is unlikely to be sufficient to account for the general preponderance of upward-sloping yield curves. It is likely that some other factor has also been at work. The second source of criticism is that the degree of forecasting ability credited to market operators is to say the least excessive. Is it really credible to assume the existence of agents able to forecast future movements of interest rates for a large number of years ahead? The third objection arises in connection with forecasting difficulties. The existence of uncertainty regarding future movements in interest rates casts doubts on the appropriateness of the assumption of risk neutrality. Casual observation of portfolios suggests diversification, rather than concentration of asset holdings in areas where the highest expected mean returns exist as would be suggested by the dominance of risk-neutral operators. Similar to the third objection is the problem of the potential existence of diverse expectations which, according to the expectations theory, would suggest an infinite amount of dealing between operators. The problem of the existence of diverse expectations can be accommodated by appealing to pragmatic considerations such as transaction costs or limitations on borrowing which, in practice, prevent unlimited dealing between operators.

We now turn to an examination of the preferred market habitat theory, which meets these objections to some extent.

9.7 The preferred market habitat theory of the term structure

The preferred market habitat theory assumes that market operators are in fact risk averse, that is, they are unwilling to incur extra risk without some extra reward in the form of a premium. Given that the risks on long-term securities are greater than those on short-term securities, it would be expected that long-term rates would be higher than short-term rates; that is, the yield curve would normally slope upwards. This does not imply that expectations of future rates are irrelevant and, as we shall see in the following explanation, these expectations will be incorporated into the yield curve.

It is believed that there is a difference between the preferences of lenders and borrowers. Lenders will prefer to hold short-term securities so that they can liquidate their loans more easily in the event of cash shortages. In contrast borrowers prefer to borrow long term so as to obtain greater security of funding. This is another illustration of the conflicting requirements of lenders and borrowers encountered generally in direct financing (see discussion on this in chapter 2). This divergence of preferences is reinforced as far as the lenders are concerned since long-term lending involves a greater degree of risk, as the future is uncertain and the market prices of long-term securities fluctuate more than those of short-term securities. Note the risk that we are considering is not one of default since the securities are identical in this respect by assumption. The logical consequence of these points is that lenders demand, and borrowers are prepared to pay, a risk premium for long-term lending over the rates for short-term lending. The risk premium is also likely to rise as the term of lending increases and may vary over time according to the degree of uncertainty present. The important point is that the risk premium is unlikely to be constant. Hence a risk premium (L) is introduced into the market clearing equilibrium discussed earlier, so that agents will enter arbitrage arrangements only if the gain is greater than the risk premium. This means that the long-term rate will be greater than the geometric average of the current actual and future expected short-term rates. More formally the equilibrium condition described by equation 9.6 has to be replaced by:

$$(1 + {}_tR_n)^n = (1 + {}_tR_1 + L_1)(1 + E_{t\,t+1}R_1 + L_2)(1 + E_{t\,t+2}R_1 + L_3) \ldots (1 + E_{t\,t+n-1}R_1 + L_n) \quad (9.8)$$

where $L_n > L_{n-1} > \ldots L_1$.

Similarly, solving for R_n, it is necessary to replace equation 9.7 with

$$R_n = \{(1 + {}_tR_1 + L_1)(1 + E_{t\,t+1}R_1 + L_2)(1 + E_{t\,t+2}R_1 + L_2) \ldots (1 + E_{t\,t+n-1}R_1 + L_n)\}^{1/n} - 1 \quad (9.9)$$

Note that in this theory expectations still play an important role but their impact is modified by the existence of a risk premium. This leads to the prediction that the normal shape of the yield curve will be upward sloping owing to the existence of the risk premium but that downward-sloping yield curves will be observed in instances when the expected fall in interest rates is sufficient to offset the risk premium. Debt of the various maturities are no longer perfect substitutes for each other, so that changing the relative supply of debt with different maturities will, according to this theory, alter the term structure and the shape of the yield curve.

Moving from postulating that debts with different maturities are imperfect substitutes to the belief that no substitution at all is possible leads to the market segmentation theory.

9.8 Market segmentation theory of the term structure

The essence of this approach to the explanation of the term structure is that there are completely separate markets for debt of different maturities. Substitution between these markets is not possible, which explains the title of market segmentation. This leads to the prediction that the shape of the yield curve reflects the differing demand and supply conditions in the various markets. Hence it would be expected that the yield on long-term debt would exceed that on short-term debt since supply will be less and demand greater at the long end of the market.

In this extreme form it is easy to be critical of the view that no substitution is possible. For example if it is felt that long-term rates are more attractive than short-term returns, it is not necessary for, say, five-year bonds to be substituted for three-month Treasury bills. All that is necessary is that portfolios go longer so that, say, five-year debt is substituted for four-year bonds in one portfolio and, say, two-year bonds for one-year bonds in another. Substitution over small but overlapping segments of the maturity spectrum means substitution over the whole spectrum. A ripple effect will occur so that in the end the more attractive (in terms of yield) longer-term debt has been substituted for shorter-term debt across portfolios in total until equilibrium is restored.

We have completed our review of the theory of the term structure and now move on to examine briefly the relevant empirical evidence.

9.9 Empirical evidence

Early empirical studies tended to favour the expectations theory. For example, Modigliani and Shiller [1973], building on earlier work by Modigliani and Sutch [1966], approached the problem of testing the role of expectations in the term structure by obtaining forecasts of short-term rates and then examining how well these forecasts explained the term structure in conjunction with a risk premium. Forecasts of future rates were based on averages of past observed nominal rates and inflation, on the grounds that the expected nominal rate could be considered to be the sum of expected real rate and the expected rate of inflation. The estimating equations were quite satisfactory, with a high degree of explanatory power and well determined coefficients. Further support for the role of expectations was obtained by Meiselman [1962], who, using an error correction model, found firm evidence of correlation between forecasting errors and the changes in the expected one-year rates implied by the expectations hypothesis. The way these are derived can easily be seen by assuming a two-year holding period and the existence of only one-year and two-year bonds. In this case, according to the expectations hypothesis, market clearing would require that:

$$(1 + {}_tR_2)^2 = (1 + {}_tR_1)(1 + E_{t\,t+1}R_1) \qquad (9.10)$$

The expected short rate implied by the expectations theory can then be obtained by solving for $E_{t\,t+1}R_1$ from equation 9.10 to obtain:

$$1 + E_{t\,t+1}R_1 = \{(1 + {}_tR_2)^2/(1 + {}_tR_1)\} \qquad (9.11)$$

Further evidence supporting the role of expectations in the determination of the term structure came indirectly from the difficulty in identifying any role for supply-side effects in the form of alterations in the available quantities of securities with differing maturities (see for example Malkiel [1966] for the US and Goodhart and Gowland [1977] for the UK). Possibly the apparent absence of these effects can be attributed to the authorities supplying debt with maturities which compensate for any changes in relative yields.

Subsequently, however, the role of expectations in the determination of the term structure has come under attack from two sources. First, similar to our discussion of excess volatility in chapter 8, section 8.4, with reference to the Stock Exchange, the volatility of long rates seems excessive (see for example Shiller [1979]). The second line of attack concerns the behaviour of short-term rates. Sargent [1972] noted that short rates exhibit a high degree of first-order correlation, so that estimation of equations of the form:

$$R_t = \beta + R_{t-1} \qquad (9.12)$$

produces estimates of β greater than 0.8 and often not significantly different from unity, thus implying a random walk. This information should be incorporated into expectations of future short-term interest rates but evidence by Sargent [1972] for the US and Goodhart and Gowland [1977] for the UK suggests that the revision of expected rates is less than that implied by the observed historical auto-regressive properties. This characteristic has more destructive implications for the expectations theory of the term structure. Since long rates under-predict changes in short rates, any movement in short rates would alter the slope of the yield curve. Thus, for example, an upward change in short-term rates would produce less than appropriate changes in long rates, so that the slope of the yield curve would tend to decrease (assuming that it was upward sloping for purposes of exposition) or even become negative if the change in short rates was sufficiently large. Goodhart [1989] points out that on balance the long rate has tended to fall when the yield curve is upward sloping and rise when it is downward sloping. In the case of a major fall in short rates this also has the implication that operators could profit from selling long-term bonds since it is likely that long rates will rise (i.e. bond prices fall) in the future. Evidence by Mankiw and Summers [1984] suggests this directional failure is also matched by an inability of the term structure to predict future short-term rates of interest.

This survey of the empirical evidence has of necessity been brief and we have merely tried to identify the important strands of the literature. For further detail the reader is referred to Goodhart [1989] and the original studies. Nevertheless, we have covered sufficient ground to indicate the main areas of controversy and to draw the conclusion yet again that the efficiency of yet another financial market, in this case the bond market, is an open question.

Chapter 10

The sterling money markets

10.1 **Introduction**

The sterling money markets located in London are markets for short-term funds and consequently provide facilities for economic units to adjust their cash position quickly. The rationale for their existence is that receipts of and payments in cash are not generally synchronised. Quite large cash balances are needed if these variations in payments made and received are to be accommodated. The problem here is that cash holdings provide either no or a very low return, so that the opportunity cost of holding large working balances is quite high. If on the other hand markets exist which can, at short notice and with low transaction costs, absorb surplus cash and also provide facilities for borrowing, then agents can economise on cash holdings and earn a higher rate of return on the deposits made in the money markets. Thus, cash positions can be adjusted by placing funds on deposit in the money markets when cash balances are temporarily too high and withdrawing or borrowing funds when the balance is too low. The success of this strategy depends on the existence of wide markets which can offer facilities for such transactions by catering for short-term deposits or lending without large fluctuations in rates of interest. This is particularly true of the banks themselves, which keep their working balances at the Bank of England and no interest is paid on these balances. Therefore the banks have a clear incentive to reduce these balances to the absolute minimum.

The London money markets are 'wholesale' markets with transactions typically for amounts considerably in excess of £500,000 or more. There are no particular central locations where members meet face to face and most of the business is conducted via the telephone (or telex) or even by personal visits. In many cases brokers act as intermediaries, bringing depositors and borrowers together. We show in table 10.1 the main London money markets, together with an estimate of their size at the end of 1993.

Table 10.1 *London sterling money markets*

	Size (£1,000 million)
The traditional discount market	9.1
The local authority market	2.1
The inter-bank market	71.3
Certificate of deposit market	69.0
Finance houses deposit market	4.2
Commercial paper market	5.5

Source: see commentary in main text.

The size of a market is not an unambiguous concept and the statistics shown in table 10.1 have been derived as follows:

(i) discount market – total borrowed funds by the discount houses (*Financial Statistics,* September 1994, table 4.2d),
(ii) local authority market – total stock of temporary money (*Financial Statistics,* September 1994, table 1.3b),
(iii) inter-bank market – total sterling time deposits of banks held with UK banks (*Financial Statistics*, September 1994, table 4.2c),
(iv) CD market – total of sterling CDs and other short-term liabilities issued by banks plus CD issues by building societies (*Financial Statistics,* September 1994, tables 4.2c and 4.3a),
(v) finance houses deposit market – total short-term funds obtained by non-bank credit companies from the banks (*Financial Statistics,* September 1994, table 5.2b),
(vi) commercial paper – total of sterling commercial paper outstanding (*Bank of England Statistical Abstract*, Part 1, 1994, tables 10.1).

The longest established market is the traditional discount market, with the markets developing alongside the discount market over the last 30 years being termed parallel or complementary money markets. The most recent development is the commercial paper money market. Using the measures of size quoted in table 10.1, the inter-bank market has, apart from the commercial paper market, shown the fastest rate of growth since 1984 (i.e. roughly doubled in size). Comparative figures for the other markets are: the traditional discount, market 22 per cent; the CD market, 41 per cent; and the local authority market, -57 per cent.

Although in the above classification we have distinguished between different markets, we would like to emphasise that these are all closely interrelated, with the same institutions operating in many of the markets. Interest rates will vary only slightly between the various markets because of the slightly differing intrinsic characteristics of the instruments involved. For example, inter-bank deposits will command a small premium over CD interest rates for comparable maturity terms because of their greater degree of liquidity. Similarly, deposits with differing terms will also attract differing rates of interest, as will deposits with institutions with lower credit worthiness. Nevertheless, these differences are likely to be fairly minor so that arbitrage will ensure that the interest rates in the various markets will tend to move together, as they reflect similar a trading environment. The basic similarity between these markets is that they all cater for short-term funds.

In the following exposition we will concentrate mainly on the traditional discount market, which is discussed in section 10.2. In section 3 we examine the parallel sterling money markets before proceeding to a brief review of the extent to which short-term rates of interest incorporate inflation expectations, in section 10.4. The institutional detail covering the banks is covered in chapters 3 and 4 and the reader may find it necessary to refer to these chapters in order to appreciate the following analysis.

10.2 The traditional discount market

The main operators in the discount market are:

(i) the Bank of England (hereafter termed the Bank),
(ii) the commercial banks,
(iii) the discount houses.

The object of the Bank's daily money market operations is either to even out the daily cash flows between the central bank, where the central government maintains its main bank account, and the commercial banks collectively and/or to enforce its interest rate policy. The commercial banks for their part use the discount market to offset daily fluctuations in their individual balances at the Bank. This is achieved by making deposits at the discount houses, with such loans being secured by collateral security in the form of asset titles. Thus, the impact of any shortage of funds is, first of all, seen in the discount market as the banks withdraw funds from the discount houses. Conversely any surplus is initially represented by an increase in funds lent to the discount houses. By custom the banks do not withdraw funds from the discount houses after midday. The discount houses operate to make the market and earn profits for themselves by purchasing assets with a yield higher than the rate of interest paid on the funds borrowed by them. Settlement for transactions in the discount market are made via electronic book entry transfers through the Central Money Markets Office, operated by the Bank of England in a similar manner to that described for gilts (chapter 9). We now discuss the operations of these parties in more detail.

In order to understand the nature of the Bank's operations in the discount market it is necessary to describe the background of the impact of payments to and by the central government on the commercial banks' cash position. Any payment by the central government to other sectors increases the banks' balances at the Bank of England. Conversely any payment to the central government by any other sector has the effect of reducing the commercial banks' balances at the Bank. Generally there is a shortage of funds (i.e. payments to the central government exceed payments by it) and such shortages arise from three sources:

(i) Exchequer transactions, that is, those necessary to finance a central government budget deficit after sales of long-term debt (a budget surplus leads to an excess supply of funds);
(ii) maturing assistance, such as loans to the discount houses and the Bank's holdings of commercial bills – in this case funds pass to the central government as the debt is repaid (see section 3.5 for a discussion of the balance sheet item representing this form of assistance); this item has been a major component of the total market shortage in recent years, and note this drain would not occur if the Bank purchased only central government rather than commercial securities;
(iii) increases in the volume of notes and coins in circulation – increased holdings of notes and coins involve a payment to the Bank for them.

The daily totals of these payments are both very large and also fluctuate widely on a daily basis. Part of this impact is netted out as some commercial banks will be withdrawing funds from the market whereas others will be lending additional funds, but overall it is likely to lead to market imbalances which are both large and difficult to predict. For example, the *Financial Times* (money market report, 24 November 1994) noted that on 23 November 1994 'the Bank of England cleared a £600 million daily shortage in UK money markets'. The size of the shortage can become extremely large in certain circumstances. For example, the defence of a specific exchange rate will lead to a large volume of payments to the government as sterling is exchanged for exchange reserves.

The impact of any shortage/surplus is seen in the discount market as the banks withdraw/deposit funds with the discount houses. The magnitude of the figures involved suggests that instability would exist in the discount market unless the Bank intervened to even out these cash flows. It does this mainly by transactions with the discount houses but also, though more rarely, directly with the banks. In the case of shortages of funds (typically the case) in the market the Bank will buy bills (Treasury bills, eligible bank bills and local authority bills) from the discount houses or make loans to them. Conversely, in the case of surpluses it would sell Treasury bills. The bills are categorised into the following bands according to the outstanding maturity of the bill:

band 1, 1–14 days;
band 2, 15–33 days;
band 3, 34–63 days;
band 4, 64–91 days.

Intervention is mainly at the short end of the maturity spectrum, that is, in bands 1 (but typically with more than seven days to maturity) and 2, so that a very small variation in the price of a bill will lead to a significant change in the annual rate of interest.

Each morning at 9.45 a.m. the Bank indicates its forecast of the daily shortage via financial news screens such as Reuters and Telerate. This prediction will be amended in the light of new information received by the Bank of England. If the shortage forecast is greater than £750 million then the Bank indicates to the discount houses that it is prepared to offer assistance (a so-called 'early round'). Otherwise there are two trading sessions a day, at midday (the 'noon' round) and 2.00 p.m. (the 'afternoon' round). However, if the shortage persists after 2 p.m., then the discount houses can apply for late assistance by way of secured loans. Their borrowing ability is defined in terms of two tranches, each of which is equal to their capital base.

Intervention is normally at or near the 'stop' rate. This rate is unannounced but the market operators are generally aware of its level and most deals occur at or slightly above the stop rate. The stop rate may be slightly different for each of the bands discussed above so as to achieve approximate equality of compound interest rates across the various maturities. The Bank invites bids and decides which bids to accept. As an alternative the Bank may also require the discount houses to offer eligible bills for sale to the Bank, with an agreement for the repurchase of the bills by the discount houses at an agreed later date. The Bank will specify terminal dates for the repurchase and the discount houses then submit offers of bills at rates of interest they are prepared to pay on the proceeds for the period indicated. The Bank responds to the bids in the manner discussed above for offers for outright purchase. Note that except in the case of secured loans by way of late assistance, intervention prices are published after the transactions have been completed by way of the financial news screens and on the following day in the financial press. In framing any bid, therefore, the discount houses will have prior knowledge of previous intervention prices and will also take into consideration the general financial environment and the likely future course of interest rates.

As an alternative to purchasing bills the Bank may decide to make loans. This practice is usually followed when the Bank wishes to give a clear signal to the market over interest rates, such as when rises are desired. For example, at the beginning of September 1990 when there was discussion over the UK joining the Exchange Rate Mechanism (ERM), with a subsequent reduction in interest rates being envisaged, the *Financial Times* money market report dated 7 September 1990 stated that 'The Bank of England indicated its concern about lower interest rates by refusing to operate in the bill market. The authorities did not offer to buy bills, but underlined the present interest rate structure by lending money to the discount houses for seven days at the clearing bank base lending rate of 15%.' In its operations in the discount market, the Bank will never refuse to supply money but, nevertheless, the rate at which intervention is carried out reflects the government's monetary policy.

The second of the Bank's motives is the evening out of flows of funds on to the market. Clearly, it would be expected that such intervention would exercise a smoothing influence on short-term rates. As noted earlier, intervention by the Bank has typically involved securities with more than seven days to maturity and no smoothing of the overnight interest rates has occurred. In fact Kasman [1992] has investigated the variability of overnight interest rates in a number of centres and the unambiguous result is that the volatility of such rates is higher in the UK than the other centres. Summary results are shown in table 10.2. Similarly, the intra-day volatility of the rates also appears to be quite high.

One source of disposing of excess or acquiring additional balances so as to meet targets is the overnight market. Hence excess volatility in this market will increase the risk and costs to operators, and this must lead to a widening (however slight) of bands by market makers in the money markets in general.

A number of reasons can be put forward as to why UK overnight interest rates exhibit the degree of volatility exhibited in table 10.2. First is the

Table 10.2 *Overnight interest rate volatility in selected countries (mean absolute deviation of daily observations, in basis points)*

	1988	*1989*	*1990*	*1991*	*Average*
Germany	15.7	18.2	13.6	13.4	15.2
Japan	8.7	8.5	7.1	8.4	8.2
UK	50.4	32.9	14.8	25.3	30.9
USA	12.3	11.9	12.3	21.1	14.4

Source: Kasman [1992].

obvious point that there is no smoothing intervention by the Bank in this market. Second, Fleming and Barr [1989] have argued that intervention rates are, in effect, points about which actual rates will pivot. Expectations of a rise in rates will cause a parallel upward shift for rates for maturities exceeding the intervention points. The converse will occur in the case of rates for maturities less than the intervention points. The reason for this seemingly perverse behaviour is that rational portfolio holders will sell longer-dated bills to avoid the capital loss and purchase shorter-dated bills. See also Schnadt and Whittaker [1993] for similar arguments. Third, UK banks are required to meet their target balances at the Bank each day. This produces greater urgency and therefore pressure on the search for funds (or disposal of excess funds). In some other countries (e.g. France, Germany and the US) required balances are based on period averages and this reduces the pressure except as the period involved draws to a close. Finally, Schnadt [1994] argues that the tactics of the Bank also exacerbate the volatility of interest rates. For example, in the case of reserve shortages, the banks will attempt to borrow the necessary funds in the money markets. The discount houses have a privileged position vis-à-vis the Bank which permits them to borrow funds from the Bank later than any other financial institution. Furthermore, the rate for these funds is not related to the overnight money market rate – whilst not published, the rate for the funds borrowed by the discount houses is normally equal to base rate for the first borrowing tranche and base rate + 0.5 per cent for the second tranche. There is therefore an incentive for the discount houses to delay depositing until as late as possible.

Various suggestions have been made to reform the system. The keystone of one set of suggested reforms is to reduce the magnitude (and the variability) of the shortages appearing in the market. It is argued that this will reduce the pressure on the system without lowering the ability of the Bank to control short-term interest rates, since this depends on the ability to supply or take up monetary base rather than the magnitudes of the imbalances. This is an institutional feature of the UK economy and could be reduced by removing the bank accounts for Exchequer transactions from the Bank to the commercial banks. This would obviate the need for smoothing of the flows of payments provided the account(s) maintained a sufficient balance to avoid overdrafts. For similar reasons, the Bank of England's portfolio of commercial bills could be significantly reduced over time, this reducing the receipts through maturing of past assistance. A second proposal would involve the Bank changing its tactics in order to smooth, or at least to take into consideration the impact of its operations on, the overnight rates as well the other interest rates.

As noted at the beginning of this chapter, the banks use the discount market to even out their cash position. In terms of the attributes discussed in chapter 1, deposits with the discount houses are liquid, short-term, capital certain and virtually free of default risk. As they earn a rate of return, they offer the perfect medium for banks to carry their first reserves against any cash shortages. Since the greater proportion of the deposits made with the discount houses originated from the banks themselves, the discount houses can themselves be considered almost as 'arm's length' departments of the banks. They borrow funds from the banks, purchase short-term monetary assets and sell such assets to the banks. They operate to make a market in Treasury bills and eligible bank and local authority bills. They underwrite the Treasury bill tender (see chapter 9) and operate facilities to borrow and lend gilt-edged stock through money brokers. As an assistance to the provision of these facilities, the discount houses have a direct dealing relationship with the Bank which involves the purchase and sale of bills to the Bank and also borrowing facilities. The discount houses are also the subject of prudential supervision by the Bank.

In order to broaden the market, the Bank indicated, during the autumn of 1988, that it was prepared to consider applications from other financial institutions for the direct dealing relationships applicable to the discount houses as described above. Such institutions would be required to accept the obligations and duties at present undertaken by the discount houses. They would further be required to conduct their business through separately capitalised entities but, in the case of existing gilt-edged market makers, would consider applications without formal separation of capital. Two institutions successfully applied for such relationships and one has since dropped out. This leaves seven pure discount houses and one gilt-edged market maker as non-bank operators within the market.

The existence of institutions operating as intermediaries between the central and commercial banks is unique to the UK financial system. It is therefore useful to list the functions of the discount market. These are:

(i) the daily adjustment by banks of their liquidity position through the placing or recall of funds with the discount houses;
(ii) daily intervention by the Bank to offset the impact of uneven flows between the central government and the rest of the economy;
(iii) the provision of a channel through which the Bank can permit, initiate or reinforce a movement in short-term interest rates;
(iv) the provision of a market for Treasury bills;
(v) the provision of a market for eligible local authority and commercial bills.

In the case of the last item, the discount houses provide expertise in assessing the quality of bills received for discount and the very act of discount assists the provision of finance for deficit units. This importance of this function has been reduced given the fact that at the end of July 1994 over 75 per cent of the total stock of eligible bills held by banks and discount houses were held by the banks themselves (*Financial Statistics,* September 1994, tables 4.2c and 4.2d).

To sum up, it is true that the facilities provided by the discount houses could be provided by the banks themselves and it remains an open question as to whether the existence of these institutions is strictly necessary. In 1959 the Radcliffe report concluded that, in relation to their function at that time, 'they are doing the work effectively, and they are doing it at a trifling cost in terms of labour and other resources'. The same conclusion is probably true today.

10.3 The parallel sterling money markets

There are a number of general points about the structure of these markets that are worth making before the more detailed discussion of the various markets themselves. These are:

(i) Lending is not secured in the manner discussed above for the traditional discount market.
(ii) There is no direct intervention by the Bank of England in these markets, so the discount market is the sole channel used by the Bank of England to enforce its short-term interest rate policy. Consequently interest rates in these markets move freely to reflect the underlying forces of supply and demand.
(iii) There are strong links between all the markets (both parallel and the discount). The same operators are involved to a considerable extent and arbitrage will ensure that interest rates move in a similar manner in all the markets.
(iv) There is no formal lender of last resort standing behind these markets in the manner that the Bank provides borrowing facilities for the discount houses. On the other hand, our discussion of prudential supervision of the banks by the Bank of England in chapter 17 suggests that the Bank would be extremely loathe to countenance the failure of any major monetary institution. This proviso suggests that this distinction between the discount and parallel money markets is superficial.
(v) Much of the volume of transactions in these markets are routed via brokers, who act as intermediaries between the ultimate borrowers and lenders.

We now turn to an examination of these markets. The discussion on each market will be much briefer than that of the discount market above. This does not mean that these markets are less important to the operation of the UK financial system but rather that they possess a relatively simple structure.

The first market we wish to discuss is the local authority money market. The requirement of local authorities to raise short-term finance arises from the different timing of their receipts and payment. Finance can be raised in a variety of ways. The first method is through the issue of bonds, normally for maturities of one to five years. The second method is through the issue of bills. Normally these are offered for tender and possess maturities of up to six months. The third method of interest in this discussion is by way of what is called temporary money. These are deposits with local authorities for varying periods up to one year but, in fact, the average maturity is for a much shorter time, with the greater proportion of deposits being for less than seven days. The minimum size of deposit is £100,000 and the deposits are non-negotiable. The sources of the deposits are monetary institutions (roughly 50 per cent), large industrial and commercial companies and overseas institutions.

The inter-bank market, as its name suggests, is a market for unsecured lending between different banks. The market grew rapidly during the 1960s when the international banks, newly located in London, extended their inter-bank lending practice from foreign currencies to sterling deposit. In fact the market now is considerably broader than just between banks (both retail and wholesale) as depositors include large industrial and commercial companies, international institutions, discount houses and other financial institutions. Deposits can be made for a variety of periods from a minimum of overnight, but are mainly for maturities of less than three months. The minimum size of transaction is usually £500,000 and, as in the case of the local authority market, deposits are non-negotiable. Borrowing in the inter-bank market provides an indication to the banks of the marginal cost of raising new funds, so that one rate in particular, the London inter-bank offer rate (LIBOR), is widely used as a basis for calculating charges on loans with variable interest rates. In addition, their own base rates are sensitive to movements in this rate.

This market provides a means for banks to balance their inflow of deposits with the demand for loans (see discussion of liability management in chapter 3). Thus, for example, a bank with a new deposit and no foreseeable immediate demand for a loan can make a deposit in the inter-bank market and earn a rate of interest. Similarly, a bank with a demand for a loan from a customer and no new deposit to hand can raise the necessary deposit in the market. In this way the market serves a smoothing function in a manner similar to that described for the discount market. A second function of the market is the provision of facilities for non-banks to make deposits for short periods as part of their cash-management techniques. The third function provided by the market is that it enables banks with less well known names to raise finance by borrowing in the inter-bank market rather than direct from customers. As a final comment it should be noted that the existence of inter-bank lending increases the connecting links between banks and raises the potential risk of systemic failure following the collapse of one institution.

A third parallel money market is the secondary market in certificates of deposit (CDs). CDs are negotiable certificates confirming that a deposit has been made with a UK office of a UK or foreign bank and, since 1983, with certain large building societies. Issues in London can be denominated in either dollars or sterling, with the latter market being the larger. They are issued in multiples of £10,000 from a minimum of £50,000 and are usually for a maturity of between three months and five years. The key advantage of a CD as distinct from a straight deposit for the holder is that it is negotiable, that is, the holder can liquidate the loan should a need for the funds arise. Consequently the rate of interest on CDs is normally slightly lower than that on deposits for the same maturity. This advantage depends critically on the existence of a secondary market in which existing CDs can be bought and sold. The market makers in this secondary market are the discount houses.

The fourth market to be considered is the market for finance house deposits. This is smaller than the other markets considered so far and refers to the raising of funds by finance houses which, in turn, use the funds for the finance of consumer credit, leasing, block discounting and factoring. Many of the institutions concerned are now classified as banks, which tends to blur the distinction between this and the inter-bank market. Much of the deposits comes from banks and other financial institutions but deposits are also made by industrial and commercial companies.

The sterling commercial paper market represents the most recent development in the sterling money markets. In its present form it dates from 1986 though an inter-company market for short-term deposits existed in the 1970s. Commercial paper is a short-term financial instrument similar to a promissory note. It is a general unsecured financial instrument with a maturity typically between seven days and three months. Commercial paper contrasts with bills of exchange since it is the liability of the issuer only, whereas bills are obligations of the drawer and the accepting house except when issued by the Treasury, banks and building societies. In terms of world markets for commercial paper, the US is the largest. The Bank of England (*Bank of England Quarterly Bulletin*, February 1987) reported that in late 1986 outstanding issues in the US amounted to $322.7 billion, compared with only $1 billion in the UK. In fact at this time it is estimated that the US market accounted for just over 80 per cent of total world outstanding issues. The recent growth in issues of commercial paper represents the general move towards securitisation. This can be attributable to a number of factors, such as financial liberalisation, and the move by banks and financial institutions towards fee-earning operations as distinct from direct lending.

In 1986 the powers conferred on the Treasury by the Banking Act 1986 to remove specified transactions from the definition of deposit taking were exercised. This relaxation permitted the issue of short-term sterling debt. Further relaxations occurred in 1987 and more fundamentally in 1990. This last revision permitted an extension to five years of the maximum permissible maturity of the paper issued under this facility. Paper issued with an original maturity of up to and including one year is termed 'commercial paper', whereas issues with an original maturity exceeding one year but less than five years are called 'medium-term notes'. It is only the first category which really forms part of the money markets. Issues can be in sterling or other currencies. Sterling issues can be made by companies with net assets valued in excess of £25 million. In addition, they must have shares and debt listed on the International Stock Exchange (ISE) in London or on the unlisted securities market (or presumably its replacement when finalised). In the case of issues by non-resident companies, the qualification is that similar criteria have to be met on an 'authorised' stock exchange in the country where the company is located. Authorisation in this case entails recognition and approval by the ISE. Issues can also be made by financial institutions. Although not a legal requirement, issues are normally restricted to investment-grade ratings (see chapter 9 for a discussion of bond rating). The Bank permitted the use of authorised intermediaries to manage the issue and the standard way of issuing such debt is to make issues via a lead bank or security house, which will manage the whole programme. The functions of the lead manager include making arrangements for the issue and redemption of the debt, offering advice on the issue and arranging the placing of the debt with other dealers. Issues are in large denominations and an indication of the size of issues can be obtained by noting that the average size of outstanding debt is £27 million (November 1994) though, of course, there will be large variations around the mean. At the moment there also appears to be no secondary market although, in some cases, the dealers are prepared to buy paper back before its maturity. Given the short-term nature of the debt generally issued, it is probably true to say that there is little need for a secondary market for the sale of existing commercial paper.

This market offers new scope for the raising of money by industrial and commercial companies. It is difficult at this stage to comment on the cost of raising finance through the issue of commercial paper because of the wide variety of issuers. The market also offers a short-term outlet for industrial and commercial firms to place surplus funds. The development of the commercial paper market contributed to the relaxation of the formerly

Table 10.3 *Value of sterling paper, 1986–93, at year end*

	Sterling commercial paper (£1,000 million)	*Sterling medium-term notes (£1,000 million)*
1986	0.5	
1987	2.1	
1988	3.3	
1989	3.5	
1990	3.8	0.4
1991	3.7	1.0
1992	3.8	3.3
1993	5.5	8.0

Source: Bank of England *Statistical Abstract* 1993, Part 1, tables 10.1 and 10.2.

close relationships between banks and their customers. Business was now being conducted on a transactional basis, where the paper was placed with financial institutions offering the lowest cost for the particular service. In addition, competition between institutions led to low rewards for dealers in the market. Nevertheless, this market has seen a fast rate of growth, as can be seen from the details shown in table 10.3, particularly in the case of medium-term sterling notes.

10.4 **Short-term interest rates and inflation**

It may be considered difficult to apply tests of market efficiency to markets for short-term deposits given the degree of intervention by the authorities. However, one interesting question was raised by Fama [1975] concerning the role of inflationary expectations in the setting of short-term rates of interest. Equation 9.2a is reproduced below for the sake of convenience:

$$R_t = i_t + E\Delta p_{t+1} \tag{9.2a}$$

where R is the nominal rate of interest, i is the real rate and $E\Delta p$ refers to the expected rate of inflation. Equation (9.3a) is often termed the 'Fisher' hypothesis and has often been tested by running a regression of the general form:

$$R_t = \alpha + \beta E_t\Delta p_{t+1} \tag{10.1}$$

Comparing equation 10.1 with equation 9.2a reveals the explicit assumption made that the real rate, i, is a constant. An estimated value for

β of unity supports the existence of complete adjustment of the nominal rate to inflation expectations – often called the strong Fisher hypothesis. A value between zero and unity supports the weak Fisher hypothesis, that inflation expectations have some role to play in the determination of short-term rates of interest but are not completely anticipated. Early evidence failed to support the view that the markets were incorporating efficient forecasts of inflation in the setting of interest rates. Various reasons were suggested, including poor price data and faulty representation of the inflation series – normally carried out by a distributed lag of past price changes.

Using US data, Fama [1975] tested whether the nominal interest rate acted as a good predictor of inflation by transforming equation 10.1 to obtain:

$$\Delta p_t = \beta' R_t - \alpha' \tag{10.2}$$

where $\alpha' = 1/\alpha$ and $\beta' = 1/\beta$.

Fama found support for the strong Fisher hypothesis since the estimate of β' was not significantly different from unity. This result was criticised by a number of investigators. The first criticism was that it was possible to obtain alternative estimators of the future rate of inflation using time series analysis and, when compared with the predictions from the rate of interest, it was found that these provided additional information. This suggested that the market's setting of short-term rates of interest failed to take into account all available information concerning future rates of inflation. The second approach followed the inclusion of additional variables to the right-hand side of equation 10.2, and it was found that these improved the fit of the equation, thus implying an improvement in the forecasts of future inflation. Fama conceded [1975] that these criticisms were correct but argued that the improvements were very small quantitatively, so that his initial result was largely intact.

Demery and Duck [1978] carried out a similar analysis based on UK data and also found support for the Fisher hypothesis but, in this case, the weak version. They concluded that nominal rates of interest rise as expectations of inflation rise but that, even in the long run, they probably fail to adjust fully for the increase in expectations of future inflation.

Chapter 11

The foreign exchange market

11.1 **Introduction**

In this chapter we first of all examine, in section 11.2, the nature of the foreign exchange market in London (forex) and in section 11.3 examine the nature of transactions carried out in the market. In section 11.4 we briefly summarise the empirical evidence concerning the efficiency of the forex.

The first step in our analysis is to clarify certain concepts with respect to the exchange rate. There are two ways in which exchange rates can be quoted. First, it is possible to define the exchange rate in terms of units of foreign currency per unit of domestic currency, for example \$1.5 per £1. Equivalently we could say the price of \$1 is £0.67, that is, in terms of units of domestic currency per unit of foreign currency. It is custom in the UK to use the first method of defining the exchange rate whereas in the rest of the world it is more usual to use the second method. We shall use the normal UK method in the rest of the text. In fact the rate we have been discussing, that is, the rate quoted in the financial media and determined in the foreign exchange markets, is termed the 'nominal' exchange rate. In practice many commercial decisions are made with respect to the 'real' exchange rate, that is, the nominal exchange rate adjusted for the relative prices of the countries concerned. This can be specified algebraically as:

$$S^{R}_{t} = S_{t} {*} (P/P^{F})_{t} \qquad (11.1)$$

where S^R is the real exchange rate, S is the nominal exchange rate (units of foreign currency per unit of domestic currency) and P and P^F are indices of domestic and foreign prices respectively. One further clarification of exchange rate definitions is appropriate. We have so far discussed exchange rates in terms of two countries and these are called 'bilateral' rates. If it is desired to measure the average level of the exchange rate against a range of representative currencies, it is necessary to construct an index of the exchange rate valued against a representative basket of currencies with weights attached to the relevant bilateral rates based on their importance in trade with the country concerned. The International Monetary Fund has developed a model for calculating effective exchange rates termed the 'multilateral exchange rate model'.

It is also useful as a prelude to the consideration of the foreign exchange markets to summarise current theories concerning the determination of exchange rates. It is an area of great controversy and it will not therefore be a great surprise to the reader to learn that there is no single theory which commands a wide degree of acceptance. All agree that, in the absence of intervention by the authorities, the exchange rate is determined by the demand and supply of currencies on the market, but there is little agreement on the factors underlying the forces of demand and supply. There are basically four main models, which differ from each other to a greater or lesser degree.

The first, the simple monetary model, assumes flexible prices and combines the purchasing-power parity view of exchange rates with a simple quantity theory. Consequently changes in the exchange rate in the case of flexible exchange rates or in the balance of payments given fixed rates are attributable to differences in the rate of monetary expansion in the two countries involved.

In contrast, the second model, commonly designated the Mundell–Flemming model, assumes fixed prices. In a regime of floating exchange rates balance-of-payments equilibrium is obtained through the sum of the current and capital accounts being zero. A zero balance on the current account is not required even in the long run and the offsetting balance on the capital account is achieved via the equilibrium rate of interest which clears the domestic goods and money markets. In the case of the fixed exchange rate regime, balance-of-payments equilibrium is achieved through changes in official reserves caused by intervention by the authorities in the foreign exchange markets.

The third model, the Dornbusch model, is an amalgam of both the previous two models. Financial markets are supposed to clear instantaneously, that is, prices are perfectly flexible. This contrasts with the goods markets, where prices are sticky. This results in the well known prediction that the exchange rate overshoots the long-run equilibrium level following a shock. The long-run equilibrium level is, however, consistent with the predictions of the simple monetary theory discussed earlier.

The fourth model is the portfolio balance model, which widens the choice of assets available rather than concentrating simply on money. Consequently the exchange rate arises from the determination of equilibrium portfolios and any shock will change the desired composition of the portfolio and therefore the equilibrium returns, including that on foreign assets, which includes expected exchange rate changes. A good detailed account of exchange rate determination is given in Copeland [1994].

Foreign exchange markets are about arbitrage and this process is likely to establish certain relationships between bilateral rates. First, it would be expected that prices in domestic or foreign currency of traded commodities would be the same whether priced in domestic or foreign currency. This is termed purchasing power parity (PPP). Second, it would also be expected that returns on financial investment in different international centres would be the same after allowing for potential exchange rate changes. This is called 'interest rate parity' (IRP). We now discuss these two propositions in more detail.

The modern doctrine of PPP is due to the work of the Swedish economist Gustav Cassel, though in fact it can be traced back to David Ricardo. The basis for the analysis is the 'law of one price'. Suppose a car sold in the UK for £10,000 and the identical model sold in the US for $15,000. Clearly, abstracting from transport costs, the equilibrium exchange rate is $1.5 per £1. At any other exchange rate arbitrage is possible. Thus, for example, if the exchange rate was $1.0 = £1, then the car could be purchased for £10,000 in the UK and transported to the US and sold for $15,000, earning a nice profit. Because cars were being purchased in the UK and sold to the US, this would set up an increased demand for pounds on the market (or equivalently and increased supply of dollars) thus causing the pound to appreciate (or equivalently the dollar to depreciate). This arbitrage would be possible until the exchange rate equalled $1.5 per £1. The converse process would occur if the $/£ exchange rate exceeded $1.5 per £1. PPP extends this relationship (i.e. the law of one price) from a single identical good to bundles of internationally traded goods. PPP also comes in two forms, absolute PPP and relative PPP. Absolute PPP contends that the bilateral exchange rate will depend on the relative prices in domestic currency of goods in the two countries. More formally:

$$S^{PPP} = P^{F}/P \tag{11.2}$$

where S^{PPP} is the PPP exchange rate (units of foreign currency per unit of domestic currency) and P and P^{F} are domestic and foreign price indices, as before. Relative PPP is a weaker concept and portrays the bilateral exchange rate changing in line with the difference between the inflation rates of the two countries concerned. More formally:

$$\Delta S^{PPP} = \Delta P^{F} - \Delta P \tag{11.3}$$

where ΔP^F and ΔP refer to the percentage rates of inflation in the two countries. Thus, for example, if inflation the UK is expected to be 5 per cent and in the US 2 per cent (both per annum) the exchange rate would be expected to depreciate at the rate of 3 per cent per annum. Given that arbitrage in goods takes time, it would be expected that an efficient market would cause the market exchange rate to tend to PPP over time rather than at each instant. We will review the evidence concerning PPP in section 11.4.

The second relationship, IRP, concerns movements of capital between financial centres. It would be expected that the total expected return in each centre would be the same or otherwise opportunities for profitable arbitrage would exist. To illustrate this point, let us suppose that the arbitrageur starts by holding sterling; the one-period return from assets in sterling ($\Pi^£$) is simply $(1+R^£)$ where $R^£$ is the relevant interest rate on sterling securities. In contrast, the one-period return from assets denoted in foreign currency (say dollars for illustrative purposes) may be defined as:

$$\Pi^\$ = S_t(1+R^\$)/(E_tS_{t+1}) \tag{11.4}$$

where the time periods are consistent and $R^\$$ represents the one-period nominal rate of interest on dollar securities and E_tS_{t+1} is the spot rate ($ per £1) expected to exist at the end of the single period. Thus, the equation represents a spot purchase of dollars at the rate of S_t, the subsequent purchase of a dollar security yielding a rate of interest equal to $R^\$$ during the period t to t+1 and the subsequent repurchase of sterling at period t+1 expected to be at the spot rate E_tS_{t+1}. Arbitrage would be expected to ensure that $\Pi^£ = \Pi^\$$, otherwise opportunities for profitable arbitrage would exist and capital flows would remove the incentive for arbitrage. For example, if the return in New York was higher than that in London, funds would flow from London to New York, thus causing the sterling spot rate (S_t) to depreciate (or equivalently the dollar to appreciate) and the rate of interest in New York to depreciate. Both of these phenomena would reduce the return in New York, so eliminating the differences in return between the two centres.

Equation 11.4 can be modified by substituting the forward rate (F_t) for the expected spot rate so that all rates (both interest and exchange rates) are known with certainty at time t. Hence equation 11.4 is rewritten as:

$$\Pi^\$ = S_t(1+R^\$)/F_t \tag{11.5}$$

where F is the forward rate (dollars per £1). Again, arbitrage should ensure that $\Pi^£ = \Pi^\$$. In this case IRP is termed covered interest parity because forward cover has been taken out against future movements in the exchange rate (see section 11.3 for a full discussion of forward and spot rates). The previous type of IRP, when no forward cover is taken out, is termed uncovered interest rate parity. The efficient markets hypothesis implies that the returns in the two centres should be equal, so that both types of IRP should exist in the foreign exchange market. The evidence for the existence of this type of efficiency will also be examined in section 11.4.

In the following section we review the nature of the London foreign exchange market. Much of the quantitative detail concerning the institutional framework about the forex is derived from Bank of England surveys of the operators within the market carried out in March 1986, April 1989 and April 1992. These were carried out at the same time as other central banks' surveys and were reported in the *Bank of England Quarterly Bulletins* of September 1986, November 1989 and November 1992 respectively. As a result of the information derived from the 1992 surveys, the Bank for International Settlements estimated that the total global foreign exchange turnover (net of all double counting) amounted to a staggering US$900 billion per day. The next set of surveys was due to be carried out in April 1995, after the time of writing of this second edition. The interested reader is therefore advised to watch the financial press for summary details and to consult the *Bank of England Quarterly Bulletin* in either September or November 1995 for more detail.

11.2 Nature of the forex

The UK forex is located in London and there is no significant market for foreign exchange elsewhere in the UK. Retail transactions are of course carried out by local financial institutions but these institutions ultimately obtain their currency mainly from transactions on the London forex. London continues to be the largest centre worldwide for foreign exchange dealing and the average dealing turnover was estimated by the Bank of England to be about US$300 billion per day in 1992. This compares with figures of US$187 and US$90 billion per day in 1986 and 1992 respectively. Other large centres were New York, Tokyo, Singapore and Switzerland, where average daily turnovers in US $billion were 192, 128, 74 and 68 respectively in 1992. Closely behind were Hong Kong ($61 billion per day), Germany ($57 billion per day) and France ($35 billion per day). It is interesting to note that the gap between London and New York and Tokyo has widened considerably, since the corresponding figures for the 1989 surveys for New York and Tokyo were $129 billion and $115 billion per day respectively. The magnitude of these flows indicates that the trading in currency in London is far greater than that warranted by trade flows into and from the UK, thus demonstrating the importance of London as a world financial market. A second feature revealed by the surveys is the very fast rate of growth in the volume of transactions. This far outweighs the growth of physical trade and no doubt is a reflection of the liberalisation of capital markets and, in particular, a general relaxation of capital controls.

The dollar is the main vehicle of exchange on the London forex and the bulk of the trading consisted of sterling/US$ (19 per cent) and US$/Deutschmark (23 per cent). The combined figure for these two types of transactions has dropped from 49 per cent of total transactions in 1989 to 42 per cent in 1992. Perhaps the most salient drop in relative shares occurred in the case of US$/yen, which fell from 14 per cent to 5 per cent of total transactions. Nevertheless, trading not involving the US$ (termed 'cross-currency') also grew, from 9 per cent in 1989 to 16 per cent in 1992 (only 3 per cent in 1986) and about 30 per cent of this business involved sterling/Deutschmark transactions. The surveys also showed that the business on the London forex was more diversified than elsewhere. For example, in Tokyo 72 per cent of the business was between the yen and US$ (1989 figures) although the Bank of Japan commented that the share of US$/yen trading had declined and trading against the Deutschmark increased, and in New York 74 per cent of the business was between the US$ and the four major currencies (DM, yen, sterling and the Swiss franc) as compared with 59 per cent in London.

The market is a continuous dealers' market and there are three types of operators within the market:

(i) *Market makers*. These are mainly the major banks, who agree to buy and sell currencies on a continuous basis. Although the detail may be finalised using other means such as the telephone, trading is carried out via quotes on screens, so there is no building serving as a market meeting place. The gap between the bid and ask prices reflects the market maker's margin to cover costs and make a profit. Profits will also accrue from taking a view of the future course of exchange rates, that is, speculation. The market maker carries a stock of currencies and he or she is the operator who incurs the risk of unanticipated changes in exchange rates. Business in the market is quite widely dispersed since 10 of the 352 principals in the Bank of England 1992 survey covered only 43 per cent of the reported business (35 per cent in 1989, so there is evidence of a drift towards a greater degree of concentration).

(ii) *Brokers*. These are institutions which act as intermediaries. They act as agents seeking out bargains and do not trade on their own account. The total share of business passing through brokers amounted to 34 per cent of the total in the 1992. The corresponding figures for 1989 and 1986 were 38 per cent and 43 per cent respectively, so there is evidence of a declining share of total business passing through brokers. It will be interesting to see whether the next survey (due April 1995) will show further decline as it is believed that the banks and Reuters were separately designing electronic trading schemes which would reduce the need for brokers.

(iii) *The Bank of England*. Apart from its role of supervising the market, the Bank will, as is true of other central banks, intervene in the foreign exchange markets to influence the exchange rate. Intervention is normally carried out via a broker, with the identity of the Bank being kept secret.

(iv) *Customers*. Customers for foreign exchange transactions on the forex are large companies and other financial institutions. The proportion of turnover reported to have been accounted for between market makers and their customers rose from 9 per cent in 1986 and 15 per cent in 1989 (9 per cent with other financial institutions and 6 per cent with non-financial institutions) to 23 per cent of total turnover (14 per cent with other financial institutions and 9 per cent with non-financial institutions).

11.3 **Nature of business**

Four types of transactions can be distinguished:

(i) spot transactions,
(ii) forward transactions,
(iii options,
(iv) futures.

The bulk of the transactions fell into the first two categories (97 per cent), with just 3 per cent consisting of the remaining two categories. We reserve discussion of both futures and options until chapter 13.

Spot transactions are required to be settled within two working days of the agreement. These fell as a proportion of total turnover from 1986 to 1992 (73 per cent to 50 per cent) and the Bank suggests that this was due to the growth in 'swaps' and other hedging instruments in the forward market. In the following discussion we will use the $/£ rate for illustrative purposes. Market makers quote two rates. The lower rate represents the rate or price at which they are prepared to buy sterling in exchange for US dollars (or, of course, sell $s in return for £s). The higher rate is the rate at which they are prepared to sell sterling in return for US dollars (or equivalently buy $s in exchange for £s). For example, the *Financial Times* in the currency market report section on 29 November 1994 gave, amongst other information, the following for the USA 'pound spot – forward against the pound' for 28 November:

(i) closing mid-point, 1.5632;
(ii) bid/offer spread, 628–636.

The spot quotation shows the best closing sterling mid-point rate, that is, the average of the buying and selling rates. On this day the spread was given by 1.5628 to 1.5636 so that market makers would buy pounds from the seller at the rate of $1.5628 for each pound. Conversely they are prepared to sell sterling at the rate of $1.5638 per £1. The bid–offer spread quoted above indicates this range in shortened form, by omitting the 1.5 from the full quote.

Forward transactions represent an agreement to purchase the currency at a later date but at a price agreed now. An outright forward transaction occurs where there is an agreement to purchase/sell a currency forward without any corresponding agreement to resell/repurchase that currency at a later date. A margin may be required by the seller of the forward contract but some market makers merely require the purchaser to hold cash in a deposit account with them. As evidenced by the Bank of England 1992 survey, the bulk of such forward contracts were for maturities up to seven days (33 percentage points out of the 47 per cent of total market turnover comprising forward contracts). Thirteen percentage points represented maturities greater than seven days but up to one year, with the remaining 1 per cent being for maturities more than one year. In some instances the trader will not be certain when the precise payment is required and he or she can, in such circumstances, arrange for an option forward contract which enables the trader to purchase (or sell) the currency at an agreed rate within a specified time period rather than on a particular date. A further type of forward contract is a 'swap', either (i) a spot purchase against a forward sale (or vice versa) or (ii) purchase and sale of currencies forward for different dates. This type of contract formed the major component of the forward transactions (33 percentage points out of the total of 47 per cent).

The forward rates at the end of trading on 28 November 1994 were shown in the same currency market report as $1.5632 for delivery in one month's time, $1.5629 in two months' time and $1.5585 in three months' time. Also quoted is the percentage premium/discount at an annualised rate.

11.4 **The efficiency of the foreign exchange market**

The question of whether the foreign exchange market is efficient (informational) is one of considerable importance for the end customer of the market. If arbitrage between sophisticated traders produces prices which do reflect instantaneously all available information, then forecasting by end customers is not a worthwhile exercise since the market has already processed the available information. In this section we provide a brief survey of the current literature on market efficiency with respect to the foreign exchange markets. This research is ongoing and the interested reader is recommended to examine the original literature.

We first of all consider the evidence concerning the existence or otherwise of PPP. Efficiency with respect to PPP is different from the types of efficiency so far examined because it involves a time element. Arbitrage in goods is not instantaneous as is the case in arbitrage in financial instruments. Hence PPP would be expected to apply in the long run (unspecified period) but not in the short run. The empirical literature on this subject is, to say the least, voluminous. It is therefore possible in this text to present only the main themes of the various studies – see Copeland [1994] and Pilbeam [1992] for further discussion and references. The main conclusions from the literature are as follows:

(i) The evidence concerning the existence of PPP is ambiguous. Some studies find support, others do not. Evidence is more supportive of the existence of PPP in the long run rather than the short run.
(ii) Evidence is more supportive of PPP for traded than non-traded goods.
(iii) The exchange rate is more volatile than national price levels. This is contrary to PPP.
(iv) Graphical presentation of bilateral exchange rates demonstrates periods of prolonged departure from PPP but also a tendency to fluctuate around the PPP level.

Reverting back to Fama's classification of types of efficiency (see chapter 7), we first of all deal with the weak tests. One type of study concerning the weak efficiency of the foreign exchange markets relates to filter rules. As noted in chapter 7, the nature of a filter rule is to buy the currency if the price rises x per cent above a recent trough and sell the currency if it falls y per cent below a recent peak. The object of the rule is to identify upturns and downturns other than small fluctuations and the values of x and y are set by the speculator in the light of previous experience of the series. Clearly, the smaller are x and y the greater the number of profitable opportunities identified but also the greater the cost of the transactions, which will offset and perhaps eliminate the profits obtained. On the other hand, large values for x and y will reduce the transaction costs but miss some profitable opportunities. Two major studies of the profitability of filter rules were carried out by Dooley and Shafer [1976] and Logue and Sweeney [1977]. Both these studies identified profits above a 'buy and hold' strategy but losses were incurred in some periods. This raises the question whether these profits were the reward for incurring risk of exchange rate losses. Taylor [1986] examined time series analysis methods of forecasting the £/$ exchange rate using daily observations for the period 1974 to 1982. He again found some improvement of the forecasts over predictions by market prices but the improvement was quite small.

One type of semi-strong test involves the forecasting ability of the forward exchange rate. If we assume that speculators are risk neutral, then their sole motivation will be to attain profits. If the forward rate for $s per £1 is below the level they expect at the end of the period in question, then they will buy sterling forward and sell the sterling spot on the maturity of the agreement. If their expectations are correct they will obtain a profit denominated in dollars. Conversely, if the risk-neutral speculators expect a lower spot rate as compared with the relevant forward rate, then they will sell sterling forward and buy spot later to cover the forward contract. Obviously if the exchange rate moves in the reverse direction to that expected, then the speculators will make a loss and the assumption of risk neutrality infers that they are not deterred from their attempt to take advantage of potential profits by the chance of a loss. Hence, given the existence of risk-neutral speculators, the forward rate should provide a good prediction of the spot rate in the future. More formally:

$$F_t = E_t S_{t+k} \tag{11.6}$$

where F_t is the forward rate observed at time t-1 for the delivery of currency at time t+k and $E_t S_{t+k}$ is the expected spot rate at time t+k with the expectation formed at time t.

It is possible to test equation 11.6 by running regressions of the form:

$$S_{t+k} = \alpha + \beta F_t \tag{11.7}$$

If the forward rate is an unbiased predictor of the spot rate, it is necessary that the estimates of α and β are not statistically different from 0 and 1 respectively. It appears conclusively that this relationship is rejected by the data – for example see Baillie *et al.* [1983] using data for the US$, sterling, the Deutschmark, lira and the French franc (1973 to 1980) and the Canadian dollar (1977–80).

An alternative approach is to examine the forward premium (i.e. $\{F_t - S_t\}/S_t$) as a predictor of the future movement in the exchange rate. This can be tested by running regressions of the form:

$$\Delta S_{t+k} = \alpha + \beta FP_t \tag{11.8}$$

where ΔS_{t+k} is the change in the spot exchange rate between time t and t+k, and FP_t refers to the forward premium at time t for delivery of currency at time t+k. Again, if the forward premium is an unbiased predictor of future movements in the spot rate, it is necessary that the estimates of α and β are not statistically different from 0 and 1 respectively. It appears conclusively that this relationship is rejected by the data – see for example Fama [1984], amongst many others.

Finally in this respect, it is possible to look at the forecasting errors e_t (defined as $S_{t+k} - F_t$) to see if they were correlated with information available to agents at time t. This can be checked by running a regression of the following form:

$$e_t = \Gamma X_t \tag{11.9}$$

where X_t is a vector of variables known at time t. If the coefficients of Γ are not all zero, then the market is not processing all available information. This requirement is known more technically as a requirement that the errors should be orthogonal to any information available to the agents.

The types of variable in X can be divided into two categories: lagged values of e, and other information additional to lagged e (i.e. weak and semi-strong tests). Tests of both type again conclusively reject the error orthogonality – see for example amongst many others Macdonald and Taylor [1989].

Two explanations are possible for this rejection of the hypothesis that the forward rate is an unbiased predictor. First, the market is inefficient and is not processing all available information correctly. Second, speculators are not risk neutral but are, in fact, risk averse, so that they require a risk premium (which may vary over time) to compensate them for the risk of a loss following an adverse movement in the exchange rate. Whatever the reason, it is apparent that the dual hypothesis of risk neutrality and market efficiency is decisively rejected by the data.

A second type of semi-strong test of market efficiency arises from covered interest arbitrage establishing interest rate parity (see equation 11.5 and related discussion). This hypothesis has been tested by a number of researchers, including Frenkel and Levich [1975, 1977] and Taylor [1987]. In general, Frenkel and Levich, using end-of-day data, found that profits were not available from covered interest arbitrage in the eurocurrency markets after taking into consideration transaction costs. In the case of domestic centres some profits were available but these could perhaps be accounted for by the greater risks involved, such as actual or potential controls on capital movements. Taylor, using high-frequency data (i.e. observations of actual rates during the day), found some departures from interest rate parity during times of turbulence on the foreign exchange markets but that in general interest rate parity held. Further casual evidence arises from the fact that many banks define the forward rate by solving equation 11.5 for F_t given the spot rate and appropriate rates of interest. The quotation indicated above from the *Financial Times* is derived in this manner.

Finally in this section we look at the performance of professional forecasting agencies. The test examines whether forecasting agencies can consistently outperform the market, that is, a 'strong' test in the Fama terminology. It is, of course, difficult to obtain information on forecasts sold to clients. However, a limited number of tests have been carried out by researchers, including Goodman [1979], Levich [1979], Bilson [1983] and Blake *et al.* [1986]. The studies by Goodman, Levich and Blake *et al.* suggested that the forward rate was at least as good a predictor as that provided by the forecasting agency. Bilson found that the gain from combining forecasts including those of a forecasting agency and adopting a portfolio approach involving more than just one currency offered the prospect of gaining substantial profits.

The question of whether the foreign exchange market conforms to the efficient markets hypothesis remains open. It seems clear that the evidence points to the rejection of the dual hypothesis of risk neutrality and efficiency.

Chapter 12

Euro-securities markets

12.1 **Introduction**

In chapter 7 we established that London is one of the main international financial centres in the world. Three main areas of international financial activity can be distinguished: (i) banking, (ii) bonds and similar types of securities and (iii) equities. We have already discussed the nature and extent of international (mainly eurocurrency) banking in chapter 4 and the extent of international equities trading through London in chapter 8. In this chapter we will examine the euro-securities markets which have developed out of the eurocurrency markets and then discuss some of the wider developments in international financing. The euro-securities markets we consider, in sections 12.2 to 12.4, are those of eurobonds, euronotes and euro-equities. These markets have been the subject of a great deal of financial innovation over the past 15 years and the new financial instruments which have emerged have tended to blur the distinction between traditional international banking and securities trading. We finish this chapter therefore with a discussion of securitisation. This process describes how changes in the financial environment and the changing preferences of borrowers and international banks have led to a move away from international financial intermediation through banks to direct financing through greater use of the international capital markets.

12.2 **Eurobonds**

Nature

A large borrower wishing to raise long-term funds through bond issues can turn to either the domestic bond market, as we saw in chapter 9, or to the international bond markets. We can distinguish between two types of international bonds. A foreign bond is one issued by a non-resident borrower on the market of a single country and denominated in that country's currency. For example, foreign bonds issued in New York in dollars, London in sterling or Tokyo in yen are known respectively as yankee, bulldog and samurai issues. The other type of international bond is the eurobond, which is a bond issued in markets other than that of the currency of issue and sold internationally. Thus, a German company which issues a US dollar bond in New York is issuing an foreign (yankee) bond, whereas if the company issues the bond in a number of national markets, other than the US, then it is classed as a eurobond.

Eurobonds are generally issued 'offshore', which means that the issue of such bonds is not subject to the rules and regulations which govern the issue of foreign bonds in that currency, such as obligations to issue detailed prospectuses and any interest-withholding taxes, that is, taxes deducted at source before interest is paid for non-resident holders of bonds. This is not to say that there are no restrictions on eurobond issues and trading, since the International Securities Markets Association (ISMA), which is a self-regulatory body, formerly the Association of International Bond Dealers (AIBD) founded in 1969, has introduced trading rules and standardised procedures in the eurobond market.

Growth of the eurobond market

The first eurobond was issued in 1963 and their use grew at a slow rate throughout the 1960s and early 1970s, and then explosively over the 1980s. Table 12.1 shows the characteristics of international bonds issued over the 1980s.

There are a number of reasons for the rapid growth of eurobond activity over the 1980s. Over this period international interest rates fell steadily, making the issue of both equities and fixed-interest bonds more attractive to borrowers. Banks have generally been reluctant to lend at fixed rates of interest over the long term. In addition, the problems of banks over the 1980s and the greater cost of borrowing through banks, described in section 12.6 on securitisation, led borrowers to look more to the international capital markets as a source of funds. Whilst international bond issues grew rapidly over the 1980s, it is clear from table 12.1 that eurobond issues, starting from a roughly equal share with foreign bonds at the beginning of the 1980s, have accounted for the majority of this growth. One reason for this is the lower cost of eurobond issues compared with domestic or foreign bond issues. The ability of buyers of bonds to escape withholding tax and income tax on interest receipts enables borrowers to issue at lower yields. Eurobonds are generally issued in bearer form, eliminating the need for registration of ownership so that ownership is vested in the holder. The anonymity this brings allows owners to avoid tax on interest. The repeal of

Table 12.1 *Growth of international bonds issues, 1979–93*

	1979	*1980*	*1981*	*1982*	*1983*	*1984*	*1985*	*1986*	*1987*	*1988*	*1989*	*1990*	*1991*	*1992*	*1993*
Total international bonds ($billion)	39.0	38.3	51.8	75.5	77.1	109.5	167.7	226.4	180.8	229.7	254.0	241.7	317.6	333.7	481.0
Eurobonds (%)	48	53	60	67	65	75	82	83	78	78	84	78	84	83	82
Foreign bonds (%)	52	47	40	33	35	26	19	17	22	22	17	22	18	17	18
Currencies (%):															
US dollar	37.8	42.7	63.0	63.9	57.0	63.5	61.1	54.9	36.2	36.8	49.8	34.8	30.2	37.7	38
Japanese yen	7.3	4.9	6.0	5.2	5.3	5.5	7.7	10.4	14.7	9.8	9.4	13.4	13.7	12.2	12.5
Swiss franc	24.9	19.5	15.7	15.0	17.5	12.0	8.9	10.3	13.4	11.5	7.5	10.1	6.8	5.4	5.6
Deutschmark	22.0	21.9	5.0	7.1	8.6	6.2	6.7	7.5	8.3	10.3	6.5	7.9	6.7	10.1	11.4
Sterling	0.7	3.0	2.8	2.6	3.9	5.1	4.1	4.8	8.4	10.4	7.4	9.2	8.7	6.9	8.9
ECU	0.8	0.2	0.8	2.6	2.6	2.8	4.2	3.1	4.1	4.9	5.2	7.8	10.7	6.3	1.5
Other	6.5	7.8	6.7	3.6	5.1	4.9	7.3	9.0	14.9	16.3	14.3	16.7	23.2	22.4	22.1

Source: OECD, *Financial Statistics* (various issues).

withholding tax on interest paid to foreign purchasers of domestic bonds in the US in 1984 together with changes to allow US residents to issue bearer bonds to non-resident borrowers may have been expected to make eurobonds less attractive. However, there are other advantages to issuing eurobonds which account for the continued growth. The lack of restrictions on eurobond trading makes it easier and therefore speedier to make issues and thus take advantage of a favourable 'window' in interest rate movements or other economic changes. Also, the liberalisation of domestic capital markets in the US, Germany and Japan and the general globalisation of capital markets that took place over the 1980s have encouraged borrowers and investors to look more to international capital markets.

International bond issues are denominated in currencies which are important for international trade. This explains the importance of dollar-denominated eurobonds. However, the dollar-denominated dominance of the eurobond market is not quite as great as the dollar dominance of the eurocurrency loans market. This is because borrowers have also tended to issue bonds to tap the savings of countries which have a high savings ratio, in particular the economies of Germany and Japan. Furthermore, investors look for securities denominated in strong currencies. As we shall see in section 12.5, the use of swap contracts allows the currency denomination of the funds raised to be swapped into a different currency if required.

It should be noted that the Swiss authorities have acted to prevent the emergence of a eurobond market in Swiss francs so as to control the international use of its currency. Swiss franc issues of international bonds are therefore solely issues of foreign bonds. The prevention of eurobonds denominated in Swiss francs together with the growth of eurobonds vis-à-vis foreign bonds partly account for the decline in international bonds denominated in Swiss francs.

One feature of recent eurobond issues, revealed in table 12.1, is the growth in ECU-denominated bonds up until 1992. (ECU stands for European Currency Unit, which is a composite currency unit made up of the currencies of the members of the European Union). Issues of ECU-denominated eurobonds grew steadily over the 1980s and early 1990s. Sovereign issues of ECU-denominated bonds provided high-quality benchmarks in the market and have promoted the introduction of ECU derivative products, for example at LIFFE and MATIF – see chapter 13. The decline in ECU eurobond issues in 1992 and 1993 reflects the turmoil in the Exchange Rate Mechanism in these years (see chapter 15).

The geographical location of borrowers in the international bond markets in recent years is shown in table 12.2. This shows the dominance of Japanese borrowers, both banks and non-banks, over the period 1987 to 1991. The growth in Japanese-based issues of bonds largely reflects the strength of the Japanese stock market over this period, with most of these issues

Table 12.2 *Main issuers of international bonds by country of origin (%)*

	1987	*1988*	*1989*	*1990*	*1991*	*1992*	*1993*
Japan	25	22	37	27	27	17	11
US	12	7	6	12	7	5	5
UK	7	12	8	11	11	10	7
Canada	5	6	5	3	8	7	7
France	5	7	5	9	10	10	9
Germany	6	5	4	0	6	6	9

Source: OECD *Financial Statistics,* various issues.

being equity-related bonds (discussed below). The decline in issues in 1992 and 1993 is related to the decline in the Japanese stock market over this period. A feature of the market not revealed by table 12.2 is the growth in issues by Latin American countries as growing investor confidence in their economies following Brady deals has permitted a return to the international bond markets – discussed further in chapter 4.

Types of eurobonds

The eurobond market has been the subject of a great deal of financial innovation over the 1980s and many different types of eurobonds have been created. It is possible though to classify eurobonds as belonging to one of three basic types:

(i) *Straight fixed-rate bonds*. These are the traditional type of bond with a fixed coupon payment.

(ii) *Floating-rate notes (FRNs)*. These are bonds issued with coupon payments made on a floating-rate basis. The coupon, which usually consists of a margin over a reference rate such as LIBOR, is paid at the end of each interest period, usually six months, and then reset in line with the reference rate for the next interest period. FRNs are generally medium-term bonds, that is, with maturities from 5 to 15 years.

(iii) *Equity-related bonds*. There are two types of equity-related bonds:

  (a) *Convertibles*. These give the holder the right to convert the bond into ordinary shares, with the terms and conditions of the conversion set at the time of issue.

  (b) *Bonds with equity warrants attached.* Warrants are options which give the holder the right to buy shares in a company at a given

Table 12.3 *Eurobond issues classified by type (%)*

	1980	*1981*	*1982*	*1983*	*1984*	*1985*	*1986*	*1987*	*1988*	*1989*	*1990*	*1991*	*1992*	*1993*
Straight fixed rate	67	64	72	59	51	52	65	68	72	60	69	81	80	78
Floating-rate notes	21	27	24	31	39	40	25	8	11	10	18	6	13	14
Equity related	9	4	9	10	8	10	8	24	17	30	14	13	7	8

Source: BIS, annual report, various issues.

price in the future. Warrants are attached to the bonds but are securities in their own right and so can be stripped from the bond and sold separately. This distinguishes them from convertibles, where the conversion rights are an integral part of the issue.

A breakdown of issue volumes by type is shown in table 12.3.

Floating-rate notes were the fastest-growing section of the eurobond markets in 1983, 1984 and 1985 and the first half of 1986. There were various innovations on the standard FRN, and issues by UK building societies and other UK financial institutions pushed sterling into the second largest currency for FRNs. The FRN market is dominated by financial institutions, banks in particular, which both issue and invest. A particular form of FRN, the perpetual floating-rate note, so called because it is never redeemed, was popular with banks as it qualified as primary capital. All these developments receded with the virtual collapse of the FRN market at the end of 1986. This was due to a variety of reasons, including (i) excess competition in the issue side of the market driving down yields on some issues to unattractive levels and (ii) concern from central bankers that perpetual FRNs both issued and held by banks did not properly spread risk outside the banking system. A further contributing factor to the demise of the FRN market, namely growing interest in the euro-commercial paper market, is discussed below. The FRN market though appeared to have recovered to some extent in 1992 and 1993 as investors looked to longer-term issues of bonds and away from short-term notes such as commercial paper (discussed below). One of the reasons for this is that investors are attracted to long-term floating-rate debt as interest rates are expected to rise and there was an expectation in the market at this time that US interest rates in particular had reached a trough. Another factor behind the renewed interest in FRNs by borrowers is the increased use of structured FRNs. These are designed to respond to investors' views of future interest rate trends but do not expose the issuer to associated interest rate risk. About 30 per cent of issues of FRNs were structured in some way in 1993. There are three principal types of structured FRNs.

(i) Reverse FRNs are structured to produce rising coupons as a floating-rate reference rate falls. The notes contain an implicit interest rate cap, with a strike price equal to the fixed-rate element, as well as non-negativity clauses to prevent rates falling below zero.

(ii) Collared FRNs contain caps and floors, thereby generating maximum and minimum returns. They contain two embedded options and in effect the issuer purchases a cap from the investor and at the same time sells the investor a floor.

(iii) Step-up recovery FRNs (SURFs) pay coupons linked to yields on comparable longer-maturity bonds. With a rising yield curve they therefore pay the higher yield available at the longer maturity.

So, in 1993, with investors' expectations that US interest rates were reaching a trough there was a high demand for collared dollar FRNs. Investors with views on the shape of the US yield curve could have alternatively purchased SURFs. However, in Europe in 1993 investors expected interest rates to fall further in many countries and thus were keen to invest in reverse FRNs. These swap-related derivative strategies are discussed further in chapter 13.

The equity-related issues of international bonds saw rapid growth over the latter part of the 1980s. These issues have been predominantly of bonds with attached warrants issued mainly by Japanese investors denominated in US dollars. As noted above, this was related to the strength of the Japanese stock market in the late 1980s, which made the issues attractive to investors. As the Japanese equity indices have fallen in the 1990s then issues of equity-related bonds which are related to these indices have fallen.

Issue of eurobonds

Since the 1980s the standard method of issuing eurobonds is by way of a bought deal. This involves a lead manager buying the entire issue at an agreed price prior to the announcement of the issue. The issue is then resold (i.e. syndicated) after the announcement.

Since the late 1980s, members of the syndicate enter into a contractual agreement not to resell at a lower price until the full issue has been completed. In US terminology this is termed a 'fixed priced re-offer' technique.

The secondary market in eurobonds is mainly over the counter, with settlement being achieved via one of the international clearing systems (i.e. Euroclear or Cedel).

12.3 **Euronotes**

In contrast to the longer-term eurobonds, the euronote markets encompass the various types of short-term securities issued to tap the eurocurrency markets. There are three basic types of euronotes, although there are many variations on these types. The original euronotes were note issuance facilities, which first appeared in 1978. The other types of euronote instruments, namely euro-commercial paper and medium-term notes, were based on the note issuance facilities and made a significant appearance in the mid-1980s. The amounts outstanding of the various types of euronotes since 1980 are shown in table 12.4.

Table 12.4 *Euronotes: amounts outstanding at year end ($billion)*

	1986	*1987*	*1988*	*1989*	*1990*	*1991*	*1992*	*1993*
Euronotes	29.4	32.8	72.3	79.2	111.3	144.6	177.1	255.8
of which:								
Euro-commercial paper	13.9	13.3	53.2	58.5	70.3	79.6	78.7	80.0
Other short-term notes	15.1	16.9	13.5	11.1	19.1	26.5	37.0	29.2
Medium-term notes	0.4	2.6	5.6	9.6	21.9	38.5	61.4	146.6

Source: BIS, annual report, various years.

Note issuance facilities (NIFs)

The original euronotes were note issuance facilities, which are formalised, syndicated, underwritten medium-term loans which enable borrowers to issue a stream of short-term bearer notes, usually of one-, three- or six-month maturity, on a rollover basis. These are generally issued through a tender panel and if the borrowers are unable to sell the notes at a given spread over LIBOR to investors in the market, then the underwriting banks guarantee to purchase the notes themselves. Thus, borrowers obtain medium-term funds, generally seven to ten years, financed by successive issues of short-term notes. NIFs are therefore transforming short-term funds into long-term funds, a transformation which is normally carried out through banks in their role as financial intermediaries. In this situation banks are, however, simply earning fee income for arranging and underwriting the facility and, as long as the notes are placed at the maturity dates without problems, then the business is off the balance sheet.

Note issuance facilities were developed as an alternative to syndicated loans and partly performed that role in 1984 and 1985 as issues of these facilities increased at a rapid rate. Their relative decline (see table 12.4 – NIFs are the main component of 'Other short-term notes') is largely explained by the action of central banks, which sought to ensure that banks increase their capital when underwriting NIFs for borrowers with low credit standing. This led to banks limiting NIFs to borrowers with high credit standing and, partly in response to this, new types of short-term credits have emerged, in particular euro-commercial paper.

Euro-commercial paper (ECP) and euro medium-term notes (EMTNs)

The issue of euro-commercial paper is a recent development in the euromarkets, making a significant appearance in late 1984, although the issuance of commercial paper dates from the mid-nineteenth century in the

US (see chapter 10 on domestic money markets for description of commercial paper). ECP programmes differ from NIFs in two important respects: first, they are not underwritten; and second, borrowers use a small group of appointed banks and dealers to distribute the notes on a 'best efforts' basis. In addition, the paper generally has more flexible maturities than NIFs, which can be tailored to investors' preferences. Dealers impart marketability to the paper by agreeing to repurchase them from holders before maturity. An important difference between US commercial paper and euro-commercial paper is that the former is always credit rated. When euro-commercial paper first appeared very few of the issues were credit rated, although by 1989 approximately 45 per cent of issues had credit ratings and recent announcements (see *Bank of England Quarterly Bulletin*, August 1990, 'International financial developments') suggest that around 90 per cent of new issues have a credit rating. This trend towards a fully credit-rated market appears to have been accelerated by defaults by some ECP issuers in 1988 and 1989. As shown in table 12.4, the greater emphasis on credit ratings appears to have had a slowing effect on the market for ECP in 1989, as lesser-rated borrowers who were originally attracted to the market in 1986–88 found it difficult to establish facilities. Another factor behind the slowdown in issues in the ECP market is competition from the newly developing domestic commercial paper markets in Europe and the more mature US market. Also, in recent years ECP has faced competition from the more flexible EMTNs.

Euro medium-term notes are borrowing facilities backed by issues of paper where the paper has a maturity over nine months. The maturity of the paper can in theory be any length of time up to infinity but in practice is limited to around ten years. The market has shown steady growth since its emergence on a significant scale in 1986, with an acceleration in growth in 1993. One factor behind the recent growth has been the relaxation of issuing constraints in several countries. Japanese companies have been permitted to tap the EMTN market directly since July 1993 and in a number of European countries deregulation measures have been taken to facilitate the use of the national currency in EMTN programmes. Another feature of the market in recent years has been that more than half the issues have been linked to derivative instruments (structured). There are a number of reasons to suggest that the EMTN market will expand in the future and in particular will take business away from the international bond markets. First, medium-term notes (MTNs) are a more flexible instrument than a bond. The maturity of the note issues together with the characteristics of the drawings under a MTN facility can be varied to meet the needs of investor and borrower. Second, the liquidity of a bond issue is to a large extent determined by its size and investors may require some minimum issue size in order to attract them to hold the bond. In contrast, the liquidity of MTNs is provided by the guarantee of dealers to buy and sell the security. Finally, recent developments in the US domestic market, where corporate borrowing appears to have shifted from bonds to MTNs, suggest that this may carry over to the international capital markets.

The sterling commercial paper market is discussed in chapter 10, section 10.3.

12.4 **Euro-equities**

Euro-equities or international equities are equities issued for sale outside the issuer's home country. The term 'international equity issues' is used to refer to both primary issues of shares and secondary placements of existing shares. The equity instrument is the same as that issued in domestic markets, so the only difference between domestic and international issues of equities is the method of distribution. One method of international equity issue is to obtain a simultaneous listing on more than one national exchange. This method has become less popular as it can be costly owing to widely different listing procedures across the various exchanges. A method that is increasingly used is the two-tranche issue, where all the issue is listed on a domestic exchange, but one tranche is targeted at foreign investors. The distribution of the foreign tranche is increasingly organised through a syndicate made up of one financial institution in each country where the issue is targeted.

There are no reliable data available on international equity issues but table 12.5 shows approximate figures for the volume of international equity issues since the mid-1980s. Up until 1987 growth of international equity issues was rapid owing to rising world stock markets and an increasing tendency towards international portfolio diversification following both liberalisation of financial markets and the abolition of capital controls in many countries. This growth was reversed following the world stock markets crash of 1987. It appears, however, that the earlier growth has resumed in

Table 12.5 *Volume of international equity issues 1984–93 ($billion)*

	1984	*1985*	*1986*	*1987*	*1988*	*1989*	*1990*	*1991*	*1992*	*1993*
International equity issues	0.2	3.5	15.5	20.0	9.0	14.9	10.0	20.3	22.4	38.7

Source: *Bank of England Quarterly Bulletin* (annual article on 'Developments in international banking and capital markets', various issues) and *Financial Times* (23 January 1995).

the 1990s and appears likely to continue, fuelled by the continuing trend towards international portfolio diversification.

There are a number of advantages to a company from an international issue of its equity. First, it has the effect of widening the ownership of the company beyond that of the domestic market. Secondly, it may be possible to issue at lower cost in foreign markets. Finally, it provides an escape from the size constraint of the domestic market. This is particularly the case for companies in some European countries with small stock markets. At present the management of international equity issues can be more profitable for a bank than an international bond issue. Greater competition in the future, however, is likely to reduce margins and therefore issue costs.

12.5 **Use of swaps in euro-securities markets**

The nature of swaps is discussed in chapter 13, on derivative instruments. Swaps are widely used in international capital market transactions and have been one of the forces behind the rapid growth of the eurobond markets over the 1980s. Swaps enable a borrower to raise funds in the market in which it has a comparative advantage and then swap into a liability with preferred characteristics. For example, a borrower, X, may have a competitive advantage in the fixed-interest bond market but a preference for floating-rate funds to match its floating-rate assets. Thus, the borrower can raise funds at a competitive cost through the issue of a fixed-rate bond but swap for a floating-rate obligation with borrower Y, which has a competitive advantage in the floating-rate market but is looking for low-cost fixed-rate funds. As long as the interest rates swapped into by the two parties are lower than the interest rates obtainable from direct borrowing through the markets where they do not have a competitive advantage then the swap is worthwhile. This fixed/floating-rate swap is a classic type of interest rate swap and, if the floating rate is one linked to LIBOR, is known as a 'plain vanilla'.

A second type of swap transaction used in the international capital markets is the currency swap. Here the swap involves an exchange of interest payments and principal denominated in one currency for payments in another. Again, borrowers will borrow in the currency in which they have a comparative advantage and then swap into the preferred currency. There are two main types of currency swap in the capital markets: fixed/fixed currency swaps, and fixed/floating currency swaps. The latter, referred to as cross-currency interest rate swaps, involve both a currency and interest rate swap. More complex swaps have been developed in recent years and the interested reader is referred to Walmsley [1988].

Table 12.6 indicates the size of the interest rate and currency swap markets in recent years. There has been a dramatic increase in the use of swap

Table 12.6 *Over-the-counter derivative markets 1988–92: notional principal outstanding ($billion)*

	1988	*1989*	*1990*	*1991*	*1992*
Interest rate swaps	1011	1503	2311	3065	3851
Currency swaps	320	449	578	807	860
Other swap-related products[a]			561	577	635

[a] Caps, collars, floors and swaptions.
Source: BIS annual report, 1994.

contracts, and interest swap contracts in particular. This growth partly reflects the growth in international bond issues, where a large proportion of fixed-rate bonds involve an interest rate or currency swap. Another factor behind this growth is the continuing volatility in interest rates and currency markets. The growth in other swap-related derivatives reflects the growing use of derivatives such as collars and caps with issues of floating-rate notes and medium-term notes (see discussion above). The US dollar market accounted for approximately 70 per cent of the interest rate swap market and 85 per cent of activity in the currency swap market involved the US dollar on one side of the transaction.

12.6 **Securitisation**

Major borrowers can raise funds in the international markets in three ways: they can borrow from the banking system, issue equities, or issue debt securities such as bonds or notes.

As we established in chapter 2, the basis of banks' existence as financial intermediaries is that of transaction and information costs. This applies as much to international financing as it does to domestic financing. Over the 1980s international banks have been beset by problems such as bank failures in the US and the sovereign debt crisis, which have reduced the credit standing of many banks and thus the competitiveness of their lending rates. It has therefore been suggested (see for example the Cross report, Bank for International Settlements [1986]) that banks have been losing their comparative advantage in international financing. In addition, information costs have fallen because of the emergence of a large number of credit rating agencies over the 1980s, providing information on credit risks. As a consequence many of the larger borrowers with good credit rating have found they can raise funds more cheaply through the international capital markets. That is, there has been a greater preference, during some periods since 1980, for direct financing rather than indirect financing through a bank intermediary. This can be seen in table 12.7, which shows the relative volumes of the various forms of international finance over the 1980s.

Net international bank lending, which is made up of syndicated credits as well as short-term lending, was a declining proportion of total net international financing over the period 1980 to 1985. This is because of a switch from bank financing to indirect financing through the capital markets, a process known as securitisation, for the reasons outlined above. Eurobonds were the main alternative long-term funding security to bank intermediation in the early 1980s. In the mid-1980s short- to medium-term direct financing through the issue of euronotes also emerged to compete with syndicated bank lending. However, this process of securitisation appears to have been halted in the latter half of the 1980s. The reason for this is principally the renewed growth in bank lending, which can be explained by the ambitious expansion of the Japanese banks over this period (discussed in chapter 7) and the increase in corporate restructuring in the US and UK financed largely by debt. In addition, issues of international securities are subject to considerable volatility owing to linkages with stock markets. The global stock market crash in 1987 halted the growth in international securities issues, with bond issues only reaching pre-crash levels again in 1989. In 1991 bank lending slowed down considerably and has only shown moderate growth since then. This slowdown can be explained by a number of factors, including a slowdown in growth in many developed countries, and related to this is banks' poor performance on the domestic front, which has constrained their international lending as a result of having to set aside high loan loss provisions.

Looking to the future, the factors which led to the expansion of bank lending in the late 1980s look unlikely to be repeated, whilst the spread of securitisation habits to Europe and the constraints on bank lending as a result of having to meet new capital adequacy requirements (discussed in chapter 17) suggest that securitisation may be a long-run trend.

It is a mistake, however, to equate securitisation with dis-intermediation. Banks are actively involved in the securities markets in arranging the issue of securities, underwriting or providing guarantees of liquidity in the euronote markets. Banks are also the important players in the derivative markets, such as swaps, futures and options, which underlie many security market transactions. Banks often act as counterparts in swap transactions or perform a transformation of characteristics as they construct tailor-made option and futures retail contracts from the wholesale standardised contracts traded on the exchanges. It can be argued then that securitisation has not led to a greater exclusion of banks from the international financing process but that banks have transferred intermediation business that appeared on the balance sheet to fee-earning business that is conducted off the balance sheet. Banks can be seen to have adapted, and more importantly innovated,

Table 12.7 *Breakdown of international financing, 1980–93 (£billion)*

	1980	*1981*	*1982*	*1983*	*1984*	*1985*	*1986*	*1987*	*1988*	*1989*	*1990*	*1991*	*1992*	*1993*
Net international bank lending[a]	160	165	95	85	90	105	206	320	260	410	465	80	195	165
Net international bond issues[b]	28	37	59	59	84	123	158	108	139	175	132	171	119	184
Net euronote issues[c]					5	10	13	23	20	8	33	35	40	73
International equity issues					0.2	4	16	20	9	15	10	20	22	39
Total international financing	188	202	154	144	174	242	392	471	428	608	640	306	376	461
minus double counting[d]	8	7	9	14	24	58	82	51	69	78	80	40	75	122
Total net international financing	180	195	145	130	150	184	310	420	361	530	560	266	301	339
Bank lending as % of total financing	89	85	66	65	60	57	66	76	72	77	83	30	65	49

[a] As defined in table 4.8 in chapter 4.
[b] Completed international bond issues (as distinct from announced bond issues recorded in table 12.1) minus redemptions and repurchases.
[c] Completed euronote placements (as distinct from announced issues recorded in table 12.4).
[d] Purchases of bonds by banks and bonds issued by banks used to underpin international lending activities.
Source: Bank for International Settlements, annual report, various years.

in response to the changing preferences of international borrowers. The innovation that has taken place has tended to blur the boundaries between traditional intermediation and securities transacting.

12.7 Conclusion

In this chapter we have looked at the development of euro-securities markets, which are the international equivalents of domestic securities markets discussed in chapters 8, 9 and 10. These have grown rapidly since the 1980s and represent one facet of the internationalisation of finance.

Chapter 13

Financial derivatives

13.1 **Introduction**

Financial derivatives can be defined as instruments whose price is derived from the underlying financial security, such as financial futures and options. Thus, for example, the price of an option to purchase ICI shares will be dependent on the price of ICI shares themselves. If, in the unlikely case, ICI shares were worthless, then the option to buy the shares would also be without value. Derivatives can be categorised according the type of trade. First, there is the category of exchange-traded instruments and in this case the instruments are purchased or sold on an organised financial exchange or market. The second category refers to those instruments bought directly from a bank or other financial institution and these are called 'over-the-counter' (OTC) derivatives.

Exchange-traded financial derivatives commenced in the US in 1972. This was followed in September 1982 with the establishment of the London International Financial Futures Exchange (LIFFE), which became the first financial futures market in Europe. In 1992, LIFFE merged with the London Traded Options Market, whose trade consisted of dealings in individual share options, but still retained the acronym LIFFE. Other markets for financial futures in Europe include the March Terme d'Instruments Financiers (MATIF) in Paris, Deutsche Terminborse (DTB), European Options Exchange in the Netherlands, Copenhagen Stock Exchange and the Irish Futures and Options Exchange. LIFFE provides facilities for dealing in financial futures and also in traded options on futures together with options on specific company shares.

As shown in table 13.1, futures and options in general have seen a very rapid rate of growth over recent years. In fact the detail in table 13.1 omits the following from the OTC contracts: forward rate agreements, currency options, forward foreign exchange contracts and equity- and

Table 13.1 *Derivative contracts traded: notional principal (US$billion)*

	1987	*1988*	*1989*	*1990*	*1991*	*1992*	*1993*
Over the counter							
Interest rate swaps	683	1,010	1,503	2,312	3,065	3,851	6,177
Currency swaps	184	320	449	578	807	860	900
Other swap-related derivatives				561	577	635	1,398
Total				3,450	4,449	5,346	8,475
Exchange traded							
Interest rate futures and options	620	1175	1,589	2,054	3,230	4,288	7,323
Currency futures and options	74	60	66	72	79	104	111
Total	694	1,234	1,654	2,126	3,309	4,392	7,434

Column totals may not agree with individual figures because of rounding.
Source: *International Banking and Financial Market Developments*, November 1994 (BIS).

commodity-related derivatives. More generally, it is estimated that about two-thirds of derivative contracts take the form of OTC contracts, so it can be seen that the total notional amount outstanding of OTC contracts is significantly underestimated by the detail in table 13.1.

One of the reasons for this spectacular rate of growth is the high degree of volatility experienced in interest rates, inflation and exchange rates since the collapse in 1971 of the fixed exchange rate regime established by the Bretton Woods agreement (see chapter 14, figures 14.1 and 14.2 for more details). In particular, the growth in the quantity of primary securities issued has led automatically to a higher volume of secondary market transactions and therefore a greater demand for hedging instruments and hence financial futures and options. The rapid growth of information technology and consequent reduction in transaction costs has also played a role by stimulating the development of new trading strategies which enabled agents to use financial futures as a means of reducing risk. This aspect of the role of financial futures and options is considered in greater detail in chapter 14.

Table 13.2 shows the relative importance of the various centres. The Chicago markets still accounted for about 46 per cent of total exchange-traded financial derivatives in the period January–September 1994. In the past, trade in the US accounted for nearly 95 per cent of the world total but this percentage has diminished because the other markets have experienced a faster rate of growth over recent years than the Chicago markets.

Table 13.2 *Top ten derivative exchanges: futures and options contract volume*

Rank	*Exchange*	*Contract volume January–September 1994 (million contracts)*
1	CBOT (Chicago)	171.1
2	CME (Chicago)	153.0
3	LIFFE (London)	118.3
4	CBOE (Chicago)	82.6
5	MATIF (Paris)	76.3
6	BM&F (Brazil)	70.6
7	NYMEX (New York)	60.2
8	DTB (Germany)	39.3
9	LME (London)	34.2
10	TIFFE (Tokyo)	29.6

Source: *Financial Times,* 16 November 1994.

In section 13.2 we will outline the general organisation of LIFFE, which, given its relative importance as indicated in table 13.2, will provide an indication of how futures markets typically operate. The role of financial futures and options will be discussed in sections 13.3 and 13.4 respectively. In sections 13.5 and 13.6 we discuss the role of other derivatives such as swaps and forward rate agreements. Section 13.7 presents a survey of the empirical evidence concerning the efficiency of this type of market.

13.2 The organisation of LIFFE

A financial futures contract can be defined as an agreement to sell or buy a quantity of a financial instrument on an organised market or exchange at a future date and at a price specified at the time of making the contract. In contrast, an option confers the right, but not the obligation, to the purchaser to buy (a 'call' option) or the right to sell (a 'put' option) financial instruments at a standard price and times in the future. The practical distinction between traded and OTC options is that the former can be bought from and sold to parties other than the original writer (i.e. seller) of the option. The market in the underlying or actual financial instrument is called the cash market and the options or futures market the derivative market. Although a range of financial instruments are the subject of futures transactions, the number is, as shown in table 13.3, limited.

A further restriction applies since the transactions are available only in specific quantities; for example, on LIFFE the standard unit of trading is £500,000 for three-month sterling deposits, US$ 1,000,000 for three-month eurodollar deposits, and £50,000 for the long gilt futures. The minimum unit of trading decreases as the maturity of the underlying cash market security increases, owing to the increase in its price volatility – this is evidenced by the difference in the notional principal of the short sterling and gilt contracts. In all futures and options exchanges delivery of the security is also made on specific dates according to a fixed sequence of months, with the cycle of March, June, September and December being the most common. The cycle usually extends up to two years in advance but in some cases the cycle can extend up to four years. These limitations reduce the flexibility of the contracts available as compared with, say, the provision of tailor-made forward foreign exchange contracts provided by the banks, as was discussed in chapter 11. On the other hand, the provision of standardised contracts enables trading to be carried out at a low cost since the buyers and sellers know precisely what they are trading.

The second general point to note is that although the transactions are originally made between two parties on the exchange, the two resulting contracts are then transferred to the London Clearing House, which clears and guarantees all transactions carried out on LIFFE and a number of other London exchanges. Consequently the Clearing House has a zero net position since it has acquired both sides of the trade. This system has a number of advantages. First, the risk of default is eliminated for both parties to the transaction since it is borne by the exchange. In order to protect itself against default, the Clearing House requires both parties to deposit cash against the transaction (the 'initial margin') and this margin is revalued on a daily basis to take account of movements in the price of the underlying security

Table 13.3 *Futures and options contracts available at LIFFE: LIFFE deals in financial futures in the following financial instruments*

Interest rate	*Stock index*	*Equity options*
Three-month sterling deposits*	FT-SE 100 Index*	On certain individual shares
Three-month eurodollar deposits*	FT-SE 250	
Three-month euromark deposits*		
Three-month ECU deposits		
Three-month eurolira deposits		
Three-month euro Swiss franc deposits*		
Long gilt		
Long German government bond (Bund)*		
Japanese government bond (JGB)		
Italian government bond (BTP)*		

Source: LIFFE.

Table 13.4 *LIFFE futures and options trading volume (million contracts)*

	1982[a]	*1983*	*1984*	*1985*	*1986*	*1987*	*1988*	*1989*	*1990*	*1991*	*1992*	*1993*
Futures												
Short interest	0.16	0.66	1.36	1.78	2.07	3.23	5.19	10.14	12.33	14.50	26.84	37.75
Bond	0.03	0.53	0.94	1.36	4.23	8.66	8.12	10.48	16.01	16.86	26.68	40.10
Currency	0.05	0.18	0.20	0.15	0.07	0.03	0.02	0.01	0.00			
Equity index			0.07	0.09	0.12	0.46	0.47	1.03	1.44	1.73	2.62	3.12
Total futures	0.24	1.37	2.57	3.38	6.49	12.38	13.80	21.66	29.78	33.09	56.14	80.97
Options												
Short interest				0.03	0.04	0.06	0.52	0.91	1.69	2.14	4.70	5.63
Bond					0.33	1.09	1.22	1.27	2.68	3.35	5.03	7.08
Currency				0.14	0.11	0.02	0.01					
Equity index						0.01					2.57	3.44
Shares											3.53	4.77
Total options	0.00	0.00	0.00	0.17	0.48	1.18	1.75	2.18	4.37	5.49	15.83	20.92
Total, all contracts	0.24	1.37	2.57	3.55	6.97	13.56	15.55	23.84	34.15	38.58	71.97	101.89

[a] September–December only.
Source: LIFFE.

(the 'variation margin'). A further protection is gained by restriction of dealing facilities to 'members' of LIFFE who, themselves, are representatives of a wide range of financial institutions. Second, it enables transactions to be 'closed out' before the maturity date since the party wishing to terminate the agreement merely takes out an exactly opposite liability. In fact over 90 per cent of agreements are closed out before the maturity date and we shall discuss the reasons for this in section 13.3.

The contracts available on LIFFE in October 1994 are shown in table 13.3. It should, however, be remembered that this list can only be indicative of what contracts will be available as it is likely that new contracts will be developed. Except for those contracts marked with an asterisk LIFFE also provides options on the futures contracts listed in table 13.3. Up to 1990, LIFFE also provided facilities for trading in futures and options in currencies but these were suspended in 1990. For the pound against the US dollar, traded options are still available (i) against cash on the Philadelphia Stock Exchange (units of £31,250 per contract) and (ii) against futures at Chicago.

The relative importance of the various contracts traded at LIFFE over the years since its formation is shown in table 13.4. The table shows the dramatic growth in total number of transactions from 0.24 million contracts in September–December 1982 to 101.9 million contracts in 1993. The statistics also demonstrate the relative importance of short-term interest rate and bond contracts. The decline of currency futures and options is also apparent. The probable reason for this is that the OTC market (i.e. the 'forward' market discussed in chapter 11) offers comparable products which are perceived by traders to be more advantageous. As far as currency futures are concerned, the forward market provides a similar and flexible opportunity to hedge against future exchange rate changes through either fixed or option dated forward contracts. This eliminates the necessity of having to sell the instrument in the market, although similar resale facilities are available if required by entering into a spot sale of the currency in the market which offsets the original forward contract. However, on 12 September 1994, the CME launched two new currency forward contracts (i.e. $/Deutschmark and $/yen) which can be used in conjunction with the currency spot contracts to replicate OTC currency swaps. As was noted in chapter 11, the swap segment of the market formed the major component of the forward market. Similarly, OTC options contracts can be arranged with banks which meet the trader's precise requirements. It is understood that such contracts have shown a considerable degree of growth, with London as an important centre, though no official statistics exist.

Dealing on LIFFE must be carried out through members. On receipt of an order from a customer, the member then transmits this order to her or his booth on the trading floor. Trading is carried out by the 'open-outcry' system during the period 8 a.m. to 4.15 p.m. and by LIFFE's automated pit trading system (APT) between 4.30 p.m. and 6.00 p.m. Whilst scenes from the trading floor or pit initially convey the impression of utter chaos, it is claimed that this system ensures that all orders receive equal treatment and that it is therefore fair. However, all this may change. Apart from the APT system discussed above, Reuters has developed a screen trading system, 'Globex', which is used as an after-hours market for some of the products traded in Chicago and other markets (see chapter 7 for further discussion). However, the Globex system has run into some difficulties and in 1994 one of its joint founders (CBOT) withdrew from the project and LIFFE declined to join. As noted earlier, the order is then transferred to the Clearing House. Immediate day-to-day supervision of the market is vested in the Board of the Exchange, which has established a market supervision department to carry out self-regulation. Ultimate supervisory authority lies with the Bank of England, which exercises general surveillance over all London exchanges.

13.3 The nature of financial futures

In order to demonstrate the nature of financial futures it is necessary to describe their function. As is the case for all traded financial instruments (see chapter 7), three uses of financial futures are traditionally identified. These are 'hedging', 'trading' (or perhaps more appropriately speculation) and 'arbitrage'. In practice, however, it may be difficult to make this a clear-cut and unambiguous distinction since financial institutions are making greater use of derivative markets for the purpose of asset/liability management.

Hedging can be considered a defensive operation by risk-averse operators to insure themselves against adverse movements in, for example, interest or exchange rates. As an outline of this function prior to consideration of particular hedging operations in detail, consider the position of an operator who buys a three-month sterling deposit financial future. If current actual interest rates fall then the value of the future will increase since it is offering higher rates than can be obtained in the market place. Conversely, if current actual interest rates rise then the value of the financial future will fall since actual deposits will earn higher rates of interest. Consequently, the price of the financial future will move in the opposite direction to the movement of interest rates. Thus, it is possible for an agent to offset – at least partially – the effects of movements in interest rates by profits or losses on the value of the financial future by selling the futures contract back to the market. The basic trading rule is that if the trader's cash position will be adversely affected by higher-than-anticipated interest rates, then a futures contract should be sold. Conversely, if it is lower rates that worry the trader, then a futures contract should be bought.

We now illustrate the procedure more precisely using as an example the three-month sterling interest rate futures contract. A company has obtained a loan of £1,000,000 at a rate of 12 per cent from the money markets which is due to be rolled over on 1 June. The company is concerned that interest rates will change with a probability that the loan will be rolled over at a higher rate. In order to protect itself the company sells two three-month sterling interest rate financial futures (each valued £500,000) which are due for delivery after 1 June – it is of critical importance that the delivery date of the futures contract is later than the date when the risk to be hedged disappears, otherwise there will be a period of time when potential changes in prices of the cash instrument are not hedged. Assuming the current interest rate is 12 per cent, the price of each contract is (100 – the annual rate of interest), that is, 88 in this example. The price of the contract will move up or down in minimum amounts of 0.01 per cent, which are known as a 'ticks' or basis points. The value of a tick varies for each type of financial future but may, in this case, be derived by applying the 0.01 per cent rate of interest to the face value of a £500,000 contract for one-quarter of a year and is therefore £12.50. On 1 June the company will buy the two contracts back from the exchange. We can now examine the effect of this transaction if interest rates had risen to 14 per cent per annum on 1 June. The first point to note is that the company will bear extra borrowing costs of £5,000 for the next quarter due to the rise in interest rates of 2 per cent per annum. We next look at the futures market transaction and we initially assume that the futures price has also moved in line with the cash market rate:

(i) sells two contracts at 88 (rate of interest 12 per cent);
(ii) buys back two futures at 86 (rate of interest 14 per cent) on 1 June;
(iii) gains 200 ticks per contract (i.e. 400) at £12.50 = £5,000.

In this case the higher cost of interest is exactly matched by the profit on the two futures transactions. If, on the other hand, interest rates had fallen, then the company's borrowing cost would have fallen but this would have been offset by the loss on buying back the futures contract. This clarifies what the company has gained from its financial futures operation, namely that the uncertainty surrounding the future interest rate on its borrowing cost has been removed. It is important to realise that the company has not necessarily made a gain on its futures transactions. In fact in the case of an interest rate fall it would have incurred a loss, but it would have reduced the uncertainty of future costs. This example also illustrates the reason why most contracts are 'closed out' (i.e. reversed) before the time for delivery of the futures contract since the offsetting gain/loss on the futures contract is realised when the futures contract is closed out.

The precision of the hedge in the above example is due to the fact we have assumed that the price of the futures contract has moved exactly in line with the cash market rate. This degree of precision is unlikely to occur in practice and, to understand why, we need to consider a concept known as basis. This may be defined as:

basis = cash price - futures price.

In the example quoted above the basis is zero at the start and the finish of the hedging operation. It is quite common, however, for a non-zero basis to exist since the cash and futures price is subject to different influences. In particular, the futures price will reflect the market's view of the level of the interest rate in the future. If we return to the above example, and consider the case where the futures price at the time the hedger sells the contracts is not 88 but rather 87.50, the existence of a futures price of 87.50 and an analogous cash price of 88.00 (100 - 12) implies that the market expects interest rates to rise in the period up to the date of the futures contract. The basis at the start of the hedge is therefore (88.0 - 87.5) or 0.5. If the basis is different at the time the hedger 'closes out' then the hedge will not be perfect. To illustrate this point, consider the position if the futures price had been 86.00 on 1 June (i.e. a zero basis given an interest rate of 14 per cent) then the gain on the hedge would have been 150 (87.50 - 86.00) ticks per contract or £3,750 in total. In this case a partial hedge has been achieved since the gain on the futures contract does not cover the additional interest charges on the rolled-over loan. It is also quite possible that the change in basis could work in favour of the hedger. For example, if the futures price was 85.00 on 1 June (i.e. a basis of 1.0) then the gain would have been 250 ticks per contract or £6,250 in total. A further point worth noting is that, if the futures contract purchased by the hedger had been for delivery in June, then it is quite likely that the basis on 1 June would have been close to zero. This is because as the delivery date on the futures contract approaches, then the cash price and the futures price tend to equality because the influences on the two contracts are identical on the delivery date. As will be shown below, any difference between the two prices would lead to arbitrage.

An existence of a non-zero basis can occur for a number of reasons. Thus, if the basis is close to zero when the contract is being taken out then it is sensible to choose futures contracts that mature soon after the disappearance of the risk to be hedged. In general, however, cash and futures prices of similar instruments do exhibit a fairly high degree of correlation, so that basis risk (the risk of movements in basis) is less than outright risk (the risk of an unhedged position) as long as the characteristics of the instrument being hedged are not very different from those of relevant futures instrument.

We now turn to examine the role of trading or speculation in the operation of financial futures markets. Providers of a hedge can protect themselves by negotiating an offsetting contract. In the example of the company quoted above, the purchaser of the futures may at that time be able to identify a customer who wishes to buy two similar contracts. In this instance the financial institution providing the hedge has incurred no risk since it has two offsetting contracts with windfall gains on one contract matching windfall losses on the other. In practice it is highly unlikely that the quantity of hedging demanded for a change in one direction will exactly match that required in the opposite direction, so traders fill the gap by making the market and therefore provide a useful economic function. Trading is basically a non-defensive activity undertaken by those agents willing to bear the risk of price changes. Their income comes from two sources which in practice may be difficult to distinguish. First, there is the reward for undertaking risk, and second the potential profits to be earned from taking a correct view of the future course of the prices of the underlying cash market securities. Financial futures are a particularly useful vehicle for speculation since (i) transaction costs are low and (ii) there is no need to purchase or sell the underlying instrument and the cash outlay is restricted to the initial margin (typically varying between 0.1 per cent and 6 per cent of the face value of the contract) and the variation margin, thus offering potential for high degrees of leverage. If the price of the underlying security is expected to rise, speculators will go long, that is, buy financial futures, or if the price is expected to fall they would go short, that is, sell financial futures. Clearly, this is a risky operation and losses will be incurred if the prices move in the opposite direction to those anticipated by the trader. We use the long gilt futures contract as an illustration of the potential for trading contracts. Again we would like to emphasise that this is just one particular example of a wide range of potential trading activities available.

As was pointed out in chapter 9, prices of gilts are sensitive to interest rate changes and the degree of sensitivity increases directly with the outstanding maturity of the stock in question. Assume that a trader feels that the next round of publications of the various official statistics will be more favourable than has hitherto been the case. He also feels that this is likely to lead to a reduction in interest rates which has not fully been reflected in the current prices of gilt-edged stock. He therefore purchases one unit of gilt futures £50,000 nominal value for the next delivery date after the publication of the last in the round of the official statistics he considers relevant. Assume that the relevant contract is trading at £102–25, that is, £102 and 25/32nds. The minimum price movement is 1/32nd with a tick valued at £15.625 for this contract. If he is correct and the statistics on balance are sufficiently favourable to permit a fall in interest rates then gilt prices will rise and so consequently will the gilt futures contract, so that the trader will make the expected profit. It should be emphasised that the profit is entirely dependent on the accuracy of the trader's forecast as against that implicit in market prices.

The third activity in futures markets refers to arbitrage to take advantage of price anomalies between either (i) the underlying cash market instruments and the futures or (ii) different futures contracts. Such price anomalies are likely to be quite small and short lived since other traders will quickly perceive the opportunity of making a profit with minimal risk. As one example we consider the position of the long gilt futures contract. This contract can be carried out by delivery of a specified gilt-edged stock. The current specification broadly refers to any stock maturing between the years 2003 and 2009 inclusive but excludes convertible and index-linked stocks. Thus, if the prices of the futures and underlying stocks are misaligned it may be possible to borrow funds, purchase the misaligned deliverable stock and sell an appropriate futures contract. This is called cash and carry arbitrage. Little risk is attached to such an operation provided all the contracts are undertaken simultaneously. Anomalies between the prices of future contracts may occur between (i) different types of contracts such as between the various three-month interest rate futures noted in section 13.2 or (ii) between different delivery dates of the same futures contract. This latter arbitrage is known as spreading. We now demonstrate the process of cash and carry arbitrage more formally.

Assuming continuous discounting, then the following condition must hold if 'no arbitrage' possibilities exist :

$$F = Se^{r(T-t)} \qquad (13.1)$$

where F is the forward price, S the price of the underlying security, r the risk-free rate of interest, T time when contract matures and t current time. If, for example, $F > Se^{r(T-t)}$, then profits can be made by borrowing £S for the period T–t, buying the asset and selling (taking a short position) the forward contract. At time T-t, a profit equal to $F - Se^{r(T-t)}$ has been obtained. The converse would apply if $F < Se^{r(T-t)}$, that is, the forward contract would be purchased and the asset sold with the proceeds from the asset being invested at the risk-free interest rate until the forward contract matures. To illustrate this point consider a share where the market price is £40, the risk-free rate of interest is 4 per cent per annum and, for sake of ease of exposition, the time period involved (T–t) is one year (note if the futures matured in three months' time, then T - t = 0.25). Given this information, the equilibrium futures price is given by equation 13.1 as (£40 × $e^{0.04}$), or £41.63. If the actual market price of the forward contract is £40, then sale of the stock would produce £40, the proceeds would be invested to obtain £40 × $e^{0.04}$, or £41.63, as compared with the £40 required to purchase the forward contract in one year's time. Conversely if the forward price is £42, then £40 is borrowed for the year at the risk-free rate of 4 per cent, and the asset purchased for £40. In one year's time the asset would be sold for £42 in accordance with the forward contract as against the cost of borrowed funds of £41.63. This analysis applies strictly for forward contracts and would also apply to futures if either the risk-free interest rate is constant and the same for all maturities or is a known function of time. The intuitive reason for differences between forward and future prices is that the latter involve margin payments whereas the former do not. Also, equation 13.1 ignores costs involved in carrying the instrument. In the case of financial assets this is likely to be very near zero, so equation 13.1 can be regarded as depicting what is known as the 'cost of carry' relationship between the spot and the futures price. This cost would be reduced if the futures instrument yielded some known dividend or return and can be described by:

$$F = Se^{(r-i)(T-t)} \tag{13.2}$$

where i is the return on the futures instrument. In the case where the dividend is not known, i will represent the average dividend.

In addition to the three traditional uses discussed above, futures markets can be used to vary a portfolio's overall maturity structure by altering the maturity of individual securities. For example, the average maturity of a portfolio can be 'synthetically' reduced by the sale of, say, a long gilt futures in five months' time and using a 'deliverable' gilt from the portfolio to complete the transaction. Thus, the maturity on the security has been changed from its previous term to five months and the new redemption value is the price implied by the futures contract. Similarly, the average length of a portfolio of short-term securities can be lengthened by purchasing a series of short-term contracts.

Before turning to a discussion of the nature of options in section 13.4, it is worthwhile examining, albeit briefly, the nature of foreign currency futures on the International Money Market (IMM) at CME. The four major currencies traded are the Deutschmark, Swiss franc, Japanese yen and sterling. The largest of these four contracts concerns the Deutschmark and the market report for this contract in the *Financial Times* (6 December 1994) quoted a latest price of $0.6351 (the equivalent of a closing price) for delivery in March. We use this quotation to demonstrate the principles of this market. As is the case for other futures contracts, settlement is made on a specific date and can be by way of cash settlement or delivery of the currency. IMM quotes the rate as $s per 1 D-Mark and the size of the contract is 125,000 D-Mark so the buyer of the contract has agreed to pay $79,387.5 for 125,000 D-Mark for delivery in March (125,000 × 0.6351). If the price of the D-Mark rises to 0.6400 the value of the contract rises to $80,0000 and the buyer has made a profit of $612.5. As in the case of LIFFE and other futures contracts, the seller of the contract would have to pay and the buyer receive additional margins.

Clearly, on the expiry date the underlying (i.e. the spot rate) and the futures price would coincide. Before this date there will be a gap between the current spot rate and the futures price and this is called the 'swap'. The level of the swap reflects the interest differentials and can be calculated according to the following formula (assuming interest is paid at discrete intervals):

$$\text{swap} = (\text{spot exchange rate}) \times (\text{eurodollar rate - euro-D-Mark rate}) \times (\text{days to delivery}/360)$$

(Most contracts are worked out on the basis of 360 days.)

Thus, for example, suppose at the close of trade on a particular day, the eurodollar and euromark three-month deposit rates were 6.5 per cent per annum and 5.5 per cent respectively and the spot exchange rate $0.6500 per 1 D-Mark. On a contract which has, say, 90 days to delivery, the swap is:

$$0.6500 \times (0.065 - 0.055) \times (90/360) = 0.0025$$

The trader could then add the swap to the current spot rate to arrive at a theoretical futures price of 0.6525. If the actual futures price were less than 0.6525, a trader could make a profit by selling D-Mark spot and buying futures. Similarly, if the futures price was above 0.6525 the trader could buy D-Mark spot and sell futures. Of course in practice the differential would have to exceed transaction costs, which in any case are likely to be low.

13.4 **The nature of options**

Options give the purchaser, in return for a premium, the right to buy (a 'call' option) or the right to sell (a 'put' option) a financial instrument at an agreed exchange rate (the 'striking' price) at a specified date or dates. No obligation is imposed on buyers to carry out the obligation so they will choose to do so only if it is profitable for them. Two classes or types of options can be distinguished. As was discussed in section 13.2, an option can be either an OTC option or a traded option. OTC options have either to be exercised or allowed to lapse. Traded options offer the additional choice to the holder of reselling them on the market. In fact, as we shall see later, it is more likely that a traded option will be resold rather than exercised. Trading on organised option markets can be for the purposes of both speculation and hedging and it is the presence of speculators which provides liquidity for the market. Options can be further categorised into American and European options. An American type of option can be exercised at any date up to the expiry of the option whereas the European type can be

Table 13.5 *Example of LIFFE equity options*

		Calls			Puts		
		January	*April*	*June*	*January*	*April*	*June*
BP	420	13	23	31½	10½	17½	24
(*421)	460	1½	8	16	39½	43	48
ICI	700	53	66½	75½	3½	20	25½
(*746)	750	19	35½	47	20	43½	49

* Underlying security price.
Source: *Financial Times,* market report dated 17 December 1994.

exercised only on a specified date. The options traded on LIFFE are generally of the American type. Premiums for traded options are quoted in market statistics and we show in table 13.5 the relevant details at the close of trading on 16 December 1994 for just two of the share options (i.e. BP and ICI) which are traded at LIFFE as reported in the *Financial Times* on 17 December 1994.

The detail contained in table 13.5 can be interpreted in the following way. A trader can purchase a call option (i.e. the right to buy BP shares) expiring in January 1995 at a strike/exercise price of 420p per share for a premium (i.e. price) of 13p per share. For April 1995 expiry and the same strike price the premium is 23p per share. Similarly, the purchase of a put option (the right to sell) with a strike price of 460p per share and June 1995 expiry would require a premium of 48p per share. A similar interpretation is easily derived for ICI shares. Shares have to be purchased in quantities of 1,000.

We use the quotation for April calls and puts at a strike price of 420p per share to derive the diagrams used to illustrate the profit and loss situation for the purchaser and the writer of the option. In the first example the purchaser of a call option will exercise it to purchase BP shares only if the market price rises above 420p per share. At market prices lower than this price it is more profitable for the trader to purchase BP equity in the market so that the loss is restricted to the 23p premium paid on taking out the option. The break-even point occurs when the actual market price is 443p per share so that the premium just matches the gain on the option contract of 23p. In effect, therefore, the purchase of the call option has fixed the maximum price to be paid for BP shares at 443p per share. As the market price rises above 443p per share the purchaser obtains profits which in theory are unlimited but in practice are limited to the likely range of market fluctuations. The position for the seller (i.e the 'writer') of the option is the mirror image of that of the purchaser. Figure 13.1 illustrates the above situation.

The position in the case of the purchase of a put option is the reverse of that in the case of a call option and is illustrated in figure 13.2. For an exercise price of 420p per share the option will be exercised only when the market price for BP equity falls below 420p per share. At prices above 420p it is more profitable to sell the shares in the market. Consequently, the break-even price for the purchaser is 402½p per share, when the profit on the sale of shares just matches the premium paid (i.e. 17½p per share). As the actual market price falls below 402½p per share the purchaser makes gains which in theory are only limited by a market price of zero but, in practice, are again limited by the likely range of fluctuations. As for the case of a call option, the position of the writer is the mirror image of that of the purchaser.

Remember, the exercise of an option lies entirely in the hands of the purchaser. The writer has no control over whether the option is exercised or not. It is in the nature of a contingent liability which may or may not be incurred. As far as the purchaser is concerned, an option contract is analogous to an insurance policy with the premium for the option representing the premium paid for the policy and the risk insured is the downside risk of an adverse movement in the share price with the purchaser taking all the benefits of a favourable movement.

The price of an option contract can be divided into two components:

(i) The *intrinsic value* is the gain which would be realised if an option were exercised immediately. In the case of a call option it is the excess of the spot price over the exercise price. This represents the gain that can be made by exercising the option immediately and selling the share in the market. For a put option the intrinsic value is the excess of the exercise price over the spot rate, which represents the profit derived from buying the share in the market and exercising the option to sell the currency at the strike price. In the above example the current market price for BP shares was 421p per share at the close of trading on 16 December 1994. For a strike price of 420p per share the intrinsic value for a call option for April 1995 delivery is 1p per share. Similarly, for a put option at a strike price of 460p per share for April delivery the intrinsic value is 39p (460 - 421). The intrinsic value is always positive or zero.

(ii) The *time value* represents that part of the premium not represented by the intrinsic value. For the call example given above, an intrinsic value of 1p per share and a premium of 23p per share (April call option), the time value is 22p per share; similarly, the time value for the put quoted above is 4p per share (43 - 39). Time value cannot be negative and will approach zero at an increasing rate as the option

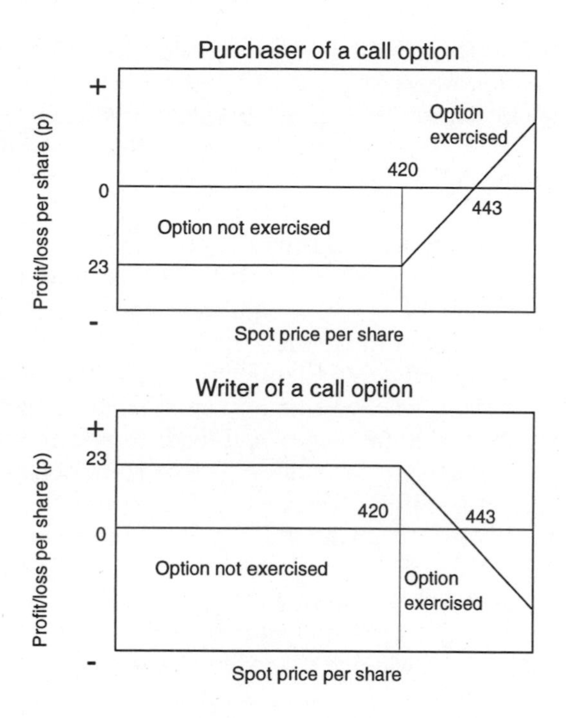

Figure 13.1

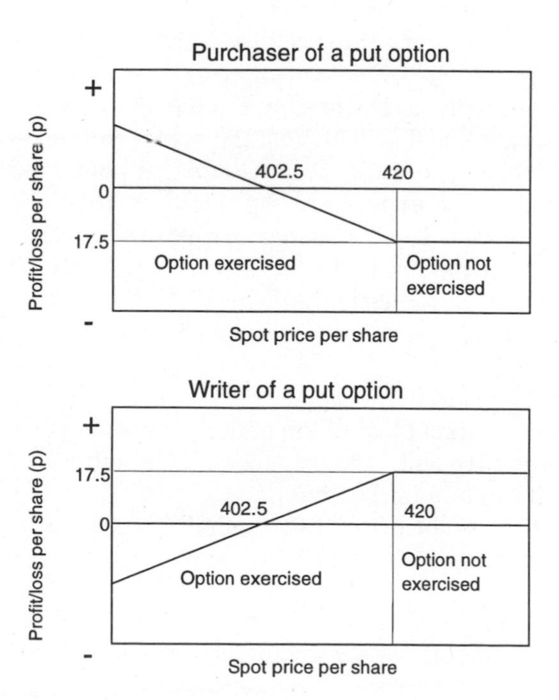

Figure 13.2

nears expiry. This can be seen from table 13.5, where the time value of a call option at a strike price for ICI shares of 700p is 7p for January delivery (current price 746, hence intrinsic value = 46 which with premium of 53 gives a time value of 7), 20½ for April delivery and 29½ for June delivery.

When a non-zero intrinsic value of an option exists the option is said to be 'in the money'. For a put option, if the strike price is less than the current spot rate, then the option is said to be 'out of the money'. A call option is said to be 'out of the money' if the strike price is more than the current price. If the exercise (strike) price is equal to the spot price then the option is 'at the money'. Time value is at its maximum for a given expiry date when an option is at the money and tends to zero for options deeply out of the money or deeply in the money. This can be rationalised intuitively by considering the position of an option deeply out of the money. The further the option is away from the strike price the more unlikely it becomes that it will be exercised. Hence both the value to the holder and the risk to the writer are reduced, thus lowering the premiums required for taking on the risk. For an in the money option, intrinsic value exists so that the holder incurs the risk of this value being eroded by adverse movements in the spot price. As far as the writer of the option is concerned, the adverse movement to the holder would be a gain for the writer. The larger the intrinsic value the greater is the risk of erosion of the intrinsic value. Thus, the premium will compensate the buyer of the option with a reduced time value in the premium and the writer will be willing to grant the lower premium owing to the lower risk involved. The presence of the time component in the price of an option means that it is likely that the holder will sell the option in the market rather than exercise it. To illustrate this point consider again the case of the call option expiring in April with a strike price of 420p per share. The premium is 23p per share, which exceeds the intrinsic value of 1p, so that sale of the option in the market would permit the holder to extract the time value for herself or himself.

The price of an option mainly depends on the factors listed below:

(i) the strike or exercise price,
(ii) the current market price of the underlying asset, in the case of BP or ICI shares 421p and 746p respectively (see table 13.5),
(iii) time to the expiry of the option,
(iv) the volatility of the price of the underlying asset,
(v) the risk-free interest rate.

The precise relationship between these factors is derived by various mathematical formulae, of which perhaps the most well known is the

Black–Scholes formula. Discussion of the mathematical methods necessary to derive such relationships is beyond the scope of this text but it is possible to identify intuitively how these factors influence the price of an option.

In the case of a call option, the lower the exercise or strike price the more likely it is to be exercised and therefore the higher the price. The second factor is the current spot price. In this case the higher the spot price the more likely the option is to be exercised. Two other factors are the volatility of the price of the underlying cash asset and the maturity of the option. The option is more likely to be exercised (i) if the price of the cash instrument is volatile and/or (ii) the greater is the length of time before the option expires. Anything which increases the probability of the option being exercised raises the price of the option, that is, the premium. In the case of a put option the premium would be raised if the direction of the first two factors is reversed; that is, the option will be more valuable (i) the lower the price of the underlying cash instrument and/or (ii) the higher the strike or exercise price. Finally, a rise in the risk-free rate of interest is likely to be accompanied by expectations of increased growth rate of the price of the share. However, the increased interest rate will reduce the present value of any future cash flows associated with the holding of the option. Both these effects will reduce the value of a put option. In the case of a call option, following a rise in the risk-free interest rate, the first effect discussed above raises its value but the second effect lowers it. However, the first effect dominates so that a rise in the risk-free rate of interest always increases the price of call options.

The effect of changes in the strike/exercise price and time can easily be seen from the detail contained in tables 13.5 and 13.6. The effect of changes in the exercise price can bc observed by looking down the columns and in time by looking along the rows.

Table 13.6 *Philadelphia Stock Exchange £/$ options as at close of trading 16 December 1994 (£31,250) (cents per £1)*

Strike price	*Calls*			*Puts*		
	December	*January*	*February*	*December*	*January*	*February*
1.500	6.17	6.18	6.35	–	–	0.18
1.525	3.67	3.84	4.24	–	0.12	0.55
1.550	1.22	1.91	2.51	–	0.64	1.29
1.575	–	0.67	1.33	1.18	1.88	2.54
1.600	–	0.15	0.60	3.62	3.80	4.23
1.625	–	–	0.22	6.12	6.13	6.33

Source: *Financial Times*, market report, 17 December 1994.

So far our exposition has been in terms of options on individual shares. Options exist however for other financial assets such as stock indices, foreign currency and futures. Options on foreign currency are mainly conducted on an over-the-counter basis but traded options are available on the Philadelphia Stock Exchange. The *Financial Times* market quotation for the end of trade on 16 December 1994 is reproduced as table 13.6.

The interpretation of the table is similar to that for share options. The exception is that the option is to purchase sterling in amounts of £31,250 with the option price quoted per £1. Thus, the total cost for an option to purchase £31,250 for February delivery at a strike price of $1.500 per £1 is $1,984.375 (31,250 × 0.0635). For the purposes of comparison, the spread for the spot exchange rate at close of trading on 16 December 1994 in the London forex was $1.5625 to $1.5635 per £1.

In addition to the standard American-type and European-type options so far discussed, a number of options with non-standard or more complicated payoffs exist. These are termed 'exotic options'. These are generally over-the-counter options and are designed by banks to meet the specific needs of their customers. A large number of such options exist and we mention only a few to illustrate their nature. One such option is called a 'Bermudan' option, which, like US-type options, can be exercised up to and including the maturity date but, unlike US-type options, such early exercise is restricted to specific dates. Another type is 'forward start options', for which payment is made now but the option does not start until a later date. Similarly, options can be made up of a package of options in the manner discussed in chapter 14, where payoffs of a combination of options are illustrated. One further example is provided by 'compound options', which are in fact options on options. As noted earlier, the types of exotic options are exceedingly numerous and our examples are designed merely to point out how departures from the standard European and US types of options can be engineered. We now turn to a discussion of swaps.

13.5 Swaps

A swap is an agreement between two parties to exchange future cash flows in accordance with a previously agreed formula. Normally such arrangements involve a bank acting as an intermediary rather than being directly between two companies. In this case the bank has entered into two contracts, one with each party. This causes the bank/financial intermediary to incur the additional risk that one party may default, leaving the bank with an open contract. It is often the case that only one customer has approached a bank to arrange a specific swap. In this case the bank may assume the position of the counter-party until such time as the second part of the swap can be arranged. In this case the bank is said to 'warehouse'

Table 13.7 *Hypothetical example of borrowing costs of two companies*

	Fixed rate	*Floating rate*
Company A	8%	0.5% above LIBOR
Company B	9%	1.0% above LIBOR

the interest rate swap. Again, additional risk is incurred by the bank until the offsetting transaction is arranged. Swaps are OTC derivatives and arise in a variety of forms. We commence our discussion with the simplest and most common form of a swap, between fixed and floating interest rate payments in the same currency. This is called a 'plain vanilla' interest rate swap.

Consider the matrix of borrowing costs for two companies, A and B, shown in table 13.7. Suppose also that B wishes to borrow at fixed rates and A at floating rates. It may appear that since A can borrow more cheaply at both fixed and floating rates that no profitable swap is possible. This is not so, since the gap between the two fixed rates is different from that for the two floating rates. Company A pays 1 per cent less than B for fixed-rate loans but only 0.5 per cent less in the case of floating-rate loans. Thus, company A has a comparative advantage in the fixed-rate loan market and company B in the floating-rate loan market. The two companies profitably exploit this situation through:

(i) A borrowing at fixed rates and lending to B at say 8.2 per cent;
(ii) B borrowing at floating rates and lending to A at say LIBOR + 0.5 per cent.

For the sake of ease of exposition we shall assume that the loan period is one year. The two companies' cash position is as follows.

Company A:
Borrows at 8 per cent,
lends to B at 8.2 per cent,
pays B LIBOR + 0.5 per cent.
Hence net cost of a floating-rate loan to A is LIBOR + 0.3 per cent.

Company B:
Borrows at LIBOR + 1 per cent,
lends to A at LIBOR + 0.5 per cent,
borrows from A at 8.2 per cent.
Hence net cost of fixed-rate loan to B is 8.7 per cent.

Note that the cost of the preferred type of borrowing is lower for both companies after the swap. This is the case even though company A has cheaper access to finance than company B in both markets. It is the existence of comparative advantage that matters.

In practice, as we have already noted, the swap would be arranged via a financial intermediary and the margins of lower cost in our hypothetical example show that the financial intermediary could easily exploit the situation to obtain a profit for itself. Also, it is important to realise that the principals themselves would not be exchanged, merely the net difference between the two streams of interest-rate payments at periodic intervals as set out in the agreement.

It is interesting to speculate why such differences would occur. One reason put forward, as illustrated in the above example, is the existence of comparative advantage. However, this view does come up against the problem of why such differences are not eliminated by arbitrage in the manner indicated above. One possible explanation centres around the term of a loan and the possibility of default. If during the period of the loan contract the default risk of a company which had borrowed at floating rates increased, the desired margin over LIBOR would also increase. Normally the lender has the option of reviewing the margin during the period of the loan. The providers of fixed-rate loans do not have this option so the comparative advantage of A in the fixed-rate loan market may reflect differing probabilities of default in the future. Thus, B has secured a fixed rate of interest lower than would otherwise be the case.

A second type of swap is a 'plain deal currency' swap. Suppose company D wished to borrow in dollars and company C in sterling but the comparative advantages favoured dollar borrowing for C and sterling for D. In this case company C would borrow in dollars and company D in sterling. They would exchange the two sums borrowed and agree to pay the interest rates associated with the swapped sums (C in dollars and D in sterling). At the end of the period of the loan they would again exchange the original principal sums so that no risk would arise from exchange rate changes. Again, the reason for this type of swap is probably differences in comparative advantage. As was the case for plain vanilla swaps, such a contract would normally be arranged via a financial intermediary who is likely to 'warehouse' the swap if a counterpart is not immediately available.

A number of variations of the simple swaps discussed above exist and we discuss below a number of such possibilities. It is possible to combine a plain vanilla swap with a plain deal currency swap so that fixed-rate borrowing in one currency is swapped for floating-rate borrowing in another currency. Another alternative is an amortising swap, whereby the notional principal is reduced in a similar manner to a scheduled amortisation on a loan. Deferred or forward swaps are available and in this case the swap is negotiated now but comes into operation at a later date. Similarly, swaps can be 'extendable' (i.e. one party has the right to extend the life of the swap) or 'puttable' (i.e. one party has the right to terminate the swap). Finally options are available on swaps and these are called 'swaptions'.

A wide range of transactions are available in futures and options markets including both defensive and speculative. It might be expected therefore that price anomalies between and within the various securities and options would be quickly eliminated so that market prices would reflect all available information; that is, the market would be efficient. It is to this aspect that we turn in section 13.7, after a consideration of forward rate agreements.

13.6 **Forward rate agreements**

A forward rate agreement (FRA) is very similar to the interest rate futures discussed in section 13.3. It is an agreement in which two parties agree on the level of an interest rate to be paid on a notional deposit for a specific maturity at some specified time in the future. For example, a contract could be arranged for an agreed interest rate to be applied for, say, a six-month deposit commencing in three months' time. This particular contract would be quoted as 'three against nine months'. As in the case of interest rate futures, the deposit itself cannot be exchanged, so cash settlement is practised. Settlement takes place at the commencement of the contract, after three months in our example. The actual settlement is the difference between the interest rate agreed in the contract and a reference rate, which is normally LIBOR. If LIBOR is higher on the settlement date than the agreed rate then the buyer of the FRA receives from the seller the gap between the two rates (assuming of course that LIBOR is the reference rate). Conversely if the agreed rate is lower than LIBOR, the buyer pays the seller the gap between LIBOR and the agreed rate. In effect then, a FRA is an OTC interest rate futures contract.

We now discuss briefly the nature of the FRA market. FRAs are usually traded for standard periods such as three, six, nine or twelve months. The market is primarily an inter-bank market although banks do conclude a number of agreements with their customers. FRAs are predominantly a US dollar market although contracts are specified in other currencies. Individual contracts are quite large, with agreements for $20 million being quite common by late 1985 and some contracts amounting to $50 million (Cross report [BIS, 1986]). London is one of the main centres of the market and the Cross report estimated that about 40 per cent of total FRA market activity occurred in London in 1985.

Forward rate agreements are popular as a means of managing interest rate risk. Thus, in the example quoted above, the buyer of the FRA has protected himself/herself against a rise in interest rates as represented by the reference rate. Whatever happens to market rates of interest in three months' time, the buyer has locked himself/herself into the agreed rate. The position for the seller is the converse. The seller has been assured of receiving the agreed rate, again irrespective of what happens to the reference rate. Both parties have purchased interest rate certainty and have given up the chance of random gains or losses. In other words it is a risk-averse strategy. For the policy to work the reference rate must be chosen to be representative of interest rates in general, hence the choice of LIBOR. Clearly, FRAs also offer the opportunity of speculating against future interest rate movements.

We now demonstrate the calculation of payments on FRAs. The standard formula is:

$$\pi = P \times (S\text{-}R) \times (m/\text{year})/(1 + S(m/\text{year}))$$

where π is the payment to be made to the buyer by the seller if S is $> R$, or to the seller if S is $< R$, S is the reference rate at the settlement date and R the agreed rate; m is the number of days in the FRA agreement. For the purpose of calculation, a year can consist of either 365 days (UK or Australia) or 360 days (e.g. US). Note that the payment is discounted by the market rate of interest (S) for the length of the FRA agreement because the payment is made at the commencement of the contract.

To illustrate this formula consider the example quoted at the beginning of this section ('three against nine months') and assume that the agreed rate was 7 per cent and LIBOR 8 per cent on the settlement day and the agreement was for $1,000,000. The buyer would receive from the seller of the FRA the following amount:

$$\pi = \frac{1{,}000{,}000 \times (0.08\text{-}0.07) \times (182/360)}{(1 + 0.08(182/360))}$$
$$= \$4859.03$$

The buyer of the FRA has successfully locked himself/herself into a rate of 7 per cent at the end of the FRA period. This can easily be seen from the following calculations:

borrowing at LIBOR:
$1,000,000 @ 8 per cent for 182 days = 40444.44
less receipt on FRA invested until end of agreement:
$4859.03 \times \{1+0.08(182/360)\}$ = 5,055.55
net payment = 35,388.89
borrowing cost at 7 per cent:
$1{,}000{,}000 \times 0.07(182/360)$ = 35,388.89

This numerical example demonstrates that the buyer of the FRA has, in effect, a fixed-rate loan at 7 per cent. Similarly, the seller has supplied a loan at a fixed rate of 7 per cent. In this example, the buyer has gained and the seller lost compared with transactions at LIBOR in three months' time. If interest rates had fallen, the loss would have been borne by the buyer of the FRA. The significant point is that both parties have guaranteed themselves the fixed rate of 7 per cent for their respective transactions.

13.7 **The efficiency of derivatives markets**

Futures and options are derivative markets, so their prices are a function of the anticipated movements in the price of the underlying cash market asset. It is therefore possible to impute equilibrium prices from the prices of options and futures. Efficiency requires that these imputed prices should provide accurate forecasts. The literature on the efficiency of these markets is more limited than that for the cash markets and so our survey of the evidence is more restricted. We describe studies of the role of options prices in the stock market and foreign currency markets, and futures in relation to the foreign currency markets and the US Treasury bill futures market.

The method adopted by Manaster and Rendleman [1982] in respect to the stock market was to use option prices to calculate the market's implied equilibrium stock price using the Black–Scholes formula for close-of-market option prices on all listed options exchanges for the period 26 April 1973 to 30 June 1976 (approximately 37,000 observations). This price was compared with another estimate of the equilibrium price given by the actual observed stock price and the divergence between these two estimates of the unobservable equilibrium price calculated. If this divergence is related to future movements in stock price then there is a suggestion that option prices contain some information not contained in the observed price. Manaster and Rendleman found that a relationship does exist between these two variables but simulation of an 'ex ante' trading rule suggested that this information was not sufficient to generate significant economic profits.

The method used by Manaster and Rendleman was adopted by Tucker [1987] for a study of the foreign exchange market using the implied exchange rates in comparison with the forward rate to derive a profitable trading strategy. The database consisted of 608 observations of options for sterling, Deutschmark, Swiss franc, and Japanese yen over the period November 1983 to August 1984. The assumption of interest rate parity and the observed forward rate were incorporated into the calculation of the implied equilibrium exchange rate. This resulted in a trading rule which suggested that when the implied spot rate is greater than the observed spot rate, then the currency options market assessment is that the forward rate is underpriced, so the currency should be bought forward. In a result similar to that obtained by Masters and Rendleman, Tucker also found that, whilst the deviation between the observed and implied spot rates was a statistically significant determinant of future returns, this information was insufficient to generate significant economic profits.

Cavanaugh [1987] looked at the potential to use futures contract prices to generate profits. The data represented daily changes in the logarithm of futures prices for delivery of currency on specific days. Fifteen series for the Canadian dollar and sterling were examined by Cavanaugh and he found evidence of serial correlation. Tests of simulated trading strategies suggested that this dependence could have been exploited by members of the exchange to generate profits in excess of those obtained by a policy of buy and hold. Because of the higher costs of trading involved, it was also suggested that these opportunities for profit could not have been exploited by non-members.

Elton *et al.* [1984] based their study on intra-day quotations for Treasury bills (cash and futures) for the period 6 January 1976 through to 22 December 1982. Elton *et al.* note that an investor can purchase an N-day Treasury bill in either of two ways using the futures market:

(i) purchase an N-day Treasury bill in the cash market,
(ii) purchase a $(91+N)$-day Treasury bill in the cash market and sell a Treasury bill in the futures market for delivery in N days, then deliver the $(91+N)$-day bill against the futures contract.

An efficient market implies that the returns on the two strategies should be the same after allowance for transaction costs. Three strategies are examined. First, there is the simple strategy of purchasing the lower-priced instrument. Second, an arbitrage strategy could be followed whereby the lower-priced instrument is purchased and this is financed by shorting the higher-priced instrument. The third strategy examined was a swap, whereby holders of the higher-priced instrument liquefied their holdings and used the proceeds to purchase the lower-priced instrument. Elton *et al.* found that profits can be made from all three strategies, which suggests that the US Treasury bill futures market is not perfectly efficient. Since the study did not depend on any assumptions concerning an equilibrium model, these are direct tests of efficiency rather than joint tests of efficiency and a particular equilibrium model as was the case for the earlier tests discussed.

Finally we mention assessment of market efficiency through an examination of the volatility of option prices. It is possible to derive an estimate of the expected volatility of option prices through use of the Black–Scholes model. All the other variables in the model are known so it is relatively easy to calculate the implied volatility and compare this figure with the actual volatility observed in the market. A number of studies have been carried out using this method and the general conclusion is that the implied measure of volatility is biased (see e.g. Beckers [1981], Gemmill [1986] and Gwylim and Buckle [1994]). While this does not prove the market is inefficient, it does tend towards the rejection of the combined hypotheses, (i) that the Black–Scholes model is appropriate for the valuation of option prices and (ii) that the market is efficient. Unfortunately it does not suggest which (or perhaps both) is irrelevant.

13.8 **Conclusion**

We have surveyed the development of the financial futures markets in London and find that these markets have grown rapidly. The conditions for this rapid growth, that is, the observed volatility of asset prices in the related cash markets, are likely to continue and use of these markets is therefore likely to grow both in volume and number of securities traded in the future as they offer traders some opportunity to hedge against adverse price movements. The question of the efficiency of these markets is, like the other markets surveyed, an open question. In this connection it is relevant that many of these markets are relatively new and that the operators may still be on a learning curve. Finally, as we have noted in the main body of the text, the development of derivative markets has increased the risk attached to the operations of banks. This raises the question of how far prudential control of banks by the authorities can control such risks. This aspect is discussed in chapter 17.

Chapter 14

Managing risk via the financial markets

14.1 **Introduction**

In this chapter we survey the various methods that are open to traders to manage risk. The risks we are concerned with arise in connection with unforeseen changes in exchange rates and interest rates. Quite obviously a rise in interest rates raises both costs to borrowers and also returns to lenders. Similarly, changes in exchange rates alter the domestic currency equivalent of foreign currency. This is easily demonstrated by reference to the sterling equivalent of $500,000 at exchange rates of $1.95 per £1 and $2.0 per £1. At the former rate the sterling equivalent is £256,410 but only £250,000 at the latter rate. Thus, a person making a payment denominated in dollars benefits as sterling appreciates from $1.95 to $2.0 per £1 but the recipient of a payment denominated in dollars loses out. This causes problems for the traders. In a similar way changes in interest rates cause problems for the borrower and lender when these are made at floating rates of interest.

In this chapter we discuss how firms may attempt to manage this risk. This type of risk has increased in severity since the beginning of the 1970s owing to the increasing volatility of prices on security markets. This is demonstrated in figures 14.1 and 14.2, which show changes in volatility in representative exchange and interest rates since 1964. In the case of figure 14.1, exchange rate volatility for the $/£ exchange rate is represented by the annual standard deviation of percentage monthly changes. The picture shown before 1970 is one of relative stability, with the exception of the

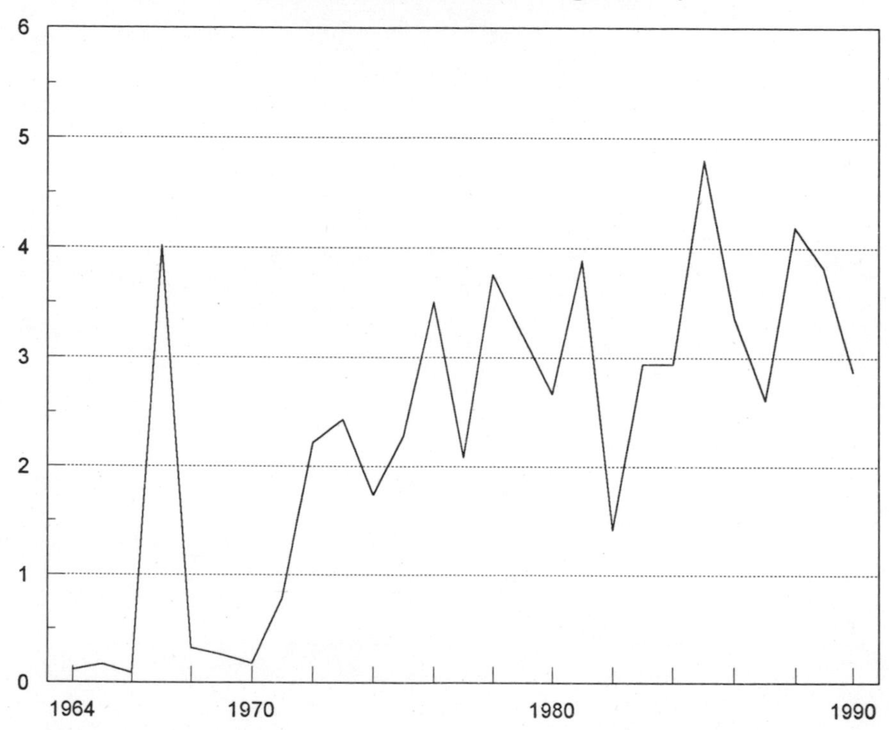

Figure 14.1

year 1967, when sterling was devalued. With the change from fixed to floating exchange rates at the beginning of the 1970s a steep increase in volatility can be observed and this increase persisted until 1990. Interest rate volatility is also measured by the annual standard deviation of monthly changes. It seems inappropriate to use percentage changes when the level of the rate itself is subject to such a range of values and the cost/benefit to the trader depends on the absolute magnitude of the change. The changes themselves depicted in figure 14.2 are more volatile than those for exchange rates shown in figure 14.1 but generally interest rate volatility was more pronounced in the 1970s and 1980s than during the 1960s. This is

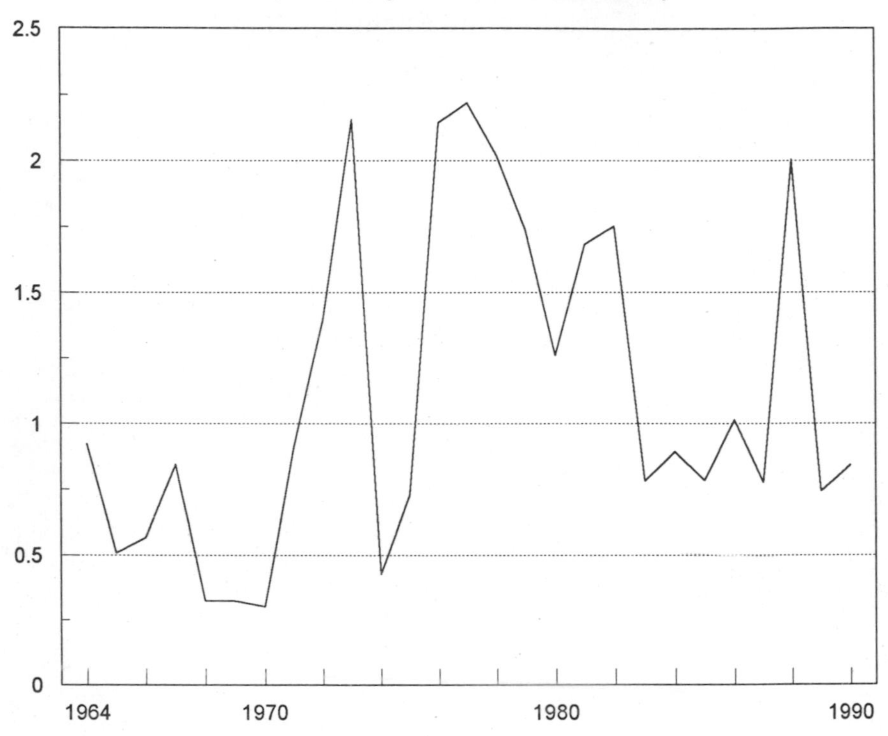

Figure 14.2

particularly true of the late 1970s and early 1980s. The general picture revealed by these two figures is then one of increasing volatility of exchange and interest rates, which in turn enhanced the uncertainties faced by firms.

In section 14.2 we discuss in more detail the precise nature of exchange and interest rate risk before proceeding in section 14.3 to discuss how firms can use internal methods of managing exchange rate risk. In section 14.4 we discuss external methods of managing exchange rate risk and in section 14.5 the management of interest rate risk. Our conclusions are presented in section 14.6.

14.2 **Nature of risk**

Exchange rate risk can arise in a number of different ways. First, there is transaction risk, which arises because the exchange rate has changed between the date of the commitment and the date the payment is made or received. For the exporter uncertainty is increased by the possibility of exchange rate changes if the commodity is invoiced in foreign currency and costs are primarily defined in terms of domestic currency. A similar problem arises for importers, who find the domestic currency costs of their inputs denominated in foreign currency rising and falling in an unpredictable manner. This raises the possibility of unforeseen windfall losses or profits, making foreign trade considerably more risky than domestic trade. It also makes it difficult for firms engaged in foreign trade to quote prices for fear of exchange rate changes altering costs. It is important to define when this risk is incurred. It arises from the date the commitment is entered into. In the case of exports, this dates from the time the price quotation has been communicated to the purchaser. This may be a special quotation or it may date from the time a price list is circulated to actual or prospective customers. In a similar manner for importers, the risk dates from the time they have communicated their acceptance of the purchase of the goods from the foreign company. It is also important to realise that, in the case when the trade is priced in one currency and payment is to be made in another, it is the currency in which the good is priced that is subject to exchange rate risk. If, for example, payment is to be made in dollars, then if both the domestic currency and that used as the unit of account move against the dollar in the same proportion, then no extra exchange rate risk is involved.

The second type of exposure to exchange rate changes is defined as translation risk. This arises when it is necessary to value overseas assets and liabilities for their incorporation into a consolidated balance sheet. If a company has a net surplus or deficit of assets defined in non-domestic currencies, then the balance sheet valuation will change as the relevant exchange rate alters. This particular exposure would not pose serious difficulties if the changes in the exchange rates were purely random around a relatively constant value. In fact since the abandonment of fixed exchange rates in 1972, long swings in exchange rates have been observed. Again, the nature of the commitment of the asset or liability is relevant. The translation exposure on a short-term liability or asset which is likely to be realised in the fairly near future (say one to five years) is similar to transaction exposure since their renewal might occur at the time of an unfavourable exchange rate. Therefore potential serious translation risk exists for the firm unless these risks are hedged. In contrast, permanent investment in subsidiaries can be treated as non-renewable and therefore impose a much lower incidence of exposure, though this could be serious if the currency in which the asset/liability is priced has shown a long-trend movement against the domestic currency.

The third type of exposure is economic exposure. In this case changes in exchange rates alter the relative prices of exports and imports. Over time this can adversely affect the position of firms where exchange rates have moved against them or alternatively help those firms whose products are made relatively cheaper by the exchange rate change. This type of exposure is of a long-term nature and is brought about by changes in the volume of sales following a change in the exchange rate. One example of this type of exposure is the pricing of oil in dollars. Thus, if the domestic currency depreciates against the dollar, the price of oil rises, adversely affecting those companies whose products have a large oil component. It should be emphasised that the exchange rate which matters for international trade is the real exchange rate, which may be defined as the nominal rate corrected for price changes. Thus, if nominal rates always moved to correct differing rates of inflation in the countries concerned then the dangers arising from economic exposure would be considerably reduced. In fact there is a considerable volume of evidence suggesting that purchasing power parity does not exist in the short run so that changes in real exchange rates do occur. There is little a company can do to protect itself against this type of risk except to diversify its products and production centres.

The final type of risk can be termed hidden exposure. A firm may not be directly affected by exchange rate changes since its products may be sold entirely to domestic customers and its raw materials bought from domestic producers. Despite this concentration on the domestic market, the firm would be exposed to indirect transaction and economic risk via one of its suppliers. Similarly, exchange rate change may beneficially affect potential competitors from abroad. An alternative form of indirect exposure can arise from the operation of a subsidiary which is itself affected by exchange rate changes in a third market even if the currencies of the principal and its subsidiary are linked together by fixed exchange rates.

So far we have concentrated on exchange rate exposure, but interest rate exposure may be analysed in the same way. Transaction exposure occurs through changing interest payments or receipts following a change in the interest rate structure. Translation exposure can occur through changes in the value of financial assets held originating from changes in interest rates. This is particularly applicable to the position of investment institutions which hold large volumes of long-term financial securities. Economic exposure arises from changes in interest rates, which affect the general business environment as well as having an impact on firms according to the degree of leverage, that is, the proportion of capital raised by way of loans as distinct from equity finance. Thus, a rise in interest rates will reduce consumer demand and therefore, generally, raise the cost of investment and impose costs on particular firms which have undertaken to raise finance by way of loans subject to interest rate adjustment.

In the following section we discuss how firms may reduce exchange rate exposure by methods internal to the firm and in section 14.4 the role of methods external to the firm.

14.3 Managing exchange rate risk: internal methods

A number of methods exist to manage exchange rate risk which are internal to the firm. These include (i) doing nothing, (ii) forecasting exchange rate movements, (iii) invoicing or accepting invoices denominated only in domestic currency, and (iv) operating a foreign currency bank account. In summary, the individual firm has a choice of doing nothing or hedging. The first option offers the lowest cost but the least protection against exchange rate exposure whereas hedging offers the highest degree of protection but also the highest cost because of the number of transactions involved.

The first method of managing exchange rate risk is therefore to do nothing and accept the spot rate at the time the payment is made or received. Appeal to the efficient markets hypothesis suggests that the current spot rate may well be the best available forecast of the future spot rate. In this case the most profitable policy for the firm would be to rely on the future spot rate for conversion of the foreign currency. Two problems arise with this approach. First, there is a distinct possibility that the foreign exchange market does not conform to the efficient markets hypothesis and that therefore the current spot rate is not the 'best' forecast of future exchange rates. Second, the firm may value certainty or near certainty of the domestic currency equivalent of the foreign currency receipt or payment, or in other words it may be risk averse in this respect. To illustrate this point, a firm is able to plan its pricing policy if it knows in advance the sterling value of future imports and exports. This may well be preferable to a trading system that lowers the average domestic currency cost of imports and raises the average domestic currency receipts for exports if this policy involves relatively large gains and losses around the average. It is quite possible that the firm, in these circumstances, may place a higher value on certainty than profitability in areas where it lacks expertise.

The policy of relying on the future spot rate to convert foreign currency into domestic currency is really nested in the second option, that of forecasting. In reality, doing nothing is equivalent to using the current spot rate as the optimal forecast of future spot exchange rates. It may, however, be the view of the firm that it can improve on the current spot rate as a predictor so that it forecasts the future pattern of spot exchange rates itself. The policy for the firm to manage exchange rate risk would then be to forecast and to choose between the use of internal and external methods of managing the risk in the light of a comparison of its internal forecasts and the constellation of market spot rates, forward rates and option prices. In a similar manner the firm could speed up payments in foreign currency (or purchase of the foreign currency) when the domestic currency was expected to depreciate and retard conversion of foreign currency receipts into domestic currency. The converse behaviour would occur when the domestic currency was expected to appreciate. This overall strategy of forecasting would be consistent with the view that the foreign exchange market does not conform to the efficient markets hypothesis. Apart from the comments made above with respect to risk aversion, the strategy of forecasting the future pattern of exchange rates also suffers from the defect that it requires resources to develop the expertise necessary to provide accurate forecasts. The firm may feel that its available resources are more profitably directed towards its primary functions.

The third internal method is to require invoices to be denominated in domestic currency. In this case there is no exchange rate exposure as far as the transaction component is concerned. However, this exposure has not been eliminated but rather transferred to the foreign purchaser or supplier of the goods. It is also more than likely that the foreign purchaser of goods would not be willing to accept invoices denominated in the domestic currency of the supplier and, given the existence of competition, this would be likely to cause loss of orders. In effect, transaction exposure has been changed into economic exposure.

The final internal method of managing exchange rate risk is to operate foreign currency bank accounts. Thus, as long as receipts and payments are in balance over a reasonable period of time, the exposure on receipts would match and offset the exposure on payments in a specific foreign currency. This type of account could also be allowed to run into deficit by way of an overdraft for a short period of time provided this overdraft was eliminated by future receipts of that currency. This type of risk management has only a limited application since it does require receipts and payments of that currency to cancel each other out over a reasonably short period of time. A persistent balance, particularly a persistently growing balance (either in deficit or surplus), leaves the firm open to exchange rate exposure on both a transaction and a translation basis.

It was seen that internal methods offer the firm only limited scope to manage exchange rate risk, so we now turn to discussing the external methods open to the firm.

14.4 Managing exchange rate risk: external methods

In this section we discuss how a firm might manage exchange rate risk by having recourse to the financial institutions and markets. A number of such methods exist and these are the use of (i) the forward exchange market, (ii) temporary foreign currency loans and deposits, (iii) forfaiting, (iv) options, (v) futures and (vi) back-to-back loans. We do not consider in this section the use of currency futures because they seem to play a less important role in the management of exchange rate risk than in the case of other financial risks. However, a brief discussion of the nature of currency futures is provided in chapter 13, section 13.3.

Forward contracts

We discussed the forward exchange market in chapter 11, where it was seen that it is possible to purchase or sell foreign currency for delivery at a future date at a rate agreed at the time of the transaction. For example, if a trader was due to receive $500,000 in three months' time, he could sell the $500,000 forward for sterling, thus fixing the rate for conversion into sterling in three months' time. Clearly, this method of managing risk provides the trader with certainty of the domestic currency equivalent of the foreign currency receipts or payments. For example, if the relevant forward rate was $1.9398 per £1, then the sterling value of the $500,000 is £257,758.53. Again, it is worthwhile emphasising that the firm does not make a profit by trading in the forward exchange market. At the time of the conversion out of or into foreign currency the spot rate may be higher or lower than the agreed forward rate of $1.9398 per £1. In fact our survey of the empirical evidence on the efficiency of the forward rate as a predictor of the future spot rate suggests that the forward rate will deviate from the future spot rate because of the existence of a risk premium. In other words, the trader will on balance pay a premium to the provider of the forward exchange as a compensation for the transfer of risk. Thus, the trader's gains arise purely from knowing what the rate will be, that is, he has purchased certainty, which, in the case of the above example, means he is sure that he can convert the $500,000 into £257,758.53. Even here a caveat must be raised. The certainty is obtained only provided the second party (i.e. the person buying or selling the goods) does not default. If she fails to complete her part of the transaction, the original trader is left with a forward contract not matched by a future spot receipt or payment so that he then has a foreign exchange rate exposure.

A further restriction on a straightforward contract is that it applies to a fixed date whereas in many commercial transactions the precise date of receipt of or payment in foreign currency is uncertain. One way around this is to choose an option date forward contract. This provides the right to buy or sell foreign currency up to a particular date. The disadvantage with this type of purchase is that the bank will offer the contract at the rate most favourable to itself. Thus, for a contract to sell sterling for an option contract for three months forward, the bank would select the highest rate out of the spot and individual outright forward rates up to three months. Conversely, in the case of an option date forward contract for the bank to purchase sterling, it would apply the lowest of the relevant rates. The trader can mitigate the impact of the adverse (from his point of view) selection of rates by entering into overlapping option date forward contracts so that, for example, receipts of foreign currency expected in instalments over the next three months might be covered by an option forward contract for one month for a proportion of the total receipts and the balance by way of an option forward contract for two to three months. A further restriction may occur because the forward market for the desired currency is very thin or, in the extreme, non-existent. This may be overcome by exercising two forward contracts. In the case of a future receipt of a thinly traded currency, for example, it may be possible, given the importance of the dollar in international financial transactions, (i) to sell dollars forward for domestic currency and (ii) simultaneously to buy dollars forward for the thinly traded currency. By this method the firm has achieved an indirect forward sale of the currency concerned.

Temporary foreign currency deposits and loans

A firm can use temporary foreign deposits and loans to achieve the same degree of protection against transaction exposure as is afforded by forward transactions. Reverting to the example of the future receipt of $500,000, the firm can achieve protection in the following manner:

(i) borrow $500,000 from a bank for three months at the time of entering into the contract leading to the receipt of dollars;
(ii) convert the dollars into sterling at the current spot exchange rate;
(iii) deposit the sterling received in a three-month interest-bearing sterling deposit.

The dollar loan is then paid off by the $500,000 receipt in three months' time. The sterling equivalent of the $500,000 depends on the two interest rates (the dollar and the sterling deposit) and the spot exchange rate. Since all these rates are known, this strategy fixes the sterling equivalent of the future receipt of dollars. In the case of a payment of $500,000 by a firm, steps (i) to (iii) above are reversed, that is:

(i) borrow for three months the sterling equivalent of the quantity of

dollars which will increase to $500,000 when invested; alternatively the firm could use any spare cash holdings to finance step (ii);
(ii) convert the sterling into dollars at the current spot rate;
(iii) invest the dollar receipts from (ii) above into a three-month interest-bearing dollar deposit.

On maturity of the deposit, the dollars are then used to make the dollar payment. In principle the cost of using this type of strategy should be the same as using the forward exchange market since it is in effect equivalent to covered interest arbitrage discussed in chapter 11 and interest rate parity would imply that no profits can be made through moving funds between various centres.

Forfaiting
The third method of avoiding transaction exposure is to use a technique known as forfaiting. This involves transferring the risk on to a bank by obtaining domestic currency from the bank in return for the transfer of the foreign currency debt to the bank. The most common types of debt instruments transferred are promissory notes and bills of exchange and the usual currencies are Deutschmarks and US dollars. The base interest rate for the transaction would be the relevant eurocurrency rate and, in addition, the bank would charge a commitment fee representing the delay between the agreement and the delivery of the instrument and the risk of exchange rate changes.

Options
Options also offer a method of managing exchange rate risk. As noted in chapter 13, options give the purchaser, in return for a premium, the right to buy (a 'call' option) or the right to sell (a 'put' option) at an agreed exchange rate (the 'striking' price) at a specified date or dates. No obligation is imposed on buyers to exercise the option so they will choose to do so only if it is profitable for them. Remember, the exercise of an option lies entirely in the hands of the purchaser. The writer has no control over whether the option is exercised or not. As was demonstrated in chapter 13, an option contract is analogous to an insurance policy, with the premium for the option representing the premium paid for the policy and the risk insured is the risk of an adverse exchange rate movement, with the purchaser taking all the benefits of a favourable movement. Options are also particularly useful in the case of contingent exposures, for example in the case of a tender in foreign currency. If the firm does not win the contract, there is no need for the foreign currency and the option will be exercised only if it offers the chance of immediate profit because it is 'in the money'. Similarly,

Table 14.1 *Philadelphia Stock Exchange £/$ options (£31,250) (cents per £1)*

Strike price	*Calls*				*Puts*			
	Oct.	*Nov.*	*Dec.*	*March*	*Oct.*	*Nov.*	*Dec.*	*March*
1.875	9.10	9.20	9.33	9.79	–	0.70	1.41	3.56
1.900	6.60	7.04	7.31	8.02	0.04	1.22	2.01	4.56
1.925	4.11	5.17	5.57	6.49	0.07	2.02	2.91	5.71
1.950	1.97	3.61	4.11	5.20	0.29	2.88	4.05	7.06
1.975	0.53	2.43	3.00	4.12	1.37	4.24	5.47	8.55
2.000	0.07	1.65	2.08	–	3.29	5.89	7.11	–
2.025	0.01	1.08	1.56	–	5.67	7.77	8.94	–

the firm may wish to take out options because the precise quantity of foreign exposure is not known, for example in the case of an uncertain volume of sales of goods abroad or in the case of domestic sales requiring imported raw materials. In such cases the firm can use options to provide a hedge against foreign currency exposure.

Over-the-counter options would be arranged as a private contract with a bank and offer the advantage that the conditions attached to the contract exactly match those required by the purchaser. In contrast traded options are standardised and may not therefore match the precise quantity requirements of the purchaser. For example, the sterling options quoted on the Philadelphia Stock Exchange are denominated in units of £31,250. On the other hand they offer the additional benefit of being able to be sold on the market rather than just being exercised or allowed to lapse. The suspension of currency options on LIFFE suggests that the disadvantage of standardised contracts outweighs the advantage of tradeability.

Various option strategies are possible and we use the quotations for December delivery on the Philadelphia Stock Exchange listed in table 14.1 to illustrate them – note in the following examples the spot rate is assumed to be $1.9750 per £1 for illustrative purposes.

In the case of options, the trader has a choice of exercise rates. If he or she purchases, for example, a call option with a strike price of $1.875 per £1 the premium is 9.33 cents, implying a maximum price for the purchase of pounds of $1.9683 per £1 (1.875 + 0.0933). Thus, the trader is sure that the minimum quantity of sterling obtained for a future receipt of $500,000 is £254,026.32. If the spot rate at the time of receipt of the dollars is less than $1.875, then the option will not be exercised and the trader will purchase the sterling in the market at the lower price but losing the option premium. Similarly, at strike prices of $1.975 and $2.025 per £1, the maximum prices rise to $2.005 and $2.0406 respectively. In a similar manner buying put options with strike prices of \$1.875, \$1.975 and \$2.025 per £1 fixes the minimum prices obtained by the sale of sterling at \$1.8609, \$1.9203 and \$1.9356 respectively. It can be seen that the analogy to insurance is very close. The higher the premium paid the greater the degree of protection against the downside risk of adverse changes in the spot exchange rate. This leaves the trader a choice of strategies in which there is a trade-off between protection and cost. More complex strategies are discussed below.

One such strategy goes by the name of a vertical spread, involving the simultaneous purchase and sale of options with different exercise prices. In the case of a vertical bull call spread (so called because of the expectation of rises in the exchange rate) the trader would buy a call option with a strike price of, say, \$1.975 per £1 at a premium of 3.0 cents and write (sell) a call with a higher strike price, say \$2.025 per £1 at a premium of 1.56 cents. Thus, the premium income incurs a loss of 1.44 cents (3.0 - 1.56) or equivalently \$0.0144. At a spot rate below \$1.975 per £1 neither option is exercised and the trader's loss is 1.44 cents. At spot rates between \$1.975 and \$2.025 only the purchased call option is exercised, so the trader benefits from the increasing profitability of this option. At the rate of \$2.025 per £1 the trader's profit (compared with the spot rate) is at a maximum since thereafter any profit on the purchase of the call option is matched on a one-for-one basis by the loss on the option sold. At a spot rate of \$2.025 per £1, the trader's profit (as compared with the spot rate) is given by the profit on the option purchased minus the loss on the premium, that is:

$$\$(2.025 - 1.975) - \$0.0144 = \$0.0356 \text{ or } 3.56 \text{ cents.}$$

In this case the trader has given up the potential unlimited gain above a spot rate of \$2.005 per £1 offered by a simple call option purchase with a strike price of \$1.975 per £1 in return for a lower premium, that is, 1.44 cents as against 3.0 cents. In terms of hedging the trader has ensured a minimum sterling equivalent, for say \$500,000, of £251,332.06 {500,000/(1.975 + 0.0144)} provided the spot exchange rate remains below \$2.025 per £1. As the rate rises above \$2.025 per £1 the trader is fully exposed to potential losses. Traders would use this strategy in the case where they thought that the exchange rate is likely to rise above the current spot rate but not by any great amount.

In an analogous manner a trader who believed that the spot rate was likely to fall from the current level but not to any great extent would buy a put, again say with a strike price of \$1.975 per £1 (premium 5.47 cents) and sell a put with a lower strike price, say \$1.950 per £1 (premium 4.05 cents). At an exchange rate greater than \$1.975 per £1 neither option would be exercised and the trader's loss is limited to the premium deficiency of 1.42 cents per £1. At rates below \$1.975 per £1 but above \$1.950 per £1

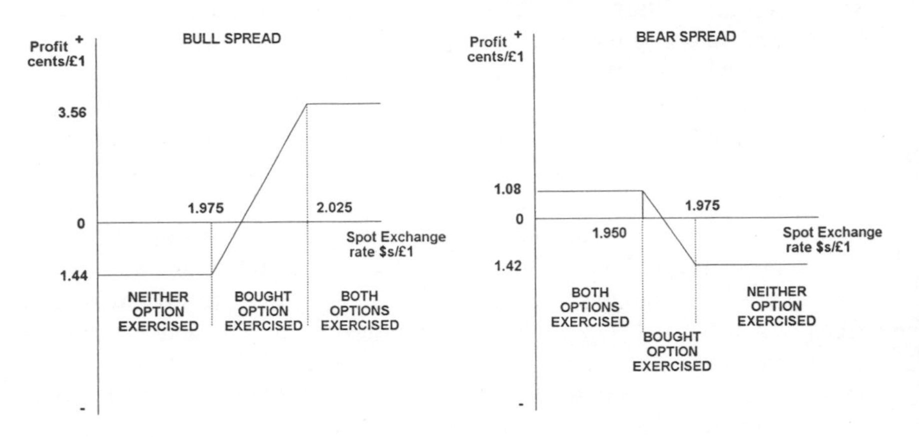

Figure 14.3

only the put option purchased is exercised and below \$1.950 per £1 both options are exercised. Thus, the trader's maximum profit at \$1.950 per £1 is \$0.0108 or 1.08 cents per £1 (\$1.975 - \$1.950 - \$0.0142). Again, the trader has given up the opportunity of obtaining an unlimited profit at rates below \$1.950 per £1 in return for the lower premium of 1.08 cents per £1. In terms of hedging, the trader, who has to make a payment of \$500,000, has ensured a maximum sterling cost of £254,556.56 provided the spot rate remains above \$1.950 per £1 {500,000/(1.975 - 0.0108)}. As the spot rate falls below \$1.950 per £1, the trader is fully exposed to potential losses. This type of strategy is called a vertical bear spread.

The vertical spread strategy is also called a 'collar' because of the restricted range of protection as compared with a traditional option. Note that this restricted range of protection is obtained through payment of a reduced premium. This type of trade can be gainfully used by either a hedger or a speculator. In the case of a hedger, it is no longer a pure hedge since the firm has taken a view on the likely direction and magnitude of future exchange rate movements. A diagrammatic presentation of profit/loss situations is shown in figure 14.3.

The concluding types of option trading strategies examined are concerned with volatility trading. These are (i) straddles, (ii) strangles and (iii) butterflies. In each case the operator takes a view on the likely course of movements in exchange rate volatility and backs this view by entering into an appropriate option strategy. For this reason these strategies are more likely to be adopted by speculators and writers of options than firms using the market as a facility to hedge.

A straddle involves writing or purchasing a call and put option at the same strike price. In the case of a sale of a straddle (sometimes called a short straddle) the writer could, for example, write (sell) a December call and a December put each with a strike price of $1.975 per £1. The combined premium received from the sale would be 8.47 cents per £1 (5.47 + 3.0). At the strike price (i.e. $1.975 per £1) neither option would be exercised. At spot exchange rates below $1.975 per £1, only the put option would be exercised and the break-even point for the writer of the option occurs where the loss on this option is just matched by the combined premium receipts. This occurs at a spot exchange rate of $1.8903 per £1. In a similar way, as the spot exchange rate rises above $1.975 per £1, only the call option is exercised and the break-even rate is $2.0597 per £1 (i.e. $1.975 + $0.0847). Whilst the rate remains within the two bounds (1.975 and 2.0597) the speculator will profit but otherwise faces unlimited loss. This type of trade is likely to be used by a speculator who believes that volatility is not likely to increase to any great extent and it is often therefore called a bear straddle. In contrast, a speculator who believes that volatility is likely to increase will buy a straddle (a 'long' or 'bull' straddle). In this case he or she would purchase a call and put option for the same delivery date and strike price. Using the above example as an illustration the speculator could purchase a December call and put with each with a strike price of $1.975 per £1. In this case he or she pays out the combined premium of 8.47 cents per £1 and this is the maximum loss. The profit is unlimited if the spot exchange rate rises above $2.0597 per £1 or falls below $1.8903 per £1. In both cases of long and short straddles, the speculator is not forming a view as to the direction of the exchange rate movement but rather its volatility or the

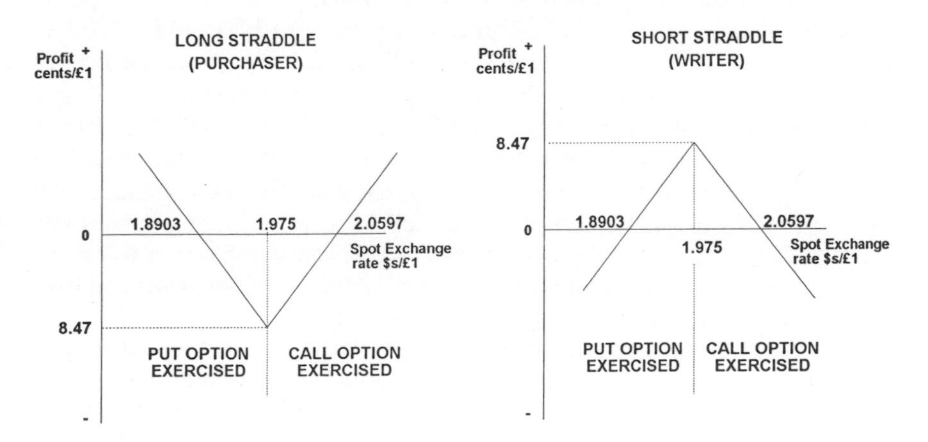

Figure 14.4

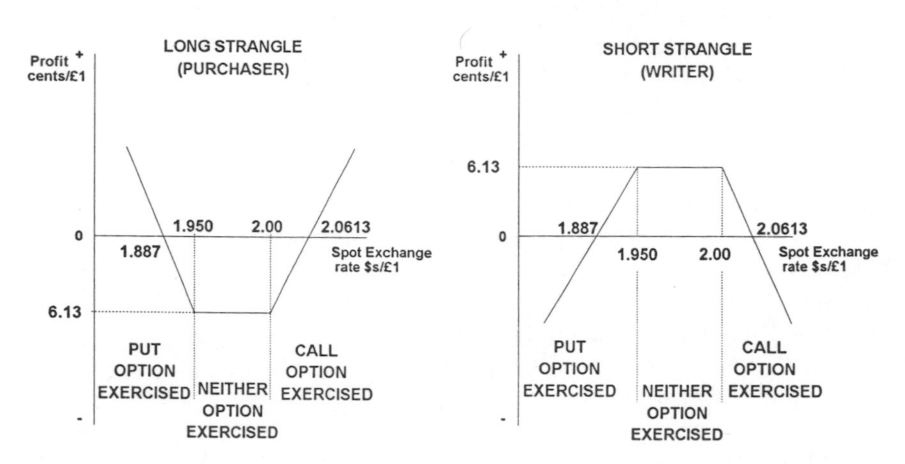

Figure 14.5

likelihood of it moving beyond specified limits. The profit and loss situations for both types of straddle are shown in figure 14.4.

The second type of volatility strategy is a strangle. It is similar to a straddle and has the same underlying rationale but two different strike prices are involved and this lengthens the area of maximum profitability in the case of a short strangle or maximum loss in the case of a long straddle. In the case of a short strangle, the speculator could write a December call with a strike price of $2.000 per £1 (premium 2.08 cents) and a December put with a strike price of $1.950 per £1 (premium 4.05 cents). The combined premium income is 6.13 cents per £1 (2.08 + 4.05). At spot rates below $1.950 per £1 only the put option is exercised so that the break-even point is $1.887 per £1 (1.950 - 0.0613). Between rates of $1.950 and $2.000 per £1, neither option is exercised so the speculator earns a profit of 6.13 cents per £1. At rates above $2.000 per £1, only the call option is exercised and the break-even point is $2.0613 per £1 (2.000 + 0.0613). The case of a long strangle can be illustrated by the same example but in this case the speculator purchases the two options. Consequently her or his maximum loss is given by the combined premium income and positions of profit are given when the spot exchange rate either falls below $1.887 per £1 or rises above $2.0613 per £1. A diagrammatic representation of the profit and loss situations for strangles are shown in figure 14.5.

The final option strategy considered is a butterfly. A butterfly strategy is also similar to a straddle and has the same underlying rationale of trading against movements in the volatility of exchange rates. In this strategy, however, a floor is provided for the maximum loss or a ceiling to the

Table 14.2 *Illustration of the purchase of a butterfly*

	Strike price ($ per £1)	*Premium (cents per £1)*	*Spot rate when exercised ($ per £1)*
In-the-money	1.925	5.57	> 1.925
At-the-money	1.975	3.00	> 1.975
Out-of-the-money	2.025	1.56	> 2.000

maximum gain. Purchase of a butterfly (a long butterfly) entails buying an out-of-the-money call, writing two at-the-money calls and buying an in-the-money call. As an illustration of this strategy the calls purchased could be as shown in table 14.2.

The combined premium income represents a net loss of 1.13 cents. At a spot rate below $1.925 no option is exercised so the maximum loss is the negative premium income, that is, 1.13 cents per £1. Up to a spot rate of $1.975 per £1, only the in-the-money option is exercised so the point of maximum gain is $(1.975 - 1.925 - 0.0113) per £1, that is, $0.0387 per £1 or 3.87 cents per £1. At rates above $1.975 per £1 but below $2.025 per £1 the two at-the-money options (written) are exercised so losses on these offset the profits gained on the in-the-money option purchased. The maximum loss occurs at a spot rate of $2.025 per £1 because after this point the out-of-the-money call is exercised. Consequently the gain on the two call options purchased is matched on a one-for-one basis by the loss on the two call options sold. The maximum loss is therefore the gain on the option with a strike price of $1.1925 per £1 less the loss on the two options written with a strike price of $2.000 less the net premium deficiency: $((2.025-1.925) - 2(2.025-1.975) - 0.0113) per £1, which is $0.0113 per £1 or 1.13 cents per £1.

Selling a butterfly (a short butterfly) would entail the reverse procedure, that is, writing an in-the-money call, buying two at-the-money calls and writing an out-of-the-money call. The profit and loss situation would be precisely opposite to that illustrated for the above example, that is, a maximum loss of 3.87 cents per £1 and a maximum profit of 1.13 cents per £1. The profit and losses for this situation are illustrated in figure 14.6.

As noted above, figures 14.5 and 14.6 illustrate the essential difference between a butterfly and a straddle, that is, the maximum loss or gain is restricted to a fixed amount.

One of the problems for traders using options, as a strategy to manage risk, is that the premium has to be paid in advance, or 'up front' in the jargon. Partly in response to the reluctance to make payments up front, a

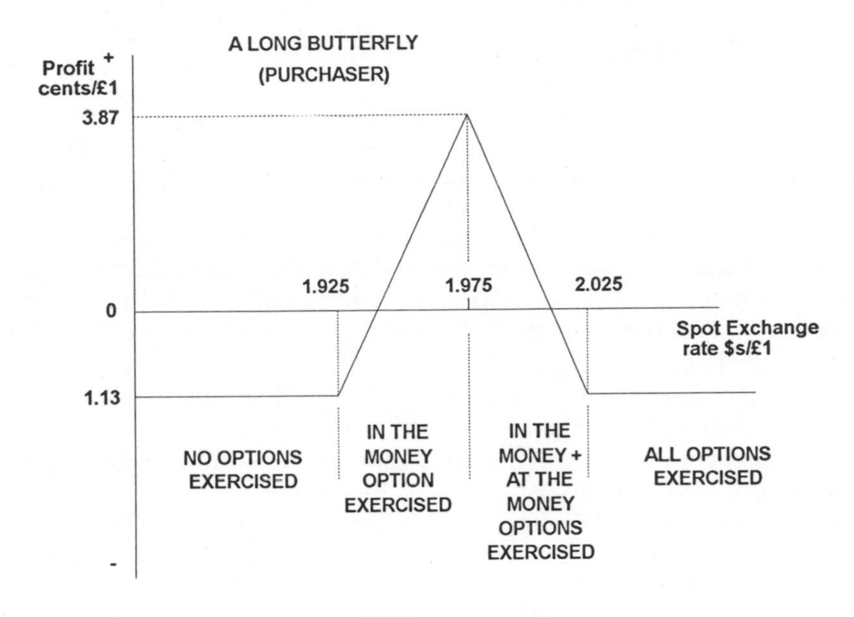
Profit and Loss for a Butterfly
A LONG BUTTERFLY
(PURCHASER)
Profit +
cents/£1
3.87
0
1.13
-
1.925
1.975
2.025
Spot Exchange
rate $s/£1
NO OPTIONS
EXERCISED
IN THE
MONEY
OPTION
EXERCISED
IN THE
MONEY +
AT THE
MONEY
OPTIONS
EXERCISED
ALL OPTIONS
EXERCISED

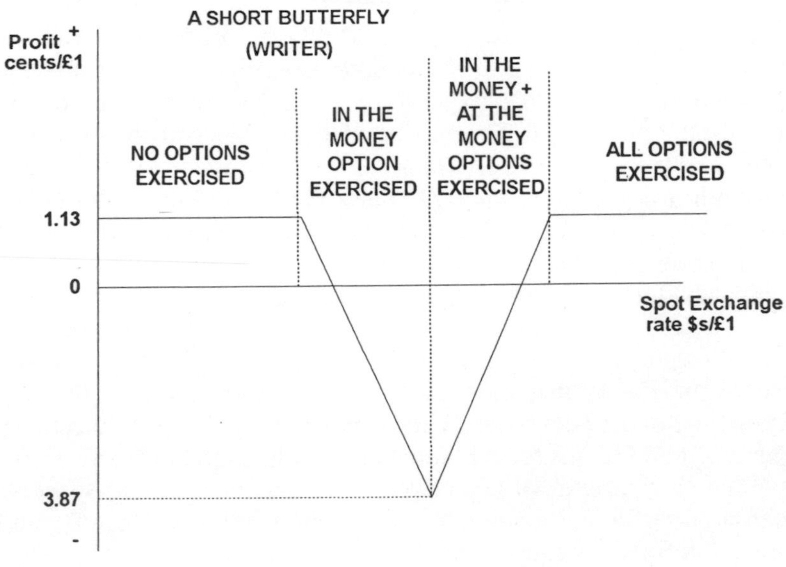
A SHORT BUTTERFLY
(WRITER)
Profit +
cents/£1
1.13
0
3.87
-
NO OPTIONS
EXERCISED
IN THE
MONEY
OPTION
EXERCISED
IN THE
MONEY +
AT THE
MONEY
OPTIONS
EXERCISED
ALL OPTIONS
EXERCISED
Spot Exchange
rate $s/£1

Figure 14.6

number of variants have been developed in the OTC sector. These variants have been given a number of names according to the marketing strategy of the institution itself, but a generic title would be 'hidden premium' options. These are a sort of hybrid between normal forward contracts and options. The trader due to receive dollars would enter into a forward contract to purchase pounds but one with a break point at which the trader could break out of the forward position and transact at the spot rate. No up-front premium is involved as the cost would be incorporated into the forward rate. Clearly, in view of the added protection, the forward rate would be less advantageous than for a standard forward contract; it would be a higher rate in the case of purchases of, or a lower rate in the case of sales of, pounds. As an illustration, consider again the situation of the receipt of $500,000. The normal forward rate discussed earlier was assumed to be $1.9398 per £1. For the illustration of the principle behind hidden premium options, we assume that the rate for a forward contract with a break at $1.90 per £1 is $1.9980 per £1. This gives the trader the right to break the contract if the spot rate at the maturity of the contract is less than $1.90 per £1. If on maturity the spot rate was $1.80 per £1 the following transactions are implied, leaving the trader with net receipts of £264,870.14:

sale of $500,000 at the forward rate (1.9980)	£250,250.25
purchase of $500,000 at the break rate (1.90)	-£263,157.89
purchase of $500,000 at the spot rate (1.80)	£277,777.70
net receipts	£264,870.14

Note that by this strategy, the trader is protected against the loss of falls in the spot rate against the forward rate below the break rate. At the same time the trader is protected against rises in the spot rate above the agreed forward rate. The protection strategy in the case of sale of sterling would be the mirror image of that discussed above for the purchase of sterling. The trader would enter into a contract with an enhanced forward rate but one which provided a break if the spot rate rose above a specified break rate.

Back-to-back loans

The final method of using the market to hedge exchange rate risk is to arrange a back-to-back loan. Back-to-back loans can take two forms: parallel loans or swaps. Multinational corporations use these types of loans for subsidiaries wishing to raise finance in foreign currencies. Assume there are two parent companies, one in the UK and one in the USA, each with a subsidiary in the country of the other parent company. Thus, the UK parent company lends in sterling to the subsidiary of the US company located in the UK and the US parent company lends in dollars to the subsidiary of the

UK company located in the US. Each subsidiary company has a loan and cash denominated in the currency where it operates and has, therefore, avoided exchange rate exposure. If each parent company had borrowed in its domestic currency it would then have to transform the loan into foreign currency for the use of its subsidiary and it would therefore be exposed to exchange rate risk. Swap loans involve the exchange of debts denominated in different currencies. Thus, a firm with easy access to the UK capital market may wish to finance an investment in the US. If it is possible for that firm to find a corresponding US firm which has easy access to the US capital market but wishes to finance a sterling investment, then it is possible for both firms to gain by swapping their respective liabilities for repayment of the debt principal and interest payments. Such parallel and swap loans may be arranged through banks.

Finally, we look at currency exchange agreements, which are in essence similar to swap loans. Returning to the example used to illustrate the parallel loan, the two parent companies would agree to lend to each other, the US company to the UK company in dollars and the UK company to the US company in sterling. These loans would then be passed on to their subsidiaries, and hence each subsidiary has a loan denominated in the desired currency. Swaps are discussed in more detail in chapter 13, section 13.5. The repayment terms including any interest differentials would be agreed at the time of the original loan, thus removing any exposure to subsequent exchange rate movements.

We now turn to examine strategies to manage interest rate risk.

14.5 **Managing interest rate risk**

We shall spend rather less time discussing interest rate risk, not because we regard this type of risk as being of less importance than exchange rate risk but rather because many of the strategies have already been discussed in the previous section. Internal methods of managing interest rate exposure take the form of doing nothing or forecasting with all the inherent problems examined at the beginning of section 14.3. External methods of managing risk include use of the futures market, of options and of interest rate swaps. In chapter 13 section 13.3 we illustrated the position of a company which wished to hedge against a rise in rates of interest by selling a financial futures short-term deposit. We also noted that the hedge may be less than perfect due to a change in basis. We also emphasised that the hedger should sell futures if the company was harmed by rising interest rates but buy futures if its position was adversely affected by falls in interest rates.

As was noted in table 13.3 of chapter 13, a range of interest rate futures are provided, including domestic and foreign rates of interest, short- and long-term rates. This provides a number of possible strategies to manage interest rate exposure. However, a single interest rate contract is likely to involve more than one instance of exposure. Thus, a loan which is to be rolled over every three months for one year involves four instances of, rather than a single, risk. This can be covered by utilising a strip hedge, that is, taking out sales of four futures contracts, one for each time the loan is to be rolled over. This may prove to be difficult if the market for distant futures is illiquid. An alternative strategy is to employ a rolling hedge. Successive hedges are obtained on the earliest interest rate revisions only. An alternative strategy is to take out a 'piled-up' hedge, in which futures amounting to a multiple of the loan would be taken out. Thus, if the interest rate on the loan is to be reassessed four times, futures contracts equal to four times the loan would be sold. These contracts would be closed out and renewed at each of the reassessment dates. The advantage of piled-up hedges is that they avoid distant futures but on the other hand they incur a large number of contracts and therefore commission charges.

Over-the-counter options are provided by some banks and LIFFE also offers options on interest rate futures on some of the most important contracts (see table 13.3 for details). This provides hedging opportunities, in the same way as was discussed for exchange rate exposure in the previous section, for fixing maximum and minimum rates of interest. An interest rate cap gives a borrower an opportunity to purchase an agreement that will compensate the borrower if interest rates rise above a specific level. Similarly, an interest rate floor gives an investor the opportunity to purchase an agreement that will compensate the investor if interest rates fall below a certain level. In return for these facilities the borrower or investor will pay a premium to the seller and this cost can be seen as an insurance against adverse interest rate movements. As an example, consider the case of a company borrowing $10 million from a bank on a floating-rate basis linked to three-month LIBOR. The treasurer is concerned that interest rates may rise over the next three years and so purchases an interest cap at 8 per cent based on three-month LIBOR for a period of three years. If three-month LIBOR rises to 10 per cent on the first settlement date the company would be paid an amount by the seller to compensate for the 2 per cent difference between the cap rate and the LIBOR rate. The cap rate will continue to be checked against LIBOR at each settlement date (every three months) until the end of the three-year period. If interest rates were to fall to say 6 per cent, then the company would receive no benefit under the cap facility but would be able to take advantage of the lower rate on the underlying loan. Thus, the advantages of the cap facility are that the borrower can quantify maximum borrowing costs over the term of the facility and that, unlike futures or fixed-rate funding, the borrower is protected from rising interest rates but is able to benefit from any downturn in rates.

An interest-rate floor is an option contract which compensates investors for falls in interest rates but allows them to take advantage of interest rate rises. A collar, as discussed in the section 14.4, on exchange rate hedging, is effectively a combination of an interest rate cap and floor. One party to the agreement will sell the cap and the other party will sell the floor. A borrower therefore will buy the cap to establish a maximum borrowing cost and simultaneously sell a floor which will set a minimum borrowing cost. The value of the floor will be used either partially or fully to offset the cost of the cap. In practice the value of the floor agreement is usually less than the value of the cap agreement and so a net payment is required. The advantage of the collar agreement over the cap is the reduction (or elimination) of charges. However, this saving is achieved by giving up some part of the gain that could be achieved if rates fall. A collar can also be used by an investor. An investor would buy a floor and sell a cap which would give protection against rates falling below the floor level but by sacrificing some of the potential gain available when rates rise above the cap level.

The preceding discussion of caps, floors and collars related to OTC option contracts. Traded options on interest rate futures can also be used to provide the same sort of protection. With a traded option, instead of the seller of the option compensating the buyer for adverse changes in interest rates, the protection is obtained by first buying an option and then selling before maturity with the net gain providing compensation. For example, a lending floor can be obtained by buying call options that will increase in value if interest rates decline. Assume the option selected is a December 89.00 call with a premium of 0.61. This option achieves a minimum effective lending rate of 10.39 per cent:

Interest rate implied by exercise price =	11.00 per cent (100-89)
less call premium,	-0.61 per cent
= minimum effective lending rate,	10.39 per cent

If the interest rate underlying the option falls before the option expires then the value (premium) of the option will rise. If, say, interest rates fall from 11 per cent to 10 per cent and the call option value increases to 1.00, then the option can be sold and a gain of 1.00 - 0.61 = 0.39 is made. This gain compensates the investor for a fall in the underlying interest rate. The effective lending rate has thus been fixed at 10.39 per cent:

lending rate	= 10.00 per cent
plus gain on option,	0.39 per cent
= effective lending rate,	10.39 per cent

Finally in this section we discuss the nature of interest rate swaps. An interest rate swap entails the exchange by two parties of interest rate payments of a different character based on a notional principal amount. Three types of swap are probably the most important. These are coupon swaps, basis swaps and cross-currency interest rate swaps. In chapter 12 we described the dramatic growth in the interest rate swap market in recent years, partly reflecting the growth in fixed-rate eurobond issues. In chapter 13 we discussed the nature of the coupon swap. The classic example of this type of swap is to exchange a floating-rate loan for a fixed-rate one. This may be carried out to eliminate the risk of changes in interest rates. Note again that the benefit of this strategy is the substitution of certainty for uncertainty. This swap may be carried out directly by the two liability holders or through a bank acting as an intermediary. In the latter case anonymity is preserved. The second type of interest rate swap is a basis swap, where a loan with interest rates based on one key rate is swapped for another loan based on an alternative key rate (e.g. a LIBOR rate for say a local authority rate). In both cases it may be possible for a borrower with a low credit rating to obtain a lower charge than would otherwise be the case. Finally we have examined the nature of the cross-currency interest rate swap in section 14.4.

14.6 **Conclusion**

We have examined a wide range of strategies for firms to manage exposure to risk. Since these risks have increased since the early 1960s it is not surprising that the number of instruments available to hedge risk has also increased. This is just one further example of financial innovation.

Although derivatives can be and are used to manage financial risk, they are not themselves inherently riskless. This is evidenced by the detail in table 14.3, which lists some well publicised examples of companies incurring losses through the use of derivative products.

Table 14.3 *Examples of companies incurring losses through the use of derivative products*

Company	*Estimated loss reported in the media*
Allied Lyons	£150 million
Atlantic Richfield	$22 million
Codelco	$200 million
Proctor and Gamble	$100 million
Metallgesellschaft	$1.3 billion
Barings	£860 million

One of the problems with regard to the use of derivative instruments occurs if such instruments are 'marked to market'. In this case, users of such instruments may incur a significant negative cash flow if the price of the instrument moves against them because margin payments have to be made. Such payments have to be made before maturity of the futures contract and hence before any profit/loss on the derivatives contracts have been offset by those on the underlying cash market transaction. The case of Metallgesellschaft (MG) is interesting in this connection. An American subsidiary of MG used futures contracts to manage the potential risk of rising oil prices in the face of fixed-price sales over a number of years in the future. In fact oil prices fell substantially and the company was faced with extremely heavy margin payments, leading to liquidity strains. These margin payments led the company to wind up the contracts and incur substantial cash losses, as indicated in table 14.3

The existence of losses on the scale noted in table 14.3 has also led to discussion over whether derivative markets should be more tightly regulated. It is a salient feature of the losses noted in table 14.3 that, with the sole exception of Barings, all were in respect of non-financial companies. It would seem reasonable to assume that companies would operate in such markets only if they possessed the necessary financial expertise to comprehend the risks involved. In any case, customers who feel they have been misled or ill-advised in any way have recourse to legal action. In fact it is reported in the media that such action is currently being undertaken by Procter and Gamble and Atlantic Richfield. It has been reported that CS First Boston has made repayments to three customers totalling $40 million in respect of derivatives advice it provided. Consequently no further prudential control would seem to be necessary to protect customers. The case of regulating banks' operations in derivative markets raises different issues, which are considered in chapter 17.

Chapter 15

The single European market in financial services

15.1 **Introduction**

The general principle of a single market for Europe was embodied in the Treaty of Rome in 1957. However, little was done in terms of achieving this over the 1960s and 1970s as the individual member states of the European Community (now European Union, EU) concentrated attention on their own domestic economic problems. The impetus for achieving the objective of a single market came in 1985 with the publication of an EU Commission white paper *Completing the Internal Market*, promoted by the then Vice President of the Commission, Lord Cockfield. Momentum was achieved by setting a target date of 1992 for completion of thc single market. To this end the white paper detailed 300 measures designed to remove physical, technical and fiscal barriers to trade within the Community. The introduction of the principle of qualified majority voting in the EU Council on most issues, whereby no individual member state can veto a proposal, also helped to speed up the decision-making process. This is illustrated by the passing of the Single European Act in 1987, soon after the white paper.

The underlying objective for a single European market is to benefit consumers and producers by a variety of methods, but most importantly by reducing costs through the removal of non-tariff barriers to trade, increased competition and the ability to operate on a larger scale, thereby obtaining the benefits of economies of scale. These developments should in turn promote greater efficiency of firms operating within the EU and thus strengthen their ability to compete in world markets, with the prospect of increased growth in EU economies.

In this chapter we will examine in section 15.2 the progress so far in achieving a single market in financial services. In section 15.3 we will discuss some of the likely effects of a single market in financial services for UK-based financial intermediaries. Finally, in section 15.4 we will briefly consider the complementary developments towards achieving economic and monetary union within the EU.

15.2 A single European market in financial services

Progress has been slower in tackling barriers to trade in financial services than in physical goods. This is despite the economic importance of financial services, which is estimated at eight per cent of EU GDP (higher in the UK – see table 2.7). Also, the removal of barriers to trade in financial services will have effects wider than those directly impinging on the financial services industry, given the important role of the financial system in encouraging and facilitating investment and hence economic growth.

The main barriers to trade in financial services are:

(i) market entrance requirements,
(ii) differences in prudential standards,
(iii) differences in rules of market conduct.

In terms of (i), a basic right of establishment already exists in the EU for providers of financial services. That is, a firm from one EU member state can set up an operation in another EU member state and compete on an equal basis with other firms in that state, provided it establishes local offices in conformity with the rules and regulations of that member state. This falls short of a true single market and recent negotiations have been aimed at giving the right to firms to trade financial services throughout the EU on the basis of a single authorisation 'passport' from their home member state. To ease doubts about the completeness or rigour of home country regulatory regimes, attention is being directed at harmonising key prudential standards. This harmonisation aims to remove (i) host country concerns about the possible failure of foreign firms and (ii) concerns about 'unlevel playing fields', whereby a firm operating in one member state but subject to lighter and therefore lower-cost regulation under its home country regulations may obtain an unfair advantage in the market in which it operates.

The main headings under which financial services are being liberalised by EU legislation are collective investments, banking, investment services and insurance. We now consider the principal developments to date in each of these areas.

Collective investments

The EU directive harmonising the laws relating to the authorisation of undertakings for collective investment in transferable securities (UCITS), which for the UK refers to unit trusts, was implemented in 1989. Once authorised at home, UCITS will be free to market their units anywhere in the EU subject only to compliance with local marketing regulations.

Banking

The first attempt at harmonisation of banking across the EU was the First Banking Directive of 1977. This laid down minimum legal requirements for credit institutions to be authorised in member states and created a basic right of establishment. The Second Banking Coordination Directive of 1989, which came fully into effect at the beginning of 1993, takes the harmonisation process considerably further. Rather than large-scale harmonisation, the aim of the Second Directive was to establish the minimum harmonisation of prudential standards to entitle a credit institution authorised in one

Table 15.1 *Business which is integral to banking and included within the scope of mutual recognition according to the Second Banking Coordination Directive*

1	Deposit taking and other forms of borrowing
2	Lending, including: consumer credit mortgage lending factoring trade finance
3	Financial leasing
4	Money transmission services
5	Issuing and administering means of payment (credit cards, travellers' cheque and banker's draft)
6	Guarantees and commitments
7	Trading for own account or for account of customers in: money market instruments (bills, CDs, etc.) foreign exchange financial futures and options exchange and interest-rate instruments securities
8	Participation in share issues and the provision of services related to such issues
9	Advice to undertakings on capital structure, industrial strategy and related issues
10	Money broking
11	Portfolio management and advice
12	Safekeeping of securities
13	Credit reference services
14	Safe custody services

Source: Annex to Second Banking Coordination Directive.

member state to provide core banking services throughout the EU under the passport scheme, outlined above. The core banking services referred to are listed in table 15.1.

In addition to the Second Banking Directive, which provides for authorisation, a number of related directives provide harmonisation of regulations. The 1989 Solvency Ratio Directive establishes an EU-wide rule that a bank's capital must be at least eight per cent of its risk-adjusted assets and off-balance-sheet transactions (in line with the Basle accord of 1988 – see chapter 17, section 17.4). Capital is defined by the 1989 Own Funds Directive. The Directive on the Monitoring and Control of Large Exposures states that from January 1994 a limit of 40 per cent of capital will be imposed for exposures to a single client, which will be reduced over time to 25 per cent. In addition, the aggregate amount of large exposures (those exceeding 10 per cent of capital) may not exceed 800 per cent of such capital. Finally, a directive on deposit guarantee schemes provides for mandatory insurance for all EU deposit-taking institutions. The coverage per depositor is set at a minimum of ECU 20,000 (ECU 15,000 until 1999).

Investment services

The Investment Services Directive (ISD) of 1993 aims to give non-bank investment firms the same opportunities for conducting business in the EU as banks already enjoy under the Second Banking Directive. In addition, the Capital Adequacy Directive (CAD) of 1993 fulfils a similar function to the bank regulatory directives listed above and provides a similar framework for regulating investment firms as well as the securities business of banks. Both these directives come into force in January 1996.

The main driving force behind the harmonisation provisions of the ISD and CAD is the need to ensure competitive equality between universal banks (where banking and investment business is mixed) and non-bank investment firms. Those countries with a long tradition of universal banking, such as Germany, favoured a conservative capital adequacy regime whereas countries such as the UK feared that if bank-style capital regulations were imposed on non-bank investment firms they would be placed at a competitive disadvantage compared with non-European firms. Indeed, there is a case for lighter capital controls for investment firms than for banks. The emphasis for banks is on solvency and hence capital is important (see chapter 17) whereas the emphasis for investment firms is on liquidity, reflecting the ability to scale down their activities.

The main structures available for a regulatory regime for banking and securities firms are set out by Dale [1994]. At one extreme we have the Glass–Steagall model: the US arrangements where banks are not permitted to undertake investment business or own securities firms. At the other extreme we have the universal bank model, which is the traditional model for much of Continental Europe. The model chosen for the EU was the trading book approach, which permits banks to engage freely either directly or through subsidiaries (as in the UK). Each bank would need to separate its securities 'trading book' from the rest of its business (securities held for investment purposes). The trading book alone would then be subject to more permissive capital adequacy rules appropriate to securities trading. This creates a number of problems, discussed by Dale [1994]. One particular problem is that the capital requirements for bank loans are much higher than those applicable to debt securities of equivalent default risk and maturity held on the trading book. The CAD regime may therefore provide an incentive for banks to shift their business from traditional bank lending towards securitised lending (see chapter 12 for further discussion of securitisation).

Insurance

Freedom of establishment was provided in 1973 for non-life insurance and 1979 for life insurance. The next main breakthrough came with the Second Non-Life Insurance Directive, which was implemented in 1990. This provided freedom to provide cross-border insurance services for large commercial risks. In 1992 the Third Life Directive along with the Third Non-Life Directive were adopted and came into force in 1994. Under these directives an insurer with its head office within the EU can, under the single passport principle, set up operations anywhere in the EU.

A complementary Directive on the Liberalisation of Capital Movements, requiring the removal of all capital controls in the EU, was adopted in June 1988 and largely put into effect during 1990. The UK has of course been free of capital controls since 1979.

15.3 Likely effects of the liberalisation of EU financial services

To examine the potential effects of a single market in financial services we draw upon the Cecchini [1988] report, *Costs of Non-Europe*, published by the European Commission. The Cecchini report's section on financial services is based on an analysis by Price Waterhouse. The methodology of the report was to make a comparison between the price charged for a particular service in one member state and the average of the four lowest member state prices. The member states considered were Belgium, France, Germany, Spain, Italy, Luxembourg, the Netherlands and the UK. A selection of the results of the study are presented in table 15.2.

The Cecchini report attempts to predict the effects of competition in financial services with the arrival of a single market by assuming that where prices are higher than the average of the four lowest then the price will fall by half the difference. Such assumptions are questionable for a number of

Table 15.2 *Percentage differences in the prices of standard financial products compared with the average of the four lowest national prices*

Service	*Description of service*	*B*	*G*	*S*	*F*	*I*	*L*	*N*	*UK*
Banking services									
Consumer credit	Annual cost to consumer of 500 ECU. Excess interest rate over money market rates	-41	136	39	n.a.	121	-26	31	121
Credit cards	Annual cost assuming 500 ECU debit. Excess interest rate over money market rates	79	60	26	-30	89	-12	43	16
Mortgages	Annual cost of home loan of 25,000 ECU. Excess interest rate over money market rates	31	57	118	78	-4	n.a.	-6	-20
Commercial loans	Annual cost (including commissions and charges) to a medium-size firm of a loan of 250,000 ECU	-5	6	19	-7	9	6	43	46
Insurance services									
Life insurance	Average annual cost of life insurance	78	5	37	33	83	66	-9	-30
Home insurance	Annual cost of fire and theft cover for house valued at 70,000 ECU with 20,000 ECU contents	-16	3	-4	39	81	57	17	90

B, Belgium; G, Germany; S, Spain; F, France; I, Italy; L, Luxembourg; N, Netherlands.
Source: Cecchini report [1988], table 6.1.

reasons. First, the figures may not be based on a comparison of like with like, so for example a consumer loan in the UK may have a different default rate, and hence a different interest rate, when compared with a consumer loan in Spain. Similarly, when comparing insurance premiums, the variation in premium rates may reflect variations in expected claims. In other words, some variation in prices may be justifiable given the idiosyncratic nature of individual markets. Also, whilst it is likely that some business will flow to low-cost producers, assuming a competitive market emerges, this process may take some time to occur because of, for example, price-insensitive consumers, cultural factors which favour the home producer and the costs involved in setting up a distribution network. With these drawbacks in mind, the figures in table 15.2 provide some indication of where UK producers face competition or where they have scope for expansion into other EU countries. One area where UK consumers face high cost is consumer credit, where interest rates are approximately nine per cent above money market rates. It should be noted though that building societies have entered into competition with banks in this market since the Price Waterhouse study was conducted, following liberalisation of building societies (discussed in chapter 5). In addition, with the four main countries of the EU at the high end of the credit price range it is doubtful that there will be much competition from other EU banks in the UK market. One area where the UK has a cost advantage is in mortgage lending. The Spanish mortgage market in particular offers the most scope to UK banks and building societies in their expansion into EU countries. However, the wide variation in legal and institutional arrangements for mortgage lending in EU countries may slow down any expansion.

The benefits of a single market in financial services are undermined by exchange rate fluctuations between EU member states' currencies, which create uncertainty and therefore would inhibit cross-border trade. Moves towards economic and monetary union between member states and in particular to closer linkage of exchange rates through the Exchange Rate Mechanism can therefore be seen as complementary to the creation of a single market. It is to these developments we now turn.

15.4 European economic and monetary union

The Delors report, prepared in 1989 by the Committee for the Study of Economic and Monetary Union, provided a broad framework for the transition towards monetary union in Europe. The report recommended three stages in a 'progressive realisation of economic and monetary union'. The first stage began in July 1990 and is aimed at accomplishing liberalisation of financial markets (in particular the removal of exchange controls), enlargement of the membership of the Exchange Rate Mechanism (ERM) of the European Monetary System (EMS) and a change in the mandate of the Committee of Central Bank Governors. The second stage envisaged the establishment of the European System of Central Banks (ESCB), which would initially operate alongside the national monetary authorities. The third stage proposed the irrevocable fixing of exchange rates, with a possible replacement by a single currency and the transfer of monetary authority to the ESCB.

Stage 1 of the report has been largely implemented and the details and timetable for implementing stages 2 and 3 were set out in the Treaty of Maastricht. The timetable is set out below:

1 January 1994	Stage 2 to begin, with the establishment of the European Monetary Institute (forerunner of the European Central Bank).
31 December 1996	United Kingdom to notify the Council whether it intends to move to stage 3, or by 1 January 1998 if no decision has yet been taken by the Council.
31 December 1996	Deadline for decision by qualified majority to launch stage 3 if a 'critical mass' of member states (majority would currently mean 7 out of 12 member states, or 6 if the UK is not taking part in stage 3) meet the convergence criteria. The date would also be fixed.
1 July 1998	European Central Bank (ECB) and the ESCB to be set up if this has not already happened. This is therefore the deadline for member states to make the national central banks independent (if the ECB and ESCB are only now being set up).
1 January 1999	European monetary union to begin 'irrevocably' if this has not yet happened.

A number of issues arise out of this timetable, which we now briefly comment upon. The European Monetary Institute (EMI) has now been set up in Frankfurt. The EMI has an advisory and consultative role and its primary aim is to develop the regulatory, organisational and logistical framework for the ESCB. The Maasticht Treaty laid down five convergence criteria to determine the degree of economic convergence by member states before commencing stage 3. The criteria are:

(i) price stability – inflation rate over one year should not exceed the average inflation rate of the three best-performing states, in terms of price stability, by more than 1.5 percentage points;
(ii) interest rates – average nominal long-term interest rate over one year

should not exceed the average interest rate of the best three states in terms of price stability by more than two percentage points;

(iii) government budget deficit – the deficit should not exceed three per cent of the ratio of planned or actual government deficit to gross domestic product at market prices;

(iv) government debt – the ratio of government debt to gross domestic product should not exceed 60 per cent;

(v) participation in the ERM – a member state should have participated in the ERM for at least two years before proceeding to stage 3 and should not have devalued or revalued its currency within the mechanism.

If a member state meets all these criteria then it is permitted to join in stage 3. The main problem in Europe in the 1990s has been the high public debt levels following a severe economic downturn in the early 1990s. This suggests that many states are not going to be able to meet the two public-debt criteria in time for the December 1996 deadline for achieving a critical mass.

It is noted in the timetable that the UK has a separate protocol, which states that the UK shall not be obliged or committed to move to stage 3 of monetary union without a separate decision to do so by Parliament.

Finally, the proposed ECB will be independent of any government interference and will have the primary objective of maintaining price stability. Its constitution is based largely on that of the Bundesbank (see chapter 3 for further discussion of the nature of independence).

The ERM plays an important role in the moves towards monetary union in Europe and we briefly review its history and some recent developments in the next section.

The Exchange Rate Mechanism

The history of the ERM can be traced back to the breakdown of the Bretton Woods system of fixed exchange rates in 1971. Attempts were made to create a European successor to Bretton Woods with the establishment of the European Currency 'Snake' in 1972. This arrangement was designed to narrow fluctuating margins between EU currencies. Sterling participated in the early months of the Snake but withdrew to follow a floating-rate regime. The Snake had mixed success, with other currencies withdrawing in its first years of operation, leaving just five currencies participating in 1978. The Snake was replaced by the more durable ERM in March 1979. A number of realignments were undertaken in the early years of the ERM but until the problems of the early 1990s, discussed below, there were no general realignments after January 1987. The ERM appeared to become more stable in the late 1980s and in 1989 the Spanish peseta joined, followed by sterling in October 1990. These two currencies were permitted fluctuations of up to 6 per cent around agreed central rates with other currencies, whilst the other currencies were allowed fluctuations of 2.25 per cent. Strains appeared in the ERM in the early 1990s, caused in particular by the reunification of Germany. The cost of raising living standards in the East towards equality with the West led to the German budget deficit increasing dramatically. The effect of this was to raise interest rates in Germany and consequently in the rest of the ERM states, as the currencies are tied through the ERM. However, this coincided with a downturn in the business cycle in Europe in the aftermath of the late 1980s boom, and the burden of high interest rates became onerous. Countries deep in recession, such as the UK and Italy, were seen by currency speculators as having unsustainable currency parities in the ERM and they believed that devaluation was inevitable. Selling pressure on the currencies of these and other ERM countries eventually proved too much for the authorities and the UK and Italy departed from the ERM in September 1992. Then in 1993 a further wave of speculative pressure led the French authorities to give up the battle to prevent the franc falling below its floor with the Deutschmark. This led to an effective abandonment of the ERM although strictly speaking the system survives in operation with 15 per cent rather than 2.25 per cent fluctuation bands.

15.5 **Conclusion**

In this chapter we have briefly summarised the main developments in the move towards greater integration amongst EU countries in terms of trade in financial services and economic and monetary union. The final outcome of these developments is uncertain, as at the time of writing the timing and extent of the moves towards integration are uncertain. What is clear though is that, given the momentum for change and the changes already agreed, a greater degree of European integration is inevitable.

Chapter 16

The efficiency of the UK financial system

16.1 **Introduction**

The criticisms of the UK financial system are generally based on the following rationale. Growth of UK gross national product (GNP) since 1945 has been less than that of many other countries. Over this period gross domestic capital formation has been lower in the UK than in other countries and this has caused the lower rate of growth of GNP. In turn this lower level of investment has been caused by deficiencies in the UK financial system. Complaints have focused on the excessive amount of resources devoted to speculation on secondary markets, inadequate provision of funds for investment, excessive cost of capital, and 'short termism', that is, excessive concentration on the short term as opposed to the long term. Such criticisms have come from a wide range of sources, not just the left in political terms. For example, a conservative chancellor referred to market operators as 'teenaged scribblers'. Nevertheless, these arguments appear to be rather tenuous in the absence of other confirmatory evidence.

It is factual to note that both the rate of growth and also the level of investment have been lower than those observed in many Continental countries. This, as any student of statistics knows, does not of necessity indicate a causal relationship flowing from the lower level of investment to the lower rate of growth. It could be plausible to argue that the lower rate of growth in the UK has led to ('caused'?) the lower level of investment or that they were both caused by a third variable. Similarly, it is a large step to assume that, in the absence of other confirmatory evidence, the lower level of investment has been caused by deficiencies in the financial system. Equally it is true to add that additional evidence may well support these criticisms.

It is as well at this stage to remind the reader of the functions of the financial system discussed in chapter 1. These are the provision of (i) a payments mechanism, (ii) a mechanism for financial intermediation between surplus and deficit units, (iii) primary and secondary markets so that portfolio holders can adjust their portfolios and (iv) various financial services, such as foreign exchange, pension provision, and insurance. As can be seen from the opening remarks, most of the complaints have centred on functions (ii) to (iv) rather than on the provision of the payments mechanism. Consequently we concentrate on these aspects of the financial system in the following assessment though, in view of the large volume of literature on this topic, we are able only to indicate the main themes of the various arguments. In section 16.2 we will examine the efficiency of the various markets and in section 16.3 discuss the nature of short termism, which is perhaps the most consistent criticism raised. In section 16.4 we review some explanations of short termism and the slower rate of growth and present our remedies in section 16.5.

16.2 **Efficiency of the financial system**

In chapter 7 we reviewed the various meanings of the word efficiency as applied to financial markets. These were (i) allocative efficiency, (ii) operational efficiency and (iii) informational efficiency.

Allocative efficiency

Allocative efficiency is a broad concept and is likely to be achieved provided the market is giving out correct signals (i.e. that informational efficiency is achieved) and that incentives exist to follow the direction of these signals. There is just one proviso to this statement and this concerns the possibility that certain types of undertaking may not be able to obtain finance owing to gaps in the market.

The proposition that it is difficult for entrepreneurs to obtain small amounts of capital to finance the start up of a company or to expand it in its early years is of long standing. In 1931 the Macmillan Committee on Finance and Industry brought attention to such a gap in the provision of finance (the 'Macmillan gap') and as a consequence the forerunner of the 3i Group (previously Investors In Industry – owned by the clearing banks and the Bank of England) was established in 1945. In 1971, the Bolton Committee in its report highlighted both an 'equity gap' in terms of raising long-term finance below £250,000 (£1 million in current prices) and an information gap where small firms were unaware of sources of finance or could not present a reasoned request for finance. The Wilson Committee also reported on the financial problems of small companies in 1979 and also highlighted the information gap and commented on the difficulties for small firms in obtaining venture capital (i.e. for high-risk ventures with little track record).

Over the 1980s there have been a number of developments which have gone some way to closing the finance and information gaps identified.

What follows is a brief summary of these developments – more detailed surveys can be found in the *Bank of England Quarterly Bulletin* (November 1990) and Boocock [1990].

With regard to the information gap, the Department of Trade and Industry has set up a number of small-firm information centres, providing free information and advice. In addition, a number of regional development agencies and other specialised agencies have been established, which also provide advice. There has also been a growth in venture capital providers which provide equity and other forms of long-term capital to small/medium-sized firms at both the early stages of development (e.g. seed capital) and later stages (e.g. expansion, management buy-outs/ins). Institutions offering this type of financing can be divided into two broad groups. First, captive funds are subsidiaries of the major UK pension funds, insurance companies and banks. These captive funds obtain their finance from the parent company. Second, independent funds raise capital for investment from a wide variety of sources, including private investors and some financial institutions. In 1988 the independents accounted for approximately 66 per cent of the amount invested by venture capital funds, with captive funds accounting for most of the rest. The distinction between captive and independent is not so clear cut though, with most independent funds having some links with financial institutions and captive funds having some degree of independence.

The finance provided by the venture capital industry substantially increased over the 1980s so that in 1988 over £1 billion was invested. However, there has been a change in the nature of the finance provided over this period, illustrated in table 16.1. There has been an increasing emphasis on financing buy-outs, buy-ins and acquisitions at the expense of start up and other early-stage financing. UK corporate restructuring over the latter half of the 1980s led to the sale of non-core businesses by many diversified companies as they reverted back to core activities. These sales were often to incumbent management (management buy-out) and financed by venture capital funds. This type of financing was attractive to venture capital funds as it was less risky than the traditional investment and usually offered a quicker exit route (i.e. realisation of the fund's investment) through a trade sale or flotation.

Two government initiatives in the early 1980s also addressed the funding gap for small companies. The first was the Loan Guarantee Scheme (LGS), which was introduced in 1981 following a recommendation of the Wilson Committee. The aim of this initiative is to encourage banks and some other credit institutions to supply medium-term (2–7 years) loan finance, up to a maximum of £100,000, where the risks involved would normally mean the loan request is rejected. The government guarantees 70 per cent of any loan approved and the borrower pays a premium on top of the normal

Table 16.1 *UK venture capital financing by financing stage (% of total invested)*

	1984	*1985*	*1986*	*1987*	*1988*
Start up	17	13	16	8	5
Other early-stage	10	6	7	4	2
Expansion	39	36	27	22	27
Buy-out/in and acquisition	28	38	44	63	62
Secondary purchase	5	6	5	3	4
Other	1	1	1	–	–
Total (£million)	228	279	396	795	1,006

Buy-out/in – the purchase of an existing company as a going concern.
Secondary purchase – the acquisition of existing shares in a company from another venture capital firm or other shareholders.
Source: *Bank of England Quarterly Bulletin*, February 1990.

interest rate. The scheme was extended indefinitely following a review by the government in 1989. This suggests that the government perceives there is a funding gap requiring a scheme of this sort. The scheme has been criticised though, as it provides loan finance whereas equity risk capital is considered more appropriate for small growing companies. The second government initiative was the Business Expansion Scheme (BES), introduced in the 1983 Finance Act. This is designed to attract investors to provide equity finance to non-quoted companies, by giving tax relief to investors at the marginal rate paid for amounts up to £40,000 per annum. This tax relief is to compensate investors for the extra risks involved. Most finance of this sort is obtained by companies making a direct issue of shares to the public. The advantage to the company is that investors cannot sell shares purchased under the scheme before five years has elapsed without losing the tax relief. BES funding can be used for a variety of activities and it is believed that investors' preferences have increasingly moved away from venture capital funding, so that in 1988 only 2 per cent of venture capital funding came from this source compared with 20 per cent in 1984.

Despite the developments in funding for small business over the 1980s and in particular the growth in venture capital providers, it is still widely believed that there exists an equity gap for amounts below £100,000. There is also some evidence to suggest that a second gap exists for funding for amounts between £100,000 to £250,000.

Operational efficiency

It is difficult to obtain hard evidence concerning operational efficiency but what we can obtain is indirect evidence from the structure of the financial system and also the cost of capital. In a competitive system we would expect to see inefficiencies competed away and, in the long run, profits to be 'normal', reflecting the degree of risk involved in the industry. As we have seen in earlier chapters, the UK financial system has certainly been subject to a large degree of liberalisation in areas of pricing and range of business conducted.

To take just a few examples, in recent years we have seen the relaxation of controls over the banking industry, and the death of some cartels, such as 'Big Bang' on the Stock Exchange removing fixed commissions and opening up the Exchange to a greater degree of competition. The building societies' interest rate cartel has also ended and, as a consequence, the mortgage market is now a 'competitive price-driven' market. The incidence of competition has increased not only in the domestic context but also on an international scale. The abolition of exchange controls allows residents to invest overseas without restraint. As we have seen in chapter 4, a large number of foreign banks now operate in London. Consequently it would be reasonable to expect that the increased competitive environment would have led to a greater degree of efficiency. We certainly have seen a fairly high degree of financial innovation, that is, the development of new markets and financial instruments. In chapter 13 we discussed the development in London of a major new financial market, LIFFE. The increased volume of trading on this market noted in chapter 13 indicates a successful development. New instruments have been developed and extended, such as in the commercial paper market together with all those available to manage risk as indicated in chapter 13.

Nevertheless, critics have pointed to the volume of trading carried out on the major markets and in particular the Stock Exchange and the foreign exchange market. With reference to the Stock Exchange we noted in chapter 8, table 8.1, the low proportion of funds raised by firms through new issues of equity and debentures and the consequent importance of internally generated funds as a source of business finance.

One other aspect of the operational efficiency of markets concerns the cost of capital. A number of commentators have argued that the cost of capital is higher in countries such as the UK and US compared with other countries such as Germany and in particular Japan. Perhaps one of the most recent and widely quoted studies was that carried out by McCauley and Zimmer [1989], who claimed that the real cost of funds after tax was some three per cent higher in the UK than in Germany and Japan. The main reasons given for this difference were (i) higher saving ratios, and (ii) lower risk premiums. These reasons are not unambiguous with respect to their theoretical underpinning. If real returns on savings are lower in some countries, then, given the current level of globalisation of the nature of finance, it would be expected that international arbitrage would lead to funds moving out of countries with a lower rate of return in favour of centres with higher real rates of return. This would tend to lead to real rates of return being equalised across international centres. The second reason put forward suggests that high levels of inflation lead to volatility of nominal returns and a higher risk premium. Marsh [1990] suggests that examination of the gap between the risk-free return and the return on equities shows that risk premiums were higher in Japan than in the UK. This is supported also by the fact that the standard deviation of stock market returns were higher in Japan than in other countries. Marsh also argues that McCauley and Zimmer have used an inappropriate measure of the cost of equity capital in their study, that is, the inverse of the price/earnings ratio. This is inappropriate because it makes no allowance for future growth potential; the correct measure is the risk-free real rate of interest plus a premium for investing in equities. However, a contrary argument must also be raised at this juncture. High nominal rates of interest can cause cash flow problems, particularly for firms with high gearing. It could be claimed that nominal interest rate stability permits firms to utilise a more highly geared capital structure with its cost advantage without the danger of a financial crisis due to restrictive monetary policy. Clearly, this has not been the case for UK firms during periods of high nominal interest rates (e.g. to take just one example, Brent Walker in 1990). All in all it seems that the cost of capital may well be higher in the UK than in other countries but that the extent of the margin has been exaggerated. Furthermore, any higher cost due to higher nominal rates of interest must be the responsibility of the government for permitting higher and more volatile rates of inflation rather than that of the financial system.

One final criticism of the operational efficiency concerns the response of the financial system to firms in difficulty. It is often claimed that the financial institutions are too keen to foreclose on debt rather than allow sufficient time for a firm to recover its former position of financial strength. This is of course the classic dilemma for banks. Do they force the firm into bankruptcy and accept the loss without a chance to recoup their losses, or do they lend additional funds, thus incurring additional risk, in the hope of obtaining repayment of all lending eventually? The criticism suggests that the banks and other lenders too often follow the first course of action. There appears to be some force in this argument since the Bank of England has been negotiating with the commercial banks to produce an agreed procedure to deal with companies with a liquidity crisis. Basically the approach is to provide funds for the company to keep it afloat until such time as a considered judgement can be made about its long-term future. The funds are to be provided by the lending banks in proportion to their existing exposure. A lead bank is to be identified to keep the other creditors informed. This is necessary because of the large number of banks often lending to a single firm. For example, in the case of the troubled Goodman International empire in Ireland, it was reported that 33 different banks were involved in lending the equivalent of £500 million. The lead bank is likely to be the bank with the largest exposure. Finally, in this interval all other lending to the company should be suspended.

Informational efficiency

It has been argued that an excessive amount of resources has been devoted to speculation as distinct from the raising of capital. A similar objection could be raised against the operation of the foreign exchange market, where the daily volume of trading dwarfs any requirement to finance UK overseas trade. The counter-argument is that the speculators are necessary to ensure that prices of the various securities reflect all available information. The aim of the speculator is to make a profit. They do this by identifying securities which are incorrectly priced in the market, purchasing those which are identified as under-priced and selling those identified as over-priced. In this manner the speculator contributes to market efficiency in the informational sense. Correct decision making will reward the speculator and, in the same way, the inefficient speculator, who makes wrong decisions, will be penalised. A 'Darwinian' process will ensure the survival of efficient speculators at the expense of the inefficient ones. Speculation will, therefore, be stabilising. However, it is of course perfectly possible to argue that the process is not as efficient as that described above. Whilst persistently inefficient speculators must leave the market through shortages of finance, it is quite possible (though improbable over a long period) that successive waves of inefficient speculators will appear on the market, leading to the existence of destabilising speculation.

A second criticism arising from the relative volume of speculative activity on financial markets points to the likelihood of increased volatility of market prices. It is quite probable that this increased volatility may have detracted from the efficiency of the market mechanism by obscuring the price signals given out by the market. Some casual empirical support for an adverse effect of market volatility on business operation is given by the rapid growth of hedging instruments such as financial futures since 1980. However, the real test of these criticisms must be whether the market conforms to the efficient markets hypothesis or not. Clearly, no market can be absolutely efficient in the sense that market prices always fully reflect all available information. The acid test is more sensibly one of examining whether market prices usually reflect all available information, so that the market approximates to the efficient markets hypothesis. In this connection we examined the efficiency of the stock market (chapter 8), the bond market (chapter 9), the foreign exchange market (chapter 11) and the financial futures market (chapter 12). Our conclusions were not decisive in either direction but it is certainly true to say that no conclusive evidence was presented against market efficiency in the informational sense.

A second aspect of informational efficiency concerns the advice given by City analysts about the advisability of purchasing equity in a company. In this connection the *Observer* (28 October 1990) provided an interesting commentary on analysts' reports on Polly Peck, which foundered in the autumn of 1990. Throughout 1990 a considerable number of analysts were recommending the purchase of Polly Peck shares on the ground that the shares were undervalued. At least ten analysts were quoted as recommending the purchase and some with a repetition of a buy and hold strategy even as late as September. It is patently obvious that the advice was ill-founded and this may raise doubts on this aspect of the City's work. This, incidentally, adds additional support to the efficient markets hypothesis since, at least in this case, market experts failed to beat the market.

We now turn to discuss short termism, which is perhaps the main thrust of common criticism of the UK financial system.

16.3 **Short termism**

In general terms, short termism can be defined as a climate in which companies concentrate on short-term profits rather than long-term investment. Associated with the concept of short termism is the view that the UK financial system suffers from myopia. One aspect of this view on short termism is the belief that the take-over mechanism contributes to companies concentrating on short-term issues because of the necessity of having to look continually over their shoulders, as it were, to identify possible predators. This is particularly true in times of falling share prices. This largely a consequence of the type of financial system that exists in the UK. As we saw in chapter 2, the financial systems in the UK and US can be broadly categorised as market based. Thus, financial markets play an important role in terms of both raising long-term capital and changing corporate control. In contrast, in bank-based financial systems, such as those of Germany and Japan, the banks play a greater role in providing external finance. The finance provided by banks consists of loans and equity so that the banks often take a more active role in the running of the companies they finance. In particular they will often initiate changes in management and sometimes ownership. However, such changes are carried out without hostile confrontation.

Certainly it is true that expenditure on take-overs has increased over the last ten years but the question remains as to whether this will have encouraged the growth of short termism. The role of the financial system in mergers and acquisitions is highlighted by the advisory fees earned from both the predators and the victims. The fact that such fees add to a bank's profitability without incurring any of the balance sheet restraints imposed through prudential control provides an additional stimulus for banks to engage in this type of business. A counter-argument would suggest that take-overs are part of the discipline of the market and are necessary to provide a spur for the stimulation of efficiency and the removal of inefficient managements. However, the discipline is rather a blunt instrument which may threaten efficient as well as inefficient companies.

Protagonists of the view that the financial system is responsible for short termism suggest that the equity of a company is subject to a dual valuation situation. First, there is what may be called the normal valuation, when the price of equity reflects the marginal trading in company shares between portfolio investors. There is, however, a second valuation, which occurs when a potential bidder is attempting to acquire control of a business and so is bidding for the whole of the company's equity. In this case the share price will rise above the normal price and the difference between the two prices is the bid premium. This provides an incentive for shareholders, particularly the institutions, to accept the bid because it is unlikely that the share price will continue to remain at that level in the absence of the predator. The source of the bid premium can be construed to be the increased efficiency with which the firm taken over is managed or alternatively increased economies of scale attributable to the integration of the firm into the predator's operations. An alternative view of the source of the bid premium is, however, that it represents the anticipated profit through asset stripping, including sale of assets and perhaps the acquisition of pension fund surpluses. In this case the bid premium represents a transfer from the other stakeholders in the firm, such as employees, to the predator company without conferring any benefit to the economy as a whole.

In the UK the investment institutions dominate holdings of equities in companies so it is their decisions which matter as far as the success of take-overs are concerned. In this connection it is also important to note that the institutions have incentives to accept take-over offers for reasons other than that described above. Fund managers prepare statistics every quarter and have therefore an additional incentive to accept bids for companies whose shares are held in their portfolios to boost the quarterly performance of the fund that they manage. This also raises the question of their commitment to the company whose securities are held in their portfolios. In general they seem quite reluctant to become involved in the management of these firms, possibly owing to a lack of expertise. A second possible reason for this is that the possession of detailed knowledge of any firms would make it more difficult for them to deal in their securities for fear of falling foul of legislation on insider trading. A further reason for a 'hands-off' approach to the management of the companies is the number of different funds which are likely to hold the equity of any one individual company. This general situation is contrasted with the position of countries where the banks provide a major source of funds for industrial and commercial companies. It appears that these banks are more firmly committed to their clients and are represented in top management and have, therefore, a voice in the firm's policy-making process.

However, changes may be taking place in the UK financial system. A number of insurance companies and issuing houses are trying to devise a new form of intermediary operating between the institutional shareholders and the company itself. This new intermediary would represent the large shareholders without holding or trading shares itself. It would be expected that such an intermediary would be able to demand management information without falling foul of the law. Logically it would also be able to change directors and call in consultants. It could obtain power to enforce its demands through being granted proxy votes by the institutional shareholders.

The general tenor of the argument above depends on the hypothesis that share prices do not reflect the long-run profit potential of the company concerned, or in other words that the efficient markets hypothesis is breached since some facets of information are not fully reflected in the price of equity. Marsh [1990] disputes this with the aid of an illustration derived from the valuation of ICI shares according to a standard valuation model. The then current share price and price of capital for ICI implied:

> that the market is expecting ICI's dividends to grow at the rate of 13% per annum. In turn this implies that of ICI's current market capitalization, only 8% is attributable to the current year's dividend, only 29% can be explained by the present value of dividends expected over the next five years and only 50% by the value of the dividends expected over the next 10 years. (Marsh [1990])

Marsh admits that analysts' judgements on the cost of capital are tentative but nevertheless the figures are not suggestive of short termism in share valuation. This point seems to us to be critical since if the price of equity is representing, albeit as an approximation, the long-term profit potential of firms then the search for short-term profits by fund managers will not provoke short-term profit decisions by firms. A fund manager will seek to identify shares which are incorrectly valued and then buy (in the case of undervalued shares) or sell from the portfolio any shares which are considered to be overvalued. Consequently even though the manager's actions are motivated by short-term gains, he or she is in fact moving share prices towards their correct price. Clearly, if the market is not efficient in an informational sense then the foregoing argument is not correct and the manager's actions will be stimulating short-term behaviour.

A further consideration concerns the influence of investment on the price of a company's shares. There is a not inconsiderable volume of evidence derived from the USA to suggest the announcement of long-term investment often enhances the value of a company's shares – see for example McConnell and Muscerella [1985]. This implies that investment is not of necessity an activity to be avoided for fear of inducing take-over bids through lower share prices. In this connection it may also be argued that the perception that investment and dividend payments are necessarily alternative sources of demand for a company's resources is incorrect. Successful investment projects will enhance a company's profit-making potential and therefore dividends in the long run.

16.4 An alternative explanation of short termism

An alternative explanation of short termism is provided by Marsh [1990]. This is based on the view that it is the management itself which is subject to myopia, or 'managerial short termism'. A number of arguments are presented to support this hypothesis. The first point concerns the system of remunerating top managers. It appears that only a small proportion of managers' remuneration is directly linked to the performance of the corporation. Furthermore, the majority of executive schemes that are in existence are based on short-term indicators, such as accounting profit. The underlying argument is that such schemes may provide an incentive for executives to pursue short-term objectives at the expense of a long-term strategy. One example would be an investment proposal which provided benefits in the long run but which is perceived to have an adverse effect on profits in the next few years.

Second, there is the role of investment appraisal. It is often argued that current profitability influences the divisional allocation of capital budgets. The problem arises because profitability is assessed via accounting profits and this may provide incorrect signals for investment appraisal, which should be based on discounting methods. It also appears that, in practice, the payback method of investment appraisal is still used by UK managers to assess investment projects – see Marsh [1990] for survey evidence. The problem with this method of investment appraisal is that it concentrates on the short term only and ignores any long-term profits which occur after the break-even time has been reached. If true, this would also provide an important explanation of short termism.

The third broad strand of the argument for managers suffering from myopia can be considered under the heading of a perceived lack of investment opportunities. One reason for this could be poor labour relations, with a heavy incidence of restrictive practices leading to a dilution of the benefits from innovation and investment. A second reason could be the uncertain economic climate due to the higher inflation rates experienced in the UK which have led to the imposition of restrictive monetary policies from time to time. The resulting uncertain economic climate would not be expected to provide a spur to the development of long-term strategies by firms. A further argument offered is the lower investment in education and training in the UK as compared with other developed nations.

In the following section, we discuss possible remedies for 'short termism'.

16.5 Remedies for short termism

Assuming that short termism is a problem for the UK economy, the proposal of adequate remedies requires identification of its causes. One reform which would draw fairly wide support is a change in the method of remuneration of managers by providing incentive schemes which link their salaries to the medium-term (say in the region of five years) market value of their companies. Sykes [1990] suggests that the rate would typically be in the range of 5–10 per cent and also that penalties should accrue for non-performance. This would require both an extension of incentive schemes and also the replacement of the role of short-term accounting profits within existing schemes. Presumably extension of such schemes would require fiscal incentives to be provided by government. Benefits would accrue in the form of an incentive directed towards the adoption of long-term strategies by firms. Furthermore, the risk element coupled with the incentives should assist the correct allocation of managerial resources within the UK economy.

A similar proposal advocates the extension of the appointment of non-executive directors and the separation of the duties of managing director and chairperson of a company. Advocates of this strategy claim that this would provide a more independent element in the board of directors and remove an element of passivity and self-selection. It would also facilitate a more objective assessment of past policies and remedies where appropriate. A basic requirement for this strategy to be successful is that the non-executive directors must be genuinely independent and not just 'old cronies' of the existing directors.

The above two proposals could presumably be facilitated by persuading shareholders to take a more active and discerning role in the management of firms. This in reality entails the investment institutions taking a more active role in the management because, in general, individuals' shareholdings are dwarfed by those held by the institutions, with the result that proposals by individuals have little chance of acceptance. The problem with institutions taking a more active role in the management of individual firms in their portfolio is, as we have seen earlier, twofold. First, they probably lack the expertise and would therefore be involved in additional expenditure recruiting the requisite qualified staff. Second, the possession of inside knowledge would inhibit share dealings and could therefore detract from market efficiency. For similar reasons it is advocated that banks should become more like banks in Germany and Japan by being closely identified with their borrowers. This would include lending by way of equity and becoming involved in management decisions.

Further remedies suggested depend on the view that short termism is attributable to the deficiencies of the financial system – for such a view see for example Cosh *et al.* [1990]. They argue that remedies such as those indicated above will require a fairly long time to implement. It is therefore suggested that some 'grit' should be introduced into the take-over mechanism. First, terms of reference to the Monopolies and Mergers Commission should be broadened so as to enable a better distinction between take-overs which result in economies of scale and greater efficiency of operation and those which are designed to gain profits by asset stripping. Currently criteria are restricted to the effect on competition, which provide a reasonably clear framework for decisions. Extension of the criteria to incorporate public interest would permit the authorities to filter out, albeit judgementally, take-overs which were not designed to increase efficiency of operation. Further restraints could be introduced by requiring all contested bids to be submitted to the Monopolies and Mergers Commission.

Another suggestion on a similar line takes the form of restricting the voting rights from newly acquired shares for a specific period of time after the acquisition, such as 12 months. Similarly, it is also suggested that the threshold at which a predator is obliged to make an offer to all shareholders is reduced from the current 29.9 per cent to a lower figure, such as 14.9 per cent (Plender [1990]). Both these measures would increase the cost and difficulty of making predatory bids, especially where they are contested.

A further proposal along these lines advocates the imposition of tax penalties on share transactions to encourage the institutions to take a longer view in their portfolio decisions. This seems to us to be a step in the wrong direction for three reasons. First, the existence of a secondary market provides liquidity, so that existing individuals as well as institutions can change the composition of their portfolios. Restriction on this important function may well reduce the willingness of individuals to hold equity in their overall portfolio of wealth. Second, as we have noted earlier, dealings by institutions is a mechanism which pushes equity prices towards their true value. Third, imposition of taxes on share dealings on the London Stock Exchange would force business away to other international stock exchanges. It is quite likely that attempts to tax dealings on other exchanges would create massive scope for evasion. It would therefore in all probability be ineffective and costly to operate.

16.6 **Conclusion**

Certain facets of the debate appear to be clear. Short termism is generally perceived to be a problem for the UK economy. Investment has been lower in the UK economy and this is presumably owing, at least in part, to short termism. Certain of the proposed remedies command fairly widespread support. These include the proposals for the introduction of long-term incentives for managers and increased representation of genuinely independent non-executive directors. Beyond this, little agreement on either the causes or the remedies exists. Those who believe that the volume of take-overs is excessive advocate legal or quasi-legal restraints on the take-over process. Believers in the efficient markets hypothesis argue that such restraints would do more harm than good.

The arguments are likely to continue. For example, Will Hutton (*Guardian*, 3 January 1995) argues strongly that the 'City' has failed UK industry over a long period of time. The main criticism, due to Professor C. Mayer, is based on the alleged failure of the City to provide either 'a stable long-term ownership base' or cheap long-term debt. Similarly, arguments continue to be made that the cost of capital is higher in the UK than elsewhere because of the alleged requirement of the City for high rates of return. The problem with these arguments is that they do not provide irrefutable evidence of the failure of the financial system. As noted earlier, arbitrage, given the current freedom of international movement of capital, should stimulate movement towards equality of risk-adjusted rates of return across national boundaries. The higher rates required by the UK financial institutions could therefore reflect higher risk in the UK due to more volatile conditions partly (or perhaps wholly) due to inappropriate government macroeconomic policy. The lack of availability to private firms of cheap long-term debt may be attributable to the size of the public sector borrowing requirement over the post-war period. It can be argued that excessive borrowing by the government 'crowded out' private sector borrowing. Finally, we have discussed the problem of short termism at some length in the previous section.

On the other hand, we would not argue that the financial system is perfect. Financial scandals such as occurred in the Lloyd's insurance market and the Maxwell raid on pension funds are pertinent in this respect. Similarly, problems have occurred in the life assurance industry, with salespersons selling inappropriate pensions. Regulation has appeared to be questionable from time to time, both in the examples quoted above and with respect to the supervision of banking – the example of BCCI is relevant here.

As in most cases discussed in this text, there is no clear-cut objective answer. It is a question of judgement and as we have stated above the arguments are likely to continue for some time.

Chapter 17

Regulation of the financial system

17.1 **Introduction**

The type of regulation which we discuss in this chapter is termed prudential regulation since it is designed to ensure prudent behaviour by financial institutions. In contrast to the rest of the financial sector, prudential regulation of banks has been the subject of analysis over quite a long period of time. Consequently the major part of the discussion in sections 17.2, 17.3 and 17.4 will be directed to prudential control of banks. We will review the system of prudential control of the investment industry in section 17.5 and present our conclusions in section 17.6. We begin with a brief survey of recent bank failures and an examination of the type of risks faced by the banking industry.

17.2 **History of bank failures**

Regulation of banks must be examined against the background of bank failures. Any major problem results in changes in the regulatory environment as the regulators try to block any loophole in the rules. Concentrating on events this century, the greatest incidence of bank failure occurred in the US between the years 1929, when then were 25,000 banking firms, and 1934, when the number had been reduced to 14,000. These failures led to the introduction of fairly restrictive bank legislation such as single-state operations, which have remained characteristic of the US banking scene until today, although these restrictions are currently under review. Broadly speaking, there were no further major problems until 1973, which saw the start of the fringe bank crisis in the UK. Over the early 1970s, following rapid credit expansion which was a consequence of the introduction of the policy of 'competition and credit control', many secondary (or 'fringe') banks increased their deposits rapidly and lent a large proportion of these funds to property-related companies. Following a slump in property values in 1973 the secondary banks began to experience difficulties. As a consequence the inter-bank market, upon which the secondary banks were heavily dependent for deposits, dried up for all but banks of good standing and in addition deposits were withdrawn from the secondary banks. At the end of 1973 the Bank of England, seeing the problem as one of illiquidity, stepped in and organised a rescue of the secondary banks which has come to be known as 'the lifeboat'. Under this operation the Bank of England sought the help of the clearing banks in recycling the deposits they had gained following the withdrawal of deposits from the secondary banks. However, the problems in the property market which had caused the loss of confidence in the secondary banks deteriorated further over 1974 and several of the banks receiving support under the 'lifeboat' moved into a position of insolvency. Whilst a few banks were allowed to fail the majority were kept going. The Bank of England's intervention was justified in the following way (*Bank of England Quarterly Bulletin*, June 1978):

> The Bank thus found themselves confronted with the imminent collapse of several deposit-taking institutions and with the clear danger of a rapidly escalating crisis of confidence. This threatened other deposit-taking institutions and if left unchecked, would have quickly passed into parts of the banking system proper. While the UK clearing banks still appeared secure from the domestic effects of any run ... their international exposure was such that the risk to external confidence was a matter of concern for themselves as well as for the Bank. The problem was to avoid a widening circle of collapse through the contagion of fear.

At the height of the rescue operations, total lending amounted to over £1,000 million. This crisis led to a rethink of banking supervision and subsequently to the introduction of the Banking Act of 1979, which provided the first legal codification of the Bank of England's regulatory powers. This Act required the licensing of banks and deposit-taking institutions and also transferred the duty of supervision entirely to the Bank of England.

Further major failures occurred in 1974, namely Bankhaus Herstatt (Germany) and the Franklin National Bank (US). The latter was the twelfth largest bank in the US. Also in the US, 1984 saw the failure of Continental Illinois Bank, which was the eighth largest bank in the US. In this year the Johnson Matthey Bank failed in the UK – this failure is discussed in detail below. Other bank failures occurred over a range of countries, including Denmark, Canada and Ireland.

The Johnson Matthey Bank (JMB) faced financial difficulties which resulted in the Bank of England purchasing the JMB for £1 on 1 October 1984 from its parent company Johnson Matthey p.l.c. with a view to rescue and subsequently resale, which has now been carried out. This was the first rescue of an ailing bank by the Bank of England since the lifeboat operation of 1974. The Bank of England sought to justify the rescue of JMB with arguments similar to those used to justify the lifeboat operation, in particular the fear of contagion if JMB were to collapse. There were also reasons put forward which were specific to the JMB case. JMB was one of a group of five gold bullion dealers which jointly fixed the price of gold on a twice-daily basis in London. It was feared that the other gold bullion price fixers may have encountered liquidity problems if JMB were allowed to collapse, which would have put in jeopardy London's position in the international bullion market. The rescue of JMB, like the lifeboat operation of 1974, involved the participation of other banks and the clearing banks in particular. These banks were persuaded by the Bank of England to provide indemnities against potential loan losses by JMB in order to keep JMB's credit lines open. This time, however, the clearing banks publicly objected to being forced into the rescue of JMB. As Goodhart [1988] argues: 'In today's more competitive conditions, the banks at the centre of the system frequently see the failing bank as being a relatively imprudent competitor. Why then, they feel, should they penalise their own shareholders for the sake of such a competitor?' Goodhart goes on to argue that the clearing banks' reaction in the JMB affair 'is a clear warning now that the Bank of England, and other central banks, may find it increasingly hard, if not impossible, to persuade other commercial banks to assist them in future rescue packages'. Goodhart suggests this should lead to a consideration of alternative strategies to deal with a future illiquidity/insolvency problem, and we consider one such alternative (namely deposit insurance) in the next section.

There are other issues highlighted by the JMB affair (see Hall [1987a] for further discussion) which merit comment. It can be argued that the act of rescuing JMB introduces moral hazard into the banking system; that is, other banks may act less prudently in the belief that the Bank of England will not allow them to fail. The Bank of England, however, has stated that the rescue of JMB is a special case and does not imply that all banks in difficulties will be rescued, but as Hall [1987a] argues, 'no amount of exhortation is likely to persuade market operators to ignore the Bank's actual deeds in the market place'. The JMB affair also opens to question the adequacy of the supervisory arrangements and authorisation procedures at that time. The supervisors of JMB did not chase up late quarterly returns and allowed JMB to postpone meetings with Bank staff. Also, the escalating problems of JMB were not seen by the supervisors, despite the breaches of the Bank's guideline on loan exposure. The Bank expects to be notified of any single non-bank exposure of over 10 per cent of the bank's capital. In its 1985 annual report the Bank of England stated that two large exposures at the end of June 1983 were reported to be 15 per cent and 12 per cent of capital (in fact these were understated and the 'true' figures were 26 per cent and 17 per cent respectively) and at the end of June 1984 were reported to be 38 per cent and 34 per cent ('true' figures being 76 per cent and 39 per cent respectively). Leaving aside the understatement, the Bank's guidelines on loan exposure were known to be breached, with the problem getting worse, well before JMB had to be rescued. The Bank, however, has stated that breaches of this guideline are commonplace and that complete observance of this rule would be too restrictive. The catalogue of incompetence by JMB management, reported in the Bank of England's report for 1985, also calls into question the adequacy of the vetting arrangements undertaken by the Bank. One final issue raised by the JMB affair is the role of auditors in the supervision process. The auditors of JMB, Arthur Young, have been criticised and successfully sued by the Bank of England. However, at the time the auditors of a bank were not allowed to express fears to supervisors without the client's permission. Therefore the only action the auditors could take was resign or qualify the accounts, both of which risked a run on the bank, thereby complicating any future rescue.

The next significant bank failure in the UK was the collapse of the Bank of Credit and Commerce International (BCCI), which was forced to close its operations in July 1991. BCCI was first registered in Luxembourg in 1972 and opened its first UK branch a year later. By 1977 it had 45 branches in the UK and planned to increase the number to 150 but the Bank of England refused this expansion because of concerns regarding its Middle Eastern connections. In 1980 the Bank of England refused BCCI full banking status but allowed it to act as a second-tier licensed deposit taker. Over the 1980s a number of incidents occurred which cast doubt on the competency of management at BCCI and revealed criminal activity in its operation. For example, in 1985 BCCI reported large losses on its futures and options trading. After this BCCI moved its treasury operations out of London to the Gulf region. In 1990 BCCI was found guilty in a Florida court of conspiring to launder money for a Colombian drug cartel. Later on that year the bank's auditors revealed the use of false accounting practices and fictitious loans. In 1990 BCCI moved its operations to Abu Dhabi, making it less accessible to its regulators. Also in that year the auditors of BCCI produced a report to the Bank of England estimating that £1.5 billion was required to cover potential losses. Early in 1991, after a tip-off to the auditors revealing fraudulent activity on a massive scale, the Bank of England initiated a further study from the auditors. This study found that accounts had been falsified for a number of years, that transactions had been disguised and that BCCI was insolvent. The Bank of England shut down BCCI in July 1991. It later emerged that BCCI had worldwide debts of $10 billion (in the UK £400 million). UK depositors were entitled to receive only 75 per cent of their deposits, up to a maximum of £20,000, under the deposit insurance scheme (see below). The main criticism of the Bank of England in this case was why it failed to close down BCCI during the 1980s when there was evidence of fraudulent activity. Indeed, the Bank of England attempted to restructure BCCI in 1990 to save it from closure. In order to investigate this and other aspects of the supervision of BCCI, the government and the Bank of England set up the Bingham inquiry, which reported in October 1992. The inquiry cleared the Bank of England of any negligence in its supervisory activities. However, the inquiry did comment on the slack supervisory regime which took too long to investigate reports of fraud and close BCCI down. The report can be summarised in the following points. (i) The auditors of BCCI may not have pursued evidence aggressively enough, nor did they pass on their concerns to the Bank of England as fully as they may have done. (ii) The Bank of England failed to understand BCCI's legal status, wrongly leading it to rely on the Luxembourg authorities' judgement. (iii) Although fraud was brought to light by other parties, the Bank of England did not investigate; the Bank did not see itself in an investigatory role. (iv) When BCCI faced closure, the Bank of England tried to restructure it and did not take enough notice of reports of lack of fitness and properness.

Among the recommendations of the Bingham inquiry was the establishment of the Special Investigations Unit in the Bank of England (now set up) to examine any warning signs received by the Bank. One of the main lessons to come out of the BCCI affair though was that banking group structures which deny supervisors a clear view of how business is conducted should be outlawed. This has since been addressed by the Basle Committee and is discussed in section 17.4.

The most recent major bank failure was that of Barings in February 1995. Barings was placed in administration following a failed attempt by the Bank of England to secure a buyer. Since then the Barings group operations have been taken over by the Dutch financial services group ING. The failure of Barings was brought on by losses incurred on unauthorised transactions in derivatives undertaken by a single trader operating in a Singapore subsidiary of the group. The size of the losses (which turned out to be £860 million) exceeded the bank's capital. The cause of failure in this case appears to be inadequate internal controls within the Barings group operations. However, the Bank of England, in its role as lead regulator, has also been criticised for its failure to heed earlier warnings of problems in the Barings Singapore subsidiary and its failure to ensure that the group had adequate internal controls. As with BCCI, when the Barings group was faced with closure the Bank of England's preferred solution was a rescue by a bank or syndicate of banks. Justification for such a rescue was weak, as the systemic risks associated with failure were relatively low. Although Barings was allowed to fail in the end, thus sending signals to the marketplace that banks in difficulty will not automatically be bailed out, the signal was not as clear as it could otherwise have been.

Other lessons to come out of the Barings collapse relate to the regulation of derivatives trading and are discussed in section 17.4.

17.3 **Reasons for the prudential control of banks**

As indicated above, the occurrence of bank failure provides the trigger for further regulation but, before looking at the detail of the system of control, we examine why financial institutions are subject to a degree of prudential regulation and supervision. This contrasts with the position of industry and commerce in general where imprudent behaviour (other than illegal activities such as fraud) likely to lead to bankruptcy is the concern of the owners and shareholders rather than any supervisory authority. In discussion of the reasons for prudential control of the financial system, we follow the direction of most of the early literature on this topic, which was focused on prudential control of the banks rather than the financial system as a whole.

First of all we need to examine the nature of the risks faced by banks. These can be categorised as (i) systemic failure arising from deposit withdrawals, (ii) price risk, (iii) default risk, (iv) fraud and mismanagement risk and (v) regulatory risk. Systemic risk arises from the fact that banks' assets and liabilities have a particular feature which may render them liable to financial difficulties even when they are basically sound. Their liabilities are very liquid, often withdrawable on demand, whereas a large proportion of their assets are in the form of loans and advances which are illiquid owing to both (i) the difficulty of securing repayment at short notice and (ii) the absence of a wide secondary market in bank debt. Consequently exercise of the right to withdraw by a large number of depositors (i.e. a run on the bank) may cause failure of a bank which is perfectly viable in the sense that the discounted value of its assets exceeds that of its liabilities. This problem is enhanced by the procedure followed by banks in the event of a run occurring. Until insolvency is declared the bank is obliged to pay out the full amount of any deposit withdrawn. Once insolvency is declared the depositors must await realisation of the bank's assets in the company of other creditors and have their claims assessed by the courts. Thus, in the event of a rumour of difficulties being faced by a bank, there is likely to be a run on that institution since it is in the interest of each depositor to be at the head of the queue. In fact the risk is wider than that so far discussed since, for similar reasons, the 'run mentality' can spread to other banks even though these banks may not be in difficulties. This is because depositors have only imperfect information about a bank's safety. If they see one bank in difficulty they do not have the information to assess whether the problems are specific to that bank or affect all banks. In such circumstances it is rational for depositors to withdraw funds from sound banks in order fully to guarantee safety for their deposits. Thus, the run can spread through the banking system. An unregulated banking system is therefore susceptible to swings in public confidence and this provides one of the main reasons why the banking system is regulated. This danger is termed 'systemic risk' or contagion.

Price risk refers to the possibility of asset prices changing in a manner which will have adverse effects on the bank's financial position. A good illustrative example of price risk is given by the current position of the savings and loans associations in the US. If assets are held with a longer maturity duration than liabilities, then unanticipated rises in interest rates will cause losses unless the lending is at floating rates of interest. It is estimated (see for example Benston and Kaufman [1988]) that at least 500 savings and loans associations were merged or failed since 1981 because of this type of risk. Open currency positions also incur a price risk since unanticipated changes in the relevant exchange rate will result in windfall gains or losses to the bank concerned. Involvement of a bank in futures or options also leaves it exposed to the risk of price changes. The final type of price risk occurs when an institution is forced to sell an asset to obtain funds quickly. The necessity of a speedy sale may prevent the bank from seeking out the most advantageous deal, thus incurring some form of loss. This is in effect a liquidity risk. Price risk in general has increased because of the rising volatility of asset prices, illustrated in figures 14.1 and 14.2.

The risk of default is endemic in bank lending and arises for example from changes in economic climate which will induce failure of some firms. The impact of monetary restraint, with its accompanying high interest rates, on firms with a large percentage of capital in the form of debt provides a good illustration of increased risk of default due to a changing economic climate. Another potential source of debt failure arises from country risk, which refers to the failure of foreign governments and other borrowers to repay loans. The problem of sovereign lending was examined in chapter 4. As was discussed in chapters 3 and 4, a bank can reduce the incidence of default risk by spreading its lending activities over a wide number of customers so that failure of any one customer imposes only a light burden on the bank. Banks can also further reduce the incidence of this type of risk by applying an adequate system of scrutiny of loan applications. Nevertheless, default risk is always present for banks.

Fraud and mismanagement offer further risks to banks. In the UK the closure of BCCI in 1991 – discussed above – was a direct consequence of fraud on a massive scale on the part of the management. In the US it seems that fraud has been the reason for the failure of some savings and loan associations. Yang [1987] reports that fraud and other misconduct was the principal reason for the failure of some 30 associations in California between 1983 and 1986. Mismanagement is a fairly general cause of difficulties for all concerns, financial or otherwise, and was probably one of the main reasons for the 1984 failure of the Johnson Matthey Bank in the UK.

The final type of risk faced by a bank is the potential impact of the regulatory environment, which may impair the safe and efficient operation of a bank. One example of this type of risk in the UK was that in the past banks were subject to imposed lending restraints as part of the government's monetary policy. Similar restraints were not imposed on lending by the building societies.

For the sake of ease of exposition, we have examined these risks as though they were independent of each other. In fact they are interdependent in a number of ways. Thus, for example, inefficient management is likely to lead to inadequate scrutiny of loan applications and hence greater default risk. Price risk can be reduced by appropriate interest-rate pricing and taking a balanced currency position. Liquidity risks can be avoided by holding a sufficient level of highly liquid assets. Fraud can be prevented by good internal supervision as well as the supervision provided by auditors.

We now turn to examining the justification for external regulation of banks in the light of the risks examined above. The first reason offered concerns systemic risk. It is argued that the financial system is subject to waves of confidence and so external regulation is necessary to prevent financial panics.

A second reason offered for the control of banks is that the social costs of a major bank failure are far more wide reaching than the failure of a single firm. Failure of any firm affects shareholders. The difference is that the customers (i.e. the depositors) of a bank are likely to be much larger in number and wider in geographical distribution than a comparable commercial undertaking. In addition, there is the adverse impact on the function of channelling savings to prospective investors which is likely to lower the aggregate level of investment within an economy.

A third reason offered for prudential control is the possible lack of sophistication of the general public. It is argued that they lack the expertise to differentiate between safe and risky investments. One consequence of this is that the public would be likely to accept a higher return offered for investment in one direction without analysing any extra risk which may be involved. This problem is reinforced by the difficulty of obtaining adequate statistics to assess the risk or safety of an individual institution. Balance sheets tend to conceal the type of lending and the risks involved. In addition, as we saw in chapter 2, banks' existence is partly based on asymmetric information since banks have access to information not available to depositors. Adequate risk assessment requires information supplementary to that contained in the financial reports. The justification of regulation under this heading may be conveniently summed up as depositor protection.

As we have seen in chapters 3 and 4, banks are currently under a considerable degree of pressure for a variety of reasons, such as the sovereign debt overhang, bad debts arising from company failure due to high interest rates and falling property values and keen competition. These facets provide a fourth reason for supervising banks, which is the prevention of banks undertaking excessively risky operations in an effort to restore their financial position. There is also the feeling that excessive competition may lead to underpricing of services which, in turn, has an adverse effect on long-run profitability and, therefore, the viability of banks. This fear is compounded by the fact that the 'correct' price for a new service may be difficult to determine without experience extending over an adequate period of time.

The final reason offered for prudential control of banks is the prevention of the entrance of 'undesirable' firms or individuals into an industry in which the preservation of confidence is so vital. A supporting argument is that the industry offers considerable scope for fraud and that, therefore, this restraint is essential.

It should be noted that the arguments so far presented favour regulation of banks. Nevertheless, certain caveats can be entered against the exercise of excessive prudential control over banks. The first consideration is the incontrovertible fact that regulation imposes costs in the form of real resources on both the regulators and the regulated. The central bank has to employ the expertise necessary to carry out the prudential control and the banks have to employ resources to complete the returns required by the controller. These costs can be relatively high and it is therefore a question of cost–benefit analysis to determine whether the benefits gained by prudential regulation outweigh the costs incurred. Second, there is the danger of the regulation becoming so excessive as to reduce competition, raising costs and lowering the pace of financial innovation. A similar argument is often presented in terms of the institutions 'capturing' the regulator by the introduction of practices favourable to themselves, as for example the introduction of a cartel restraining competition and raising profits. A further argument against regulation is that the form of the regulations will distort the market mechanism by diverting resources to fields of activity favoured by the regulators.

Finally by way of arguments opposed to regulation is the danger that onerous regulations imposed in one centre will merely lead to the movement of the activity to centres where regulation is more relaxed. This is of course one of the main reasons for the development of offshore banking and is perhaps the main incentive for a common regulation system across banks operating in different countries, often termed a 'level playing field'. This aspect of prudential control is discussed in the following section. In recent years a small but growing group of economists have argued that banking markets are no different to any other markets and so the principle of laissez-faire should also apply. These 'free-bankers' believe that banks should be allowed to operate in a truly competitive market environment with no restrictions on the types of assets they hold or the liabilities they issue and in addition no protective restrictions such as restrictions on entry to banking, deposit insurance (see later) or lender of last resort. In such a competitive banking system depositors would be aware that they would lose their funds if the bank failed. Depositors would want reassurance that their funds were safe. Bank managers would want to keep depositors' confidence because if depositors had any doubts about the safety of the bank they would start to withdraw deposits. Bank managers would therefore want to reassure depositors that they were not taking excessive risks and would expose their policies to outside scrutiny. Bank managers would also want to maintain adequate capital, again to reassure depositors. Competition would ensure that bankers struck the right balance between return to investors and depositor protection. According to Dowd [1993] history shows us that banks in relatively unregulated systems maintained strong capital. Dowd also argues that bank runs were usually constructive events that weeded out the weaker banks. One interesting suggestion put forward by Benston (see e.g. Benston and Kaufman [1988]) is for a bank's assets and liabilities to be revalued at market prices and that, when economic capital becomes negative (or perhaps positive but only by a small margin), the bank should be reorganised or taken over. One of the main advantages claimed for this system is that the cost of any bank rescue would be quite small. Second, it is argued that depositors would have increased confidence in the banking system, so that runs on banks would become less frequent. Third, the requirement for much of the system of prudential control would be removed. Implementation of such a system would require periodic revaluation of assets and this would cause major difficulty given the high proportion of UK bank assets in the form of loans which, as we have already seen, are difficult to recall or sell on a secondary market.

In summing up the arguments for and against prudential regulation of banks, perhaps the most telling argument is the lack of expertise and knowledge possessed by the individual depositor to assess the quality of the bank. The argument in favour of prudential regulation of the financial industry has been framed in terms of banks but most of the arguments can easily be extended to incorporate prudential regulation of financial institutions in general. The remainder of this chapter will concentrate on the regulation of banks (section 17.4) followed by the investment institutions (section 17.5).

17.4 The UK system of prudential control of banks

The Banking Acts of 1979 and 1987 require banks to be licensed by the Bank of England before operating as a bank. The 1979 Act divided the industry into banks and deposit-taking institutions, which were seen by many as first- and second-division banking institutions. This distinction was removed by the 1987 Act. The licensing procedure requires the Bank of England to be satisfied that the quality of management, range of services and reputation are consistent with the banking status. There is also provision for removal of the licence but this has not yet been carried out for a bank though licences were terminated for a number of licensed deposit-taking institutions under the 1979 Act. The connection between this requirement and the danger of undesirable firms/individuals entering the banking industry is obvious. Other components of the UK system of prudential control are (i) deposit insurance, (ii) the role of auditors, (iii) liquidity controls and (iv) capital adequacy. These are dealt with in the following sections together with the problem of international coordination of supervision of banks.

Deposit insurance

The second component of the UK system of prudential control is the existence of insurance of deposits. In the event of failure, depositors would have 75 per cent of their deposits refunded, up to a maximum of £20,000. The scheme is financed by a flat-rate contribution by banks in proportion to their deposits and is administered by the Bank of England. The advantages claimed for deposit insurance are threefold. First, such schemes are designed to provide for speedy compensation for depositors, who then have no need to wait for the completion of the winding up of the institution. Second, systemic risk should be reduced since the incentive to be first in the queue to withdraw deposits is reduced. This point is critically dependent on the public being aware that deposits are insured in this manner. This is far from evident. As an interesting exercise the reader should try asking friends or a class of students if they know that their deposits are insured! Third, perhaps the hidden rationale for the scheme is that it provides the finance for compensation of depositors without recourse to the government.

Deposit insurance is not without its critics since it is open to a number of objections. It can be argued that the existence of deposit insurance increases the problem of 'moral hazard'. As far as the banks are concerned the wrath of the depositors may be averted because of the knowledge that they will obtain compensation for any deposit loss. This could act as an incentive to the bank managers to take excessive risks since any profits gained will be theirs but any loss will be borne by the insurer. For similar reasons the depositors may be less careful in their assessment of risk and may select institutions which offer the highest rate of interest on deposits regardless of the risks involved because they know any loss will be reimbursed by the insurer. Presumably the restriction of reimbursement to 75 per cent and a maximum of £20,000 is both an attempt to overcome the moral hazard problem and a recognition that large deposits are likely to be made by persons or institutions with an awareness of the financial risks involved. There is some doubt, however, as to whether a 25 per cent 'haircut' will prevent a 'run' developing. Apart from the question of moral hazard, there is doubt over the precise form of insurance charge levied in the UK and most other countries. The charge is levied on the quantity of deposits at a flat rate. Many argue that the charge should be linked to the risk involved, in the manner of car insurance. The problem with this suggestion is who is going to make the risk assessment? It is likely that a central bank would baulk at that type of decision for fear of complaints of discrimination. It also remains a moot point whether ratings provided by private agencies would be satisfactory for the purpose of fixing deposit insurance rates. Nevertheless, the Federal Insurance Corporation in the US has submitted a proposal for discussion whereby premiums would be cut for banks rated as well capitalised and well managed, from 23 cents per $100 of deposits to 4 cents. In contrast, banks regarded as risky would have to pay the much higher premium of 31 cents. This would provide a rough and ready approximation to a risk-related premium.

The last point to be made about deposit insurance is that it is not likely to be an adequate substitute for prudential control unless central banks are prepared to permit banks to become bankrupt so that insurance would be seen as protection rather than compensation. The evidence is mixed as far as the Bank of England is concerned, as the JMB bank was rescued whilst BCCI and Barings were allowed to fail. Schemes for the overhaul of the UK system of deposit insurance are suggested by Hall [1987b] and Goodhart [1988].

In the 1980s the US system of banks and particularly thrift institutions has seen a dramatic increase in the number of institutions failing, putting the Federal Deposit Insurance Scheme under a tremendous strain. The Federal Savings and Loan Insurance Fund was overwhelmed and federal taxpayers had to bail the fund out to the tune of several hundred billion dollars. This has prompted a lively debate in the US about reform of the deposit insurance system and the interested reader is referred to a series of essays which examine reform from a variety of angles (Russell [1993]).

Liaison with auditors

Auditors provide a potentially fruitful source of information concerning the financial position of banks. However, a conflict of duty may arise since the auditors have a prime responsibility to the shareholders of the banks whereas the role of the supervisors is the protection of the depositors. Following the Banking Act 1987, a relationship between the auditors and the Bank was provided for. The relationship is to be based on trilateral meetings between the auditors, the institution and the supervisors at the Bank. Matters to be discussed include the statutory accounts and the auditors' reports. The reporting accountants are also required to report on the institution's accounting and other internal control systems and the returns provided for prudential control purposes. Meetings are normally to be called by the Bank or by the auditors via the institution concerned. In exceptional cases, however, the auditors or reporting accountants could report direct to the Bank. Such exceptional circumstances would have to be of a serious nature, such as situations where the integrity of the directors or senior management is being questioned.

The connection between the role of auditors and the failure of management in connection with JMB failure, accompanied by inadequate internal systems of control and provision of inaccurate returns, is self-evident.

Liquidity control

As we have discussed above, one feature of the asset and liability structure of banks which suggests prudential control is the liquid nature of their liabilities and illiquid nature of their assets. A bank can fail through inability to meet deposit withdrawals through lack of liquidity even though it is viable in the long run. Liquidity can be provided in a number of ways, including:

(i) holding sufficient cash or assets which are easily liquefied,
(ii) holding an appropriately matching portfolio of cash flows from maturing assets,
(iii) maintaining an adequately diversified deposit base in terms of maturities and mix of depositors.

The bank supervisors have the duty to ensure that banks maintain an appropriate mix of all three. With specific reference to the liquidity position, no minimum overall liquidity ratio is applied to all banks because it is felt that the allocation of specific assets to a liquidity category is bound to be arbitrary. Banks engage in maturity transformation, so that the term structure of their assets is longer than that of their liabilities. Hence control of the liquidity position of banks can be achieved by preparing a maturity ladder, showing the accumulated mismatch of short-term assets and liabilities over a variety of time periods up to one year. In this ladder marketable assets are shown as maturing immediately but are subject to a discount for valuation in the liquidity ladder so as to reflect potential variations in market price; for example, CDs with less than six months remaining to maturity are subject to five per cent discount and those up to five years ten per cent discount. The time periods of this maturity ladder are (i) sight to eight days; (ii) eight days to one month; (iii) one to three months; (iv) three to six months; and (v) six to twelve months. It would be expected that the maximum point of excess of liabilities over assets will occur in the first six months. No standards are imposed for any of the periods involved and the position of each bank will be considered in the environment in which it operates.

A further control exists since the Bank is concerned with individual banks' holdings of 'high-class' liquidity. High-class liquidity is defined as instruments with which the Bank of England is prepared to deal in its daily operations in the London discount market (see chapter 10), such as eligible bills, local authority bills, and so on. No general requirement is imposed on all banks but the Bank will discuss with each bank its holdings of high-class liquidity. Assessment of its adequacy will be considered against the individual circumstances of each bank

Capital adequacy

As we have noted in the last section, liquidity is essentially a short-term concept referring to the ability of an institution to meet day-to-day cash outflows, whereas solvency is a longer-term concept referring to the prospective ability of a bank to meet all its liabilities as they fall due. The distinction between liquidity and solvency is not as clear cut as these definitions imply. There is a view that if a financial institution is confidently believed to be solvent then it should be able to borrow through the markets to meet any short-term liquidity difficulties. It follows therefore that the existence of liquidity problems that cannot be resolved through the markets implies that other market participants believe the risk of insolvency for that institution to be high. The reverse is generally not the case as it is possible to face insolvency problems without any illiquidity problems first showing up, as was the case with the Johnson Matthey Bank. The view that 'banks with liquidity problems that cannot be solved through the markets implies the bank is likely to be insolvent' is seen by Quinn, the Executive Director of the Bank of England with responsibility for banking supervision, to be one which is 'absolutist and neglects the vital role that time plays in assessing the quality of a bank's assets, quite apart from being a high risk strategy' (*Bank of England Quarterly Bulletin*, May 1988). Quinn argues that there are great difficulties in establishing the value of a bank's assets and that it is possible for assets to gain or lose value very quickly, thus creating liquidity problems. A bank's management may be able to turn round the problem over time or the problem may disappear through an improvement in external circumstances. However, if a bank is denied short-term funding, its capacity to recover claims is put in doubt and other debtors may then stop paying, believing that the institution is likely to become insolvent, thus compounding the problem. Thus, the Bank of England has placed increasing emphasis on banks managing their liquidity as part of the overall policy of minimising the risk of insolvency. However, the most important aspect of the Bank's policy in this regard relates to its monitoring of each bank's capital adequacy.

The capital of a bank is seen as financing the infrastructure of the business and providing a cushion to absorb any losses on its assets. As we saw in chapter 2, a bank can minimise any default losses with regard to its loans by (i) limiting the risk of default on individual loans through appropriate selection of borrowers, (ii) reducing the overall risk of its loan portfolio by diversifying and (iii) pooling its risk so as to make the overall risk of default more predictable. This last point enables the bank to cover its expected losses by incorporating a premium in its loan rate of interest. Unexpected loan losses are then covered by the bank's profits in the first instance and ultimately by its capital. Thus, the level of a bank's capital is important in assessing the solvency of a bank in adverse circumstances. The underlying principle is that it is the shareholders rather than the depositors who should bear the risks of the business undertaking.

The question of capital adequacy was first addressed by a working party set up by the Bank of England in 1974, which reported in 1975 (see *Bank of England Quarterly Bulletin*, September 1975). This working party recommended the use of two ratios: the free resources (gearing) ratio and the risk assets ratio. These ratios were further revised in 1979 and the system of assessing capital adequacy that operated throughout most of the 1980s is set out in the *Bank of England Quarterly Bulletin* of September 1980. The gearing ratio is a very simple measure, essentially relating the value of a bank's free resources, that is broadly the bank's capital minus the value of its infrastructure, to the value of its deposits. Thus, it takes no account of the riskiness of the bank's assets and as a consequence is rarely referred to nowadays for supervisory purposes. The risk assets ratio has become the key ratio in monitoring capital adequacy and this relates the value of a bank's capital to the value of its assets weighted according to their inherent riskiness. Whilst this approach related an individual bank's capital to the riskiness of its activities, it did so only to the extent that these activities appeared on the balance sheet. As we have discussed in chapter 4, over the 1980s banks have increasingly undertaken activities which do not result in a balance sheet entry under normal accounting procedures ('off-balance-sheet' business). Thus, in order to measure the adequacy of a bank's capital to all, or at least most, of the default risks it is exposed to, the risk assets ratio has recently been modified to incorporate 'off-balance-sheet' business.

The new system of risk weightings and capital definitions were proposed in an agreement reached by the Basle Committee in 1988. This accord, which provides for a common system of prudential control for banks operating in the major industrial countries, came into effect at the beginning of 1993. Under this approach banks' assets are divided into various categories and each category is given a weighting according to its perceived relative riskiness. Each asset is multiplied by this risk factor and the total of the risk-adjusted assets then related to the bank's capital. For example, cash has a risk weight of 0, loans to discount houses 10 per cent and commercial loans 100 per cent. A two-step process is involved for off-balance-sheet items. First, they are transformed into an on-balance-sheet item using standard conversion ratios. Second, the risk weightings are then applied to the converted values. The capital base itself consists of two components: (i) core capital, or tier 1, and (ii) supplementary capital, or tier 2. The first component broadly represents equity, reserves and retained profits and the second consists of other types of capital liabilities such as subordinated debt instruments (i.e. debt ranking after all other debt for winding up purposes), general provisions and revaluation reserves. Three restrictions are imposed. First, the total of tier 2 components should not exceed a maximum of 100 per cent of the total of tier 1 items. Second, subordinated debt should not exceed a maximum of 50 per cent of the total of tier 1 items. Third, general provisions should not exceed 1.25 per cent of weighted risk assets. A minimum level for the risk assets ratio of eight per cent is prescribed but it is not expected that all banks will work to this figure and capital adequacy will be considered for each bank against the background of its operations. Sometimes an informal distinction is made between upper tier 2 capital and lower tier 2 capital. Lower tier 2 capital refers to subordinated term debt which, as noted above, is restricted to a maximum of 50 per cent of tier 1 capital. All other types of tier 2 capital fall into the upper category.

The theoretical basis of the risk-adjusted asset ratio is perhaps suspect since is based on the assumption that the risks are independent, otherwise it would not be possible to add the risk-adjusted assets together. Portfolio theory suggests that risks may be interdependent in some instances; for example, a general recession will induce failures of a number of companies. It is difficult, however, to design a scheme which would take this factor into consideration. A second problem arises if the risk factors do not accurately measure the relative degree of risk in each asset. This problem is made worse because the effect of the risk weightings is likely to induce lending favourable to the arbitrarily imposed risk factors and may therefore distort the market mechanism. Another serious concern with the new system relates to the 100 per cent risk weighting applicable to commercial loans to the private sector. The implication is that the capital requirement for a loan to an AAA-rated multinational company (see section on credit ratings in chapter 9) is precisely the same for a loan of the same size to a small company with a lower credit rating. As banks' main assets are loans it is not clear why the designers of the system did not allow for differential risk weightings in this area. One consequence may be that aggressively managed banks may be tempted to shift their lending towards high-risk (high-return) borrowers while cautiously managed banks are not rewarded for their prudence.

Heavy exposure to individual companies imposes a risk over and above that captured by comparing asset risks and capital, as evidenced in the failure of JMB. A bank is therefore required to notify exposure to any individual customer in excess of 10 per cent of its capital (calculated in the same manner as for the risk-adjusted asset ratio). Any exposure in excess of 25 per cent of the capital base requires prior permission of the Bank of England.

Foreign currency exposure provides an additional source of danger to banks since exchange rates can change quickly, imposing potential losses of a major nature. Consequently banks' open dealing positions are restricted to a maximum of:

(i) 10 per cent of capital base for net open position in any one currency;
(ii) 15 per cent of capital base for net open short position of all currencies taken together.

The precise position for each bank would depend on its experience in dealing in foreign currency assets/liabilities and management skills, so it would not be likely that each bank could deal up to the positions discussed above. Again, it is notable that the control is based on ensuring that the capital position of a bank is adequate to cover potential losses incurred through open foreign currency dealing positions, so as to protect depositors rather than shareholders from losses.

International cooperation

Banking is an international function, with many banks operating outside the country where their head office is located. Types of foreign banking establishments comprise (i) branches, (ii) subsidiaries and (iii) joint ventures or consortia. Thus, some difficulties could occur for effective prudential control because of ambiguities as to the precise division of the responsibility for supervision. In 1975 the Basle concordat set out guidelines defining the responsibilities of the parent and the host country for supervision. This was reformulated again in 1983. The main principle of these guidelines was that no foreign banking establishment should escape adequate supervision. It was agreed that supervision of consortia should be exercised by the authorities in the country of incorporation. With respect to the remaining two categories, host authorities are primarily responsible for supervision of their liquidity and foreign currency positions. Capital adequacy is the responsibility of the parent country. As described above, in July 1988 the Basle Committee launched a major new regulatory initiative with an agreement by the Group of 10 industrial countries (G-10) to establish minimum capital adequacy standards for international banks. A reassessment of the Basle approach to banking regulation was prompted by the supervisory weaknesses revealed by the collapse of BCCI in the summer of 1991. In particular, the BCCI collapse demonstrated the ease with which a fraudulent bank could exploit weakly regulated offshore centres. This led in July 1992 to the Basle Committee issuing a new set of minimum standards for the supervision of international banks. The main requirement is that all international banks should be supervised by a home-country authority 'that capably performs consolidated supervision'. That is, the authority concerned should (i) monitor banks' global operations on the basis of verifiable consolidated data, (ii) be able to prohibit the creation of corporate structures that impede consolidated supervision and (iii) be able to prevent banks from establishing a presence in a suspect jurisdiction. In April 1993 the Basle Committee issued new proposals to extend the 1988 accord. The 1988 accord was principally concerned with credit risk. The new proposals extend this to cover the supervisory treatment of market risk and interest rate risk. These proposals, agreed in 1995, provide for the use of banks' own internal models for measuring market risks. Those firms that do not have a comprehensive internal model will apply a standardised measurement framework. Such models measure the sensitivity of a bank to loss from adverse movements in the market. Under these proposals, specific capital charges would be applied to banks' trading positions, including derivative positions, in debt and equity instruments. In addition, a measurement system is proposed to identify where banks have significant interest rate exposure. One issue raised by the proposed market risk proposals is that it requires a bank to separate its long-term investments in securities from its trading book. The long-term investments would then be subject to the original credit risk capital requirements under the 1988 accord. The trading book positions would be subject to lighter capital requirements. This is designed to create a level playing field in regulation for all institutions undertaking securities business. An obvious problem with this proposal is where the cut-off between an investment and a trading position should occur. This raises the possibility of regulatory circumvention, as a bank may categorise some of its investments as trading book positions to benefit from lighter regulation. The aim of the interest rate risk proposals is simply to develop a measurement system which will allow supervisors to identify high-risk banks. Appropriate action on dealing with excessive risk taking in this area is then left to the discretion of the supervisory authority. It is likely though that once agreement is reached on a measurement system further arrangements to discourage excessive risk taking are likely to follow.

Finally in this section, regulatory agencies around the world have become increasingly concerned by the rapid growth in derivatives trading by banks (see chapters 13 and 14 for discussion) and the potential risks arising out of this. The main concerns are that the complexity of these instruments may impede effective risk control by bank management and supervisors and the market linkages created by derivatives increases the potential for financial contagion. This latter concern is another form of the systemic risk problem discussed in section 17.3. A number of regulatory authorities, including the US Federal Reserve, the Bank of England and the Bank for International Settlements, have undertaken reviews of the derivatives situation and each has expressed concern. These concerns have been heightened by the collapse of Barings bank in February 1995 following losses sustained in derivatives trading (discussed in section 17.2). The capital adequacy regime arising out of the Basle accord covers the credit risk side of derivatives and the new market risk proposals, agreed in 1995, will cover derivatives market risk. Differences may exist between exchange-traded derivatives, which are transparent, and OTC derivatives, which are more opaque. Hence further developments in this area are likely to focus on encouraging institutions to disclose more information about their risk positions and risk control systems. This control refers to banks, not customers. The latter may be assumed to have expertise in assessing risks although recent examples of losses made by companies through misuse of derivatives (e.g. Mettalgesellshaft and Procter and Gamble) may suggest otherwise.

We now turn to an examination of the supervision of investment institutions.

17.5 **Control of investment business**

Before 1986, the control of investment business was carried out under the provisions of Prevention of Fraud (Investments) Act 1958. However, at the beginning of the 1980s doubts were being expressed concerning the effectiveness of this Act and these led to the appointment of Professor Gower to review the protection of investors. The Financial Services Act 1986 was based on the Gower report. In this section we briefly review the general nature of the machinery of control.

In general the 1986 Act provided for the legislation of investment business. An investment was widely defined to include securities issued by companies, public corporations, central and local government. Units in collective investment schemes were also included, as were futures, options and long-term insurance. Investment business was also widely defined and included dealing, arranging deals, managing collective investment schemes and investment advice. Basically the legislation requires that any person or company carrying out such investment business must obtain authorisation. Certain institutions and persons can gain exemption from the need to be authorised, as 'exempted persons'. Exempted persons include Lloyd's underwriters, the Bank of England and recognised investment exchanges (see below). Provision was included for removal of authorisation in the case of wrongdoing. A compensation fund was set up and provisions made for dealing with complaints by the general public.

The overall regulatory function was delegated to the Securities and Investment Board (SIB). Second-tier regulatory bodies were also set up for the various subdivisions of the investment business and these were called self-regulatory organisations (SROs). The SROs require approval from the SIB before they can operate. The SROs currently recognised by the SIB are:

(i) the Securities and Futures Authority (SFA),
(ii) the Personal Investment Authority (PIA),
(iii) the Financial Intermediaries, Managers and Brokers Regulatory Association (FIMBRA),
(iv) the Investment Management Regulatory Organisation (IMRO),
(v) the Life Assurance and Unit Trust Regulatory Organisation (LAUTRO).

The Personal Investment Authority (PIA) was set up in 1994 and regulates investment business conducted with private investors chiefly relating to 'packaged products' such as life assurance policies and unit trusts. In late 1995 the PIA will completely take over the regulatory tasks currently undertaken by LAUTRO and FIMBRA and these two bodies will have their recognition terminated by the SIB. Supervision of the conduct of business is entrusted to these SROs and they have had to produce rule books for operations within their trade which are at least equivalent to the rule book of the SIB. In this connection it has proved difficult to reach a compromise between broad coverage and a lack of complexity.

Investment exchanges may also apply for recognition by the SIB. A recognised investment exchange (RIE) is classed as an exempted person as regards investment business done in its capacity and therefore does not require authorisation. RIEs currently recognised include the London Stock Exchange, LIFFE and the main commodities exchanges in London. A second category of investment exchange created under the SIB's rules is the designated investment exchange (DIE). This is an investment exchange engaged in the dealing of international securities but not subject to UK regulation. An example of a DIE is the International Securities Markets Association, which organises a market in international bonds from London. Transactions effected on a DIE by an authorised person need not be reported to the SIB. Finally, overseas exchanges can also be recognised under the Financial Services Act. Once recognised, an overseas exchange is classed as an exempted person in respect of investment business done in the UK. Examples of overseas exchanges obtaining such recognition are NASDAQ and the Sydney Futures Exchange.

The other main part of the investment regulatory environment is the Criminal Justice Act 1993, which deals, among other things, with insider dealing and money laundering offences.

The overall objective of the legislation is to achieve protection for investors with involvement of government being the minimum necessary to achieve an operation of a financial system which provides fair rewards without fraud. The strategy adopted was one of self-regulation within a statutory framework. Some felt that a more legal approach would have been desirable, on the lines of the US Securities and Exchange Commission. The opposing argument is based on the idea that practitioners are better placed to spot abuses and breaches of rules than an external body carrying out legal obligations. It is probable that the system adopted will be more flexible and faster in the provision of remedies than a court.

17.6 **Conclusion**

We have surveyed the UK system of prudential control of financial institutions. The main thrust of our argument has been concerned with the banks. Because of the central position of financial institutions as intermediaries between lenders and borrowers, it is generally (but not always) agreed that some form of external control should be exercised over their behaviour to ensure that they act in a 'prudential' or careful manner. However, all financial behaviour involves risk and prudential control should not be too excessive otherwise competition may be restrained in a manner which leads to excessive operating costs and a lack of financial innovation.

Chapter 18

Conclusions

18.1 Nature of the UK financial system

In this section we provide a brief summary of the nature of the UK financial system and in section 18.2 we discuss the extent to which the financial system impinges on the operation of monetary policy.

In chapter 2, we defined the financial system as a set of markets and institutions which provide the means of raising finance and which supply various financial services. The institutions we have considered in this book can be usefully subdivided as follows:

(i) the monetary sector – wholesale and retail banks (chapters 3 and 4 respectively), and discount houses (section 10.2),
(ii) other deposit-taking institutions – building societies and finance houses (chapter 5),
(iii) long-term investment institutions – pension funds, life assurance companies, investment and unit trusts (chapter 6).

In a similar manner, discussion of markets proceeded as follows:

(i) introduction to markets (chapter 7)
(ii) equity markets (chapter 8)
(iii) the bond market, including the term structure of interest rates (chapter 9),
(iv) the sterling money markets (chapter 10),
(v) the foreign exchange markets (chapter 11)
(vi) the euro-securities markets (chapter 12),
(vii) the newer derivative markets, that is, financial futures and options markets (chapter 13); this was followed by a discussion of the role of these markets in the management of risk (chapter 14).

The operation of the financial system raises a number of issues. The first concerns how far prudential control should be exercised over the institutions/markets. This was considered in chapter 17. The impact of a single European market and economic and monetary union between member states of the European Union was discussed in chapter 15. Efficiency of the system was examined in two ways. First, consideration of the application of the efficient markets hypothesis (EMH) took place against the background of each of the markets. An agnostic conclusion was reached for all markets, implying that the EMH was still an open question. Second, the broader aspect of the efficiency of the UK financial system was discussed in chapter 16, and here again our conclusions were not firm but tended to point towards efficiency.

By any standard, the UK financial system described above is a sophisticated system. It is also an open financial system, without restriction of flows of funds into or out of the country for either residents or non-residents. It is also a financial system which has seen a considerable degree of change in recent years in the development of both (i) new markets (e.g. financial futures) and new instruments (e.g. commercial paper) and (ii) liberalisation in the sense of the removal of controls restricting competition between institutions. At the same time, the incidence of prudential control has increased. It is an interesting question whether such a sophisticated financial system impedes or reinforces monetary policy, and we now turn to consider this.

18.2 The financial system and monetary policy

Clearly, monetary policy operates through the financial system. For example, if it is desired to raise rates of interest, the initial change is introduced by the Bank of England through its daily operations in the discount market, as described in section 10.2. In a similar way, intervention in the foreign exchange markets to influence exchange rates also affects the market makers in the forex. Policy changes may have an adverse effect on the financial institutions involved. The first way in which a problem may arise for the operation of the monetary policy is attributable to the dual function of the central bank, that is, the Bank of England. As we saw in chapter 3, the Bank has the responsibility of (i) supporting the financial system in its function as a lender of last resort and (ii) operating monetary policy. A fear is sometimes expressed that if the Bank pressed too hard in its operation of monetary policy, this would cause difficulties for financial institutions such as the banks and discount houses, causing them problems which could lead to a possibility of failure. In a similar way, recent worldwide increases in rates of interest caused problems for debtor nations and led to the sovereign lending problem discussed in section 4.5. Fear of default by debtor nations raises the spectre of bank failure on a large scale. For this type of reason it is sometimes argued that the wellbeing of the financial system imposes restraints on the operation of monetary policy.

The nature of the financial system may also impose restraints on the effectiveness of different monetary instruments. This is particularly true of the UK system, which, as we have seen, is very open, so that restraint in the UK may be avoided by borrowing overseas, or by the movement of institutions to offshore locations.

In the last decade, UK monetary policy has been operated via interest rate changes. A restrictive policy has raised nominal interest rates (and often real rates) quite sharply with a view to dampening down expenditure. An interest rate policy will also alter the cost of borrowing overseas through adjustments to the expected exchange rate as compared with the current rate so as to maintain interest rate parity (if only approximately), as discussed in section 11.4 (see, in particular, equation 11.3). A problem of course arises with respect to the UK's membership of the ERM (section 15.4) since only limited exchange rate movements are feasible. If domestic policy actions are deemed by market operators to be inconsistent with maintenance of the current exchange rate, then speculative flows will occur on a massive scale. This will happen because market operators have been presented with what has been termed a 'one-way option'. In the case of a probable devaluation, speculators know that an appreciation of the exchange rate is not possible, so that their losses from speculation in favour of a devaluation will be minimal whereas their gains will be substantial if the devaluation occurs. Consequently, the operation of a sophisticated financial system may force devaluation of a fixed exchange rate on an unwilling government and frustrate any attempts by monetary policy to protect the exchange rate at its agreed level.

This concentration of monetary policy has been criticised in the past and, in particular, credit controls have been suggested as an alternative/supplement to interest rate policy. For example, a restrictive monetary policy would entail increasing the severity of credit controls so that the resulting restriction of the supply of funds would reduce the level of aggregate demand. The efficacy of such controls depends critically on the extent to which they can be circumvented. This can occur in two ways. First, new types of domestic financial institutions and/or lending can develop which are outside the area of the controls. This is likely to be quite a slow process, so that it may well be that the authorities have little to fear from it in the short run. The potentially more serious frustration of credit controls occurs as a consequence of the very openness of the UK financial system. Capital controls no longer exist for domestic residents of the UK and their reimposition is incompatible with EU regulations (stage 1 of European monetary union). Consequently, imposition of credit controls within the

UK could be easily frustrated by overseas institutions or UK institutions operating offshore branches. For example, restraint on mortgage lending can be avoided by borrowing from a non-resident institution or an overseas branch of a UK institution. Similarly, restrictions on hire purchase on, say, cars within the UK could be avoided by the purchase of the car from an alternative centre within Europe with finance organised at the point of purchase. In the former case it only needs the opening of a UK office to channel lending to the head office overseas. It may be argued that such developments would take some time to come into being, but, on the other hand, sophisticated financial systems are likely to take advantage quickly of perceived profitable opportunities. It would seem therefore that credit controls could provide only an extremely short-term alternative to rising interest rates. They also suffer from the disadvantage that their impact is arbitrary and likely to discriminate unfairly between different classes of people. For example, the economically literate will perceive the opportunities offered by borrowing abroad in the face of domestic credit restraints, whereas those who are not so well informed will be slow to take up that opportunity. Furthermore, such controls interfere with the operation of the price mechanism, the efficiency of which has been one of the main objectives of the policy of liberalisation of the financial system.

Our conclusion is, therefore, that a developed and open financial system does make it difficult to operate non-market types of monetary policy, as the imposition of direct controls is likely to be quite quickly frustrated by the development of new financial instruments and/or sources of funds.

Glossary

ADRs American Depositary Receipts – confer ownership rights to British shares and traded in their own right. Avoids the need to register change in share ownership and transactions do not involve stamp duty.

Arbitrage Buying and selling securities in order to profit from price differences without incurring risk.

Ask price The price at which a market maker is prepared to sell a security.

Banker's acceptance A bill of exchange endorsed by a bank, i.e. the bank is guaranteeing the bill. It commands a low rate of discount – see under *bill of exchange*.

Basis The spread or difference between two rates, such as the difference between the futures price and that of the underlying cash instrument.

Basis-point One one-hundredth of 1 per cent.

Bearer bond A bond which is owned by whoever holds it. No registration of ownership is involved – see under *bond*.

BES Business Expansion Scheme – a scheme set up by the government in 1983 whereby investors can claim tax relief for investment in unquoted companies.

Bill of exchange An order in writing telling a person to pay a certain sum of money to another at a specific time in the future. Bills are mainly used in foreign trade. The person who promises to pay is said to accept the bill. A prime bank bill is a bill accepted by a high-class bank. A fine trade bill is a bill accepted by a trader with a first-class reputation. A bill bears no interest rate and is said to be discounted when it is sold for a price less than its maturity value.

BIS	Bank for International Settlements – a bank for European central banks.
Bond	A title issued by the public sector or a company acknowledging the existence of debt. Normally a bond commands a fixed rate of interest based on its nominal value.
Broker	A person who arranges deals between buyers and sellers on behalf of a third party. A broker is not trading on her/his own account but earns a commission on the deal called a brokerage fee.
Cap	A derivative instrument designed to fix a maximum level to which a price or interest rate can rise.
CD	A certificate of deposit – a negotiable instrument issued by a bank or building society acknowledging an interest-bearing time deposit.
CHAPS	Clearing House Automated Payments System – automated end-of-day net settlement system for sterling wholesale payments.
Collar	A derivative instrument designed to fix both a maximum and minimum level to which a price or interest rate can rise or fall.
Collateral	Security given for the repayment of a loan.
Commercial paper	An unsecured promissory note issued by commercial firms promising to pay a fixed sum of money normally with a maturity of less than 270 days. This security is usually sold at a discount, i.e. for less than its nominal or face value.
Consortium banks	A subsidiary set up by a number of banks for the purpose of making a large loan(s).
Contingent liability	Debt which comes into existence on the occurrence of some contingency.
Coupon	Fixed rate of interest payable on bonds.
Covered interest arbitrage	Investing in a security denominated in a foreign currency and covering against the exchange rate risk by taking out an offsetting forward transaction.
Cross default clause	A condition of a loan which permits the lender to demand immediate repayment if the borrower defaults on another loan.
Debt rescheduling	Formal rearrangement of both debt service payments and repayment of the principal with new maturities.
Default	Failure of a borrower to make a payment of either interest or principal on the due date.
Discount	The payment of an immediate sum in settlement of a sum due at a later date.
Discount houses	A group of institutions whose main function is to discount bills of exchange and other short-term financial instruments.

Dividend	Income return on ordinary shares.
ECU	The European Currency Unit. It is made up of a weighted total of the currencies of the member states of the European Union.
EMH	The efficient markets hypothesis, which puts forward the view that market prices reflect all available information.
EMI	European Monetary Institute – forerunner of the European Central Bank.
ERM	Exchange Rate Mechanism. The system of semi-fixed exchange rates of participating countries of the European Union.
Equity	The part of total capital of a company belonging to the shareholders. In terms of a company's balance sheet it is the residual after deducting liabilities except those due to shareholders from total assets.
ESCB	European System of Central Banks – the central banks of Europe all acting independently of domestic governments under an agreement on monetary union, under the control of the European Central Bank.
Eurobank	Financial institutions that accept deposits and make loans in currencies other than that of the country where they are located (i.e. the 'host country').
Eurobond	A bond issued in a currency other than that of the country where it is issued, for example a bond denominated in dollars issued in London.
Eurodollar	Dollar deposits held at banks located outside the US. More broadly the terms can be used for a deposit denominated in any currency other than that of the host country.
Euronote	Short-term notes or debts issued in the syndicated loan market. Short term usually refers to one-, three- or six-month maturities.
Exercise price	The specified price at which *options* can be taken up or exercised.
Factoring	The act of a financial institution taking over the debts owed to a firm. The price paid for the debts would be less than the nominal amount outstanding, i.e. the debts are discounted and the rate of discount will reflect the relevant interest charge and an allowance for the riskiness of the debt.
Financial futures	A standardised contract providing for the purchase or sale of a fixed quantity of a financial commodity such as foreign exchange, bank deposit, etc. The underlying financial instrument is known as the cash instrument.

Floating rate An interest rate which is reset at regular intervals – the adjustment usually being made with reference to a key rate such as *LIBOR*.

Floor A derivative instrument designed to fix a minimum level below which a price or interest rate cannot fall.

Foreign bond A *bond* issued by a borrower in the capital market of another country.

Forfaiting Buying a client's debts without the right to reclaim in the event of a *default*.

Forward contract A contract specifying a price for the delivery of a commodity or financial instrument at an agreed date in the future. This contract differs from a futures contract since the contract is not standardised and can be adjusted according to the needs of the purchaser.

Forward premium The gap between the forward exchange rate and the ruling *spot rate*. If the forward rate is less than the current spot rate then the currency is at a discount. The premium/discount can be expressed as an annual percentage or in the form of cents, etc., per £1.

FRN A floating-rate *note*, i.e. a note issued with provision for revision of the rate of interest at periodic intervals (normally three or six months) in line with a key market rate such as *LIBOR*.

Gilt-edged security A *bond* issued by the UK government.

Hedge The reduction of risk on exposure to changes in market prices/rates through taking an offsetting position.

Hedge fund An investment fund drawn up in such a manner as to avoid the main investment protection legislation. It is usually highly leveraged.

IMF International Monetary Fund. A multilateral agency that assists countries with payments difficulties by arranging rescheduling of debts or new credits.

Index fund An investment fund which is constructed to track an appropriate stock market index, e.g. the FT-SE All-Share Index.

Interest rate parity The requirement that the difference in interest rates between two countries should be matched by the forward exchange rate premium/discount.

Investment bank A bank that is involved in the commencement, underwriting and distribution of new issues of securities.

Junk bonds High-risk, high-return *bonds*. Substantial volumes were issued to finance buy-outs (leveraged buy-outs) in the US during a wave of corporate restructuring in the late 1980s. A junk bond has a credit rating of less than BBB.

Lender of last resort An institution, normally the central bank, which underpins the financial system by lending to banks, or more occasionally domestic firms, which are facing a liquidity crisis but are basically sound in the long run.

LIBID The London Interbank Bid Rate, i.e. the rate of interest paid on deposits in the London inter-bank market.

LIBOR The London Interbank Offer Rate, i.e. the rate at which banks are willing to lend funds in the London inter-bank market.

LIFFE London International Financial Futures and Options Exchange.

Market maker An institution which undertakes to sell and buy a commodity(ies) or financial instrument(s) on a continuous basis. This ensures that others can always buy or sell, thus providing liquidity.

Matching The practice of securing a distribution of assets which is equal to that of the liabilities in respect of characteristics such as maturity or currency denomination.

Maturity The time to the expiry of a loan/debt. Original maturity is the time to expiry when the loan was issued.

MBO Management buy-out. The purchase of an existing company by its incumbent management, usually financed by a venture capital fund.

Merchant bank Banks which make profits from carrying out services for corporate customers in addition to lending. The types of services are portfolio advice, new issues advice and underwriting, accepting bills of exchange, advising on takeovers and mergers, foreign currency services, etc.

NASDAQ National Association of Securities Dealers Automated Quotations – the computerised price information system used by dealers in the over-the-counter market (*OTC*) in the US.

NAV Net asset value per share. The value of assets less liabilities divided by the number of issued shares.

NIF A note-issuing facility whereby a bank (or more commonly a syndicate of banks) arranges and guarantees the availability of funds from the issue of a succession of short-term notes (commonly three or six months). In the case of these notes not being taken up by the market, the banks will provide the funds.

Note A short-term financial instrument similar to a *bond*. Unlike a bond, a note is essentially a short-term instrument.

OECD The Organization for Economic Co-operation and Development. Membership includes Australia, Austria, Belgium, Canada, Denmark, Finland, France, Germany, Greece, Iceland, Ireland, Italy, Japan, Luxembourg, Netherlands, New Zealand, Norway, Portugal, Spain, Sweden, Switzerland, Turkey, UK and US.

Off-balance-sheet business A type of business which does not create liabilities or assets for banks (or other businesses). Fees are usually generated along with contingent liabilities. Examples are *NIF*, forward exchange contracts, option writing, etc.

Offer price The price at which a *market maker* is prepared to sell securities.

Off-shore bank A subsidiary bank, such as a *eurobank*, which operates in a currency other than that of the host country. An alternative definition emphasises business carried out with non-residents in addition to the currency definition.

Options The right *but not* the obligation to buy (a 'call' option) or sell (a 'put' option) a commodity or financial instrument in return for the payment of a premium. The seller of an option is called the 'writer'. An over-the-counter (*OTC*) option is an option which is tailor-made for the purchaser and which cannot be sold. A traded option is an option in the form of a standardised agreement which the purchaser can sell on an organised market. A European-type option can be exercised only on a specific date and an American-type option can be exercised on any date prior to the expiry date.

OTC Over-the-counter market. An informal dealer-based market.

Perpetual FRN A *note* issued without provision for redemption.

Primary market A market for new issues of securities.

PSBR Public-sector borrowing requirement. The amount of money required by the public sector not otherwise raised by taxation.

PSDR Public-sector debt repayment. Repayment of debt by the public sector when it has a surplus.

Repurchase agreement (repo) An agreement to sell securities and repurchase them at a later date, both prices being agreed at the time of the initial sale. This is in effect an agreement to lend money with *collateral* and the two prices would reflect this.

Rollover credit A loan that is renewed (rolled over) at fixed intervals, with the interest rate being altered in line with a key rate such as *LIBOR*.

Savings and Loans Association In the US, an institution which accepts deposits and makes loans, the bulk of which are in the form of mortgages. The equivalent of building societies in the UK.

SEAQ Stock Exchange Automatic Quotation System.

SEC Securities and Exchange Commission. US investment regulatory body.

Secondary market A market for the sale and purchase of existing securities, as opposed to a market for the sale (or issue) of new securities, which is termed the *primary market*.

Securitisation The process by which existing non-negotiable debt (such as bank loans) is changed into a security which is marketable. The term can also be used in a broader sense to indicate the change of procedure through which debt which was formerly obtained by bank lending (i.e. non-negotiable) is issued in marketable forms such as *NIF* etc.

SIB Securities and Investment Board. Regulatory body set up by the Financial Services Act to oversee regulation of the investment industry. Delegates to *SROs*.

Spot rate The rate (most commonly exchange) which refers to transactions completed now rather than at some future time. In the case of foreign exchange rate transactions, settlement must be completed within two days.

Spread The gap between the institution's buying and selling rates for financial securities and foreign exchange. It can also refer to the margin above the base rate, such as *LIBOR*, at which a specific loan is priced.

SRO Self-regulatory organisation. Body authorised by the *SIB* to undertake regulation of a designated part of the investment industry.

Subordinated debt Debt which ranks after all other debt for repayment in the event of liquidation.

Swap An exchange of currencies or of debt with different characteristics such as interest rate type.

Syndicated loan A loan which is made by a group of banks. Normally one bank or banks act as the lead bank(s) and then arrange to sell all or some of the debt to other banks, who are termed participating banks.

Underwriting A process whereby financial institutions guarantee that a debt or *equity* issue will be taken up at a specified price. In the event of the market not purchasing all the issue, the institutions will purchase the balance.

USM Unlisted stock market. Second-tier stock market set up in 1980.

Withholding tax A tax which is deducted at source prior to payment of the interest or *dividends*.

References

Akerlof, G. [1970] 'The market for "lemons": qualitative uncertainty and market mechanism', *Quarterly Journal of Economics*, 89, 488–500.

Alesina, A. [1989] 'Politics and business cycles in industrial democracies', *Economic Policy*, 8, 55–98.

Alesina, A. and Summers, L. [1993] 'Central bank independence and macroeconomic performance: some comparative evidence', *Journal of Money, Credit and Banking*, May, 151–63.

Alexander, S. S. [1954] 'Price movements in speculative markets: trends or random walks', *Industrial Management Review*, V, 25–46.

Allen, T. J. [1990] 'Developments in the international syndicated loan market in the 1980's', *Bank of England Quarterly Bulletin*, February, 71–83.

Arrow, K. J. and Hahn, F. H. [1971] *General Equilibrium Analysis*, Holden Day Inc.

Bade, R. and Parkin, M. [1988] *Central Bank Laws and Monetary Policy*, University of Western Ontario, mimeograph.

Baillie, R. T., Lippens, R. E. and McMahon, P. C. [1983] 'Testing rational expectations and efficiency in the foreign exchange market', *Econometrica*, 51, 553–64.

Bank for International Settlements (BIS) [1986] *Recent Innovations in International Banking* (the Cross report), BIS.

Beckers, S. [1981] 'Standard deviations implied in option prices as predictors of future stock price variability', *Journal of Banking and Finance*, 5, 363–81

Benston, G. J. and Kaufman, G. G. [1988] *Risk and Solvency Regulation of Depository Institutions: Past Policies and Current Options*, Monograph 1 in Finance and Economics, Saloman Brothers Centre for the Study of Financial Institutions.

Bilson, J. F. O. [1983] 'The evaluation and use of foreign exchange rate forecasting services', in R. J. Herring (ed.), *Managing Foreign Exchange Risk*, Cambridge University Press.

Bjerring, J. H., Lakonishok, J. and Vermaelen, T. [1983] 'Stock prices and financial analysts' recommendations', *Journal of Finance*, 38, 187–204.

Blake, D., Beenstock, M. and Brasse, V. [1986] 'The performance of UK exchange rate forecasters', *Economic Journal*, 96, 986–99.
Blume, M. E. and Friend, I. [1974] 'Risk, investment strategies and the long-run rates of return', *Review of Economics and Statistics*, 56, 259–69.
Boocock, J. G. [1990] 'An examination of non-bank funding for small and medium sized enterprises in the UK', *Service Industries Journal*, 124–45.
Brady Commission [1988] *Report of the Presidential Task Force on Market Mechanisms*, US Government Printing Office
Bryant, C. [1987] 'National and sector balance sheets 1957–1985', *Economic Trends*, no. 403, May, 92–119.
Building Societies Association [1993] *The Future Constitution and Powers of Building Societies*, Building Societies Association.
Building Societies Association [1994] *New Legislation for Building Societies*, Building Societies Association
Cantor, R. and Packer, F. [1994] 'The credit rating industry', *Federal Reserve Bank of New York Review*, 19, no. 2, 1–26.
Cavanaugh, K. L. [1987] 'Price dynamics in the foreign currency futures market', *Journal of International Money and Finance*, 6, 295–314.
Cecchini, P. [1988] *The European Challenge 1992: The Benefits of a Single Market*, Gower Publishing Group.
Clark, J. [1993] 'Debt reduction and market reentry under the Brady Plan', *Federal Reserve Bank of New York Quarterly Review*, 18, no. 4, 38–62
Copeland, L. [1994] *Exchange Rates and International Finance*, 2nd edition, Addison-Wesley.
Cosh, A., Carty, J., Hughes, A., Plender, J. and Singh, A. [1990] *Take-Overs and Short-Termism in the UK*, Institute of Public Policy Research, Industrial Policy Paper no. 3.
Cukierman, A. [1992] *Central Bank Strategy, Credibility and Independence*, MIT Press.
Dale, R. [1994] 'Regulating investment business in the single market', *Bank of England Quarterly Bulletin*, November, 333–40.
Davis, E. P. [1990] *International Financial Centres – An Industrial Analysis*, Bank of England Discussion Paper no. 51.
Davis, E. P. and Latter, A. R. [1989] 'London as an international financial centre', *Bank of England Quarterly Bulletin*, November, 516–28.
Delors, J. [1989] *Report on Economic and Monetary Union in the European Community*, Committee for the Study of Economic and Monetary Union.
Demery, D. and Duck, N. W. [1978] 'The behaviour of nominal interest rates in the United Kingdom 1961–1973', *Economica*, 45, 23–37.
Diamond, D. [1984] 'Financial intermediation and delegated monitoring', *Review of Economic Studies*, 51, 393–414.
Diamond, D. [1989] 'Reputation acquisition in debt markets', *Journal of Political Economy*, 97, 728–62.
Diamond, D. [1991] 'Monitoring and reputation: the choice between bank loans and directly placed debt', *Journal of Political Economy*, 99, 689–721.
Dimson, E. and Marsh, P. [1984] 'Unpublished forecasts of UK stock returns', *Journal of Finance*, 39, 1257–92.

Dooley, M. P. and Shafer, J. R. [1976] *Analysis of Short-Run Exchange Rate Behavior: March 1973 to September 1975*, International Finance Discussion Papers no. 76, Federal Reserve System.

Dooley, M. P., Fernandez-Arias, E. and Kletzer, K. M. [1994] 'Recent private capital inflows to developing countries: is the debt crisis history?', *NBER Working Paper No. 4792.*

Dowd, K. [1993] 'Deposit insurance: a skeptical view', *Federal Reserve Bank of St Louis Review*, January/February, 14–17.

Elton E. J., Gruber, M. J. and Rentzler, J. [1984] 'Intra-day tests of the efficiency of the treasury bills futures market', *Review of Economics and Statistics*, 129–37.

Fama, E. F. [1970] 'Efficient capital markets: a review of theory and empirical evidence', *Journal of Finance*, 84, 499–522.

Fama, E. F. [1975] 'Short term interest rates as predictors of inflation', *American Economic Review*, 65, 269–82.

Fama, E. F. [1980] 'Banking in the theory of finance', *Journal of Monetary Economics*, 6, 7–28.

Fama, E. F. [1984] 'Forward and spot exchange rates', *Journal of Monetary Economics*, 14, no. 3, 319–39.

Fama, E. F. and Blume, M. E. [1966] 'Filter rules and stock market trading', *Journal of Business*, 39, 226–41.

Fleming, J. S. and Barr, D. G. [1989] *Modelling Money Market Interest Rates*, Bank of England Technical Paper series, no. 24.

Flood, M. D. [1991] 'An introduction to complete markets', *Federal Reserve Bank of St Louis*, 73, no. 2, 32–57.

Frenkel, J. A. and Levich, R. M. [1975] 'Covered interest arbitrage: unexploited profits?' *Journal of Political Economy,* 83, 325–38.

Frenkel, J. A. and Levich, R. M. [1977] 'Transactions costs and interest arbitrage: tranquil versus turbulent periods', *Journal of Political Economy*, 85, 1209–24.

Gemmill, G. [1986] 'The forecasting performance of stock options on the London Traded Options market', *Journal of Business, Finance and Accounting*, 13, 535–46.

Gibbons, M. and Hess, P. [1980] 'Day of the week effects and asset returns', *Journal of Business*, 54, 579–96.

Giovannini, A. [1990] *The Transition to Economic and Monetary Union*, Essays in International Finance no. 178, Department of Economics, Princeton University.

Goodhart, C. [1988] 'Bank insolvency and deposit insurance: a proposal', in P. Arestis (ed.), *Contemporary Issues in Money and Banking*, Macmillan.

Goodhart, C. A. E. [1989] *Money, Information and Uncertainty*, 2nd edition, Macmillan.

Goodhart, C. A. E. and Gowland, D. [1977] 'The relationship between yields on short and long-dated gilt-edged stock', *Bulletin of Economic Research*, 29.

Goodman, S. J. [1979] Foreign exchange forecasting techniques: implications for business and policy', *Journal of Finance*, 34, 415–27.

Grilli, V., Masciandaro, D. and Tabellini, G. [1991] 'Political and monetary institutions and public financial policies in the industrial countries', *Economic Policy*, 13, 341–92.
Gurley, J. and Shaw, E. [1960] '*Money in a Theory of Finance*', Brookings Institute.
Gwylim, O. and Buckle, M. [1994] *Volatility Forecasting in the Framework of the Option Expiry Cycle*, European Business Management School Discussion Paper, University of Wales.
Haldane, A. G. [1991] 'The exchange rate mechanism of the European monetary system: a review of the literature', *Bank of England Quarterly Bulletin*, February, 73–82.
Hall, M. [1987a] 'UK banking supervision and the Johnson Mathey affair', in C. Goodhart, D. Currie and D. Llewellyn (eds), *The Operation and Regulation of Financial Markets*, Macmillan.
Hall, M. [1987b] 'The deposit protection scheme: a case for reform', *National Westminster Bank Quarterly Review*, 45–53.
Hirschleifer, J. [1958] 'On the theory of optimal investment analysis', *Journal of Political Economy*, August, 329–52.
Kasman, B. [1992] 'A comparison of monetary policy operating procedures in six industrial countries, *Federal Reserve Bank of New York*, 17, no. 3, 5–24.
Keim, D. B. [1986] 'The CAPM and equity return regularities', *Financial Analyst Journal*, 42, 19–34.
Kindleberger, C. P. [1978] *Manias, Panics and Crashes: A History of Financial Crises*, Basic Books.
Kleidon, A. W. [1986] 'Variance bounds tests and stock price valuation models', *Journal of Political Economy*, 74, 639–55.
Lancaster, K. [1966] 'A new approach to consumer theory', *Journal of Political Economy*, 74, 132–57.
Leland, H. E. and Pyle, D. H. [1977] 'Information assymetries, financial structure and financial intermediation', *Journal of Finance*, 32, 371–87.
Lever, H. and Huhne, C. [1985] *Debt and Danger: The World Financial Crisis*, Penguin Books.
Levich, R. M. [1979] 'On the efficiency of markets for foreign exchange', in R. Dornbusch and J. A. Frenkel (eds), *International Economic Policy*, John Hopkins University Press.
Lewis, M. K. [1987] 'Off-balance sheet activities and financial innovation in banking', *Banca Nationale del Lavoro*, 387–410.
Lewis, M. K. and Davis, K. T. [1987] *Domestic and International Banking*, Philip Allan.
Llewellyn, D. [1985] *The Evolution of the British Financial System*, Gilbart Lectures on Banking, Institute of Bankers.
Llewellyn, D. T. [1991] 'Structural change in the British financial system' in C. J. Green and D. T. Llewellyn (eds), *Surveys in Monetary Economics, 2, Financial Markets and Institutions*, Blackwell.
Logue, D. E. and Sweeney, R. J. [1977] 'White noise in imperfect markets: the case of the franc/dollar exchange rate', *Journal of Finance*, 32, 761–8.

Macdonald, R. and Taylor, M. P. [1989] 'Economic analysis of foreign exchange markets: an expository survey', in R. Macdonald and M. P. Taylor (eds), *Innovations in Open Economy Macroeconomics*, Basil Blackwell.

Malkiel, B. G. [1966] *The Term Structure of Interest Rates*, Princeton University Press.

Manaster, S. and Rendleman, R. J. [1982] 'Options prices as predictors of equilibrium stock prices', *Journal of Finance*, 37, 1043–57.

Mankiw, G. and Summers, L. H. [1984] 'Do long-term interest rates overreact to short-term interest rates?' *Brookings Papers on Economic Activity*, 1.

Marsh, P. [1990] *Short Termism on Trial*, IFMA.

Massimb, M. and Phelps, B. [1993] 'Electronic trading, market structure and liquidity', *Financial Analysts Journal*, 50, no. 1, 39–50.

Mayer, C. and Alexander, I. [1990] *Bank and Securities Markets: Corporate Financing in Germany and the UK*, Centre for Economic Policy Research Discussion Paper no. 433.

McCauley, R. N. and Zimmer, S. A. [1989] 'Explaining international differences in the cost of capital', *Quarterly Review Federal Reserve Bank of New York*, summer, 7–21.

McConnell, J. J. and Muscerella, C. S. [1985] 'Corporate capital expenditure decisions and the market value of the firm', *Journal of Financial Economics*, 14, 399–422.

McCulloch, J. H. [1981] 'Misintermediation and macroeconomic fluctuations', *Journal of Monetary Economics*, 8, 103–15.

Meiselman, D. [1962] *The Term Structure of Interest Rates*, Prentice-Hall.

Miles, D. [1989] *Financial Liberalisation, the Housing Market and the Current Account*, Birkbeck College mimeo.

Modigliani, F. and Shiller, R. J. [1973] 'Inflation, rational expectations and the term structure of interest rates', *Economica*, 40, 12–43.

Modigliani, F. and Sutch, R. C. [1966] 'Innovations in interest rate policy', *American Economic Review*, 56, 178–97.

Newberry, D. J. [1989] 'Futures markets, hedging and speculation', in J. Eatwell, M. Milgate and P. Newman (eds), *The New Palgrave Dictionary of Finance*, Macmillan.

Pilbeam, K. [1992] *International Finance*, Macmillan.

Plender, J. [1990] 'Throw sand in the take over machine', *Financial Times*, 24 July.

Pollard, P. S. [1993] 'Central bank independence and economic performance', *Federal Reserve Bank of St Louis*, July/August, 21–36.

Russell, S. [1993] 'The government's role in deposit insurance', *Federal Reserve Bank of St Louis Review*, January/February, 3–9.

Rybczynski, T. [1988] 'Financial systems and industrial restructuring', *National Westminster Bank Quarterly Review*, 3–13.

Sachs, J. [1986] 'Managing the LDC debt crisis', *Brookings Papers on Economic Activity*, 397–440.

Sachs, J. and Huizinga, H. [1987] 'US commercial banks and the developing-country debt crisis', *Brookings Papers on Economic Activity*, 555–606.

Santoni, G. J. [1987] 'The great bull markets 1924–1929 and 1982–1987:

speculative bubbles or economic fundamentals', *Federal Reserve Bank of St Louis Review,* November, 16–30.

Sargent, T. [1972] 'Rational expectations and the term structure of interest rates', *Journal of Money Credit and Banking*, 4.

Schnadt, N. [1994] 'Domestic money markets of the UK, France, Germany and the US', *The City Research Project: Key Issues for the Square Mile*, City Corporation of London.

Schnadt, N. and Whittaker, J. [1993] 'Optimal money market behaviour and sterling interest rates', Paper presented to the Money, Macro and Finance Research Group annual conference at St Andrew's University.

Securities and Investments Board (SIB) [1994] *Regulation of the United Kingdom Equity Markets*, Discussion Paper of SIB.

Shiller, R. J. [1979] 'The volatility of long-term interest rates and expectations models of the term structure', *Journal of Political Economy*, 87, 1190–2119.

Shiller, R. J. [1981] 'Do stock prices move too much to be justified by subsequent changes in dividends?', *American Economic Review*, 71, 421–36.

Stickel, S. E. [1985] 'The effect of value line investment survey rank changes on common stock prices', *Journal of Financial Economics*, 14, 121–43.

Sykes, A. [1990] 'Bigger carrots and sticks', *Financial Times*, 31 October.

Taylor, M. P. [1987] 'Covered interest parity: a high-frequency, high-quality data study', *Economica*, 54, 429–38.

Taylor, S. [1986] *Modelling Financial Time Series*, John Wiley.

Tobin, J. [1984] 'On the efficiency of the financial system', *Lloyds Bank Review*, 153, 1–15.

Tucker, A. L. [1987] 'Foreign exchange option prices as predictors of equilibrium forward exchange rates', *Journal of International Money and Finance*, 6, 283–94.

Twinn, C. [1994] 'Asset backed securitisation in the UK', *Bank of England Quarterly Bulletin*, May, 134–43.

Walmsley, J. [1988] *The New Financial Instruments: An Investors' Guide*, Wiley.

Yang, J. E. [1987] 'Fraud is the main cause of failure at S&Ls in California, Congress says', *Wall Street Journal*, 15 June, 6.

Index